THE GIANT BOOK OF
CLASSIC GHOST STORIES

D1347191

THE GIANT BOOK OF
CLASSIC GHOST STORIES

Edited by Richard Dalby

This edition published and distributed by Magpie Books,
an imprint of Robinson Publishing Ltd, London, 1997

Magpie Books
7 Kensington Church Court,
London W8 4SP

This collection first published in the UK as
The Mammoth Book of Victorian & Edwardian Ghost Stories
by Robinson Publishing 1995

A copy of the British Library Cataloguing in Publication Data
is available from the British Library

ISBN 1 85487 672 4

Printed and bound by Firmin-Didot (France),
Group Herissey. No d'impression : 37145.

Contents

viii CONTENTS

Publisher's Note:

Every effort has been made to trace copyright holders but the publishers would be interested to hear from anyone not here acknowledged.

Introduction

> "Besides this earth, and besides the race of men,
> there is an invisible world and a kingdom of spirits;
> that world is round us, for it is everywhere."

These lines come from Charlotte Brontë's *Jane Eyre* and are spoken by Helen, the character said to be based on Charlotte's elder sister who died young.

In the early nineteenth century most of the greatest British writers, notably Lord Byron, Percy and Mary Shelley, Sir Walter Scott, Ann Radcliffe, and the young Brontës, were fascinated by the supernatural, and their countless readers shared this obsession with the "invisible world".

The beginning of the Victorian era in 1837 coincided exactly with Richard Barham's first series of *The Ingoldsby Legends* in *Bentley's Miscellany*, which included many classics like "The Spectre of Tappington" and "The Hand of Glory" and were constantly reprinted (and much recited) during the rest of the century, and Charles Dickens's first excursions into the supernatural, such as "The Story of the Goblins who Stole a Sexton" (which originally formed chapter 28 of *The Pickwick Papers*).

Apart from these light-hearted pieces, the first great wholly macabre Victorian classic short stories were "Schalken the Painter" and "The Ghost and the Bone-Setter" by Joseph Sheridan Le Fanu. Regarded by many connoisseurs of the genre as the most outstanding ghost story writer of the century, his literary career climaxed with a stunning collection, *In a Glass Darkly* (1872), containing, in M. R. James's words, "four stories of paramount excellence" – "Green Tea", "The Familiar", "Mr Justice Harbottle", and "Carmilla" – plus a fine thriller "The Room in the Dragon Volant".

After Dickens's *A Christmas Carol* first appeared in 1843, ghost stories became an ever-popular and essential ingredient of weekly and monthly magazines, especially the Christmas Numbers. Dickens himself commissioned many noted tales from writers like Wilkie Collins, Bulwer Lytton and Mrs Gaskell, several contained in "round robin" collections for *Household Words* (from 1850) and *All the Year Round* which followed nine years later. The best of his own later stories, "No. 1 Branch Line: The Signalman", formed part of *Mugby Junction*, the 1866 Christmas Number of *All the Year Round*.

A huge number of contemporary magazines followed the example of these two magazines, flourishing and expanding rapidly in the 1860s and beyond, some of the best early examples being the *Cornhill*, *Blackwoods*, *Belgravia*, *Temple Bar*, *Argosy* and *Tinsleys*. Many of the stories in the present anthology originally appeared in these magazines, including those by Braddon (*Belgravia*), Broughton (*Temple Bar*) and Cowper (*Blackwoods*).

The majority of the stories in these magazines were first printed anonymously, and were only credited to a specific author when published in book form by such popular names as D. M. Mulock, later Mrs Craik (*Nothing New*), Amelia B. Edwards (*Miss Carew; Monsieur Maurice*), Mary E. Braddon (*Weavers and Weft; Ralph the Bailiff*), J. Sheridan Le Fanu (*Ghost Stories and Tales of Mystery*, 1851), Rhoda Broughton (*Tales for Christmas Eve*) and Mrs J. H. Riddell (*Weird Stories*); but several others continued to remain nameless between hard covers like the versatile John Berwick Harwood (*Major Peter*).

Countless others were not so lucky as the leading lights, being doomed to permanent anonymity, as with the entertaining contributors to *Tinsley's Annuals*, notably the ghost-filled *Stable for Nightmares* in 1868 (from which I have taken "Haunted" for the present volume), and the unknown writers who accompanied a young Arthur Conan Doyle in the similarly anonymous anthology *Ghost Stories and Presentiments* in 1887.

The ghost story became equally popular in America, following the success of Dickens and his disciples, and early examples by Henry James, Fitz-James O'Brien and Harriet Beecher Stowe, with later tales by Ralph Adams Cram, Robert W. Chambers, W. C. Morrow, Thomas Nelson Page, and F. Marion Crawford, are all included in this anthology.

At least half of the best practitioners in the genre were women, and several of them are represented here, including the children's writers E. Nesbit and "Theo Gift" (Dora Havers).

The French writers Erckmann and Chatrian (usually combined with a hyphen) also enjoyed a great vogue in Britain during the last half of the century. Their bizarre supernatural tales were much admired by a youthful M. R. James whose own first ghost stories were published in 1895 magazines. His magnificent *Ghost Stories of an Antiquary* (1904) was a seminal work – the greatest ghost story collection of the Edwardian (or any other) era, which uniquely invigorated the whole genre. It has been reprinted up to the present more often than any other supernatural volume.

In the present anthology, I have included not only some unavoidable well-known classics by Dickens, Le Fanu, Bram Stoker and M. R. James, but also a wide choice of less familiar tales by Mary E. Braddon, Dinah M. Mulock, Amelia B. Edwards, Alice Perrin, Tom Gallon, S. Baring-Gould, Richard Marsh (creator of *Dracula*'s eminent rival bestseller, *The Beetle*) and many more.

I hope even the most avid collector of ghostly fiction will find several new and unknown tales here, alongside old favourites worth savouring again.

Richard Dalby

THE GIANT BOOK OF
CLASSIC GHOST STORIES

Ghosts

A characteristic Victorian poem on the subject of ghosts (from the anonymously edited and written anthology Ghost Stories and Presentiments, *1887).*

Creatures of mist, half credited;
Our faint form flings
No shadow in moonlight on the bed
We visit; noiseless is our tread,
Who come from deserts of the dead,
Where no bird sings.

For ever, in dark and cold forlorn,
We wander there;
Pale spectres, wondrous pale and worn,
As privet flowers at even shorn
Are pale when Phosphor fails with morn,
We who once were.

Who now nor see the sunny day,
Nor waving wheat
Hear whisper in its autumn play;
The sweet world's face is never gay
For us, who see no flowers of May;
But night is sweet.

Night brings us back to earth again,
Again we fill
Our old familiar homes, a train
Of dead men out of mind, who fain
To be remembered, long, in vain,
To linger still.

In vain. Dawn's dated herald shows
Dawn comes apace.
On the orient heaven ere Morning throws
Broadcast her buds of white and rose,
Each sad unwilling phantom goes
To its own place.

Ah, why are these, when we appear,
Our children, frayed?
Could they once feel how very dear
We find their faces, none would fear
Us, so far distant, yet so near,
Dim folk of shade.

Do these not know their children's toys,
Long years ago,
Were ours; their lovers' woes and joys,
Their prayers, their faith, their fame, their noise,
Know they not this, these girls and boys,
Nor care to know?

As sights, which memory endears,
Seen once more, please;
As sounds, unheard for many years,
Heard once more waken joys and tears –
So are we moved by hopes and fears
And cares of these.

Oft at their births we intervene;
The stray ears strown
In their loves' harvest-home we glean

And garner; in their deaths we lean
Over them, kindred shadows seen
By them alone.

Would we might help them, though abhorred,
From harm and wrong!
From plague and famine, fire and sword,
In weal and woe, at bed and board,
Would our weak hands might work to ward
Their whole life long!

Would we might say the things we know,
A little say
Of all the gods conceal! But, lo,
Our very dumb lips bid men go
Eat bread, and let the wine's blood flow
While it is day.

Bid them, while yet they see the light,
Ere the black pall
Cover them, let their robes be white,
Perfumed their heads in death's despite;
We know what wisdom is in night,
What end for all.

We watch the moon's far choral band
Fade in the blue;
We watch the sinking grains of sand,
And yearn for voices to command,
"Do with your might what deed your hand
May find to do."

We watch the unheeded hours, which yet
Return no more;
We watch them wane with long regret.
Ye fools! what meed have faces met
With fasting gaunt, with weeping wet,
Sealed up in store?

Warm tender hands with last touch close
The dead's dull eyes;
For ever from you to us he goes,
To our waste land where no wind blows.
Whither beyond? What wise man knows,
However wise?

Tossed for a while in life's mad foam,
A bubble at best,
His body lies long wrapped in loam;
With us his weary ghost must roam
Always: men call it going home
To perfect rest.

Home! rest! words laughed by us to scorn.
Is, then, rest there
Indeed? But we away are torn:
We see the glow-worm's glimmer born,
We smell the mild sweet breath of morn,
And mix with air.

Joseph Sheridan Le Fanu

Schalken the Painter

This was the first important ghost story to be published in the Victorian era, and is still regarded as among the finest of the whole century. Joseph Sheridan Le Fanu (1814–73) was acclaimed by M. R. James (and many others) as the greatest ghost-story writer of the nineteenth century, bar none. "Schalken the Painter" originally appeared in The Dublin University Magazine *of May 1839.*

YOU WILL NO DOUBT be surprised, my dear friend, at the subject of the following narrative. What had I to do with Schalken, or Schalken with me? He had returned to his native land, and was probably dead and buried before I was born; I never visited Holland, nor spoke with a native of that country. So much I believe you already know. I must, then, give you my authority, and state to you frankly the ground upon which rests the credibility of the strange story which I am about to lay before you.

I was acquainted, in my early days, with a Captain Vandael, whose father had served King William in the Low Countries, and also in my own unhappy land during the Irish campaigns. I know not how it happened that I liked this man's society, spite of his politics and religion: but so it was; and it was by means of the free intercourse to which our intimacy gives rise that I became possessed of the curious tale which you are about to hear.

I had often been struck, while visiting Vandael, by a remarkable picture, in which, though no connoisseur myself, I could not fail to discern some very strong peculiarities, particularly in the distribution of light and shade, as also a certain oddity in the design itself, which interested my curiosity. It represented the interior of what might be a chamber in some antique religious building – the foreground was occupied by a female figure, arrayed in a species of white robe, part of which was arranged so as to form a veil. The dress, however, was not strictly that of any religious order. In its hand the figure bore a lamp, by whose light alone the form and face were illuminated; the features were marked by an arch smile, such as pretty women wear when engaged in successfully practising some roguish trick; in the background, and (excepting where the dim red light of an expiring fire serves to define the form) totally in the shade, stood the figure of a man equipped in the old fashion, with doublet and so forth, in an attitude of alarm, his hand being placed upon the hilt of his sword, which he appeared to be in the act of drawing.

"There are some pictures," said I to my friend, "which impress one, I know not how, with a conviction that they represent not the mere ideal shapes and combinations which have floated through the imagination of the artist, but scenes, faces and situations which have actually existed. When I look upon that picture, something assures me that I behold the representation of a reality."

Vandael smiled, and, fixing his eyes upon the painting musingly, he said –

"Your fancy has not deceived you, my good friend, for that picture is the record, and I believe a faithful one, of a remarkable and mysterious occurrence. It was painted by Schalken, and contains, in the face of the female figure which occupies the most prominent place in the design, an accurate portrait of Rose Velderkaust, the niece of Gerard Douw, the first and, I believe, the only love of Godfrey Schalken. My father knew the painter well, and from Schalken himself he learned the story of the mysterious drama, one scene of which the picture has embodied. This painting, which is accounted a fine specimen of Schalken's style, was bequeathed to my father by the artist's will, and, as you have observed, is a very striking and interesting production."

I had only to request Vandael to tell the story of the painting in order to be gratified; and thus it is that I am enabled to submit to you a faithful recital of what I heard myself, leaving you to reject or to allow the evidence upon which the truth of the tradition depends – with this one assurance, that Schalken was an honest, blunt Dutchman, and, I believe, wholly incapable of committing a flight of imagination; and further, that Vandael, from whom I heard the story, appeared firmly convinced of its truth.

There are few forms upon which the mantle of mystery and romance could seem to hang more ungracefully than upon that of the uncouth and clownish Schalken – the Dutch boor – the rude and dogged, but most cunning worker in oils, whose pieces delight the initiated of the present day almost as much as his manner disgusted the refined of his own; and yet this man, so rude, so dogged, so slovenly, I had almost said so savage in mien and manner, during his after successes, had been selected by the capricious goddess, in his early life, to figure as the hero of a romance by no means devoid of interest or of mystery.

Who can tell how meet he may have been in his young days to play the part of the lover or of the hero? who can say that in early life he had been the same harsh, unlicked, and rugged boor that, in his maturer age, he proved? or how far the neglected rudeness which afterwards marked his air, and garb, and manners, may not have been the growth of that reckless apathy not unfrequently produced by bitter misfortunes and disappointments in early life?

These questions can never now be answered.

We must content ourselves, then, with a plain statement of facts, leaving matters of speculation to those who like them.

When Schalken studied under the immortal Gerard Douw, he was a young man; and in spite of the phlegmatic constitution and excitable manner which he shared, we believe, with his countrymen, he was not incapable of deep and vivid impressions, for it is an established fact that the young painter looked with considerable interest upon the beautiful niece of his wealthy master.

Rose Velderkaust was very young, having, at the period of which we speak, not yet attained her seventeenth year; and if tradition speaks truth, she possessed all the soft dimpling charms of the fair, light-haired Flemish maidens. Schalken had not studied long in the school of Gerard Douw when he felt this interest deepening into something of a keener and intenser feeling than was quite consistent with the tranquillity of his honest Dutch heart; and at the same time he perceived or thought he perceived, flattering symptoms of a reciprocal attachment, and this was quite sufficient to determine whatever indecision he might have heretofore experienced, and to lead him to devote exclusively to her every hope and feeling of his heart. In short, he was as much in love as a Dutchman could be. He was not long in making his passion known to the pretty maiden herself, and his declaration was followed by a corresponding confession upon her part.

Schalken, howbeit, was a poor man, and he possessed no counterbalancing advantages of birth or position to induce the old man to consent to a union which must involve his niece and ward in the strugglings and difficulties of a young and nearly friendless artist. He was, therefore, to wait until time had furnished him with opportunity, and accident with success; and then, if his labours were found sufficiently lucrative, it was to be hoped that his proposals might at least be listened to by her jealous guardian. Months passed away, and, cheered by the smiles of the little Rose, Schalken's labours were redoubled, and with such effect and improvement as reasonably to promise the realization of his hopes, and no contemptible eminence in his art, before many years should have elapsed.

The even course of this cheering prosperity was, unfortunately, destined to experience a sudden and formidable interruption, and that, too, in a manner so strange and mysterious as to baffle all investigation, and throw upon the events themselves a shadow of almost supernatural horror.

Schalken had one evening remained in the master's studio considerably longer than his more volatile companions, who had gladly availed themselves of the excuse which the dusk of evening afforded to withdraw from their several tasks, in order to finish a day of labour in the jollity and conviviality of the tavern.

But Schalken worked for improvement, or rather for love. Besides, he was now engaged merely in sketching a design, an operation which, unlike that of colouring, might be continued as long as there was light sufficient to distinguish between canvas and charcoal. He had not then, nor, indeed until long after, discovered the peculiar powers of his pencil; and he was engaged in composing a group of extremely roguish-looking and grotesque imps and demons, who were inflicting various ingenious torments upon a perspiring and pot-bellied St Anthony, who reclined in the midst of them, apparently in the last stage of drunkenness.

The young artist, however, though incapable of executing or even of appreciating, anything of true sublimity, had nevertheless discernment enough to prevent his being by any means satisfied with his work; and many were the patient erasures and corrections which the limbs and features of saint and devil underwent, yet all without producing in their new arrangement anything of improvement or increased effect.

The large, old-fashioned room was silent, and, with the exception of himself, quite deserted by its usual inmates. An hour had passed – nearly two – without any improved result. Daylight had already declined, and twilight was fast giving way to the darkness of night. The patience of the young man was exhausted, and he stood before his unfinished production, absorbed in no very pleasing ruminations, one hand buried in the folds of his long dark hair, and the other holding the piece of charcoal which had so ill executed its office, and which he now rubbed, without much regard to the sable streaks which it produced, with irritable pressure upon his ample Flemish inexpressibles.

"Pshaw!" said the young man aloud, "would that picture, devils, saint, and all, were where they should be – in hell!"

A short, sudden laugh, uttered startlingly close to his ear, instantly responded to the ejaculation.

The artist turned sharply round, and now for the first time became aware that his labours had been overlooked by a stranger.

Within about a yard and a half, and rather behind him, there stood what was, or appeared to be, the figure of an elderly man: he wore a short cloak, and a broad-brimmed hat with a conical crown, and in his hand, which was protected with a heavy, gauntlet-shaped glove, he carried a long ebony walking-stick, surmounted with what appeared, as it glittered dimly in the twilight to be a massive head of gold; and upon his breast, through the folds of the cloak, there shone the links of a rich chain of the same metal.

The room was so obscure that nothing further of the appearance of the figure could be ascertained, and the face was altogether overshadowed by the heavy flap of the beaver which overhung it, so that no feature could be clearly discerned. A quantity of dark hair escaped from beneath this sombre hat, a circumstance which, connected with the firm, upright carriage of the intruder, proved that his years could not exceed threescore or thereabouts.

There was an air of gravity and importance about the garb of this person, and something indescribably odd – I might say awful – in the perfect, stone-like movelessness of the figure, that effectually checked the testy comment which had at once risen to the lips of the irritated artist. He therefore, as soon as he had sufficiently recovered the surprise, asked the stranger, civilly, to be seated, and desired to know if he had any message to leave for his master.

"Tell Gerard Douw," said the unknown, without altering his attitude in the smallest degree, "that Mynher Vanderhausen, of Rotterdam, desires to speak with him tomorrow evening at this hour, and, if he please, in this room, upon matters of weight; that is all. Goodnight."

The stranger, having finished this message, turned abruptly, and, with a quick but silent step quitted the room before Schalken had time to say a word in reply.

The young man felt a curiosity to see in what direction the burgher of Rotterdam would turn on quitting the studio, and for that purpose he went directly to the window which commanded the door.

A lobby of considerable extent intervened between the inner door of the painter's room and the street entrance, so that Schalken occupied the post of observation before the old man could possibly have reached the street.

He watched in vain, however. There was no other mode of exit.

Had the old man vanished, or was he lurking about the recesses of the lobby for some bad purpose? This last suggestion filled the mind of Schalken with a vague horror, which was so unaccountably intense as to make him alike afraid to remain in the room alone and reluctant to pass through the lobby.

However, with an effort which appeared very disproportioned to the occasion, he summoned resolution to leave the room, and, having double-locked the door, and thrust the key in his pocket, without looking at the right or left, he traversed the passage which had so recently, perhaps still, contained the person of his mysterious visitant, scarcely venturing to breathe till he had arrived in the open street.

"Mynher Vanderhausen," said Gerard Douw, within himself, as the appointed hour approached; "Mynher Vanderhausen of Rotterdam! I never heard of the man till yesterday. What can he want of me? A portrait, perhaps, to be painted; or a younger son of a poor relation to be apprenticed; or a collection to be valued; or – pshaw! there's no one in Rotterdam to leave me a legacy. Well, whatever the business may be, we shall soon know it all."

It was now the close of day, and every easel, except that of Schalken, was deserted. Gerard Douw was pacing the apartment with the restless step of impatient expectation, every now and then humming a passage from a piece of music which he was himself composing for, though no great proficient, he admired the art; sometimes pausing to glance over the work of one of his absent pupils, but more frequently placing himself at the window, from whence he might observe the passengers who threaded the obscure by-street in which his studio was placed.

"Said you not, Godfrey," exclaimed Douw, after a long and fruitless gaze from his post of observation, and turning to Schalken – "said you not the hour of appointment was at about seven by the clock of the Stadhouse?"

"It had just told seven when I first saw him, sir," answered the student.

"The hour is close at hand, then," said the master, consulting a horologe as large and as round as a full-grown orange. "Mynher Vanderhausen, from Rotterdam – is it not so?"

"Such was the name."

"And an elderly man, richly clad?" continued Douw.

"As well as I might see," replied his pupil. "He could not be young, nor yet very old neither, and his dress was rich and grave, as might become a citizen of wealth and consideration."

At this moment the sonorous boom of the Stadhouse clock told, stroke after stroke, the hour of seven; the eyes of both master and student were directed to the door; and it was not until the last peal of the old bell had ceased to vibrate, that Douw exclaimed –

"So, so; we shall have his worship presently – that is, if he means to keep his hour; if not, thou mayst wait for him, Godfrey, if you court the acquaintance of a capricious burgomaster. As for me, I think our old Leyden contains a sufficiency of such commodities, without an importation from Rotterdam."

Schalken laughed, as in duty bound; and, after a pause of some minutes, Douw suddenly exclaimed, –

"What if it should all prove a jest, a piece of mummery got up by Vankarp, or some such worthy! I wish you had run all risks, and cudgelled the old burgomaster, stadholder, or whatever else he may be, soundly. I would wager a dozen of Rhenish, his worship would have pleaded old acquaintance before the third application."

"Here he comes, sir," said Schalken, in a low, admonitory tone; and instantly, upon turning towards the door, Gerard Douw observed the same figure which had, on the day before, so unexpectedly greeted the vision of his pupil Schalken.

There was something in the air and mien of the figure which at once satisfied the painter that there was no mummery in the case, and that he really stood in the presence of a man of worship; and so, without hesitation, he doffed his cap, and courteously saluting the stranger, requested him to be seated.

The visitor waved his hand slightly, as if in acknowledgement of the courtesy, but remained standing.

"I have the honour to see Mynher Vanderhausen, of Rotterdam?" said Gerard Douw.

"The same," was the laconic reply.

"I understood your worship desires to speak with me," continued Douw, "and I am here by appointment to wait your commands."

"Is that a man of trust?" said Vanderhausen, turning towards Schalken, who stood at a little distance behind his master.

"Certainly," replied Gerard.

"Then let him take this box and get the nearest jeweller or goldsmith to value its contents, and let him return hither with a certificate of the valuation."

At the same time he placed a small case, about nine inches square, in the hands of Gerard Douw, who was as much amazed at its weight as at the strange abruptness with which it was handed to him.

In accordance with the wishes of the stranger, he delivered it into the hands of Schalken, and repeating his directions, despatched him upon the mission.

Schalken disposed his precious charge securely beneath the folds of his cloak, and rapidly traversing two or three narrow streets, he stopped at a corner house, the lower part of which was then occupied by the shop of a Jewish goldsmith.

Schalken entered the shop, and calling the little Hebrew into the obscurity of its back recesses, he proceeded to lay before him Vanderhausen's packet.

On being examined by the light of a lamp, it appeared entirely cased with lead, the outer surface of which was much scraped and soiled, and nearly white with age. This was with difficulty partially removed, and disclosed beneath a box of some dark and singularly hard wood; this, too, was forced, and after the removal of two or three folds of linen, its contents proved to be a mass of golden ingots, close packed, and, as the Jew declared, of the most perfect quality.

Every ingot underwent the scrutiny of the little Jew, who seemed to feel an epicurean delight in touching and testing these morsels of the glorious metal; and each one of them was replaced in the box with the exclamation –

"*Mein Gott*, how very perfect! Not one grain of alloy – beautiful, beautiful!"

The task was at length finished, and the Jew certified under his hand that the value of the ingots submitted to his examination amounted to many thousand rix-dollars.

With the desired document in his bosom, and the rich box of gold carefully pressed under his arm, and concealed by his cloak, he retraced the way, and, entering the studio, found his master and the stranger in close conference.

Schalken had no sooner left the room, in order to execute the commission he had taken in charge, than Vanderhausen addressed Gerard Douw in the following terms:

"I may not tarry with you tonight more than a few minutes, and so I shall briefly tell you the matter upon which I come. You visited the town of Rotterdam some four months ago, and then I saw in the church of St Lawrence your niece, Rose Velderkaust. I desire to marry her, and if I satisfy you as to the fact that I am very wealthy – more wealthy than any husband you could dream of for her – I expect that you will forward my views to the utmost of your authority. If you approve my proposal, you must close with it at once, for I cannot command time enough to wait for calculations and delays."

Gerard Douw was, perhaps, as much astonished as anyone could be by the very unexpected nature of Mynher Vanderhausen's communication; but he did not give vent to any unseemly expression of surprise. In addition to the motives supplied by prudence and politeness, the painter experienced a kind of chill and oppressive sensation – a feeling like that which is supposed to affect a man who is placed unconsciously in immediate contact with something to which he has a natural antipathy – an undefined horror and dread – while standing in the presence of the eccentric stranger, which made him very unwilling to say anything that might reasonably prove offensive.

"I have no doubt," said Gerard, after two or three prefatory hems, "that the connection which you propose would prove alike advantageous and honourable to my niece; but you must be aware that she has a will of her own, and may not acquiesce in what we may design for her advantage."

"Do not seek to deceive me, Sir Painter," said Vanderhausen; "you are her guardian – she is your ward. She is mine if you like to make her so."

The man of Rotterdam moved forward a little as he spoke, and Gerard Douw, he scarce knew why, inwardly prayed for the speedy return of Schalken.

"I desire," said the mysterious gentleman, "to place in your hands at once an evidence of my wealth, and a security for my liberal dealing with your niece. The lad will return in a minute or two with a sum in value five times the fortune which she has a right to expect from a husband. This shall lie in your hands, together with her dowry, and you may apply the united sum as suits her interest best; it shall be all exclusively hers while she lives. Is that liberal?"

Douw assented, and inwardly thought that fortune had been extraordinarily kind to his niece. The stranger, he deemed, must be most wealthy and generous, and such an offer was not to be despised, though made by a humorist, and one of no very prepossessing presence.

Rose had no very high pretensions, for she was almost without dowry; indeed, altogether so, excepting so far as the deficiency had been supplied by the generosity of her uncle. Neither had she any right to raise any scruples against the match on the score of birth, for her own origin was by no means elevated; and as to other objections, Gerard resolved, and, indeed, by the usages of the time was warranted in resolving, not to listen to them for a moment.

"Sir," said he, addressing the stranger, "your offer is most liberal, and whatever hesitation I may feel in closing with it immediately, arises solely from my not having the honour of knowing anything of your family or station. Upon these points you can, of course, satisfy me without difficulty?"

"As to my respectability," said the stranger drily, "you must take that for granted at present; pester me with no inquiries; you can discover nothing more about me than I choose to make known. You shall have sufficient security for my respectability – my word, if you are honourable: if you are sordid, my gold."

"A testy old gentleman," thought Douw; "he must have his own way. But, all things considered, I am justified in giving my niece to him. Were she my own daughter, I would do the like by her. I will not pledge myself unnecessarily, however."

"You will not pledge yourself unnecessarily," said Vanderhausen, strangely uttering the very words which had just floated through the mind of his companion: "but you will do so if it is necessary, I presume; and I will show you that I consider it indispensable. If the gold I mean to leave in your hands satisfies you, and if you desire that my proposal shall not be at once withdrawn, you must, before I leave this room, write your name to this engagement."

Having thus spoken, he placed a paper in the hands of Gerard, the contents of which expressed an engagement entered into by Gerard Douw, to give to Wilken Vanderhausen, of Rotterdam, in marriage, Rose Velderkaust, and so forth, within one week of the date hereof.

While the painter was employed in reading this covenant, Schalken, as we have stated, entered the studio, and having delivered the box and the valuation of the Jew into the hands of the stranger, he was about to retire, when Vanderhausen called him to wait; and, presenting the case and the certificate to Gerard Douw, he waited in silence until he had satisfied himself by an inspection of both as to the value of the pledge left in his hands. At length he said:

"Are you content?"

The painter said "he would fain have another day to consider."

"Not an hour," said the suitor, coolly.

"Well, then," said Douw, "I am content; it is a bargain."

"Then sign at once," said Vanderhausen; "I am weary."

At the same time he produced a small case of writing materials, and Gerard signed the important document.

"Let this youth witness the covenant," said the old man; and Godfrey Schalken unconsciously signed the instrument which bestowed upon another that hand which he had so long regarded as the object and reward of all his labours.

The compact being thus completed, the strange visitor folded up the paper, and stowed it safely in an inner pocket.

"I will visit you tomorrow night, at nine of the clock, at your house, Gerard Douw, and will see the subject of our contract. Farewell." And so saying, Wilken Vanderhausen moved stiffly, but rapidly out of the room.

Schalken, eager to resolve his doubts, had placed himself by the window in order to watch the street entrance; but the experiment served only to support his suspicions, for the old man did not issue from the door. This was very strange, very odd, very fearful. He and his master returned together, and talked but little on the way, for each had his own subjects of reflection, of anxiety, and of hope.

Schalken, however, did not know the ruin which threatened his cherished schemes.

Gerard Douw knew nothing of the attachment which had sprung up between his pupil and his niece; and even if he had, it is doubtful whether he would have regarded its existence as any serious obstruction to the wishes of Mynher Vanderhausen.

Marriages were then and there matters of traffic and calculation; and it would have appeared as absurd in the eyes of the guardian to make a mutual attachment an essential element in a contract of marriage, as it would have been to draw up his bonds and receipts in the language of chivalrous romance.

The painter, however, did not communicate to his niece the important step which he had taken in her behalf, and his resolution arose not from any anticipation of opposition on her part, but solely from a ludicrous consciousness that if his ward were, as she very naturally might do, to ask him to describe the appearance of the bridegroom whom he destined for her, he would be forced to confess that he had not seen his face, and, if called upon, would find it impossible to identify him.

Upon the next day, Gerard Douw having dined, called his niece to him, and having scanned her person with an air of satisfaction, he took her hand, and looking upon her pretty innocent face with a smile of kindness, he said:

"Rose, my girl, that face of yours will make your fortune." Rose blushed and smiled. "Such faces and such tempers seldom go together, and, when they do, the compound is a love-potion which few heads or hearts can resist. Trust me, thou wilt soon be a bride, girl. But this is trifling, and I am pressed for time, so make ready the large room by eight o'clock tonight, and give directions for supper at nine. I expect a friend tonight; and observe me, child, do thou trick thyself out handsomely, I would not have him think us poor or sluttish."

With these words he left the chamber, and took his way to the room to which we have already had occasion to introduce our readers – that in which his pupils worked.

When the evening closed in, Gerard called Schalken, who was about to take his departure to his obscure and comfortable lodgings, and asked him to come home and sup with Rose and Vanderhausen.

The invitation was of course accepted, and Gerard Douw and his pupil soon found themselves in the handsome and somewhat antique-looking room which had been prepared for the reception of the stranger.

A cheerful wood-fire blazed in the capacious hearth; a little at one side an old-fashioned table, with richly-carved legs, was placed – destined, no doubt, to receive the supper, for which preparations were going forward; and ranged with exact regularity stood the tall-backed chairs whose ungracefulness was more than counterbalanced by their comfort.

The little party consisting of Rose, her uncle, and the artist, awaited the arrival of the expected visitor with considerable impatience.

Nine o'clock at length came, and with it a summons at the street-door, which, being speedily answered, was followed by a slow and emphatic tread upon the staircase; the steps moved heavily across the lobby, the door of the room in which the party which we have described were assembled slowly opened and there entered a figure which startled, almost appalled, the phlegmatic Dutchmen, and nearly made Rose scream with affright; it was the form, and arrayed in the garb, of Mynher Vanderhausen; the air, the gait, the height was the same, but the features had never been seen by any of the party before.

The stranger stopped at the door of the room, and displayed his form and face completely. He wore a dark coloured cloth cloak, which was short and full, not falling quite to the knees; his legs were cased in dark purple silk stockings, and his shoes were adorned with roses of the same colour. The opening of the cloak in front showed the undersuit to consist of some very dark, perhaps sable material, and his hands were enclosed in a pair of heavy leather gloves which ran up considerably above the wrist, in the manner of a gauntlet. In one hand he carried his walking-stick and his hat, which he had removed, and the other hung heavily by his side. A quantity of grizzled hair descended in long tresses from his head, and its folds rested upon the plaits of a stiff ruff, which effectually concealed his neck.

So far all was well; but the face! – all the flesh of the face was coloured with the bluish leaden hue which is sometimes produced by the operation of metallic medicines administered in excessive quantities; the eyes were enormous, and the white appeared both above and below the iris, which gave to them an expression of insanity, which was heightened by their glassy redness; the nose was well enough, but the mouth was writhed considerably to one side, where it opened in order to give egress to two long, discoloured fangs, which projected from the upper jaw, far below the lower lip; the hue of the lips themselves bore the usual relation to that of the face, and was consequently nearly black. The character of the face was malignant, even satanic, to the last degree; and, indeed, such a combination of horror could hardly be accounted for, except by supposing the corpse of some atrocious malefactor, which had long hung blackening upon the gibbet, to have at length become the habitation of a demon – the frightful sport of satanic possession.

It was remarkable that the worshipful stranger suffered as little as possible of his flesh to appear, and that during his visit he did not once remove his gloves.

Having stood for some moments at the door, Gerard Douw at length found breath and collectedness to bid him welcome, and, with a mute inclination of the head, the stranger stepped forward into the room.

There was something indescribably odd, even horrible about all his motions, something undefinable, something unnatural, unhuman – it was as if the limbs were guided and directed by a spirit unused to the management of bodily machinery.

The stranger said hardly anything during his visit, which did not exceed half an hour; and the host himself could scarcely muster courage enough to utter the few necessary salutations and courtesies: and, indeed, such was the nervous terror which the presence of Vanderhausen inspired, that very little would have made all his entertainers fly bellowing from the room.

They had not so far lost all self-possession, however, as to fail to observe two strange peculiarities of their visitor.

During his stay he did not once suffer his eyelids to close, nor even to move in the slightest degree; and further, there was death-like stillness in his whole person, owing to the total absence of the heaving motion of the chest caused by the process of respiration.

These two peculiarities, though when told they may appear trifling, produced a very striking and unpleasant effect when seen and observed. Vanderhausen at length relieved the painter of Leyden of his inauspicious presence; and with no small gratification the little party heard the street door close after him.

"Dear uncle," said Rose, "what a frightful man! I would not see him again for the wealth of the States!"

"Tush, foolish girl!" said Douw, whose sensations were anything but comfortable. "A man may be as ugly as the devil, and yet if his heart and actions are good, he is worth all the pretty-faced, perfumed puppies that walk the Mall. Rose, my girl, it is very true he has not thy pretty face, but I know him to be wealthy and liberal; and were he ten times more ugly – "

"Which is inconceivable," observed Rose.

"These two virtues would be sufficient," continued her uncle, "to counterbalance all his deformity; and if not of power sufficient actually to alter the shape of the features, at least of efficacy enough to prevent one thinking them amiss."

"Do you know, uncle," said Rose, "when I saw him standing at the door, I could not get it out of my head that I saw the old, painted, wooden figure that used to frighten me so much in the church of St Lawrence at Rotterdam."

Gerard laughed, though he could not help inwardly acknowledging the justness of the comparison. He was resolved, however, as far as he could, to check his niece's inclination to ridicule the ugliness of her intended bridegroom, although he was not a little pleased to observe that she appeared totally exempt from that mysterious dread of the stranger, which, he could not disguise it from himself, considerably affected him, as it also did his pupil Godfrey Schalken.

Early on the next day there arrived from various quarters of the town, rich presents of silks, velvets, jewellery, and so forth, for Rose; and also a packet directed to Gerard Douw, which, on being opened, was found to contain a contract of marriage, formally drawn up, between Wilken Vanderhausen of the Boom-quay, in Rotterdam, and Rose Velderkaust of Leyden, niece to Gerard Douw, master in the art of painting, also of the same city; and containing engagements on the part of Vanderhausen to make settlements upon his bride far more splendid than he had before led her guardian to believe likely, and which were to be secured to her use in the most unexceptionable manner possible – the money being placed in the hands of Gerard Douw himself.

I have no sentimental scenes to describe, no cruelty of guardians or magnanimity of wards, or agonies of lovers. The record I have to make is one of sordidness, levity, and interest. In less than a week after the first interview which we have just described, the contract of marriage was fulfilled, and Schalken saw the prize which he would have risked anything to secure, carried off triumphantly by his formidable rival.

For two or three days he absented himself from the school; he then returned and worked, if with less cheerfulness, with far more dogged resolution than before; the dream of love had given place to that of ambition.

Months passed away, and, contrary to his expectation, and, indeed, to the direct promise of the parties, Gerard Douw heard nothing of his niece or her worshipful spouse. The interest of the money, which was to have been demanded in quarterly sums, lay unclaimed in his hands. He began to grow extremely uneasy.

Mynher Vanderhausen's direction in Rotterdam he was fully possessed of. After some irresolution he finally determined to journey thither – a trifling undertaking, and easily accomplished – and thus to satisfy himself of the safety and comfort of his ward, for whom he entertained an honest and strong affection.

His search was in vain, however. No one in Rotterdam had ever heard of Mynher Vanderhausen.

Gerard Douw left not a house in the Boom-quay untried; but all in vain. No one could give him any information whatever touching the object of his inquiry; and he was obliged to return to Leyden, nothing wiser than when he had left it.

On his arrival he hastened to the establishment from which Vanderhausen had hired the lumbering, though, considering the times, most luxurious vehicle which the bridal party had employed to convey them to Rotterdam. From the driver of this machine he learned, that having proceeded by slow stages, they had late in the evening approached Rotterdam; but that before they entered the city, and while yet nearly a mile from it, a small party of men, soberly clad, and after the old fashion, with peaked beards and moustaches, standing in the centre of the road, obstructed the further progress of the carriage. The driver reined in his horses, much fearing, from the obscurity of the hour, and the loneliness of the road, that some mischief was intended.

His fears were, however, somewhat allayed by his observing that these strange men carried a large litter, of an antique shape, and which they immediately set down upon the pavement, whereupon the bridegroom, having opened the coach door from within, descended, and having assisted his bride to do likewise, led her, weeping bitterly and wringing her hands, to the litter, which they both entered. It was then raised by the men who surrounded it, and speedily carried towards the city, and before it had proceeded many yards the darkness concealed it from the view of the Dutch chariot.

In the inside of the vehicle he found a purse, whose contents more than thrice paid the hire of the carriage and man. He saw and could tell nothing more of Mynher Vanderhausen and his beautiful lady. This mystery was a source of deep anxiety and almost of grief to Gerard Douw.

There was evidently fraud in the dealing of Vanderhausen with him, though for what purpose committed he could not imagine. He greatly doubted how far it was possible for a man possessing in his countenance so strong an evidence of the presence of the most demoniac feelings to be in reality anything but a villain; and every day that passed without his hearing from or of his niece, instead of inducing him to forget his fears, tended more and more to intensify them.

The loss of his niece's cheerful society tended also to depress his spirits; and in order to dispel this despondency, which often crept upon his mind after his daily employment was over, he was wont frequently to prevail upon Schalken to accompany him home, and by his presence to dispel, in some degree, the gloom of his otherwise solitary supper.

One evening, the painter and his pupil were sitting by the fire, having accomplished a comfortable supper. They had yielded to that silent pensiveness sometimes induced by the process of digestion, when their reflections were disturbed by a loud sound at the street-door, as if occasioned by some person rushing forcibly and repeatedly against it. A domestic had run without delay to ascertain the cause of the disturbance, and they heard him twice or thrice interrogate the applicant for admission, but without producing an answer or any cessation of the sounds.

They heard him then open the hall door, and immediately there followed a light and rapid tread upon the staircase. Schalken laid his hand on his sword, and advanced towards the door. It opened before he reached it, and Rose rushed into the room. She looked wild and haggard, and pale with exhaustion and terror; but her dress surprised them as much even as her unexpected appearance. It consisted of a kind of white woollen wrapper, made close about the neck, and descending to the very ground. It was much deranged and travel-soiled. The poor creature had hardly entered the chamber when she fell senseless on the floor. With some difficulty they succeeded in reviving her, and, on recovering her senses she instantly exclaimed in a tone of eager, terrified impatience –

"Wine, wine, quickly, or I'm lost!"

Much alarmed at the strange agitation in which the call was made, they at once administered to her wishes, and she drank some wine with a haste and eagerness which surprised them. She had hardly swallowed it, when she exclaimed with the same urgency –

"Food, food, at once, or I perish!"

A considerable fragment of a roast joint was upon the table, and Schalken immediately proceeded to cut some, but he was anticipated; for no sooner had she become aware of its presence than she darted at it with the rapacity of a vulture, and, seizing it in her hands, she tore off the flesh with her teeth and swallowed it.

When the paroxysm of hunger had been a little appeased, she appeared suddenly to become aware how strange her conduct had been, or it may have been that other more agitating thoughts recurred to her mind, for she began to weep bitterly, and to wring her hands.

"Oh! Send for a minister of God," said she; "I am not safe till he comes; send for him speedily."

Gerard Douw despatched a messenger instantly, and prevailed on his niece to allow him to surrender his bedchamber to her use; he also persuaded her to retire to it at once and to rest; her consent was extorted upon the condition that they would not leave her for a moment.

"Oh that the holy man were here!" she said; "he can deliver me. The dead and the living can never be one – God has forbidden it."

With these mysterious words she surrendered herself to their guidance, and they proceeded to the chamber which Gerard Douw had assigned to her use.

"Do not – do not leave me for a moment," said she. "I am lost for ever if you do."

Gerard Douw's chamber was approached through a spacious apartment, which they were now about to enter. Gerard Douw and Schalken each carried a wax candle, so that sufficient degree of light was cast upon all surrounding objects. They were now entering the large chamber, which, as I have said, communicated with Douw's apartment, when Rose suddenly stopped, and, in a whisper which seemed to thrill with horror, she said –

"O God! he is here – he is here! See, see – there he goes!"

She pointed towards the door of the inner room, and Schalken thought he saw a shadowy and ill-defined form gliding into that apartment. He drew his sword, and raising the candle so as to throw its light with increased distinctness upon the objects in the room, he entered the chamber into which the figure had glided. No figure was there – nothing but the furniture which belonged to the room, and yet he could not be deceived as to the fact that something had moved before them into the chamber.

A sickening dread came upon him, and the cold perspiration broke out in heavy drops upon his forehead; nor was he more composed when he heard the increased urgency, the agony of entreaty, with which Rose implored them not to leave her for a moment.

"I saw him," said she. "He's here! I cannot be deceived – I know him. He's by me – he's with me – he's in the room. Then, for God's sake, as you would save me, do not stir from beside me!"

They at length prevailed upon her to lie down upon the bed, where she continued to urge them to stay by her. She frequently uttered incoherent sentences, repeating again and again, "The dead and the living cannot be one – God has forbidden it!" and then again, "Rest to the wakeful – sleep to the sleep-walkers."

These and such mysterious and broken sentences she continued to utter until the clergyman arrived.

Gerard Douw began to fear, naturally enough, that the poor girl, owing to terror or ill-treatment, had become deranged; and he half suspected, by the suddenness of her appearance, and the unseasonableness of the hour, and, above all, from the wildness and terror of her manner, that she had made her escape from some place of confinement for lunatics, and was in immediate fear of pursuit. He resolved to summon medical advice as soon as the mind of his niece had been in some measure set at rest by the offices of the clergyman whose attendance she had so earnestly desired; and until this object had been attained, he did not venture to put any questions to her, which might possibly, by reviving painful or horrible recollections, increase her agitation.

The clergyman soon arrived – a man of ascetic countenance – and venerable age – one whom Gerard Douw respected much, forasmuch as he was a veteran polemic, though one, perhaps, more dreaded as a combatant than beloved as a Christian – of pure morality, subtle brain, and frozen heart. He entered the chamber which communicated with that in which Rose reclined, and immediately on his arrival she requested him to pray for her, as for one who lay in the hands of Satan, and who could hope for deliverance only from Heaven.

That our readers may distinctly understand all the circumstances of the event which we were about imperfectly to describe, it is necessary to state the relative positions of the parties who were engaged in it. The old clergyman and Schalken were in the ante-room of which we have already spoken; Rose lay in the inner chamber, the door of which was open; and by the side of the bed, at her urgent desire, stood her guardian; a candle burned in the bedchamber, and three were lighted in the outer apartment.

The old man now cleared his voice, as if about to commence; but before he had time to begin, a sudden gust of air blew out the candle which served to illuminate the room in which the poor girl lay, and she with hurried alarm, exclaimed:

"Godfrey, bring in another candle; the darkness is unsafe."

Gerard Douw, forgetting for the moment her repeated injunctions in the immediate impulse, stepped from the bedchamber into the other, in order to supply what she desired.

"O God! do not go, dear uncle!" shrieked the unhappy girl; and at the same time she sprang from the bed and darted after him, in order, by her grasp, to detain him.

But the warning came too late, for scarcely had he passed the threshold, and hardly had his niece had time to utter the startling exclamation, when the door which divided the two rooms closed violently after him, as if swung to by a strong blast of wind.

Schalken and he both rushed to the door, but their united and desperate efforts could not avail so much as to shake it.

Shriek after shriek burst from the inner chamber, with all the piercing loudness of despairing terror. Schalken and Douw applied every energy and strained every nerve to force open the door; but all in vain.

There was no sound of struggling from within, but the screams seemed to increase in loudness, and at the same time they heard the bolts of the latticed window withdrawn, and the window itself grated upon the sill as if thrown open.

One last shriek, so long and piercing and agonized as to be scarcely human, swelled from the room, and suddenly there followed a death-like silence.

A light step was heard crossing the floor, as if from the bed to the window; and almost at the same instant the door gave way, and yielding to the pressure of the external applicants, they were nearly precipitated into the room. It was empty. The window was open, and Schalken sprang to a chair and gazed out upon the street and at the canal below. He saw no form, but he beheld, or thought he beheld, the waters of the broad canal beneath settling ring after ring in heavy circular ripples, as if a moment before disturbed by the immersion of some large and heavy mass.

No trace of Rose was ever after discovered, nor was anything certain respecting her mysterious wooer detected or even suspected; no clue whereby to trace the intricacies of the labyrinth, and to arrive at a distinct conclusion was to be found. But an incident occurred, which, though it will not be received by our rational readers as at all approaching to evidence upon the matter, nevertheless produced a strong and a lasting impression upon the mind of Schalken.

Many years after the events which we have detailed, Schalken, then remotely situated, received an intimation of his father's death, and of his intended burial upon a fixed day in the church of Rotterdam. It was necessary that a very considerable journey should be performed by the funeral procession, which, as it will readily be believed, was not very numerously attended. Schalken with difficulty arrived in Rotterdam late in the day upon which the funeral was appointed to take place. The procession had not then arrived. Evening closed in, and still it did not appear.

Schalken strolled down to the church – he found it open; notice of the arrival of the funeral had been given, and the vault in which the body was to be laid had been opened. The official who corresponds to our sexton, on seeing a well-dressed gentleman, whose object was to attend the expected funeral, pacing the aisle of the church, hospitably invited him to share with him the comforts of a blazing wood fire, which as was his custom in winter time upon such occasions, he had kindled on the hearth of a chamber which communicated by a flight of steps with the vault below.

In this chamber Schalken and his entertainer seated themselves; and the sexton, after some fruitless attempts to engage his guest in conversation, was obliged to apply himself to his tobacco-pipe and can to solace his solitude.

In spite of his grief and cares, the fatigues of a rapid journey of nearly forty hours gradually overcame the mind and body of Godfrey Schalken, and he sank into a deep sleep, from which he was awakened by someone shaking him gently by the shoulder. He first thought that the old sexton had called him, but he was no longer in the room.

He roused himself, and as soon as he could clearly see what was around him, he perceived a female form, clothed in a kind of light robe of muslin, part of which was so disposed as to act as a veil, and in her hand she carried a lamp. She was moving rather away from him, and towards the flight of steps which conducted towards the vaults.

Schalken felt a vague alarm at the sight of this figure, and at the same time an irresistible impulse to follow its guidance. He followed it towards the vaults, but when it reached the head of the stairs, he paused; the figure paused also, and turning gently round, displayed, by the light of the lamp it carried, the face and features of his first love, Rose Velderkaust. There was nothing horrible, or even sad, in the countenance. On the contrary, it wore the same arch smile which used to enchant the artist long before in his happy days.

A feeling of awe and of interest, too intense to be resisted, prompted him to follow the spectre, if spectre it were. She descended the stairs – he followed; and, turning to the left through a narrow passage she led him, to his infinite surprise, into what appeared to be an old-fashioned Dutch apartment, such as the pictures of Gerard Douw have served to immortalize.

Abundance of costly antique furniture was disposed about the room, and in one corner stood a four-post bed, with heavy black cloth curtains around it. The figure frequently turned towards him with the same arch smile; and when she came to the side of the bed, she drew the curtains, and by the light of the lamp which she held towards its contents, she disclosed to the horror-stricken painter, sitting bolt upright in the bed, the livid and demoniac form of Vanderhausen. Schalken had hardly seen him when he fell senseless upon the floor, where he lay until discovered, on the next morning, by persons employed in closing the passages into the vaults. He was lying in a cell of considerable size, which had not been disturbed for a long time, and he had fallen beside a large coffin which was supported upon small stone pillars, a security against the attacks of vermin.

To his dying day Schalken was satisfied of the reality of the vision which he had witnessed, and he has left behind him a curious evidence of the impression which it wrought upon his fancy, in a painting executed shortly after the event we have narrated, and which is valuable as exhibiting not only the peculiarities which have made Schalken's pictures sought after, but even more so as presenting a portrait, as close and faithful as one taken from memory can be, of his early love, Rose Velderkaust, whose mysterious fate must ever remain a matter of speculation.

The picture represents a chamber of antique masonry, such as might be found in most old cathedrals, and is lighted faintly by a lamp carried in the hand of a female figure, such as we have above attempted to describe; and in the background, and to the left of him who examines the painting, there stands the form of a man apparently aroused from sleep, and by his attitude, his hand being laid upon his sword, exhibiting considerable alarm; this last figure is illuminated only by the expiring glare of a wood or charcoal fire.

The whole production exhibits a beautiful specimen of that artful and singular distribution of light and shade which has rendered the name of Schalken immortal among the artists of his country. This tale is traditionary, and the reader will easily perceive, by our studiously omitting to heighten many points of the narrative, when a little additional colouring might have added effect to the recital, that we have desired to lay before him, not a figment of the brain, but a curious tradition connected with, and belonging to, the biography of a famous artist.

Dinah Maria Mulock

M. Anastasius

Dinah Maria Mulock (1826–87) is best remembered for her novel John Halifax – Gentleman *(1856), an immediate success both in Britain and America. She was a prolific writer of novels, fairy tales, essays, poems and short stories. She became Mrs Craik in 1864, the same year that she was awarded a Civil List Pension – which she put aside for authors less fortunate and successful than herself.*

This tale is taken from her collection Nothing New *(1857).*

I

I WILL RELATE to you, my friend, the whole history, from the beginning to – nearly – the end.

The first time that – *that it happened*, was on this wise.

My husband and myself were sitting in a private box at the theatre – one of the two large London theatres. The performance was, I remember well, an Easter piece in which were introduced live dromedaries and an elephant, at whose clumsy feats we were considerably amused. I mention this to show how calm and even gay was the state of both our minds that evening, and how little there was in any of the circumstances of the place or time to cause, or render us liable to – what I am about to describe.

I liked this Easter piece better than any serious drama. My life had contained enough of the tragic element to make me turn with a sick distaste from all imitations thereof in books or plays. For months, ever since our marriage, Alexis and I had striven to lead a purely childish,

commonplace existence, eschewing all stirring events and strong
emotions, mixing little in society, and then, with one exception, making
no associations beyond the moment.

It was easy to do this in London; for we had no relations – we two were
quite alone and free. Free – free! How wildly I sometimes grasped Alexis'
hand as I repeated that word.

He was young – so was I. At times, as on this night, we would sit
together and laugh like children. It was so glorious to know of a surety
that now we could think, feel, speak, act – above all, love one another –
haunted by no counteracting spell, responsible to no living creature for
our life and our love.

But this had been our lot only for a year – I had recollected the date,
shuddering, in the morning – for one year, from this same day.

We had been laughing very heartily, cherishing mirth, as it were, like
those who would caress a lovely bird that had been frightened out of its
natural home and grown wild and rare in its visits, only tapping at the
lattice for a minute, and then gone. Suddenly, in the pause between the
acts, when the house was half-darkened, our laughter died away.

"How cold it is," said Alexis, shivering. I shivered too; but not with
cold, it was more like the involuntary sensation at which people say,
"Someone is walking over my grave." I said so, jestingly.

"Hush, Isbel," whispered my husband, and again the draught of cold
air seemed to blow right between us.

I should describe the position in which we were sitting, both in front of
the box, but he in full view of the audience, while I was half hidden by the
curtain. Between us, where the cold draught blew, was a vacant chair.
Alexis tried to move this chair, but it was fixed to the floor. He passed
behind it, and wrapped a mantle over my shoulders.

"This London winter is cold for you, my love. I half wish we had taken
courage, and sailed once more for Hispaniola."

"Oh, no – oh, no! No more of the sea!" said I, with another and
stronger shudder.

He took his former position, looking round indifferently at the audience. But neither of us spoke. The mere word "Hispaniola" was enough
to throw a damp and a silence over us both.

"Isbel," he said at last, rousing himself, with a half-smile, "I think you
must have grown remarkably attractive. Look! half the glasses opposite
are lifted to our box. It cannot be to gaze at me, you know. Do you
remember telling me I was the ugliest fellow you ever saw?"

"Oh, Alex!" Yet it was quite true – I had thought him so, in far back, strange, awful times, when I, a girl of sixteen, had my mind wholly filled with one idea! – one insane, exquisite dream; when I brought my innocent child's garlands, and sat me down under one spreading magnificent tree, which seemed to me the king of all the trees of the field, until I felt its dews dropping death upon my youth, and my whole soul withering under its venomous shade.

"Oh, Alex!" I cried once more, looking fondly on his beloved face, where no unearthly beauty dazzled, no unnatural calm repelled; where all was simple, noble, manly, true. "Husband, I thank heaven for that dear 'ugliness' of yours. Above all, though blood runs strong, they say, I thank heaven that I see in you no likeness to – "

Alexis knew what name I meant, though for a whole year past – since God's mercy made it to us only a name – we had ceased to utter it, and let it die wholly out of the visible world. We dared not breathe to ourselves, still less to one another, how much brighter, holier, happier, that world was, now that the Divine wisdom had taken – *him* – into another. For he had been my husband's uncle, likewise, once my guardian. He was now dead.

I sat looking at Alexis, thinking what a strange thing it was that his dear face should not have always been as beautiful to me as it was now. That loving my husband now so deeply, so wholly, clinging to him heart to heart in the deep peace of satisfied, all-trusting, and all-dependent human affection, I could ever have felt that emotion, first as an exquisite bliss, then as an ineffable terror, which now had vanished away, and become – nothing.

"They are gazing still, Isbel."

"Who, and where?" For I had quite forgotten what he said about the people staring at me.

"And there is Colonel Hart. He sees us. Shall I beckon him?"

"As you will."

Colonel Hart came up into our box. He shook hands with my husband, bowed to me, then looked round, half-curiously, half-uneasily.

"I thought there was a friend with you."

"None. We have been alone all evening."

"Indeed? How strange!"

"What! That my wife and I should enjoy a play alone together?" said Alexis, smiling.

"Excuse me, but really I was surprised to find you alone. I have certainly seen for the last half-hour a third person sitting on this chair, between you both."

We could not help starting; for, as I stated before, the chair had in truth been left between us, empty.

"Truly our unknown friend must have been invisible. Nonsense, Colonel; how can you turn Mrs Saltram pale, by thus peopling with your fancies the vacant air?"

"I tell you, Alexis," said the Colonel (he was my husband's old friend, and had been present at our hasty and private marriage), "nothing could be more unlike a fancy, even were I given to such. It was a very remarkable person who sat here. Even strangers noticed him."

"Him!" I whispered.

"It was a man, then," said my husband, rather angrily.

"A very peculiar-looking and extremely handsome man. I saw many glasses levelled at him."

"What was he like?" said Alexis, rather sarcastically. "Did he speak? or we to him?"

"No – neither. He sat quite still, in this chair."

My husband turned away. If the Colonel had not been his friend, and so very simple-minded, honest, and sober a gentleman, I think Alexis would have suspected some drunken hoax, and turned him out of the box immediately. As it was, he only said:

"My dear fellow, the third act is beginning. Come up again at its close, and tell me if you again see my invisible friend, who must find so great an attraction in viewing, gratis, a dramatic performance."

"I perceive – you think it a mere hallucination of mine. We shall see. I suspect the trick is on your side, and that you are harbouring some proscribed Hungarian. But I'll not betray him. Adieu."

"The ghostly Hungarian shall not sit next you, love, this time," said Alexis, trying once more to remove the chair. But possibly, though he jested, he was slightly nervous, and his efforts were vain. "What nonsense this is! Isbel, let us forget it. I will stand behind you, and watch the play."

He stood – I clasping his hand secretly and hard; then I grew quieter; until, as the drop-scene fell, the same cold air swept past us. It was as if someone fresh from the sharp sea-wind had entered the box. And just at that moment we saw Colonel Hart's and several other glasses levelled as before.

"It is strange," said Alexis.

"It is horrible," I said. For I had been cradled in Scottish, and then

filled with German superstition; besides the events of my own life had
been so wild, so strange, that there was nothing too ghastly or terrible for
my imagination to conjure up.

"I will summon the Colonel. We must find out this," said my husband,
speaking beneath his breath, and looking round, as if he thought he was
overheard.

Colonel Hart came up. He looked very serious; so did a young man
who was with him.

"Captain Elmore, let me introduce you to Mrs Saltram. Saltram, I
have brought my friend here to attest that I have played off on you no
unworthy jest. Not ten minutes since, he, and I, and some others saw the
same gentleman whom I described to you half an hour ago, sitting as I
described – in this chair."

"Most certainly – in this chair," added the young captain.

My husband bowed; he kept a courteous calmness, but I felt his hand
grow clammy in mine.

"Of what appearance, sir, was this unknown acquaintance of my
wife's and mine, whom everybody appears to see, except ourselves?"

"He was of middle-age, dark-haired, pale. His features were very still,
and rather hard in expression. He had on a cloth cloak with a fur collar,
and wore a long, pointed Charles-the-First Beard."

My husband and I clung hand to hand with an inexpressible horror.
Could there be another man – a living man, who answered this description?

"Pardon me," Alexis said faintly. "The portrait is rather vague; may I
ask you to repaint it as circumstantially as you can."

"He was, I repeat, a pale, or rather a sallow-featured man. His eyes
were extremely piercing, cold, and clear. The mouth close-set – a very
firm but passionless mouth. The hair dark, seamed with gray – bald on
the brow – "

"O heaven!" I groaned in an anguish of terror. For I saw again – clear
as if he had never died – the face over which, for twelve long months, had
swept the merciful sea-waves, off the shores of Hispaniola.

"Can you, Captain Elmore," said Alexis, "mention no other distinguishing mark? This countenance might resemble many men."

"I think not. It was a most remarkable face. It struck me the more –
because – " and the young man grew almost as pale as we – "I once saw
another very like it."

"You see – a chance resemblance only. Fear not, my darling," Alexis breathed in my ear. "Sir, have you any reluctance to tell me who was the gentleman?"

"It was no living man, but a corpse that we last year picked up off a wreck, and again committed to the deep – in the Gulf of Mexico. It was exactly the same face, and had the same mark – a scar, cross-shape, over one temple."

" 'Tis he! He can follow and torture us still; I knew he could!"

Alexis smothered my shriek on his breast.

"My wife is ill. This description resembles slightly a – a person we once knew. Hart, will you leave us? But no, we must probe this mystery. Gentlemen, will you once more descend to the lower part of the house, whilst we remain here, and tell me if you still see the – the figure, sitting in this chair."

They went. We held our breaths. The lights in the theatre were being extinguished, the audience moving away. No one came near our box; it was perfectly empty. Except our two selves, we were conscious of no sight, no sound. A few minutes after Colonel Hart knocked.

"Come in," said Alexis, cheerily.

But the Colonel – the bold soldier – shrunk back like a frightened child.

"I have seen him – I saw him but this minute, sitting there."

I swooned away.

II

It is right I should briefly give you my history up to this night's date.

I was a West Indian heiress – a posthumous, and, soon after birth, an orphan child. Brought up in my mother's country, until I was sixteen years old, I never saw my guardian. Then he met me in Paris, with my governess, and for the space of two years we lived under the same roof, seeing one another daily.

I was very young; I had no father or brother; I wished for neither lover nor husband; my guardian became to me the one object of my existence.

It was no love-passion; he was far too old for that, and I comparatively too young, at least too childish. It was one of those insane, rapturous adorations which young maidens sometimes conceive, mingling a little of the tenderness of the woman with the ecstatic enthusiasm of the devotee. There is hardly a prophet or leader noted in the world's history who has not been followed and worshipped by many such women.

So was my guardian, M. Anastasius – not his true name, but it sufficed then, and will now.

Many may recognize him as a known leader in the French political and moral world – as one who, by the mere force of intellect, wielded the most irresistible and silently complete power of any man I ever knew, in every circle into which he came; women he won by his polished gentleness – men by his equally polished strength. He would have turned a compliment and signed a death-warrant, with the same exquisitely calm grace. Nothing was to him too great or too small. I have known him, on his way to advise that the President's soldiers should sweep a cannonade down the thronged street – stop to pick up a strayed canary-bird, stroke its broken wing, and confide it with beautiful tenderness to his bosom.

Oh how tender! – how mild! – How pitiful he could be!

When I say I loved him, I use, for want of a better, a word which ill expresses that feeling. It was – Heaven forgive me if I err in using the similitude – the sort of feeling the Shunamite woman might have had for Elisha. Religion added to its intensity; for I was brought up a devout Catholic; and he, whatever his private opinions might have been, adhered strictly to the forms of the same Church. He was unmarried, and most people supposed him to belong to that Order called – though often, alas! how unlike Him from whom they assume their name – the Society of Jesus.

We lived thus – I entirely worshipping, he guiding, fondling, watching, and ruling by turns, for two whole years. I was mistress of a large fortune, and, though not beautiful, had, I believe, a tolerable intellect and a keen wit. With both he used to play, according as it suited his whim – just as a boy plays with fireworks, amusing himself with their glitter – sometimes directing them against others, and smiling as they flashed or scorched – knowing that against himself they were utterly powerless and harmless. Knowing, too, perhaps, that were it otherwise, he had only to tread them out under foot, and step aside from the ashes, with the same unmoved, easy smile.

I never knew – nor know I to this day, whether I was in the smallest degree dear to him. Useful I was, I think, and pleasant, I believe. Possibly he liked me a little, as the potter likes his clay, and the skilful mechanician his tools – until the clay hardened, and the fine tools refused to obey the master's hand.

I was the brilliant West Indian heiress. I did not marry. Why should I? At my house – at least it was called mine – all sorts and societies met, carrying on their separate games; the quiet, soft hand of M. Anastasius playing his game – in, and under, and through them all. Mingled with this grand game of the world was a lesser one – to which he turned sometimes, just for amusement, or because he could not cease from his *métier* – a simple, easy, domestic game, of which the battledore was the same ingenious hand, and the shuttlecock my foolish child's heart.

Thus much have I dilated on him, and on my own life, during the years when all its strong wild current flowed towards him; that, in what followed when the tide turned, no one may accuse me of fickleness, or causeless aversion, or insane terror of one who after all was only man, "whose breath is in his nostrils."

At seventeen I was wholly passive in his hands; he was my sole arbiter of right and wrong – my conscience – almost my God. As my character matured, and in a few things I began to judge for myself, we had occasional slight differences – begun, on my part, in shy humility, continued with vague doubt, but always ending in penitence and tears. Since one or other erred, of course it must be I. These differences were wholly on abstract points of truth or justice.

It was his taking me by a persuasion that was like compulsion, to the ball at the Tuileries, which was given after Louis Napoleon Bonaparte had seized the Orleans property, and it was my watching my cousin's conduct there, his diplomatic caution of speech; his smooth smiling reverence to men whom I knew, and fancied he knew, to be either knaves or fools – that first startled me concerning him. Then it was I first began to question, in a trembling, terrified way – like one who catches a glimpse of the miracle-making priest's hands behind the robe of the worshipped idol – whether, great as M. Anastasius was, as a political ruler, as a man of the world, as a faithful member of the Society of Jesus, he was altogether so great when viewed beside any one of those whose doctrines he disseminated, whose faith he professed.

He had allowed me the New Testament, and I had been reading it a good deal lately. I placed him, my spiritual guide, at first in adoring veneration, afterwards with an uneasy comparison, beside the Twelve Fishermen of Galilee – beside the pattern of perfect manhood, as exemplified in their Divine Lord – and ours.

There was a difference.

The next time we came to any argument – always on abstract questions – for my mere individual will never have any scruple in resigning itself to his – instead of yielding I ceased open contest, and brought the matter afterwards privately to the One infallible Rule of right and wrong.

The difference grew.

Gradually, I began to take my cousin's wisdom – perhaps, even his virtues – with certain reservations, feeling that there was growing in me some antagonistic quality which prevented my full understanding or sympathising with the idiosyncrasies of his character.

"But," I thought, "he is a Jesuit; he only follows the law of his Order, which allows temporising, and diplomatising, for noble ends. He merely dresses up the Truth, and puts it in the most charming and safest light, even as we do our images of the Holy Virgin, adorning them for the adoration of the crowd, but ourselves spiritually worshipping them still. I do believe, much as he will dandle and play with the truth, that, not for his hope of heaven, would Anastasius stoop to a lie."

One day, he told me he should bring to my salons an Englishman, his relative, who had determined on leaving the world and entering the priesthood.

"Is he of our faith?" asked I indifferently.

"He is, from childhood. He has a strong, fine intellect; this, under fit guidance, may accomplish great things. Once of our Society, he might be my right hand in every Court in Europe. You will receive him?"

"Certainly."

But I paid very little heed to the stranger. There was nothing about him striking or peculiar. He was the very opposite of M. Anastasius. Besides, he was young, and I had learnt to despise youth – my guardian was fifty years old.

Mr Saltram (you will already have guessed it was he) showed equal indifference to me. He watched me, sometimes did little kindnesses for me, but always was quiet and silent – a mere cloud floating in the brilliant sky, which M. Anastasius lit up as its gorgeous sun. For me, I became moonlike, appearing chiefly at my cousin's set and rise.

I was not happy. I read more in my Bible and less in my breviary; I watched with keener, harder eyes my cousin Anastasius, weighed all his deeds, listened to and compared his words. My intellect worshipped him, my memoried tenderness clung round him still, but my conscience had fled out of his keeping, and made for itself a higher and purer ideal.

Measured with common men, he was godlike yet – above all passions, weaknesses, crimes; but viewed by the one perfect standard of man – Christian man – in charity, humility, single-mindedness, guilelessness, truth – my idol was no more. I came to look for it, and found only the empty shrine.

He went on a brief mission to Rome. I marvelled that instead as of yore wandering sadly through the empty house from the moment he quitted it, I breathed freer, as if a weight were taken out of the air. His absence used to be like wearisome ages – now it seemed hardly a week before he came back.

I happened to be sitting with his nephew Alexis when I heard his step down the corridor – the step which had once seemed at every touch to draw music from the chords of my prostrate heart, but which now made it shrink into itself, as if an iron-shod footfall had passed along its strings.

Anastasius looked slightly surprised at seeing Alexis and myself together, but his welcome was very kind to us both.

I could not altogether return it. I had just found out two things which, to say the least, had startled me. I determined to prove them at once.

"My cousin, I thought you were aware that, though a Catholic myself, my house is open, and my friendship likewise, to honest men of every creed. Why did you give your nephew so hard an impression of me, as to suppose I would dislike him on account of his faith? And why did you not tell me that Mr Saltram has for some years been a Protestant?"

I know not what reply he made; I know only that it was ingenious, lengthy, gentle, courteous – that for the time being it seemed entirely satisfactory, that we spent all three together a most pleasant evening. It was only when I lay down on my bed, face to face with the solemn Dark, in which dwelt conscience, truth, and God, that I discovered how Anastasius had, for some secret – doubtless blameless, nay even justifiable purpose, told of me, and to me, two absolute Lies!

Disguise it as he might, excuse it as I might, and did, they were Lies. They haunted me – flapping their black wings like a couple of fiends, mopping and mowing behind him when he came – sitting on his shoulders, and mocking his beautiful, calm, majestic face – for days. That was the beginning of my sorrows; gradually they grew until they blackened my whole world.

M. Anastasius was bent, as he had (for once truly) told me, on winning his young nephew back into the true fold, making him an instrument of that great purpose which was to bring all Europe, the Popedom itself,

under the power of the Society of Jesus. Not this alone – a man may be
forgiven, nay, respected, who sells his soul for an abstract cause in which
he himself is to be absorbed and forgotten – but in this case it was not –
though I long, believed it – it was not so. Carefully as he disguised it, I
slowly found out that the centre of all things – the one grand pivot upon
which this vast machinery for the improvement, or rather government,
of the world, was to be made to turn, was M. Anastasius.

Alexis Saltram might be of use to him. He was rich, and money is
power; an Englishman, and Englishmen are usually honourable and
honoured. Also there was in him a dogged directness of purpose that
would make him a strong, if carefully guided, tool.

However, the young man resisted. He admired and revered his
kinsman; but he himself was very single-hearted, staunch, and true.
Something in that Truth, which was the basis of his character, struck
sympathy with mine. He was far inferior in most things to Anastasius –
he knew it, I knew it, but through all, this divine element of Truth was
patent, beautifully clear. It was the one quality I had ever worshipped,
ever sought for, and never found.

Alexis and I became friends – equal, earnest friends. Not in the way of
wooing or marriage – at least, he never spoke of either; and both were
far, oh how far! from my thought – but there was a great and tender
bond between us, which strengthened day by day.

The link which riveted it was religion. He was as I said, a Protestant,
not adhering to any creed, but simply living – not preaching, but living –
the faith of our Saviour. He was not perfect – he had his sins and short-
comings even as I. We both struggled on towards the glimmering light.
So, after a season, we clasped hands in friendship, and with eyes stead-
fastly upward, determined to press on together towards the one goal, and
along the self-same road.

I put my breviary aside, and took wholly to the New Testament,
assuming no name either of Catholic or Protestant, but simply that of
Christian.

When I decided on this, of course I told Anastasius. He had ceased to
be my spiritual confessor for some time; yet I could see he was
surprised.

"Who has done this?" was all he said.

Was I a reed, then, to be blown about with every wind? Or a toy, to be
shifted from hand to hand, and set in motion just as my chance-master
chose? Had I no will, no conscience of my own?

He knew where he could sting me – and did it – but I let the words pass.

"Cousin, when you ask, 'Who did it?' I answer, Desdemona-like, 'Nobody': I myself. In my change of faith I have had no book but this – which you gave me; no priest, except the inward witness of my own soul."

"And Alexis Saltram."

Not said in any wrath, or suspicion, or inquiry – simply as the passive statement of a fact. When I denied it, he accepted my denial; when I protested, he suffered me to protest. My passionate arguments he took in his soft passionless hold – melted and moulded them – turned and twisted them – then reproduced them to me so different that I failed to recognize either my own meaning or even my own words.

After that, on both sides the only resource was silence.

III

"I wish," said I to my guardian one day, "as I shall be twenty-one next year, to have more freedom. I wish even" – for since the discovery of my change of faith he had watched me so closely, so quietly, so continually, that I had conceived a vague fear of him, and a longing to get away – to put half the earth between me and his presence – "I wish even if possible this summer, to visit my estates in Hispaniola?"

"Alone?"

"No; Madam Gradelle will accompany me. And Mr Saltram will charter one of his ships for my use."

"I approve the plan. Alexis is going too, I believe?"

How could he have known that which Alexis had never told me? But he knew everything. "Madame Gradelle is not sufficient escort. I, as your guardian, will accompany and protect you."

A cold dread seized me. Was I never to be free? Already I began to feel my guardian's influence surrounding me – an influence once of love, now of intolerable distaste, and even fear. Not that he was ever harsh or cruel – not that I could accuse him of any single wrong towards me or others: but I knew I had thwarted him, and, through him, his cause – that cause whose strongest dogma is, that any means are sacred; any evil consecrated to good, if furthering the one great end – Power.

I had opposed him, and I was in his hand – that hand which I had once believed to have almost superhuman strength. In my terror I half believed so still.

"He will go with us – we cannot escape from him," I said to Alexis. "He will make you a priest and me a nun, as he once planned – I know he did. Our very souls are not our own."

"What, when the world is so wide, and life so long, and God's kindness over all – when, too, I am free, and you will be free in a year – when" –

"I shall never be free. He is my evil genius. He will haunt me till my death."

It was a morbid feeling I had, consequent on the awful struggle which had so shaken body and mind. The very sound of his step made me turn sick and tremble; the very sight of his grand face – perhaps the most beautiful I ever saw, with its faultless features, and the half-melancholy cast given by the high bald forehead and the pointed beard – was to me more terrible than any monster of ugliness the world every produced.

He held my fortune – he governed my house. All visitors there came and went under his control, except Alexis. Why this young man still came – or how – I could not tell. Probably because in his pure singleness of heart and purpose, he was stronger even than M. Anastasius.

The time passed. We embarked on board the ship *Argo*, for Hispaniola.

My guardian told me, at the last minute, that business relating to his Order would probably detain him in Europe – that we were to lie at anchor for twelve hours, off Havre – and, if he then came not, sail.

He came not – we sailed.

It was a glorious evening. The sun, as he went down over the burning sea, beckoned us with a finger of golden fire, westward – to the free, safe, happy West.

I say us, because on that evening we first began unconsciously to say it too – as if vaguely binding our fates together – Alexis and I. We talked for a whole hour – till long after France, with all our old life therein, had become a mere line, a cloudy speck on the horizon – of the new life we should lead in Hispaniola. Yet all the while, if we had been truly as the priest and nun Anastasius wished to make us, our words, and I believe our thoughts, could not have been more angel-pure, more free from any bias of human passion.

Yet, as the sun went down, and the sea breeze made us draw nearer together, both began, I repeat, instinctively to say "we", and talk of our future as if it had been the future of one.

"Good evening, friends!"

He was there – M. Anastasius!

I stood petrified. That golden finger of hope had vanished. I shuddered, a captive on his courteously compelling arm – seeing nothing but his terrible smiling face and the black wilderness of sea. For the moment I felt inclined to plunge therein – as I had often longed to plunge penniless into the equally fearsome wilderness of Paris – only I felt sure he would follow me still. He would track me, it seemed, through the whole world.

"You see I have been able to accomplish the voyage; men mostly can achieve any fixed purpose – at least some men. Isbel, this sea-air will bring back your bloom. And, Alexis, my friend, despite those close studies you told me of, I hope you will bestow a little of your society at times on my ward and me. We will bid you a good evening now."

He transferred to his nephew my powerless hand; that of Alexis, too, felt cold and trembling. It seemed as if he likewise were succumbing to the fate which, born out of one man's indomitable will, dragged us asunder. Ere my guardian consigned me to Madame Gradelle, he said, smiling, but looking me through and through.

"Remember, my fair cousin, that Alexis is to be – must be – a priest."

"It is impossible!" said I, stung to resistance. "You know he has altogether seceded from the Catholic creed; he will never return to it. His conscience is his own."

"But not his passions. He is young – I am old. He will be a priest yet."

With a soft hand-pressure, M. Anastasius left me.

Now began the most horrible phase of my existence. For four weeks we had to live in the same vessel; bounded and shut up together, – Anastasius, Alexis, and I; meeting continually, in the soft bland atmosphere of courteous calm; always in public – never alone.

From various accidental circumstances, I discovered how M. Anastasius was now bending all the powers of his enormous intellect, his wonderful moral influence, to compass his cherished ends with regard to Alexis Saltram.

An overwhelming dread took possession of me. I ceased to think of myself at all – my worldly hopes, prospects, or joys – over which this man's influence had long hung like an accursed shadow; a sun turned

into darkness – the more terrible because it had once been a sun. I
seemed to see M. Anastasius only with relation to this young man, over
whom I knew he once had so great power. Would it return – and in what
would it result? Not merely in the breaking off any feeble tie to me. I
scarcely trembled for that, since, could it be so broken, it was not worth
trembling for. No! I trembled for Alexis' soul.

It was a soul, I had gradually learnt – more than ever perhaps in this
voyage, of which every day seemed a life, full of temptation, contest, trial
– a soul pure as God's own heaven, that hung over us hour by hour in its
steady tropic blue; and deep as the seas that rolled everlastingly around
us. Like then, stirring with the lightest breath, often tempest-tossed, liable
to adverse winds and currents; yet keeping far, far below the surface a
divine tranquillity – diviner than any mere stagnant calm. And this soul,
full of all rich impulses, emotions, passions, – a soul which, because it
could strongly sympathise with, might be able to regenerate its kind, M.
Anastasius wanted to make into a Catholic Jesuit priest – a mere
machine, to work as he, the head machine, chose!

This was why (the thought suddenly struck me, like lightning) he had
told each of us severally, concerning one another, those two lies. Because
we were young; we might love – we might marry; there was nothing
externally to prevent us. And then what would become of his scheme?

I think there was born in me – while the most passive slave to lawful,
loving rule – a faculty of savage resistance to all unlawful and unjust
power. Also, a something of the female wild-beast, which, if alone, will lie
tame and coward in her solitary den, to be shot at by any daring hunter;
whereas if she be not alone – if she have any love-instinct at work for cubs
or mate – her whole nature changes from terror to daring, from
cowardice to fury.

When, as we neared the tropics, I saw Alexis' cheek growing daily
paler, and his eye more sunken and restless with some secret struggle, in
the which M. Anastasius never left him for a day, an hour, a minute, I
became not unlike that poor wild-beast mother. It had gone ill with the
relentless hunter of souls if he had come near me then.

But he did not. For the last week of our voyage M. Anastasius kept
altogether out of my way.

It was nearly over – we were in sight of the shores of Hispaniola. Then
we should land. My estates lay in this island. Mr Saltram's business, I was
aware, called him to Barbados; thence again beyond seas. Once parted, I
well knew that if the power and will of my guardian could compass

anything, and it seemed to me that they were able to compass everything in the whole wide earth – Alexis and I should never meet again.

In one last struggle after life – after the fresh, wholesome, natural life which contact with this young man's true spirit had given me – I determined to risk all.

It was a rich tropic twilight. We were all admiring it, just as three ordinary persons might do who were tending peacefully to their voyage-end.

Yet Alexis did not seem at peace. A settled, deadly pallor dwelt on his face – a restless anxiety troubled his whole mien.

M. Anastasius said, noticing the glowing tropic scenery which already dimly appeared in our shoreward view,

"It is very grand: but Europe is more suited to us grave Northerns. You will think so, Alexis, when you are once again there."

"Are you returning?" I asked of Mr Saltram.

My cousin answered for him, "Yes, immediately."

Alexis started; then leaned over the poop in silence, and without denial.

I felt profoundly sad. My interest in Alexis Saltram was at this time – and but for the compulsion of opposing power, might have ever been – entirely apart from love. We might have gone on merely as tender friends for years and years – at least I might. Therefore no maidenly consciousness warned me from doing what my sense of right impelled, towards one who held the same faith as I did, and whose life seemed strangled in the same mesh of circumstances which had nearly paralysed my own.

"Alexis, this is our last evening; you will sail for Europe – and we shall be friends no more. Will you take one twilight stroll with me?" – and I extended my hand.

If he had hesitated, or shrunk back from me, I would have flung him to the winds, and fought my own battle alone; I was strong enough now. But he sprang to me, clung to my hand, looked wildly in my face, as if there were the sole light of truth and trust left in the world; and as if even there, he had begun – or been taught – to doubt. He did not, now.

"Isbel, tell me! You still hold our faith – you are not going to become a nun?"

"Never! I will offer myself to Heaven as Heaven gave me to myself – free, bound by no creed, subservient to no priest. What is he, but a man that shall die, whom the worms shall cover?"

I said the words out loud. I meant M. Anastasius to hear. But he

looked as if he heard not; only when we turned up the deck, he slowly
followed.

I stood at bay. "Cousin, leave me. I wish to speak to Mr Saltram.
Cannot I have any friend but you?"

"None, whom I believe you would harm and receive harm from."

"Dare you – "

"I myself dare nothing; but there is nothing which my church does
not dare. Converse, my children. I hinder you not. The deck is free for
all."

He bowed, and let us pass, then followed. Every sound of that slow,
smooth step seemed to strike on my heart like the tracking tread of doom.

Alexis and I said little or nothing. A leaden despair seemed to bind us
closely round, allowing only one consciousness, that for a little, little
time, it bound us together! He held my arm so fast that I felt every
throbbing of his heart. My sole thought was how to say some words that
should be fixed eternally there, so that nothing might make him swerve
from his Christian faith. That faith, which was my chief warranty of
meeting him – never, or never in this world! but in the world
everlasting.

Once or twice in turning we came face to face with M. Anastasius. He
was walking at his usual slow pace, his hands loosely clasped behind him
– his head bent; a steely repose, even pensiveness, which was his natural
look – settled in his grave eyes. He was a man of intellect too great to
despise, of character too spotless to loathe. The one sole feeling he
inspired was that of unconquerable fear. Because you saw at once that *he*
feared nothing either in earth or heaven, that he owed but one influence,
and was amenable but to one law, which he called "the Church", but
which was, himself.

Men like M. Anastasius, one-idea'd, all-engrossed men, are according
to slight variations in their temperaments, the salvation, the laughing-
stock, or the terror of the world.

He appeared in the latter form to Alexis and me. Slowly, surely came
the conviction, that there was no peace for us on this earth while he stood
on it; so strong, so powerful, that at times I almost yielded to a vague
belief in his immortality. On this night, especially, I was stricken with a
horrible – curiosity, I think it was – to see whether he *could* die, whether
the grave could open her mouth to swallow him, and death have power
upon his flesh, like that of other men.

More than once, as he passed under a huge beam, I thought – should it fall? as he leaned against the ship's side – should it give way? But only, I declare solemnly, out of a frenzied speculative curiosity, which I would not for worlds have breathed to a human soul! I never once breathed it to Alexis Saltram, who was his sister's son, and whom he had been kind to as a child.

Night darkened, and our walk ceased. We had said nothing – nothing; except that on parting, with a kind of desperation Alexis buried my hand tightly in his bosom, and whispered, "Tomorrow?"

That midnight a sudden hurricane came on. In half an hour all that was left of the good ship *Argo* was a little boat, filled almost to sinking with half-drowned passengers, and a few sailors clinging to spars and fragments of the wreck.

Alexis was lashed to a mast, holding me partly fastened to it, and partly sustained in his arms. How he had found and rescued me I know not; but love is very strong. It has been sweet to me afterwards to think that I owed my life to him – and him alone. I was the only woman saved.

He was at the extreme end of the mast; we rested, face to face, my head against his shoulder. All along to its slender point, the sailors were clinging to the spar like flies; but we two did not see anything in the world, save one another.

Life was dim, death was near, yet I think we were not unhappy. Our heaven was clear, for between us and Him to whom we were going came no threatening image, holding in its remorseless hand life, faith, love. Death itself was less terrible than M. Anastasius.

We had seen him among the saved passengers swaying in the boat; then we thought of him no more. We clung together with closed eyes, satisfied to die.

"No room – off there! No room!" I heard shouted, loud and savage, by the sailor lashed behind me.

I opened my eyes. Alexis was gazing on me only. I gazed, transfixed, over his shoulder, into the breakers beyond.

There, in the trough of a wave, I saw, clear as I see my own right hand now, the up-turned face of Anastasius, and his two white stretched-out hands, on one finger of which was his well-known diamond ring – for it flashed that minute in the moon.

"Off!" yelled the sailor, striking at him with an oar. "One man's life's as good as another's. Off!"

The drowning face rose above the wave, the eyes fixed themselves full on me, without any entreaty in them, or wrath, or terror – the long-familiar, passionless, relentless eyes.

I see them now; I shall see them till I die. Oh, would I had died!

For one brief second I thought of tearing off the lashings and giving him my place; for I had loved him. But youth and life were strong within me, and my head was pressed to Alexis' breast.

A full minute, or it seemed so, was that face above the water; then I watched it sink slowly, down, down.

IV

We, and several others, were picked up from the wreck of the *Argo* by a homeward-bound ship. As soon as we reached London I became Alexis' wife.

That which happened at the theatre was exactly twelve months after – as we believed – Anastasius died.

I do not pretend to explain, I doubt if any reasoning can explain, a circumstance so singular – so impossible to be attributed to either imagination or illusion. For, as I must again distinctly state, we ourselves saw nothing. The apparition, or whatever it was, was visible only to other persons, all total strangers.

I had a fever. When I arose from it, and things took their natural forms and relations, this strange occurrence became mingled with the rest of my delirium, of which my husband persuaded me it was a part. He took me abroad – to Italy – Germany. He loved me dearly! He was, and he made me, entirely happy.

In our happiness we strove to live, not merely for one another, but for all the world; all who suffered and had need. We did – nor shrunk from the doing – many charities which had first been planned by Anastasius, with what motives we never knew. While carrying them out, we learnt to utter his name without trembling; remembering only that which was beautiful in him and his character, and which we had both so worshipped once.

In the furtherance of these schemes of good, it became advisable that we should go to Paris, to my former hotel, which still remained empty there.

"But not, dear wife, if any uneasiness or lingering pain rests in your mind in seeing the old spot. For me, I love it! since there I loved Isbel, before Isbel knew it, long."

So I smiled; and went to Paris.

My husband proposed, and I was not sorry, that Colonel Hart and his newly-married wife should join us there, and remain as our guests. I shrunk a little from re-inhabiting the familiar rooms, long shut up from the light of day; and it was with comfort I heard my husband arranging that a portion of the hotel should be made ready for us, namely, two salons *en suite*; leading out of the farther one of which, were a chamber and dressing-room for our own use – opposite two similar apartments for the Colonel and his lady.

I am thus minute for reasons that will appear.

Mrs Hart had been travelling with us some weeks. She was a mild sweet-faced English girl, who did not much like the Continent, and was half shocked at some of my reckless foreign ways, on board steamboats and on railways. She said I was a little – just a little – too free. It might have seemed so to her; for my southern blood rushed bright and warm, and my manner of life in France had completely obliterated early impressions. Faithful and fond woman, and true wife as I was, I believe I was in some things unlike an English woman or an English wife, and that Mrs Hart thought so.

Once – for being weak of nature and fast of tongue, she often said things she should not – there was even some hint of the kind dropped before my husband. He flashed up – but laughed the next minute; for I was his, and he loved me!

It seemed uncourteous to retire for the night; so I merely threw my dressing-gown over my evening toilette, and lay down outside the bed dreamily watching the shadows which the lamp threw. This lamp was in my chamber, but its light extended faintly into the boudoir, showing the tall mirror there, and a sofa which was placed opposite. Otherwise, the little room was half in gloom, save for a narrow glint streaming through the not quite closed door of the salon.

I lay broad awake, but very quiet, contented, and happy. I was thinking of Alexis. In the midst of my reverie, I heard, as I thought, my maid trying the handle of the door behind me.

"It is locked," I said; "come another time."

The sound ceased; yet I almost thought Fanchon had entered, for there came a rift of wind which made the lamp sway in its socket. But when I looked, the door was closely shut, and the bolt still fast.

I lay, it might be, half an hour longer. Then, with a certain compunction at my own discourtesy in leaving her, I saw the salon door open, and Mrs Hart appear.

She looked into the boudoir, drew back hurriedly, and closed the door after her.

Of course I immediately rose to follow her. Ere doing so, I remember particularly standing with the lamp in my hand, arranging my dress before the mirror in the boudoir, and seeing reflected in the glass, with my cashmere lying over its cushions, the sofa, unoccupied.

Eliza was standing thoughtful.

"I ought to ask pardon for my long absence, my dear Mrs Hart."

"Oh no – but I of you, for intruding in your apartment; I did not know Mr Saltram had returned. Where is my husband?"

"With mine, no doubt! We need not expect them for an hour yet, the renegades."

"You are jesting," said Mrs Hart, half offended. "I know they are come home. I saw Mr Saltram in your boudoir not two minutes since."

"How?"

"In your boudoir, I repeat. He was lying on the sofa."

"Impossible!" and I burst out laughing. "Unless he has suddenly turned into a cashmere shawl. Come and look."

I flung the folding doors open, and poured a blaze of light into the little room.

"It is very odd," fidgeted Mrs Hart; "very odd indeed. I am sure I saw a gentleman here. His face was turned aside – but of course I concluded it was Mr Saltram. Very odd, indeed."

I still laughed at her, though an uneasy feeling was creeping over me. To dismiss it, I showed her how the door was fastened, and how it was impossible my husband could have entered.

"No; for I distinctly heard you say, 'It is locked – come another time.' What did you mean by that?"

"I thought it was Fanchon."

To change the subject I began showing her some parures my husband had just bought me. Eliza Hart was very fond of jewels. We remained looking at them some time longer in the inner-room where I had been lying on my bed; and then she bade me good night.

"No light, thank you. I can find my way back through the boudoir. Goodnight. Do not look so pale tomorrow, my dear."

She kissed me in the friendly English fashion, and danced lightly away, out at my bedroom door and into the boudoir adjoining – but instantly I saw her reappear, startled and breathless, covered with angry blushes.

"Mrs Saltram, you have deceived me! You are a wicked French woman."

"Eliza!"

"You know it – you knew it all along. I will go and seek my husband. He will not let me stay another night in your house!"

"As you will," – for I was sick of her follies. "But, explain yourself."

"Have you no shame? Have you foreign women never any shame? But I have found you out at last."

"Indeed!"

"There is – I have seen him twice with my own eyes – there is a man lying this minute in your boudoir, – and he is – *not* Mr Saltram!"

Then indeed I sickened – a deadly horror came over me. No wonder the young thing, convinced of my guilt, fled from me, appalled.

For, I knew now *whom* she had seen.

Hour after hour I must have lain where I fell. There was some confusion in the house – no one came near me. It was early daylight when I woke and saw Fanchon leaning over me, and trying to lift me from the floor.

"Fanchon – is it morning?"

"Yes, Madame."

"What day is it?"

"The twenty-sixth of May."

It had been *he*, then. He followed us still.

Shudder after shudder convulsed me. I think Fanchon thought I was dying.

"Oh, Madame! oh, poor Madame! And Monsieur not yet come home."

I uttered a terrible cry – for my heart foreboded what either had happened or assuredly would happen.

Alexis never came home again.

An hour after, I was sent for to the little woodcutter's hut, outside Paris gates, where he lay dying.

Anastasius had judged clearly; my noble generous husband had in him but one thing lacking – his passions were "not in his hand". When Colonel Hart, on the clear testimony of his wife, impugned *his* wife's honour, Alexis challenged him – fought and fell.

It all happened in an hour or two, when their blood was fiery hot. By daylight the Colonel stood, cold as death, pale as a shadow, by Alexis' bedside. He had killed him, his old friend whom he loved.

No one thought of me. They let me weep near my husband – unconscious as he was – doubtless believing mine the last contrite tears of an adulteress. I did not heed nor deny that horrible name – Alexis was dying.

Towards evening he revived a little, and his senses returned. He opened his eyes and saw me – they closed with a shudder.

"Alexis – Alexis!"

"Isbel, I am dying. You know the cause. In the name of God – are you – "

"In the name of God, I am your pure wife, who never loved any man but you."

"I am satisfied. I thought it was so."

He looked at Colonel Hart, faintly smiling; then opened his arms and took me into them, as if to protect me with his last breath.

"Now," he said, still holding me, "My friends, we must make all clear. Nothing must harm her when I am gone. Hart, fetch your wife here."

Mrs Hart came, trembling violently. My husband addressed her.

"I sent for you – to ask you a question. Answer, as to a dying person, who tomorrow will know all secrets. Who was the man you saw in my wife's chamber?"

"He was a stranger to me. I never met him before, anywhere. He lay on the sofa, wrapped in a fur cloak."

"Did you see his face?"

"Not the first time. The second time I did."

"What was he like? Be accurate, for the sake of more than life – honour."

My husband's voice sank. There was terror in his eyes, but not *that* terror – he held me to his bosom still.

"What was he like, Eliza?" repeated Colonel Hart.

"He was middle-aged; of a pale, grave countenance, with keen, large eyes, high forehead, and a pointed beard."

"Heaven save us! I have seen him too," cried the Colonel, horror-struck. "It was no living man."

"It was M. Anastasius!"

My husband died that night. He died, his lips on mine, murmuring how dearly he loved me, and how happy he had been.

For many months after then I was quite happy, too; for my wits wandered, and I thought I was again a little West Indian girl, picking gowans in the meadows about Dumfries.

The Colonel and Mrs Hart were, I believe, very kind to me. I always took her for a little playfellow I had, who was called Eliza. It is only lately, as the year has circled round again to the spring, that my head has become clear, and I have found out who she is, and – ah, me! – who I am.

This coming to my right senses does not give me so much pain as they thought it would; because great weakness of body has balanced and soothed my mind.

I have but one desire: to go to my own Alexis – and before the twenty-fifth of May.

Now I have been able nearly to complete our story; which is well. My friend, judge between us – and *him*. Farewell.

ISBEL SALTRAM

POSTSCRIPT

I think it necessary that I, Eliza Hart, should relate, as simply as vera-ciously, the circumstances of Mrs Saltram's death, which happened on the night of the twenty-fifth of May.

She was living with us at our house, some miles out of London. She had been very ill and weak during May, but towards the end of the month she revived. We thought if she could live till June she might even recover. My husband desired that on no account might she be told the day of the month – she was indeed purposely deceived on the subject. When the twenty-fifth came she thought it was only the twenty-second. For some weeks she had kept her bed, and Fanchon never left her. Fanchon, who knew the whole history, and was strictly charged, whatever delusions might occur to take no notice whatever of the subject to her mistress. For my husband and myself were again persuaded that it must be some delusion. So was the physician, who nevertheless determined to visit us himself on the night of the twenty-fifth of May.

It happened that the Colonel was unwell, and I could not remain constantly in Mrs Saltram's room. It was a large but very simple suburban bedchamber, with white curtains and modern furniture, all of which I myself arranged in such a manner that there should be no dark corners, no shadows thrown by hanging draperies, or anything of the kind.

About ten o'clock at night Fanchon accidentally quitted her mistress for a few minutes, sending in her place a nursemaid who had lately come into our family.

This girl tells me that she entered the room quickly, but stopped, seeing, as she believed, the physician sitting by the bed, on the further side, at Mrs Saltram's right hand. She thought Mrs Saltram did not see him, for she turned and asked her, the nursemaid – "Susan, what o'clock is it?"

The gentleman did not speak. She says, he appeared sitting with his elbows on his knees, and his face partly concealed in his hands. He wore a long coat or cloak – she could not distinguish which, for the room was rather dark, but she could plainly see on his little finger the sparkle of a diamond ring.

She is quite certain that Mrs Saltram did not see the gentleman at all, which rather surprised her, for the poor lady moved from time to time, and spoke complainingly of its being "very cold." At length she called Susan to sit by her side, and chafe her hands.

Susan acquiesced – "But did not Mrs Saltram see the gentleman?"

"What gentleman?"

"He was sitting beside you, not a minute since. I thought he was the doctor, or the clergyman. He is gone now."

And the girl, much terrified, saw that there was no one in the room.

She says, Mrs Saltram did not seem terrified at all. She only pressed her hands on her forehead; her lips slightly moving – then whispered: "Go, call Fanchon and them all, tell them what you saw."

"But I must leave you. Are you not afraid?"

"No. Not now – not now."

She covered her eyes, and again her lips began moving.

Fanchon entered, and I too, immediately.

I do not expect to be credited. I can only state on my honour, what we both then beheld.

Mrs Saltram lay, her eyes open, her face quite calm, as that of a dying person; her hands spread out on the counterpane. Beside her sat erect the same figure I had seen lying on the sofa in Paris, exactly a year ago. It appeared more life-like than she. Neither looked at each other. When we brought a bright lamp into the room, the appearance vanished.

Isbel said to me, "Eliza, he is come."

"Impossible! You have not seen him?"

"No, but you have?" She looked me steadily in the face. "I knew it. Take the light away, and you will see him again. He is here, I want to speak to him. Quick, take the light away."

Alarmed as I was, I could not refuse, for I saw by her features that her last hour was at hand.

As surely as I write this, I, Eliza Hart, saw, when the candles were removed, that figure grow again, as out of air, and become plainly distinguishable, sitting by her bedside.

She turned herself with difficulty, and faced it. "Eliza, is he there? I see nothing but the empty chair. Is he there?"

"Yes."

"Does he look angry or terrible?"

"No."

"Anastasius!" She extended her hand towards the vacant chair. "Cousin Anastasius!"

Her voice was sweet, though the cold drops stood on her brow.

"Cousin Anastasius, I do not see you, but you can see and hear me. I am not afraid of you now. You know, once, I loved you very much."

Here – overcome with terror, I stole back towards the lighted staircase. Thence I still heard Isbel speaking.

"We erred, both of us, Cousin. You were too hard upon me – I had too great love first, too great terror afterwards, of you. Why should I be afraid of a man that shall die, and of the son of man, whose breath is in his nostrils? I should have worshipped, have feared, not you, but only God."

She paused – drawing twice or thrice, heavily, the breath that could not last.

"I forgive you – forgive me also! I loved you. Have you anything to say to me, Anastasius?"

Silence.

"Shall we ever meet in the boundless spheres of heaven?"

Silence – a long silence. We brought in candles, for she was evidently dying.

"Eliza – thank you for all! Your hand. It is so dark – and" – shivering –

"I am afraid of going into the dark. I might meet Anastasius there. I wish my husband would come."

She was wandering in her mind, I saw. Her eyes turned to the vacant chair.

"Is there anyone sitting by me?"

"No. Dear Isbel; can you see anyone?"

"No one – yes" – and with preternatural strength she started right up in bed, extending her arms. "Yes! There – close behind you – I see – my husband. I am quite safe – now!"

So, with a smile upon her face, she died.

Fitz-James O'Brien

The Lost Room

Fitz-James O'Brien (1828–62), Irish-born son of a lawyer, emigrated in 1852 to America, where he quickly became recognized as the leading writer of horror stories in the decade immediately following the death of Edgar Allan Poe. The year 1858 saw the first publication not only of his best-known story, "The Diamond Lens", but also his surreal fantasies "From Hand to Mouth" and "The Lost Room" (which made its debut in Harper's New Monthly Magazine, *September 1858).*

IT WAS OPPRESSIVELY warm. The sun had long disappeared, but seemed to have left its vital spirit of heat behind it. The air rested; the leaves of the acacia trees that shrouded my windows hung plumb-like on their delicate stalks. The smoke of my cigar scarce rose above my head, but hung about me in a pale blue cloud, which I had to dissipate with languid waves of my hand. My shirt was open at the throat, and my chest heaved laboriously in the effort to catch some breath of fresher air. The noises of the city seemed to be wrapped in slumber, and the shrilling of the mosquitoes was the only sound that broke the stillness.

As I lay with my feet elevated on the back of a chair, wrapped in that peculiar frame of mind in which thought assumes a species of lifeless motion, the strange fancy seized me of making a languid inventory of the principal articles of furniture in my room. It was a task well suited to the mood in which I found myself. Their forms were duskily defined in the dim twilight that floated shadowily through the chamber; it was no labour to note and particularize each, and from the place where I sat I could command a view of all my possessions without even turning my head.

There was, *imprimis*, that ghostly lithograph by Calame. It was a mere black spot on the white wall, but my inner vision scrutinized every detail of the picture. A wild, desolate, midnight heath, with a spectral oak tree in the centre of the foreground. The wind blows fiercely, and the jagged branches, clothed scantily with ill-grown leaves, are swept to the left continually by its giant force. A formless wrack of clouds streams across the awful sky, and the rain sweeps almost parallel with the horizon. Beyond, the heath stretches off into endless blackness, in the extreme of which either fancy or art has conjured up some undefinable shapes that seem riding into space. At the base of the huge oak stands a shrouded figure. His mantle is wound by the blast in tight folds around his form, and the long cock's feather in his hat is blown upright, till it seems as if it stood on end with fear. His features are not visible, for he has grasped his cloak with both hands, and drawn it from either side across his face. The picture is seemingly objectless. It tells no tale, but there is a weird power about it that haunts one, and it was for that I bought it.

Next to the picture comes the round blot that hangs below it, which I know to be a smoking-cap. It has my coat of arms embroidered on the front, and for that reason I never wear it; though, when properly arranged on my head, with its long blue silken tassel hanging down by my cheek, I believe it becomes me well. I remember the time when it was in the course of manufacture. I remember the tiny little hands that pushed the coloured silks so nimbly through the cloth that was stretched on the embroidery-frame – the vast trouble I was put to to get a colored copy of my armorial bearings for the heraldic work which was to decorate the front of the band – the pursings up of the little mouth, and the contractions of the young forehead, as their possessor plunged into a profound sea of cogitation touching the way in which the cloud should be represented from which the armed hand, that is my crest, issues, the heavenly moment when the tiny hands placed it on my head, in a position that I could not bear for more than a few seconds, and I, king-like, immediately assumed my royal prerogative after the coronation, and instantly levied a tax on my only subject, which was, however, not paid unwillingly. Ah! the cap is there, but the embroiderer has fled; for Atropos was severing the web of life above her head while she was weaving that silken shelter for mine!

How uncouthly the huge piano that occupies the corner at the left of the door looms out in the uncertain twilight! I neither play nor sing, yet I own a piano. It is a comfort to me to look at it, and to feel that the music is there, although I am not able to break the spell that binds it. It is pleasant to know that Bellini and Mozart, Cimarosa, Porpora, Glück, and all such – or at least their souls – sleep in that unwieldy case. There lie embalmed, as it were, all operas, sonatas, oratorios, notturnos, marches, songs, and dances, that ever climbed into existence through the four bars that wall in melody. Once I was entirely repaid for the investment of my funds in that instrument which I never use. Blokeeta, the composer, came to see me. Of course his instincts urged him as irresistibly to my piano as if some magnetic power lay within it compelling him to approach. He tuned it, he played on it. All night long, until the gray and spectral dawn rose out of the depths of the midnight, he sat and played, and I lay smoking by the window listening. Wild, unearthly, and sometimes insufferably painful, were the improvisations of Blokeeta. The chords of the instrument seemed breaking with anguish. Lost souls shrieked in his dismal preludes; the half-heard utterances of spirits in pain, that groped at inconceivable distances from anything lovely or harmonious, seemed to rise dimly up out of the waves of sound that gathered under his hands. Melancholy human love wandered out on distant heaths, or beneath dank and gloomy cypresses, murmuring its unanswered sorrow, or hateful gnomes sported and sang in the stagnant swamps, triumphing in unearthly tones over the knight whom they had lured to his death. Such was Blokeeta's night's entertainment; and when he at length closed the piano, and hurried away through the cold morning, he left a memory about the instrument from which I could never escape.

Those snow-shoes that hang in the space between the mirror and the door recall Canadian wandering – a long race through the dense forests, over the frozen snow, through whose brittle crust the slender hoofs of the caribou that we were pursuing sank at every step, until the poor creature despairingly turned at bay in a small juniper coppice, and we heartlessly shot him down. And I remember how Gabriel, the *habitant*, and François, the half-breed, cut his throat, and how the hot blood rushed out in a torrent over the snowy soil; and I recall the snow *cabane* that Gabriel built, where we all three slept so warmly; and the great fire that glowed at our feet, painting all kinds of demoniac shapes on the black screen of forest that lay without; and the deer-steaks that we roasted for our breakfast; and the savage drunkenness of Gabriel in the morning, he having been privately drinking out of my brandy-flask all the night long.

That long, haftless dagger that dangles over the mantelpiece makes

my heart swell. I found it, when a boy, in a hoary old castle in which one
of my maternal ancestors once lived. That same ancestor – who, by the
way, yet lives in history – was a strange old sea-king, who dwelt on the
extremest point of the southwestern coast of Ireland. He owned the
whole of that fertile island called Inniskeiran, which directly faces Cape
Clear, where between them the Atlantic rolls furiously, forming what the
fishermen of the place call "the sound". An awful place in winter is that
same Sound. On certain days no boat can live there for a moment, and
Cape Clear is frequently cut off for days from any communication with
the mainland.

This old sea-king – Sir Florence O'Driscoll by name – passed a stormy
life. From the summit of his castle he watched the ocean, and when any
richly laden vessels, bound from the south to the industrious Galway
merchants, hove in sight, Sir Florence hoisted the sails of his galley, and it
went hard with him if he did not tow into harbour ship and crew. In this
way he lived; not a very honest mode of livelihood, certainly, according
to our modern ideas, but quite reconcilable with the morals of the time.
As may be supposed, Sir Florence got into trouble. Complaints were laid
against him at the English court by the plundered merchants, and the
Irish viking set out for London, to plead his own cause before good
Queen Bess, as she was called. He had one powerful recommendation:
he was a marvellously handsome man. Not Celtic by descent, but half
Spanish, half Danish in blood, he had the great northern stature with the
regular features, flashing eyes, and dark hair of the Iberian race. This
may account for the fact that his stay at the English court was much
longer than was necessary, as also for the tradition, which a local histo-
rian mentions, that the English Queen evinced a preference for the Irish
chieftain, of other nature than that usually shown by monarch to subject.

Previous to his departure, Sir Florence had entrusted the care of his
property to an Englishman named Hull. During the long absence of the
knight, this person managed to ingratiate himself with the local authorities, and gain their favor so far that they were willing to support him in
almost any scheme. After a protracted stay, Sir Florence, pardoned of all
his misdeeds, returned to his home. Home no longer. Hull was in possession, and refused to yield an acre of the lands he had so nefariously
acquired. It was no use appealing to the law, for its officers were in the
opposite interest. It was no use appealing to the Queen, for she had
another lover, and had forgotten the poor Irish knight by this time; and
so the viking passed the best portion of his life in unsuccessful attempts to

reclaim his vast estates, and was eventually, in his old age, obliged to content himself with his castle by the sea and the island of Inniskeiran, the only spot of which the usurper was unable to deprive him. So this old story of my kinsman's fate looms up out of the darkness that enshrouds that haftless dagger hanging on the wall.

It was somewhat after the foregoing fashion that I dreamily made the inventory of my personal property. As I turned my eyes on each object, one after the other – or the places where they lay, for the room was now so dark that it was almost impossible to see with any distinctness – a crowd of memories connected with each rose up before me, and, perforce, I had to indulge them. So I proceeded but slowly, and at last my cigar shortened to a hot and bitter morsel that I could barely hold between my lips, while it seemed to me that the night grew each moment more insufferably oppressive. While I was revolving some impossible means of cooling my wretched body, the cigar stump began to burn my lips. I flung it angrily through the open window, and stooped out to watch it falling. It first lighted on the leaves of the acacia, sending out a spray of red sparkles, then, rolling off, it fell plump on the dark walk in the garden, faintly illuminating for a moment the dusky trees and breath-less flowers. Whether it was the contrast between the red ash of the cigar-stump and the silent darkness of the garden, or whether it was that I detected by the sudden light a faint waving of the leaves, I know not; but something suggested to me that the garden was cool. I will take a turn there, thought I, just as I am; it cannot be warmer than this room, and however still the atmosphere, there is always a feeling of liberty and spaciousness in the open air, that partially supplies one's wants. With this idea running through my head, I arose, lit another cigar, and passed out into the long, intricate corridors that led to the main staircase. As I crossed the threshold of my room, with what a different feeling I should have passed it had I known that I was never to set foot in it again!

I lived in a very large house, in which I occupied two rooms on the second floor. The house was old-fashioned, and all the floors communi-cated by a huge circular staircase that wound up through the centre of the building, while at every landing long, rambling corridors stretched off into mysterious nooks and corners. This palace of mine was very high, and its resources, in the way of crannies and windings, seemed to be interminable. Nothing seemed to stop anywhere. Cul-de-sacs were unknown on the premises. The corridors and passages, like mathemat-ical lines, seemed capable of indefinite extension, and the object of the architect must have been to erect an edifice in which people might go ahead forever. The whole place was gloomy, not so much because it was large, but because an unearthly nakedness seemed to pervade the structure. The staircases, corridors, halls, and vestibules all partook of a desert-like desolation. There was nothing on the walls to break the sombre monotony of those long vistas of shade. No carvings on the wainscoting, no moulded masks peering down from the simply severe cornices, no marble vases on the landings. There was an eminent dreariness and want of life – so rare in an American establishment – all over the abode. It was Hood's haunted house put in order and newly painted. The servants, too, were shadowy, and chary of their visits. Bells rang three times before the gloomy chambermaid could be induced to present herself; and the negro waiter, a ghoul-like looking creature from Congo, obeyed the summons only when one's patience was exhausted or one's want satisfied in some other way. When he did come, one felt sorry that he had not stayed away altogether, so sullen and savage did he appear. He moved along the echoless floors with a slow, noiseless shamble, until his dusky figure advancing from the gloom, seemed like some reluctant afreet, compelled by the superior power of his master to disclose himself. When the doors of all the chambers were closed, and no light illuminated the long corridor save the red, unwholesome glare of a small oil lamp on a table at the end, where late lodgers lit their candles, one could not by any possibility conjure up a sadder or more desolate prospect.

Yet the house suited me. Of meditative and sedentary habits, I enjoyed the extreme quiet. There were but few lodgers, from which I infer that the landlord did not drive a very thriving trade; and these, probably oppressed by the sombre spirit of the place, were quiet and ghost-like in their movements. The proprietor I scarcely ever saw. My bills were deposited by unseen hands every month on my table, while I was out walking or riding, and my pecuniary response was entrusted to the attendant afreet. On the whole, when the bustling, wide-awake spirit of New York is taken into consideration, the sombre, half-vivified character of the house in which I lived was an anomaly that no one appreciated better than I who lived there.

I felt my way down the wide, dark staircase in my pursuit of zephyrs. The garden, as I entered it, did feel somewhat cooler than my own room, and I puffed my cigar along the dim, cypress-shrouded walks with a sensation of comparative relief. It was very dark. The tall-growing flowers that bordered the path were so wrapped in gloom as to present the aspect of solid pyramidal masses, all the details of leaves and blossoms being buried in an embracing darkness, while the trees had lost all form, and seemed like masses of overhanging cloud. It was a place and time to excite the imagination; for in the impenetrable cavities of endless gloom there was room for the most riotous fancies to play at will. I walked and walked, and the echoes of my footsteps on the ungravelled and mossy path suggested a double feeling. I felt alone and yet in company at the same time. The solitariness of the place made itself distinct enough in the stillness, broken alone by the hollow reverberations of my step, while those very reverberations seemed to imbue me with an undefined feeling that I was not alone. I was not, therefore, much startled when I was suddenly accosted from beneath the solid darkness of an immense cypress by a voice saying, "Will you give me a light, sir?"

"Certainly," I replied, trying in vain to distinguish the speaker amidst the impenetrable dark.

Somebody advanced, and I held out my cigar. All I could gather definitively about the individual who thus accosted me was that he must have been of extremely small stature; for I, who am by no means an over-grown man, had to stoop considerably in handing him my cigar. The vigorous puff that he gave his own lighted up my Havana for a moment, and I fancied that I caught a glimpse of a pale, weird countenance, immersed in a background of long, wild hair. The ash was, however, so momentary that I could not even say certainly whether this was an actual impression or the mere effort of imagination to embody that which the senses had failed to distinguish.

"Sir, you are out late," said this unknown to me, as he, with half-uttered thanks, handed me back my cigar, for which I had to grope in the gloom.

"Not later than usual," I replied, drily.

"Hum! you are fond of late wanderings, then?"

"That is just as the fancy seizes me."

"Do you live here?"

"Yes."

"Queer house, isn't it?"

"I have only found it quiet."

"Hum! But you *will* find it queer, take my word for it." This was earnestly uttered; and I felt at the same time a bony finger laid on my arm, that cut it sharply like a blunted knife.

"I cannot take your word for any such assertion," I replied; rudely, shaking off the bony finger with an irrepressible motion of disgust.

"No offence, no offence," muttered my unseen companion rapidly, in a strange, subdued voice, that would have been shrill had it been louder; "your being angry does not alter the matter. You will find it a queer house. Everybody finds it a queer house. Do you know who lives there?"

"I never busy myself, sir, about other people's affairs," I answered sharply, for the individual's manner, combined with my utter uncertainty as to his appearance, oppressed me with an irksome longing to be rid of him.

"O, you don't? Well, I do. I know what they are, – well, well, well!" and as he pronounced the three last words his voice rose with each, until, with the last, it reached a shrill shriek that echoed horribly among the lonely walks. "Do you know what they eat?" he continued.

"No, sir – nor care."

"O, but you will care. You must care. You shall care. I'll tell you what they are. They are enchanters. They are ghouls. They are cannibals. Did you never remark their eyes, and how they gloated on you when you passed? Did you never remark the food that they served up at your table? Did you never in the dead of night hear muffled and unearthly footsteps gliding along the corridors, and stealthy hands turning the handle of your door? Does not some magnetic influence fold itself continually around you when they pass, and send a thrill through spirit and body, and a cold shiver that no sunshine will chase away? O, you have! You have felt all these things! I know it!"

The earnest rapidity, the subdued tones, the eagerness of accent, with which all this was uttered, impressed me most uncomfortably. It really seemed as if I could recall all those weird occurrences and influences of which he spoke; and I shuddered in spite of myself in the midst of the impenetrable darkness that surrounded me.

"Hum!" said I, assuming, without knowing it, a confidential tone, "may I ask how you know these things?"

"How I know them? Because I am their enemy; because they tremble at my whisper; because I hang upon their track with the perseverance of a bloodhound and the stealthiness of a tiger; because – because – I was *of* them once!"

"Wretch!" I cried excitedly, for involuntarily his eager tones had wrought me up to a high pitch of spasmodic nervousness "then you mean to say that you – "

As I uttered this word, obeying an uncontrollable impulse, I stretched forth my hand in the direction of the speaker and made a blind clutch. The tips of my fingers seemed to touch a surface as smooth as glass, that glided suddenly from under them. A sharp, angry hiss sounded through the gloom, followed by a whirring noise, as if some projectile passed rapidly by, and the next moment I felt instinctively that I was alone.

A most disagreeable feeling instantly assailed me – a prophetic instinct that some terrible misfortune menaced me; an eager and overpowering anxiety to get back to my own room without loss of time. I turned and ran blindly along the dark cypress alley, every dusky clump of flowers that rose blackly in the borders making my heart each moment cease to beat. The echoes of my own footsteps seemed to redouble and assume the sounds of unknown pursuers following fast upon my track. The boughs of lilac-bushes and syringas, that here and there stretched partly across the walk, seemed to have been furnished suddenly with hooked hands that sought to grasp me as I flew by, and each moment I expected to behold some awful and impassable barrier fall across my track and wall me up forever.

At length I reached the wide entrance. With a single leap I sprang up the four or five steps that formed the stoop, and dashed along the hall, up the wide, echoing stairs, and again along the dim, funereal corridors until I paused, breathless and panting, at the door of my room. Once so far, I stopped for an instant and leaned heavily against one of the panels, panting lustily after my late run. I had, however, scarcely rested my whole weight against the door, when it suddenly gave way, and I staggered in head-foremost. To my utter astonishment the room I had left in profound darkness was now a blaze of light. So intense was the illumination that, for a few seconds while the pupils of my eyes were contracting under the sudden change, I saw absolutely nothing save the dazzling glare. This fact in itself, coming on me with such utter suddenness, was sufficient to prolong my confusion, and it was not until after several minutes had elapsed that I perceived the room was not only illuminated, but occupied. And such occupants! Amazement at the scene took such possession of me that I was incapable of either moving or uttering a word. All that I could do was to lean against the wall, and stare blankly at the strange picture.

It might have been a scene out of Faublas, or Grammont's Memoirs, or happened in some palace of Minister Fouquet.

Round a large table in the centre of the room, where I had left a student-like litter of books and papers, were seated half a dozen persons. Three

were men and three were women. The table was heaped with a prodigality
of luxuries. Luscious eastern fruits were piled up in silver filigree vases,
through whose meshes their glowing rinds shone in the contrasts of a thousand hues. Small silver dishes that Benvenuto might have designed, filled
with succulent and aromatic meats, were distributed upon a cloth of snowy
damask. Bottles of every shape, slender ones from the Rhine, stout fellows
from Holland, sturdy ones from Spain, and quaint basket-woven flasks
from Italy, absolutely littered the board. Drinking-glasses of every size and
hue filled up the interstices, and the thirsty German flagon stood side by
side with the aerial bubbles of Venetian glass that rest so lightly on their
threadlike stems. An odor of luxury and sensuality floated through the
apartment. The lamps that burned in every direction seemed to diffuse a
subtle incense on the air, and in a large vase that stood on the floor I saw
a mass of magnolias, tuberoses, and jasmines grouped together, stifling
each other with their honeyed and heavy fragrance.

The inhabitants of my room seemed beings well suited to so sensual an
atmosphere. The women were strangely beautiful, and all were attired in
dresses of the most fantastic devices and brilliant hues. Their figures were
round, supple, and elastic; their eyes dark and languishing; their lips full,
ripe, and of the richest bloom. The three men wore half-masks, so that all
I could distinguish were heavy jaws, pointed beards, and brawny throats
that rose like massive pillars out of their doublets. All six lay reclining on
Roman couches about the table, drinking down the purple wines in large
draughts, and tossing back their heads and laughing wildly.

I stood, I suppose, for some three minutes, with my back against the
wall staring vacantly at the bacchanal vision, before any of the revellers
appeared to notice my presence. At length, without any expression to
indicate whether I had been observed from the beginning or not, two of
the women arose from their couches, and, approaching, took each a
hand and led me to the table. I obeyed their motions mechanically. I sat
on a couch between them as they indicated. I unresistingly permitted
them to wind their arms about my neck.

"You must drink," said one, pouring out a large glass of red wine,
"here is Clos Vougeot of a rare vintage; and here," pushing a flask of
amber-hued wine before me, "is Lachryma Christi."

"You must eat," said the other, drawing the silver dishes toward her.
"here are cutlets stewed with olives, and here are slices of a *filet* stuffed
with bruised sweet chestnuts" – and as she spoke, she, without waiting for
a reply, proceeded to help me.

The sight of the food recalled to me the warnings I had received in the garden. This sudden effort of memory restored to me my other faculties at the same instant. I sprang to my feet, thrusting the women from me with each hand.

"Demons!" I almost shouted, "I will have none of your accursed food. I know you. You are cannibals, you are ghouls, you are enchanters. Begone, I tell you! Leave my room in peace!"

A shout of laughter from all six was the only effect that my passionate speech produced. The men rolled on their couches, and their half-masks quivered with the convulsions of their mirth. The women shrieked, and tossed the slender wine-glasses wildly aloft, and turned to me and flung themselves on my bosom fairly sobbing with laughter.

"Yes," I continued, as soon as the noisy mirth had subsided, "yes, I say, leave my room instantly! I will have none of your unnatural orgies here!"

"His room!" shrieked the woman on my right.

"His room!" echoed she on my left.

"His room! He calls it his room!" shouted the whole party, as they rolled once more into jocular convulsions.

"How know you that it is your room?" said one of the men who sat opposite to me, at length, after the laughter had once more somewhat subsided.

"How do I know?" I replied, indignantly. "How do I know my own room? How could I mistake it, pray? There's my furniture – my piano – "

"He calls that a piano!" shouted my neighbors, again in convulsions as I pointed to the corner where my huge piano, sacred to the memory of Blokeeta, used to stand. "O, yes! It is his room. There – there is his piano!"

The peculiar emphasis they laid on the word "piano" caused me to scrutinize the article I was indicating more thoroughly. Up to this time, though utterly amazed at the entrance of these people into my chamber, and connecting them somewhat with the wild stories I had heard in the garden, I still had a sort of indefinite idea that the whole thing was a masquerading freak got up in my absence, and that the bacchanalian orgy I was witnessing was nothing more than a portion of some elaborate hoax of which I was to be the victim. But when my eyes turned to the corner where I had left a huge and cumbrous piano, and beheld a vast and sombre organ lifting its fluted front to the very ceiling, and

convinced myself, by a hurried process of memory, that it occupied the
very spot in which I had left my own instrument, the little self-possession
that I had left forsook me. I gazed around me bewildered.

In like manner everything was changed. In the place of that old haftless
dagger, connected with so many historic associations personal to myself,
I beheld a Turkish yataghan dangling by its belt of crimson silk, while the
jewels in the hilt blazed as the lamplight played upon them. In the spot
where hung my cherished smoking-cap, memorial of a buried love, a
knightly casque was suspended, on the crest of which a golden dragon
stood in the act of springing. That strange lithograph by Calame was no
longer a lithograph, but it seemed to me that the portion of the wall
which it had covered, of the exact shape and size, had been cut out, and,
in place of the picture, a real scene on the same scale, and with real
actors, was distinctly visible. The old oak was there, and the stormy sky
was there; but I saw the branches of the oak sway with the tempest, and
the clouds drive before the wind. The wanderer in his cloak was gone; but
in his place I beheld a circle of wild figures, men and women, dancing
with linked hands around the bole of the great tree, chanting some wild
fragment of a song, to which the winds roared an unearthly chorus. The
snow-shoes, too, on whose sinewy woof I had sped for many days amidst
Canadian wastes, had vanished, and in their place lay a pair of strange
up-curled Turkish slippers, that had, perhaps, been many a time shuffled
off at the doors of mosques, beneath the steady blaze of an orient sun.

All was changed. Wherever my eyes turned they missed familiar
objects, yet encountered strange representatives. Still, in all the substi-
tutes there seemed to me a reminiscence of what they replaced. They
seemed only for a time transmuted into other shapes, and there lingered
around them the atmosphere of what they once had been. Thus I could
have sworn the room to have been mine, yet there was nothing in it that I
could rightly claim. Everything reminded me of some former possession
that it was not. I looked for the acacia at the window, and, lo! long, silken
palm-leaves swayed in through the open lattice; yet they had the same
motion and the same air of my favorite tree, and seemed to murmur to
me, "Though we seem to be palm-leaves, yet are we acacia-leaves; yea,
those very ones on which you used to watch the butterflies alight and the
rain patter while you smoked and dreamed!" So in all things the room
was, yet was not, mine; and a sickening consciousness of my utter
inability to reconcile its identity with its appearance overwhelmed me,
and choked my reason.

"Well, have you determined whether or not this is your room?" asked the girl on my left, proffering me a huge tumbler creaming over with champagne, and laughing wickedly as she spoke.

"It is mine," I answered, doggedly, striking the glass rudely with my hand, and dashing the aromatic wine over the white cloth. "I know that it is mine; and ye are jugglers and enchanters who want to drive me mad."

"Hush! hush!" she said, gently, not in the least angered at my rough treatment. "You are excited. Alf shall play something to soothe you."

At her signal, one of the men sat down at the organ. After a short, wild, spasmodic prelude, he began what seemed to me to be a symphony of recollections. Dark and sombre, and all through full of quivering and intense agony, it appeared to recall a dark and dismal night, on a cold reef, around which an unseen but terribly audible ocean broke with eternal fury. It seemed as if a lonely pair were on the reef, one living, the other dead; one clasping his arms around the tender neck and naked bosom of the other, striving to warm her into life, when his own vitality was being each moment sucked from him by the icy breath of the storm. Here and there a terrible wailing minor key would tremble through the chords like the shriek of sea-birds, or the warning of advancing death. While the man played I could scarce restrain myself. It seemed to be Blokeeta whom I listened to, and on whom I gazed. That wondrous night of pleasure and pain that I had once passed listening to him seemed to have been taken up again at the spot where it had broken off, and the same hand was continuing it. I stared at the man called Alf. There he sat with his cloak and doublet, and long rapier and mask of black velvet. But there was something in the air of the peaked beard, a familiar mystery in the wild mass of raven hair that fell as if wind-blown over his shoulders which riveted my memory.

"Blokeeta! Blokeeta!" I shouted, starting up furiously from the couch on which I was lying, and bursting the fair arms that were linked around my neck as if they had been hateful chains – "Blokeeta! my friend! speak to me, I entreat you! Tell these horrid enchanters to leave me. Say that I hate them. Say that I command them to leave my room."

The man at the organ stirred not in answer to my appeal. He ceased playing, and the dying sound of the last note he had touched faded off into a melancholy moan. The other men and the women burst once more into peals of mocking laughter.

"Why will you persist in calling this your room?" said the woman next me, with a smile meant to be kind, but to me inexpressibly loathsome. "Have we not shown you by the furniture, by the general appearance of the place, that you are mistaken, and that this cannot be your apartment? Rest content, then, with us. You are welcome here, and need no longer trouble yourself about your room."

"Rest content!" I answered, madly; "live with ghosts! eat of awful meats, and see awful sights! Never, never! You have cast some enchantment over the place that has disguised it; but for all that I know it to be my room. You shall leave it!"

"Softly, softly!" said another of the sirens. "Let us settle this amicably. This poor gentleman seems obstinate and inclined to make an uproar. Now we do not want an uproar. We love the night and its quiet; and there is no night that we love so well as that on which the moon is coffined in clouds. Is it not so, my brothers?"

An awful and sinister smile gleamed on the countenances of her unearthly audience, and seemed to glide visibly from underneath their masks.

"Now," she continued, "I have a proposition to make. It would be ridiculous for us to surrender this room simply because this gentleman states that it is his; and yet I feel anxious to gratify, as far as may be fair, his wild assertion of ownership. A room, after all, is not much to us; we can get one easily enough, but still we should be loath to give this apartment up to so imperious a demand. We are willing, however, to *risk* its loss. That is to say," – turning to me – "I propose that we play for the room. If you win, we will immediately surrender it to you just as it stands; if, on the contrary, you lose, you shall bind yourself to depart and never molest us again."

Agonized at the ever-darkening mysteries that seemed to thicken around me, and despairing of being able to dissipate them by the mere exercise of my own will, I caught almost gladly at the chance thus presented to me. The idea of my loss or my gain scarce entered into my calculation. All I felt was an indefinite knowledge that I might, in the way proposed, regain, in an instant, that quiet chamber and that peace of mind of which I had so strangely been deprived.

"I agree!" I cried, eagerly; "I agree. Anything to rid myself of such unearthly company!"

The woman touched a small golden ball that stood near her on the table, and it had scarce ceased to tinkle when a negro dwarf entered with a silver tray on which were dice-boxes and dice. A shudder passed over me as I thought in this stunted African I could trace a resemblance to the ghoul-like black servant to whose attendance I had been accustomed.

"Now," said my neighbor, seizing one of the dice-boxes and giving me the other, "the highest wins. Shall I throw first?"

I nodded assent. She rattled the dice, and I felt an inexpressible load lifted from my heart as she threw fifteen.

"It is your turn," she said, with a mocking smile; "but before you throw, I repeat the offer I made you before. Live with us. Be one of us. We will initiate you into our mysteries and enjoyments – enjoyments of which you can form no idea unless you experience them. Come; it is not too late yet to change your mind. Be with us!"

My reply was a fierce oath, as I rattled the dice with spasmodic nervousness and flung them on the board. They rolled over and over again, and during that brief instant I felt a suspense, the intensity of which I have never known before or since. At last they lay before me. A shout of the same horrible, maddening laughter rang in my ears. I peered in vain at the dice, but my sight was so confused that I could not distinguish the amount of the cast. This lasted for a few moments. Then my sight grew clear, and I sank back almost lifeless with despair as I saw that I had thrown but *twelve*!

"Lost! lost!" screamed my neighbor, with a wild laugh. "Lost! lost!" shouted the deep voices of the masked men. "Leave us, coward!" they all cried; "you are not to be one of us. Remember your promise; leave us!"

Then it seemed as if some unseen power caught me by the shoulders and thrust me toward the door. In vain I resisted. In vain I screamed and shouted for help. In vain I implored them for pity. All the reply I had was those mocking peals of merriment, while, under the invisible influence, I staggered like a drunken man toward the door. As I reached the threshold the organ pealed out a wild, triumphal strain. The power that impelled me concentrated itself into one vigorous impulse that sent me blindly staggering out into the echoing corridor, and, as the door closed swiftly behind me, I caught one glimpse of the apartment I had left forever. A change passed like a shadow over it. The lamps died out, the siren women and masked men vanished, the flowers, the fruits, the bright silver and bizarre furniture faded swiftly, and I saw again, for the tenth of a second, my own old chamber restored. There was the acacia waving darkly; there was the table littered with books; there was the ghostly lithograph, the dearly beloved smoking-cap, the Canadian snow-shoes, the ancestral dagger. And there, at the piano, organ no longer, sat Blokeeta playing.

The next instant the door closed violently, and I was left standing in the corridor stunned and despairing.

As soon as I had partially recovered my comprehension I rushed madly to the door, with the dim idea of beating it in. My fingers touched a cold and solid wall. There was no door! I felt all along the corridor for many yards on both sides. There was not even a crevice to give me hope. I rushed downstairs shouting madly. No one answered. In the vestibule I met the negro; I seized him by the collar, and demanded my room. The demon showed his white and awful teeth, which were filed into a saw-like shape, and, extricating himself from my grasp with a sudden jerk, fled down the passage with a gibbering laugh. Nothing but echo answered to my despairing shrieks. The lonely garden resounded with my cries as I strode madly through the dark walks, and the tall funereal cypresses seemed to bury me beneath their heavy shadows. I met no one – could find no one. I had to bear my sorrow and despair alone.

Since that awful hour I have never found my room. Everywhere I look for it, yet never see it. Shall I ever find it?

Charles Dickens

No. 1 Branch Line: The Signalman

This is the best – and most famous – of the many short ghost stories written by Charles Dickens (1812–70) in the twenty-five years following A Christmas Carol *(1843). He originally wrote this classic tale for inclusion in* Mugby Junction, *the 1866 Christmas Number of his popular magazine* All the Year Round.

"HALLOA! BELOW THERE!"

When he heard a voice thus calling to him, he was standing at the door of his box, with a flag in his hand, furled round its short pole. One would have thought, considering the nature of the ground, that he could not have doubted from what quarter the voice came; but instead of looking up to where I stood on the top of the steep cutting nearly over his head, he turned himself about, and looked down the Line. There was something remarkable in his manner of doing so, though I could not have said for my life what. But I know it was remarkable enough to attract my notice, even though his figure was foreshortened and shadowed, down in the deep trench, and mine was high above him, so steeped in the glow of an angry sunset, that I had shaded my eyes with my hand before I saw him at all.

"Halloa! Below!"

From looking down the Line, he turned himself about again, and, raising his eyes, saw my figure high above him.

"Is there any path by which I can come down and speak to you?"

He looked up at me without replying, and I looked down at him without pressing him too soon with a repetition of my idle question. Just then there came a vague vibration in the earth and air, quickly changing into a violent pulsation, and an oncoming rush that caused me to start back, as though it had force to draw me down. When such vapour as rose to my height from this rapid train had passed me, and was skimming away over the landscape, I looked down again, and saw him refurling the flag he had shown while the train went by.

I repeated my inquiry. After a pause, during which he seemed to regard me with fixed attention, he motioned with his rolled-up flag towards a point on my level, some two or three hundred yards distant. I called down to him, "All right!" and made for that point. There, by dint of looking closely about me, I found a rough zigzag descending path notched out, which I followed.

The cutting was extremely deep, and unusually precipitate. It was made through a clammy stone, that became oozier and wetter as I went down. For these reasons, I found the way long enough to give me time to recall a singular air of reluctance or compulsion with which he had pointed out the path.

When I came down low enough upon the zigzag descent to see him again, I saw that he was standing between the rails on the way by which the train had lately passed, in an attitude as if he were waiting for me to appear. He had his left hand at his chin, and that left elbow rested on his right hand, crossed over his breast. His attitude was one of such expectation and watchfulness that I stopped a moment, wondering at it.

I resumed my downward way, and stepping out upon the level of the railroad, and drawing nearer to him, saw that he was a dark sallow man, with a dark beard and rather heavy eyebrows. His post was in as solitary and dismal a place as ever I saw. On either side, a dripping-wet wall of jagged stone, excluding all view but a strip of sky; the perspective one way only a crooked prolongation of this great dungeon; the shorter perspective in the other direction terminating in a gloomy red light, and the gloomier entrance to a black tunnel, in whose massive architecture there was a barbarous, depressing, and forbidding air. So little sunlight ever found its way to this spot, that it had an earthy, deadly smell; and so much cold wind rushed through it, that it struck chill in me, as if I had left the natural world.

Before he stirred, I was near enough to him to have touched him. Not even then removing his eyes from mine, he stepped back one step, and lifted his hand.

This was a lonesome post to occupy (I said), and it had riveted my attention when I looked down from up yonder. A visitor was a rarity, I should suppose; not an unwelcome rarity, I hoped? In me, he merely saw a man who had been shut up within narrow limits all his life, and who, being at last set free, had a newly-awakened interest in these great works. To such purpose I spoke to him; but I am far from sure of the terms I used; for, besides that I am not happy in opening any conversation, there was something in the man that daunted me.

He directed a most curious look towards the red light near the tunnel's mouth, and looked all about it, as if something were missing from it, and then looked at me.

That light was part of his charge? Was it not?

He answered in a low voice, "Don't you know it is?"

The monstrous thought came into my mind, as I perused the fixed eyes and the saturnine face, that this was a spirit, not a man. I have speculated since, whether there may have been infection in his mind.

In my turn I stepped back. But in making the action, I detected in his eyes some latent fear of me. This put the monstrous thought to flight.

"You look at me," I said, forcing a smile, "as if you had a dread of me."

"I was doubtful," he returned, "whether I had seen you before."

"Where?"

He pointed to the red light he had looked at.

"There?" I said.

Intently watchful of me, he replied (but without sound), "Yes."

"My good fellow, what should I do there? However, be that as it may, I never was there, you may swear."

"I think I may," he replied. "Yes; I am sure I may."

His manner cleared, like my own. He replied to my remarks with readiness, and in well-chosen words. Had he much to do there? Yes; that was to say, he had enough responsibility to bear; but exactness and watchfulness were what was required of him, and of actual work — manual labour — he had next to none. To change that signal, to trim those lights, and to turn this iron handle now and then, was all he had to do under that head. Regarding those many long and lonely hours of which I seemed to make so much, he could only say that the routine of his life had shaped itself into that form, and he had grown used to it. He had taught himself a language down here — if only to know it by sight, and to have formed his own crude ideas of its pronunciation, could be called learning it. He had also worked at fractions and decimals, and tried a little algebra; but he was, and had been as a boy, a poor hand at figures. Was it necessary for him when on duty always to remain in that channel of damp air, and could he never rise into the sunshine from between those high stone walls? Why, that depended upon times and circumstances. Under some conditions there would be less upon the Line than under others, and the same held good as to certain hours of the day and night. In bright weather, he did choose occasions for getting a little above these lower shadows; but, being at all times liable to be called by his electric bell, and at such times listening for it with redoubled anxiety, the relief was less than I would suppose.

He took me into his box, where there was a fire, a desk for an official book in which he had to make certain entries, a telegraphic instrument with its dial, face, and needles, and the little bell of which he had spoken. On my trusting that he would excuse the remark that he had been well educated, and (I hoped I might say without offence), perhaps educated above that station, he observed that instances of slight incongruity in such wise would rarely be found wanting among large bodies of men, that he had heard it was so in workhouses, in the police force, even in that last desperate resource, the army; and that he knew it was so, more or less, in any great railway staff. He had been, when young (if I could believe it, sitting in that hut – he scarcely could), a student of natural philosophy, and had attended lectures; but he had run wild, misused his opportunities, gone down, and never risen again. He had no complaint to offer about that. He had made his bed, and he lay upon it. It was far too late to make another.

All that I have here condensed he said in a quiet manner, with his grave dark regards divided between me and the fire. He threw in the word, "Sir," from time to time, and especially when he referred to his youth – as though to request me to understand that he claimed to be nothing but what I found him. He was several times interrupted by the little bell, and had to read off messages, and send replies. Once he had to stand without the door, and display a flag as a train passed, and make some verbal communication to the driver. In the discharge of his duties, I observed him to be remarkably exact and vigilant, breaking off his discourse at a syllable, and remaining silent until what he had to do was done.

In a word, I should have set this man down as one of the safest of men to be employed in that capacity, but for the circumstance that while he was speaking to me he twice broke off with a fallen colour, turned his face towards the little bell when it did *not* ring, opened the door of the hut (which was kept shut to exclude the unhealthy damp), and looked out towards the red light near the mouth of the tunnel. On both of those occasions, he came back to the fire with the inexplicable air upon him which I had remarked, without being able to define, when we were so far asunder.

Said I, when I rose to leave him, "You almost make me think that I have met with a contented man."

(I am afraid I must acknowledge that I said it to lead him on.)

"I believe I used to be so," he rejoined, in the low voice in which he had first spoken, "but I am troubled, Sir, I am troubled."

He would have recalled the words if he could. He had said them, however, and I took them up quickly.

"With what? What is your trouble?"

"It is very difficult to impart, Sir. It is very, very difficult to speak of. If ever you make me another visit, I will try to tell you."

"But I expressly intend to make you another visit. Say, when shall it be?"

"I go off early in the morning, and I shall be on again at ten tomorrow night, Sir."

"I will come at eleven."

He thanked me, and went out at the door with me. "I'll show my white light, Sir," he said, in his peculiar low voice, "till you have found the way up. When you have found it, don't call out! And when you are at the top, don't call out!"

His manner seemed to make the place strike colder to me, but I said no more than, "Very well."

"And when you come down tomorrow night, don't call out! Let me ask you a parting question. What made you cry, 'Halloa! Below there!' tonight?"

"Heaven knows," said I, "I cried something to that effect – "

"Not to that effect, Sir. Those were the very words. I know them well."

"Admit those were the very words. I said them, no doubt, because I saw you below."

"For no other reason?"

"What other reason could I possibly have?"

"You had no feeling that they were conveyed to you in any supernatural way?"

"No."

He wished me good night, and held up his light. I walked by the side of the down Line of rails (with a very disagreeable sensation of a train coming behind me) until I found the path. It was easier to mount than to descend, and I got back to my inn without any adventure.

Punctual to my appointment, I placed my foot on the first notch of the zigzag next night, as the distant clocks were striking eleven. He was waiting for me at the bottom, with his white light on. "I have not called out," I said, when we came close together; "may I speak now?"

"By all means, Sir."

"Good night, then, and here's my hand."

"Good night, Sir, and here's mine." With that we walked side by side to his box, entered it, closed the door, and sat down by the fire.

"I have made up my mind, Sir," he began, bending forward as soon as we were seated, and speaking in a tone but a little above a whisper, "that you shall not have to ask me twice what troubles me. I took you for some one else yesterday evening. That troubles me."

"That mistake?"

"No. That some one else."

"Who is it?"

"I don't know."

"Like me?"

"I don't know. I never saw the face. The left arm is across the face, and the right arm is waved – violently waved. This way."

I followed his action with my eyes, and it was the action of an arm gesticulating, with the utmost passion and vehemence, "For God's sake, clear the way!"

"One moonlight night," said the man, "I was sitting here, when I heard a voice cry, 'Halloa! Below there!' I started up, looked from that door, and saw this someone else standing by the red light near the tunnel, waving as I just now showed you. The voice seemed hoarse with shouting, and it cried, 'Look out! Look out!' And then again, 'Halloa! Below there! Look out!' I caught up my lamp, turned it on red, and ran towards the figure, calling, 'What's wrong? What has happened? Where?' It stood just outside the blackness of the tunnel. I advanced so close upon it that I wondered at its keeping the sleeve across its eyes. I ran right up at it, and had my hand stretched out to pull the sleeve away, when it was gone."

"Into the tunnel?' said I.

"No. I ran on into the tunnel, five hundred yards. I stopped, and held my lamp above my head, and saw the figures of the measured distance, and saw the wet stains stealing down the walls and trickling through the arch. I ran out again faster than I had run in (for I had a mortal abhorrence of the place upon me), and I looked all round the red light with my own red light, and I went up the iron ladder to the gallery atop of it, and I came down again, and ran back here. I telegraphed both ways. 'An alarm has been given. Is anything wrong?' The answer came back, both ways, 'All well.' "

Resisting the slow touch of a frozen finger tracing out my spine, I showed him how that this figure must be a deception of his sense of sight; and how that figures, originating in disease of the delicate nerves that minister to the functions of the eye, were known to have often troubled patients, some of whom had become conscious of the nature of their affliction, and had even proved it by experiments upon themselves. "As to an imaginary cry," said I, "do but listen for a moment to the wind in this unnatural valley while we speak so low, and to the wild harp it makes of the telegraph wires."

That was all very well, he returned, after we had sat listening for a while, and he ought to know something of the wind and the wires – he who so often passed long winter nights there, alone and watching. But he would beg to remark that he had not finished.

I asked his pardon, and he slowly added these words, touching my arm –

"Within six hours after the appearance, the memorable accident on this Line happened, and within ten hours the dead and wounded were brought along through the tunnel over the spot where the figure had stood."

A disagreeable shudder crept over me, but I did my best against it. It was not to be denied, I rejoined, that this was a remarkable coincidence, calculated deeply to impress his mind. But it was unquestionable that remarkable coincidences did continually occur, and they must be taken into account in dealing with such a subject. Though to be sure I must admit, I added (for I thought I saw that he was going to bring the objection to bear upon me), men of common sense did not allow much for coincidences in making the ordinary calculations of life.

He again begged to remark that he had not finished.

I again begged his pardon for being betrayed into interruptions.

"This," he said, again laying his hand upon my arm, and glancing over his shoulder with hollow eyes, "was just a year ago. Six or seven months passed, and I had recovered from the surprise and shock, when one morning, as the day was breaking, I, standing at the door, looked towards the red light, and saw the spectre again." He stopped, with a fixed look at me.

"Did it cry out?"

"No. It was silent."

"Did it wave its arm?"

"No. It leaned against the shaft of the light, with both hands before the face. Like this."

Once more I followed his action with my eyes. It was an action of mourning. I have seen such an attitude on stone figures on tombs.

· "Did you go up to it?"

"I came in and sat down, partly to collect my thoughts, partly because it had turned me faint. When I went to the door again, daylight was above me, and the ghost was gone."

"But nothing followed? Nothing came of this?"

He touched me on the arm with his forefinger twice or thrice, giving a ghastly nod each time –

"That very day, as a train came out of the tunnel, I noticed, at a carriage window on my side, what looked like a confusion of hands and heads, and something waved. I saw it just in time to signal the driver, Stop! He shut off, and put his brake on, but the train drifted past here a hundred and fifty yards or more. I ran after it, and, as I went along, heard terrible screams and cries. A beautiful young lady had died instantaneously in one of the compartments, and was brought back in here, and laid down on this floor between us."

Involuntarily I pushed my chair back, as I looked from the boards at which he pointed to himself.

"True, Sir. True. Precisely as it happened, so I tell it you."

I could think of nothing to say, to any purpose, and my mouth was very dry. The wind and the wires took up the story with a long lamenting wail.

He resumed, "Now, Sir, mark this, and judge how my mind is troubled. The spectre came back a week ago. Ever since, it has been there, now and again, by fits and starts."

"At the light?"

"At the Danger-light."

"What does it seem to do?"

He repeated, if possible with increased passion and vehemence, that former gesticulation of "For God's sake, clear the way!"

Then he went on. "I have no peace or rest for it. It calls to me, for many minutes together, in an agonised manner, 'Below there! Look out! Look out!' It stands waving to me. It rings my little bell – "

I caught at that. "Did it ring your bell yesterday evening when I was here, and you went to the door?"

"Twice."

"Why, see," said I, "how your imagination misleads you. My eyes were on the bell, and my ears were open to the bell, and if I am a living man, it did not ring at those times. No, nor at any other time, except when it was rung in the natural course of physical things by the station communicating with you."

He shook his head. "I have never made a mistake as to that yet, Sir. I have never confused the spectre's ring with the man's. The ghost's ring is a strange vibration in the bell that it derives from nothing else, and I have not asserted that the bell stirs to the eye. I don't wonder that you failed to hear it. But I heard it."

"And did the spectre seem to be there when you looked out?"

"It *was* there."

"Both times?"

He repeated firmly: "Both times."

"Will you come to the door with me, and look for it now?"

He bit his under lip as though he were somewhat unwilling, but arose. I opened the door, and stood on the step, while he stood in the doorway. There was the Danger-light. There was the dismal mouth of the tunnel. There were the high, wet stone walls of the cutting. There were the stars above them.

"Do you see it?" I asked him, taking particular note of his face. His eyes were prominent and strained, but not very much more so, perhaps than my own had been when I had directed them earnestly towards the same spot.

"No," he answered. "It is not there."

"Agreed," said I.

We went in again, shut the door, and resumed our seats. I was thinking how best to improve this advantage, if it might be called one, when he took up the conversation in such a matter-of-course way, so assuming that there could be no serious question of fact between us, that I felt myself placed in the weakest of positions.

"By this time you will fully understand, Sir," he said, "that what troubles me so dreadfully is the question, What does the spectre mean?"

I was not sure, I told him, that I did fully understand.

"What is its warning against?" he said, ruminating, with his eyes on the fire, and only by times turning them on me. "What is the danger? Where is the danger? There is danger overhanging somewhere on the Line. Some dreadful calamity will happen. It is not to be doubted this third time, after what has gone before. But surely this is a cruel haunting of me. What can I do?"

He pulled out his handkerchief, and wiped the drops from his heated forehead.

"If I telegraph Danger, on either side of me, or on both, I can give no reason for it," he went on, wiping the palms of his hands. "I should get into trouble and do no good. They would think I was mad. This is the way it would work – Message: 'Danger! Take care!' Answer: 'What Danger? Where?' Message: 'Don't know. But, for God's sake, take care!' They would displace me. What else could they do?"

His pain of mind was most pitiable to see. It was the mental torture of a conscientious man, oppressed beyond endurance by an unintelligible responsibility involving life.

"When it first stood under the Danger-light," he went on, putting his dark hair back from his head, and drawing his hands outward across and across his temples in an extremity of feverish distress, "why not tell me where that accident was to happen – if it must happen? Why not tell me how it could be averted – if it could have been averted? When on its second coming it hid its face, why not tell me, instead, 'She is going to die. Let them keep her at home'? If it came, on those two occasions, only to show me that its warnings were true, and so to prepare me for the third, why not warn me plainly now? And I, Lord help me! A mere poor signalman on this solitary station! Why not go to somebody with credit to be believed, and power to act?"

When I saw him in this state, I saw that for the poor man's sake, as well as for the public safety, what I had to do for the time was to compose his mind. Therefore, setting aside all question of reality or unreality between us, I represented to him that whoever thoroughly discharged his duty must do well, and that at least it was his comfort that he understood his duty, though he did not understand these confounding Appearances. In this effort I succeeded far better than in the attempt to reason him out of his conviction. He became calm; the occupations incidental to his post as the night advanced began to make larger demands on his attention: and I left him at two in the morning. I had offered to stay through the night, but he would not hear of it.

That I more than once looked back at the red light as I ascended the pathway, that I did not like the red light, and that I should have slept but poorly if my bed had been under it, I see no reason to conceal. Nor did I like the two sequences of the accident and the dead girl. I see no reason to conceal that either.

But what ran most in my thoughts was the consideration how ought I to act, having become the recipient of this disclosure? I had proved the man to be intelligent, vigilant, painstaking, and exact; but how long might he remain so, in his state of mind? Though in a subordinate position, still he held a most important trust, and would I (for instance) like to stake my own life on the chances of his continuing to execute it with precision?

Unable to overcome a feeling that there would be something treacherous in my communicating what he had told me to his superiors in the Company, without first being plain with himself and proposing a middle course to him, I ultimately resolved to offer to accompany him (otherwise keeping his secret for the present) to the wisest medical practitioner we could hear of in those parts, and to take his opinion. A change in his time of duty would come round next night, he had apprised me, and he would be off an hour or two after sunrise, and on again soon after sunset. I had appointed to return accordingly.

Next evening was a lovely evening, and I walked out early to enjoy it. The sun was not yet quite down when I traversed the field-path near the top of the deep cutting. I would extend my walk for an hour, I said to myself, half an hour on and half an hour back, and it would then be time to go to my signalman's box.

Before pursuing my stroll, I stepped to the brink and mechanically looked down, from the point from which I had first seen him. I cannot describe the thrill that seized upon me, when, close at the mouth of the tunnel, I saw the appearance of a man, with his left sleeve across his eyes, passionately waving his right arm.

The nameless horror that oppressed me passed in a moment, for in a moment I saw that this appearance of a man was a man indeed, and that there was a little group of other men, standing at a short distance, to whom he seemed to be rehearsing the gesture he made. The Danger-light was not yet lighted. Against its shaft a little low hut, entirely new to me, had been made of some wooden supports and tarpaulin. It looked no bigger than a bed.

With an irresistible sense that something was wrong – with a flashing self-reproachful fear that fatal mischief had come of my leaving the man there, and causing no one to be sent to overlook or correct what he did – I descended the notched path with all the speed I could make.

"What is the matter?" I asked the men.

"Signalman killed this morning, Sir."

"Not the man belonging to that box?"

"Yes, Sir."

"Not the man I know?"

"You will recognize him, Sir, if you knew him," said the man who spoke for the others, solemnly uncovering his own head, and raising an end of the tarpaulin, "for his face is quite composed."

"O, how did this happen, how did this happen?" I asked, turning from one to another as the hut closed in again.

"He was cut down by an engine, Sir. No man in England knew his work better. But somehow he was not clear of the outer rail. It was just at broad day. He had struck the light, and had the lamp in his hand. As the engine came out of the tunnel, his back was towards her, and she cut him down. That man drove her, and was showing how it happened. Show the gentleman, Tom."

The man, who wore a rough dark dress, stepped back to his former place at the mouth of the tunnel.

"Coming round the curve in the tunnel, Sir," he said, "I saw him at the end, like as if I saw him down a perspective-glass. There was no time to check speed, and I knew him to be very careful. As he didn't seem to take heed of the whistle, I shut it off when we were running down upon him, and called to him as loud as I could call."

"What did you say?"

"I said, 'Below there! Look out! Look out! For God's sake, clear the way!'"

I started.

"Ah! it was a dreadful time, Sir. I never left off calling to him. I put this arm before my eyes not to see, and I waved this arm to the last; but it was no use."

Without prolonging the narrative to dwell on any one of its curious circumstances more than on any other, I may, in closing it, point out the coincidence that the warning of the engine-driver included, not only the words which the unfortunate signalman had repeated to me as haunting him, but also the words which I myself – not he – had attached, and that only in my own mind, to the gesticulation he had imitated.

Haunted.

Ghost stories were invariably part of "Christmas Numbers" during the Victorian era, more so than now. The large majority were published anonymously, though some appeared in collections later credited to specific writers. "Haunted" is taken from a bumper Christmas volume, Tinsley's Annual *(December 1868), with the splendid title* A Stable for Nightmares. *Among the other delights in this rare number are "An American Ghost", "Mrs Brown's Ghost Story", "The Phantom Fourth", "Doctor Feversham's Story", and "The Spirit's Whisper".*

SOME FEW YEARS ago one of those great national conventions which draw together all ages and conditions of the sovereign people of America was held in Charleston, South Carolina.

Colonel Demarion, one of the State Representatives, had attended that great national convention; and, after an exciting week, was returning home, having a long and difficult journey before him.

A pair of magnificent horses, attached to a light buggy, flew merrily enough over a rough country road for a while; but towards evening stormy weather reduced the roads to a dangerous condition, and compelled the Colonel to relinquish his purpose of reaching home that night, and to stop at a small wayside tavern, whose interior illuminated by blazing wood-fires, spread a glowing halo among the dripping trees as he approached it, and gave promise of warmth and shelter at least.

Drawing up to this modest dwelling, Colonel Demarion saw through its uncurtained windows that there was no lack of company within. Beneath the trees, too, an entanglement of rustic vehicles, giving forth red gleams from every dripping angle, told him that beasts as well as men were cared for. At the open door appeared the form of a man who, at the sound of wheels, but not seeing in the outside darkness whom he addressed, called out, "'Tain't no earthly use a-stoppin' here."

Caring more for his chattels than for himself, the Colonel paid no further regard to this address than to call loudly for the landlord.

At the tone of authority, the man in outline more civilly announced himself to be the host; yet so far from inviting the traveller to alight, insisted that the house was "as full as it could pack"; but that there was a place a little farther down the road where the gentleman would be certain to find excellent accommodation.

"What stables have you here?" demanded the traveller, giving no more heed to this than to the former announcement; but bidding his servant to alight, and preparing to do so himself.

"Stables!" repeated the baffled host, shading his eyes so as to scrutinize the newcomer, "*stables*, Cap'n?"

"Yes, *stables*. I want you to take care of my horses; I can take care of myself. Some shelter for cattle you must have by the look of these traps," pointing to the wagons. "I don't want my horses to be kept standing out in this storm, you know."

"No, Major. Why no, certn'y; Marions ain't over a mile, and – "

"Conf – !" muttered the Colonel; "but it's over the *river*, which I don't intend to ford tonight under any consideration."

So saying, the Colonel leaped to the ground, directing his servant to cover the horses and then get out his valise; while the host, thus defeated, assumed the best grace he could to say that he would see what could be done "for the *horses*."

"I am a soldier, my man," added the Colonel in a milder tone, as he stamped his cold feet on the porch and shook off the rain from his travelling gear; "I am used to rough fare and a hard couch: all we want is shelter. A corner of the floor will suffice for me and my rug; a private room I can dispense with at such times as these."

The landlord seemed no less relieved at this assurance than mollified by the explanation of a traveller whom he now saw was of a very different stamp from those who usually frequented the tavern. "For the matter of *stables*, his were newly put up, and first-rate," he said; and "cert'n'y the Gen'ral was welcome to a seat by the fire while 'twas a-storming so fierce."

Colonel Demarion gave orders to his servant regarding the horses, while the landlord, kicking at what seemed to be a bundle of sacking down behind the door, shouted – "Jo! Ho, Jo! Be alive, boy, and show this gentleman's horses to the stables." Upon a repetition of which charges a tall, gaunt, dusty figure lifted itself from out of the dark corner, and grew taller and more gaunt as it stretched itself into waking with a grin which was the most visible part of it, by reason of two long rows of ivory gleaming in the red glare. The hard words had fallen as harmless on Jo's ear-drum as the kicks upon his impassive frame. To do Jo's master justice, the kicks were not vicious kicks, and the rough language was but an intimation that despatch was needed.

"Splendid pair, sir," said the now conciliating landlord. "Shove some o' them mules out into the shed, Jo (which your horses'll feel more to hum in my new stalls, Gen'ral)."

Again cautioning his man Plato not to leave them one moment, Colonel Demarion turned to enter the house.

"You'll find a rough crowd in here, sir," said the host, as he paused on the threshold; "but a good fire, anyhow. 'Tain't many of these loafers as understands this convention business – I *pre*sume, Gen'ral, you've attended the convention – they all on em *thinks* they does, tho'. Fact most on 'em thinks they'd orter be on the committee theirselves. Good many on 'em is from Char'ston today, but is in the same fix as yerself, Gen'ral – can't get across the river tonight."

"I see, I see," cried the statesman, with a gesture towards the sitting-room. "Now what have you got in your larder, Mr Landlord? and send some supper out to my servant; he must make a bed of the carriage-mats tonight."

The landlord introduced his guest into a room filled chiefly with that shiftless and noxious element of Southern society known as "mean whites." Pipes and drinks, and excited arguments, engaged these people as they stood or sat in groups. The host addressed those who were gathered round the log fire, and they opened a way for the newcomer, some few, with republican freedom, inviting him to be seated, the rest giving one furtive glance, and then, in antipathy born of envy, skulking away.

The furniture of this comfortless apartment consisted of sloppy, much-jagged deal tables, dirty whittled benches, and a few uncouth chairs. The walls were dingy with accumulated tobacco-stains, and so moist and filthy was the floor, that the sound only of scraping seats and heavy foot-steps told that it was of boards and not bare earth.

Seated with his back towards the majority of the crowd, and shielded by his newspaper, Colonel Demarion sat awhile unobserved; but was presently recognized by a man from his own immediate neighbourhood, when the information was quickly whispered about that no less a person than their distinguished congressman was among them.

This piece of news speedily found its way to the ears of the landlord, to whom Colonel Demarion was known by name only, and forthwith he reappeared to overwhelm the representative of his State with apologies for the uncourteous reception which had been given him, and to express his now very sincere regrets that the house offered no suitable accommodation for the gentleman. Satisfied as to the safety of his chattels, the Colonel generously dismissed the idea of having anything either to resent or to forgive; and assured the worthy host that he would accept of no exclusive indulgences.

In spite of which the landlord bustled about to bring in a separate table, on which he spread a clean coarse cloth, and a savoury supper of broiled ham, hot corncakes, and coffee; every few minutes stopping to renew his apologies, and even appearing to grow confidentially communicative regarding his domestic economies; until the hungry traveller cut him short with "Don't say another word about it, my friend; you have not a spare sleeping-room, and that is enough. Find me a corner – a clean corner – " looking round upon the most unclean corners of that room – "perhaps upstairs somewhere, and – "

"Ah! *upsta'rs*, Gen'ral. Now, that's jest what I had in my mind to ax you. Fact is, ther' *is* a spar' room upsta'rs, as comfortable a room as the best of folks can wish; but – "

"But it's crammed with sleeping folks, so there's an end of it," cried the senator, thoroughly bored.

"No, sir, ain't no person in it; and ther' ain't no person likely to be in 'cept 'tis *yerself*, Colonel Demarion. Leastways – "

After a good deal of hesitation and embarrassment, the host, in mysterious whispers, imparted the startling fact that this most desirable sleeping-room was *haunted*; that the injury he had sustained in consequence had compelled him to fasten it up altogether; that he had come to be very suspicious of admitting strangers, and had limited his custom of late to what the bar could supply, keeping the matter hushed up in the hope that it might be the sooner forgotten by the neighbours; but that in the case of Colonel Demarion he had now made bold to mention it; "as I can't but think, sir," he urged, "you'd find it prefer'ble to sleepin' on the floor or sittin' up all night along ov these loafers. Fer if 'tis any deceivin' trick got up in the house, maybe they won't try it on, sir, to a gentleman of your reputation."

Colonel Demarion became interested in the landlord's confidences, but could only gather in further explanation that for some time past all travellers who had occupied that room had "made off in the middle of the night, never showin' their faces at the inn again"; that on endeavouring to arrest one or more in their nocturnal flight, they – all more or less terrified – had insisted on escaping without a moment's delay, assigning no other reason than that they had seen a ghost. "Not that folks seem to get much harm by it, Colonel – not by the way they makes off without paying a cent of money!"

Great indeed was the satisfaction evinced by the victim of unpaid bills on the Colonel's declaring that room for him. "If to be turned out of my bed at midnight is all I have to fear, we will see who comes off master in my case. So, Mr Landlord, let the chamber be got ready directly, and have a good fire built there at once."

The exultant host hurried away to confide the great news to Jo, and with him to make the necessary preparations. "Come what will, Jo, Colonel Demarion ain't the man to make off without paying down good money for his accommodations."

In reasonable time, Colonel Demarion was beckoned out of the public room, and conducted upstairs by the landlord, who, after receiving a cheerful "goodnight," paused on the landing to hear his guest bolt and bar the door within, and then push a piece of furniture against it. "Ah," murmured the host, as a sort of misgiving came over him, "if a apparishum has a mind to come thar, 'tain't all the bolts and bars in South Carlina as 'll kip'en away."

But the Colonel's precaution of securing his door, as also that of placing his revolvers in readiness, had not the slightest reference to the reputed ghost. Spiritual disturbances of such kind he feared not. Spirits *tangible* were already producing ominous demonstrations in the rooms below, nor was it possible to conjecture what troubles these might evolve. Glad enough to escape from the noisy company, he took a survey of his evil-reputed chamber. The only light was that of the roaring, crackling, blazing wood-fire, and no other was needed. And what storm-benighted traveller, when fierce winds and rains are lashing around his lodging, can withstand the cheering influences of a glorious log-fire? especially if, as in that wooden tenement, that fire be of abundant pine-knots. It rivals the glare of gas and the glow of a furnace; it charms away the mustiness and fustiness of years, and causes all that is dull and dead around to laugh and dance in its bright light.

By the illumination of just such a fire, Colonel Demarion observed that the apartment offered nothing worthier of remark than that the furniture was superior to anything that might be expected in a small wayside tavern. In truth, the landlord had expended a considerable sum in fitting up this, his finest chamber, and had therefore sufficient reason to bemoan its unprofitableness.

Having satisfied himself as to his apparent security, the senator thought no more of spirits palpable or impalpable; but to the far graver issues of the convention his thoughts reverted. It was yet early; he lighted a cigar, and in full appreciation of his retirement, took out his notebook and plunged into the affairs of state. Now and then he was recalled to the circumstances of his situation by the swaggering tread of unsteady feet about the house, or when the boisterous shouts below raged above the outside storm; but even then he only glanced up from his papers to congratulate himself upon his agreeable seclusion.

Thus he sat for above an hour, then he heaped fresh logs upon the hearth, looked again to his revolvers, and retired to rest.

The house-clock was striking twelve as the Colonel awoke. He awoke suddenly from a sound sleep, flashing, as it were, into full consciousness, his mind and memory clear, all his faculties invigorated, his ideas undisturbed, but with a perfect conviction that he was not alone.

He lifted his head. A man was standing a few feet from the bed, and between it and the fire, which was still burning, and burning brightly enough to display every object in the room, and to define the outline of the intruder clearly. His dress also and his features were plainly distinguishable: the dress was a travelling-costume, in fashion somewhat out of date; the features wore a mournful and distressed expression – the eyes were fixed upon the Colonel. The right arm hung down, and the hand, partially concealed, might, for aught the Colonel knew, be grasping one of his own revolvers; the left arm was folded against the waist. The man seemed about to advance still closer to the bed, and returned the occupant's gaze with a fixed stare.

"Stand, or I'll fire!" cried the Colonel, taking in all this at a glance, and starting up in his bed, revolver in hand.

The man remained still.

"What is your business here?" demanded the statesman, thinking he was addressing one of the roughs from below.

The man was silent.

"Leave this room, if you value your life," shouted the indignant soldier, pointing his revolver.

The man was motionless.

"RETIRE! or by heaven I'll send a bullet through you!"

But the man moved not an inch.

The Colonel fired. The bullet lodged in the breast of the stranger, but he started not. The soldier leapt to the floor and fired again. The shot entered the heart, pierced the body, and lodged in the wall beyond; and the Colonel beheld the hole where the bullet had entered, and the fire-light glimmering through it. And yet the intruder stirred not. Astounded, the Colonel dropped his revolver, and stood face to face before the unmoved man.

"Colonel Demarion," spake the deep solemn voice of the perforated stranger, "in vain you shoot me – I am dead already."

The soldier, with all his bravery, gasped, spellbound. The firelight gleamed through the hole in the body, and the eyes of the shooter were riveted there.

"Fear nothing," spake the mournful presence; "I seek but to divulge my wrongs. Until my death shall be avenged my unquiet spirit lingers here. Listen."

Speechless, motionless was the statesman; and the mournful apparition thus slowly and distinctly continued:

"Four years ago I travelled with one I trusted. We lodged here. That night my comrade murdered me. He plunged a dagger into my heart while I slept. He covered the wound with a plaster. He feigned to mourn my death. He told the people here I had died of heart-complaint; that I had long been ailing. I had gold and treasures. With my treasure secreted beneath his garments he paraded mock grief at my grave. Then he departed. In distant parts he sought to forget his crime; but his stolen gold brought him only the curse of an evil conscience. Rest and peace are not for him. He now prepares to leave his native land for ever. Under an assumed name that man is this night in Charleston. In a few hours he will sail for Europe. Colonel Demarion, you must prevent it. Justice and humanity demand that a murderer roam not at large, nor squander more of the wealth that is by right my children's."

The spirit paused. To the extraordinary revelation the Colonel had listened in rapt astonishment. He gazed at the presence, at the firelight glimmering through it – through the very place where a human heart would be – and he felt that he was indeed in the presence of a supernatural being. He thought of the landlord's story; but while earnestly desiring to sift the truth of the mystery, words refused to come to his aid.

"Do you hesitate?" said the mournful spirit. "Will *you* also flee, when my orphan children cry for retribution?" Seeming to anticipate the will of the Colonel, "I await your promise, senator," he said. "There is not time to lose."

With a mighty effort, the South Carolinian said, "I promise. What would you have me do?"

In the same terse, solemn manner, the ghostly visitor gave the real and assumed names of the murderer, described his person and dress at the present time, described a certain curious ring he was then wearing, together with other distinguishing characteristics: all being carefully noted down by Colonel Demarion, who, by degrees, recovered his self-possession, and pledged himself to use every endeavour to bring the murderer to justice.

Then, with a portentous wave of the hand, "It is well," said the apparition. "Not until the spirit of my murderer shall be separated from the mortal clay can *my* spirit rest in peace." And vanished.

Half-past six in the morning was the appointed time for the steamer to leave Charleston; and the Colonel lost not a moment in preparing to depart. As he hurried down the stairs he encountered the landlord, who – his eyes rolling in terror – made an attempt to speak. Unheeding, except to demand his carriage, the Colonel pushed past him, and effected a quick escape towards the back premises, shouting lustily for "Jo" and "Plato," and for his carriage to be got ready immediately. A few minutes more, and the bewildered host was recalled to the terrible truth by the noise of the carriage dashing through the yard and away down the road; and it was some miles nearer Charleston before the unfortunate man ceased to peer after it in the darkness – as if by so doing he could recover damages – and bemoan to Jo the utter ruin of his house and hopes.

Thirty miles of hard driving had to be accomplished in little more than five hours. No great achievement under favourable circumstances; but the horses were only half refreshed from their yesterday's journey, and though the storm was over, the roads were in a worse condition than ever.

Colonel Demarion resolved to be true to his promise; and fired by a curiosity to investigate the extraordinary communication which had been revealed to him, urged on his horses, and reached the wharf at Charleston just as the steamer was being loosed from her moorings.

He hailed her. "Stop her! Business with the captain! STOP HER!"

Her machinery was already in motion; her iron lungs were puffing forth dense clouds of smoke and steam; and as the Colonel shouted – the crowd around, from sheer delight in shouting, echoing his "Stop her! stop her!" – the voices on land were confounded with the voices of the sailors, the rattling of chains, and the hauling of ropes.

Among the passengers standing to wave farewells to their friends on the wharf were some who recognized Colonel Demarion, and drew the captain's attention towards him; and as he continued vehemently to gesticulate, that officer, from his post of observation, demanded the nature of the business which should require the ship's detention. Already the steamer was clear of the wharf. In another minute she might be beyond reach of the voice; therefore, failing by gestures and entreaties to convince the captain of the importance of his errand, Colonel Demarion, in desperation, cried at the top of his voice, "A murderer on board! For God's sake, STOP!" He wished to have made this startling declaration in private, but not a moment was to be lost; and the excitement around him was intense.

In the midst of the confusion another cry of "Man overboard!" might have been heard in a distant part of the ship, had not the attention of the crowd been fastened on the Colonel. Such a cry was, however, uttered, offering a still more urgent motive for stopping; and the steamer being again made fast, Colonel Demarion was received on board.

"Let not a soul leave the vessel!" was his first and prompt suggestion; and the order being issued, he drew the captain aside, and concisely explained his grave commission. The captain thereupon conducted him to his private room, and summoned the steward, before whom the details were given, and the description of the murderer was read over. The steward, after considering attentively, seemed inclined to associate the description with that of a passenger whose remarkably dejected appearance had already attracted his observation. In such a grave business it was, however, necessary to proceed with the utmost caution, and the "passenger-book" was produced. Upon reference to its pages, the three gentlemen were totally dismayed by the discovery that the name of this same dejected individual was that under which, according to the apparition, the murderer had engaged his passage.

"I am here to charge that man with murder," said Colonel Demarion. "He must be arrested."

Horrified as the captain was at this astounding declaration, yet, on account of the singular and unusual mode by which the Colonel had become possessed of the facts, and the impossibility of proving the charge, he hesitated in consenting to the arrest of a passenger. The steward proposed that they should repair to the saloons and deck, and while conversing with one or another of the passengers, mention – as it were casually – in the hearing of the suspected party his own proper name, and observe the effect produced on him. To this they agreed, and without loss of time joined the passengers, assigning some feasible cause for a short delay of the ship.

The saloon was nearly empty, and while the steward went below, the other two repaired to the deck, where they observed a crowd gathered seaward, apparently watching something over the ship's side.

During the few minutes which had detained the captain in this necessarily hurried business, a boat had been lowered, and some sailors had put off in her to rescue the person who was supposed to have fallen overboard; and it was only now, on joining the crowd, that the captain learned the particulars of the accident. "Who was it?" "What was he like?" they exclaimed simultaneously. That a man had fallen overboard was all that could be ascertained. Someone had seen him run across the deck, looking wildly about him. A splash in the water had soon afterwards attracted attention to the spot, and a body had since been seen struggling on the surface. The waves were rough after the storm, and thick with seaweed, and the sailors had as yet missed the body. The two gentlemen took their post among the watchers, and kept their eyes intently upon the waves, and upon the sailors battling against them. Ere long they see the body rise again to the surface. Floated on a powerful wave, they can for the few moments breathlessly scrutinize it. The colour of the dress is observed. A face of agony upturned displays a peculiar contour of forehead; the hair, the beard; and now he struggles – an arm is thrown up, and a remarkable ring catches the Colonel's eye. "Great heavens! The whole description tallies!" The sailors pull hard for the spot, the next stroke and they will rescue –

A monster shark is quicker than they. The sea is tinged with blood. The man is no more!

Shocked and silent, Colonel Demarion and the captain quitted the deck and resummoned the steward, who had, without success, visited the berths and various parts of the ship for the individual in question. Every hole and corner was now, by the captain's order, carefully searched, but in vain; and as no further information concerning the missing party could be obtained, and the steward persisted in his statement regarding his general appearance, they proceeded to examine his effects. In these he was identified beyond a doubt. Papers and relics proved not only his guilt but his remorse; remorse which, as the apparition had said, permitted him no peace in his wanderings.

Those startling words, "A murderer on board!" had doubtless struck fresh terror to his heart; and, unable to face the accusation, he had thus terminated his wretched existence.

Colonel Demarion revisited the little tavern, and on several occasions occupied the haunted chamber; but never again had he the honour of receiving a midnight commission from a ghostly visitor, and never again had the landlord to bemoan the flight of a non-paying customer.

Henry James

The Romance of Certain Old Clothes

Henry James (1843–1916) declared – early in his career – that a good ghost story must be connected at a hundred points with the common objects of life. He wrote over a dozen classic ghostly tales (including the legendary novel, The Turn of the Screw *and "Owen Wingrave"), and "The Romance of Certain Old Clothes" was his first experiment in this genre. It originally appeared in the* Atlantic Monthly *(February 1868). James revised the text for its inclusion in his first collection,* A Passionate Pilgrim *(1875); and further extensive revisions were made by the author for* Stories Revived *(1885). Among the alterations was the change of the family name from Willoughby to Wingrave. The text which follows here is taken from the "definitive" 1885 version.*

I

TOWARDS THE MIDDLE of the eighteenth century there lived in the Province of Massachusetts a widowed gentlewoman, the mother of three children, by name Mrs Veronica Wingrave. She had lost her husband early in life, and had devoted herself to the care of her progeny. These young persons grew up in a manner to reward her tenderness and to gratify her highest hopes. The first-born was a son, whom she had called Bernard, after his father. The others were daughters – born at an interval of three years apart. Good looks were traditional in the family, and this youthful trio were not likely to allow the tradition to perish. The boy was of that fair and ruddy complexion and that athletic structure which in those days (as in these) were the sign of good English descent – a frank, affectionate young fellow, a deferential son, a patronizing brother, a steadfast friend. Clever, however, he was not; the wit of the family had been apportioned chiefly to his sisters. The late Mr Wingrave had been a great reader of Shakespeare, at a time when this pursuit implied more freedom of thought than at the present day, and in a community where it required much courage to patronize the drama even in the closet; and he had wished to call attention to his admiration of the great poet by calling his daughters out of his favourite plays. Upon the elder he had bestowed the romantic name of Rosalind, and the younger he had called Perdita, in memory of a little girl born between them, who had lived but a few weeks.

　When Bernard Wingrave came to his sixteenth year his mother put a brave face upon it and prepared to execute her husband's last injunction. This had been a formal command that, at the proper age, his son should be sent out to England, to complete his education at the university of Oxford, where he himself had acquired his taste for elegant literature. It was Mrs Wingrave's belief that the lad's equal was not to be found in the two hemispheres, but she had the old traditions of literal obedience. She swallowed her sobs, and made up her boy's trunk and his simple provincial outfit, and sent him on his way across the sea. Bernard presented himself at his father's college, and spent five years in England, without great honour, indeed, but with a vast deal of pleasure and no discredit. On leaving the university he made the journey to France. In his twenty-fourth year he took ship for home, prepared to find poor little New England (New England was very small in those days) a very dull, unfashionable residence. But there had been changes at home, as well as in Mr Bernard's opinions. He found his mother's house quite habitable, and his sisters grown into two very charming young ladies, with all the accomplishments and graces of the young women of Britain, and a certain native-grown originality and wildness, which, if it was not an accomplishment, was certainly a grace the more. Bernard privately assured his mother that his sisters were fully a match for the most genteel young women in the old country; whereupon poor Mrs Wingrave, you may be sure, bade them hold up their heads. Such was Bernard's opinion, and such, in a tenfold higher degree, was the opinion of Mr Arthur Lloyd. This gentleman was a college mate of Mr Bernard, a young man of reputable family, of a good person and a handsome inheritance; which latter appurtenance he proposed to invest in trade in the flourishing colony. He and Bernard were sworn friends; they had crossed the ocean together, and the young American had lost no time in presenting him at his mother's house, where he had made quite as good an impression as that which he had received and of which I have just given a hint.

The two sisters were at this time in all the freshness of their youthful bloom; each wearing, of course, this natural brilliancy in the manner that became her best. They were equally dissimilar in appearance and character. Rosalind, the elder – now in her twenty-second year – was tall and white, with calm gray eyes and auburn tresses; a very faint likeness to the Rosalind of Shakespeare's comedy, whom I imagine a brunette (if you will), but a slender, airy creature, full of the softest, quickest impulses. Miss Wingrave, with her slightly lymphatic fairness, her fine arms, her majestic height, her slow utterance, was not cut out for adventures. She would never have put on a man's jacket and hose; and, indeed, being a very plump beauty, she may have had her reasons apart from her natural dignity. Perdita, too, might very well have exchanged the sweet melancholy of her name against something more in consonance with her aspect and disposition. She had the cheek of a gipsy and the eye of an eager child, as well as the smallest waist and lightest foot in all the country of the Puritans. When you spoke to her she never made you wait, as her handsome sister was wont to do (while she looked at you with a cold fine eye), but gave you your choice of a dozen answers before you had uttered half your thought.

The young girls were very glad to see their brother once more; but they found themselves quite able to spare part of their attention for their brother's friend. Among the young men and their friends and neighbours, the *belle jeunesse* of the Colony, there were many excellent fellows, several devoted swains, and some two or three who enjoyed the reputation of universal charmers and conquerors. But the homebred arts and somewhat boisterous gallantry of these honest colonists were completely eclipsed by the good looks, the fine clothes, the punctilious courtesy, the perfect elegance, the immense information, of Mr Arthur Lloyd. He was in reality no paragon; he was a capable, honourable, civil youth, rich in pounds sterling, in his health and complacency and his little capital of uninvested affections. But he was a gentleman; he had a handsome person; he had studied and travelled; he spoke French, he played the flute, and he read verses aloud with very great taste. There were a dozen reasons why Miss Wingrave and her sister should have thought their other male acquaintance made but a poor figure before such a perfect man of the world. Mr Lloyd's anecdotes told our little New England maidens a great deal more of the ways and means of people in fashion in European capitals then he had any idea of doing. It was delightful to sit by and hear him and Bernard talk about the fine people and fine things they had seen. They would all gather round the fire after tea, in the little wainscoted parlour, and the two young men would remind each other, across the rug, of this, that and the other adventure. Rosalind and Perdita would often have given their ears to know exactly what adventure it was, and where it happened, and who was there, and what the ladies had on; but in those days a well-bred young woman was not expected to break into conversation of her elders, or to ask too many questions; and the poor girls used therefore to sit fluttering behind the more languid – or more discreet – curiosity of their mother.

II

That they were both very fine girls Arthur Lloyd was not slow to discover; but it took him some time to make up his mind whether he liked the big sister or the little sister best. He had a strong presentiment – an emotion of a nature entirely too cheerful to be called a foreboding – that he was destined to stand up before the parson with one of them; yet he was unable to arrive at a preference, and for such a consummation a preference was certainly necessary, for Lloyd had too much young blood in his veins to make a choice by lot and be cheated of the satisfaction of falling in love. He resolved to take things as they came – to let his heart speak. Meanwhile he was on a very pleasant footing. Mrs Wingrave showed a dignified indifference to his "intentions", equally remote from a carelessness of her daughters' honour and from that sharp alacrity to make him come to the point, which, in his quality of young man of property, he had too often encountered in the worldly matrons of his native islands. As for Bernard, all that he asked was that his friend should treat his sisters as his own; and as for the poor girls themselves, however each may have secretly longed that their visitor should do or say something "marked", they kept a very modest and contented demeanour.

Towards each other, however, they were somewhat more on the

offensive. They were good friends enough, and accommodating bedfellows (they shared the same four poster), betwixt whom it would take more than a day for the seeds of jealousy to sprout and bear fruit; but they felt that the seeds had been sown on the day that Mr Lloyd came into the house. Each made up her mind that, if she should be slighted, she would bear her grief in silence, and that no one should be any the wiser; for if they had a great deal of ambition, they had also a large share of pride. But each prayed in secret, nevertheless, that upon her the selection, the distinction, might fall. They had need of a vast deal of patience, of self control, of dissimulation. In those days a young girl of decent breeding could make no advances whatever, and barely respond, indeed, to those that were made. She was expected to sit still in her chair, with her eyes on the carpet, watching the spot where the mystic handkerchief should fall. Poor Arthur Lloyd was obliged to carry on his wooing in the little wainscoted parlour, before the eyes of Mrs Wingrave, her son, and his prospective sister-in-law. But youth and love are so cunning that a hundred signs and tokens might travel to and fro, and not one of these three pairs of eyes detect them in their passage. The two maidens were almost always together, and had plenty of chances to betray themselves. That each knew she was being watched, however, made not a grain of difference in the little offices they mutually rendered, or in the various household tasks they performed in common. Neither flinched nor fluttered beneath the silent battery of her sister's eyes. The only apparent change in their habits was that they had less to say to each other. It was impossible to talk about Mr Lloyd, and it was ridiculous to talk about anything else. By tacit agreement they began to wear all their choice finery, and to devise such little implements of conquest, in the way of ribbons and top-knots and kerchiefs, as were sanctioned by indubitable modesty. They executed in the same inarticulate fashion a contract of fair play in this exciting game. "Is it better so?" Rosalind would ask, tying a bunch of ribbons on her bosom, and turning about from her glass to her sister. Perdita would look up gravely from her work and examine the decoration. "I think you had better give it another loop," she would say, with great solemnity, looking hard at her sister with eyes that added, "upon my honour!" So they were for ever stitching and trimming their petticoats, and pressing out their muslins, and contriving washes and ointments and cosmetics, like the ladies in the household of the vicar of Wakefield. Some three or four months went by; it grew to be midwinter, and as yet Rosalind knew that if Perdita had nothing more to boast of than she, there was not much to be feared from her rivalry. But Perdita by this time – the charming Perdita – felt that her secret had grown to be tenfold more precious than her sister's.

One afternoon Miss Wingrave sat alone – that was a rare accident – before her toilet-glass, combing out her long hair. It was getting too dark to see; she lit the two candles in their sockets, on the frame of her mirror, and then went to the window to draw her curtains. It was a grey December evening; the landscape was bare and bleak, and the sky heavy with snow-clouds. At the end of the large garden into which her window looked was a wall with a little postern door, opening into a lane. The door stood ajar, as she could vaguely see in the gathering darkness, and moved slowly to and fro, as if someone were swaying it from the lane without. It was doubtless a servant-maid who had been having a tryst with her sweetheart. But as she was about to drop her curtain Rosalind saw her sister step into the garden and hurry along the path which led to the house. She dropped the curtain, all save a little crevice for her eyes. As Perdita came up the path she seemed to be examining something in her hand, holding it close to her eyes. When she reached the house she stopped a moment, looked intently at the object, and pressed it to her lips.

Poor Rosalind slowly came back to her chair and sat down before her glass, where, if she had looked at it less abstractedly, she would have seen her handsome features sadly disfigured by jealousy. A moment afterwards the door opened behind her and her sister came into the room, out of breath, her cheeks aglow with the chilly air.

Perdita started. "Ah," she said, "I thought you were with our mother." The ladies were to go to a tea-party, and on such occasions it was the habit of one of the girls to help their mother to dress. Instead of coming in, Perdita lingered at the door.

"Come in, come in," said Rosalind. "We have more than an hour yet. I should like you very much to give a few strokes to my hair." She knew that her sister wished to retreat, and that she could see in the glass all her movements in the room. "Nay, just help me with my hair," she said, "and I will go to mamma."

Perdita came reluctantly, and took the brush. She saw her sister's eyes, in the glass, fastened hard upon her hands. She had not made three passes when Rosalind clapped her own right hand upon her sister's left, and started out of her chair. "Whose ring is that?" she cried, passionately, drawing her towards the light.

On the young girl's third finger glistened a little gold ring, adorned with a very small sapphire. Perdita felt that she need no longer keep her secret, yet that she must put a bold face on her avowal. "It's mine," she said proudly.

"Who gave it to you?" cried the other.

Perdita hesitated a moment. "Mr Lloyd."

"Mr Lloyd is generous, all of a sudden."

"Ah no," cried Perdita, with spirit, "not all of a sudden! He offered it to me a month ago."

"And you needed a month's begging to take it?" said Rosalind, looking at the little trinket, which indeed was not especially elegant, although it was the best that the jeweller of the Province could furnish. "I wouldn't have taken it in less than two."

"It isn't the ring," Perdita answered, "it's what it means!"

"It means that you are not a modest girl!" cried Rosalind. "Pray, does your mother know of your intrigue? does Bernard?"

"My mother has approved my 'intrigue', as you call it. Mr Lloyd has asked for my hand, and mamma has given it. Would you have had him apply to you, dearest sister?"

Rosalind gave her companion a long look, full of passionate envy and sorrow. Then she dropped her lashes on her pale cheeks and turned away. Perdita felt that it had not been a pretty scene; but it was her sister's fault. However, the elder girl rapidly called back her pride, and turned herself about again. "You have my very best wishes," she said, with a low curtsey. "I wish you every happiness, and a very long life."

Perdita gave a bitter laugh. "Don't speak in that tone!" she cried. "I would rather you should curse me outright. Come, Rosy," she added, "he couldn't marry both of us."

"I wish you very great joy," Rosalind repeated, mechanically, sitting down to her glass again, "and a very long life, and plenty of children."

There was something in the sound of these words not at all to Perdita's taste. "Will you give me a year to live at least?" she said. "In a year I can have one little boy – or one little girl at least. If you will give me your brush again I will do your hair."

"Thank you," said Rosalind. "You had better go to mamma. It isn't becoming that a young lady with a promised husband should wait on a girl with none."

"Nay," said Perdita, good-humouredly, "I have Arthur to wait upon me. You need my service more than I need yours."

But her sister motioned her away, and she left the room. When she had gone poor Rosalind fell on her knees before her dressing-table, buried her head in her arms, and poured out a flood of tears and sobs. She felt very much the better for the effusion of sorrow. When her sister came back she insisted on helping her to dress – on her wearing her prettiest things. She forced upon her acceptance a bit of lace of her own, and declared that now she was to be married she should do her best to appear worthy of her lover's choice. She discharged these offices in stern silence; but, such as they were, they had to do duty as an apology and an atonement; she never made any other.

Now that Lloyd was received by the family as an accepted suitor nothing remained but to fix the wedding day. It was appointed for the following April, and in the interval preparations were diligently made for the marriage. Lloyd, on his side, was busy with his commercial arrangements, and with establishing a correspondence with the great mercantile house to which he had attached himself in England. He was therefore not so frequent a visitor at Mrs Wingrave's as during the months of his diffidence and irresolution, and poor Rosalind had less to suffer than she feared from the sight of the mutual endearments of the young lovers. Touching his future sister-in-law Lloyd had a perfectly clear conscience. There had not been a particle of love-making between them, and he had not the slightest suspicion that he had dealt her a terrible blow. He was quite at his ease; life promised so well, both domestically and financially. The great revolt of the Colonies was not yet in the air, and that his connubial felicity should take a tragic turn it was absurd, it was blasphemous, to apprehend. Meanwhile, at Mrs Wingrave's, there was a greater rustling of silks, a more rapid clicking of scissors and flying of needles, than ever. The good lady had determined that her daughter should carry from home the genteelest outfit that her money could buy or that the country could furnish. All the sage women in the Province were convened, and their united taste was brought to bear on Perdita's wardrobe. Rosalind's situation, at this moment, was assuredly not to be envied. The poor girl had an inordinate love of dress, and the very best taste in the world, as her sister knew perfectly well. Rosalind was tall, she was stately and sweeping, she was made to carry stiff brocade and masses of heavy lace, such as belong to the toilet of a rich man's wife. But Rosalind sat aloof, with her beautiful arms folded and her head averted, while her mother and sister and the venerable women aforesaid worried and wondered over their materials, oppressed by the multitude of their resources. One day there came in a beautiful piece of white silk,

brocaded with heavenly blue and silver, sent by the bridegroom himself –
it not being thought amiss in those days that the husband-elect should
contribute to the bride's trousseau. Perdita could think of no form or
fashion which would do sufficient honour to the splendour of the material.

"Blue's your colour, sister, more than mine," she said, with appealing
eyes. "It's a pity it's not for you. You would know what to do with it."

Rosalind got up from her place and looked at the great shining fabric,
as it lay spread over the back of the chair. Then she took it up in her
hands and felt it – lovingly, as Perdita could see – and turned about
toward the mirror with it. She let it roll down to her feet, and flung the
other end over her shoulder, gathering it in about her waist with her
white arm, which was bare to the elbow. She threw back her head and
looked at her image, and a hanging tress of her auburn hair fell upon the
gorgeous surface of the silk. It made a dazzling picture. The women
standing about uttered a little "Look, look!" of admiration. "Yes,
indeed," said Rosalind, quietly, "blue is my colour." But Perdita could
see that her fancy had been stirred, and that she would now fall to work
and solve all their silken riddles. And indeed she behaved very well, as
Perdita, knowing her insatiable love of millinery, was quite ready to
declare. Innumerable yards of lustrous silk and satin, of muslin, velvet
and lace, passed through her cunning hands, without a jealous word
coming from her lips. Thanks to her industry, when the wedding day
came Perdita was prepared to espouse more of the vanities of life than
any fluttering young bride who had yet received the sacramental blessing
of a New England divine.

It had been arranged that the young couple should go out and spend
the first days of their wedded life at the country house of an English
gentleman – a man of rank and a very kind friend to Arthur Lloyd. He
was a bachelor; he declared he should be delighted to give up the place to
the influence of Hymen. After the ceremony at church – it had been
performed by an English clergyman – young Mrs Lloyd hastened back to
her mother's house to change her nuptial robes for a riding-dress.
Rosalind helped her to effect the change, in the little homely room in
which they had spent their undivided younger years. Perdita then
hurried off to bid farewell to her mother, leaving Rosalind to follow. The
parting was short; the horses were at the door, and Arthur was impatient
to start. But Rosalind had not followed, and Perdita hastened back to her
room, opening the door abruptly. Rosalind, as usual, was before the

glass, but in a position which caused the other to stand still, amazed. She had dressed herself in Perdita's cast-off wedding veil and wreath, and on her neck she had hung the full string of pearls which the young girl had received from her husband as a wedding gift. These things had been hastily laid aside, to await their possessor's disposal on her return from the country. Bedizened in this unnatural garb Rosalind stood before the mirror, plunging a long look into its depths and reading heaven knows what audacious visions. Perdita was horrified. It was a hideous image of their old rivalry come to life again. She made a step toward her sister, as if to pull off the veil and the flowers. But catching her eyes in the glass, she stopped.

"Farewell, sweetheart," she said. "You might at least have waited till I had got out of the house!" And she hurried away from the room.

Mr Lloyd had purchased in Boston a house which to the taste of those days appeared as elegant as it was commodious; and here he very soon established himself with his young wife. He was thus separated by a distance of twenty miles from the residence of his mother-in-law. Twenty miles, in that primitive era of roads and conveyances, were a serious matter as a hundred at the present day, and Mrs Wingrave saw but little of her daughter during the first twelvemonth of her marriage. She suffered in no small degree from Perdita's absence; and her affliction was not diminished by the fact that Rosalind had fallen into terribly low spirits and was not to be roused or cheered but by change of air and company. The real cause of the young lady's dejection the reader will not be slow to suspect. Mrs Wingrave and her gossips, however, deemed her complaint a mere bodily ill, and doubted not that she would obtain relief from the remedy just mentioned. Her mother accordingly proposed, on her behalf, a visit to certain relatives on the paternal side, established in New York, who had long complained that they were able to see so little of their New England cousins. Rosalind was despatched to these good people, under a suitable escort, and remained with them for several months. In the interval her brother Bernard, who had begun the practice of law, made up his mind to take a wife. Rosalind came home to the wedding, apparently cured of her heartache, with bright roses and lilies in her face and a proud smile on her lips. Arthur Lloyd came over from Boston to see his brother-in-law married, but without his wife, who was expecting very soon to present him with an heir. It was nearly a year since Rosalind had seen him. She was glad – she hardly knew why – that Perdita had stayed at home. Arthur looked happy, but he was more grave and important than before his marriage. She thought he looked "interesting" – for although the word, in its modern sense, was not then invented, we may be sure that the idea was. The truth is, he was simply anxious about his wife and her coming ordeal. Nevertheless, he by no means failed to observe Rosalind's beauty and splendour, and to note how she effaced the poor little bride. The allowance that Perdita had enjoyed for her dress had now been transferred to her sister, who turned it to wonderful account. On the morning after the wedding he had a lady's saddle put on the horse of the servant who had come with him from town, and went out with the young girl for a ride. It was a keen, clear morning in January; the ground was bare and hard, and the horses in good condition – to say nothing of Rosalind, who was charming in her hat and plume, and her dark blue riding coat, trimmed with fur. They rode all the morning, they lost their way, and were obliged to stop for dinner at a farmhouse. The early winter dusk had fallen when they got home. Mrs Wingrave met them with a long face. A messenger had arrived at noon from Mrs Lloyd; she was beginning to be ill, she desired her husband's immediate return. The young man, at the thought that he had lost several hours, and that by hard riding he might already have been with his wife, uttered a passionate oath. He barely consented to stop for a mouthful of supper, but mounted the messenger's horse and started off at a gallop.

He reached home at midnight. His wife had been delivered of a little girl. "Ah, why weren't you with me?" she said, as he came to her bedside.

"I was out of the house when the man came. I was with Rosalind," said Lloyd, innocently.

Mrs Lloyd made a little moan, and turned away. But she continued to do very well, and for a week her improvement was uninterrupted. Finally, however, through some indiscretion in the way of diet or exposure, it was checked, and the poor lady grew rapidly worse. Lloyd was in despair. It very soon became evident that she was breathing her last. Mrs Lloyd came to a sense of her approaching end, and declared that she was reconciled with death. On the third evening after the change took place she told her husband that she felt she should not get through the night. She dismissed her servants, and also requested her mother to withdraw – Mrs Wingrave having arrived on the preceding day. She had had her infant placed on the bed beside her, and she lay on her side, with the child against her breast, holding her husband's hands. The night lamp was hidden behind the heavy curtains of the bed, but the room was illumined with a red glow from the immense fire of logs on the hearth.

"It seems strange not to be warmed into life by such a fire as that," the young woman said, feebly trying to smile. "If I had but a little of it in my veins! But I have given all my fire to this little spark of mortality." And she dropped her eyes on her child. Then raising them she looked at her husband with a long, penetrating gaze. The last feeling which lingered in her heart was one of suspicion. She had not recovered from the shock which Arthur had given her by telling her that in the hour of her agony he had been with Rosalind. She trusted her husband very nearly as well as she loved him; but now that she was called away forever she felt a cold horror of her sister. She felt in her soul that Rosalind had never ceased to be jealous of her good fortune; and a year of happy security had not effaced the young girl's image, dressed in her wedding garments, and smiling with simulated triumph. Now that Arthur was to be alone, what might not Rosalind attempt? She was beautiful, might she not make upon the young man's saddened heart? Mrs Lloyd looked at her husband in silence. It seemed hard, after all, to doubt of his constancy. His fine eyes were filled with tears; his face was convulsed with weeping; the clasp of his hands was warm and passionate. How noble he looked, how tender, how faithful and devoted! "Nay," thought Perdita, "he's not such a one for Rosalind. He'll never forget me. Nor does Rosalind truly care for him; she cares only for vanities and finery and jewels." And she lowered her eyes on her white hands, which her husband's liberality had covered with rings, and on the lace ruffles which trimmed the edge of her nightdress. "She covets my rings and my laces more than she covets my husband."

At this moment the thought of her sister's rapacity seemed to cast a dark shadow between her and the helpless figure of her little girl. "Arthur," she said, "you must take off my rings. I shall not be buried in them. One of these days my daughter shall wear them – my rings and my laces and silks. I had them all brought out and shown me today. It's a great wardrobe – there's not such another in the Province; I can say it without vanity, now that I have done with it. It will be a great inheritance for my daughter when she grows into a young woman. There are things there that a man never buys twice, and if they are lost you will never again see the like. So you will watch them well. Some dozen things I have left to Rosalind; I have named them to my mother. I have given her that blue and silver; it was meant for her; I wore it only once, I looked ill in it. But the rest are to be sacredly kept for this little innocent. It's such a providence that she should be my colour; she can wear my gowns; she has her mother's eyes. You know the same fashions come back every twenty years. She can wear my gowns as they are. They will lie there quietly waiting till she grows into them – wrapped in camphor and rose leaves, and keeping their colours in the sweet-scented darkness. She shall have black hair, she shall wear my carnation satin. Do you promise me, Arthur?"

"Promise you what, dearest?"

"Promise me to keep your poor little wife's old gowns."

"Are you afraid I shall sell them?"

"No, but that they may get scattered. My mother will have them properly wrapped up, and you shall lay them away under a double lock. Do you know the great chest in the attic, with the iron bands? There is no end to what it will hold. You can put them all there. My mother and the housekeeper will do it, and give you the key. And you will keep the key in your secretary, and never give it to anyone but your child. Do you promise me?"

"Ah, yes, I promise you," said Lloyd, puzzled at the intensity with which his wife appeared to cling to this idea.

"Will you swear?" repeated Perdita.

"Yes, I swear."

"Well – I trust you – I trust you," said the poor lady, looking into his eyes with eyes in which, if he had suspected her vague apprehensions, he might have read an appeal quite as much as an assurance.

Lloyd bore his bereavement rationally and manfully. A month after his wife's death, in the course of business, circumstances arose which offered him an opportunity of going to England. He took advantage of it, to change the current of his thoughts. He was absent nearly a year, during which his little girl was tenderly nursed and guarded by her grandmother. On his return he had his house again thrown open, and announced his intention of keeping the same state as during his wife's lifetime. It very soon came to be predicted that he would marry again, and there were at least a dozen young women of whom one may say that it was by no fault of theirs that, for six months after his return, the prediction did not come true. During this interval he still left his little daughter in Mrs Wingrave's hands, the latter assuring him that a change of residence at so tender an age would be full of danger for her health. Finally, however, he declared that his heart longed for his daughter's presence and that she must be brought up to town. He sent his coach and his housekeeper to fetch her home. Mrs Wingrave was in terror lest something should befall her on the road; and, in accordance with this feeling, Rosalind offered to accompany her. She could return the next day. So she went up to town with her little niece, and Mr Lloyd met her on the threshold of his house, overcome with her kindness and with paternal joy. Instead of returning the next day Rosalind stayed out the week; and when at last she reappeared, she had only come for her clothes. Arthur would not hear of her coming home, nor would the baby. That little person cried and choked if Rosalind left her; and at the sight of her grief Arthur lost his wits, and swore that she was going to die. In fine, nothing would suit them but that the aunt should remain until the little niece had grown used to strange faces.

It took two months to bring this consummation about; for it was not until this period had elapsed that Rosalind took leave of her brother-in-law. Mrs Wingrave had shaken her head over her daughter's absence; she had declared that it was not becoming, that it was the talk of the whole country. She had reconciled herself to it only because, during the girl's visit, the household enjoyed an unwonted term of peace. Bernard Wingrave had brought his wife home to live, between whom and her sister-in-law there was as little love as you please. Rosalind was perhaps no angel; but in the daily practice of life she was a sufficiently good-natured girl, and if she quarrelled with Mrs Bernard, it was not without provocation. Quarrel, however, she did, to the great annoyance not only of her antagonist, but of the two spectators of these constant altercations. Her stay in the household of her brother-in-law, therefore, would have been delightful, if only because it removed her from contact with the object of her antipathy at home. It was doubly – it was ten times – delightful, in that it kept her near the object of her early passion. Mrs Lloyd's sharp suspicions had fallen very far short of the truth. Rosalind's sentiment had been a passion at first, and a passion it remained – a passion of whose radiant heat, tempered to the delicate state of his feelings, Mr Lloyd very soon felt the influence. Lloyd, as I have hinted, was not a modern Petrarch; it was not in his nature to practice an ideal constancy. He had not been many days in the house with his sister-in-law before he began to assure himself that she was, in the language of that day, a devilish fine woman. Whether Rosalind really practised those insidious arts that her sister had been tempted to impute to her it is needless to inquire. It is enough to say that she found means to appear to the very best advantage. She used to seat herself every morning before the big fireplace in the dining room, at work upon a piece of tapestry, with her little niece disporting herself on the carpet at her feet, or on the train of her dress, and playing with her woollen balls. Lloyd would have been a very stupid fellow if he had remained insensible to the rich suggestions of this charming picture. He was exceedingly fond of his little girl, and was never weary of taking her in his arms and tossing her up and down, and making her crow with delight. Very often, however, he would venture upon greater liberties than the young lady was yet prepared to allow, and then she would suddenly vociferate her displeasure. Rosalind, at this, would drop her tapestry, and put out her handsome hands with the serious smile of the young girl whose virgin fancy has revealed to her all a mother's healing arts. Lloyd would give up the child, their eyes would meet, their hands would touch, and Rosalind would extinguish the little girl's sobs upon the snowy folds of the kerchief that crossed her bosom. Her dignity was perfect, and nothing could be more discreet than the manner in which she accepted her brother-in-law's hospitality. It may almost be said, perhaps, that there was something harsh in her reserve. Lloyd had a provoking feeling that she was in the house and yet was unapproachable. Half an hour after supper, at the very outset of the long winter evenings, she would light her candle, make the young man a most respectful curtsey, and march off to bed. If these were arts, Rosalind was a great artist. But their effect was so gentle, so gradual, they were calculated to work upon the young widower's fancy with a crescendo so finely shaded, that, as the reader has seen, several weeks elapsed before Rosalind began to feel sure that her returns would cover her outlay. When this became morally certain she packed up her trunk and returned to her mother's house. For three days she waited; on the fourth Mr Lloyd made his appearance – a respectful but pressing suitor. Rosalind heard him to the end, with great humility, and accepted him with infinite modesty. It is hard to imagine that Mrs Lloyd would have forgiven her husband; but if anything might have disarmed her resentment it would have been the ceremonious continence of this interview. Rosalind imposed upon her lover but a short probation. They were married, as was becoming, with great privacy – almost with secrecy – in the hope perhaps, as was waggishly remarked at the time, that the late Mrs Lloyd wouldn't hear of it.

The marriage was to all appearance a happy one, and each party obtained what each had desired – Lloyd "a devilish fine woman," and Rosalind – but Rosalind's desires, as the reader will have observed, had remained a good deal of a mystery. There were, indeed, two blots upon their felicity, but time would perhaps efface them. During the first three years of her marriage Mrs Lloyd failed to become a mother, and her husband on his side suffered heavy losses of money. This latter circumstance compelled a material retrenchment in his expenditure, and Rosalind was perforce less of a fine lady than her sister had been. She contrived, however, to carry it like a woman of considerable fashion. She had long since ascertained that her sister's copious wardrobe had been sequestrated for the benefit of her daughter, and that it lay languishing in thankless gloom in the dusty attic. It was a revolting thought that these exquisite fabrics should await the good pleasure of a little girl who sat in a high chair and ate bread and milk with a wooden spoon. Rosalind had the good taste, however, to say nothing about the matter until several months had expired. Then, at last, she timidly broached it to her husband. Was it not a pity that so much finery should be lost? – for lost it would be, what with colours fading, and moths eating it up, and the change of fashions. But Lloyd gave her so abrupt and peremptory a refusal, that she saw, for the present, her attempt was vain. Six months went by, however, and brought with them new seeds and new visions. Rosalind's thoughts hovered lovingly about her sister's relics. She went up and looked at the chest in which they lay imprisoned. There was a sullen defiance in its three great padlocks and its iron bands which only quickened her cupidity. There was something exasperating in its incorruptible immobility. It was like a grim and grizzled old household servant, who locks his jaws over a family secret. And then there was a look of capacity in its vast extent, and a sound as of dense fullness, when Rosalind knocked its side with the toe of her little shoe, which caused her to flush with baffled longing. "It's absurd," she cried; "it's improper, it's wicked"; and she forthwith resolved upon another attack upon her husband. On the following day, after dinner, when he had had his wine, she boldly began it. But he cut her short with great sternness.

"Once for all, Rosalind," said he, "it's out of the question. I shall be gravely displeased if you return to the matter."

"Very good," said Rosalind. "I am glad to learn the esteem in which I am held. Gracious heaven," she cried, "I am a very happy woman! It's an agreeable thing to feel one's self sacrificed to a caprice!" And her eyes filled with tears of anger and disappointment.

Lloyd had a good-natured man's horror of a woman's sobs, and he attempted – I may say he condescended – to explain. "It's not a caprice, dear, it's a promise," he said – "an oath."

"An oath? It's a pretty matter for oaths! and to whom, pray?"

"To Perdita," said the young man, raising his eyes for an instant, but immediately dropping them.

"Perdita – ah, Perdita!" and Rosalind's tears broke forth. Her bosom heaved with stormy sobs – sobs which were the long deferred sequel of the violent fit of weeping in which she had indulged herself on the night when she discovered her sister's betrothal. She had hoped, in her better moments, that she had done with her jealousy; but her temper, on that occasion, had taken an ineffaceable hold. "And pray, what right had Perdita to dispose of my future?" she cried. "What right had she to bind you to meanness and cruelty? Ah, I occupy a dignified place, and I make a very fine figure! I am welcome to what Perdita has left! And what has she left? I never knew till now how little! Nothing, nothing, nothing."

This was very poor logic, but it was very good as a "scene." Lloyd put his arm around his wife's waist and tried to kiss her, but she shook him off with magnificent scorn. Poor fellow! he had coveted a "devilish fine woman," and he had got one. Her scorn was intolerable. He walked away with his ears tingling – irresolute, distracted. Before him was his secretary, and in it the sacred key which with his own hand he had turned in the triple lock. He marched up and opened it, and took the key from a secret drawer, wrapped in a little packet which he had sealed with his own honest bit of glazonry. *Je garde*, said the motto – "I keep." But he was ashamed to put it back. He flung it upon the table beside his wife.

"Put it back!" she cried. "I want it not. I hate it!"

"I wash my hands of it," cried her husband. "God forgive me!"

Mrs Lloyd gave an indignant shrug of her shoulders, and swept out of the room, while the young man retreated by another door. Ten minutes later Mrs Lloyd returned, and found the room occupied by her little step-daughter and the nursery maid. The key was not on the table. She glanced at the child. Her little niece was perched on a chair, with the packet in her hands. She had broken the seal with her own small fingers. Mrs Lloyd hastily took possession of the key.

At the habitual supper hour Arthur Lloyd came back from his counting room. It was the month of June, and supper was served by daylight. The meal was placed on the table, but Mrs Lloyd failed to make her appearance. The servant whom his master sent to call her came back with the assurance that her room was empty, and that the women informed him that she had not been since dinner. They had, in truth, observed her to have been in tears, and, supposing her to be shut up in her chamber, had not disturbed her. Her husband called her name in various parts of the house, but without response. At last it occurred to him that he might find her by taking the way to the attic. The thought gave him a strange feeling of discomfort, and he bade his servants remain behind, wishing no witness in his quest. He reached the foot of the staircase leading to the topmost flat, and stood with his hand on the banisters, pronouncing his wife's name. His voice trembled. He called again louder and more firmly. The only sound which disturbed the absolute silence was a faint echo of his own tones, repeating his question under the great eaves. He nevertheless felt irresistibly moved to ascend the staircase. It opened upon a wide hall, lined with wooden closets, and terminating in a window which looked westward, and admitted the last rays of the sun. Before the window stood the great chest. Before the chest, on her knees, the young man saw with amazement and horror the figure of his wife. In an instant he crossed the interval between them, bereft of utterance. The lid of the chest stood open, exposing, amid their perfumed napkins, its treasure of stuffs and jewels. Rosalind had fallen backward from a kneeling posture, with one hand supporting her on the floor and the other pressed to her heart. On her limbs was the stiffness of death, and on her face, in the fading light of the sun, the terror of something more than death. Her lips were parted in entreaty, in dismay, in agony; and on her blanched brow and cheeks there glowed the marks of ten hideous wounds from two vengeful ghostly hands.

Mary E. Braddon

John Granger

Mary Elizabeth Braddon (1835–1915) was the Victorian era's most popular "sensation" novelist, outselling even Wilkie Collins and Charles Dickens. Her first great success came with Lady Audley's Secret *(1862), followed by* Aurora Floyd *(1863) and over eighty more novels in similar vein. She also wrote a number of fine ghost stories, including "The Cold Embrace", "Eveline's Visitant" and the less familiar "John Granger" (which originally appeared in the* Belgravia Annual, *1870).*

I

"THEN THERE IS no hope for me, Susy?"

The speaker was a stalwart young fellow of the yeoman class, with a grave, earnest face, and a frank, fearless manner. He was standing by the open window of a pleasant farmhouse parlour, by the side of a bright-eyed girl, who was leaning with folded arms upon the broad window-sill, looking shyly downwards as he talked to her.

"Is there no chance, Susy! none? Is it all over between us?"

"If you mean that I shall ever cease to think of you as one of the best friends I have in this world, John, no," she answered; "or that I shall ever cease to look up to you as the noblest and truest of men, no, John – a hundred times no."

"But I mean something more than that, Susy, and you know it as well as I do. I want you to be my wife by-and-by. I'm not in a hurry, you know, my dear. I can bide my time. You're very young yet, and may be you scarcely know your own mind. I can wait, Susy. My love will stand wear and tear. Let me have the hope of winning you by-and-by. I'm not a poor man at this present time, you know, Susy. There are three thousand pounds of old uncle Tidman's on deposit in my name in Hillborough Bank. I've been a lucky fellow in having an industrious father and a rich bachelor uncle, and with this chance of you for my wife, a few years would make me a rich man."

"That can never be, John. I know how proud I ought to be that you should think of me like this. I'm not worthy of so much love. It isn't that I don't appreciate your merits, John; but – "

"There's someone else, eh, Susy?"

"Yes, John," she faltered, in a very low voice, and with a vivid blush on her drooping face.

"Someone who has asked you to be his wife?"

"No, John; but I think he likes me a little, and – "

Here she stopped suddenly, finding the sentence difficult to continue.

John Granger gave a long, heavy sigh, and stood for some minutes looking at the ground in dead silence.

"I think I can guess who it is," he said at last; "Robert Ashley – eh, Susy?" The blush grew deeper, and the girl's silence was a sufficient answer. "Well, he's a fine handsome young fellow, and more likely to take a pretty girl's fancy than such a blunt, plain-spoken chap as I am; and he's a good fellow enough, as far as I know; I've nothing to say against him, Susy. But there's one man in the world I should have liked to warn you against, Susan, if I'd thought there was a shadow of a chance you'd ever listen to any love-making of his."

"Who is that, John?"

"Your cousin, Stephen Price."

"You needn't fear that I should ever listen to him, John. There's little love lost between Stephen and me."

"Isn't there? I've heard him swear that he'd have you for his wife some day, Susan. I don't like him, my dear, and I don't trust him either. It isn't only that he bears a bad character up town, as a dissipated, pleasure-loving spendthrift; there's something more than that; something below the surface that I can't find words for. I know that he's very clever. Folks say that Mr Vollair the lawyer looks over all his faults on account of his cleverness, and that he never had a clerk to serve him so well as Stephen does. But cleverness and honesty don't always go together, Susy, and I fear that cousin of yours will come to a bad end."

Susan Lorton did not attempt to dispute the justice of this opinion. Stephen Price was no favourite of hers, in spite of those good looks and that showy cleverness which had won him a certain amount of popularity elsewhere.

John Granger lingered at the sunny window, where the scent of a thousand roses came floating in upon the warm summer air. He lingered as if loth to go and make an end of that interview; though the end must come, and the last words must needs be spoken very soon.

"Well, well, Susy," he said presently, "a man must teach himself to bear these things, even when they seem to break his life up somehow, and make an end of every hope and dream he ever had. I can't tell you how I've loved you, my dear – how I shall love you to the end of my days. Bob Ashley is a good fellow, and God grant he may make you a good husband! But I don't believe it's in him to love you, as I do, Susan. He takes life pleasantly and has his mind full of getting on in the world, you see, and he has father and mother and sisters to care for. I've got no one but you to love, Susan. I've stood quite alone in the world ever since I was a boy, and you've been all the world to me. It's bitter to bear, my dear; but it can't be helped. Don't cry, Susy darling. I'm a selfish brute to talk like this, and bring the tears into those pretty eyes. It can't be helped, my dear. Providence orders these things, you see, and we must bear them quietly. Goodbye, dear."

He gave the girl his big honest hand. She took it in both her own, bent over it, and kissed it tearfully.

"You'll never know how truly I respect you John," she said. "But don't say goodbye like that. We are to be friends always, aren't we?"

"Friends always? Yes, my dear; but friends at a distance. There's some things I couldn't bear to see. I can wish for your happiness, and pray for it – honestly; but I couldn't stop at Friarsgate to see you Robert Ashley's wife. My lease of the old farm is out. I'm to call on Mr Vollair this afternoon to talk about renewing it. I fancied you'd be mistress of the dear old place, Susy. That's been my dream for the last three years. I couldn't bear the look of the empty rooms now that dream's broken. I shall surrender the farm at once, and go to America, I've got capital that'll start me anywhere, and I'm not afraid of work. I've old friends out there too; my first cousin, Jim Lomax, and his wife. They went out five years ago, and have been doing wonders with a farm in New England. I shan't feel quite strange there."

"Go to America, John, and never come back?" said Susan, despondently.

She had a sincere regard for this honest yeoman, and was grieved to the heart at the thought of the sorrow that had come to him through his unfortunate desire to be something more to her than a friend.

"Never's a long word, Susy," he answered, in his serious straightforward way. "Perhaps when a good many years have gone over all our heads, and when your children are beginning to grow up, I may come back and take my seat beside your hearth, and smoke my pipe with your husband. Not that I should ever cease to love you, my dear; but time would take the sting out of the old pain, and it would be only a kind of placid sorrow, like the thought of one that's long been dead. Yes, I shall come back to England after ten or fifteen years, if I live, if it's only for the sake of seeing your children – and I'll wager there'll be one amongst them that'll take to me almost as if it was my own, and will come to be like a child to me in my old age. I've seen such things. And now I must say goodbye, Susy; for I've got to be up town at three o'clock to see Mr Vollair, and I've a deal of work to do before I leave."

"Shall you go soon, John!"

"As soon as ever I can get things settled – the farm off my hands, and so on. But I shall come to say goodbye to you and your father before I go."

"Of course, you will, John. It would be unfriendly to go without seeing father. Goodbye!"

They shook hands once more and parted. The yeoman walked slowly along the little garden path, and across a patch of furze-grown common land, on the other side of which there was a straggling wood of some extent, broken up here and there by disused gravel-pits and pools of stagnant water – a wild kind of place to pass at night, yet considered safe enough by the country people about Hillborough as there was scarcely any part of it that was not within earshot of the high road. The narrow footpath across this wood was a short-cut between Matthew Lorton's farm and Hillborough, and John Granger took it.

He walked with a firm step and an upright bearing, though his heart was heavy, as he went townwards that afternoon. He was a man to bear his trouble in a manly spirit, whatever it might be, and there were no traces of his disappointment in his looks or manner when he presented himself at the lawyer's house.

Mr Vollair had a client with him; so John Granger was ushered into the clerk's office, where he found Stephen Price hard at work at a desk, in company with a smaller and younger clerk.

"Good afternoon, Granger," he said, in a cool patronizing manner that John Granger hated; "come about your lease, of course?"

"There is nothing else for me to come about."

"Ah, you see, you're one of those lucky fellows who never want the help of the law to get you out of a scrape. And you're a devilish lucky fellow, too, in the matter of this lease, if you can get Friarsgate for a new term at the rent you've been paying hitherto, as I dare say you will, if you play your cards cleverly with our governor presently."

"I am not going to ask for a new lease," answered John Granger; "I am going to leave Friarsgate."

"Going to leave Friarsgate! You astound me. Have you got a better farm in your eye?"

"I am going to America."

Stephen Price gave expression to his astonishment by a prolonged whistle, and then twisted himself round upon his stool, the better to regard Mr Granger.

"Why, Granger, how is this?" he asked. "A fellow like you, with plenty of money, going off to America! I thought that was the refuge for the destitute."

"I'm tired of England, and I've a fancy for a change. I hear that a man may do very well in America, with a good knowledge of farming and a tidy bit of capital."

"Ah, and you've got that," said Stephen Price, with an envious sigh. "And so you're thinking of going to America? That's very strange. I used to fancy you were sweet upon a certain pretty cousin of mine. I've seen you hanging about old Lorton's place a good deal of late years."

John Granger did not reply to this remark. Mr Vollair's client departed a few minutes later, and Mr Granger was asked to step into the lawyer's office. He found his business very easy to arrange in the manner he wished. Mr Vollair had received more than one offer for Friarsgate farm, and there was an applicant who would be glad to get the place as soon as John Granger could relinquish it, without waiting for the expiration of his lease. This incoming tenant would no doubt be willing to take his furniture and live and dead stock at a valuation, Mr Vollair told John. So the young farmer left the office in tolerable spirits, pleased to find there were no obstacles to his speedy departure from a home that had once been dear to him.

II

John Granger's preparations and arrangements, the disposal of his property, and the getting together of his simple outfit, occupied little more than three weeks; and it was still bright midsummer weather when he took his last walk round the pastures of Friarsgate and, for the first time since he had resolved to leave those familiar scenes, realized how great a hold they had upon his heart.

'It'll be dreary work in a strange country," he thought, as he leaned upon a gate, looking at the lazy cattle which were no longer his, and wondering whether they would miss him when he was gone; "and what pleasure can I ever take in trying to get rich! – I who have no one to work for, no one to take pride in my success! Perhaps it would have been better to stay here, even though I had to hear her wedding bells some fine summer morning, and see her leaning on Robert Ashley's arm, and looking up in his face as I used to fancy she would look up to me in all the years to come. O God, how I wish I was dead! What an easy end that would make of everything!"

He thought of the men and women who had died of a fever last autumn round about Hillborough – people who had wished to live, for whom life was full of duties and household joys; whose loss left wide gaps among their kindred, not to be filled again upon this earth. If death would come to him, what a glad release! It was not that he suffered from any keen or violent agony; it was the dull blankness of his existence which he felt – an utter emptiness and hopelessness; nothing to live for in the present, nothing to look forward to in the future.

This was the last day. His three great sea chests, containing his clothes, books, and other property which he could not bring himself to part with, had gone on to London by that morning's luggage train. He had arranged to follow himself by the night mail which left Hillborough Station at half-past nine, and would be in London at two o'clock next morning. At the last he had been seized with a fancy for prolonging his time to the uttermost, and it was for this reason, he had chosen the latest train by which he could leave Hillborough. He had a good many people to take leave of, and it was rather trying work. He had always been liked and respected, and on this last day it surprised him to find how fond the people were of him, and how general was the regret caused by his departure. Little children clung about his knees, matronly eyes were dried in lavender cotton aprons, pretty girls offered blushingly to kiss him at parting; stalwart young fellows, his companions of old, declared they would never have a friend they could trust and honour as they had trusted and honoured him. It touched the poor fellow to the heart to find himself so much beloved. And he was going to sacrifice all this, because he could not endure to live in the old home now his dream was broken.

He had put off his visit to Matthew Lorton's house to the very last. His latest moments at Hillborough should be given to Susan, he told himself. He would drain to the last drop the cup of that sweet, sad parting. His last memory of English soil should be her bright tender face looking at him compassionately, as she had looked the day she broke his heart.

It was half-past seven when he went in at the little garden gate. A warm summer evening, the rustic garden steeped in the low western sunshine; the birds singing loud in hawthorn and sycamore; a peaceful vesper calm upon all things. John Granger had been expected. He could see that at a glance. The best tea-things were set out in the best parlour, and Mr Lorton and his daughter were waiting tea for him. There was a great bunch of roses on the table, and Susan was dressed in light blue muslin, with a rose in her bosom. He thought how often in the dreary time to come she would arise before him like a picture, with the sunshine flickering about her bright hair, and the red rose at her breast.

She was very sweet to him that evening, tender and gentle and clinging, as she might have been with a fondly loved brother who was leaving her for ever. The farmer asked him about his plans, and gave his approval of them heartily. It was well for a sturdy fellow with a bit of money to push his way in a new country, where he might make fifty per cent upon his capital, instead of dawdling on in England, where it was quite as much as a man could do to make both ends meet at the close of a year's hard work.

"My little Susy is going to be married to young Bob Ashley," Mr Lorton said by-and-by. "He asked her last Tuesday was a week; but they've been courting in a kind of way this last twelvemonth. I couldn't well say no, for Bob's father and I have been friends for many a year, and the young man's a decent chap enough. He's going to rent that little dairy farm of Sir Marmaduke Halliday's on the other side of Hillborough Road. Old Ashley has promised to stock it for him, and he hopes to do well. It isn't much of a match for my girl, you know, John; but the young people have made up their minds, so it's no use setting my face against it."

They had been sitting at the tea-table nearly half an hour, when the sunny window was suddenly darkened by the apparition of Mr Stephen Price looking in upon them in an easy familiar manner, with his folded arms upon the sill.

"Good evening, uncle Lorton," he said. "Good evening, Susy. How do, Granger? I didn't know there was going to be a tea-party, or I shouldn't have come."

"It isn't a tea-party," answered Susan; "it is only John Granger, who has come to bid us goodbye, and we are very, very sorry he is going away."

"Oh, we are, are we?" said the lawyer's clerk with a sneer; "what would Bob Ashley say to that, I wonder?"

"Come in, Steph, and don't be a fool," growled the old man.

Mr Price came in, and took his seat at the tea-table. He was flashily dressed, wore his hair long and had a good deal of whisker, which he was perpetually caressing with a hand of doubtful cleanliness, whereon the inky evidence of his day's work was unpleasantly obvious.

He did not care much for such womanish refreshment as tea, which he denounced in a sweeping manner as "cat-lap," but he took a cup from his cousin nevertheless, and joined freely in the conversation while he drank it.

He asked John Granger a good many questions about his plans – whether he meant to buy land, and when, and where, and a great deal more in the same way – to all of which John replied as shortly as was consistent with the coldest civility.

"You take all your capital with you, of course!" asked Stephen Price.

"No; I take none of my capital with me."

"Why, hang it all, man, you must take some money!"

"I take the money I received for my furniture and stock."

"Ah, to be sure; you came to the office yesterday afternoon to receive it? Over six hundred pounds, wasn't it? I drew up the agreement between you and the new man; so I ought to know."

"It was over six hundred pounds."

"And you take that with you? Quite enough to start with, of course. And the rest of your money is as safe as houses in old Lawler's bank. No fear of any smash there. I wish I was going with you, Granger. I'm heartily sick of Hillborough. I shall cut old Vollair's office before very long, come what may. I can't stand it much longer. I've got a friend on the look-out for a berth for me up in London, and directly I hear of anything I shall turn my back upon this dismal old hole."

"You'll have to pay your debts before you do that, I should think, Steph," his uncle remarked, bluntly.

Stephen Price shrugged his shoulders, and pushed his teacup away with a listless air. He got up presently and lounged out of the house, after a brief good evening to all. He made no attempt to take leave of John Granger, and seemed in his careless way to have forgotten that he was parting with him for the last time. No one tried to detain him. They seemed to breathe more freely when he was gone.

John and Susan wandered out into the garden after tea, while the farmer smoked his pipe by the open window. The sun was low by this time, and the western sky flooded with rosy light. The garden was all abloom with roses and honeysuckle. John Granger fancied he should never look upon such flowers or such a garden again.

They walked up and down the narrow path once or twice almost in silence, and then Susan began to tell him how much she regretted his departure.

"I don't know how it is, John," she said, "but I feel tonight as if I would give all the world to keep you here. I cannot tell you how sorry I am you are going. Oh, John, I wish with all my heart I could have been what you asked me to be. I wish I could have put aside all thoughts of Robert."

"Could you have done that, Susan?" he cried, with sudden energy.

His fate trembled upon a breath in that moment. A word from Susan, and he would have stayed; a word from her, and he would never have taken the path across the common and through the wood to Hillborough on that fair summer evening. He was her valued friend of many years; dearer to her than she had known until that moment. It seemed to her all at once that she had thrown away the gold, and had chosen – not dross, but something less precious than that unalloyed gold.

It was too late now for any change.

"I have promised Robert to be his wife," she said; "but oh, John, I wish you were not going away."

"My dear love, I could not trust myself to stay here; I love you too much for that. But I will come back when I am a sober elderly man, and ask for a corner beside your hearth."

"Promise me that. And you will write to me from America, won't you,

John? I shall be so anxious, and father too, to know that you are safe and well."

"Yes, my dear, I will write."

"What is the name of the steamer you are to go in?"

"The *Washington*, bound for New York."

"I shall not forget that – the *Washington*."

John Granger looked at his watch. The sun had gone down, and there was a long line of crimson yonder in the west above the edge of the brown furze-grown common. Beyond it, the wood dipped down, and the tops of the trees made a black line against that red light. Above, the sky was of one pale tender green, with stars faintly shining here and there.

"What a lovely night!" said Susan.

John Granger sighed as he looked at that peaceful landscape.

"I did not know how much I loved this place and all belonging to it," he said. "Good night, Susy; Good night, and goodbye."

"Won't you kiss me the last time, John?" she said, shyly.

She scarcely knew what she had asked. He took her in his arms, strained her to his breast, and pressed one passionate, despairing kiss upon her brow. It was the first and last in his life.

"Time's up, Susy," he said, gently releasing her.

He went to the window, shook hands with the farmer, and took leave of him in that quiet, undemonstrative way which means a good deal with a man of John Granger's mould. A minute more, and he was gone.

Susan stood at the garden gate, watching the tall dark figure crossing the common. Twice he turned and waved his hand to her – the last time upon the edge of the common, before he took the path down to the wood. After this night the still twilight hour seldom came without bringing the thought of him to Susan Lorton.

It seemed to grow dark all at once when he was gone, and the house had a dreary look to Susan when she went indoors. What was it that made her shiver as she crossed the threshold? Something – some nameless, shapeless fancy shook her with a sudden fear. Her father had strolled out to the garden through the wide open back door. The house seemed quite empty, and the faint sound of the summer wind sighing in the parlour chimney was like the lamentation of a human creature in pain.

III

The summer passed, and in the late autumn came Susan's wedding day. She was very fond of her good-looking generous-hearted young suitor, and yet even on the eve of her marriage her heart had turned a little regretfully towards absent John Granger. She was not a coquette, to glory in the mischief her beauty had done. It seemed to her a terrible thing that a good man should have been driven from his home for love of her.

She had thought of him a great deal since that summer night upon which he had looked back at her on the verge of Hawley Wood – all the more because no letter had come from him yet, and she was beginning to be a little anxious about his safety. She thought of him still more, by and by, as the winter months passed without bringing the promised letter. Her husband made light of her fears, telling her that John Granger would find plenty to do in a new country, without wasting his time in scribbling letters to old friends. But this did not convince Susan.

"He promised to write, Robert," she said; "and John Granger is not the man to break his promise."

Susan was very happy in her new home, and Robert Ashley declared he had the handiest, brightest, and most industrious wife in all Woodlandshire, to say nothing of her being the prettiest. She had been used to keeping her father's house since her early girlhood, and her matronly duties came very easy to her. The snug little farmhouse, with its neat furniture and fresh dimity draperies, was the prettiest thing possible in the way of rustic interiors; the Dutch-tiled dairy was like a temple dedicated to some pastoral divinity, and Susan took a natural womanly pride in this bright home. She had come from as good a house; but then this was quite her own, and young Robert Ashley was a more romantic figure in the foreground of the picture than her good humdrum old father.

Stephen Price did not stay at Hillborough long enough to see his cousin's wedding. He left Mr Vollair's employment about three weeks after John Granger's departure, and left without giving his employer any notice of his intention.

He went away from Hillborough as deeply in debt as it was practicable for a young man in his position to be, and the tradesmen to whom he owed money were loud in their còmplaints about him.

He was known to have gone to London, and there were some attempts made to discover his whereabouts. But in that mighty metropolis it was no easy thing to find an obscure lawyer's clerk, and nothing resulted from the endeavours of his angry creditors, except the mortification of defeat, which made them still more angry. No one, except those to whom he owed money, cared what had become of him. He had been considered pleasant company in a tavern parlour, and his manners and dress had been copied by some aspiring clerks and apprentices in Hillborough; but he had never been known to do anyone a kindness, and his disappearance left no empty place in any heart.

The new year came, and still there was no letter from John Granger. But early in January Robert Ashley came home from Hillborough market one afternoon, and told his wife she needn't worry herself about her old friend any longer.

"John Granger's safe enough, my lass," he said. "I was talking to Simmons, the cashier at Lawler's bank, this morning, and he told me that Granger wrote to them for a thousand pounds last November from New York, and he has written five hundred more since. He is buying land somewhere – I forget the name of the place – and he's well and hearty, Simmons tells me."

Susan clapped her hands joyfully.

"Oh, Robert, how glad I am!" she cried. "It isn't kind of John to have forgotten his promise; but I don't care about that as long as he's safe."

"I don't know why you should ever take it into your head that there was anything amiss with him," said Robert Ashley, who did not regard John Granger's exile from a sentimental point of view.

"Well, I'm afraid I'm rather fanciful, Bob; but I could never explain to you what a strange feeling came over me the night John Granger went away from Hillborough. It was after I had said goodbye to him, and had gone back into the house, where all was dark and quiet. I sat in the parlour thinking of him, and it seemed as if a voice was saying in my ear that neither I, nor anyone that cared for him, would ever see John Granger again. There wasn't any such voice, of course, you know, Robert, but it seemed like that in my mind; and whenever I've thought of poor John Granger since that time, it has seemed to me like thinking of the dead. Often and often I've said to myself, 'Why, Susan, you foolish thing, you ought to know that he's safe enough in America. Ill news travels fast; and if there'd be anything wrong, we should have heard of it somehow.' But, reason with myself as I would, I have never been able to feel comfortable about him; and thank God for your good news, Robert, and thank you for bringing it to me."

She raised herself on tiptoe to kiss her husband, who looked down at her in a fond, protecting way from the height of his own wisdom.

"Why, Susy, what a timid, nervous little puss you are!" he said. "I should have been getting jealous of John Granger by this time if I'd known you thought so much of him."

The winter days lengthened, and melted into early spring. It was bright March weather, and Susan had an hour of daylight after tea for her needlework, while Robert attended to his evening duties out of doors. They had fires still, though the days were very mild; and Susan used to sit at the open window, with a jug of primroses on the wide wooden ledge before her, executing some dainty little repairs upon her husband's shirts.

One evening Robert Ashley was out later than usual, and when it had grown too dark for her to work any longer, Susan sat with her hands lying idle in her lap thinking – thinking of her wedded life, and the years that had gone before it – years that she could never recall without the image of John Granger, who had been in a manner mixed up with all her girlish days. It had been very unkind of him not to write. It seemed as if his love for her could not have been very much after all, or he would have been pleased to comply with her request. She could not quite forgive him for his neglect, glad as she was to know that he was safe.

The room was rather a large one; an old-fashioned room, with a low ceiling crossed by heavy beams; half parlour, half kitchen, with a wide open fireplace at one end, on which the logs had burnt to a dullish red just now, only brightening up with a faint flash of light now and then. The old chintz-covered armchair, in which Robert Ashley was wont to smoke his evening pipe, stood by the hearth ready for him.

Susan had been sitting with her face towards the open window, looking absently out at the garden, where daffodils and early primroses glimmered through the dusk. It was only the striking of the eight day clock in the corner that roused her from her reverie. She stooped to pick up her work, which had fallen to the ground. She was standing folding this in a leisurely way, when she looked towards the fireplace, and gave a little start at seeing that her husband's armchair was no longer empty.

"Why, Robert," she cried, "how quietly you must have come into the place! I never heard you."

There was no answer, and her voice sounded strange to her in the empty room.

"Robert!" she repeated, a little louder; but the figure in the chair neither answered nor stirred.

Then a sudden fright seized her, and she knew that it was not her husband. The room was almost dark; it was quite impossible that she could see the face of that dark figure seated in the armchair, with the shoulders bent a little over the fire. Yet she knew, as well as ever she had known anything in her life, that it was not Robert Ashley.

She went slowly towards the fireplace, and stood within a few paces of that strange figure. A little flash of light shot up from the smouldering logs, and shone for an instant on the face.

It was John Granger!

Susan Ashley tried to speak to him; but the words would not come. And yet it was hardly so appalling a thing to see him there that she need have felt what she did. England is not so far from America that a man may not cross the sea and drop in upon his friends unexpectedly.

The logs fell together with a crashing noise, and broke into a ruddy flame, lighting up the whole room. The chair was empty.

Susan uttered a loud cry, and almost at the same time Robert Ashley came in at the door.

"Why, Susy!" he exclaimed, "What's amiss lass?"

She ran to him, and took shelter in his arms, sobbing hysterically, and then, calming herself with an effort, told him how she had seen John Granger's ghost.

Robert laughed her to scorn.

"Why, my pet, what fancies will you be having next? Granger is safe enough over in Yankee land. It was some shadow that took the shape of your old friend, to your fancy. It's easy enough to fancy such a thing when your mind's full of anyone."

"There's no use in saying that, Robert," Susan answered, resolutely. "It was no fancy. John Granger is dead, and I have seen his ghost."

"He wasn't dead on the 10th of last December, anyhow. They had a letter from him at Lawler's bank, dated that day. Simmons told me so."

Susan shook her head mournfully.

"I've a feeling that he never got to America alive, Robert," she said. "I can't explain how it is, but I've a feeling that it was so."

"Dead men don't write letters, Susy, or send for their money out of the bank."

"Someone else might write the letters."

"Nonsense, lass! They know John Granger's handwriting and signature well enough at the bank, depend upon it. It would be no easy matter to deceive them. But I'll look in upon Simmons tomorrow. He and I are uncommonly friendly, you know, and there's nothing he wouldn't do to oblige me, in a reasonable way. I'll ask him if there have been any more letters from Granger, and get him to give me the address."

Susan did not say much more about that awful figure in the armchair. It was no use trying to convince her husband that the thing which she had seen was anything more than a creation of her own brain. She was very quiet all the rest of the evening, though she tried her uttermost to appear as if nothing had happened.

Robert Ashley saw Mr Simmons the cashier next day, and came back to his wife elated by the result of his inquiries. John Granger had written for another five hundred pounds by the very last post from America, and reported himself well and thriving. He was still in New York, and Mr Simmons had given Robert Ashley his address in that city.

Susan wrote to her old friend that very afternoon, telling him what she had seen, and begging him to write and set her mind at ease. After all, it was very consoling to hear what she had heard from her husband, and she tried to convince herself that the thing she had seen was only a trick of her imagination.

Another month went by, and again in the twilight the same figure appeared to her. It was standing this time, with one arm leaning on the high mantlepiece; standing facing her as she came back to the room, after having quitted it for a few minutes for some slight household duty.

There was a better fire and more light in the room than there had been before. The logs were burning with a steady blaze that lit up the well-known figure and unforgotten face. John Granger was looking at her with an expression that seemed half reproachful, half beseeching. He was very pale, much paler than she had ever seen him in life; and as he looked, she standing just within the threshold of the door, she saw him lift his hand slowly and point to his forehead. The firelight showed her a dark red stain upon the left temple, like the mark of a contused wound.

She covered her face with her hands, shuddering and uttering a little cry of terror, and then dropped half fainting upon a chair. When she uncovered her face the room was empty, the firelight shining cheerily upon the walls, no trace of that ghostly visitant. Again when her husband came in she told him of what she had seen for the first time that night. He heard her very gravely. This repetition of the business made it serious. If it were, as Robert Ashley fully believed it was, a delusion of his wife's, it was a dangerous delusion, and he knew not how to charm it away from her mind. She had conjured up a new fancy now, this notion of a blood-stained temple; the ghastly evidence of some foul play that had been done to John Granger.

And the man was alive and well in America all the time; but how convince a woman of that fact when she preferred to trust her own sick fancies?

This time Susan Ashley brooded over the thoughts of the thing she had seen, firmly believing that she had looked upon the shadow of the dead, and that there was some purpose to be fulfilled by that awful vision. In the day, however busy she might be with her daily work, the thought of this was almost always in her mind; in the dead silence of the night, when her husband was sleeping by her side, she would often lie awake for hours thinking of John Granger.

No answer had come to her letter, though there had been more than time for her to receive one.

"Robert," she said to her husband one day, "I do not believe that John Granger ever went to America."

"Oh, Susy, Susy, I wish you could get John Granger out of your head. Who is it that writes for his money, if it isn't he?"

"Anybody might know of the money – people know everything about their neighbours' affairs in Hillborough – and anybody that knew John Granger's hand might be able to forge a letter. I don't believe he ever went to America, Robert. I believe some accident – some fatal accident – happened to him on the night he was to leave Hillborough."

"Why, Susy, what should happen to him, and we not hear of it?"

"He might have been waylaid and murdered. He had a good deal of money about him, I know, that night; he was to sail from London by the *Washington*, and his luggage was all sent to an inn near the Docks. I wish you'd write to the people, Robert, and ask if he arrived there at the time he was expected; and I wish you'd find out at the station whether anyone saw him go away by the train that night."

"It's easy enough to do as much as that to please you, Susy. But I wish you wouldn't dwell upon these fancies about Granger; it's all nonsense, as you'll find out sooner or later."

He wrote the letter which his wife wanted written, asking the landlord of the Victoria Hotel, London Docks, whether a certain Mr John Granger, whose travelling chests had been forwarded from Hillborough, had arrived at his house on the 24th of July last, and when and how he had quitted it. He also took the trouble to go to the Hillborough Station, in order to question the station master and his subordinates about John Granger's departure.

Neither the station master nor the porters were able to give Robert Ashley any satisfactory information on this point. One or two of the men were not quite clear that they knew John Granger by sight; another knew him very well indeed, but could not swear to having seen him that night. The station master was quite clear that he had not seen him.

"I'm generally pretty busy with the mail bags at that time," he said, "and a passenger might very well escape my notice. But it would only have been civil in Granger to bid me goodbye; I've known him ever since he was a lad."

This was not a satisfactory account to carry back to Susan; nor was the letter that came from London in a day or two much more satisfactory. The landlord of the Victoria Hotel begged to inform Mr Ashley that the owner of the trunks from Hillborough had not arrived at his house until the middle of August. He was not quite sure about the date; but he knew the luggage had been lying in his place for something over three weeks, and he was thinking of advertising it, when the owner appeared.

Three weeks! and John Granger had left Susan Lorton that July night, intending to go straight to London. Where could he have been? What could he have been doing in the interval?

Robert Ashley tried to make light of the matter. Granger might have changed his mind at the last moment – at the railway station, perhaps – and might have gone off to visit friends in some other part of the country. But Susan told her husband that John Granger had no friends except at Hillborough, and that he was not given to changing his mind upon any occasion. She had now a settled conviction that some untimely fate had befallen her old friend, and that the letters from America were forgeries.

Ashley told his friend Simmons the story of the ghost rather reluctantly, but it was necessary to tell it in explaining how the letter to the London hotel keeper came to be written. Of course Mr Simmons was quite ready to agree with him that the ghostly part of the business was no more than a delusion of Susan's; but he was a good deal puzzled, not to say disturbed, by the hotel keeper's letter. He had talked over John

Granger's plans with him on that last day, and he remembered that John had been perfectly decided in his intention of going straight to London. The three weeks interval between his departure from Hillborough and his arrival in that city was a mystery not easily to be explained.

Mr Simmons referred to the letters from New York, and compared the signatures of them with previous signatures of John Granger's. If they were forgeries, they were very clever forgeries; but Granger's was a plain commercial hand by no means difficult to imitate. There was one thing noticeable in the signatures to the American letters – they were all exactly alike, line for line and curve for curve. This rather discomposed Mr Simmons; for it is a notorious fact that a man rarely signs his name twice in exactly the same manner. There is almost always some difference.

"I'm going up to London in a month," said the cashier; "I'll call at the Victoria Hotel when I'm there, and make a few enquiries about John Granger. We can make some excuse for keeping back the money in the meantime, if there should be any more written for."

Before the month was out, John Granger's ghost appeared for the third time to Susan Ashley. She had been to Hillborough alone to make some little purchases in the way of linen drapery, and came home through Hawley Wood in the tender May twilight. She was thinking of her old friend as she walked along the shadowy winding footpath. It was just such a still, peaceful evening as that upon which he had stood on the edge of the common looking back at her, and waving his hand, upon that last well remembered night.

He was so much in her thoughts, and the conviction that he had come from among the dead to visit her was so rooted in her mind, that she was scarcely surprised when she looked up presently, and saw a tall familiar figure moving slowly among the trees a little way before her. There seemed to be an awful stillness in the wood all at once, but there was nothing awful in that well-known figure.

She tried to overtake it; but it kept always in advance of her, and at a sudden turn in the path she lost it altogether. The trees grew thicker, and there was a solemn darkness at the spot where the path took this sharp turn, and on one side of the narrow footpath there was a steep declivity and a great hollow, made by a disused gravel pit.

She went home quietly enough, with a subdued sadness upon her, and told her husband what had happened to her. Nor did she rest until there had been a search made in Hawley Wood for the body of John Granger.

They searched, and found him lying at the bottom of the gravel pit, half buried in loose sand and gravel, and quite hidden by a mass of furze and bramble that grew over the spot. There was an inquest, of course. The tailor who had made the clothes found upon the body identified them, and swore to them as those he had made for John Granger. The pockets were all empty. There could be little doubt that John Granger had been waylaid and murdered for the sake of the money he carried upon him that night. His skull had been shattered by a blow from a jagged stick on the left temple. The stick was found lying at the bottom of the pit a little way from the body, with human hair and stains of blood upon it.

John Granger had never left Hillborough; and the person who had contrived to procure so much of his money, by sending the deposit receipts and forged letters from America, was, in all probability, his murderer. There was a large reward offered for the discovery of the guilty party; the police were hard at work; and the inquest was adjourned several times, in the hope that new facts might be elicited.

Susan Ashley and her father were examined closely as to the events of that fatal evening of July the 24th. Susan told everything: her cousin Stephen Price dropping in while they were at tea, the questions and answers about the money John Granger carried upon him – to the most minute particular.

"Then Price knew of the money Granger had about him?" suggested the coroner.

"He did, sir."

"And did he know that he had money on deposit in Hillborough Bank?"

"Yes, sir."

"Did Price leave your father's house after Granger, or before him?"

"Before him, sir: nearly an hour before him."

The inquest was adjourned; and, within a week of this examination, Matthew Lorton received an application from the police, asking for a photograph of his nephew Stephen Price, if he happened to possess such a thing.

He did possess one, and sent it to London by return of post.

The landlord of the Victoria Hotel identified this portrait as that of the person who represented himself to be John Granger, and who carried away John Granger's luggage.

After this the work was easy. Little links in the chain were picked up one by one. A labouring man turned up who had seen Stephen Price sitting on a stile hard by Hawley Wood, hacking at a thick jagged looking stake with his clasp knife, on the night of the 24th of July. The woman at whose house Price lodged gave evidence that he broke an appointment to play billiards with a friend of his on that night; the friend had called at his lodgings for him twice, and had been angry about the breaking of the appointment; and Stephen Price came in about half past ten o'clock, looking very white and strange. The lad who was his fellow clerk was ready to swear to his having been disturbed and strange in his manner during the two or three weeks before he left Hillborough; but the boy had thought very little of this, he said, knowing how deeply Stephen was in debt.

The final examination resulted in a verdict of wilful murder; and a police officer started for New York by the next steamer, carrying a warrant for the apprehension of Stephen Price.

He was not found very easily, but was ultimately apprehended, with some of John Granger's property still in his possession. He was brought home, tried, found guilty, and hung, much to the satisfaction of Hillborough. Shortly afterwards, Mr Vollair produced a will, which John Granger had executed a few days before his intended departure, bequeathing all he possessed to Susan Lorton – the interest for her sole use and benefit, the principal to revert to her eldest son after her death, the son to take the name of Granger. The bank had to make good the money drawn from them by Stephen Price. The boy came in due course, and was christened after the dead man, above whose remains a fair white monument has been erected in the rustic churchyard near Hawley Wood, at the expense of Robert and Susan Ashley; a handsomer tomb than is usually given to a man of John Granger's class, but it was the only thing Susan could do to show how much she had valued him who had loved her so dearly.

She often sits beside that quiet resting place in the spring twilight, with her children busy making daisy chains at her knee; but she has never seen John Granger's ghost since that evening in the wood, and she knows she will never see it again.

Harriet Beecher Stowe

The Ghost in the Mill
and
The Ghost in the Cap'n Brown House

Harriet Beecher Stowe (1811–96) achieved literary immortality with her classic Uncle Tom's Cabin *(1852) which became such a powerful and influential force for antislavery in the years leading up to the American Civil War. The following two stories, related by Sam Lawson, both appeared in her collection of* Oldtown Fireside Stories *(1871).*

The Ghost in the Mill

"COME, SAM, TELL us a story," said I, as Harry and I crept to his knees, in the glow of the bright evening firelight; while Aunt Lois was busily rattling the tea things, and grandmamma, at the other end of the fireplace, was quietly setting the heel of a blue-mixed yarn stocking.

In those days we had no magazines and daily papers, each reeling off a serial story. Once a week, *The Columbian Sentinel* came from Boston with its slender stock of news and editorial; but all the multiform devices – pictorial, narrative, and poetical – which keep the mind of the present generation ablaze with excitement, had not then even an existence. There was no theatre, no opera; there were in Oldtown no parties or balls, except, perhaps, the annual election, or Thanksgiving festival; and when winter came, and the sun went down at half past four o'clock; and left the long, dark hours of evening to be provided for, the necessity of amusement became urgent. Hence, in those days, chimney-corner story-telling became an art and an accomplishment. Society was then full of traditions and narratives which had all the uncertain glow and shifting mystery of the firelit hearth upon them. They were told to sympathetic audiences, by the rising and falling light of the solemn embers, with the hearth-crickets filling up every pause. Then the aged told their stories to the young – tales of early life; tales of war and adventure, of forest days, of Indian captivities and escapes, of bears and wildcats and panthers, of rattlesnakes, of witches and wizards, and strange and wonderful dreams and appearances and providences.

In those days of early Massachusetts, faith and credence were in the very air. Two-thirds of New England was then dark, unbroken forests, through whose tangled paths the mysterious winter wind groaned and shrieked and howled with weird noises and unaccountable clamors. Along the iron bound shore, the stormful Atlantic raved and thundered, and dashed its moaning waters, as if to deaden and deafen any voice that might tell of the settled life of the old civilized world, and shut us for ever into the wilderness. A good story-teller, in those days, was always sure of a warm seat at the hearth stone, and the delighted homage of children; and in all Oldtown there was no better story-teller than Sam Lawson.

"Do, do, tell us a story," said Harry, pressing upon him, and opening very wide blue eyes, in which undoubting faith shone as in a mirror; "and let it be something strange, and different from common."

"Wal, I know lots o' strange things," said Sam, looking mysteriously into the fire. "Why, I know things, that ef I should tell – why, people might say they wa'n't so; but then they is so for all that."

"Oh, *do*, do, tell us!"

"Why, I should scare ye to death, mebbe," said Sam doubtingly.

"Oh, pooh! no, you wouldn't," we both burst out at once.

But Sam was possessed by a reticent spirit, and loved dearly to be wooed and importuned; and so he only took up the great kitchen tongs, and smote on the hickory forestick, when it flew apart in the middle, and scattered a shower of clear bright coals all over the hearth.

"Mercy on us, Sam Lawson!" said Aunt Lois in an indignant voice, spinning round from her dish washing.

"Don't you worry a grain, Miss Lois," said Sam composedly. "I see that are stick was e'en a'most in two, and I thought I'd jest settle it. I'll sweep up the coals now," he added, vigorously applying a turkey wing to the purpose, as he knelt on the hearth, his spare, lean figure glowing in the blaze of the firelight, and getting quite flushed with exertion.

"There, now!" he said, when he had brushed over and under and between the fire irons, and pursued the retreating ashes so far into the red, fiery citadel, that his finger ends were burning and tingling, "that are's done now as well as Hepsy herself could 'a' done it. I allers sweeps up the haarth: I think it's part o' the man's bisness when he makes the fire. But Hepsy's so used to seein' me a-doin' on't, that she don't see no kind o' merit in't. It's just as Parson Lothrop said in his sermon – folks allers overlook their common marcies."

"But come, Sam, that story," said Harry and I coaxingly, pressing upon him, and pulling him down into his seat in the corner.

"Lord massy, these 'ere young uns!" said Sam. "There's never no contentin' on 'em: ye tell 'em one story, and they jest swallows it as a dog does a gob o' meat; and they're all ready for another. What do ye want to hear now?"

Now, the fact was, that Sam's stories had been told us so often, that they were all arranged and ticketed in our minds. We knew every word in them, and could set him right if he varied a hair from the usual track; and still the interest in them was unabated. Still we shivered, and clung to his knee, at the mysterious parts, and felt gentle, cold chills run down our spines at appropriate places. We were always in the most receptive and sympathetic condition. Tonight, in particular, was one of those thundering stormy ones, when the winds appeared to be holding a perfect mad carnival over my grandfather's house. They yelled and squealed round the corners; they collected in troops, and came tumbling and roaring down the chimney; they shook and rattled the buttery door and the sinkroom door and the cellar door and the chamber door, with a constant undertone of squeak and clatter, as if at every door were a cold, discontented spirit, tired of the chill outside, and longing for the warmth and comfort within.

"Wal, boys," said Sam confidentially, "what'll ye have?"

"Tell us 'Come down, come down'!" we both shouted with one voice. This was, in our mind, an "A No. 1" among Sam's stories.

"Ye mus'n't be frightened now," said Sam paternally.

"Oh, no! we ar'n't frightened *ever*," said we both in one breath.

"Not when ye go down the cellar arter cider?" said Sam with severe scrutiny. "Ef ye should be down cellar, and the candle should go out, now?"

"I ain't," said I; "I ain't afraid of anything. I never knew what it was to be afraid in my life."

"Wal, then," said Sam, "I'll tell ye. This 'ere's what Cap'n Eb Sawin told me when I was a boy about your bigness, I reckon.

"Cap'n Eb Sawin was a most respectable man. Your gran'ther knew him very well; and he was a deacon in the church in Dedham afore he died. He was at Lexington when the fust gun was fired agin the British. He was a dreffle smart man, Cap'n Eb was, and driv team a good many years atween here and Boston. He married Lois Peabody, that was cousin to your gran'ther then. Lois was a rael sensible woman; and I've heard her tell the story as he told her, and it was jest as he told it to me – jest exactly; and I shall never forget it if I live to be nine hundred years old, like Mathuselah.

"Ye see, along back in them times, there used to be a fellow come round these 'ere parts, spring and fall, a-peddlin' goods, with his pack on his back; and his name was Jehiel Lommedieu. Nobody rightly knew where he come from. He wasn't much of a talker; but the women rather liked him, and kind o' liked to have him round. Women will like some fellows, when men can't see no sort o' reason why they should; and they liked this 'ere Lommedieu, though he was kind o' mournful and thin and shadbellied, and hadn't nothin' to say for himself. But it got to be so, that the women would count and calculate so many weeks afore 'twas time for Lommedieu to be along; and they'd make up ginger snaps and preserves and pies, and make him stay to tea at the houses, and feed him up on the best there was and the story went round, that he was a-courtin' Phebe Ann Parker, or Phebe Ann was a-courtin' him – folks didn't rightly know which. Wal, all of a sudden, Lommedieu stopped comin' round; and nobody knew why – only jest he didn't come. It turned out that Phebe Ann Parker had got a letter from him, sayin' he'd be along afore Thanksgiving; but he didn't come, neither afore nor at Thanksgiving time, nor arter; nor next spring: and finally the women they gin up lookin' for him. Some said he was dead; some said he was gone to Canada; and some said he he'd gone over to the Old Country.

"Wal, as to Phebe Ann, she acted like a gal o' sense, and married 'Bijah Moss, and thought no more about it. She took the right view on't, and said she was sartin that all things was ordered out for the best; and it was jest as well folks couldn't always have their own way. And so, in time, Lommedieu was gone out o' folk's minds, much as a last year's apple blossom.

"It's relly affectin' to think how little these 'ere folk is missed that's so much sot by. There ain't nobody, ef they's ever so important, but what the world gets to goin' on without 'em, pretty much as it did with 'em, though there's some little flurry at fust. Wal, the last thing that was in anybody's mind was, that they ever should hear from Lommedieu agin. But there ain't nothin' but what has its time o' turnin' up; and it seems his turn was to come.

"Wal, ye see, 'twas the 19th o' March, when Cap'n Eb Sawin started with a team for Boston. That day, there come on about the biggest snowstorm that there'd been in them parts sence the oldest man could remember. 'Twas this 'ere fine, siftin' snow, that drives in your face like needles, with a wind to cut your nose off: it made teamin' pretty tedious work. Cap'n Eb was about the toughest man in them parts. He'd spent days in the woods-a-loggin', and he'd been up to the deestrict o' Maine a-lumberin', and was about up to any sort o' thing a man gen'ally could be up to; but these 'ere March winds sometimes does set on a fellow so, that neither natur' nor grave can stan' 'em. The cap'n used to say he could stan' any wind that blew one way't time for five minutes; but come to winds that blew all four p'nts at the same minit – why, they flustered him.

"Wal, that was the sort o' weather it was all day: and by sundown Cap'n Eb he got clean bewildered, so that he lost his road; and, when night came on, he didn't know nothin' where he was. Ye see the country was all under drift, and the air so thick with snow, that he couldn't see a foot afore him; and the fact was, he got off the Boston road without knowin' it, and came out at a pair o' bars nigh upon Sherburne, where old Cack Sparrock's mill is.

'Your gran'ther used to know old Cack, boys. He was a drefful drinkin' old crittur, that lived there all alone in the woods by himself a-tendin' saw and girst mill. He wa'n't allers just what he was then. Time was that Cack was a pretty consid'ably likely young man, and his wife was a very respectable woman – Deacon Amos Petengall's dater from Sherburn.

"But ye see, the year arter his wife died, Cack he gin up goin' to meetin' Sundays, and, all the tithingmen and selectmen could do, they couldn't get him out to meetin'; and, when a man neglects means o' grace and sanctuary privileges, there ain't no sayin' *what* he'll do next. Why, boys, jist think on't! An immortal crittur lyin' round loose all day Sunday, and not puttin' on so much as a clean shirt, when all 'spectable folks has on their best close, and is to meetin' worshippin' the Lord! What can you spect to come of it, when he lies idlin' round in his old week-day close, fishing, or some sich, but what the Devil should be arter him at last, as he was arter old Cack?"

Here Sam winked impressively to my grandfather in the opposite corner, to call his attention to the moral which he was interweaving with his narrative.

"Wal, ye see, Cap'n Eb he told me, that when he come to them bars and looked up, and saw the dark a-comin' down, and the storm a-thick-enin' up, he felt that things was gettin' pretty consid'able serious. There was a dark piece o' woods on ahead of him inside the bars; and he knew, come to get in there, the light would give out clean. So he jest thought he'd take the hoss out o' the team, and go ahead a little, and see where he was. So he driv his oxen up ag'in the fence, and took out the hoss, and got on him, and pushed along through the woods, not rightly known' where he was goin'.

"Wal, afore long he see a light through the trees; and, sure enough, he come out to Cack Sparrock's old mill.

"It was a pretty consid'able gloomy sort of a place, that are old mill was: There was a great fall of water that come rushin' down the rocks, and fell in a deep pool; and it sounded sort o' wild and lonesome: but Cap'n Eb he knocked on the door with his whip-handle, and got in.

"There, to be sure, sot old Cack beside a great blazin' fire, with his rum-jug at his elbow. He was a dreffel fellow to drink, Cack was! For all that, there was some good in him, for he was pleasant-spoken and 'bliging; and he made the cap'n welcome.

"Ye see, Cack," said Cap'n Eb, "I'm off my road, and got snowed up down by your bars," says he.

"Want ter know!" says Cack. "Calculate you'll jest have to camp down here till mornin'," says he.

"Wal, so old Cack he got out his tin lantern, and went with Cap'n Eb back to the bars to help him fetch along his critturs. He told him he could put 'em under the mill-shed. So they got the critturs up to the shed, and got the cart under; and by that time the storm was awful.

"But Cack he made a great roarin' fire, 'cause, ye see, Cack allers had slab-wood a plenty from his mill; and a roarin' fire is jest so much company. It sort o' keeps a fellow's spirits up, a good fire does. So Cack he sot on his old teakettle, and made a swingeing lot o' toddy; and he and Cap'n Eb were havin' a tol'able comfortable time there. Cack was a pretty good hand to tell stories; and Cap'n Eb warn't no way backward in that line, and kep' up his end pretty well; and pretty soon they was a-roarin' and haw-hawin' inside about as loud as the storm outside; when all of a sudden, 'bout midnight, there come aloud rap on the door.

" 'Lordy massy! what's that?' says Cack. Folks is rather startled allers to be checked up sudden when they are a-carryin' on an laughin'; and it was such an awful blowy night, it was a little scary to have a rap on the door.

"Wal, they waited a minit, and didn't hear nothin' but the wind a-screechin' round the chimbley; and old Cack was jest goin' on with his story, when the rap come ag'in, harder'n ever, as if it'd shook the door open.

" 'Wal,' says old Cack, 'if 'tis the Devil, we'd jest as good's open, and have it out with him to onst,' says he; and so he got up and opened the door, and, sure enough, there was old Ketury there. Expect you've heard your grandma tell about old Ketury. She used to come to meetin's sometimes, and her husband was one o' the prayin' Indians; but Ketury was one of the real wild sort, and you couldn't no more convert *her* than you could convert a wild-cat or a painter [panther]. Lordy massy! Ketury used to come to meetin', and sit there on them Indian benches; and when the second bell was a-tollin', and when Parson Lothrop and his wife was comin' up the broad aisle, and everybody in the house ris' up and stood, Ketury would sit there, and look at 'em out o' the corner o' her eyes; and folks used to say she rattled them necklaces o' rattlesnakes' tails and wild-cat teeth, and sich like heathen trumpery, and looked for all the world as if the spirit of the old Sarpent himself was in her. I've seen her sit and look at Lady Lothrop out o' the corner o' her eyes; and her old brown baggy neck would kind o' twist and work; and her eyes they looked so, that 'twas enough to scare a body. For all the world, she looked jest as if she was a-workin' up to spring at her. Lady Lothrop was jest as kind to Ketury as she always was to every poor crittur. She'd bow and smile as gracious to her when meetin' was over, and she come down the aisle, passin' out o' meetin'; Ketury's father was one o' them great powwows down to Martha's Vineyard; and people used to say she was set apart, when she was a child, to the sarvice o' the Devil: any way, she never could be made nothin' of in a Christian way. She come down to Parson

Lothrop's study once or twice to be catechised; but he couldn't get a word out o' her, and she kind o' seemed to sit scornful while he was a-talkin'. Folks said, if it was in old times, Ketury wouldn't have been allowed to go on so; but Parson Lothrop's so sort o' mild, he let her take pretty much her own way. Everybody thought that Ketury was a witch: at least, she knew consid'able more'n she ought to know, and so they was kind o' 'fraid of her. Cap'n Eb says he never see a fellow seem scareder than Cack did when he see Ketury a-standin' there.

"Why, ye see, boys, she was as withered and wrinkled and brown as an old frosted punkin-vine; and her little snaky eyes sparkled and snapped, and it made her head kind o' dizzy to look at 'em; and folks used to say that anybody that Ketury got mad at was sure to get the worst of it fust or last. And so, no matter what day or hour Ketury had a mind to rap at anybody's door, folks gen'lly thought it was best to let her in; but then, they never thought her coming was for any good, for she was just like the wind – she came when the fit was on her, she staid jest so long as it pleased her, and went when she got ready, and not before. Ketury understood English, and could talk it well enough, but always seemed to scorn it, and was allers mowin' and mutterin' to herself in Indian, and winkin' and blinkin' as if she saw more folks round than you did, so that she wa'n't no way pleasant company; and yet everybody took good care to be polite to her.

"So old Cack asked her to come in, and didn't make no question where she come from, or what she come on; but he knew it was twelve good miles from where she lived to his hut, and the snow was drifted above her middle: and Cap'n Eb declared that there wa'n't no track, nor sign o' track, of anybody's coming through that snow next morning.

" 'How did she get there then?' said I.

"Didn't ye never see brown leaves a-ridin' on the wind? Well, Cap'n Eb he says 'she came on the wind,' and I'm sure it was strong enough to fetch her. But Cack he got her down into the warm corner, and he poured her out a mug o' hot toddy, and give her: but ye see her bein' there sort o' stopped the conversation; for she sat there a-rockin' back'ards and for'ards, a-sippin' her toddy, and a-mutterin', and lookin' up chimbley.

"Cap'n Eb says in all his born days he never hearn such screeches and yells as the wind give over that chimbley; and old Cack got so frightened, you could fairly hear his teeth chatter.

"But Cap'n Eb he was a putty brave man, and he wa'n't goin' to have conversation stopped by no woman, witch or no witch; and so, when he see her mutterin' and lookin' up chimbley, he spoke up, and says he, 'Well, Ketury, what do you see?' says he. 'Come, out with it; don't keep it to yourself.' Ye see Cap'n Eb was a hearty fellow, and then he was a leetle warmed up with the toddy.

"Then he said he see an evil kind o' smile on Ketury's face, and she rattled her necklace o' bones and snakes' tails; and her eyes seemed to snap; and she looked up the chimbley, and called out, 'Come down, come down! let's see who ye be?'

"Then there was a scratchin' and a rumblin' and a groan; and a pair of feet come down the chimbley, and stood right in the middle of the hearth, the toes pi'ntin' out'rds, with shoes and silver buckles a-shinin' in the firelight. Cap'n Eb says he never come so near bein' scared in his life; and, as to old Cack, he jest wilted right down in his chair.

"Then old Ketury got up, and reached her stick up chimbley, and called out louder, 'Come down, come down! let's see who ye be.' And, sure enough, down came a pair o' legs, and j'ined right on to the feet: good fair legs they was,with ribbed stockings and leather breeches.

" 'Wal, we're in for it now,' says Cap'n Eb. 'Go it, Ketury, and let's have the rest on him.'

"Ketury didn't seem to mind him: she stood there as stiff as a stake, and kep' callin' out, 'Come down, come down! let's see who ye be.' And then come down the body of a man with a brown coat and yellow vest, and j'ined right on to the legs; but there wasn't no arms to it. Then Ketury shook her stick up chimbley, and called '*Come down, come down!*' And there came down a pair o' arms, and went on each side o' the body; and there stood a man all finished, only there wa'n't no head on him.

" 'Wal, Ketury,' says Cap'n Eb, 'this 'ere's getting serious. I 'spec' you must finish him up, and let's see what he wants of us.'

"Then Ketury called out once more, louder'n ever, 'Come down, come down! let's see who ye be.'' And, sure enough, down comes a man's head, and settled on the shoulders straight enough; and Cap'n Eb, the minit he set eyes on him, knew he was Jehiel Lommedieu.

"Old Cack knew him too; and he fell flat on his face, and prayed the Lord to have mercy on his soul: but Cap'n Eb he was for gettin' to the bottom of matters, and not have his scare for nothin'; so he says to him, 'What do you want, now you hev come?'

"The man he didn't speak; he only sort o' moaned, and p'inted to the chimbley. He seemed to try to speak, but couldn't; for ye see it isn't often that this sort o' folks is permitted to speak: but just then there came a screechin' blast o' wind, and blowed the door open, and blowed the smoke and fire all out into the room, and there seemed to be a whirlwind and darkness and moans and screeches; and, when it all cleared up, Ketury and the man was both gone, and only old Cack lay on the ground, rolling and moaning as if he'd die.

"Wal, Cap'n Eb he picked him up, and built up the fire, and sort o' comforted him up, 'cause the crittur was in distress o' mind that was drefful. The awful Providence, ye see, had awakened him, and his sin had been set home to his soul; and he was under such conviction, that it all had to come out how old Cack's father had murdered poor Lommedieu for his money, and Cack had been privy to it, and helped his father build the body up in that very chimbley; and he said that he hadn't had neither peace nor rest since then, and that was what had driv' him away from ordinances; for ye know sinnin' will always make a man leave prayin'. Wal, Cack didn't live but a day or two. Cap'n Eb he got the minister o' Sherburn and one o' the selectmen down to see him; and they took his deposition. He seemed railly quite penitent; and Parson Carryl he prayed with him, and was faithful in settin' home the providence to his soul: and so, at the eleventh hour poor old Cack might have got in; at least it looks a leetle like it. He was distressed to think he couldn't live to be hung. He sort o' seemed to think that if he was fairly tried, and hung, it would make it all square. He made Parson Carryl promise to have the old mill pulled down, and bury the body; and after he was dead, they did it.

"Cap'n Eb he was one of a party o' eight that pulled down the chimbley; and there, sure enough, was the skeleton of poor Lommedieu.

"So there you see, boys, there can't be no iniquity so hid but what it'll come out. The wild Indians of the forest, and the stormy winds and tempests, j'ined together to bring out this 'ere.'

"For my part," said Aunt Lois sharply, "I never believed that story."

"Why, Lois," said my grandmother, "Cap'n Eb Sawin was a regular church-member, and a most respectable man."

"Law, mother! I don't doubt he thought so. I suppose he and Cack got drinking toddy together, till he got asleep, and dreamed it. I wouldn't believe such a thing if it did happen right before my face and eyes. I should only think I was crazy, that's all."

"Come, Lois, if I was you, I wouldn't talk so like a Sadducce," said my grandmother. "What would become of all the accounts in Dr Cotton Mather's 'Magnilly' if folks were like you?"

"Wal," said Sam Lawson, drooping contemplatively over the coals, and gazing into the fire, "there's a putty consid'able sight o' things in this world that's true; and then ag'in there's a sight o' things that ain't true. Now, my old gran'ther used to say, 'Boys,' says he, 'if ye want to lead a pleasant and prosperous life, ye must contrive allers to keep jest the happy medium between truth and falsehood.' Now, that are's my doctrine."

Aunt Lois knit severely.

"Boys," said Sam, "don't you want ter go down with me and get a mug o' cider?"

Of course we did, and took down a basket to bring up some apples to roast.

"Boys," says Sam mysteriously, while he was drawing the cider, "you jest ask your Aunt Lois to tell you what she knows 'bout Ruth Sullivan."

"Why, what is it?"

"Oh! you must ask her. There 'ere folks that's so kind o' toppin' about sperits and sich, come sift 'em down, you gen'lly find they knows one story that kind o' puzzles 'em. Now you mind, and jist ask your Aunt Lois about Ruth Sullivan."

The Ghost in the Cap'n Brown House

"Now, Sam, tell us certain true, is there any such things as ghosts?"

"Be there ghosts?" said Sam, immediately translating into his vernacular grammar: "Wal, now, that are's jest the question, ye see."

"Well, grandma thinks there are, and Aunt Lois thinks it's all nonsense. Why, Aunt Lois don't even believe the stories in Cotton Mather's 'Magnalia'."

"Wanter know?" said Sam, with a tone of slow, languid meditation.

We were sitting on a bank of the Charles River, fishing. The soft melancholy red of evening was fading off in streaks on the glassy water, and the houses of Oldtown were beginning to loom through the gloom, solemn and ghostly. There are times and tones and moods of nature that make all the vulgar, daily real seem shadowy, vague, and supernatural, as if the outlines of this hard material present were fading into the invisible and unknown. So Oldtown, with its elm-trees, its great square white houses, its meeting-house and tavern and blacksmith's shop and mill, which at high noon seem as real and as commonplace as possible, at this hour of the evening was dreamy and solemn. They rose up blurred, indistinct, dark; here and there winking candles sent long lines of light through the shadows, and little drops of unforseen rain rippled the sheeny darkness of the water.

"Wal, you see, boys, in them things it's jest as well to mind your granny. There's a consid'able sight o' gumption in grandmas. You look at the folks that's allus tellin' you what they don't believe – they don't believe this, and they don't believe that – and what sort o' folks is they? Why, like yer Aunt Lois, sort o' stringy and dry. There ain't no 'sorption got out o' not believin' nothin'.

"Lord a massy! we don't know nothin' 'bout them things. We hain't ben there, and can't say that there ain't no ghosts and sich, can we, now?"

We agreed to that fact, and sat a little closer to Sam in the gathering gloom.

"Tell us about the Cap'n Brown house, Sam.'

"Ye didn't never go over the Cap'n Brown house?"

No, we had not that advantage.

"Wal, yer see, Cap'n Brown he made all his money to sea, in furrin parts, and then come here to Oldtown to settle down.

"Now, there ain't no known' 'bout these 'ere old ship-masters, where they's ben, or what they's ben a doin', or how they got their money. Ask me no questions, and I'll tell ye no lies, is 'bout the best philosophy for them. Wal, it didn't do no good to ask Cap'n Brown questions too close, 'cause you didn't git no satisfaction. Nobody rightly knew 'bout who his folks was, or where they come from; and, ef a body asked him, he used to say that the very fust he know'd 'bout himself he was a young man walkin' the streets in London.

'But, yer see, boys, he he'd money, and that is about all folks wanter know when a man comes to settle down. And he bought that 'are place, and built that 'are house. He built it alla sea-cap'n fashion, so's to feel as much at home as he could. The parlor was like a ship's cabin. The table and chairs was fastened down to the floor, and the closets was made with

holes to set the casters and the decanters and bottles in, jest's they be at
sea; and there was stanchions to hold on by; and they say that blowy
nights the cap'n used to fire up pretty well with his grog, till he he'd about
all he could carry, and then he'd set and hold on, and hear the wind
blow, and kind o' feel out to sea right there to hum. There wasn't no Mis'
Cap'n Brown, and there didn't seem like to be none. And whether there
ever he'd been one, nobody know'd. He he'd an old black Guinea
nigger-woman, names Quassia, that did his work. She was shaped pretty
much like one o' these 'ere great crookneck-squashes. She wa'n't no gret
beauty, I can tell you; and she used to wear a gret red turban and a yaller
short gown and red petticoat, and a gret string o' gold beads round her
neck, and gret big gold hoops in her ears, made right in the middle o'
Africa among the heathen there. For all she was black, she thought a
heap o' herself, and was consid'able sort o' predominative over the cap'n.
Lordy massy! boys, it's allus so. Get a man and a woman together – any
sort o' woman you're a mind to, don't care who 'tis – and one way or
another she gets the rule over him, and he jest has to train to her fife.
Some does it one way, and some does it another; some does it by jawin'
and some does it by kissin', and some does it by faculty and contrivance;
but one way or another they allers does it. Old Cap'n Brown was a good
stout, stocky kind o' John Bull sort o' fellow, and a good judge o' sperits,
and allers kep' the best in them 'are cupboards o' his'n; but, fust and last,
things in his house went pretty much as old Quassia said.

"Folks got to kind o' respectin' Quassia. She come to meetin' Sunday
regular, and sot all fixed up in red and yaller and green, with glass beads
and what not, lookin' for all the world like one o' them ugly Indian idols;
but she was well-behaved as any Christian. She was a master hand at
cookin'. Her bread and biscuits couldn't be beat, and no couldn't her
pies, and there wa'n't no such pound-cake as she made nowhere. Wal,
this 'ere story I'm goin' to tell you was told me by Cinthy Pendleton.
There ain't a more respectable gal, old or young, than Cinthy nowheres.
She lives over to Sherburne now, and I hear tell she's sot up a manty-
makin' business; but then she used to do tailorin' in Oldtown. She was a
member o' the church, and a good Christian as ever was. Wal, ye see,
Quassia she got Cinthy to come up and spend a week to the Cap'n
Brown house, a doin' tailorin' and fixin' over his close: 'twas along
toward the fust o' March. Cinthy she sot by the fire in the front parlor
with her goose and her press-board and her work: for there wa'n't no
company callin', and the snow was drifted four feet deep right across the

front door· so there wa'n't much danger o' anybody comin' in. And the cap'n he was a perlite man to wimmen; and Cinthy she liked it jest as well not to have company, 'cause the cap'n he'd make himself entertainin' tellin' on her sea-stories, and all about his adventures among the Ammonites, and Perresites, and Jebusites, and all sorts o' heathen people he'd been among.

"Wall, that 'are week there come on the master snow-storm. Of all the snow-storms that he'd ben, that 'are was the beater; and I tell you the wind blew as if 'twas the last chance it was ever goin' to have. Wal, it's kind o' scary like to be shet up in a lone house with all natur' a kind o' breaking' out, and goin' on so, and the snow a comin' down so thick ye can't see 'cross the street, and the wind a pipin' and a squeelin' and a rumblin' and a tumblin' fust down this chimney and then down that. I tell you, it sort o' sets a feller thinkin' o' the three great things – death, judgment, and etarnaty; and I don't care who the folks is, nor how good they be, there's times when they must be feelin' putty consid'able solemn.

"Wal, Cinthy she said she kind o' felt so along, and she he'd a sort o' queer feelin' come over her as if there was somebody or somethin' round the house more'n appeared. She said she sort o' felt it in the air; but it seemed to her silly, and she tried to get over it. But two or three times, she said, when it got to be dusk, she felt somebody go by her up the stairs. The front entry wa'n't very light in the daytime and in the storm, come five o'clock, it was so dark that all you could see was jest a gleam o' some-thing, and two or three times when she started to go up stairs she see a soft white suthin' that seemed goin' up before her, and she stopped with her heart a beatin' like a trip-hammer, and she sort o' saw it go up and along the entry to the cap'n's door, and then it seemed to go right through, 'cause the door didn't open.

"Wal, Cinthy says she to old Quassia, says she, 'Is there anybody lives in this house but us?'

" 'Anybody lives here?' says Quassia: 'what you mean?' says she.

"Says Cinthy, 'I thought somebody went past me on the stairs last night and tonight.'

"Lordy massy! how old Quassia did screech and laugh. 'Good Lord!' says she, 'how foolish white folks is! Somebody went past you? was't the capt'in?'

" 'No, it wa'n't the cap'n,' says she: 'it was somethin' soft and white, and moved very still; it was like somethin' in the air,' says she.

"Then Quassia she haw-hawed louder. Says she, 'It's hy-sterikes, Miss Cinthy; that's all it is.'

"Wal, Cinthy she was kind o' 'shamed, but for all that she couldn't help herself. Sometimes evenin's she'd be a settin' with the cap'n, and she'd think she'd hear somebody a movin' in his room overhead; and she knowed it wa'n't Quassia, 'cause Quassia was ironin' in the kitchen. She took pains once or twice to find out that 'are.

"Wal, ye see, the cap'n's room was the gret front upper chamber over the parlor, and then right opposite to it was the gret spare chamber where Cinthy slept. It was jest as grand as could be, with a gret four-post mahogany bedstead and damask curtains brought over from England; but it was cold enough to freeze a white bear solid – the way spare chambers allers is. Then there was the entry between, run straight through the house: one side was old Quassia's room, and the other was a sort o' store-room, where the old cap'n kep' all sorts o' traps.

"Wal, Cinthy she kep' a hevin' things happen and a seein' things, till she didn't railly know what was in it. Once when she come into the parlor jest at sundown, she was sure she see a white figure a vanishin' out o' the door that went towards the side entry. She said it was so dusk, that all she could see was jest this white figure, and it jest went out still as a cat as she come in.

"Wal, Cinthy didn't like to speak to the cap'n about it. She was a close woman, putty prudent, Cinthy was.

"But one night, 'bout the middle o' the week, there 'ere thing kind o' come to a crisis.

"Cinthy said she'd ben up putty late a sewin' and a finishin' off down in the parlor, and the cap'n he sot up with her, and was consid'able cheerful and entertainin', tellin' her all about things over in the Bermudys, and off to Chiny and Japan, and round the world ginerally. The storm that he'd been a blowin' all the week was about as furious as ever; and the cap'n he stirred up a mess o' flip, and he'd it for her hot to go to bed on. He was a good-natured critter, and allers had feelin's for lone women; and I s'pose he knew 'twas sort o' desolate for Cinthy.

"Wal, takin' the flip so right the last thing afore goin' to bed, she went right off to sleep as sound as a nut, and slep' on till somewhere about mornin', when she said somethin' waked her broad awake in a minute. Her eyes flew wide open like a spring, and the storm had gone down and the moon come out; and there, standin' right in the moonlight by her bed, was a woman jest as white as a sheet, with black hair hangin' down to her waist, and the brightest, mournfullest black eyes you ever see. She stood there lookin' right at Cinthy; and Cinthy thinks that was what waked her up; 'cause, you know, ef anybody stands and looks steady at folks asleep it's apt to wake 'em.

"Anyway, Cinthy said she felt jest as ef she was turnin' to stone. She couldn't move nor speak. She lay a minute, and then she shut her eyes, and begun to say her prayers; and a minute after she opening 'em, and it was gone.

"Cinthy was a sensible gal, and one that allers he'd her thoughts about her; and she jest got up and put a shawl round her shoulders, and went first and looked at the doors, and they was both on 'em locked jest as she left 'em when she went to bed. Then she looked under the bed and in the closet, and felt all round the room: where she couldn't see she felt her way, and there wa'n't nothin' there.

"Wal, next mornin' Cinthy got up and went home, and she kep' it to herself a good while. Finally, one day when she was workin' to our house she told Hepsy about it, and Hepsy she told me."

"Well, Sam," we said, after a pause, in which we heard only the rustle of leaves and the ticking of branches against each other, "what do you suppose it was?"

"Wal, there 'tis: you know jest as much about it as I do. Hepsy told Cinthy it might 'a ben a dream; so it might, but Cinthy she was sure it wa'n't a dream, 'cause she remembers plain hearin' the old clock on the stairs strike four while she had her eyes open lookin' at the woman; and then she only shet 'em a minute, jest to say 'Now I lay me,' and opened 'em and she was gone.

"Wall, Cinthy told Hepsy, and Hepsy she kep' it putty close. She didn't tell it to nobody except Aunt Sally Dickerson and the Widder Bije Smith and your Grandma Badger and the minister's wife; and they every one o' 'em make talk. Wal, come spring, somehow or other it seemed to 'a' got all over Oldtown. I heard on 't to the store and up to the tavern; and Jake Marshall he says to me one day, 'What's this 'ere about the cap'n's house?' And the Widder Loker she says to me, 'There's ben a ghost seen in the cap'n's house;' and I heard on't clear over to Needham and Sherburne.

"Some o' the women they drew themselves up putty stiff and proper. Your Aunt Lois was one on 'em.

" 'Ghost,' says she; 'don't tell me! Perhaps it would be best ef 'twas a ghost,' says she. She didn't think there ought to be no sich doin's in nobody's house; and your grandma she shet her up, and told her she didn't oughter talk so."

"Talk how?" said I, interrupting Sam with wonder. "What did Aunt Lois mean?"

"Why, you see," said Sam mysteriously, "there allers is folks in every town that's jest like the Sadducees in old times: they won't believe in angel nor sperit, no way you can fix it; and ef things is seen and done in a house, why, they say, its 'cause there's somebody there; there's some sort o' deviltry or trick about it.

"So the story got round that there was a woman kep' private in Cap'n Brown's house, and that he brought her from furrin parts; and it growed and growed, till there was all sorts o' ways o' tellin on 't.

"Some said they'd seen her a settin' at an open winder. Some said that moonlight nights they'd seen her a walkin' out in the back garden kind o' in and out 'mong the bean-poles and squash-vines.

"You see, it come on spring and summer; and the winders o' the Cap'n Brown house stood open, and folks was all a watchin' on 'em day and night. Aunt Sally Dickerson told the minister's wife that she'd seen in plain daylight a woman a settin' at the chamber winder atween four and five o'clock in the mornin' – jist a settin' a lookin' out and a doin' nothin', like anybody else. She was very white and pale, and had black eyes.

"Some said that it was a nun the cap'n had brought away from a Roman Catholic convent in Spain, and some said he'd got her out o' the Inquisition.

"Aunt Sally said she thought the minister ought to call and inquire why she didn't come to meetin', and who she was, and all about her: 'cause, you see, she said it might be all right enough ef folks only know'd jest how things was; but ef they didn't, why, folks will talk."

"Well, did the minister do it?"

"What, Parson Lothrop? Wal, no, he didn't. He made a call on the cap'n in a regular way, and asked arter his health and all his family. But the Cap'n he seemed jest as jolly and chipper as a spring robin, and he gin the minister some o' his old Jamaiky; and the minister he come away and said he didn't see nothin'; and no he didn't. Folks never does see nothin' when they aint lookin' where 'tis. Fact is, Parson Lothrop wa'n't fond o' interferin'; he was a master hand to slick things over. Your grandma she used to mourn about it, 'cause she said he never gin on p'int to the doctrines; but 'twas all of a piece, he kind o' took every thing the smooth way.

"But your grandma she believed in the ghost, and so did Lady Lothrop. I was up to her house t'other day fixin' a door-knob, and says she, 'Sam, your wife told me a strange story about the Cap'n Brown house.'

" 'Yes, ma'am, she did,' says I.

" 'Well, what do you think of it?' says she.

" 'Wall, sometimes I think, and then agin I don't know,' says I. 'There's Cinthy she's a member o' the church and a good pious gal,' says I.

" 'Yes, Sam,' says Lady Lothrop, says she; 'and Sam,' says she, 'it is jest like something that happened once to my grandmother when she was livin' in the old Province House in Bostin.' Says she, 'These 'ere things is the mysteries of Providence, and it's jest as well not to have 'em too much talked about.'

" 'Jest so,' says I – 'jest so. That 'are's what every woman I've talked with says; and I guess, fust and last, I've talked with twenty – good, safe church-members – and they's every one o' opinion that this 'ere oughtn't to be talked about. Why, over to the deakin's t'other night we went it all over as much as two or three hours, and we concluded that the best way was to keep quite still about it; and that's jest what they say over to Needham and Sherburne. I've been all round a hushin' this 'ere up, and I hain't found but a few people that hedn't the particulars one way or another.' The fact was, I never did see no report spread so, nor make sich sort o' surchin's o' heart, as this 'ere. It railly did beat all; 'cause, ef 'twas a ghost, why there was the p'int proved, ye see. Cinthy's a church-member, and she see it, and got right up and sarched the room: but then agin, ef 'twas a woman, why that are was kind o' awful; it give cause, ye see, for thinkin' all sorts o' things. There was Cap'n Brown, to be sure, he wa'n't a church-member; but yet he was as honest and regular a man as any goin', as fur as any one us could see. To be sure, nobody know'd where he come from, but that wa'n't no reason agin' him: this 'ere might a ben a crazy sister, or some poor crittur that he took out o' the best o' motives; and the Scriptur' says, 'Charity hopeth all things.' But then, ye see, folks will talk – that are's the pester of all these things – and they did some on 'em talk consid'able strong about the cap'n; but somehow or other, there didn't nobody come to the p'int o' facin' on him down, and sayin' square out, 'Cap'n Brown, have you got a woman in your house, or hain't you? or is it a ghost, or what is it?' Folks somehow never does come to that. Ye see, there was the cap'n so respectable, a settin' up every

Sunday there in his pew, with his ruffles round his hands and his red broadcloth cloak and his cocked hat. Why, folks' hearts sort o' failed 'em when it come to sayin' any thing right to him. They thought and kind o' whispered round that the minister or the deakins oughter do it: but Lordy massy! ministers, I s'pose, has feelin's like the rest on us; they don't want to eat all the hard cheeses that nobody else won't eat. Anyhow, there wasn't nothin' said direct to the cap'n; and jest for want o' that all the folks in Oldtown kep' a bilin' and a bilin' like a kettle o' soap, till it seemed all the time as if they'd bile over.

"Some o' the wimmen tried to get somethin' out o' Quassy. Lordy massy! you might as well 'a' tried to get it out an old tom-turkey, that'll strut and gobble and quitter, and drag his wings on the ground, and fly at you, but won't say nothin'. Quassy she screeched her queer sort o' laugh; and she told 'em that they was a makin' fools o' themselves, and that the cap'n's matters wa'n't none o' their bus'ness; and that was true enough. As to goin' into Quassia's room, or into any o' the store-rooms or closets she kep' the keys of, you might as well hev gone into a lion's den. She kep' all her places locked up tight; and there was no gettin' at nothin' in the Cap'n Brown house, else I believe some o' the wimmen would 'a' sent a sarch-warrant."

"Well," said I, "what came of it? Didn't anybody ever find out?"

"Wal," said Sam, "it come to an end sort o', and didn't come to an end. It was jest this 'ere way. You see, along in October, jest in the cider-makin' time, Abel Flint he was took down with dysentery and died. You 'member the Flint house: it stood on a little rise o' ground jest lookin' over towards the Brown house. Wal, there was Aunt Sally Dickerson and the Widder Bije Smith, they set up with the corpse. He was laid out in the back chamber, you see, over the milk-room and kitchen; but there was cold victuals and sich in the front chamber, where the watchers sot. Wal, now, Aunt Sally she told me that between three and four o'clock she heard wheels a rumblin', and she went to the winder, and it was clear starlight; and she see a coach come up to the Cap'n Brown house; and she see the cap'n come out bringin' a woman all wrapped in a cloak, and old Quassy came after with her arms full of bundles; and he put her into the kerridge, and shet her in, and it driv off; and she see old Quassy stand lookin' over the fence arter it. She tried to wake up the widder, but 'twas towards mornin', and the widder allers was a hard sleeper; so there wa'n't no witness but her."

"Well, then, it wasn't a ghost," said I, "after all, and it was a woman."

"Wal, there 'tis, you see. Folks don't know that 'are yit, 'cause there it's jest as broad as 'tis long. Now, look at it. There's Cinthy, she's a good, pious gal: she locks her chamber-doors, both on 'em, and goes to bed, and wakes up in the night and there's a woman there. She jest shets her eyes, and the woman's gone. She gits up and looks, and both doors is locked jest as she left 'em. That 'ere woman wa'n't flesh and blood as we knows on; but then they say Cinthy might have dreamed it!

"Wal, now, look at it t'other way. There's Aunt Sally Dickerson; she's a good woman and a church-member: wal, she sees a woman in a cloak with all her bundles brought out o' Cap'n Brown's house, and put into a kerridge, and driv off, atween three and four o'clock in the mornin'. Wal, that 'ere shows there must 'a' ben a real live woman kep' there privately, and so what Cinthy saw wasn't a ghost.

"Wal, now, Cinthy says Aunt Sally might 'a' dreamed it – that she got her head so full o' stories about the Cap'n Brown house, and watched it till she got asleep, and he'd this 'ere dream; and, as there didn't nobody else see it, it might 'a' ben, you know. Aunt Sally's clear she didn't dream; but which on 'em was awake or which on 'em was asleep, is what ain't settled in Oldtown yet."

Rhoda Broughton

Poor Pretty Bobby

Rhoda Broughton (1840–1920) – like Mary Braddon – was virtually "a national institution" in the late Victorian era. Her earlier novels horrified the censorious mid-Victorians and the (anonymous) critics, but she soon became second only to Braddon in popularity with the wide English (and American) public. Her ghost stories were collected as Tales for Christmas Eve *in 1873, and later reprinted as* Twilight Stories. *"Poor Pretty Bobby" originally appeared in* Temple Bar *in December 1872.*

I

"YES, MY DEAR, you may not believe me, but I can assure you that you cannot dislike old women more, nor think them more contemptible supernumeraries, than I did when I was your age."

This is what old Mrs Hamilton says – the old lady so incredibly tenacious of life (incredibly as it seems to me at eighteen) as to have buried a husband and five strong sons, and yet still to eat her dinner with hearty relish, and laugh at any such jokes as are spoken loudly enough to reach her dulled ears. This is what she says, shaking the while her head, which – poor old soul – is already shaking a good deal involuntarily. I am sitting close beside her arm-chair, and have been reading aloud to her; but as I cannot succeed in pitching my voice so as to make her hear satisfactorily, by mutual consent the book has been dropped in my lap, and we have betaken ourselves to conversation.

"I never said I disliked old women, did I?" reply I evasively, being too truthful altogether to deny the soft impeachment. "What makes you think I do? They are infinitely preferable to old men; I do distinctly dislike *them*."

"A fat, bald, deaf old woman," continues she, not heeding me, and speaking with slow emphasis, while she raises one trembling hand to mark each unpleasant adjective; "if in the year 1802 anyone had told me that I should have lived to be that, I think I should have killed them or myself! and yet now I am all three."

"You are not *very* deaf," say I politely – the fatness and baldness admit of no civilities consistent with veracity – but I raise my voice to pay the compliment.

"In the year 1802, I was seventeen," she says, wandering off into memory. "Yes, my dear, I am just fifteen years older than the century, and it is getting into its dotage, is not it? The year 1802 – ah! that was just about the time that I first saw my poor Bobby! Poor pretty Bobby."

"And who *was* Bobby?" ask I, pricking up my ears, and scenting, with the keen nose of youth, a dead-love idyll; an idyll of which this poor old hill of unsteady flesh was the heroine.

'I must have told you the tale a hundred times, have not I?" she asks, turning her old dim eyes towards me. "A curious tale, say what you will, and explain it how you will. I think I *must* have told you; but indeed I forget to whom I tell my old stories and to whom I do not. Well, my love, you must promise to stop me if you have heard it before, but to me, you know, these old things are so much clearer than the things of yesterday."

"You never told me, Mrs Hamilton," I say, and say truthfully; for being a new acquaintance, I really have not been made acquainted with Bobby's history. "Would you mind telling it me now, if you are sure that it would not bore you?"

"Bobby," she repeats softly to herself, "Bobby. I dare say you do not think it a very pretty name?"

"N-not particularly," reply I honestly. "To tell you the truth, it rather reminds me of a policeman."

"I dare say," she answers quietly; "and yet in the year I grew to think it the handsomest, dearest name on earth. Well, if you like, I will begin at the beginning and tell you how that came about."

"Do," say I, drawing a stocking out of my pocket, and thriftily beginning to knit to assist me in the process of listening.

"In the year 1802 we were at war with France – you know that, of course. It seemed then as if war were our normal state; I could hardly remember a time when Europe had been at peace. In these days of stagnant quiet it appears as if people's kith and kin always lived out their full time and died in their beds. *Then* there was hardly a house where there was not one dead, either in battle, or of his wounds after battle, or of some dysentery or ugly parching fever. As for us, we had always been a soldier family – always; there was not one of us that had ever worn a black gown or sat upon a high stool with a pen behind his ear. I had lost uncles and cousins by the half-dozen and dozen, but, for my part, I did not much mind, as I knew very little about them, and black was more becoming wear to a person with my bright colour than anything else."

At the mention of her bright colour I unintentionally lift my eyes from my knitting, and contemplate the yellow bagginess of the poor old cheek nearest me. Oh, Time! Time! what absurd and dirty turns you play us! What do you do with all our fair and goodly things when you have stolen them from us? In what far and hidden treasure-house do you store them?

"But I did care very much – very exceedingly – for my dear old father – not so old either – younger than my eldest boy was when he went; he would have been forty-two if he had lived three days longer. Well, well, child, you must not let me wander; you must keep me to it. He was not a soldier, was not my father; he was a sailor, a post-captain in His Majesty's navy, and commanded the ship *Thunderer* in the Channel fleet.

"I had struck seventeen in the year 1802, as I said before, and had just come home from being finished at a boarding school of repute in those days, where I had learnt to talk the prettiest *ancien régime* French, and to hate Bonaparte with unchristian violence, from a little ruined *émigre maréchale*; had also, with infinite expenditure of time, labour, and Berlin wool, wrought out *Abraham's Sacrifice of Isaac*, and *Jacob's First Kiss to Rachel* in finest cross-stitch. Now I had bidden adieu to learning; had inly resolved never to disinter *Télémaque* and Thomson's *Seasons* from the bottom of my trunk; had taken a holiday from all my accomplishments, with the exception of cross-stitch, to which I still faithfully adhered – and, indeed, on the day I am going to mention, I recollect that I was hard at work on Judas Iscariot's face in Leonardo da Vinci's *Last Supper* – hard at work at it, sitting in the morning sunshine, on a straight-backed chair. We had flatter backs in those days; our shoulders were not made round by lolling in easy-chairs; indeed, no then upholsterer made a chair that it was possible to loll in. My father rented a house near Plymouth at that time, an in-and-out nooky kind of old house – no doubt it has fallen to pieces long years ago – a house all set round with unnumbered flowers, and about which the rooks clamoured all together from the windy elm tops. I was labouring in flesh-coloured wool on Judas's left cheek, when the door opened and my mother entered. She looked as if something had freshly pleased her, and her eyes were smiling. In her hand she held an open and evidently just-read letter.

" 'A messenger has come from Plymouth,' she says, advancing quickly and joyfully towards me. 'Your father will be here this afternoon.'

" '*This afternoon!*' cry I, at the top of my voice, pushing away my heavy work-frame. 'How delightful! But how – how can that happen?'

" 'They have had a brush with a French privateer,' she answers, sitting down on another straight-backed chair, and looking again over the large square letter, destitute of envelope, for such things were not in those days, 'and then they succeeded in taking her. Yet they were a good deal knocked about in the process, and have had to put into Plymouth to rest; so he will be here this afternoon for a few hours.'

" 'Hurrah!' cry I, rising, holding out my scanty skirts, and beginning to dance.

" 'Bobby Gerard is coming with him,' continues my mother, again glancing at her despatch. 'Poor boy, he has had a shot through his right arm, which has broken the bone! So your father is bringing him here for us to nurse him well again.'

"I stop in my dancing.

" 'Hurrah again!' I say brutally. 'I do not mean about his arm; of course, I am very sorry for that; but, at all events, I shall see him at last. I shall see whether he is like his picture, and whether it is not as egregiously flattered as I have always suspected.'

"There was no photographs you know in those days – not even hazy daguerreotypes – it was fifty good years too soon for them. The picture to which I allude is a miniature, at which I had stolen many a deeply longing admiring glance in its velvet case. It is almost impossible for a miniature not to flatter. To the most coarse-skinned and mealy-potato-faced people it cannot help giving cheeks of the texture of a rose-leaf, and brows of the grain of finest marble.

" 'Yes,' replies my mother, absently, 'so you will. Well, I must be going to give orders about his room. He would like one looking on the garden best, do not you think Phoebe? – one where he could smell the flowers and hear the birds?'

"Mother goes, and I fall into a meditation. Bobby Gerard is an orphan. A few years ago his mother, who was an old friend of my father's – who knows! perhaps an old love – feeling her end drawing nigh, had sent for father, and had asked him, with eager dying tears, to take as much care of her pretty forlorn boy as he could, and to shield him a little in his tender years from the evils of this wicked world, and to be to him a wise and kindly guardian, in the place of those natural ones that God had taken. And father had promised, and when he promised there was small fear of his not keeping his word.

"This was some years ago, and yet I had never seen him nor he me; he had been almost always at sea and I at school. I had heard plenty about him – about his sayings, his waggeries, his mischievousness, his soft-heartedness, and his great and unusual comeliness; but his outward man, save as represented in that stealthily peeped-at miniature, had I never seen. They were to arrive in the afternoon; but long before the hour at which they were due I was waiting, with expectant impatience to receive them. I had changed my dress, and had (though rather ashamed of myself) put on everything of most becoming that my wardrobe afforded. If you were to see me as I stood before the glass on that summer after-noon, you would not be able to contain your laughter; the little boys in the street would run after me throwing stones and hooting; but *then* – according to the then fashion and standard of gentility – I was all that was most elegant and *comme il faut*. Lately it has been the mode to puff one's self out with unnatural and improbable protuberances; *then* one's great life-object was to make one's self appear as scrimping as possible – to make one's self look as if one had been ironed. Many people *damped* their clothes to make them stick more closely to them, and to make them define more distinctly the outline of form and limbs. One's waist was under one's arms; the sole object of which seemed to be to outrage nature by pushing one's bust up into one's chin, and one's legs were revealed through one's scanty drapery with startling candour as one walked or sat. I remember once standing with my back to a bright fire in our long drawing-room, and seeing myself reflected in a big mirror at the other end. I was so thinly clad that I was transparent, and could see through myself. Well, in the afternoon in question I was dressed quite an hour and a half too soon. I had a narrow little white gown, which clung successfully tight and close to my figure, and which was of so moderate a length as to leave visible my ankles and my neatly-shod and cross-sandalled feet. I had long mittens on my arms, black, and embroidered on the backs in coloured silks; and above my hair, which at the back was scratched up to the top of my crown, towered a tremendous tortoise-shell comb; while on each side of my face modestly dropped a bunch of curls, nearly meeting over my nose.

"My figure was full – ah! my dear, I have always had a tendency to fat, and you see what it has come to – and my pink cheeks were more deeply brightly rosy than usual. I had looked out at every upper window, so as to have the furthest possible view of the road.

"I had walked in my thin shoes half-way down the drive, so as to command a turn, which, from the house, impeded my vision, when, at last, after many tantalising false alarms, and just five minutes later than the time mentioned in the letter, the high-swung, yellow-bodied, post-chaise hove in sight, dragged – briskly jingling – along by a pair of galloping horses. Then, suddenly, shyness overcame me – much as I loved my father, it was more as my personification of all knightly and noble qualities than from much personal acquaintance with him – and I fled.

"I remained in my room until I thought I had given them ample time to get through the first greetings and settle down into quiet talk. Then, having for one last time run my fingers through each ringlet of my two curl bunches, I stole diffidently downstairs.

"There was a noise of loud and gay voices issuing from the parlour, but, as I entered, they all stopped talking and turned to look at me."

" 'And so this is Phoebe!' cries my father's jovial voice, as he comes towards me, and heartily kisses me. 'Good Lord, how time flies! It does not seem more than three months since I saw the child, and yet then she was a bit of a brat in trousers, and long bare legs!'

"At this allusion to my late mode of attire, I laugh, but I also feel myself growing scarlet.

" 'Here, Bobby!' continues my father, taking me by the hand, and leading me towards a sofa on which a young man is sitting beside my mother; 'this is my little lass that you have so often heard of. Not such a very little one, after all, is she? Do not be shy, my boy; you will not see such a pretty girl every day of your life – give her a kiss.'

"My eyes are on the ground, but I am aware that the young man rises, advances (not unwillingly, as it seems to me), and bestows a kiss some-where or other on my face. I am not quite clear *where*, as I think the curls impede him a good deal.

"Thus, before ever I saw Bobby, before ever I knew what manner of man he was, I was kissed by him. That was a good beginning, was not it?

"After these salutations are over, we subside again into conversation –
I sitting beside my father, with his arm round my waist, sitting modestly
silent, and peeping every now and then under my eyes, as often as I think
I may do so safely unobserved, at the young fellow opposite me. I am
instituting an inward comparison between nature and art: between the
real live man and the miniature that undertakes to represent him. The
first result of this inspection is disappointment, for where are the lovely
smooth roses and lilies that I have been wont to connect with Bobby
Gerard's name? There are no roses in his cheek, certainly; they are
paleish – from his wound, as I conjecture; but even before that accident,
if there were roses at all, they must have been mahogany-coloured ones,
for the salt sea winds and the high summer sun have tanned his fair face
to a rich reddish, brownish, copperish hue. But in some things the picture
lied not. There is the brow more broad than high; the straight fine nose;
the brave and joyful blue eyes, and the mouth with its pretty curling
smile. On the whole, perhaps, I am not disappointed.

"By-and-by father rises, and steps out into the verandah, where the
canary birds hung out in their cages are noisily praising God after their
manner. Mother follows him. I should like to do the same; but a sense of
good manners, and a conjecture that possibly my parents may have some
subjects to discuss, on which they would prefer to be without the help of
my advice, restrain me. I therefore remain, and so does the invalid.

II

"For some moments the silence threatens to remain unbroken between
us; for some moments the subdued sound of father's and mother's talk
from among the rosebeds and the piercing clamour of the canaries – fish-
wives among birds – are the only noises that salute our ears. Noise we
make none ourselves. My eyes are reading the muddled pattern of the
Turkey carpet; I do not know what his are doing. Small knowledge have
I had of men, saving the dancing master at our school; a beautiful new
youth is almost as great a novelty to me as to Miranda, and I am a good
deal gawkier than she was under the new experience. I think he must
have made a vow that he would not speak first. I feel myself swelling to
double my normal size with confusion and heat; at last, in desperation, I

look up, and say sententiously, 'You have been wounded, I believe?'

" 'Yes, I have.'

"He might have helped me by answering more at large, might not he? But now that I am having a good look at him, I see that he is rather red too. Perhaps he also feels gawky and swollen; the idea encourages me.

" 'Did it hurt very badly?'

" 'N – not so very much.'

" 'I should have thought that you ought to have been in bed,' say I, with a motherly air of solicitude.

" 'Should you, why?'

" 'I thought that when people broke their limbs they had to stay in bed till they were mended again.'

" 'But mine was broken a week ago,' he answers, smiling and showing his straight white teeth – ah the miniature was silent about *them*! 'You would not have had me stay in bed a whole week, like an old woman?'

" 'I expected to have seen you much *iller*,' said I, beginning to feel more at my ease, and with a sensible diminution of that unpleasant swelling sensation. 'Father said in his note that we were to nurse you well again; that sounded as if you were *quite* ill.'

" 'Your father always takes a great deal too much care of me,' he says, with a slight frown and darkening of his whole bright face. 'It might be sugar or salt.'

" 'And very kind of him, too,' I cry, firing up. 'What motive beside your own good can he have for looking after you? I call you rather ungrateful.'

" 'Do you?' he says calmly, and without apparent resentment. 'But you are mistaken. I am not ungrateful. However, naturally, you do not understand.'

" 'Oh, indeed!' reply I, speaking rather shortly, and feeling a little offended, 'I dare say not.'

"Our talk is taking a somewhat hostile tone; to what further amenities we might have proceeded is unknown; for at this point father and mother reappear through the window, and the necessity of conversing with each other at all ceases.

"Father stayed till evening, and we all supped together, and I was called upon to sit by Bobby, and cut up his food for him, as he was disabled from doing it for himself. Then, later still, when the sun had set, and all his evening reds and purples had followed him, when the night flowers were scenting all the garden, and the shadows lay about, enor-

mously long in the summer moonlight, father got into the post-chaise
again, and drove away through the black shadows and the faint clear
shine, and Bobby stood at the hall door watching him, with his arm in a
sling and a wistful smile on lips and eyes.

" 'Well, we are not left *quite* desolate this time,' says mother, turning
with rather tearful laughter to the young man. 'You wish that we were,
do not you, Bobby?'

" 'You would not believe me, if I answered "No," would you?' he asks,
with the same still smile.

" 'He is not very polite to us, is he, Phoebe?'

" 'You would not wish me to be polite in such a case,' he replies,
flushing. 'You would not wish me to be glad at missing the chance of
seeing any of the fun?'

"But Mr Gerard's eagerness to be back at his post delays the probability of his being able to return thither. The next day he has a feverish
attack, the day after he is worse; the day after that worse still, and in fine,
it is between a fortnight and three weeks before he also is able to get into
a post-chaise and drive away to Plymouth. And meanwhile mother and I
nurse him and cosset him, and make him odd and cool drinks out of
herbs and field flowers, whose uses are now disdained or forgotten. I do
not mean any offence to you, my dear, but I think that young girls in
those days were less squeamish and more truly delicate than they are
nowadays. I remember once I read *Humphrey Clinker* aloud to my father,
and we both highly relished and laughed over its jokes; but I should not
have understood one of the darkly unclean allusions in that French book
your mother left here one day. *You* would think it very unseemly to enter
the bedroom of a strange young man, sick or well; but as for me, I spent
whole nights in Bobby's, watching him and tending him with as little
false shame as if he had been my brother. I can hear *now*, more plainly
than the song you sang me an hour ago, the slumberous buzzing of the
great brown coated summer bees in his still room, as I sat by his bedside
watching his sleeping face, as he dreamt unquietly, and clenched, and
again unclenched, his nervous hands. I think he was back in the
Thunderer. I can see *now* the little close curls of his sunshiny hair straggling
over the white pillow. And then there came a good and blessed day,
when he was out of danger, and then another, a little further on, when he
was up and dressed, and he and I walked forth into the hayfield beyond
the garden – reversing the order of things – *he*, leaning on my arm; and a
good plump solid arm it was. We walked out under the heavy leaved

horse chestnut trees, and the old and rough barked elms. The sun was shining all this time, as it seems to me. I do not believe that in those days there were the same cold unseasonable rains as now; there were soft showers enough to keep the grass green and the flowers undrooped; but I have no association of overcast skies and untimely deluges with those long and azure days. We sat under a haycock, on the shady side, and indolently watched the hot haymakers – the shirt-sleeved men, and burnt and bare armed women, tossing and raking; while we breathed the blessed country air, full of adorable scents, and crowded with little happy and pretty winged insects.

" 'In three days,' says Bobby, leaning his elbow in the hay, and speaking with an eager smile, 'three days at the furthest, I may go back again, may not I, Phoebe?'

" 'Without doubt,' reply I, stiffly, pulling a dry and faded ox-eye flower out of the odorous mounds beside me; 'for my part, I do not see why you should not go tomorrow, or indeed – if we could send into Plymouth for a chaise – this afternoon; you are so thin that you look all mouth and eyes, and you can hardly stand, without assistance, but these, of course, are trifling drawbacks, and I daresay would be rather an advantage on board ship than otherwise.'

" 'You are angry!' he says, with a sort of laugh in his deep eyes. 'You look even prettier when you are angry than when you are pleased.'

" 'It is no question of my looks,' I say, still in some heat, though mollified by the irrelevant compliment.

" 'For the second time you are thinking me ungrateful,' he says, gravely; 'you do not tell me so in so many words, because it is towards yourself that my ingratitude is shown. The first time you told me of it, it was almost the first thing that you ever said to me.'

" 'So it was,' I answer quickly; 'and if the occasion were to come over again, I should say it again. I daresay you did not mean it, but it sounded exactly as if you were complaining of my father for being too careful of you.'

" 'He *is* too careful of me!' cries the young man, with a hot flushing of cheek and brow. 'I cannot help if it makes you angry again; I *must* say it, he is more careful of me than he would be of his own son, if he had one.'

" 'Did he not promise your mother that he would look after you?' ask I, eagerly. 'When people make promises to people on their death beds, they are in no hurry to break them; at least such people as father are not.'

" 'You do not understand,' he says, a little impatiently, while that hot flush still dwells on his pale cheek. 'My mother was the last person in the world to wish him to take care of my body at the expense of my honour.'

" 'What are you talking about?' I say, looking at him, with a lurking suspicion that, despite the steady light of reason in his blue eyes, he is still labouring under some form of delirium.

" 'Unless I tell you all my grievance, I see that you will never comprehend,' he says, sighing. 'Well, listen to me, and you shall hear it; and if you do not agree with me when I have done, you are not the kind of girl I take you for.'

" 'Then I am sure I am not the kind of girl you take me for,' reply I, with a laugh; 'for I am fully determined to disagree with you entirely.'

" 'You know,' he says, raising himself a little from his hay couch, and speaking with clear rapidity, 'that, whenever we take a French prize a lot of the French sailors are ironed, and the vessel is sent into port, in the charge of one officer and several men. There is some slight risk attending it – for my part, I think very slight – but I suppose that your father looks at it differently, for – *I have never been sent.*'

" 'It is accident,' say I, reassuringly. 'Your turn will come in good time.'

" 'It is *not* an accident!' he answers firmly. 'Boys younger than I am – much less trustworthy, and of whom he has not half the opinion that he has of me – have been sent; but I, *never*. I bore it as well as I could for a long time, but now I can bear it no longer; it is not, I assure you, my fancy; but I can see that my brother officers, knowing how partial your father is to me – what influences I have with him in many things – conclude that my not being sent is my own choice; in short, that I am – *afraid.*' (His voice sinks with a disgusted and shamed intonation at the last word.) 'Now – I have told you the sober facts – look me in the face' (putting his hand, with boyish familiarity, under my chin, and, turning round my curls, my features, and the front view of my big comb towards him), 'and tell me whether you agree with me, as I said you would, or not – whether it is not cruel kindness on his part to make me keep a whole skin on such terms?'

"I look him in the face for a moment, trying to say that I do not agree with him, but it is more than I can manage.

" 'You were right,' I say, turning my head away. 'I *do* agree with you; I wish to heaven that I could honestly say that I did not.'

" 'Since you do, then,' he cries excitedly – 'Phoebe! I knew you would; I knew you better than you know yourself – I have a favour to ask of you, a *great* favour, and one that will keep me all my life in debt to you.'

" 'What is it?' ask I, with sinking heart.

" 'Your father is very fond of you – '

" 'I know it,' I answer curtly.

" 'Anything that you asked, and that was within the bounds of possibility, he would do,' he continues, with eager gravity. 'Well, this is what I ask of you: to write him a line, and let me take it when I go, asking him to send me home in the next prize.'

" 'And if,' say I, with a trembling voice, 'you lost your life in this service, you will have to thank me for it; I shall have your death on my head all through my life.'

" 'The danger is infinitesimal, as I told you before,' he says, impatiently; 'and even if it were greater than it is – well, life is a good thing, very good, but there are better things; and even if I come to grief, which is most unlikely, there are plenty of men as good as – better than – I, to step into my place.'

" 'It will be small consolation to the people who are fond of you that someone better than you is alive, though you are dead,' I say, tearfully.

" 'But I do not mean to be dead,' he says, with a cheery laugh. 'Why are you so determined on killing me? I mean to live to be an admiral. Why should I not?'

" 'Why indeed?' say I, with a feeble echo of his cheerful mirth, and feeling rather ashamed of my tears.

" 'And meanwhile you will write?' he says with an eager return to the charge; 'and *soon*? Do not look angry and pouting, as you did just now, but I *must* go! What is there to hinder me? I am getting up my strength as fast as it is possible for any human creature to do, and just think how I should feel if they were to come in for something really good while I am away.'

"So I wrote.

III

"I often wished afterwards that my right hand had been cut off before its fingers had held the pen that wrote that letter. You wonder to see me moved at what happened so long ago – before your parents were born – and certainly it makes not much difference now; for even if he had prospered then, and come happily home to me, yet, in the course of nature he would have gone long before now. I should not have been so cruel as to have wished him to have lasted to be as I am. I did not mean to hint at the end of my story before I have reached the middle. Well – and so he went, with the letter in his pocket, and I felt something like the king in the tale, who sent a messenger with a letter, and wrote in the letter, 'Slay the bearer of this as soon as he arrives!' But before he went – the evening before, as we walked in the garden after supper, with our monstrously long shadows stretching before us in the moonlight – I do not think he said in so many words, 'Will you marry me?' but somehow, by some signs or words on both our parts, it became clear to us that, by-and-by, if God left him alive, and if the war ever came to an end, he and I should belong to one another. And so, having understood this, when he went he kissed me, as he had done when he came, only this time no one bade him; he did it of his own accord, and a hundred times instead of one; and for my part, this time, instead of standing passive like a log or a post, I kissed him back again, most lovingly.

"Ah! parting in those days, when the last kiss to one's beloved ones was not unlikely to be an adieu until the great Day of Judgment, was a different thing to the listless, unemotional goodbyes of these stagnant times of peace!

"And so Bobby also got into a post-chaise and drove away, and we watched him too, till he turned the corner out of our sight, as we had watched father; and then I hid my face among the jessamine flowers that clothed the wall of the house, and wept as one that would not be comforted. However, one cannot weep for ever, or, if one does, it makes one blind and blear, and I did not wish Bobby to have a wife with such defects; so in process of time I dried my tears.

"And the days passed by, and nature went slowly and evenly

through her lovely changes. The hay was gathered in, and the fine new grass and clover sprang up among the stalks of the grass that had gone; and the wild roses struggled into odorous bloom, and crowned the hedges, and then their time came, and they shook down their faint petals, and went.

"And now the corn harvest had come, and we had heard once or twice from our beloveds, but not often. And the sun still shone with broad power, and kept the rain in subjection. And all morning I sat at my big frame, and toiled on the *Last Supper*. I had finished Judas Iscariot's face and the other Apostles. I was engaged now upon the table-cloth, which was not interesting and required not much exercise of thought. And mother sat near me, either working too or reading a good book, and taking snuff – every lady snuffed in those days: at least in trifles, if not in great things, the world mends. And at night, when ten o'clock struck, I covered up my frame and stole listlessly upstairs to my room. There, I knelt at the open window, facing Plymouth and the sea, and asked God to take good care of father and Bobby. I do not know that I asked for any spiritual blessings for them, I only begged that they might be alive.

"One night, one hot night, having prayed even more heartily and tearfully than my wont for them both, I had lain down to sleep. The windows were left open, and the blinds up, that all possible air might reach me from the still and scented garden below. Thinking of Bobby, I had fallen asleep, and he is still mistily in my head, when I seem to wake. The room is full of clear light, but it is not morning: it is only the moon looking right in and flooding every object. I can see my own ghostly figure sitting up in bed, reflected in the looking-glass opposite. I listen: surely I heard some noise: yes – certainly, there can be no doubt of it – someone is knocking loudly and perseveringly at the hall-door. At first I fall into a deadly fear; then my reason comes to my aid. If it were a robber, or person with any evil intent, would he knock so openly and clamorously as to arouse the inmates? Would not he rather go stealthily to work, to force a silent entrance for himself? At worst it is some drunken sailor from Plymouth; at best it is a messenger with news of our dear ones. At this thought I instantly spring out of bed, and hurrying on my stockings and shoes and whatever garments come most quickly to hand – with my hair spread all over my back, and utterly forgetful of my big comb, I open my door, and fly down the passages, into which the moon is looking with her ghostly smile, and down the broad and shallow stairs.

"As I near the hall-door I meet our old butler also rather dishevelled, and evidently on the same errand as myself.

" 'Who can it be, Stephens?' I ask, trembling with excitement and fear.

" 'Indeed, ma'am, I cannot tell you,' replies the old man, shaking his head, 'it is a very odd time of night to choose for making such a noise. We will ask them their business, whoever they are, before we unchain the door.'

"It seems to me as if the endless bolts would never be drawn – the key never be turned in the stiff lock; but at last the door opens slowly and cautiously, only to the width of a few inches, as it is still confined by the strong chain. I peep out eagerly, expecting I know not what.

"Good heavens! What do I see? No drunken sailor, no messenger, but, oh joy! oh blessedness! my Bobby himself – my beautiful boy-lover! Even *now*, even after all these weary years, even after the long bitterness that followed, I cannot forget the unutterable happiness of that moment.

" 'Open the door, Stephens, quick!' I cry, stammering with eagerness. 'Draw the chain; it is Mr Gerard; do not keep him waiting.'

"The chain rattles down, the door opens wide and there he stands before me. At once, ere anyone has said anything, ere anything has happened, a feeling of cold disappointment steals unaccountably over me – a nameless sensation, whose nearest kin is chilly awe. He makes no movement towards me; he does not catch me in his arms, nor even hold out his right hand to me. He stands there still and silent, and though the night is dry, equally free from rain and dew, I see that he is dripping wet; the water is running down from his clothes, from his drenched hair, and even from his eyelashes, on to the dry ground at his feet.

" 'What has happened?' I cry, hurriedly, 'How wet you are!' and as I speak I stretch out my hand and lay it on his coat sleeve. But even as I do it a sensation of intense cold runs up my fingers and my arm, even to the elbow. How is it that he is so chilled to the marrow of his bones on this sultry, breathless, August night? To my extreme surprise he does not answer; he still stands there, dumb and dripping. 'Where have you come from?' I ask, with that sense of awe deepening. 'Have you fallen into the river? How is it that you are so wet?'

" 'It was cold,' he says, shivering, and speaking in a slow and strangely altered voice, 'bitter cold. I could not stay there.'

" 'Stay where?' I say, looking in amazement at his face, which, whether owing to the ghastly effect of moonlight or not, seems to me ash white. 'Where have you been? What is it you are talking about?'

"But he does not reply.

" 'He is really ill, I am afraid, Stephens,' I say, turning with a forlorn feeling towards the old butler. 'He does not seem to hear what I say to him. I am afraid he has had a thorough chill. What water can he have fallen into? You had better help him up to bed, and get him warm between the blankets. His room is quite ready for him, you know – come in,' I say, stretching out my hand to him, 'you will be better after a night's rest.'

"He does not take my offered hand, but he follows me across the threshold and across the hall. I hear the water drops falling drip, drip, on the echoing stone floor as he passes; then upstairs, and along the gallery to the door of his room, where I leave him with Stephens. Then everything becomes blank and nil to me.

"I am awoke as usual in the morning by the entrance of my maid with hot water.

" 'Well, how is Mr Gerard this morning?' I ask, springing into a sitting posture.

"She puts down the hot water tin and stares at her leisure at me.

" 'My dear Miss Phoebe, how should *I* know? Please God he is in good health and safe, and that we shall have good news of him before long.'

" 'Have not you asked how he is?' I ask impatiently. 'He did not seem quite himself last night; there was something odd about him. I was afraid he was in for another touch of fever.'

" 'Last night – fever,' repeats she, slowly and disconnectedly echoing some of my words. 'I beg your pardon, ma'am, I am sure, but I have not the least idea in life what you are talking about.'

" 'How stupid you are!' I say, quite at the end of my patience. 'Did not Mr Gerard come back unexpectedly last night, and did not I hear him knocking, and run down to open the door, and did not Stephens come too, and afterwards take him up to bed?

"The stare of bewilderment gives way to a laugh.

" 'You have been dreaming, ma'am. Of course I cannot answer for what you did last night, but I am sure that Stephens knows no more of the young gentleman than I do, for only just now, at breakfast, he was saying that he thought it was about time for us to have some tidings of him and master.'

" 'A dream!' cry I indignantly. 'Impossible! I was no more dreaming then than I am now.'

But time convinces me that I am mistaken, and that during all the time that I thought I was standing at the open hall-door, talking to my beloved, in reality I was lying on my own bed in the depths of sleep, with no other company than the scent of the flowers and the light of the moon. At this discovery a great and terrible depression falls on me. I go to my mother to tell her of my vision, and at the end of my narrative I say:

" 'Mother, I know well that Bobby is dead, and that I shall never see him any more. I feel assured that he died last night, and that he came himself to tell me of his going. I am sure that there is nothing left for me now but to go too.'

"I speak thus far with great calmness, but when I have done I break out into loud and violent weeping. Mother rebukes me gently, telling me that there is nothing more natural than that I should dream of a person who constantly occupies my waking thoughts, nor that, considering the gloomy nature of my apprehensions about him, my dream should be of a sad and ominous kind; but that, above all dreams and omens, God is good, that He has preserved him hitherto, and that, for her part, no devil-sent apparition shall shake her confidence in His continued clemency. I go away a little comforted, though not very much, and still every night I kneel at the open window facing Plymouth and the sea, and pray for my sailor boy. But it seems to me, despite all my self-reasonings, despite all that mother says, that my prayers for him are prayers for the dead.

IV

"Three more weeks pass away; the harvest is garnered, and the pears are growing soft and mellow. Mother's and my outward life goes on in its silent regularity, nor do we talk much to each other of the tumult that rages – of the heartache that burns, within each of us. At the end of the three weeks, as we are sitting as usual, quietly employed, and buried each in our own thoughts, in the parlour, towards evening we hear wheels approaching the hall-door. We both run out as in my dream I had run to the door, and arrive in time to receive my father as he steps out of the carriage that has brought him. Well! at least one of our wanderers has come home, but where is the other?

"Almost before he has heartily kissed us both – wife and child – father cries out, 'But where is Bobby?'

" 'That is just what I was going to ask you,' replies mother quickly.

" 'Is not he *here* with you?' returns he anxiously.

" 'Not he,' answers mother, 'we have neither seen nor heard anything of him for more than six weeks.'

" 'Great God!' exclaims he, while his face assumes an expression of the deepest concern, 'what *can* have become of him? what can have happened to the poor fellow?'

" 'Has not he been with you, then? – has not he been in the *Thunderer*?' asks mother, running her words into one another in her eagerness to get them out.

" 'I sent him home three weeks ago in a prize, with a letter to you, and told him to stay with you till I came home, and what can have become of him since, God only knows!' he answers with a look of the profoundest sorrow and anxiety.

There is a moment of forlorn and dreary silence; then I speak. I have been standing dumbly by, listening, and my heart growing colder and colder at every dismal word.

" 'It is all my doing!' I cry passionately, flinging myself down in an agony of tears on the straight-backed old settle in the hall. 'It is my fault – no one else's! The very last time that I saw him, I told him that he would have to thank me for his death, and he laughed at me, but it has come true. If I had not written *you*, father, that accursed letter, we should have had him here *now* this *minute*, safe and sound, standing in the middle of us – as we never, *never*, shall have him again!'

"I stop, literally suffocated with emotion.

"Father comes over, and lays his kind brown hand on my bent prone head. 'My child,' he says, 'my dear child' (and tears are dimming the clear grey of his own eyes), 'you are wrong to make up your mind to what is the worst at once. I do not disguise from you that there is cause for grave anxiety about the dear fellow, but still God is good; He has kept both him and me hitherto; into His hands we must trust our boy.'

"I sit up, and shake away my tears.

" 'It is no use,' I say. 'Why should I hope? There is no hope! I know it for a certainty! He is *dead*' (looking round at them both with a sort of calmness); 'he died on the night that I had that dream – mother, I told you so at the time. Oh, my Bobby! I knew that you could not leave me for ever without coming to tell me!'

"And so speaking, I fall into strong hysterics and am carried upstairs to bed. And so three or four more lagging days crawl by, and still we hear nothing, and remain in the same state of doubt and uncertainty; which to me, however, is hardly uncertainty; so convinced am I, in my own mind, that my fair-haired lover is away in the land whence never letter or messenger comes – that he has reached the Great Silence. So I sit at my frame, working my heart's agony into the tapestry, and feebly trying to say to God that He has done well, but I cannot. On the contrary, it seems to me, as my life trails on through the mellow mist of the autumn mornings, through the shortened autumn evenings, that, whoever has done it, it is most evilly done. One night we are sitting round the crackling little wood fire that one does not need for warmth, but that gives a cheerfulness to the room and the furniture, when the butler Stephens enters, and going over to father, whispers to him. I seem to understand in a moment what the purport of his whisper is.

" 'Why does he whisper?' I cry, irritably. 'Why does not he speak out loud? Why should you try to keep it from me? I know that it is something about Bobby.'

"Father has already risen, and is walking towards the door.

" 'I will not let you go until you tell me,' I cry wildly, flying after him.

" 'A sailor has come over from Plymouth,' he answers, hurriedly; 'he says he has news. My darling, I will not keep you in suspense a moment longer than I can help, and meanwhile pray – both of you pray for him!'

"I sit rigidly still, with my cold hands tightly clasped, during the moments that next elapse. Then father returns. His eyes are full of tears, and there is small need to ask for his message; it is most plainly written on his features – death, and not life.

" 'You were right, Phoebe,' he says, brokenly, taking hold of my icy hands; 'you knew best. He is gone! God has taken him.'

"My heart dies. I had thought that I had no hope, but I was wrong. 'I knew it!' I say, in a dry stiff voice. 'Did not I tell you so? But you would not believe me – go on! – tell me how it was – do not think I cannot bear it – make haste!'

"And so he tells me all that there is now left for me to know – after what manner, and on what day my darling took his leave of this pretty and cruel world. He had had his wish, as I already know, and had set off blithely home in the last prize they had captured. Father had taken the precaution of having a larger proportion than usual of the Frenchmen ironed, and had also sent a greater number of Englishmen. But to what purpose? They were nearing port, sailing prosperously along on a smooth blue sea, with a fair, strong wind, thinking of no evil, when a great and terrible misfortune overtook them. Some of the Frenchmen who were not ironed got the sailors below and drugged their grog; ironed them, and freed their countrymen. Then one of the officers rushed on deck, and holding a pistol to my Bobby's head bade him surrender the vessel or die. Need I tell you which he chose? I think not – well" (with a sigh) "and so they shot my boy – ah me! how many years ago – and threw him overboard! Yes – threw him overboard – it makes me angry and grieved even now to think of it – into the great and greedy sea, and the vessel escaped to France."

There is a silence between us: I will own to you that I am crying, but the old lady's eyes are dry.

"Well," she says, after a pause, with a sort of triumph in her tone, "they never could say again that Bobby Gerard was *afraid*!"

"The tears were running down my father's cheeks, as he told me," she resumes presently, "but at the end he wiped them and said, 'It is well! He was as pleasant in God's sight as he was in ours, and so He has taken him.'

"And for me, I was glad that he had gone to God – none gladder. But you will not wonder that, for myself, I was, past speaking sorry. And so the years went by, and, as you know, I married Mr Hamilton, and lived with him forty years, and was happy in the main, as happiness goes; and when he died I wept much and long, and so I did for each of my sons when in turn they went. But looking back on all my long life, the event that I think stands out most clearly from it is my dream and my boy-lover's death-day. It *was* an odd dream, was it not?"

Amelia B. Edwards

The New Pass

Amelia Ann Blandford Edwards (1831–92) is best remembered for her book A Thousand Miles Up the Nile, *and also for her invaluable work in creating the Egypt Exploration Fund. She was an inveterate traveller, and a gifted novelist and writer of ghost stories. 1873 saw both the first editions of her classic travel book* Untrodden Peaks and Unfrequented Valleys: A Midsummer Ramble in the Dolomites; *and the not unrelated tale "The New Pass" in her three-volume collection* Monsieur Maurice.

THE CIRCUMSTANCES I am about to relate happened just four autumns ago, when I was travelling in Switzerland with my old school and college friend, Egerton Wolfe.

Before going further, however, I wish to observe that this is no dressed-up narrative. I am a plain, prosaic man, by name Francis Legrice; by profession a barrister; and I think it would be difficult to find many persons less given to look upon life from a romantic or imaginative point of view. By my enemies, and sometimes, perhaps, by my friends, I am supposed to push my habit of incredulity to the verge of universal scepticism; and indeed I admit that I believe in very little that I do not hear and see for myself. But for these things that I am going to relate, I can vouch; and in so far as mine is a personal narrative, I am responsible for its truth. What I saw, I saw with my own eyes in the broad daylight. I offer nothing, therefore, in the shape of a story; but simply a plain statement of facts, as they happened to myself.

I was travelling, then, in Switzerland with Egerton Wolfe. It was not our first joint long-vacation tour by a good many, but it promised to be our last; for Wolfe was engaged to be married the following Spring to a very beautiful and charming girl, the daughter of a north-country baronet.

He was a handsome fellow, tall, graceful, dark-haired, dark-eyed; a poet, a dreamer, an artist – as thoroughly unlike myself, in short, as one man having arms, legs, and a head, can be unlike another. And yet we suited each other capitally, and were the fastest friends and best travelling companions in the world.

We had begun our holiday on this occasion with a week's idleness at a place which I will call Oberbrunn – a delightful place, wholly Swiss, consisting of one huge wooden building, half water-cure establishment, half hotel; two smaller buildings called *Dépendances*; a tiny church with a bulbous steeple painted green; and a handful of village – all perched together on a breezy mountain-plateau some three thousand feet above the lake and valley. Here, far from the haunts of the British tourist and the Alpine Club-man, we read, smoked, climbed, rose with the dawn, rubbed up our rusty German, and got ourselves into training for the knapsack work to follow.

At length, our week being up, we started – rather later on the whole than was prudent, for we had a thirty miles' walk before us, and the sun was already high.

It was a glorious morning, however; the sky flooded with light, and a cool breeze blowing. I see the bright scene now, just as it lay before us when we came down the hotel steps and found our guide waiting for us outside. There were the water-drinkers gathered round the fountain on the lawn; the usual crowd of itinerant vendors of stag-horn ornaments and carved toys in wood and ivory squatted in a semi-circle about the door; some half-dozen barefooted little mountain children running to and fro with wild raspberries for sale; the valley so far below, dotted with hamlets and traversed by a winding stream, like a thread of flashing silver; the black pine-wood half-way down the slope; the frosted peaks glittering on the horizon.

"*Bon voyage!*" said our good host, Dr Steigl, with a last hearty shake of the hand.

"*Bon voyage!*" echoed the waiters and miscellaneous hangers-on.

Some three or four of the water-drinkers at the fountain raised their hats – the ragged children pursued us with their wild fruits as far as the gate – and so we departed.

For some distance our path lay along the mountain side, through pine woods and by cultivated slopes where the Indian corn was ripening to gold, and the late hay-harvest was waiting for the mower. Then the path wound gradually downwards – for the valley lay between us and the pass we had laid out for our day's work – and then, through a succession of soft green slopes and ruddy apple-orchards, we came to a blue lake fringed with rushes, where we hired a boat with a striped awning, like the boats on Lago Maggiore, and were rowed across by a boatman who rested on his oars and sang a *jodel*-song when we were half way across.

Being landed on the opposite bank, we found our road at once begin to trend upwards; and here, as the guide informed us, the ascent of the Hohenhorn might be said to begin.

"This, however, *meine Herren*," said he, "is only part of the old pass. It is ill-kept; for none but country folks and travellers from Oberbrunn come this way now. But we shall strike the New Pass higher up. A grand road, *meine Herren* – as fine a road as the Simplon, and good for carriages all the way. It has only been open since the Spring."

"The old pass is good enough for me, anyhow!" said Egerton, crowding a handful of wild forget-me-nots under the ribbon of his hat. "It's like a stray fragment of Arcadia."

And in truth it was wonderfully lovely and secluded – a mere rugged path winding steeply upwards in a soft green shade, among large forest trees and moss-grown rocks covered with patches of velvety lichen. A little streamlet ran singing beside it all the way – now gurgling deep in ferns and grasses; now feeding a rude trough made of a hollow trunk; now crossing our road like a broken flash of sunlight; now breaking away in a tiny fall and foaming out of sight, only to reappear a few steps further on.

Then overhead, through the close roof of leaves, we saw patches of blue sky and golden shafts of sunshine, and small brown squirrels leaping from bough to bough; and in the deep rich grass on either hand, thick ferns, and red and golden mosses, and blue campanulas, and now and then a little wild strawberry, ruby red. By-and-by, when we had been following this path for nearly an hour, we came upon a patch of clearing, in the midst of which stood a rough upright monolith, antique, weather-stained, covered with rude carvings like a Runic monument – the primitive boundary-stone between the Cantons of Uri and Unterwalden.

"Let us rest here!" cries Egerton, flinging himself at full length on the grass. "*Eheu, fugaces!* – and the hours are shorter than the years. Why not enjoy them?"

But the guide, whose name is Peter Kauffmann, interposes after the manner of guides in general, and will by no means let us have our own way. There is a mountain inn, he urges, now only five minutes distant – "an excellent little inn, where they sell good red wine." So we yield to fate and Peter Kauffmann and pursue our upward way, coming presently, as he promised and predicted, upon a bright open space and a brown chalet on a shelf of plateau overhanging a giddy precipice. Here, sitting under a vine-covered trellis built out on the very brink of the cliff, we find three mountaineers discussing a flask of the good red wine aforesaid.

In this picturesque eyrie we made our mid-day halt. A smiling *Mädchen* brought us coffee, brown bread, and goats'-milk cheese; while our guide, pulling out a huge lump of the dry black bread from his wallet, fraternized with the mountaineers over a half-flask of his favourite vintage.

The men chattered merrily in their half-intelligible patois. We sat silent, looking down into the deep misty valley and across to the great amethyst mountains, streaked here and there with faint blue threads of slender waterfalls.

"There must surely be moments," said Egerton Wolfe after a while, "when even such men as you, Frank – men of the world, and lovers of it – feel within them some stirrings of the primitive Adam; some vague longing for that idyllic life of the woods and fields that we dreamers are still, in our inmost souls, insane enough to sigh after as the highest good."

"You mean, don't I sometimes wish to be a Swiss peasant-farmer, with *sabots*; a *goître*; a wife without form as regards her person, and void as regards her head; and a *crétin* grandfather a hundred and three years old? Why, no. I prefer myself as I am."

My friend smiled, and shook his head.

"Why take it for granted," said he, "that no man can cultivate his brains and his paternal acres at the same time? Horace, with none of the adjuncts you name, loved a country life and turned it to immortal poetry."

"The world has gone round once or twice since then, my dear fellow," I replied, philosophically. "The best poetry comes out of cities nowadays."

"And the worst. Do you see those avalanches over yonder?"

Following the direction of his eyes, I saw something like a tiny puff of white smoke gliding over the shoulder of a huge mountain on the opposite side of the valley. It was followed by another and another. We could see neither whence they came nor whither they went. We were too far away to hear the sullen thunder of their fall. Silently they flashed into sight, and as silently they vanished.

Wolfe sighed heavily.

"Poor Lawrence!" said he. "Switzerland was his dream. He longed for the Alps as ardently as other men long for money or power."

Lawrence was a younger brother of his whom I had never seen – a lad of great promise whose health had broken down at Addiscombe some ten or twelve years before, and who had soon after died of rapid consumption at Torquay.

"And he never had that longing gratified?"

"Ah, no – he was never out of England. They prescribe bracing climates now, I am told, for lung disease; but not so then. Poor dear fellow! I sometimes fancy he might have lived, if only he had had his heart's desire."

"I would not let such a painful thought enter my head, if I were you," said I, hastily.

"But I can't help it! My mind has been running on poor Lawrence all the morning; and, somehow, the grander the scenery gets, the more I keep thinking how he would have exulted in it. Do you remember those lines by Coleridge, written in the Valley of Chamouni? He knew them by heart. 'Twas the sight of yonder avalanches that reminded me . . . Well! I will try not to think of these things. Let us change the subject."

Just at this moment, the landlord of the châlet came out – a bright-eyed, voluble young mountaineer about five or six-and-twenty, with a sprig of Edelweiss in his hat.

"Good day, *meine Herren*," he said, including all alike in his salute, but addressing himself especially to Wolfe and myself. "Fine weather for travelling – fine weather for the grapes. These *Herren* are going on by the New Pass? *Ach, Herr Gott!* a grand work! a wonderful work! – and all begun and completed in less than three years. These *Herren* see it today for the first time? Good. They have probably been over the Tête Noire? No! Over the Splugen? Good – good. If these *Herren* have been over the Splugen, they can form an idea of the New Pass. The New Pass is very like the Splugen. It has a gallery tunnelled in the solid rock, just like the gallery on the Via Mala, with this difference that the gallery in the New Pass is much longer, and lighted by loop-holes at regular intervals. These *Herren* will please to observe the view looking both up and down the pass, before entering the mouth of the tunnel – there is not a finer view in all Switzerland."

"It must be a great advantage to the people hereabouts, having so good a road carried from valley to valley," said I, smiling at his enthusiasm.

"Oh, it is a fine thing for us, *mein Herr*!" he replied. "And a fine thing for all this part of the Canton. It will bring visitors – floods of visitors! By the way, these *Herren* must not omit to look out for the waterfall above the gallery. Holy St Nicholas! the way in which that waterfall has been arranged!"

"Arranged!" echoed Wolfe, who was as much amused as myself. "*Diavolo!* Do you arrange the waterfalls in your country?"

"It was the Herr Becker," said the landlord, unconscious of banter; "the eminent engineer who planned the New Pass. The waterfall, you see, *meine Herren,* could not be suffered to follow its old course down the face of the rock through which the gallery is tunnelled, or it would have flowed in at the loopholes and flooded the road. What, therefore, did the Herr Becker do?"

"Turned the course of the fall, and brought it down a hundred yards further on," said I somewhat impatiently.

"No so, *mein Herr* – not so! The Herr Becker attempts nothing so expensive. He permits the fall to keep its old couloir and come down its old way – but instead of letting it wash the outside of the gallery, he pierces the rock in another direction – vertically – behind the tunnel; constructs an artificial shoot, or conduit in the heart of the rock, and brings the fall out below the gallery, just where the cliff overhangs the valley. Now what do the English *Herren* say to that?"

"That it must certainly be a clever piece of engineering," replied Wolfe.

"And that having rested long enough, we will push on and see it," added I, glad to cut short the thread of our host's native eloquence.

So we paid our reckoning; took a last look at the view; and, plunging back into the woods, went on our way refreshed.

The path still continued to ascend, till we suddenly came upon a burst of daylight and found ourselves on a magnificent high road some thirty feet in breadth, with the forest and the telegraph wires on the one hand, and the precipice on the other. Massive granite posts at close intervals protected the edge of the road, and the cantonniers were still at work here and there, breaking and laying fresh stones, and clearing débris. We did not need to be informed that this was the New Pass.

Always ascending, we continued now to follow the road which at every turn commanded finer and finer views across the valley. Then by degrees the forest dwindled, and was at last left far below; and the giddy precipices to our left grew steeper, and the mountain slopes above became more and more barren, till the last Alp-roses vanished and there remained only a carpet of brown and tan moss scattered over here and there with great boulders – some freshly broken away from the heights above – others thickly coated with lichen, as if they might have been lying there for centuries.

We seemed here to have reached the highest point of the New Pass, for our road continued at this barren level for some miles. An immense panorama of peaks, snow-fields, and glaciers lay out-stretched before us to the left, with an unfathomable gulf of misty valley between. The hot air simmered in the sun. The heat and silence were intense. Once, and once only, we came upon a party of travellers. They were three in number, lying at full length in the shade of a huge fragment of fallen rock, their heads comfortably pillowed on their knapsacks, and all fast asleep.

And now the grey rock began to crop out in larger masses close beside our path, encroaching nearer and nearer, till at last the splintered cliffs towered straight above our heads and the road became a mere broad shelf along the face of the precipice. Presently, on turning a sharp angle of rock, we saw before us a vista of road, cliff, and valley – the road now perceptibly on the decline, and vanishing about a mile ahead into the mouth of a small cavernous opening (no bigger, as it seemed from that distance, than a good-sized rabbit hole) pierced through a huge projecting spur, or buttress, of the mountain.

"Behold the famous gallery!" said I. "Mine host was right – it is something like the Splugen, barring the much greater altitude of the road, and the still greater width of the valley. But where is the waterfall?"

"Well, it's not much of a waterfall," said Wolfe. "I can just see it – a tiny thread of mist wavering down the cliff a long way on, beyond the mouth of the tunnel."

"Ay; I see it now – a sort of inferior Staubbach. Heavens! what power the sun has up here! At what time did Kauffmann say we should get to Schwartzenfelden?"

"Not before seven, at the earliest – and it is now nearly four."

"Humph! three hours more – say three and a half. Well, that will be a pretty good first day's pedestrianizing, heat and all considered!"

Here the conversation dropped, and we plodded on again in silence.

Meanwhile the sun blazed in the heavens, and the light, struck back from white rock and whiter road, was almost blinding. And still the hot air danced and shimmered before us; and a windless stillness, as of death, lay upon all the scene.

Suddenly – quite suddenly, as if he had started out of the rock – I saw a man coming towards us with rapid and eager gesticulations. He seemed to be waving us back; but I was so startled for the moment by the unexplained way in which he made his appearance, that I scarcely took in the meaning of his gestures.

"How odd!" I exclaimed, coming to a halt. "How did he get there?"

"How did who get there?" said Wolfe.

"Why, that fellow yonder. Did you see where he came from?"

"What fellow, my dear boy? I see no one but ourselves."

And he stared vaguely round, while all the time the man between us and the gallery was waving his right arm above his head, and running on to meet us.

"Good heavens! Egerton," I said impatiently, "where are your eyes? Here – straight before us – not a quarter of a mile off – making signs as hard as he can. Perhaps we had better wait till he comes up."

My friend drew his race-glass from its case, adjusted it carefully, and took a long, steady look down the road. Seeing him do this, the man stood still; but kept his right hand up all the same.

"You see him now, surely?" said I.

"*No.*"

I turned and looked him in the face. I could not believe my ears.

"Upon my honour, Frank," he said earnestly, "I see only the empty road and the mouth of the tunnel beyond. Here, Kauffmann!"

Kauffmann, who was standing close by, stepped up and touched his cap.

"Look down the road," said Wolfe.

The guide shaded his eyes with his hand, and looked.

"What do you see?"

"I see the entrance to the gallery, *mein Herr*."

"Nothing else?"

"Nothing else, *mein Herr*."

And still the man stood there in the road – even came a step or two nearer! Was I mad?

"You still think you see someone yonder?" said Egerton, looking at me very seriously.

"I *know* that I do."

He handed me his race-glass.

"Look through that," he said, "and tell me if you still see him."

"I see him more plainly than before."

"What is he like?"

"Very tall – very slender – fair – quite young – no more, I should say, than fifteen or sixteen – evidently an Englishman."

"How is he dressed?"

"In a grey suit – his collar open, and his throat bare. Wears a Scotch cap with a silver badge in it. He takes his cap off, and waves it! He has a whitish scar on his right temple. I can see the motion of his lips – he seems to say, 'Go back! go back!' Look for yourself – you *must* see him!"

I turned to give him the glass, but he pushed it away.

"No, no," he said, hoarsely. "It's of no use. Go on looking . . . What more, for God's sake?"

I looked again – the glass all but dropped from my hand.

"Gracious heavens!" I exclaimed breathlessly, "he is gone!"

"Gone!"

Ay, gone. Gone as suddenly as he came – gone as though he had never been! I could not believe it. I rubbed my eyes. I rubbed the glass on my sleeve. I looked, and looked again; and still, though I looked, I doubted.

At this moment, with a wild unearthly cry, and a strange sound as of some heavy projectile cleaving the stagnant air, an eagle plunged past us upon mighty wings, and swooped down into the valley.

"*Ein Adler! ein Adler!*" shouted the guide, flinging up his cap and running to the brink of the precipice.

Wolfe laid his hand upon my arm, and drew a deep breath.

"Legrice," he said very calmly, but with a white, awe-struck look in his face, "you described my brother Lawrence – age, height, dress, everything; even to the Scotch cap he always wore, and the silver badge my uncle Horace gave him on his birthday. He got that scar in a cricket-match at Harrogate."

"Your brother Lawrence?" I faltered.

"Why you should be the one permitted to see him is strange," he went on, speaking more to himself than to me. "Very strange! I wish . . . but there! perhaps I should not have believed my own eyes. I *must* believe yours."

"I will never believe that my eyes saw your brother Lawrence," I said resolutely.

"We must turn back, of course," he went on, taking no notice of my answer. "Look here, Kauffmann – can we get to Schwartzenfelden tonight by the old pass, if we turn back at once?"

"Turn back!" I interrupted. "My dear Egerton, you are not serious?"

"I was never more serious in my life," he said, gravely.

"If these *Herren* wish to take the old pass," said the astonished guide, "we cannot get to Schwartzenfelden before midnight. We have already come seven miles out of the way, and the old pass is twelve miles farther round."

"Twelve and fourteen are twenty-six," said I. "We cannot add twenty-six miles to our original thirty. It is out of the question."

"These *Herren* can sleep at the châlet where we halted," suggested the guide.

"True – I had not thought of that," said Wolfe. "We can sleep at the châlet, and go on as soon as it is day."

"Turn back, sleep at the châlet, go on in the morning, and lose full half a day, with one of the finest passes in Switzerland before us, and our journey two-thirds done!" I cried. "The idea is too absurd."

"Nothing shall induce me to go on, in defiance of a warning from the dead," said Wolfe hastily.

"And nothing," I replied, "shall induce me to believe that we have received any such warning. I either saw that man, or I laboured under some kind of optical illusion. But ghosts I do not believe in."

"As you please. You can go on if you prefer it, and take Kauffmann with you. I know my way back."

"Agreed – except as regards Kauffmann. Let him take his choice."

Kauffmann, having the matter explained to him, elected at once to go back with Egerton Wolfe.

"If the *Herr* Englishman has been warned in a vision," he said, crossing himself devoutly, "it is suicide to go on. Obey the blessed spirit, *mein Herr!*"

But nothing now would have induced me to turn back, even if I had felt inclined to do so; so, agreeing to meet next day at Schwartzenfelden, my friend and I said goodbye.

"God grant you may come to no harm, dear old fellow," said Wolfe, as he turned away.

"I don't feel like harm, I assure you," I replied, laughing.

And so we parted.

I stood still and watched them till they were out of sight. At the turn of the road they paused and looked back. When Wolfe waved his hand for the last time and finally disappeared, I could not repress a sudden thrill – he looked so like the figure of my illusion!

For that it was an illusion, I did not doubt for a moment. Such phenomena, though not common, are by no means unheard-of. I had talked with more than one eminent physician on this very subject, and I remembered that each had spoken of cases within his own experience. Besides, there was the famous case of Nicolai, the bookseller of Berlin; not to mention many others, equally well attested. That I must have been temporarily in the condition of persons so affected, I took for granted; and yet I felt well – never better; my head cool – my mind clear – my pulse regular. Well – I would never disbelieve in hallucinations again. To that I made up my mind; but as for ghosts . . . pshaw! how could any sane man, above all, such a man as Egerton Wolfe, believe in ghosts?

Reasoning thus, and smiling to myself, I tightened the shoulder-straps of my knapsack, took a pull at my wine-flask, and set off towards the tunnel.

It was still half a mile distant; for I had stopped on first sight of the figure, before we were half across the space that lay between that dark opening and the turn of the road above. And now, plodding steadily towards it, I examined the ground at every step (especially on the side of the precipice) for any path or rocky projection of which a man could possibly have availed himself for retreat or shelter; but the smooth upright wall of solid limestone on the one hand, and the sheer, inaccessible, giddy depths on the other, made all such explanation impossible. Thrown back thus on the illusion theory, I paused once or twice, and tried to conjure up the figure before my eyes, but in vain.

And now with every step that I took the mouth of the tunnel grew larger, and the depth of shade within it blacker and more mysterious. I was by this time near enough to see that it was faced with brickwork – that it spanned the full width of the road – and that it was more than lofty enough for an old-fashioned, top-heavy diligence to pass under it. The next moment, being within half a dozen yards of it, I distinctly heard the cool murmur of the more distant waterfall (now hidden by the great mountain spur through which the gallery was carried); and the next moment after that, I had plunged into the tunnel.

It was like the transition from an orchid-house to an ice-house – from midday to midnight. The darkness was profound, and so intense the sudden chill, that for the first second it almost took my breath away.

The roof and sides of the gallery, and the road beneath my feet, were all hewn in the solid rock. A sharp, arrowy gleam of light, shooting athwart the gloom about fifty yards ahead, marked the position of the first loop-hole. A second, a third, a fourth, as many perhaps as eight or ten, gleamed faintly in the distance. The tiny blue speck which showed where the gallery opened out again upon the day, looked at least a mile away. The path underfoot was wet and slippery; and as I went on, my eyes becoming accustomed to the darkness, I saw that every part of the tunnel was streaming with moisture.

I pushed on rapidly. The first and second loop-holes were soon left behind, but at the third I paused to breathe the outer air. Then, for the first time, I observed that every rut in the road beneath my feet was filled with running water.

I hurried on faster and faster. I shivered. I felt the cold seizing me. The arched entrance through which I had just passed had dwindled already to a shining patch no bigger than my hand, while the tiny blue speck on ahead seemed far off as ever. Meanwhile the tunnel was dripping like a shower-bath.

All at once, my attention was arrested by a sound – a strange indescribable sound – heavy, muffled, as of mighty forces at work in the heart of the mountain. I stood still – I held my breath – I fancied I felt the solid rock vibrate beneath my feet! Then it flashed upon me that I must now be approaching that part of the gallery behind which the waterfall was conducted, and that what I heard was the muffled roar of its descent. At the same moment, chancing to look down at my feet, I saw that the road was an inch deep in running water from wall to wall.

Now, lawyer as I am, and ignorant of the first principles of civil engineering, I felt sure that this much-praised Herr Becker should, at least, have made his tunnel water-tight. That it leaked somewhere was plain, and that it should be suffered to go on leaking to the discomfort of travellers was simply intolerable. An inch of water, for instance, was more than . . . an inch did I say? Gracious heavens! since the moment I looked, it had risen to three – it was closing over my boots – it was becoming a rushing torrent!

In that instant a great horror fell upon me – the horror of darkness and sudden death. I turned, flung away my Alpenstock, and fled for my life.

Fled blindly, breathlessly, wildly, with the horrible grinding sound of the imprisoned waterfall in my ears, and the gathering torrent at my heels!

Never while I live shall I forget the agony of those next few seconds – the icy numbness seizing on my limbs – the sudden, frightful sense of impeded respiration – the water rising, eddying, clamouring, pursuing me, passing me – the swirl of it, as it flashed past each loop-hole in succession – the rush with which (as I strained on to the mouth of the gallery, now not a dozen yards distant) it leaped out into the sunlight like a living thing, and dashed to the edge of the precipice!

At that supreme instant, just as I had darted out through the echoing arch and staggered a few paces up the road, a deafening report, crackling, hurried, tremendous, like the explosion of a mine, rent the air and roused a hundred echoes. It was followed by a moment of strange and terrible suspense. Then, with a deep and sullen roar, audible above all the rolling thunders of the mountains round, a mighty wave – smooth, solid, glassy, like an Atlantic wave on an English western coast – came gleaming up the mouth of the tunnel, paused as it were, upon the threshold, reared its majestic crest, curved, trembled, burst in a cataract of foam, flooded the road for yards beyond the spot where I was clinging to the rock like a limpet, and rushing back again, as the wave rushes down the beach, hurled itself over the cliff, and vanished in a cloud of mist.

After this, the imprisoned flood came pouring out tumultuously for several minutes, bringing with it fragments of rock and masonry, and filling the road with debris; but even this disturbance presently subsided, and almost as soon as the last echoes of the explosion had died away, the liberated waters were rippling pleasantly along their new bed, sparkling out into the sunshine as they emerged from the gallery, and gliding in a smooth continuous stream over the brink of the precipice, thence to fall, in multitudinous wavy folds and wreaths of prismatic mist, into the valley two thousand feet below.

For myself, drenched to the skin as I was, I could do nothing but turn back and follow meekly in the track of Egerton Wolfe and Peter Kauffmann. How I did so, dripping and weary, and minus my Alpenstock; how I arrived at the châlet about sunset, shivering and hungry, just in time to claim my share of a capital omelette and a dish of mountain trout; how the Swiss press rang with my escape for, at least, nine days after the event; how the Herr Becker was liberally censured for his defective engineering; and how Egerton Wolfe believes to this day that his brother Lawrence came back from the dead to save us from utter destruction, are matters upon which it were needless to dwell in these pages. Enough that I narrowly escaped with my life, and that had we gone on, as we doubtless should have gone on but for the delay consequent upon my illusion, we should most probably have been in the heart of the tunnel at the time of the explosion, and not one left to tell the tale.

Nevertheless, my dear friends, I do not believe, and I have made up my mind never to believe – in ghosts.

Erckmann-Chatrian

The White and the Black
("*Le Blanc et le noir*")

"Erckmann-Chatrian" was the collaborative name of the most successful and popular writing team in France during the late nineteenth century: Emile Erckmann (1822–99) and Alexandre Chatrian (1826–90). Their most famous work, The Polish Jew, *was adapted for the London stage by Sir Henry Irving as* The Bells; *and many of their historical tales became accepted reading texts in British schools. "The White and the Black" is one of a large number of Erckmann-Chatrian's thrilling weird tales originally gathered together as* Histoires et Contes Fantastiques.

M. R. James was an enthusiastic admirer of their stories: "I should feel myself ungrateful if I did not pay a tribute to the supernatural tales of Erckmann-Chatrian. The blend of French with German in them (compared to the French–Irish blend in Le Fanu) has produced some quite first-class romance of this kind. Among longer stories, "La Maison forestière" (and, if you will, "Hugues le loup"); among shorter ones "Le Blanc et le noir", "Le Rêve du Cousin Elof" and "L'Oeil invisible" have for years delighted and alarmed me. It is high time that they were made more accessible than they are."

I

AT THAT TIME we passed our evenings at Brauer's alehouse, which opens upon the square of Vieux-Brisach. After eight o'clock there used to drop in, one by one, Frederick Schultz the notary; Frantz Martin the burgomaster; Christopher Ulmett the magistrate; the counsellor Klers; the engineer Rothan; the young organist Theodore Blitz; and some others of the chief townsfolk, who all sat around the same table and drank their foaming *bok-bier* like brothers.

The apparition of Theodore Blitz, who came to us from Jena with a letter of recommendation from Harmosius – his dark eyes, his brown dishevelled hair, his thin white nose, his metallic voice, and his mystic ideas, occasioned us some little disquiet. It used to trouble us to see him rise abruptly and pace two or three times up and down the room, gesticulating the while, mocking with a strange air the Swiss landscapes with which the walls were adorned – lakes of indigo blue, mountains of apple green, paths of brilliant red. Then he would seat himself down again, empty his glass at a gulp, and commence a discussion about the music of Palestrina, about the lute of the Hebrews, about the introduction of the organ into our churches, about the shophar, the sabbatic epochs, etc. He would knit his brows, plant his sharp elbows on the edge of the table, and lose himself in deep thought. Yes, he perplexed us not a little – we others who were grave and accustomed to methodical ideas. However, it was necessary to put up with it; and the engineer Rothan himself, in spite of his bantering spirit, in the end grew calm and no longer continued to contradict the young organist when he was right.

Theodore Blitz was plainly one of those nervously organized beings who are affected by every change of temperature. The year of which I speak was extremely warm; we had several heavy storms towards the autumn, and folk began to fear for the wine harvest.

One evening all our little world was gathered, according to custom, around the table, with the exception of the magistrate Ulmett and the organist. The burgomaster talked about the weather and great hydraulic works. As for me I listened to the wind gambolling without amongst the plane trees of the Schlossgarten, to the drip of the water from the spouts, and to its dashing against the windows. From time to time one could hear a tile blown off a roof, a door shut to with a bang, a shutter beat against a wall. Then would arise the great clamour of the storm, sweeping, sighing, and groaning in the distance, as if all the invisible powers were seeking and calling on one another in the darkness, while living things hid themselves, sitting in corners, in order to escape a fearful meeting with them.

From the church of Saint-Landolphe nine o'clock sounded, when Blitz hurriedly entered, shaking his hat like one possessed, and saying in his husky voice –

"Surely the Evil One is about his work! The white and the black are having a tussle. The nine times nine thousand nine hundred and ninety thousand spirits of Envy battle and tear themselves. Go, Ahriman! Walk! Ravage! Lay waste! The Amschaspands are in flight! Oromage veils her face! What a time, what a time!"

And so saying he walked round the room, stretching his long skinny limbs, and laughing by jerks.

We were all astounded at such an entry, and for some seconds no one spoke a word. Then, however, the engineer Rothan, led on by his caustic humour, said –

"What nonsense is that you are singing there, Organist? What do Amschaspands signify to us? or the nine times nine thousand nine hundred and ninety thousand spirits of Envy? Ha! ha! ha! It is really comic. Where on earth did you pick up such strange language?"

Theodore Blitz stopped suddenly short in his walk and shut one eye, while the other, wide open, shone with a diabolic irony.

When Rothan had finished –

"Oh, engineer," said he; "oh! Sublime spirit, master of the trowel and mortar, director of stones, he who orders right angles, angles acute, angles obtuse, you are right – a hundred times right."

He bent himself with a mocking air, and went on –

"Nothing exists but matter – the level, the rule, and the compass. The revelations of Zoroaster, of Moses, of Pythagoras, of Odin – the harmony, the melody, art, sentiment, they are all dreams unworthy of an enlightened intellect such as yours. To you belongs the truth, the eternal truth. Ha! ha! ha! I bow myself before you; I salute you; I prostrate myself before your glory, imperishable as that of Nineveh and of Babylon."

Finishing his speech, he made two little turns on his heels, and uttered a laugh so piercing that it was more like the crowing of a cock at daybreak.

Rothan was getting angry, when at that moment the old magistrate Ulmett came in, his head protected by a great otter-skin cap, his shoulders covered by his bottle green greatcoat bordered with fox skin. His hands hung down beside him, his back was bent, his eyes were half-closed, his big nose was red, and his large cheeks were wet with rain. He was as wet as a drake.

Outside the rain fell in torrents, the gutters gushed over, the spouts disgorged themselves, and the ditches were swollen into little rivers.

"Ah, heavens!" cried the good fellow. "Perhaps it was foolish to come out on such a night, and after such work too – two inquests, verbal processes, interrogatories! The *bok-bier* and old friends, though, would make me swim across the Rhine."

And muttering these words he put off his otter-skin cap and opened his great pelisse to take out his long tobacco pipe and his pouch, which he carefully laid down upon the table. After that he hung his greatcoat and his hat up beside the window, and called out –

"Brauer!"

"Well, Magistrate, what do you want?"

"You would do well to put to the shutters. Believe me, this storm will wind up with some thunder."

The innkeeper went out and put the shutters to, and the old magistrate, sitting down in his corner, heaved a deep sigh.

"You know what has happened, burgomaster?" he asked in a solemn voice.

"No. What has occurred, my old Christopher?"

Before he replied – Ulmett threw a glance around the room.

"We are here alone, my friends," said he, "so I am able to tell you. About three o'clock this afternoon someone found poor Gredel Dick under the sluice of the miller at Holderloch."

"Under the sluice at Holderloch?" cried all.

"Yes; a cord round her neck."

In order to understand how these words affected us it is necessary that you should know that Gredel Dick was one of the prettiest girls in Vieux-Brisach; a tall brunette, with blue eyes and red cheeks; the only daughter of an old anabaptist, Petrus Dick, who farmed considerable portions of the Schlossgarten. For some time she had seemed sad and melancholy – she who had beforetime been so merry in the morning at the washing place, and in the evening at the well in the midst of her friends. She had been seen crying, and her sorrow had been ascribed to the incessant pursuit of her by Saphéri Mutz, the postmaster's son – a big fellow, thin, vigorous, with an aquiline nose and curling black hair. He followed her like a shadow, and never let her off his arm at the dances.

There had been some talk about their marriage, but old Mutz, his wife, Karl Bremer his son-in-law, and his daughter Saffayel, were opposed to the match, all agreeing that a "heathen" should not be introduced into the family.

For three days past nothing had been seen of Gredel. No one knew what had become of her. You may imagine the thousand different thoughts which crowded upon us when we heard that she was dead. No one thought any longer of the discussion between Theodore Blitz and the engineer Rothan touching invisible spirits. All eyes were fixed on – Christopher Ulmett, who, his large bald head bent, his heavy white eyebrows knit, gravely filled his pipe, with a meditative air.

"And Mutz – Saphéri Mutz?" asked the burgomaster. "What has become of him?"

A slight flush coloured the cheeks of the old man as he answered, after some seconds of thought –

"Saphéri Mutz? He has gone."

"Gone!" cried little Klers. "Then he acknowledges his guilt?"

"It certainly seems so to me," said the old magistrate simply. "One does not scamper off for nothing. As for the rest, we have searched his father's place, and found all the house upset. The folk seemed struck with consternation. The mother raved and tore her hair; the daughter wore her Sunday clothes, and danced about like a fool. It was impossible to get anything out of them. As to Gredel's father, the poor fellow is in the deepest despair. He does not wish to say anything against his child, but it is certain that Gredel Dick left the farm of her own accord on Tuesday last in order to meet Saphéri. That fact is attested by all the neighbours. Now the gendarmes are scouring the country. We shall see, we shall see!"

Then there was a long silence. Outside the rain fell heavily.

"It is abominable!" cried the burgomaster suddenly. "Abominable! To think that every father of a family, even such as bring up their children in the fear of God, are exposed to such misfortunes."

"Yes," replied Ulmett, lighting his pipe. "It is so. They say, no doubt rightly, that heaven orders all things; but the spirit of darkness seems to me to meddle a good deal more than is necessary in them. For one good fellow how many villains do we find, without faith or law? And for one good action how many evil ones? I tell you, my friends, if the Evil One were to count his flock –"

He had not time to finish, for at that moment a terrific flash of lightning glared in through the chinks of the shutters, making the lamp burn dim. It was immediately followed by a clap of thunder, crashing, jerky – one of those claps which make you tremble. One might have thought that the world was coming to an end.

The clock of the church of Saint-Landolphe just then struck the half hour. The tolling bells seemed to be just hard by one. From far, very far off, there came a trembling plaintive voice, crying –

"Help, help!"

"Someone cries for help," said the burgomaster.

"Yes," said the others, turning pale, and listening.

While we were all thus in fright, Rothan, curling his lips in a joking fashion, broke out –

"Ha! ha! ha! It is Mademoiselle Roesël's cat singing its love story to Monsieur Roller, the young first tenor."

Then dropping his voice and lifting his hand with a tragic gesture, he went on –

"The time has sounded from the belfry of the chateau!"

"Ill-luck to those who laugh at such a cry," said old Christopher, rising.

He went towards the door with a solemn step, and we all followed him, even the fat innkeeper, who held his cotton cap in his hand and murmured a prayer very low. Rothan alone did not stir from his seat. As for me, I was behind the others, with outstretched neck, looking over their shoulders.

The glass door was scarcely opened when there came another flash of lightning. The street, with its white flags washed by the rain, its flushed gutters, its multitude of windows, its old gables, its signboards, glared out from the night, and then was swallowed up in the darkness.

That glance of the eye allowed me to see the steeple of Saint-Landolphe with its innumerable little carvings all clothed in white light. In the steeple were the bells hanging to black beams, with their clappers, and their ropes hanging down to the body of the church. Below that was a stork's nest, half torn in pieces by the wind, – the young ones with their beaks out, the mother at her wits' end, her wings extended, while the male bird flew about the shining steeple, his breast thrown forward, his neck bent, his long legs thrown out behind as if defying the thunder peals.

It was a strange sight, a veritable Chinese picture – thin, delicate, light, something strange, terrible, upon a black background of clouds broken with streaks of gold.

We stood, with open mouths, upon the threshold of the inn, and asked –

"What did you hear – Ulmett? What can you see – Klers?"

At that moment a lugubrious mewing commenced above us, and a whole regiment of cats set to work springing about in the gutter. At the same time a peal of laughter filled the room –

"Ah well! ah well!" cried the engineer. "Do you hear them? Was I wrong?"

"It was nothing," murmured the old magistrate. "Thank heaven, it was nothing. Let us go in again. The rain is recommencing."

As we took our places again, he said –

"Is it astonishing – Rothan, that the imagination of a poor old fellow, such as myself, goes astray at a time when earth and heaven confound themselves, while good and bad are struggling together, while such mysterious crimes occur around us even at this day? Is it strange?"

We all took our places with a feeling of annoyance with the engineer, who had alone remained quiet, and had seen us disconcerted. We turned our backs on him as we emptied our glasses without saying a word, while he, his elbow on the edge of the window ledge, hummed between his teeth I know not what military march, the time of which he beat with his fingers on the ledge, without deigning to notice our ill-humour.

So things went on for some minutes, when Theodore Blitz said laughingly –

"Monsieur Rothan triumphs. He does not believe in invisible spirits. Nothing troubles him. He has a good foot, good eyes, and good ear. What more is wanting to convict us of ignorance and folly?"

"Ha," replied Rothan, "I should not have dared to say it, but you express things so well, Monsieur Organist, that one cannot disagree with you, especially in any matter that concerns yourself. As for my old friends Schultz, Ulmett, Klers, and the others, it is different, very different. Any one may at times be led astray by a dream, only one must see that it does not become a custom."

Instead of answering to this direct attack, Blitz, his head bent down, seemed to be listening to some noise without.

"Hush," said he, looking at us. "Hush."

He lifted his finger, and the expression of his face was so striking that we all listened with an indefinable feeling of fear.

The same instant heavy steps were heard in the street without; a hand was laid on the catch of the door, and the organist said to us in a trembling voice –

"Be calm – listen and see. Heaven be with us."

The door opened and Saphéri Mutz appeared.

Should I live to be a thousand years old the figure of that man will never be erased from my memory. He is there – I see him. He advances reeling, pale – his hair hanging about his face – his eye dull, glassy – his blouse tight to his body – a big stick in his hand. He looks upon us without seeing us, like a man in a dream. A winding track of mud is left behind him. He stops, coughs, and says in a low voice, as if speaking to himself –

"Well! what if they arrest me ! What if they kill me! I would rather be here!"

Then, recollecting himself, and looking at us, one after another, he cried with a movement of terror –

"I have spoken! What did I say! Ah! the burgomaster – the magistrate Ulmett."

He made a bound as if he would fly, and I know not what he saw in the darkness of the night without which drove him once more from it into the room.

Theodore Blitz slowly arose. After he had looked at us, he walked up to Mutz, and, with an air of confidence, he asked him in a low voice, pointing to the dark street –

"Is it there?"

"Yes," said the man, in the same mysterious tone.

"It follows you?"

"From Fischbach."

"Behind you?"

"Yes, behind me."

"That is so, it is surely so," said the organist, throwing another look upon us. "It is always thus. Well then, stop here, Saphéri; sit down by the fire. Brauer, go and look for the gendarmes."

At the word gendarmes the wretched fellow grew fearfully pale, and seemed to think again of flight, but the same horror beat him back once more, and he sank down at the corner of the table, his head between his hands.

"Oh! had I but known – had I but known!" he moaned.

We were more dead than alive. The innkeeper went out. Not a breath was heard in the room. The old magistrate had put down his pipe, the burgomaster looked at me with a stupefied air. Rothan no longer whistled. Theodore Blitz, sitting at the end of a bench, looked at the rain streaking the darkness.

So we remained for a quarter of an hour, fearful all the time that the man would take it into his head to attempt to fly. But he did not stir. His long hair coiled from between his fingers, and the rain dripped from his clothes on to the floor.

At length the clatter of arms was heard without, and the gendarmes Werner and Keltz appeared upon the step. Keltz, darting a side glance at the man, lifted his great hat, saying –

"Good evening, Monsieur Magistrate."

Then he came in and coolly put the handcuffs on Saphéri's wrists, while Saphéri covered his face with his hands.

"Come, follow me, my son," said he. "Werner close up."

A third gendarme, short and fat, appeared in the darkness, and all the troop set off.

The wretched man made no resistance.

We looked at one another's pale faces.

"Good evening, gentlemen," said the organist, and he went off.

Then each of us, lost in his own thoughts, rose and departed to his home in silence.

As for me, I turned my head more than twenty times before I came to my door, fearful that I should see the other that had followed Saphéri Mutz, ready to lay its hands upon me.

And when at last, thank heaven, I was safe in my room, before I got into bed and blew out my light I took the wise precaution of looking under my bed to convince myself that *it* was not hidden there. I even said a prayer that *it* would not strangle me during the night. Well, what then? One is not a philosopher at all times.

II

Until then I had considered Theodore Blitz as a species of visionary imbecile. His maintaining the possibility of holding correspondence with invisible spirits by means of the music composed by all the sounds of nature, by the rustling of the leaves, by the murmur of the winds, by the hum of the insects, had appeared to me very ridiculous, and I was not the only one in that opinion.

It seemed all very well to tell us that if the grave sound of the organ awoke in us religious sentiments, that if martial music swept us on to war, and the simple melodies led us into reveries, it was because the different melodies were the invocation of the genii of the earth, who came suddenly into our midst, acted on our organs, and made us participants of their own proper essence. All that, however, appeared to me to be very obscure, and I had never doubted that the organist was just a little mad.

Now, however, my opinions changed respecting him. I said to myself that man is not a purely material being, that we are composed of body and soul; that to attribute all to the body, and to endeavour to ascribe all significance to it, is not rational; that the nervous fluid, agitated by the undulations of the air, is almost as difficult to comprehend as the direct action of occult powers; that we know not how it is that even a mere tickling of our ears, regulated by the rules of counter points excites in us a thousand agreeable or terrible emotions, elevates the soul to heaven, melts us, awakens in us the ardour of life, enthusiasm, love, fear, pity. No, the first theory was not satisfactory. The ideas of the organist appeared to me more sublime, more weighty, more just, and more acceptable, looking at things all round.

Then how could one explain, by means of mere nervous sensation, the arrival of Saphéri Mutz at the inn; how could one explain the terror of the unhappy man, which forced him to yield himself up; and the marvellous foresight of Blitz when he said to us –

"Hush! Listen! He comes! Heaven be with us!"

In the end all my prejudices against an invisible world disappeared, and new facts occurred to confirm me in this fresh manner of thinking.

About five days after the scene I have described, Saphéri Mutz had been transported by the gendarmes to the prison of Stuttgart. The thousand tales which had been set afloat respecting the death of Gredel Dick died away. The poor girl slept in peace at the back of the hill of the Trois-Fontaines, and folk were busied in looking after the wine harvest.

One evening about nine o'clock, as I left the great warehouse of the custom-house – where I had been tasting some samples of wine on behalf of Brauer, who had more confidence in my judgment in such a matter than in his own – my head a little heavy, I chanced to direct my steps towards the great Alley des Plantanes, behind the church of Saint-Landolphe.

The Rhine displayed to my right its azure waters, in which some fishermen were letting down their nets. To my left rose the old fortifications of the town. The air began to grow cool; the river murmured its eternal song; the fir trees of the Black Forest were softly ruffled; and as I walked on the sound of a violin fell on my ear.

I listened.

The black-headed linnet never threw more grace, more delicacy, into the execution of his rapid trills, nor more enthusiasm into the stream of his inspiration. It was like nothing I had heard. It had no repose, no measure. It was a torrent of notes, delirious, admirably symphonizing, but void of order or method.

Then, clashing with the thread of the inspiration, came some sharp incisive notes, piercing the ear.

"Theodore Blitz is here," said I to myself, putting aside the high branches of an elder hedge at the foot of a slope.

I looked around me, and my eyes fell upon a horse-pond covered with duck-weed, where the big frogs showed their flat noses. A little farther off rose some stables, with their big sheds, and an old dwelling-house. In the court, surrounded by a wall breast-high in which was a worm-eaten door, walked five or six fowls, and under the great stall ran the rabbits, their croups in the air, their tails up. When they saw me they disappeared under the gate of the grange like shadows.

No noise save the flow of the river and the bizarre fantasy of the violin could be heard.

Where on earth was Theodore Blitz?

The idea occurred to me that he was perhaps making trial of his music on the family of the Mutzes, and, curiosity impelling me, I glided into a hiding-place beside the wall to see what would happen in the farm.

The windows were all wide open, and in a room on the ground floor, long, with brown beams, level with the court, I perceived a long table furnished with all the sumptuousness of a village feast. Twenty or thirty covers were there. But what most astonished me was to see but five persons in front of this grand display. There was old Mutz, sombre and thoughtful, clad in a suit of black velvet with metal buttons. His large osseous head, gray, his forehead contracted in fixed thought, his eyes sunken, staring before him. There was the son-in-law, thin, insignificant, the neck of his shirt coming up almost to his ears. There was the mother in a great tulle cap, with a distracted look; the daughter – a rather pretty brunette, in a cap of black taffeta with spangles of gold and silver, her bosom covered with a silk neckerchief of a thousand colours. Lastly, there was Theodore Blitz, his three-cornered hat over his ear, the violin held between his shoulder and chin, his little eyes sparkling, his cheeks standing out in relief from a deep wrinkle, and his elbows thrown out and drawn in, like a grasshopper scraping its shrill aria on the heath.

The shades of the setting sun, the old clock with its delf dial with red and blue flowers, and above all the music, which grew more and more discordant, produced an indefinable impression upon me. I was seized with a truly panic terror. Was it the effect of my having breathed too long the *rudesheim*? Was it the effect of the pale tints of the falling night? I do not know; but without looking farther I glided away as quietly as possible, bending down, creeping by the wall in order to regain the road, when all of a sudden a large dog darted the length of his chain towards me, and made me utter a cry of surprise.

"Tirik!" cried the old postmaster.

And Theodore, perceiving me, jumped out of the room, crying –

"Ah! it is Christian Species! Come in, my dear Christian! You have come most opportunely." He strode across the court, and came and took my hands.

"My dear friend," said he to me, with strange animation. "This is a time when the *black* and the *white* engage with one another. Come in, come in."

His excitement frightened me, but he would accept none of my excuses, and dragged me on without my being able to make any resistance.

"You must know, dear Christian," said he, "that we have this morning baptized an angel of heaven, the little Nickel Saphéri Brêmer. I have celebrated her coming into the world by the chorus of the 'Séraphins.' Nevertheless, you may imagine that three-fourths of those who were invited have not come. Ha! ha! ha! Come in then! You will be welcome."

He pushed me on by the shoulders, and willing or unwilling, I stepped across the threshold. All the members of the Mutz family turned their heads. I should have liked not to have sat down, but those enthusiasts surrounded me. "This will be the sixth!" cried Blitz. "The number six is a good number!"

The old postmaster took my hands with emotion, saying –

"Thanks, Monsieur Species, thanks for having come! They say that honest folk fly from us! That we are abandoned alike by God and by man! You will stop to the end?"

"Yes," mumbled the old woman, with a supplicating look. "Surely Monsieur Species will stay to the end. He will not refuse us that?"

Then I understood why the table was set in such grand fashion, and why the guests were so few. All of those invited to the baptism, thinking of Gredel Dick, had made excuses for not coming.

The idea of a like desertion went against my heart.

"Oh, certainly," I said. "Certainly! I will stay – with pleasure – with great pleasure!"

The glasses were refilled, and we drank of a rough strong wine, of an old *markobrünner*, the austere flavour of which filled me with melancholy thoughts.

The old woman, putting her long hand upon my shoulder, murmured –

"Just a drop more, Monsieur Species, just a drop more."

And I dared not say no.

At that moment Blitz, passing his bow over the vibrating cords, made a cold shudder pass through all my limbs.

"This, my friends," said he, "is Saul's invocation to the Pythoness."

I should have liked to run away, but in the court the dog was lamentably howling, the night was coming on, and the room was full of shadows. The harsh features of old Mutz, his keen eyes, the sorrowful compression of his big jaws, did not reassure one.

Blitz went on scraping, scraping away at that invocation of his, with great sweeps of his arm. The wrinkle which ploughed itself deep down his left cheek grew deeper and deeper, the perspiration stood on his forehead.

The postmaster filled up our glasses again, and said to me in a low imperious voice –

"Your health."

"Yours, Monsieur Mutz," responded I, trembling.

All of a sudden the child in the cradle commenced to cry, and Blitz, with a diabolical irony, accompanied its shrill wailing with piercing notes, saying –

"It is the hymn of life – ha! ha! ha! Really little Nickel sings it as if she were already old – ha! ha! ha!" The old clock at the same time commenced to strike in its walnut-tree case; and when I raised my eyes, astonished by the noise, I saw a little figure advance from the background, bony, bald, hollow-eyed, a mocking smile on its lips – Death, in short. He came out a few steps and set himself to gather, by jerks, some bits of flowers painted in green on the edge of the clock-case. Then, at the last stroke of the hour, he turned half round and went back to his den as he had come out.

"Why the deuce did the organist bring me here?" said I to myself. "This is a nice baptism! And these are merry folk – ha! ha! ha!"

I filled my glass and drank it in order to gain courage.

"Well, let us go on, let us go on. The die is cast. No one escapes his destiny. I was destined before the commencement of the ages to go this evening to the custom-house; to walk in the alley of Saint-Landolphe; to come in spite of myself to this abominable cut-throat place, attracted by the music of Blitz; to drink *markobrünner* which smacks of cypress and vervain; and to see Death gathering painted flowers! Well, it is droll – truly droll!"

So I dreamed, laughing at men who, thinking themselves free, are dragged on by threads attached to the stars. So astrologers have told us, and we must believe them.

I laughed then amongst the shadows as the music ceased.

A great silence fell around. The clock alone broke the stillness with its regular tick-tack; outside the moon, slowly rising over the Rhine, behind the trembling foliage of a poplar, threw its pale light over innumerable ripples. I noticed it, and saw a black boat pass along in the moon's reflected light.

On it was a man, all dark like the boat. He had a loose cloak around him, and wore a large hat with wide brim, from which hung streamers.

He went by like a figure in a dream. I felt my eyelids heavy.

"Let us drink," cried the organist.

The glasses clattered.

"How well the Rhine sings! It sings the air of Barthold Gouterolf," said the son-in-law, "*ave-ave-stella!*"

No one made reply.

Far off, far off, we could hear the rhythmic beat of two oars. "Today," cried the old postmaster suddenly, in a hoarse voice, "Saphéri makes expiation."

No doubt he had long been thinking, thinking of that. It was that which had rendered him so sad. My flesh crept. "He thinks of his son," said I to myself, "of his son who dies today!"

And a cold shiver ran through me.

"His expiation," cried the daughter with a harsh laugh, "yes – his expiation!"

Theodore touched my shoulder, and, bending to my ear, said –

"The spirits are coming – they are at hand!"

"If you speak like that," cried the son-in-law, whose teeth were chattering. "If you speak like that I shall be off!"

"Go then, go then, coward!" said the daughter. "No one has need of you."

"Very well, I will be off," said he, rising.

And taking his hat off the hook in the wall, he went away with long strides. I saw him pass rapidly before the windows, and I envied him.

How could I get away?

Something was walking upon the wall in front. I stared – my eyes wide open with surprise, and at length saw that it was a cock. Far off between the old palings the river shone, and its ripples slowly beat upon the sand of the shore. The light upon it danced like a cloud of sea-gulls with great white wings. My head was full of shadows and weird reflections.

"Listen, Peter," cried the old woman, at the end of a moment. "Listen, you have been the cause of all that has happened to us."

"I," cried the old man huskily, angrily, "I! of what have I been the cause?"

"Yes," she went on. "You never took pity on our lad. You forgave nothing. It was you who prevented his marrying that girl!"

"Woman," cried the old man, "instead of accusing others, remember that his blood is on your own head. During twenty years you have done naught but hide his faults from me. When I punished him for his evil disposition, for his temper, for his drunkenness, you – you would console him, you would weep with him, you would secretly give him money, you would say to him, "your father does not love you; he is a harsh man!" And you lied to him that you might have the greater portion of his love. You robbed me of the confidence and respect that a child should have for those who love him and correct him. So then, when he wanted to marry that girl, I had no power to make him obey me."

"You should have said 'yes,' " howled the woman.

"But," said the old man, "I had rather say no, because my mother, my grandmother, and all the men and women of my family would not be able to receive that pagan in heaven."

"In heaven," chattered the woman. "In heaven!" And the daughter added in a shrill voice –

"From the earliest time I can remember, our father has only bestowed upon us blows!"

"Because you deserved them," cried the old man. "They gave me more pain than they did you."

"More pain! ha! ha! ha! more pain!"

At that moment, a hand touched my arm. It was Blitz. A ray of the moon, falling on the window-panes, scattered its light around. His face was white, and his stretched-out hand pointed to the shadows. I followed his finger with my eyes, for he evidently was directing my attention to something, and I saw the most terrible sight of which I have a memory – a shadow, motionless, appeared before the window, against the light surface of the river. This shadow had a man's shape, and seemed suspended between heaven and earth. Its head hung down upon its breast, its elbows stood out square beside the body, and its legs straight down tapered to a point.

As I looked on, my eyes round, wide opened with astonishment, every feature developed in that wan figure. I recognized Saphéri Mutz; and above his bent shoulders I saw the cord, the beam, and the outline of the gibbet. Then, at the foot of this deathly apparition, I saw a white figure, kneeling, with long dishevelled hair. It was Gredel Dick, her hands joined in prayer.

It would seem as though all the others, at the same time, saw that strange apparition as well as myself, for I heard them breathe –

"Heaven! Heaven have mercy on us!"

And the old woman, in a low choking voice, murmured –

"Saphéri is dead!"

She commenced to sob.

And the daughter cried –

"Saphéri! Saphéri!"

Then all disappeared, and Theodore Blitz, taking me by the hand, said –

"Let us go."

We set off. The night was fine. The leaves fluttered with a sweet murmur.

As we went on, horrified, along the great Alley des Plantanes, a mournful voice from afar off sang upon the river the old German song –

> "The grave is deep and silent,
> Its borders are terrible!
> It throws a sombre mantle
> It throws a sombre mantle
> Over the kingdom of the dead."

"Ah!" said Blitz, "if Gredel Dick had not been there we should have seen the *other* – the fearful one take Saphéri. But she prayed for him! The poor soul! she prayed for him. What is *white* remains *white*!"

The voice afar off, growing feebler and feebler, answered the murmur of the tide –

> "Death does not find an echo
> For the song of the thrush,
> The roses which grow on the grave,
> The roses which grow on the grave,
> Are the roses of grief."

The horrible scene which had unfolded itself to my eyes, and that far-off melancholy voice which, growing fainter and fainter, at length died away in the distance, remain with me as a confused mirage of the infinite, of that infinite which pitilessly absorbs us, and engulfs us without possibility of our escape. Some may laugh at the idea of such an infinity, like the engineer Rothan; some may tremble at it, as did the burgomaster; some may groan with a pitiable voice; and others may, like Theodore Blitz, crane themselves over the abyss in order to see what passes in the depths. It all, however, comes to the same thing in the end, and the famous inscription over the temple of Isis is always true –

> *I am he that is.*
> *No one has ever penetrated the mystery which envelops me.*
> *No one shall ever penetrate it.*

John Berwick Harwood

The Underground Ghost

John Berwick Harwood (1828–86?) contributed many (usually anonymous) stories and articles – some of them about his experiences in China – to Blackwoods *and the* Cornhill Magazine. *He wrote around twenty novels including* The Bridal and the Bridle *(1851 – celebrating his own honeymoon!),* Lord Lynn's Wife *(1864 – dealing with bigamy),* Lady Flavia *(1865) and* The Serf Sisters *(1885 – a novel on modern Russia). He also penned several exciting Christmas horror tales including* "Horror: A True Tale" *(1861) and* "The Painted Room at Blackston Manor".*

The following unusual story, set in a Cheshire salt-mine, appeared in his 3-volume collection of mystery tales, Major Peter *(1866).*

"BEG PARDON SIR; you'd like to go underground this morning, Missis thought. Large party, sir, in the Dolphin room, going down at eleven; and our Cheshire mines are thought very curious, particularly Setton Bassett, sir. Supply half Europe, they do, sir; and uncommon pretty the galleries look by torch-light. Very celebrated mine, ours, sir, and worth notice; and only half-a-crown charge for each person, when many go at one time with the guides. Shall I say you'll go, sir?"

I should have had some curiosity, in any case, to explore one of those noted Cheshire salt-mines, which, if dwarfish in their proportions, when compared with those of Poland, are still worth visiting; but in the present case, though the waiter did not know it, since he did not know me, there was an especial attraction for me to accept his invitation. The mine was the property of my mother's uncle, and *might* one day be my own; might, that is, if three healthy cousins should die off before my delicate and ailing self. Still there was enough of contingent ownership in the thing, to give it an interest in my eyes. I was what is called a rising junior at the bar; but overwork and late hours had combined to sap what was a weakly constitution from the first. My health had given way, after a struggle, and symptoms of consumption, which fell disease was hereditary in my family, had at last begun to manifest themselves. The doctors were peremptory in ordering me to a warm climate, for at least a couple of years, and I had chosen Malta as the place of my reluctant exile. My passage was taken on board the *Astarte*, a fine steamer plying between Liverpool and the principal Mediterranean ports. When I reached Liverpool, however, on the eve of the day of sailing, I found to my annoyance, that a vexatious delay must intervene. Some accident had happened, while in the Mersey, to the *Astarte*'s machinery, and it would take five, or more probably six days, to repair the damage. There was nothing for it but to wait; my berth was taken, and my fare paid; and thus it fell out that, after killing time by a short tour through the more accessible parts of North Wales, I thought I would visit Setton Bassett, and behold with my own eyes that famous salt-mine, of which as much had been talked in our family, as though it had been one of the seven wonders of the world. I was not on the best of terms with my uncle, so I had put up at the little inn *incognito*.

I stood at the sitting-room window, after the waiter left me, looking out at the dull gray of the November sky and the yellowing pastures of the dairy county. There was no rain, but also no gleam of sunshine; and the still waters of the mere within rifle-shot of the hotel – the pike-fishing in which attracted many an angler to the district – looked as dark as lead. The canal, with the green and red barges sleeping on its weedy surface; the marshy meadows; the ugly factory chimneys, peeping out among the bare tree-tops afar off – these things made up anything but an enlivening prospect. My mind wandered off to the orange-groves and cloudless skies of Malta, to the pleasant voyage up the storied Mediterranean – I was a good sailor, and had no dread of sea-sickness to dash the enjoyment of the trip – and then my thoughts strayed back to my abandoned chambers in Hare Court, Temple. It had not been without a pang that I had wrenched myself away from law and equity, musty black-letter commentaries and brand new reports; and I sighed involuntarily as I thought how I had been forced to drop behind in the race of life, and to yield the palm to others. But life itself was in the balance, and I had no choice in the matter.

"Only waiting for you, sir," said the napkin-bearing attendant, jerking the door open, and poking the fire as waiters will, when no other exercise for their restless activity presents itself. I declare that I had forgotten the salt-mine, the proposed excursion, and my own consent to make one among the pilgrims. But I could not be always reading yesterday's newspaper; and I had seen Llangollen and Valle Crucis and Rows of Chester, and the castles of Chirk and Bran; and however little attractive the dive might prove, it would be as well to have seen the family salt-mine, while a couple of hours at least would thus be got rid of. It was Saturday; and on Monday at noon, the splendid screw steamship *Astarte*, with her freight and passengers, was to drop down to the Mersey, and carry me along with her. I had but two days, therefore, to kill, and this underground exploring would answer as well as anything else. I put on my great-coat, therefore, and followed William the waiter.

There were a good many sight-seers going down, besides the large and rather noisy family party occupying the Dolphin room, and which included three or four young ladies. Besides these, there were three or four recruits from the commercial, and as many from the coffee-room – all of whom had been impressed into the service by the eloquence of the glib waiter, who, I rather think, must have received some fee from the head-guide for each visitor to the mine. This guide, like his two subordinates, was a plain, shrewd-faced miner, in a rough suit of unbleached flannel, well provided with torches, lanterns, and other requisites for such an expedition. He assured us, with gruff civility, that there was no sort of danger, if we only kept together, took care of the lights, and minded what he told us; and after this exordium, he led the way to the pit, which was half a mile off. A gin, turned by an old wall-eyed white horse, sufficed to lower the cage which held us, in detachment, and we were soon underground.

A pretty sight was that mine, though I suspect it was not by any means so superior a specimen of its class as the waiter's interested panegyrics would have led us to believe. But it was pretty and curious withal, to see the stretch of long galleries running away to the dim distance, to see the "halls" and "chambers" into which we suddenly emerged, and whose roofs were propped on columns of salt, and decked with frieze and cornice never carved by earthly chisel. Part of the mine was in full yield; the picks and shovels of the workmen rang against the rocky walls and floor, awakening a thousand sullen echoes from the excavations; and shaggy ponies came clattering and stumbling past, dragging trucks laden with corves of salt, some in block, and some in splinters, along the tram-ways. There were a good many men and boys busy in the regular routine of the mine, and the sight of this industry seemed the main attraction in the eyes of my fellow-pilgrims. They were all hearty, hale, north-country folks, except myself; the Dolphin party in especial being from Yorkshire, as they told everybody, and who had previously seen no mines but coal-pits. My own experience was still more restricted; but I did not take the same interest in the details of the labour of extracting salt as my tempo-rary companions, most of whom so loudly evinced their interest in "clay-stones" or "jewels".

Besides, somehow, I felt the loud blithe mirth of the rest, who seemed as frolicsome as school children on a holiday, jar a little with my own highly-wrought and irritable nerves. I was sickly and peevish, I dare say; but at any rate, I shrank instinctively away from the laughter and conver-sation of the rest of the party, and turned off into one of the lateral galleries of the mine. I had a lantern – we all carried lanterns or torches – and it was wonderful how the light which it gave was reflected back from the pellucid walls, which might have been hewn in rock crystal, so bright and pure was the salt through which the passage had been cut. The rough facets of the great crystalline lumps sparkled like monstrous gems, and the floor was rough with glittering fragments. This passage was intersected by others of varying width, some of which were broad corri-dors, with grooved floors, where trams had once been laid; while others were mere fissures, in the forming of which spade and pick could have played but a secondary part. I wandered on, and on, and still on, musing as I went, and taking little heed to my course.

Suddenly I stumbled, tripped over some loose masses of salt, and fell on my hands and knees, managing – and only just managing – to save the lantern which I carried from being extinguished in the fall. The floor of the cavern was very uneven in that part, and I had inadvertently walked into a sort of pit or basin of no great depth, and half filled with sand and moist salt, more or less pulverised. I rose and looked about me. Evidently, I had strayed from the direct track, thanks to my old habit of indulging in reverie, and had mechanically taken a wrong turning among some of the many passages. The place where I now found myself was by no means similar to the part of the mine that was in full yield, and from which I had wandered. Instead of being dry, airy, and full of life and bustle, the passage where I stood was damp, and quite silent, not a sound being audible except the drip, drip of the water that oozed through the roof in fifty places, and fell sullenly splashing into the little pools of dark green brine that lay among the stones. The floor was of stones, not of salt; and what salt was left in heaps was mixed with sand and loam, so as to be worthless for marketable purposes. It was plain that I was in some neglected corner of the mine; it was plain, too, that I had lost my way.

I am not, I think, more timid at heart than other Englishmen of my age and habits, but I must own that the first sensation I experienced was one of actual alarm. I remembered the words of the guide, when he told us that there was no danger so long as we kept together and near him. I had smiled when I heard this gruff caution, regarding it as a mere common-place speech, or perhaps a phrase designed to enhance the value of our conductor's services; but now the warning came back to me with unwelcome emphasis, and as I breathed with difficulty the clammy and heavy air of the vault, a shudder ran through my whole frame. In the next instant, I rallied my courage, laughed contemptuously at my own fears, and stepped out manfully along the passage. The abandoned salt pit, the moist and sticky brine of which adhered to my clothes, showed me at least what to avoid, and I knew that I must have entered the passage from the right. But, alas! On emerging from the passage into a sort of square chamber, in which some rude benches, carved out of the rock-salt for the miners' use in bygone times, were cut in the gleaming walls, I found that no less than six openings gave access to different parts of the mine, and I was fairly at fault.

How I had strayed so far without paying any attention to the bearings of my heedless course, is what, perhaps, none but an absent man can understand; and I, unluckily, was an absent man. It was not the first time, by many, that I had lost my way; but my former escapades had all occurred under the free sky, in the blessed summer sunlight, and the worst that had ever come of them was the temporary inconvenience of losing my dinner. But it is one thing to range about a mazy wood, or to roam in circles among the great purple moors, and another to be lost underground, in the dank air and darkness of a living tomb. I remarked, too, that the candle in my lantern would not last very long – from one to two hours perhaps, but certainly not longer. It was annoying, very annoying, to be left thus alone. I did not like to own to myself that it was dangerous.

How strange it was, I thought, that I did not hear the very faintest sound from the scene of all those busy labours in the mine. I listened –

listened intently. Not a sound; not so much as the faint click of a distant pickaxe, or the crash of a falling block of salt; not the welcome sound of a human voice; not the tramp of one of those shaggy ponies that drew the corves. I had never before realised what the weight of solitude – enforced solitude – could be. I listened; I waited. Not the faintest indication that any other mortal but myself was below ground, reached my ears. Angry with my own fears, vexed with my own carelessness, that had brought me to this pass, I selected at hazard one of the passages opening into the chamber, and entered it, walking fast, but holding the lantern well in front, to avoid any fresh pitfalls which might lie in wait for the unwary foot. The passage was but some ten yards long, and then it branched off into two narrower corridors, the widest of which led me to a wide but low-browed cave of mixed salt and stone. I entered it stooping, but soon found that I should be obliged to proceed on hands and knees, if at all, so I retraced my steps: and, tracing the other corridor to its extremity, found myself once more in the square chamber which I had left a few minutes before.

And now I began to own to myself that I felt anything but hopeful of a speedy deliverance. My best chance was, that I might be missed, and sought for, since it was evident that I might wander aimlessly, as in a labyrinth, until my candle was spent, and then I should be indeed in sorry case. But should I be missed? I had no friend among the party of blithe sight-seers. If they remembered the existence of the pale, taciturn stranger who had seemed to shrink from their companionship, no doubt they would think that he had made his way back to the shaft, and got some of the miners to draw him up "to bank"; and the guides were only too likely to think so too. I should be inquired for at the inn, of course, but not till dinner-time, and my absence might very probably be misinterpreted. The people knew nothing of me; my luggage was of the lightest; I might be thought of merely as a bilking scamp, who had levanted without paying his bill. And even a night spent in that cheerless place would, to one in my failing health, be no trifling misfortune. Already my feet were cold and wet with the tenacious brine; the cold moist air had brought back my cough, and I shivered in the chill atmosphere of the vault where I stood. Yet perhaps there were people near me, within earshot all the time, for I could not believe that the mine had been suddenly deserted. I shouted, and shouted again, the many crevices and passages giving back the sound of my voice with strange and sullen dissonance.

Presently, though no answering call was returned, I saw a light, far off and dim, but rapidly advancing towards me along the gallery that lay on my left, and which was one of the six I have mentioned. Nearer and nearer it came; no flare of torches, but the steady gleam of a small lamp; and then, to my surprise, I saw that the human figure that soon became visible was not that of a miner. The light of the lantern fell faintly on the pale face, colourless as marble, but delicate and pretty enough, of a young and slender girl – a lady, evidently, by her dress, and whom I instantly conjectured to have been one of the party of explorers. But how came she there, and alone? Was she lost, like me? or – "Did you not call a minute ago? I can show you the way, if you like."

Common-place words these; but they were spoken with a peculiar quiet intonation, that impressed me in spite of myself. The voice was sweet and low, but almost solemn in its calm. There was something strange, too, in the composure and the unsmiling gravity of one so young, while her very presence in that out-of-the-way part of the mine perplexed me. My first idea was, that the young lady, like myself, had lost her way in the intricacies of the pit; but this supposition her confidence of bearing seemed to contradict. No doubt she knew the mine well, or she would scarcely have offered to guide me to safety. This was an additional proof that she could not have been one of the merry, rosy-cheeked Yorkshire girls who had made part of the explorers that morning. Most likely, some fresh party had descended to see the mine, and this young lady – some resident in the neighbourhood – had accompanied her friends to a place which she knew well. And yet, why alone?

Then I snapped the thread of my thoughts rather abruptly, as I remembered that I had not uttered a single syllable of thanks or explanation to my fair rescuer, who had, no doubt, been the only member of the party to which she belonged who had happened to hear the cries for aid, of which I was beginning to be heartily ashamed. A man's self-love is easily piqued, and I felt a hot flush of shame rise to my cheek as I thought in how pitiful a light I probably appeared to the sole spectator of what must seem my poltroonery in shouting for help. I therefore put on a bold front, and made a few remarks in as sprightly a tone as I could adopt upon the absurdity of my position, and went so far as to express my regret for any trouble or inconvenience I might have occasioned the fair damsel on behalf of so insignificant a person as myself. At the same time, I thanked her for her kindness, and admitted that I should not be sorry to regain the upper air.

She bowed her head slightly, and in the same grave, unsmiling manner as before, and turned towards the passage whence she had come, merely replying in answer to my speech: "This is the way we must take."

I followed her as she swiftly and steadily glided forward, traversing the long and narrow passage lamp in hand. At the end of the passage was a sort of hexagonal vault, full of openings in its dull, white walls, where the salt was much corroded by the moisture that dripped from the roof. The floor was covered with white incrustations, and several of the entrances were more or less choked with earth and rocks. My guide selected one of the narrowest of the galleries, without a moment's hesitation, and entered it with the same quick but light step. It was a mere fissure of irregular width, so very narrow in parts that it seemed as if the rocks were closing their stony jaws to bar our egress, while the height was considerable. Once I fancied, as I looked up, that I could see a faint glimmer of daylight filtered down through the overlying rocks, but it may have been mere fancy. For some moments, not a word was spoken. I was the first to break the silence.

"I had no idea," said I, in a lively tone that cost me an effort, for I could scarcely keep my teeth from chattering as I spoke, so chilly and moist was the atmosphere of the unsunned caves – "I had no idea that I had wandered so far, or indeed that the mine was so large. I can recognise none of these objects by which we are passing, and yet some of them are worth looking at. How pretty is this, for instance!" And I came to a stop, glancing about me with involuntary admiration, as I found myself in a large natural grotto into which the fissure led. The lofty but broken roof was of rock-salt, but stained of many hues, green and crimson, orange, brown, scarlet, by the infiltration of water, which dripped abundantly from the cracks in the rough ceiling, and which probably contained metallic oxides in greater or less amount. The floor was of stone, wet and furrowed by the trickling of fifty tiny rivulets, which meandered over the honey-combed surface, till they were lost over the smooth lip of a long and narrow chasm that intersected the grotto. But the beauty of the place was in the infinite variety of fantastic columns, some of pure white salt, some of the same salt discoloured and crumbling, that composed the walls. As the feeble light of the lanterns flashed on the pellucid surfaces of these fairy pillars, some simple and rude as the Doric, some slender and frail, some more elaborate in the intricacies of their mouldings than the Corinthian or Byzantine, I could not restrain my exclamations of surprise and delight. For a moment I forgot the cold, the damp, the discomfort, and said, half to myself: "What a wonderful sight! If a human artist had carved those delicate capitals and rich decorations, what a rush would there be to see his handiwork! But I dare say even the county handbook does not condescend to describe this place, which is worthy to be the palace of the king of the gnomes."

"Few know of this place," said my conductress, in the same measured, passionless voice as before. She had stopped when I stopped, and she stood motionless as a statue, and as pale as if she had been a figure hewn out of alabaster, rather than a creature of flesh and blood. It was the first word of the nature of a remark which had fallen from her, and I tried to draw her into conversation by descanting on the beauty of the singular grotto, and the spaciousness of the mine. She said very little, but her reticence did not seem to be caused by any poverty of intellect. There was, however, a peculiar want of warmth or enthusiasm, whether the subject were art or nature, in what little my fair guide could be induced to say. Nor was she by any means communicative as to herself. My attempts to discover whether she really lived in the neighbourhood, were quietly baffled, and when I said that "doubtless her friends would begin to be alarmed at her long absence for which I feared that my own stupid blundering was to blame," she merely bowed, and led the way as before. On we went, through a network of passages, that only seemed to grow more Daedalian every moment, but through which my companion glided along as unswervingly as if she held in her hand an unfailing clue. Many of these galleries were evidently the work of man, hearing traces of pick and spade; while others, heaped with rubbish, and obstructed by rude columns of salt, were as plainly natural caves. In all, however, the air was heavy, chill, and moist, and water dripped from the walls, and fell gurgling down hidden fissures into some unseen depths below. I was confident that I had passed none of these places that day, and began to suspect that my guide was leading me a long round, so as to shew me all the lions of the mine, instead of taking a short-cut to the workings. At another time, this desire to impress a stranger with a full notion of local marvels would have amused me; but my cough got worse; I shivered, and longed for the excursion to come to a close. Yet there was an awkwardness in suggesting this. I ventured on a safe remark.

"It is bitterly cold," said I, with a shudder, for the damp seemed to be piercing to the very marrow of my bones. "Do you not find it so?"

"Very cold!" She said no more; but those two common-place words were spoken in a voice that awed me, somehow, in spite of myself, and

seemed to freeze me into silence. On we went, and I trusted that we must
be approaching the working-part of the mine, for the candle in my
lantern was reduced to a mere morsel, and must soon be burned out. But
ill as I felt, and hard as it was for my weak lungs to endure the unwholesome air, I almost forgot this in my perplexity as to my conductress. I
could not make her out at all. I had met with romantic young ladies, silly
young ladies, sensible young ladies, even haughty and vain young ladies,
but never with any one like my guide. Why was she leading me thus,
what I felt must be a circuitous course through the mine? Why –

She came to a dead stop, slowly-turned, and confronted me. The hood
of her grey cloak, an old-fashioned article of attire, such as I had not seen
for many years, was drawn over her head, and it threw her face partly
into shadow; but her eyes were bright and clear, though there was something in their cold steady look that made me shiver afresh, as if the air of
the mine had grown even more icy and oppressive than before.

"Tell me about yourself. Tell me what you are going to do. What are
your plans, I mean," she said in the same manner as before, like a sleep-
walker unconsciously uttering words that volition does not prompt.

I laughed, and blundered out some would-be witty rejoinder on my
own good-fortune in having inspired so charming a person with sufficient
interest in my fate to suggest the question; but the flippant words died
away on my lips half spoken, as she waved her hand, not impatiently, not
coquettishly, but with a calm dignity of bearing that matched well her
bloodless cheek and the carriage of her proud head. "You are to sail in
the *Astarte* – is it not so?" said this singular girl, without a smile or a falter
in her low but very distinctive voice. I owned the fact, in no slight
surprise. I had mentioned to no one at Setton Bassett the name of the
ship in which my passage was taken. The idea of a mystification, of a
trick, dawned upon me, but I was at a loss to guess how my strange guide
could have obtained the information she evidently possessed. Did she
know more of me than this? My name, for instance, my profession, and
my reason for quitting England? If so, at any rate she made no parade of
her knowledge. She merely raised her hand for a moment – it was
ungloved, and there were rings of price sparkling on the thin white
fingers – and her eyes seemed to gather a new expression of sadness and
warning as she said: "Beware of the *Astarte*! If you love your life – and oh,
it is bitter to die young – do not sail in that ship."

Slowly the hand she had lifted in warning fell to her side, and holding
up the lamp as before, she turned away, and preceded me along the

galleries. I followed her, perplexed, half angry, half alarmed. I began to fear that I was the sport of a mad woman. And then a new fancy seized me. Perhaps I myself might be delirious, and the mine, the endless galleries, and my strange guide, were visions of a disordered brain, a frightful dream, from which I vainly strove to awake. Presently, it occurred to me for the first time that my new-found friend's feet made no sound as they trod the broken and rugged pavement, slippery and heaped with rubbish. Certain it was that she moved firmly and swiftly on, without any sign of difficulty or fatigue, while I stumbled and splashed, splashed and stumbled, and at times found it hard to keep up with her. But as regarded the noiselessness of her tread, I could not solve the doubt. If I stopped, she stopped too, not after a pause, but instantly. And I heard nothing but my own labouring breath and hacking cough, and the sound of my own weary feet crunching the splinters of salt.

A little while, and even this was forgotten in a new source of apprehension. I had for some time vaguely conceived the idea that, as in a labyrinth, we were walking in a circle; and gradually I began to fancy that I had seen this or that block of salt or darkling arch before, and that I had passed through some of the corridors at least once before. But suspicion was changed to certainty when I suddenly espied, lying on the ground in one of the galleries, one of my own gloves. I had dropped this glove some time before, for I had missed it soon after the arrival of the Unknown. As I picked it up, I glanced keenly around me, and thought I recognised the opening that led into the square chamber. I was right; in another moment I had followed my mysterious guide into the square chamber itself. More than an hour's weary toil, for my candle was all but spent, had brought us back to the point from which we had started. I was angry at last; all my involuntary awe for my strange conductress was lost, and I stamped my foot hard upon the floor as I asked if she had been amusing herself at my expense, or whether she, too, were ignorant of the topography of the mine, and had misled me by accident. I spoke in wrath, and almost in menace; but there was no reply, save one long moan, as from a child in pain, that rang sadly through the vault. I turned my head, but I could see nothing; and when I again confronted what I now deemed my treacherous guide, a sort of mist seemed to dim my eyes, and I saw, or thought I saw, her form grow faint and indistinct, fading and fading like breath upon a mirror, but with still the same calm face, the same grave look of sorrow and warning, until that too faded, and nothing was left opposite to me – nothing but the rocky wall. I sprang forward, incredulous, and touched the wall with my hand. As I did so, a repetition of the moaning cry made me start, and far down the passage where I had seen her first, I saw her again – the pure, pale outline of the young face, the tall, slender form in the grey mantle, with the hood drawn over the head, the lamp shining in the outstretched hand. How came she there?

"This is too much!" cried I passionately, and convinced that I was the victim of a trick, though how such a trick could have been effected, I did not care to consider. "I will not bear this juggling. I will not – "

As I spoke, I darted forward to overtake the receding figure, and my foot tripping among the loose stones of the floor, as I ran, I fell heavily, crushing the lantern beneath me, and being instantly involved in Egyptian darkness. Bruised and hurt, I gave no heed to the pain of the fall, but sprang up, and strained my eyes in the direction where the lamp had been last seen. There was not a spark – not a sound. No light, no rustle of her dress, no faint sound of a distant footfall, nothing but darkness and silence. Eagerly I listened, eagerly I watched, but in vain. I tried to call aloud, but my tongue refused its office; and when I did raise a weak shout, I felt my natural repugnance to the darkness deepen as no answer came.

"She is doing this to frighten me," I murmured; "she is hiding behind some pillar. Whoever she is, she never could be cruel enough to leave me here in the dark alone, to perish."

Silence, still silence. Any sound, even that moan, at which my very heartstrings had quivered, would have been better than that. Darkness, blank, blank darkness. I tried to shout, tried to grope my way out, but the sides of the rocky vault were slippery to the touch, and when I found an opening, I stumbled and fell again, and had not strength to rise. Oh, it was very cold, cold and dark. This must be death.

"A drop more brandy, Jem; the last did him good, I can't feel any pulse yet, though. Don't crowd so about him, lads. Give him air! That's enough of the brandy, but don't leave off chafing the hands. He'll come round!"

With my dulled ear, I heard these words, but scarcely understood them, and from between the half-closed lids my weak eyes could feebly distinguish a glare of torches, and several rough men in miners' garb, and one in black with a kind, shrewd face – the doctor, no doubt. I saw all his, in a stupid sort of indifferent way, as if it had been a pageant, and then I seemed to sink down into a black sea of roaring water, and fainted for the second time.

I was in bed at last. I had been in bed some days, very ill, and with a brain too deadened, and a frame too exhausted, to take note of time. When my senses returned, I asked what was the date, and hearing it, knew that the *Astarte* had sailed without me, and that my passage-money was lost. It was not for weeks, and until my slow convalescence had ripened into recovery from the illness brought on by cold and the wetting I had experienced, that the doctor asked me how I came to separate myself from the rest of the company, and to get lost in the mine.

"It so happened," said he, "that work was suspended unusually early on that day, as there was a wake at Swivelsby, and the miners had a sort of half-holiday by annual custom. The mine was therefore abandoned, and but for the lucky chance, that when you were missed at the inn, and inquiries were made, an intelligent boy, the son of a miner, declared that you had never come up to bank at all, it is probable that no search would have taken place. As it was, long hours passed before a party started in quest of you; and it is fortunate that they were in time. Setton Bassett mine has witnessed more than one tragic incident, even in my day."

"To what do you allude, doctor?" asked I eagerly.

"Eighteen years ago, a young lady, a Miss Walcott, became separated from her friends, as you did, in that mine," answered the doctor. "I had not as yet settled in the district, and only know the details from report, and very imperfectly. I believe, however, that the poor girl, who had made one of a large family party, was bound on a visit to an aunt who lived a few miles off; her own parents then residing at Hallings Court, near here. The day was a stormy one; the carriages drove off in a heavy fall of rain; and I believe the missing one was understood by her mother to be staying at her aunt's, and vice versa, for there was no alarm till help was impossible. The poor girl's body was found – for she perished of cold and hunger in that maze of galleries – in the very spot where we found you, and – Bless me, how pale you look, my dear sir. Take some cordial, and lie down, and no more talking – not a word more, I insist."

I have no explanation of the above facts to offer. I have endeavoured, far from England, to set down every detail of the occurrence as simply and succinctly as possible. I should be thankful if I could disabuse my mind of the ghastly doubt and horror that cling to it, and which haunt me when I recall the events of that day in the Cheshire salt-mine. The good doctor, when he heard my statement, did his best to convince me that what I saw was a mere hallucination, due to my disordered health and excited nerves. I wish I could think so; but further inquiries, made before I left England, served to assure me that I was not the only person who was supposed to have seen the presence that I had beheld in the disused portion of the mine.

One word more. The warning was no idle one, though I doubt whether I should not have been ashamed to have heeded it, had not illness chained me to my sick-bed. Before I was able to quit Setton Bassett, news came that the fine steamship *Astarte* had been cast away on the rocks of Cape Spartel, and that most of the crew and passengers had perished miserably in the surf.

Frank Cowper

Christmas Eve on a Haunted Hulk

*Frank Cowper (1849–1930) spent much of his life on boats along English canals,
and in the North Sea and the English Channel. He compiled five volumes of* Sailing
Tours, *and his popular collection,* Cruising Sails and Yachting Tales *(1921),
was reprinted several times. His occasional grim supernatural and horror tales usually
reflected his love of small boats and remote places. This atmospheric tale originally
appeared in the January 1889 number of* Blackwood's Magazine.

I SHALL NEVER FORGET that night as long as I live.

It was during the Christmas vacation 187– . I was staying with an old
college friend who had lately been appointed the curate of a country
parish, and had asked me to come and cheer him up, since he could not
get away at that time.

As we drove along the straight country lane from the little wayside
station, it forcibly struck me that a life in such a place must be dreary
indeed. I have always been much influenced by local colour; above all
things, I am depressed by a dead level, and here was monotony with a
vengeance. On each side of the low hedges, lichen-covered and wind-
cropped, stretched bare fields, the absolute level of the horizon being
only broken at intervals by some mournful tree that pointed like a
decrepit finger-post towards the east, for all its western growth was
nipped and blasted by the roaring south-west winds. An occasional black
spot, dotted against the grey distance, marked a hay-rick or labourer's
cottage, while some two miles ahead of us the stunted spire of my friend's

church stood out against the wintry sky, amid the withered branches of a few ragged trees. On our right hand stretched dreary wastes of mud, interspersed here and there with firmer patches of land, but desolate and forlorn, cut off from all communication with the mainland by acres of mud and thin streaks of brown water.

A few sea-birds were piping over the waste, and this was the only sound, except the grit of our own wheels and the steady step of the horse, which broke the silence.

"Not lively is it?" said Jones: and I couldn't say it was. As we drove "up street", as the inhabitants fondly called the small array of low houses which bordered the highroad, I noticed the lack-lustre expression of the few children and untidy women who were loitering about the doors of their houses.

There was an old tumbledown inn, with a dilapidated sign-board, scarcely held up by its rickety ironwork. A daub of yellow and red paint, with a dingy streak of blue, was supposed to represent the Duke's head, although what exalted member of the aristocracy was thus distinguished it would be hard to say. Jones inclined to think it was the Duke of Wellington; but I upheld the theory that it was the Duke of Marlborough, chiefly basing my arguments on the fact that no artist who desired to convey a striking likeness would fail to show the Great Duke in profile, whereas this personage was evidently depicted full face, and wearing a three-cornered hat.

At the end of the village was the church, standing in an untidy church-yard, and opposite it was a neat little house, quite new, and of that utilitarian order of architecture which will stamp the Victorian age as one of the least imaginative of eras. Two windows flanked the front door, and three narrow windows looked out overhead from under a slate roof; variety and distinction being given to the façade by the brilliant blending of the yellow bricks with red, so bright as to suggest the idea of their having been painted. A scrupulously clean stone at the front door, together with the bright green of the little palings and woodwork, told me what sort of landlady to expect, and I was not disappointed. A kindly featured woman, thin, cheery, and active, received us, speaking in that encouraging tone of half-compassionate, half-proprietary patronage, which I have observed so many women adopt towards lone beings of the opposite sex.

"You will find it precious dull, old man," said Jones, as we were eating our frugal dinner. "There's nothing for you to do, unless you care to try a shot at the duck over the mud-flats. I shall be busy on and off nearly all tomorrow."

As we talked, I could not help admiring the cheerful pluck with which Jones endured the terrible monotony of his life in this dreary place. His rector was said to be delicate, and in order to prolong a life, which no doubt he considered valuable to the Church, he lived with his family either at Torquay or Cannes in elegant idleness, quite unable to do any duty, but fully equal to enjoying the pleasant society of those charming places, and quite satisfied that he had done his duty when he sacrificed a tenth of his income to provide for the spiritual needs of his parish. There was no squire in the place; no "gentlefolk", as the rustics called them, lived nearer than five miles; and there was not a single being of his own class with whom poor Jones could associate. And yet he made no complaint. The nearest approach to one being the remark that the worst of it was, it was so difficult, if not impossible, to be really understood. "The poor being so suspicious and ignorant, they look at everything from such a low standpoint, enthusiasm and freshness sink so easily into formalism and listlessness."

The next day, finding that I really could be of no use, and feeling awkward and bored, as a man always is when another is actively doing his duty, I went off to the marshes with a gun to see if I could get any sport.

I took some sandwiches and a flask with me, not intending to return until dinner. After wandering about for some time, crossing dyke after dyke by treacherous rails more or less rotten, I found myself on the edge of a wide mere. I could see some duck out in the middle, and standing far out in the shallow water was a heron. They were all out of shot, and I saw I should do no good without a duck-punt. I sat down on an old pile left on the top of the sea-wall, which had been lately repaired. The duck looked very tempting; but I doubted if I should do much good in broad daylight, even if I had a duck-punt, without a duck-gun. After sitting disconsolately for some time, I got up and wandered on.

The dreariness of the scene was most depressing: everything was brown and grey. Nothing broke the monotony of the wide-stretching mere; the whole scene gave me the impression of a straight line of interminable length, with a speck in the centre of it. That speck was myself. At last, as I turned an angle in the sea-wall, I saw something lying above high-water mark, which looked like a boat.

Rejoiced to see any signs of humanity, I quickened my pace. It was a boat, and, better still, a duck-punt. As I came nearer I could see that she was old and very likely leaky; but here was a prospect of adventure, and I was not going to be readily daunted. On examination, the old craft seemed more watertight than I expected. At least she held water very well, and if she kept it in, she must equally well keep it out. I turned her over to run the water out, and then dragging the crazy old boat over the line of seaweed, launched her. But now a real difficulty met me. The paddles were nowhere to be seen. They had doubtless been taken away by the owner, and it would be little use searching for them. But a stout stick would do to punt her over the shallow water; and after some little search, I found an old stake which would answer well. This was real luck. I had now some hope of bagging a few duck; at any rate, I was afloat, and could explore the little islets, which barely rose above the brown water. I might at least find some rabbits on them. I cautiously poled myself towards the black dots; but before I came within range, up rose first one, then another and another, like a string of beads, and the whole flight went, with outstretched necks and rapidly beating wings, away to my right, and seemed to pitch again beyond a low island some half-mile away. The heron had long ago taken himself off; so there was nothing to be done but pole across the mud in pursuit of the duck. I had not gone many yards when I found that I was going much faster than I expected, and soon saw the cause. The tide was falling, and I was being carried along with it. This would bring me nearer to my ducks, and I lazily guided the punt with the stake.

On rounding the island I found a new source of interest. The mere opened out to a much larger extent, and away towards my right I could see a break in the low land, as if a wide ditch had been cut through; while in this opening ever and anon dark objects rose up and disappeared again in a way I could not account for. The water seemed to be running off the mud-flats, and I saw that if I did not wish to be left high, but not dry, on the long slimy wastes, I must be careful to keep the little channels or "lakes" which acted as natural drains to the acres of greasy mud.

A conspicuous object attracted my attention some mile or more towards the opening in the land. It was a vessel lying high up on the mud, and looking as if she was abandoned.

The ducks had pitched a hundred yards or so beyond the island, and I approached as cautiously as I could; but just as I was putting down the stake to take up my gun, there was a swift sound of beating wings and splashing water, and away my birds flew, low over the mud, towards the old hulk.

Here was a chance, I thought. If I could get on board and remain hidden, I might, by patiently waiting, get a shot. I looked at my watch; there was still plenty of daylight left, and the tide was only just beginning to leave the mud. I punted away, therefore, with renewed hope, and was not long in getting up to the old ship.

There was just sufficient water over the mud to allow me to approach within ten or twelve feet, but farther I could not push the punt. This was disappointing; however, I noticed a deep lake ran round the other side, and determined to try my luck there. So with a slosh and a heave I got the flat afloat again, and made for the deeper water. It turned out quite successful, and I was enabled to get right under the square overhanging counter, while a little lane of water led alongside her starboard quarter. I pushed the nose of the punt into this, and was not long in clambering on board by the rusty irons of her fore-chains.

The old vessel lay nearly upright in the soft mud, and a glance soon told she would never be used again. Her gear and rigging were all rotten, and everything valuable had been removed. She was a brig of some two hundred tons, and had been a fine vessel, no doubt. To me there is always a world of romance in a deserted ship. The places she has been to, the scenes she has witnessed, the possibilities of crime, of adventure – all these thoughts crowd upon me when I see an old hulk lying deserted and forgotten, left to rot upon the mud of some lonely creek.

In order to keep my punt afloat as long as possible, I towed her round and moored her under the stern, and then looked over the bulwarks for the duck. There they were, swimming not more than a hundred and fifty yards away and they were coming towards me. I remained perfectly concealed under the high bulwark, and could see them paddling and feeding in the greasy weed. Their approach was slow, but I could afford to wait. Nearer and nearer they came; another minute, and they would be well within shot. I was already congratulating myself upon the success of my adventure, and thinking of the joy of Jones at this large accession to his larder, when suddenly there was a heavy splash, and with a wild sputtering rush the whole pack rose out of the water, and went skimming over the mud towards the distant sea. I let off both barrels after them, and tried to console myself by thinking that I saw the feathers fly from one; but not a bird dropped, and I was left alone in my chagrin.

What could have caused the splash, I wondered. There was surely no one else on board the ship, and certainly no one could get out here without mud-pattens or a boat. I looked round. All was perfectly still. Nothing broke the monotony of the grey scene – sodden and damp and lifeless. A chill breeze came up from the south-west, bringing with it a raw mist, which was blotting out the dark distance, and fast limiting my horizon. The day was drawing in, and I must be thinking of going home. As I turned round, my attention was arrested by seeing a duck-punt glide past me in the now rapidly falling water, which was swirling by the mud-bank on which the vessel lay. But there was no one in her. A dreadful thought struck me. It must be my boat, and how shall I get home? I ran to the stern and looked over. The duck-punt was gone.

The frayed and stranded end of the painter told me how it had happened. I had not allowed for the fall of the tide, and the strain of the punt, as the water fell away, had snapped the line, old and rotten as it was. I ran to the bows and, jumping on to the bits, saw my punt peace-fully drifting away, some quarter of a mile off. It was perfectly evident I could not hope to get her again.

It was beginning to rain steadily. I could see that I was in for dirty weather, and became a little anxious about how I was to get back, espe-cially as it was now rapidly growing dark. So thick was it that I could not see the low land anywhere, and could only judge of its position by remembering that the stern of the vessel pointed that way.

The conviction grew upon me that I could not possibly get away from this doleful old hulk without assistance; and how to get it, I could not for the life of me see. I had not seen a sign of a human being the whole day. It was not likely any more would be about at night. However, I shouted as loud as I could, and then waited to hear if there were any response. There was not a sound, only the wind moaned slightly through the stumps of the masts, and something creaked in the cabin.

Well, I thought, at least it might be worse. I shall have shelter for the night; while had I been left on one of these islands, I should have had to spend the night exposed to the pelting rain. Go below before it gets too dark, and see what sort of a berth can be got, if the worst comes to the worst. So thinking, I went to the booby-hatch, and found as I expected that it was half broken open, and anyone could go below who liked.

As I stepped down the rotting companion, the air smelt foul and dank. I went below very cautiously, for I was not at all sure that the boards would bear me. It was fortunate I did so, for as I stepped off the lowest step the floor gave way under my foot, and had I not been holding on to the stair-rail, I should have fallen through. Before going any farther, I took a look around.

The prospect was not inviting. The light was dim; I could scarcely make out objects near me, all else was obscurity. I could see that the whole of the inside of the vessel was completely gutted. What little light there was came through the stern ports. A small round speck of light looked at me out of the darkness ahead, and I could see that the flooring had either given way or been taken out of her. At my feet a gleam of water showed me what to expect if I should slip through the floor-joists. Altogether, a more desolate, gloomy, ghostly place it would be difficult to find.

I could not see any bunk or locker where I could sit down, and everything moveable had been taken out of the hulk. Groping my way with increasing caution, I stepped across the joists, and felt along the side of the cabin. I soon came to a bulkhead. Continuing to grope, I came to an opening. If the cabin was dim, here was blackness itself. I felt it would be useless to attempt to go farther, especially as a very damp foul odour came up from the bilge-water in her hold. As I stood looking into the darkness, a cold chilly shudder passed over me, and with a shiver I turned round to look at the cabin. My eyes had now become used to the gloom. A deeper patch of darkness on my right suggested the possibility of a berth, and groping my way over to it, I found the lower bunk was still entire. Here at least I could rest, if I found it impossible to get to shore. Having some wax vestas in my pocket, I struck a light and examined the bunk. It was better than I expected. If I could only find something to burn, I should be comparatively cheerful.

Before reconciling myself to my uncomfortable position, I resolved to see whether I could not get to the shore, and went up the rickety stairs again. It was raining hard, and the wind had got up. Nothing could be more dismal. I looked over the side and lowered myself down from the main-chains, to see if it were possible to walk over the mud. I found I could not reach the mud at all; and fearful of being unable to climb back if I let go, I clambered up the side again and got on board.

It was quite clear I must pass the night here. Before going below I once more shouted at the top of my voice, more to keep up my own spirits than with any hope of being heard, and then paused to listen. Not a sound of any sort replied. I now prepared to make myself as comfortable as I could.

It was a dreary prospect. I would rather have spent the night on deck than down below in that foul cabin; but the drenching driving rain, as well as the cold, drove me to seek shelter below. It seemed so absurd to be in the position of a shipwrecked sailor, within two or three miles of a prosy country hamlet, and in a landlocked harbour while actually on land, if the slimy deep mud could be called land. I had not many matches left, but I had my gun cartridges. The idea occurred to me to fire off minute-guns. "That's what I ought to do, of course. The red flash will be seen in this dark night", for it was dark now and no mistake. Getting up on to the highest part of the vessel, I blazed away. The noise sounded to me deafening; surely the whole countryside would be aroused. After firing off a dozen cartridges, I waited. But the silence only seemed the more oppressive, and the blackness all the darker. "It's no good; I'll turn in," I thought dejectedly.

With great difficulty I groped my way to the top of the companion-ladder, and bumped dismally down the steps. If only I had a light I should be fairly comfortable, I thought. "Happy thought, make a 'spit-devil!'" as we used when boys to call a little cone of damp gunpowder.

I got out my last two cartridges, and emptying the powder carefully into my hand, I moistened it and worked it up to a paste. I then placed it on the smooth end of the rail, and lighted it. This was brilliant: at least so it seemed by contrast with the absolute blackness around me. By its light I was able to find my way to the bunk, and it lasted just long enough for me to arrange myself fairly comfortably for the night. By contriving a succession of matches, I was enabled to have enough light to see to eat my frugal supper; for I had kept a little sherry and a few sandwiches to meet emergencies, and it was a fortunate thing I had. The light and the food made me feel more cheery, and by the time the last match had gone out, I felt worse might have happened to me by a long way.

As I lay still, waiting for sleep to come, the absurdity of the situation forced itself upon me. Here was I, to all intents and purposes as much cut off from all communication with the rest of the world as if I were cast away upon a desert island. The chances were that I should make someone see or hear me the next day. Jones would be certain to have the country searched, and at the longest I should only endure the discomfort of one night, and get well laughed at for my pains; but meanwhile I was absolutely severed from human contact, and was as isolated as Robinson Crusoe, only "more so", for I had no other living thing whatever to share my solitude. The silence of the place was perfect; and if silence can woo sleep, sleep ought very soon to have come. But when one is hungry and wet, and in a strange uncanny kind of place, besides being in one's clothes, it is a very difficult thing to go to sleep. First, my head was too low; then, after resting it on my arms, I got cramp in them. My back seemed all over bumps; when I turned on my side, I appeared to have got a rather serious enlargement of the hip-joint; and I found my damp clothes' smell very musty. After sighing and groaning for some time, I sat up for change of position, and nearly fractured my skull in so doing, against the remains of what had once been a berth above me. I didn't dare to move in the inky blackness, for I had seen sufficient to know that I might very easily break my leg or my neck in the floorless cabin.

There was nothing for it but to sit still, or lie down and wait for daylight. I had no means of telling the time. When I had last looked at my watch, before the last match had gone out, it was not more than six o'clock; it might be now about eight, or perhaps not so late. Fancy twelve long hours spent in that doleful black place, with nothing in the world to do to pass away the time! I must go to sleep; and so, full of this resolve, I lay down again.

I suppose I went to sleep. All I can recollect, after lying down, is keeping my mind resolutely turned inwards, as it were, and fixed upon the arduous business of counting an imaginary and interminable flock of sheep pass one by one through an ideal gate. This meritorious method of compelling sleep had, no doubt, been rewarded; but I have no means of knowing how long I slept. All I know is that the next thing I can remember after getting my five-hundredth sheep through the gate is that I heard two most horrible yells ring through the darkness. I sat bolt-upright; and as a proof that my senses were "all there", I did not bring my head this time against the berth overhead, remembering to bend it outwards so as to clear it.

There was not another sound. The silence was as absolute as the darkness. "I must have been dreaming," I thought; but the sounds were ringing in my ears, and my heart was beating with excitement. There must have been some reason for this. I never was "taken this way" before. I could not make it out, and felt very uncomfortable. I sat there listening for some time. No other sound breaking the deathly stillness, and becoming tired of sitting, I lay down again. Once more I set myself to get my interminable flocks through that gate, but I could not help myself listening.

There seemed to me a sound growing in the darkness, a something gathering in the particles of the air, as if molecules of the atmosphere were rustling together, and with stilly movement were whispering something. The wind had died down, and I would have gone on deck if I could move; but it was hazardous enough moving about in the light: it would have been madness to attempt to move in that blackness. And so I lay still and tried to sleep.

But now there was a sound, indistinct, but no mere fancy; a muffled sound, as of some movement in the forepart of the ship.

I listened intently and gazed into the darkness.

What was the sound? It did not seem like rats. It was a dull, shuffling kind of noise, very indistinct, and conveying no clue whatever as to its cause. It lasted for only a short time. But now the cold damp air seemed to have become more piercingly chilly. The raw iciness seemed to strike into the very marrow of my bones, and my teeth chattered. At the same time a new sense seemed to be assailed: the foul odour which I had noticed arising from the stagnant water in the bilge appeared to rise into more objectionable prominence, as if it had been stirred.

"I cannot stand this," I muttered, shivering in horrible aversion at the disgusting odour. "I will go on deck at all hazards."

Rising to put this resolve in execution, I was arrested by the noise beginning again. I listened. This time I distinctly distinguished two separate sounds: one, like a heavy soft weight being dragged along with difficulty; the other like the hard sound of boots on boards. Could there be others on board after all? If so, why had they made no sound when I clambered on deck, or afterwards, when I shouted and fired my gun?

Clearly, if there were people, they wished to remain concealed, and my presence was inconvenient to them. But how absolutely still and quiet they had kept! It appeared incredible that there should be anyone. I listened intently. The sound had ceased again, and once more the most absolute stillness reigned around. A gentle swishing, wobbling, lapping noise seemed to form itself in the darkness. It increased, until I recognized the chattering and bubbling of water. "It must be the tide which is rising," I thought. "It has reached the rudder, and is eddying round the stern-post." This also accounted, in my mind, for the other noises, because, as the tide surrounded the vessel, and she thus became waterborne, all kinds of sounds might be produced in the old hulk as she resumed her upright position.

However, I could not get rid of the chilly horrid feeling those two screams had produced, combined with the disgusting smell, which was getting more and more obtrusive. It was foul, horrible, revolting, like some carrion, putrid and noxious. I prepared to take my chances of damage, and rose up to grope my way to the companion-ladder.

It was a more difficult job than I had any idea of. I had my gun, it was true, and with it I could feel the joists; but when once I let go of the edge of the bunk I had nothing to steady me, and nearly went headlong at the first step. Fortunately I reached back in time to prevent my fall; but this attempt convinced me that I had better endure the strange horrors of the unknown, than the certain miseries of a broken leg or neck.

I sat down, therefore, on the bunk.

Now that my own movements had ceased, I became aware that the shuffling noise was going on all the time. "Well," thought I, "they may shuffle. They won't hurt me, and I shall go to sleep again." So reflecting, I lay down, holding my gun, ready to use as a club if necessary.

Now it is all very well to laugh at superstitious terrors. Nothing is easier than to obtain a cheap reputation for brilliancy, independence of thought, and courage, by deriding the fear of the supernatural when comfortably seated in a drawing-room well lighted, and with company. But put those scoffers in a like situation with mine, and I don't believe they would have been any more free from a feeling the reverse of bold, mocking, and comfortable, than I was.

I had read that most powerful ghost-story, "The Haunted and the Haunters", by the late Lord Lytton, and the vividness of that weird tale had always impressed me greatly. Was I actually now to experience in my own person, and with no possibility of escape, the trying ordeal that bold ghost-hunter went through, under much more favourable circumstances? He at least had his servant with him. He had fuel and a light, and above all, he could get away when he wanted to. I felt I could face any number of spiritual manifestations, if only I had warmth and light. But the icy coldness of the air was eating into my bones, and I shivered until my teeth chattered.

I could not get to sleep. I could not prevent myself listening, and at last I gave up the contest, and let myself listen. But there seemed now nothing to listen to. All the time I had been refusing to let my ears do their office, by putting my handkerchief over one ear, and lying on my arm with the other, a confused noise appeared to reach me, but the moment I turned round and lay on my back, everything seemed quiet. "It's only my fancy after all; the result of cold and want of a good dinner. I will go to sleep." But in spite of this I lay still, listening a little longer. There was the sound of trickling water against the broad bilge of the old hulk, and I knew the tide was rising fast; my thoughts turned to the lost canoe, and to reproaching myself with my stupidity in not allowing enough rope, or looking at it more carefully. Suddenly I became all attention again. An entirely different sound now arrested me. It was distinctly a low groan, and followed almost immediately by heavy blows – blows which fell on a soft substance, and then more groans, and again those sickening blows.

"There must be men here. Where are they, and what is it?" I sat up, and strained my eyes towards where the sound came from. The sounds had ceased again. Should I call out, and let the man or men know that I was here? What puzzled me was the absolute darkness. How could anyone see to hit an object, or do anything else in this dense obscurity? It appalled me. Anything might pass at an inch's distance, and I could not tell who or what it was. But how could anything human find its way about, any more than I could? Perhaps there was a solid bulkhead dividing the forecastle from me. But it would have to be very sound, and with no chink whatever, to prevent a gleam or ray of light finding its way out somewhere. I could not help feeling convinced that the whole hull was open from one end to the other. Was I really dreaming after all? To convince myself that I was wide awake, I felt in my pockets for my note-book, and pulling out my pencil, I opened the book, and holding it in my left hand, wrote as well as I could, by feel alone: "I am wide awake; it is about midnight – Christmas Eve, 187–." I found I had got to the bottom of the page, so I shut the book up, resolving to look at it the next morning. I felt curious to see what the writing looked like by daylight.

But all further speculation was cut short by the shuffling and dragging noise beginning again. There was no doubt the sounds were louder, and were coming my way.

I never in all my life felt so uncomfortable – I may as well at once confess it – so frightened. There in that empty hull, over that boardless floor, over these rotting joists, somebody or something was dragging some heavy weight. What, I could form no conjecture; only the shrieks, the blows, the groans, the dull thumping sounds, compelled me to suspect the worse – to feel convinced that I was actually within some few feet of a horrible murder then being committed. I could form no idea of who the victim was, or who was the assassin. That I actually heard the sounds I had no doubt; that they were growing louder and more distinct I felt painfully aware. The horror of the situation was intense. If only I could strike a light, and see what was passing close there – but I had no matches. I could hear a sound as of someone breathing slowly, stertorously, then a dull groan. And once more the cruel sodden blows fell again, followed by a drip, drip, and heavy drop in the dank water below, from which the sickening smell rose, pungent, reeking, horrible.

The dragging, shuffling noise now began again. It came quite close to me, so close that I felt I had only to put out my hand to touch the thing. Good heavens! was it coming to my bunk? The thing passed, and all the time the dull drip, as of some heavy drops, fell into the water below. It was awful. All this time I was sitting up, and holding my gun by its barrel, ready to use it if I were attacked. As the sound passed me at the closest, I put out the gun involuntarily; but it touched nothing, and I shuddered at the thought that *there was no floor over which the weight could be drawn.*

I must be dreaming some terribly vivid dream. It could not be real. I pinched myself. I felt I was pinching myself. It was no dream. The sweat poured off my brow, my teeth chattered with the cold. It was terrific in its dreadful mystery.

And now the sounds altered. The noises had reached the companion-ladder. Something was climbing them with difficulty. The old stairs creaked. Bump, thump, the thing was dragged up the steps with many pauses, and at last it seemed to have reached the deck. A long pause now followed. The silence grew dense around. I dreaded the stillness – the silence that made itself be heard almost more than the sounds. What new horror would that awful quiet bring forth?

The absolute silence was broken by a dull drip from the stairs, and then the dragging began again. Distant and less distinct, but the steps were louder. They came nearer – over my head – the old boards creaked, and the weight was dragged right over me. I could hear it above my head; for the steps stopped, and two distinct raps, followed by a third heavier one, sounded so clearly above me that it seemed almost as if it was something striking the rotten woodwork of the berth over my head. The sounds were horribly suggestive of the elbows and head of a body being dropped on the deck.

And now, as if the horrors had not been enough, a fresh ghastliness was added. So close were the raps above me that I involuntarily moved, as if I had been struck by what caused them. As I did so, I felt something drop on to my head and slowly trickle over my forehead. I sprang up in my disgust, and with a wild cry I stepped forward, and instantly fell between the joists into the rank water below.

The shock was acute. Had I been asleep and dreaming before, this must inevitably have roused me up. I found myself completely immersed in water, and, for a moment, was absolutely incapable of thinking. As it was pitch-dark and my head had gone under, I could not tell whether I was above water or not, as I felt the bottom and struggled and splashed on to my legs. It was only by degrees I knew I must be standing with my head out of the foul mixture, because I was able to breathe easily, although the wet running down from my hair dribbled into my mouth as I stood shivering and gasping.

It was astonishing how a physical discomfort overcame a mental terror. Nothing could be more miserable than my present position, and my efforts were at once directed to getting out of this dreadful place. But let anyone who has ever had the ill-luck to fall out of bed in his boyhood try and recollect his sensations. The bewildering realization that he is not in bed, that he does not know where he is, which way to go, or what to do to get back again; everything he touches seems strange, and one piece of furniture much the same as any other.

If, then, one is so utterly at fault in a room every inch of which one knows intimately, how much more hopeless was my position at the bottom of this old vessel, half immersed in water, and totally without any clue which could help me to get out! I had not the least idea which was the ship's stern or which her stem, and every movement I made with my feet only served to unsteady me, as the bottom was covered with slime, and uneven with the great timbers of the vessel.

My first thought on recovering my wits was to stretch my arms up over my head, and I was relieved to find that I could easily reach the joists above me. I was always fairly good at gymnastics, and I had not much difficulty in drawing myself up and sitting on the joist, although the weight of my wet clothes added to my exertions considerably. Having so far succeeded, I sat and drained, as it were, into the water below. The smell was abominable. I never disliked myself so much, and I shivered with cold.

As I could not get any wetter, I determined to go on deck somehow, but where was the companion-ladder? I had nothing to guide me. Strange to say, the reality of my struggles had almost made me forget the mysterious phenomena I had been listening to. But now, as I looked round, my attention was caught by a luminous patch which quivered and flickered on my right, at what distance from me I could not tell. It was like the light from a glow-worm, only larger and changing in shape; sometimes elongated like a lambent oval, and then it would sway one way or another, as if caught in a draught of air. While I was looking at it and wondering what could cause it, I heard the steps over my head; they passed above me, and then seemed to grow louder on my left. A creeping dread again came over me. If only I could get out of this horrible place – but where were the stairs? I listened. The footfall seemed to be coming down some steps; then the companion-ladder must be on my left. But if I moved that way I should meet the thing, whatever it was, that was coming down. I shuddered at the thought. However, I made up my mind. Stretching out my hand very carefully, I felt for the next joist, reached it, and crawled across. I stopped to listen. The steps were coming nearer. My hearing had now become acute; I could almost tell the exact place of each footfall. It came closer – closer – quite close, surely – on the very joist on which I was sitting. I thought I could feel the joist quiver, and involuntarily moved my hand to prevent the heavy tread falling on it. The steps passed on, grew fainter, and ceased, as they drew near the pale lambent light. One thing I noticed with curious horror, and that was that although the thing must have passed between me and the light, yet it was never for a moment obscured, which it must have been had any body or substance passed between, and yet I was certain that the steps went directly from me to it.

It was all horribly mysterious; and what had become of the other sound – the thing that was being dragged? An irresistible shudder passed over me; but I determined to pursue my way until I came to something. It would never do to sit still and shiver there.

After many narrow escapes of falling again, I reached a bulkhead, and cautiously feeling along it, I came to an opening. It was the companion-ladder. By this time my hands, by feeling over the joists, had become dry again. I felt along the step to be quite sure that it was the stairs, and in so doing I touched something wet, sticky, clammy. Oh, horror! what was it? A cold shiver shook me nearly off the joist, and I felt an unutterable sense of repulsion to going on. However, the fresher air which came down the companion revived me, and, conquering my dread, I clambered on to the step. It did not take long to get upstairs and stand on the deck again.

I think I never in all my life experienced such a sense of joy as I did on being out of that disgusting hole. It was true I was soaking wet, and the night wind cut through me like a knife; but these were things I could understand, and were matters of common experience. What I had gone through might only be a question of nerves, and had no tangible or visible terror; but it was none the less very dreadful, and I would not go through such an experience again for worlds. As I stood cowering under the lee of the bulwark, I looked round at the sky. There was a pale light as if of daybreak, and it seemed as if all my troubles would be over with the dawn. It was bitterly cold. The wind had got round to the north, and I could faintly make out the low shore astern.

While I stood shivering there, a cry came down the wind. At first I thought it was a sea-bird, but it sounded again. I felt sure it was a human voice. I sprang up on to the taffrail, and shouted at the top of my lungs, then paused. The cry came down clearer and distinct. It was Jones's voice – had he heard me? I waved my draggled pocket-handkerchief and shouted again. In the silence which followed, I caught the words "We are coming". What joyful words! Never did shipwrecked mariner on a lonely isle feel greater delight. My misery would soon be over.

Unfortunately the tide was low, and was still falling. Nothing but a boat could reach me, I thought, and to get a boat would take some time. I therefore stamped up and down the deck to get warm; but I had an instinctive aversion for the companion-ladder, and the deep shadows of the forepart of the vessel.

As I turned round in my walk, I thought I saw something moving over the mud. I stopped. It was undoubtedly a figure coming towards me. A voice hailed me in gruff accents –

"*Lily*, ahoy! Be anyone aboard?"

What an absurd question! and here I had been shouting myself hoarse. However, I quickly reassured him, and then understood why my rescuer did not sink in the soft mud. He had mud-pattens on. Coming up as close as he could, he shouted to me to keep clear, and then threw first one, then the other, clattering wooden board on to the deck. I found them, and under the instructions of my friend, I did not take long in putting them on. The man was giving me directions as to how to manage; but I did not care how much wetter I got, and dropped over the side into the slime. Sliding and straddling, I managed to get up to my friend, and then together we skated, as it were, to the shore – although skating very little represents the awkward splashes and slips I made on my way to land. I found quite a little crowd awaiting me on the bank; but Jones, with ready consideration, hurried me off to a cart he had in a lane nearby, and drove me home.

I told him the chief points of the adventure on our way; but did not say anything of the curious noises. It is odd how shy a man feels at telling what he knows people will never believe. It was not until the evening of the next day that I began to tell him, and then only after I was fortified by an excellent dinner, and some very good claret. Jones listened attentively. He was far too kindly and well-bred to laugh at me; but I could see he did not believe one word as to the reality of the occurrence. "Very strange!" "How remarkable!" "Quite extraordinary!" he kept saying, with evident interest. But I was sure he put it all down to my fatigue and disordered imagination. And so, to do him justice, has everybody else to whom I have told the tale since.

The fact is, we cannot, in this prosaic age, believe in anything the least approaching the supernatural. Nor do I. But nevertheless I am as certain as I am that I am writing these words, that the thing did really happen, and will happen again, may happen every night for all I know. I have a theory which of course will be laughed at, and as I am not in the least scientific, I cannot bolster it up by scientific arguments. It is this. As Mr Edison has now discovered that by certain simple processes human sounds can be reproduced at any future date, so accidentally, and owing to the combination of most curious coincidences, it might happen that the agonized cries of some suffering being, or the sounds made by one at a time when all other emotions are as nothing compared to the supreme sensations of one committing some awful crime, could be impressed on the atmosphere or surface of an enclosed building, which could be reproduced by a current of air passing into that building under the same atmospheric conditions. This is the vague explanation I have given to myself.

However, be the explanation what it may, the facts are as I have stated them. Let those laugh who did not experience them. To return to the end of the story. There were two things I pointed out to Jones as conclusive that I was not dreaming. One was my pocket-book. I showed it him, and the words were quite clear – only, of course, very straggling. This is a facsimile of the writing, but I cannot account for the date being 1837–

I am wide a wake it is about midnight Christmas Eve 1837

The other point was the foul-smelling dark chocolate stains on my hair, hands, and clothes. Jones said, of course, this was from the rust off the mouldering ironwork, some of which no doubt had trickled down, owing to the heavy rain, through the defective caulking of the deck. The fact is, there is nothing that an ingenious mind cannot explain; but the question is, is the explanation the right one?

I could easily account for the phosphorescent light. The water was foul and stagnant, and it was no doubt caused by the same gases which produce the well-known *ignis fatuus* or will-o'-the-wisp.

We visited the ship, and I recovered my gun. There were the same stains on the deck as there were on my clothes; and curiously enough they went in a nearly straight line over the place where I lay from the top of the companion to the starboard bulwark. We carefully examined the fore-part of the ship; it was as completely gutted as the rest of her. Jones was glad to get on deck again, as the atmosphere was very unpleasant, and I had no wish to stay.

At my request Jones made every inquiry he could about the old hulk. Not much was elicited. It bore an evil name, and no one would go on board who could help it. So far it looked as if it were credited with being haunted. The owner, who had been the captain of her, had died about three years before. He bore an ill reputation; but as he had left his money to the most influential farmer in the district, the country-people were unwilling to talk against him.

I went with Jones to call on the farmer, and asked him point-blank if he had ever heard whether a murder had been committed on board the *Lily*. He stared at me, and then laughed. "Not as I know of" was all his answer – and I never got any nearer than that.

I feel that this is all very unsatisfactory. I wish I could give some thrilling and sensational explanation. I am sorry I cannot. My imagination suggests many, as no doubt it will to each of my readers who possess that faculty; but I have written this only to tell the facts, not to add to our super-abundant fiction.

If ever I come across any details bearing upon the subject, I will not fail to communicate them at once.

The vessel I found was the *Lily of Goole*, owned by one Master Gad Earwaker, and built in 1801.

Theo Gift

Dog or Demon?

"Theo Gift" was a pseudonym employed by Dora Havers (1847–1923), who, like her great friend E. Nesbit, penned several very grim horror tales under a male alias, while achieving larger fame for popular children's stories, notably Cape Town Dicky; Or, Colonel Jack's Boy. *"Dog or Demon?" is taken from her very scarce collection aptly named* Not for the Night-time *(1889).*

The following pages came into my hands shortly after the writer's death. He was a brother officer of my own, had served under me with distinction in the last Afghan campaign, and was a young man of great spirit and promise. He left the army on the occasion of his marriage with a very beautiful girl, the daughter of a Leicestershire baronet; and I partially lost sight of him for some little time afterwards. I can, however, vouch for the accuracy of the principal facts herein narrated, and of the story generally; the sad fate of the family having made a profound impression, not only in the district in Ireland where the tragedy occurred, but throughout the country.

(signed) William J. Porlock,
Lieut.-Col. – Regt.
The Curragh, Co. Kildare

AT LAST SHE is dead!

It came to an end today: all that long agony, those heart-rending cries and moans, the terrified shuddering of that poor wasted body, the fixed and maddening glare, more awful for its very unconsciousness. Only this very day they faded out and died one by one, as death crept at last up the tortured and emaciated limbs, and I stood over my wife's body, and tried to thank God for both our sakes that it was all over.

And yet it was I who had done it. I who killed her – not meaningly or of intent (I will swear that), not even so that the laws of this earth can punish me; but truly, wilfully all the same; of my own brutal, thoughtless selfishness. I put it all down in my diary at the time. I tear out the pages that refer to it now, and insert them here, that when those few friends who still care for me hear of the end they may know how it came about.

June 10th, 1878. Castle Kilmoyle, Kerry – Arrived here today with Kilmoyle after a hard battle to get away from Lily, who couldn't bear me going, and tried all manner of arguments to keep me from leaving her.

"What have *you* to do with Lord Kilmoyle's tenants?" she would keep on asking. "They owe no rent to you. Oh, Harry, do let them alone and stay here. If you go with him you'll be sure to come in for some of the ill-feeling that already exists against himself; and I shall be so miserably anxious all the time. Pray don't go."

I told her, however, that I must; first, because I had promised, and men don't like going back from their word without any cause; and secondly, because Kilmoyle would be desperately offended with me if I did. The fact is, I hadn't seen him for three years till we met at that tennis-party at the FitzHerbert's last week; and when he asked me if I would like to run over for a week's fishing at his place in Ireland, and help him to enforce the eviction of a tenant who declined either to pay for the house he lived in or leave it, I accepted with effusion. It would be a spree. I had nothing to do, and I really wanted a little change and waking up. As for Lily, her condition naturally makes me rather nervous and fanciful at present, and to have me dancing attendance on her does her more harm than good. I told her so, and asked her, with half a dozen kisses, if she'd like to tie me to her apron-string altogether. She burst out crying, and said she would! There is no use in reasoning with the dear little girl at present. She is better with her sisters.

June 12th – We have begun the campaign by giving the tenant twenty-four hours' notice to quit or pay. Kilmoyle and I rode down with the bailiff to the cottage, a well-built stone one in the loveliest glen ever dreamt of out of fairyland, to see it served ourselves. The door was shut and barred, and as no answer save a fierce barking from within responded to our knocks, we were beginning to think that the tenant had saved us the trouble of evicting him by decamping of his own accord, when, on crossing round the side of the house where there was a small unglazed window, we came in full view of him, seated as coolly as possible beside a bare hearthstone, with a pipe in his mouth and a big brown dog between his knees. His hair, which was snow-white, hung over his shoulders, and his face was browned to the colour of mahogany by exposure to sun and wind; but he might have been carved out of mahogany too for all the sign of attention that he gave while the bailiff repeated his messages, until Kilmoyle, losing patience, tossed a written copy of the notice into him through the open window, with a threat that, unless he complied with it, he would be smoked out of the place like a rat; after which we rode off, followed by a perfect pandemonium of barks and howls from the dog, a lean and hideous mongrel, who seemed to be only held by force from flying at our throats.

We had a jolly canter over the hills afterwards, selected the bit of river that seemed most suitable for our fishing on the morrow; and wound up the day with a couple of bottles of champagne at dinner, after which Kilmoyle was warmed up into making me an offer which I accepted on the spot – i.e., to let me have the identical cottage we had been visiting rent free, with right of shooting and fishing, for two years, on condition only of my putting and keeping it in order for that time. I wonder what Lily will say to the idea. She hates Ireland almost as much as Kilmoyle's tenants are supposed to hate him, but really it would cost mighty little to make a most picturesque little place of the cabin in question, and I believe we should both find it highly enjoyable to run down here for a couple of months' change in the autumn, after a certain and much-looked-forward-to event is well over.

June 19th – The job is done, and the man out; and Kilmoyle and I shook hands laughingly today over our victory as he handed me the key in token of my new tenantship. It has been rather an exciting bit of work, however; for the fellow – an ill-conditioned old villain, who hasn't paid a stiver of rent for the last twelve months, and only a modicum for the three previous years – *wouldn't* quit; set all threats, persuasions, and warnings at defiance, and simply sat within his door with a loaded gun in his hand, and kept it pointed at anyone who tried to approach him. In the end, and to avoid bloodshed, we had to smoke him out. There was nothing else for it, for though we took care that none of the neighbours should come near the house with food, he was evidently prepared to starve where he was rather than budge an inch; and on the third day, Donovan, the bailiff, told Kilmoyle that if he didn't want it to come to that, he must have in the help either of the "peelers" or a bit of smoke.

Kilmoyle vowed he wouldn't have the peelers anyhow. He had said he'd put the man out himself, and he'd do it; and the end of it was, we first had the windows shuttered up from outside, a sod put in the chimney, and then the door taken off its hinges while the tenant's attention was momentarily distracted by the former operations. Next, a good big fire of damp weeds which had been piled up outside was set alight, and after that there was nothing to do but wait.

It didn't take long. The wind was blowing strongly in the direction of the house, and the dense volume of thick, acrid smoke would have driven me out in about five minutes. As for the tenant, he was probably more hardened on the subject of atmosphere generally, for he managed to stand it for nearly half an hour, and until Kilmoyle and I were almost afraid to keep it up lest he should let himself be smothered out of sheer obstinacy. Just as I was debating, however, whether I wouldn't brave his gun, and make a rush for him at all costs, nature or vindictiveness got the better of his perversity; a dark figure staggered through the stifling vapour to the door, fired wildly in the direction of Kilmoyle (without hitting him, thank God!), and then dropped, a miserable object, purple with suffocation and black with smoke, upon the threshold, whence some of the keepers dragged him out into the fresh air and poured a glass of whisky down his throat, just too late to prevent his fainting away.

Five minutes later the fire was out, the windows opened, and two stalwart Scotch keepers put in charge of the dwelling, while Kilmoyle and I went home to dinner, and the wretched old man, who had given us so much trouble for nothing, was conveyed in a handcart to the village by some of his neighbours, who had been looking on from a distance, and beguiling the time by hooting and groaning at us.

"Who wants the police in these cases?" said Kilmoyle triumphantly. "To my mind, Glennie, it's more cowardice to send for those poor fellows to enforce orders we ought to be able to carry out for ourselves, and so get them into odium with the whole neighbourhood. We managed this capitally by ourselves" – and, upon my word, I couldn't help agreeing heartily with him. Indeed, the whole affair had gone off with only one trifling accident, and that was no one's fault but the tenant's.

It seems that for the last two days his abominable dog had been tied up in a miserable little pigsty a few yards from the house, Donovan having threatened him that if the brute flew at or bit anyone it would be shot instantly. Nobody was aware of this, however, and unfortunately, when the bonfire was at its height, a blazing twig fell on the roof of this little shelter and set it alight; the clouds of smoke which were blowing that way hiding what had happened until the wretched animal inside was past rescue; while even its howls attracted no attention, from the simple fact that not only it, but a score of other curs belonging to the neighbours round had been making as much noise as they could from the commencement of the affair.

Now, of course, we hear that the evicted tenant goes about swearing that we deliberately and out of malice burnt his only friend alive, and calling down curses on our heads in consequence. I don't think we are much affected by them, however. Why didn't he untie the poor brute himself? . . .

June 22nd – A letter from Lady FitzHerbert, Lily's eldest sister, telling me she thinks I had better come back at once! L. not at all well, nervous about me, and made more, instead of less so, by my account of our successful raid. What a fool I was to write it! I thought she would be amused; but the only thing now is to get back as quickly as possible, and I started this morning, Kilmoyle driving me to the station. We were bowling along pretty fast, when, as we turned a bend in the road, the horse swerved suddenly to one side, and the off-wheel of the trap went over something with that sickening sort of jolt, the meaning of which some of us know, by experience, and which made Kilmoyle exclaim:

"Good heavens, we've run over something!"

Fortunately nothing to hurt! Nothing but the carcass of a dead dog, whose charred and blackened condition would have sufficiently identified it with the victim of Tuesday's bonfire, even if we had not now perceived its late owner seated among the heather near the roadside, and occupied in pouring forth a string of wailing sounds, which might have been either prayers or curses for aught we could tell; the while he waved his shaggy white head and brown claw-like hands to and fro in unison. I yelled at him to know why he had left his brute of a dog there to upset travellers, but he paid no attention, and did not seem to hear, and as we were in a hurry to catch the train we could not afford to waste words on him, but drove on.

June 26th. Holly Lodge, West Kensington – This day sees me the proud father of a son and heir, now just five hours old, and, though rather too red for beauty, a very sturdy youngster, with a fine pair of lungs of his own. Lily says she is too happy to live, and as the dread of losing her has been the one thought of the last twenty-four hours, it is a comfort to know from the doctor that this means she has got through it capitally, and is doing as well as can be expected. Thank God for all His mercies!

July 17th – Lily has had a nasty fright this evening, for which I hope she won't be any the worse. She was lying on a couch out in the veranda for the first time since her convalescence, and I had been reading to her till she fell asleep, when I closed the book, and leaving the bell beside her in case she should want anything, went into my study to write letters. I hadn't been there for half an hour, however, when I was startled by a cry from Lily's voice and a sharp ringing of the bell, which made me fling open the study window and dart round to the veranda at the back of the house. It was empty, but in the drawing-room within, Lily was standing upright, trembling with terror and clinging to her maid, while she tried to explain to her that there was someone hidden in the veranda or close by, though so incoherently, owing to the state of agitation she was in, that it was not until I and the man-servant had searched the veranda, garden, and outbuildings, and found nothing, that I was even able to understand what had frightened her.

It appeared then that she had suddenly been awakened from sleep by the pressure of a heavy hand on her shoulder, and a hot breath – so close, it seemed as if someone were about to whisper in her ear – upon her cheek. She started up, crying out, "Who's that? What is it?" but was only answered by a hasty withdrawal of the pressure, and the pit-pat of heavy but shoeless feet retreating through the dusk to the further end of the veranda. In a sudden access of ungovernable terror she screamed out, sprang to her feet, ringing the bell as she did so, and rushed into the drawing-room, where she was fortunately joined by her maid, who had been passing through the hall when the bell rang.

Well, as I said, we searched high and low, and not a trace of any intruder could we find; nay, not even a stray cat or dog, and we have none of our own. The garden isn't large, and there is neither tree nor shrub in it big enough to conceal a boy. The gate leading into the road was fastened inside, and the wall is too high for easy climbing; while the maid having been in the hall, could certify that no one had passed out through the drawing-room. Finally I came to the conclusion that the whole affair was the outcome of one of those very vivid dreams which sometimes come to us in the semi-conscious moment between sleep and waking; and though Lily, of course, wouldn't hear of such an idea, for a long while, I think even she began to give into it after the doctor had been sent for, and had pronounced it the only rational one, and given her a composing draught before sending her off to bed. At present she is sleeping soundly, but it has been a disturbing evening, and I'm glad it's over.

September 20th – Have seen Dr C— today, and he agrees with me – that there is nothing for it but change and bracing air. He declares that the fright Lily had in July must have been much more serious than we imagined, and that she has never got over it. She *seemed* to do so. She was out and about after her confinement as soon as other people; but I remember now her nerves seemed gone from the first. She was always starting, listening, and trembling without any cause, except that she appeared in constant alarm lest something should happen to the baby; and as I took that to be a common weakness with young mothers over their first child, I'm afraid I paid no attention to it. We've a very nice nurse for the boy, a young Irishwoman named Bridget McBean (not that she's ever seen Ireland herself, but her parents came from there, driven by poverty to earn their living elsewhere, and after faithfully sending over every farthing they could screw out of their own necessities to "the ould folks at home", died in the same poverty here). Bridget is devoted to the child, and as long as he is in her care Lily generally seems easy and peaceful. Otherwise (and some strange instinct seems to tell her when this is the case) she gets nervous at once, and is always restless and uneasy.

Once she awoke with a scream in the middle of the night, declaring, "Something was wrong with the baby. Nurse had gone away and left it; she was sure of it!" To pacify her I threw on my dressing-gown and ran up to the nursery to see; and, true enough, though the boy was all right and sound asleep, Nurse was absent, having gone up to the cook's room to get something for her toothache. She came back the next moment and I returned to satisfy Lily, but she would scarcely listen to me.

"Is it gone?" she asked. "Was the nursery door open? Oh, if it had been! Thank God, you were in time to drive the thing down. But how – how could it have got into the house?"

"*It?* What?" I repeated, staring.

"The dog you passed on the stairs. I saw it as it ran past the door – *a big black dog!*"

"My dear, you're dreaming. I passed no dog; nothing at all."

"Oh, Harry, didn't you see it then? I did, though it went by so quietly. Oh, is it in the house still?"

I seized the candle, went up and down the stairs and searched the whole house thoroughly; but again found nothing. The fancied dog must have been a shadow on the wall only, and I told her so pretty sharply; yet on two subsequent occasions when, for some reason or another, she had the child's cot put beside her own bed at night, I was awoken by finding her sitting up and shaking with fright, while she assured me that something – *some animal* – had been trying to get into the room. She could hear its breathing distinctly as it scratched at the door to open it! Dr C – is right. Her nerves are clearly all wrong, and a thorough change is the only thing for her. How glad I am that the builder writes me my Kerry shooting-box is finished! We'll run over there next week . . .

September 26th, The Cabin, Kilmoyle Castle, Kerry – Certainly this place is Paradise after London, and never did I imagine that by raising the roof so as to transform a garret into a large, bright attic, quite big enough for a nursery, throwing out a couple of bay windows into the two rooms below, and turning an adjoining barn into a kitchen and servants' room, this cottage could ever have been made into such a jolly little box. As for Lily, she's delighted with it, and looks ever so much better already. Am getting my guns in order for tomorrow, anticipating a pleasant day's shooting.

September 27th – Here's an awful bother! Bridget has given warning and declares she will leave today! It seems she knew her mother came from Kerry, and this morning she has found out that the old man who lived in this very cottage was her own grandfather, and that he died of a broken heart within a week of his eviction, having first called down a solemn curse on Kilmoyle and me, and all belonging to us, in this world and the next. They also say that he managed to scoop out a grave for his dog, and bury it right in front of the cabin door; and now Bridget is alternately tearing her hair for ever having served under her "grandfather's murtherer", and weeping over the murderer's baby the while she packs her box for departure. That wouldn't matter too much, though it's awfully unpleasant; for the housekeeper at the Castle will send us someone to mind the boy till we get another nurse; but the disclosure seems to have driven Lily as frantic as Bridget. She entreated me with tears and sobs to give up the cabin, and take her and baby back to England before "the curse could fall upon us", and wept like one broken-hearted when I told her she must be mad even to suggest such a thing after all the expense I had been to. All the same, it's a horrid nuisance. She has been crying all day, and if this fancy grows on her the change will do her no good, and I shan't know what to do. I'm sorry I was cross to her, poor child, but I was rather out of sorts myself, having been kept awake all night by the ceaseless mournful howling of some unseen cur. Besides, I'm bothered about Kilmoyle. He arranged long ago to be here this week; but the bailiff says he has been ill and is travelling, and speaks in a mysterious way as if the illness were D.T. I hope not! I had no idea before that my old chum was even addicted to drink. Anyhow, I won't be baulked of a few days shooting, at all events, and perhaps by that time Lily will have calmed down.

October 19th, The Castle – It is weeks since I opened this, and I only do so now before closing it for ever. I shall never dare to look at it again after writing down what I must today. I did go out for my shooting on the morning after my last entry, and my wife, with the babe in her arms, stood at the cabin door to see me off. The sunlight shone full on them – on the tear-stains still dark under her sweet blue eyes, and the downy head and tiny face of the infant on her breast. But she smiled as I kissed my hand to her. I shall never forget that – the last smile that *ever* . . . The woman we had brought with us as servant told me the rest. She said her mistress went on playing with the child in the sunshine till it fell asleep and then laid it in its cot inside, and sat beside it rocking it. By-and-by, however, the maid went in and asked her to come and look at something that was wrong with the new kitchen arrangements, and Lily came out with her. They were in the kitchen about ten minutes, when they heard a wail from the cabin, and both ran out. Lily was first, and cried out:

"Oh, Heaven! Look! what's that – that great dog, *all black and burnt-looking*, coming out of the house? Oh, my baby! My baby!"

The maid saw no dog, and stopped for an instant to look round for it, letting her mistress run on. Then she heard one wild shriek from within – such a shriek as she had never heard in all her life before – and followed. She found Lily lying senseless on the floor, and in the cradle the child – stone dead! Its throat had been torn open by some strange savage animal, and on the bedclothes and the fresh white matting covering the floor were the blood-stained imprints of a dog's feet!

That was three weeks ago. It was evening when I came back; came back to hear my wife's delirious shrieks piercing the autumn twilight – those shrieks which, from the moment of her being roused from the merciful insensibility which held her for the first hours of her loss, she has never ceased to utter. We have moved her to the Castle since then; but I can hear them now. She has never regained consciousness once. The doctors fear she never will.

And she never did! That last entry in my diary was written two years ago. For two years my young wife, the pretty girl who loved me so dearly, and whom I took from such a happy home, has been a raving lunatic – obliged to be guarded, held down, and confined behind high walls. They have been my own walls, and I have been her keeper. The doctors wanted me to send her to an asylum; said it would be for her good, and on that I consented; but she grew so much worse there, her frantic struggles and shrieks for me to come to her, to "save her from the dog, to keep it off", were so incessant and heart-rending that they sent for me; and I have never left her again. God only knows what that means; what the horror and agony of those two years, those ceaseless, piteous cries for her child, our child, those agonized entreaties to me "not to go with Kilmoyle; to take her away, away"; those – oh! how have I ever borne it! . . .
 Today it is over. She is dead; and – I scarce dare leave her even yet! Never once in all this time have I been tempted to share the horrible delusion which, beginning in a weak state of health, and confirmed by the awful coincidence of our baby's death, upset my darling's brain; and yet now – now that it is over, I feel as if the madness which slew her were coming on me also. As she lay dying last night, and I watched by her alone, I seemed to hear a sound of snuffing and scratching at the door outside, as though some animal were there. Once, indeed, I strode to it and threw it open, but there was nothing – nothing but a dark, fleeting shadow seen for one moment, and the sound of soft, unshod feet going pit, pat, pit, pat, upon the stairs as they retreated downwards. It was but fancy; my own heartbeats, as I knew; and yet – yet if the women who turned me out an hour ago should have left her alone – if that sound now –

* * *

Here the writing came to an abrupt end, the pen lying in a blot across it. At the inquest held subsequently the footman deposed that he heard his master fling open the study door, and rush violently upstairs to the death-chamber above. A loud exclamation, and the report of a pistol-shot followed almost immediately; and on running to the rescue he found Captain Glennie standing inside the door, his face livid with horror, and the revolver in his outstretched hand still pointed at a corner of the room on the other side of the bier, the white covering on which had in one place been dragged off and torn. Before the man could speak, however, his master turned round to him, and exclaiming:

"Williams, *I have seen it*! It was there! *On her!* Better this than a madhouse! There is no other escape," put the revolver to his head, and fired. He was dead ere even the servant could catch him.

J. E. P. Muddock
A Ghost from the Sea

Joyce Emmerson Preston Muddock (1843–1934) was better known under his alter ego of "Dick Donovan", author of more than fifty mystery and detective volumes – many starring Donovan himself. He was credited under both names in equal measures, and his best short horror and ghost stories were published in two volumes: Tales of Terror *by Dick Donovan (1899) and* Stories Weird and Wonderful *by J. E. Muddock (1889; from which the following story is taken).*

TOWARDS THE LATTER half of the fifties, Melbourne, in Australia, was startled by an extraordinary and terrible crime. It was at the very height of what was known as the "gold fever". A year or two before, news had spread like wildfire that gold had been discovered in enormous quantities in various parts of the country. That news literally seemed to turn people mad, and young and old, the halt, the lame, and even the blind, rushed away for the fabled regions of El Dorado. Whole families, who had been content to jog on quietly year after year, earning fair wages, and getting all the necessaries of life, were seized with the fever, and, selling up their belongings rump and stump, invested in billies,[1] tomahawks, spades, pick-axes, washing-pans,[2] and other etceteras, and shouldering their swags set off for the mysterious regions, where it was rumoured gold was lying on the surface of the ground in big nuggets. Fortunate, indeed, were those who had any belongings to sell in order to provide themselves with the plant required for roughing it in the bush; for many had nothing at all,

[1] Billies – tin cans for cooking.
[2] Washing-pans – the primitive mode of washing gold.

save what they stood upright in, but, imagining that they were going to
gather in the precious metal in sackfulls, they started off with the rest,
only to perish, it may be, miserably of starvation, disappointment, and
broken hearts. This period in the history of our Australian colonies is a
startling record of human credulity, human folly, wickedness, despair
and death. The fever was confined to no particular class of people.
Clergymen, bankers, landowners, shipowners, merchants, shopkeepers,
sailors, labourers, classical scholars and ignoramuses alike fell under
the fascination. The worst passions of our nature manifested
themselves; hatred, envy, jealousy, greed, uncharitableness. The
parsons were no better than the paupers; the classical scholars than the
ignoramuses. The thin veneering of so-called civilization was rubbed
off, and the savage appeared in all his fierceness at the cry of "Gold!
Gold!"

It is at such periods as these that the moralist finds his pabulum, and
those good but weak-minded people who think that human nature has
improved with the advance of time have only to get on the house-tops
and utter the cry of "Gold!" again, to prove that we are not a whit better
than our ancestors were three thousand years ago. This may not be very
flattering to us, but alas! it is true. In those days of Australian gold rushes
the bush was a veritable *terra incognita*. Explorers had attempted to penetrate into the mystic interior, but many never came back again, and to
this day it is not known where their bones moulder. Those who did
return were gaunt, famine-stricken, hollow-eyed, for they had looked
upon death, and the stories they told were calculated to appal everyone
but the most daring and reckless. But the report of the gold finds so
turned the heads of people that, forgetting all about the dangers and
privations they would have to endure, they started off into those
unknown regions, and thousands literally perished by the way. The experiences of some of these unfortunate people are in themselves amongst
the most pathetic and moving of human stories.

Melbourne at the time of this narrative was not the Melbourne of
today. It was then simply a collection of canvas and wooden huts and
houses, with a few buildings of a more substantial character. One of the
most imposing houses in the place was that known as "Jackson's
Boarding-house." It was built partly of wood and partly of stone, and was
kept by a man and his wife named Jackson. Very little, if anything, was
known of the Jacksons' history, beyond that they had come to the colony
a few years previously. Jackson was a nautical man, and had purchased a

schooner with which he traded up and down the coast, though with indifferent success.

At last his schooner was wrecked, and Jackson and his wife, who had always sailed with him, built a wooden shanty, in what was then known as Canvas Town – now Melbourne – where they sold liquors and provisions. They seemed to have done fairly well, for very soon they erected what was then quite an imposing building, and they called it "Jackson's Boarding-house."

Jackson was remarkable for an extraordinarily powerful physique. He stood about six feet high, and his muscular development was so great that it was said he could lift a cask of split peas, weighing nearly three hundredweight, from the ground, and raise it at arm's length above his head. He was an ill-favoured man, however, for he had a low brow, small cunning sort of eyes, and was exceedingly passionate in his temper. But it was notable that he seemed to be strongly attached to his wife, and they were never known to disagree.

Mrs Jackson was a striking contrast to her husband, for she was a slightly built little woman, with a pink and white face, sickly blue eyes, and a mass of tow-like hair that was almost the colour of flax, whereas her husband was as dark as a raven.

Soon after these people had opened their boarding-house, there came to lodge with them a Mr and Mrs Harvey, who had recently arrived from England. They had, like many others, come out to try and improve their fortunes. A warm intimacy seemed to spring up between the two couples, and they lived apparently in the greatest harmony. It was understood that Mr Harvey was a mechanic by trade. He was a strong, healthy man, very handy and useful, and did odd jobs for the community. His wife was a pretty, agreeable woman, and soon became a great favourite, for she played the piano and sang well, and was always ready to afford amusement or render assistance to anyone needing it, where it lay in her power. Her husband acquired the character of a rather indolent, good-natured sort of fellow, whose aim seemed to be to suddenly accumulate wealth without doing much labour for it.

At length the gold fever set in, and amongst those who started off in the first rush for the regions of fabulous wealth was Harvey, his wife remaining behind at Jackson's boarding-house. Some eight months later Harvey returned, and soon the report spread that he had brought thousands of pounds' worth of nuggets and gold dust. He remained in the town for four weeks, during which he and his wife denied themselves nothing, and it was evident that the report about his wealth was in the main true. Then, having furnished himself with an extensive outfit in the shape of tent, cooking-stove, digging and washing utensils, he started up the country again, Mrs Harvey still remaining at the boarding-house. She purchased a horse and buggy, provided herself with fine clothes and jewellery, and common gossip had it that this little, blue-eyed flaxen-haired woman was the richest person in Melbourne. Two months later, her husband still being absent at the diggings, the community was startled one morning by a report that Mrs Harvey had been murdered. The report proved to be only too true, and the story told by a female servant in the boarding-house was this. She went to the lady's room to see why she had not appeared, it being an hour and a half after her usual time of rising. She found the door locked, and, repeated knocking having failed to elicit a response, she informed her master, and expressed fears that something was wrong. Jackson at once went upstairs with some of the lodgers, and, failing to get an answer, he at once broke open the door, and then a terrible sight revealed itself.

Lying across the bed was the body of Mrs Harvey. She was dressed only in her night-dress, which was disarranged and torn as if she had struggled desperately, as in fact she had, for further evidence of this was forthcoming. She was on her back, her head hanging over the farthest side of the bed. Twisted tightly round her neck until it had cut into the flesh was a crimson cord sash or belt, such as in those days was common – these sashes, or, more correctly speaking scarves, being worn by men round their waists to keep their trousers up, instead of braces. The horribly distorted features showed that the poor woman had been strangled, and subsequent medical examination brought to light that her head had been forced back with such tremendous force that the neck was absolutely broken. Discolorations about the mouth indicated that a heavy hand had been pressed there to keep her from screaming. There were also deep indents and bruises on the wrists, which proved that she had struggled and been firmly grasped there by the murderer. Other parts of the body were also terribly bruised, as if in the struggle she had been banged repeatedly against the massive wooden bedstead.

Murder had been done, that was certain. That the murderer was a man was equally certain, for no female could have exerted such tremendous force as had evidently been used. It was no less certain that robbery had been the motive, for a very large travelling trunk or box had been forced open, in spite of an unusually strong lock, and two iron bands round it which were secured with padlocks. All the poor creature's clothes had been turned out of the box, and were scattered about the floor, as well as her jewellery, nothing in that way being taken. Now what did that prove? It proved this: the murderer, with the cunning of a devil, knew that in such a place to possess himself of her jewellery, valuable as it was, would almost certainly lead to his detection. No, it was neither her jewellery nor her clothes he wanted, but the nuggets and gold dust her husband had brought from the diggings. No one could swear to gold dust or nuggets, and both were plentiful, for diggers, especially sailors, were constantly arriving from the diggings with hoards of gold, which they sold for ready cash far below their value: for at this early period there was no regular exchange or agency for the purchase of the precious metal.

The next question was: How did the murderer get into the room? Not by the door, for a dozen witnesses vowed that it was locked on the inside, the key still in the lock, when Jackson broke open the door. The only other entrance, then, was by the window, twenty-five feet from the ground. There was no indication that a ladder had been used, and so the theory was that the murderer had secreted himself under the bed, and when his fiendish work was completed he had gone out by the window, climbed up by means of an iron gutter pipe to the roof, and had then descended into the house through a skylight.

Now came the most important question of all: Who was the murderer? At the time of the crime there were nearly forty people staying in the boarding-house, mostly men, a good many of them being sailors. The police arrangements of the town were very primitive, and by no means equal to coping with such a mysterious tragedy, and unfortunately not an atom of evidence could be got that would have justified the arrest of any individual. The result was the mystery was destined to remain a mystery for ever; and the times were too exciting and too changing for such a crime even as that to long occupy the public mind, and so, almost with the burying of the flaxen-haired woman who had been so cruelly done to death, the tragedy was forgotten for a time. Three months later, however, its memory was revived by the arrival of Mr Harvey. He had written two or three times to his wife, had received no answer, had got alarmed, and had come to see what was the matter. The news almost drove him off his mind, for he had been passionately attached to his wife. He stated that he had left her with about ten thousand pounds' worth of gold; and he now offered to give anyone five thousand pounds' worth of gold who would bring the murderer to justice. The offer, however, proved of no avail; not the faintest clue could be obtained. Jackson had taken charge of the murdered woman's effects, and these he handed to the husband, who certified his belief that they were all correct except the gold, which was in nuggets and dust, one nugget alone being valued at between two and three thousand pounds. And so the poor husband departed, an utterly changed and broken man.

Another person in the community had also changed considerably. This was Jackson, the boarding-house keeper. He generally bore the character of being a steady, industrious man, but he suddenly developed a craving for drink, and as a consequence neglected his business, which, of course, declined, the result being an opposition house was started, and Jackson's once flourishing boarding establishment lost all its custom. Jackson drank harder than ever then, and even his wife gave way to the vice. At length, a year after the murder, Jackson sold off his effects, and he and his wife took their passage for England, in a ship called the *Gloriana*.

This ends the first part of the record, but the sequel – startling and inexplicable – has yet to be told.

The *Gloriana* was a large, full-rigged, clipper ship, one of a line trading between the mother country and the colonies. She was commanded by a hard-headed Scotchman, Captain Norman Douglas, who was well known in the trade, and, in fact, was one of the most popular skippers on that route. He bore the reputation of being a singularly conscientious and truthful man, and utterly without sentiment or superstition. There are no doubt plenty of people still living who were acquainted with him, who would unhesitatingly endorse this statement.

The *Gloriana* had a fair complement of passengers, first and second class. Amongst the first class were Jackson and his wife. It is necessary, in order to make what follows more clearly intelligible, to describe one portion of the ship. She was fitted with what was known in the old days as a "monkey poop", with an alloway or passage running on each side. This passage was reached from the main deck by three or four wooden steps. Right aft a short flight of steps led to the poop, on which was a hurricane house, with a companion way going down to the cuddy, or, as it is now called, the saloon. In the break of the poop, flush with the main deck, so that his window and door faced the bows of the vessel, was the captain's state-room, and alongside of his door was the entrance to the cuddy from the main deck. The Jacksons' cabin was the first in the cuddy on the left-hand side on entering, and next to the captain's, though it must be remembered that the captain had to come out of the cuddy to get into his room. That is, his door opened from the main deck, whereas the Jackson's opened from the cuddy, and consequently at right angles with the captain's.

The vessel made a splendid passage through Bass's Straits, the weather being magnificent, but it was noted with some astonishment that the Jacksons rarely appeared on deck, but remained in their cabin, and it was whispered about that Mr Jackson was almost constantly muddled more or less with drink. He and his wife kept to themselves, and seemed to carefully avoid their fellow passengers. One night, when the ship was well out in the South Pacific, and bowling along under double-reefed top-sails, Captain Douglas was sleeping soundly in the middle watch, when his door was suddenly opened, and Jackson precipitated himself into his room, dressed only in his night shirt. He was ghastly pale, was trembling like an aspen leaf, and seemed to be suffering from the effects of a terrible fright.

Naturally thinking that something was the matter, the captain sprang from his bed, and was surprised to find Jackson on his knees, his lips blanched, his face streaming with a cold perspiration.

"What is the meaning of this?" the captain demanded.

"For God's sake save me!" Jackson moaned in terror. "Save you from what and whom?" asked the captain, thinking that his passenger was suffering from delirium tremens.

"From her," groaned the man. "She all but lured me into the sea, but I broke the spell in time, and rushed in here."

This extraordinary remark naturally tended to confirm the captain's idea about the delirium, and so he soothed his passenger as well as he could, and then led him back to his cabin, where he noted that Mrs Jackson was soundly asleep in her bunk. He helped Jackson into his bunk, tucked him well up with the clothes, and left him; and as he came out of the cuddy on to the deck to reach his own room again, he started back until he all but fell, for it seemed to him that a flash of brilliant light had almost blinded him, while something soft touched his face. He thought that this might be a sea-bird, but what was the light?

It was the second mate's watch, and that officer was walking the poop, while the portion of the crew on duty were lying or sitting about in the waist of the vessel.

"Mr Harrington," sang out the captain to the second mate, "what was that light?"

"What light, sir?" asked the officer in astonishment.

"Why, didn't you see a brilliant flash of light?"

"No, sir," answered the officer, thinking the captain must have been indulging in a little too much grog.

"Ahoy, there, you fellows," roared the skipper to the watch on deck. "Where did that light come from?"

"What light, sir?" asked several voices.

"Good heavens! did you not see a flash of bright light?" exclaimed the captain angrily, for he thought he was being made a fool of.

"No, sir, we saw no light," answered the crew unanimously.

Captain Douglas was mystified. What did this mean? Was it a delusion? Had he been made a fool of by his senses, or what?

He went into his cabin again with his mind strangely disturbed. The ship was sailing splendidly, a heavy sea running after her, a gale was blowing, the sky was clear, the stars shining brightly, and neither in sea nor sky was there anything to account for that flash of light, or that *something* that had touched him. His officer and his men could not have been in collusion, and therefore Captain Douglas came to the conclusion that he had been made a fool of by his own senses, though, taken in connection with Jackson's strange remarks, Captain Douglas was affected as he had never been affected before.

Next day the crew told one another that "the old man" had been "soaking himself."

Captain Douglas was unusually thoughtful. He invited Jackson into his cabin and asked him what had been the matter with him during the night. Jackson appeared to be very ill, with a scared, cowed expression in his face. "I don't know," he replied a little sullenly, "I think I must have been dreaming."

"Well, I hope you won't dream again like that," remarked the captain, and then he told his own experience. As he heard this Jackson seemed to grow terrified again, and he groaned between chattering teeth:

"Heaven pity me then, it's a reality!"

"What is?" asked the astonished captain.

Jackson covered his face with his hands as he answered:

"Three times since we left Melbourne I have seen the vision of a woman, and she tries to lure me into the sea." He shuddered like one who was seized with palsy.

A few hours before this Captain Douglas would have roared with incredulous laughter had he been told such a thing. Now he was solemnly silent, for his own experience – the touch and the flash of light – permitted of no explanation that he could furnish. And so this tough old sailor, who had sailed the salt seas from his youth, and braved the perils of the deep in all parts of the world, was seized with a nameless fear that he could not allay.

The good ship continued to bowl along before favouring gales until she drew into the stormy ocean that roars around Cape Horn. During this time Jackson was seldom seen except for an hour or two in the early part of the day, when he and his wife would promenade the poop. He seemed to have changed very much. Everyone on board said that he looked ten years older since leaving Melbourne. His hair had blanched, his face was pallid and wrinkled, his eyes were restless as if from fear.

The vessel fell in with terrific weather off the Horn. Monstrous icebergs and field ice made navigation perilous, while the hurricane's wrath lashed the ice-strewn ocean into mountainous waves. The ship could only pursue her course under storm sails, and only then by ceaseless vigilance being exercised on the part of all the crew. For nearly a week the captain was on deck, snatching an hour or two's sleep as best he could during the twenty-four.

One night, when the *Gloriana* had nearly doubled the Horn, the weather seemed to grow worse, so that it became necessary to heave the ship to under a close-reefed main topsail. The sky was inky in its blackness. Not a star shone out from the ebony vault; but over the sea were vast flashing fields of phosphorescent foam as the giant waves broke with an awful roar; while looming in the blackness were ponderous icebergs in whose hollows the sea thundered. Now and again unusually terrific squalls came howling up from the south, bringing showers of jagged ice and hailstones as big as marbles. It was a night of horror and danger such as those who have never sailed in that stormy southern ocean can form but a faint conception of.

Vigilant and anxious, and clad in heavy sea-boots and oilskins, Captain Douglas stood on the poop with the chief mate; the second mate and several of the crew being on the forecastle straining their eyes on the look-out for the ice, while both in the main and foretop a man was lashed also on the look-out. Suddenly as the captain and chief officer stood together at the break of the poop sheltering themselves under the lee of a tarpaulin lashed in the rigging, the captain staggered, and seizing the officer's arm exclaimed hoarsely:

"My God! what is that?"

And well might he so exclaim, for to his horrified gaze there appeared on the main deck a mass of trembling light that in an instant seemed to change into a woman's figure, a woman with long, streaming fair hair, while round her white neck a scarf was twisted. The captain and his mate were transfixed with horror, for they both saw it. But they were to see even a more fearsome sight yet. The apparition rose, waving her arms the while, and floating out over the howling waste of black, writhing waters; and as she rose there suddenly darted from the cabin doorway the half-naked Jackson, his hair streaming in the wind. The apparition still waved her arm, still floated out away from the ship, and then, before the terror-stricken men who witnessed the awful sight could move to stop him, the wretched man uttered a scream of despair and fear that froze the blood of those who heard it, and with one bound he leapt into the boiling waters, and at that instant the apparition disappeared like a flash of lightning.

It was some moments before either of the two men had sufficiently recovered to speak. Then they asked each other if their senses had fooled them. But the captain, remembering his former experience, rushed to Jackson's cabin. Mrs Jackson alone was in it, and she was sleeping. It was no delusion then. Jackson had jumped overboard, lured by that ghost from the sea. It was impossible to make the slightest attempt to save him; he had gone down into the black and boiling waters never to rise again.

Mrs Jackson was not informed of her husband's suicide until the following day, and when she heard of it she fell down in a swoon; and, on recovering, it was found that she had lost her reason, so that it was necessary to watch and guard her for the rest of the voyage. On arrival in England it was deemed prudent to place her in an asylum, where she died six months later. No word ever escaped her lips that would have tended to elucidate the awful mystery. She seemed to be tortured with some indescribable anguish, and from morning till night she paced to and fro, wringing her hands and moaning piteously. But to those who witnessed that appalling scene off Cape Horn when Jackson went to his doom, the mystery required no explanation, for it explained itself: and that explanation was that it was he who had murdered poor Mrs Harvey, and the phantom of his victim had lured him to a terrible death.

Richard Marsh

A Set of Chessmen

"Richard Marsh", pseudonym of Richard Bernard Heldmann (1857–1915), was a prolific novelist whose greatest success was the horror novel The Beetle *(1897) which outsold its contemporary rival, Bram Stoker's* Dracula, *for several years, and was also adapted for stage and screen in England (long before the renaissance of* Dracula*)! "A Set of Chessmen" was the first of many dozens of weird and supernatural stories by Marsh which appeared in various popular magazines, and a few collections, over twenty-five years. It first appeared in* Cornhill Magazine *in April 1890, and was later included in his rare collection,* Both Sides of the Veil *(1901).*

I

"BUT, MONSIEUR, PERCEIVE how magnificent they are! There is not in Finistère, there is not in Brittany, nay, it is certain there is not in France so superb a set of chessmen. And ivory! And the carving – observe, for example, the variety of detail."

They certainly were a curious set of chessmen, magnificent in a way, but curious first of all. As M. Bobineau remarked, holding a rook in one hand and a knight in the other, the care paid to details by the carver really was surprising. But two hundred and fifty francs! For a set of chessmen!

"So, so, my friend. I am willing to admit that the work is good – in a kind of way. But two hundred and fifty francs! If it were fifty, now?"

"Fifty!" Up went M. Bobineau's shoulders, and down went M. Bobineau's head between them, in the fashion of those toys which are pulled by a string. "Ah, mon Dieu! Monsieur laughs at me!"

And there came another voluble declaration of their merits. They certainly were a curious set. I really think they were the most curious set I ever saw. I would have preferred them, for instance, to anything they have at South Kensington, and they have some remarkable examples there. And, of course, the price was small – I even admit it was ridiculously small. But when one has only five thousand francs a year for everything, two hundred and fifty being taken away – and for a set of chessmen – do leave a vacancy behind. I asked Bobineau where he got them. Business was slack that sunny afternoon – it seemed to me that I was the only customer he ever had, but that must have been a delusion on my part. Report said he was a warm man, one of Morlaix's warmest men, and his queer old shop in the queer old Grande Rue – Grande Rue! what a name for an alley! – contained many things which were valuable as well as queer. But there, at least, was no other customer in sight just then, so Bobineau told me all the tale.

It seemed there had been a M. Funichon – Auguste Funichon – no, not a Breton, a Parisian, a true Parisian, who had come and settled down in the commune of Plouigneau, over by the *gare*. This M. Funichon was, for example, a little – well, a little – a little *exalted*, let us say. It is true that the country people said he was stark mad, but Bobineau, for his part, said non, no, no! It is not necessary, because one is a little eccentric, that one is mad. Here Bobineau looked at me out of the corner of his eye. Are not the English, of all people, the most eccentric, and yet is it not known to all the world that they are not, necessarily, stark mad? This M. Funichon was not rich, quite the contrary. It was a little place he lived in – the merest cottage, in fact. And in it he lived alone, and, according to report, there was only one thing he did all day and all night long, and that was, play chess. It appears that he was that rarest and most amiable of imbeciles, a chess-maniac. Is there such a word?

"What a life!" said M. Bobineau. "Figure it to yourself! To do nothing – nothing! – but play chess! They say" – M. Bobineau looked round him with an air of mystery – "they say he starved himself to death. He was so besotted by his miserable chess that he forgot – absolutely forgot, this imbecile – to eat."

That was what M. Bobineau said they said. It required a vigorous effort of the imagination to quite take it in. To what a state of forgetfulness must a man arrive before he forgets to eat! But whether M. Funichon forgot to eat, or whether he didn't, at least he died, and being dead they sold his goods – why they sold them was not quite clear, but at the sale M. Bobineau was the chief purchaser. One of the chief lots was the set of ivory chessmen which had caught my eye. They were the dead man's favourite set, and no wonder! Bobineau was of the opinion that if he had had his way he would have had them buried with him in his grave.

"It is said," he whispered, again with the glance of mystery around, "that they found him dead, seated at the table, the chessmen on the board, his hand on the white rook, which was giving mate to the adversary's king."

Either what a vivid imagination had Bobineau or what odd things the people said! One pictures the old man, seated all alone, with his last breath finishing his game.

Well, I bought the set of ivory chessmen. At this time of day I freely admit that they were cheap at two hundred and fifty francs – dirt cheap, indeed; but a hundred was all I paid. I knew Bobineau so well – I daresay he bought them for twenty-five. As I bore them triumphantly away my mind was occupied by thoughts of their original possessor. I was filled by quite a sentimental tenderness as I meditated on the part they had played, according to Bobineau, in that last scene. But St Servan drove all those things away. Philippe Henri de St Servan was rather a difficult person to get on with. It was with him I shared at that time my apartment on the *place*.

"Let us see!" I remarked when I got in, "what have I here?"

He was seated, his country pipe in his mouth, at the open window, looking down upon the river. The Havre boat was making ready to start – at Morlaix the nautical event of the week. There was quite a bustle on the quay. St Servan just looked round, and then looked back again. I sat down and untied my purchase.

"I think there have been criticisms – derogatory criticisms – passed by a certain person upon a certain set of chessmen. Perhaps that person will explain what he has to say to these."

St Servan marched up to the table. He looked at them through his half-closed eyelids.

"Toys!" was all he said.

"Perhaps! Yet toys which made a tragedy. Have you ever heard of the name of Funichon?" By a slight movement of his grisly grey eyebrows he intimated that it was possible he had. "These chessmen belonged to him. He had just finished a game with them when they found him dead – the winning piece, a white rook, was in his hand. Suggest an epitaph to be placed over his grave. There's a picture for a painter – eh?"

"Bah! He was a Communist!"

That was all St Servan said. And so saying, St Servan turned away to look out of the window at the Havre boat again. There was an end of M. Funichon for him. Not that he meant exactly what he said. He simply meant that M. Funichon was not Legitimist – out of sympathy with the gentlemen who met, and decayed, visibly, before the naked eye, at the club on the other side of the *place*. With St Servan not to be Legitimist meant to be nothing at all – out of his range of vision absolutely. Seeing that was so, it is strange he should have borne with me as he did. But he was a wonderful old man.

II

We played our first game with the ivory chessmen when St Servan returned from the club. I am free to confess that it was an occasion for me. I had dusted all the pieces, and had the board all laid when St Servan entered, and when we drew for choice of moves the dominant feeling in my mind was the thought of the dead man sitting all alone, with the white rook in his hand. There was an odour of sanctity about the affair – a whiff of air from the land of the ghosts.

Nevertheless, my loins were girded up, and I was prepared to bear myself as a man in the strife. We were curiously well matched, St Servan and I. We had played two hundred and twenty games, and, putting draws aside, each had scored the same number of wins. He had his days, and so had I. At one time I was eleven games ahead, but since that thrice blessed hour I had not scored a single game. He had tracked me steadily, and eventually had made the scores exactly tie. In these latter days it had grown with him to be an article of faith that as a chess-player I was quite played out – and there was a time when I had thought the same of him!

He won the move, and then, as usual, there came an interval for reflection. The worst thing about St Servan – regarded from a chess-playing point of view – was, that he took such a time to begin. When a man has opened his game it is excusable – laudable, indeed – if he pauses to reflect, a reasonable length of time. But I never knew a man who was so fond of reflection before a move was made. As a rule, that absurd habit of his had quite an irritating effect upon my nerves, but that evening I felt quite cool and prepared to sit him out.

There we sat, both smoking our great pipes, he staring at the board, and I at him. He put out his hand, almost touched a piece, and then, with a start, he drew it back again. An interval – the same pantomime again. Another interval – and a repetition of the pantomime. I puffed a cloud of smoke into the air, and softly sighed. I knew he had been ten minutes by my watch. Possibly the sign had a stimulating effect, for he suddenly stretched out his hand and moved queen's knight's pawn a single square.

I was startled. He was great at book openings, that was the absurdest part of it. He would lead you to suppose that he was meditating something quite original, and then would perhaps begin with fool's mate after all. He, at least, had never tried queen's knight's pawn a single square before.

I considered a reply. Pray let it be understood – though I would not have confessed it to St Servan for the world – that I am no player. I am wedded to the same for an hour or two at night, or, peradventure, of an afternoon at times; but I shall never be admitted to its inner mysteries – never! Not if I outspan Methuselah. I am not built that way. St Servan and I were two children who, loving the sea, dabble their feet in the shallows left by the tide. I have no doubt that there are a dozen replies to that opening of his, but I did not know one then. I had some hazy idea of developing a game of my own, while keeping an eye on his, and for that purpose put out my hand to move the queen's pawn two, when I felt my wrist grasped by – well, by what felt uncommonly like an invisible hand. I was so startled that I almost dropped my pipe. I drew my hand back again, and was conscious of the slight detaining pressure of unseen fingers. Of course it was hallucination, but it seemed so real, and was so expected, that – well, I settled my pipe more firmly between my lips – it had all but fallen from my mouth, and took a whiff or two to calm my nerves. I glanced up, cautiously, to see if St Servan noticed my unusual behaviour, but his eyes were fixed stonily upon the board.

After a moment's hesitation – it was absurd! – I stretched out my hand again. The hallucination was repeated, and in a very tangible form. I was distinctly conscious of my wrist being wrenched aside and guided to a piece I had never meant to touch, and almost before I was aware of it, instead of the move I had meant to make, I had made a servile copy of St Servan's opening – I had moved queen's knight's pawn a single square!

To adopt the language of the late Dick Swiveller, that was a staggerer. I own that for an instant I was staggered. I could do nothing else but stare. For at least ten seconds I forgot to smoke. I was conscious that when St Servan saw my move he knit his brows. Then the usual interval for reflection came again. Half unconsciously I watched him. When, as I supposed, he had decided on his move, he stretched out his hand, as I had done, and also, as I had done, he drew it back again. I was a little startled – he seemed a little startled too. There was a momentary pause; back went his hand again, and, by way of varying the monotony, he moved – king's knight's pawn a single square.

I wondered, and held my peace. There might be a gambit based upon these lines, or there might not; but since I was quite clear that I knew no reply to such an opening I thought I would try a little experiment, and put out my hand, not with the slightest conception of any particular move in my head, but simply to see what happened. Instantly a grasp fastened on my wrist; my hand was guided to – king's knight's pawn a single square.

This was getting, from every point of view, to be distinctly interesting. The chessmen appeared to be possessed of a property of which Bobineau had been unaware. I caught myself wondering if he would have insisted on a higher price if he had known of it. Curiosities nowadays do fetch such fancy sums – and what price for a ghost? They appeared to be automatic chessmen, automatic in a sense entirely their own.

Having made my move, or having had somebody else's move made for me, which is perhaps the more exact way of putting it, I contemplated my antagonist. When he saw what I had done, or what somebody else had done – the things are equal – St Servan frowned. He belongs to the bony variety, the people who would not loll in a chair to save their lives – his aspect struck me as being even more poker-like than usual. He meditated his reply an unconscionable length of time, the more unconscionable since I strongly doubted if it would be his reply after all. But at last he showed signs of action. He kept his eyes fixed steadily upon the board, his frown became pronounced, and he began to raise his hand. I write "began," because it was a process which took some time. Cautiously he brought it up, inch by inch. But no sooner had he brought it over the board than his behaviour became quite singular. He positively glared, and to my eyes seemed to be having a struggle with his own right hand. A struggle in which he was worsted, for he leant back in his seat with a curiously discomfited air.

He had moved queen's rook's pawn two squares – the automatic principle which impelled these chessmen seemed to have a partiality for pawns.

It was my turn for reflection. I pressed the tobacco down in my pipe, and thought – or tried to think – it out. Was it an hallucination, and was St Servan the victim of hallucination too? Had I moved those pawns spontaneously, actuated by the impulse of my own free will, or hadn't I? And what was the meaning of the little scene I had just observed? I am a tolerably strong man. It would require no slight exercise of force to compel me to move one piece when I had made up my mind that I would move another piece instead. I have been told, and I believe not altogether untruly told, that the rigidity of my right wrist resembles iron. I have not spent so much time in the tennis-court and fencing-room for nothing. I had tried one experiment. I thought I would try another. I made up my mind that I would move queen's pawn two – stop me who stop can.

I felt that St Servan in his turn was watching me. Preposterously easy though the feat appeared to be as I resolved on its performance, I was conscious of an unusual degree of cerebral excitement – a sort of feeling of do or die. But as, in spite of the feeling, I didn't do, it was perhaps as well I didn't die. Intending to keep complete control over my own muscles, I raised my right hand, probably to the full as cautiously as St Servan had done. I approached the queen's pawn. I was just about to seize the piece when that unseen grasp fastened on my wrist. I paused, with something of the feeling which induces the wrestler to pause before entering on the veritable tug of war. For one thing, I was desirous to satisfy myself as to the nature of the grasp – what it was that seemed to grasp me.

It seemed to be a hand. The fingers went over the back of my wrist, and the thumb beneath. The fingers were long and thin – it was altogether a slender hand. But it seemed to be a man's hand, and an old man's hand at that. The skin was tough and wrinkled, clammy and cold. On the little finger there was a ring, and on the first, about the region of the first joint, appeared to be something of the nature of a wart. I should say that it was anything but a beautiful hand, it was altogether too attenuated and clawlike, and I would have betted that it was yellow with age.

At first the pressure was slight, almost as slight as the touch of a baby's hand, with a gentle inclination to one side. But as I kept my own hand firm, stiff, resolved upon my own particular move, with, as it were, a

sudden snap, the pressure tightened and, not a little to my discomfiture, I felt my wrist held as in an iron vice. Then, as it must have seemed to St Servan, who, I was aware, was still keenly watching me, I began to struggle with my own hand. The spectacle might have been fun to him, but the reality was, at that moment, anything but fun to me. I was dragged to one side. Another hand was fastened upon mine. My fingers were forced open – I had tightly clenched my fist to enable me better to resist – my wrist was forced down, my fingers were closed upon a piece, I was compelled to move it forward, my fingers were unfastened to replace the piece upon the board. The move completed, the unseen grasp instantly relaxed, and I was free, or appeared to be free, again to call my hand my own.

I had moved queen's rook's pawn two squares. This may seem comical enough to read about, but it was anything but comical to feel. When the thing was done I stared at St Servan, and St Servan stared at me. We stared at each other, I suppose a good long minute, then I broke the pause.

"Anything the matter?" I inquired. He put up his hand and curled his moustache, and, if I may say so, he curled his lip as well. "Do you notice anything odd about – about the game?" As I spoke about the game I motioned my hand towards my brand-new set of chessmen. He looked at me with hard suspicious eyes.

"Is it a trick of yours?" he asked.

"Is what a trick of mine?"

"If you do not know, then how should I?"

I drew a whiff or two from my pipe, looking at him keenly all the time, then signed towards the board with my hand.

"It's your move," I said.

He merely inclined his head. There was a momentary pause. When he stretched out his hand he suddenly snatched it back again, and half started from his seat with a stifled execration.

"Did you feel anything upon your wrist?" I asked.

"Mon Dieu! It is not what I feel – see that!"

He was eyeing his wrist as he spoke. He held it out under the glare of the lamp. I bent across and looked at it. For so old a man he had a phenomenally white and delicate skin – under the glare of the lamp the impressions of finger-marks were plainly visible upon his wrist. I whistled as I saw them.

"Is it a trick of yours?" he asked again.

"It is certainly no trick of mine."

"Is there anyone in the room besides us two?"

I shrugged my shoulders and looked round. He too looked round, with something I thought not quite easy in his glance.

"Certainly no one of my acquaintance, and certainly no one who is visible to me!"

With his fair white hand – the left, not the one which had the finger-marks upon the wrist – St Servan smoothed his huge moustache.

"Someone, or something, has compelled me – yes, from the first – to move, not as I would, but – bah! I know not how."

"Exactly the same thing has occurred to me."

I laughed. St Servan glared. Evidently the humour of the thing did not occur to him, he being the sort of man who would require a surgical operation to make him see a joke. But the humorous side of the situation struck me forcibly.

"Perhaps we are favoured by the presence of a ghost – perhaps even by the ghost of M. Funichon. Perhaps, after all, he has not yet played his last game with his favourite set. He may have returned – shall we say from – where? – to try just one more set-to with us! If, my dear sir" – I waved my pipe affably, as though addressing an unseen personage – "it is really you, I beg you will reveal yourself – materialize is, I believe, the expression now in vogue – and show us the sort of ghost you are!"

Somewhat to my surprise, and considerably to my amusement, St Servan rose from his seat and stood by the table, stiff and straight as a scaffold-pole.

"These, Monsieur, are subjects on which one does not jest."

"Do you, then, believe in ghosts?" I knew he was a superstitious man – witness his fidelity to the superstition of right divine – but this was the first inkling I had had of how far his superstition carried him.

"Believe! – In ghosts! In what, then, do you believe? I, Monsieur, am a religious man."

"Do you believe, then, that a ghost is present with us now – the ghost, for instance, of M. Funichon?"

St Servan paused. Then he crossed himself – actually crossed himself before my eyes. When he spoke there was a peculiar dryness in his tone.

"With your permission, Monsieur, I will retire to bed."

There was an exasperating thing to say! There must be a large number of men in the world who would give – well, a good round sum, to light even on the trail of a ghost. And here were we in the actual presence of

something – let us say apparently curious, at any rate, and here was St
Servan calmly talking about retiring to bed, without making the slightest
attempt to examine the thing! It was enough to make the members of the
Psychical Research Society turn in their graves. The mere suggestion
fired my blood.

, "I do beg, St Servan, that you at least will finish the game." I saw he
hesitated, so I drove the nail well home. "Is it possible that you, a brave
man, having given proofs of courage upon countless fields, can turn tail
at what is doubtless an hallucination after all?"

"Is it that Monsieur doubts my courage?"

I knew the tone – if I was not careful I should have an affair upon my
hands.

"Come, St Servan, sit down and finish the game."

Another momentary pause. He sat down, and – it would not be
correct to write that we finished the game, but we made another effort to
go on. My pipe had gone out. I refilled and lighted it.

"You know, St Servan, it is really nonsense to talk about ghosts."

"It is a subject on which I never talk."

"If something does compel us to make moves which we do not intend,
it is something which is capable of a natural explanation."

"Perhaps Monsieur will explain it, then?"

"I will! Before I've finished! If you only won't turn tail and go to bed! I
think it very possible, too, that the influence, whatever it is, has gone – it
is quite on the cards that our imagination has played us some subtle trick.
It is your move, but before you do anything just tell me what move you
mean to make."

"I will move" – he hesitated – "I will move queen's pawn."

He put out his hand, and, with what seemed to me hysterical suddenness, he moved king's rook's pawn two squares.

"So! our friend is still here then! I suppose you did not change your
mind?"

There was a very peculiar look about St Servan's eyes.

"I did not change my mind."

I noticed, too, that his lips were uncommonly compressed.

"It is my move now. *I* will move queen's pawn. We are not done yet.
When I put out my hand you grasp my wrist – and we shall see what we
shall see."

"Shall I come round to you?"

"No, stretch out across the table – now!"

I stretched out my hand; that instant he stretched out his, but spontaneous though the action seemed to be, another, an unseen hand, had fastened on my wrist. He observed it too.

"There appears to be another hand between yours and mine."

"I know there is."

Before I had the words well out my hand had been wrenched aside, my fingers unclosed, and then closed, then unclosed again, and I had moved king's rook's pawn two squares. St Servan and I sat staring at each other – for my part I felt a little bewildered.

"This is very curious! Very curious indeed! But before we say anything about it we will try another little experiment, if you don't mind. I will come over to you." I went over to him. "Let me grasp your wrist with both my hands." I grasped it, as firmly as I could, as it lay upon his knee. "Now try to move queen's pawn."

He began to raise his hand, I holding on to his wrist with all my strength. Hardly had he raised it to the level of the table when two unseen hands, grasping mine, tore them away as though my strength were of no account. I saw him give a sort of shudder – he had moved queen's bishop's pawn two squares.

"This is a devil of a ghost!" I said.

St Servan said nothing. But he crossed himself, not once, but half a dozen times.

"There is still one little experiment that I would wish to make."

St Servan shook his head.

"Not I!" he said.

"Ah but, my friend, this is an experiment which I can make without your aid. I simply want to know if there is nothing tangible about our unseen visitor except his hands. It is my move." I returned to my side of the table. I again addressed myself, as it were, to an unseen auditor. "My good ghost, my good M. Funichon – if it is you – you are at liberty to do as you desire with my hand."

I held it out. It instantly was grasped. With my left hand I made several passes in the air up and down, behind and before, in every direction so far as I could. It met with no resistance. There seemed to be nothing tangible but those invisible fingers which grasped my wrist – and I had moved queen's bishop's pawn two squares.

St Servan rose from his seat.

"It is enough. Indeed it is too much. This ribaldry must cease. It had been better had Monsieur permitted me to retire to bed."

"Then you are sure it is a ghost – the ghost of M. Funichon, we'll say?"

"This time Monsieur must permit me to wish him a good night's rest."

He bestowed on me, as his manner was, a stiff inclination of the head, which would have led a stranger to suppose that we had met each other for the first time ten minutes ago, instead of being the acquaintances of twelve good years. He moved across the room.

"St Servan, one moment before you go! You are surely not going to leave a man alone at the post of peril?"

"It were better that Monsieur should come too."

"Half a second, and I will. I have only one remark to make, and that is to the ghost."

I rose from my seat. St Servan made a half-movement towards the door, then changed his mind and remained quite still.

"If there is any other person with us in the room, may I ask that person to let us hear his voice, or hers? Just to speak one word."

Not a sound.

"It is possible – I am not acquainted with the laws which govern – eh – ghosts that the faculty of speech is denied to them. If that be so, might I ask for the favour of a sign – for instance, move a piece while my friend and I are standing where we are?"

Not a sign; not a chessman moved.

"Then M. Funichon, if it indeed be you, and you are incapable of speech, or even of moving a piece of your own accord, and are only able to spoil our game, I beg to inform you that you are an exceedingly ill-mannered and foolish person, and had far better have stayed away."

As I said this I was conscious of a current of cold air before my face, as though a swiftly moving hand had shaved my cheek.

"By jove, St Servan, something has happened at last. I believe our friend the ghost has tried to box my ears!"

St Servan's reply came quietly stern.

"I think it were better that Monsieur came with me."

For some reason St Servan's almost contemptuous coldness fired my blood. I became suddenly enraged.

"I shall do nothing of the kind! Do you think I am going to be fooled by a trumpery conjuring trick which would disgrace a shilling séance? Driven to bed at this time of day by a ghost! And such a ghost! If it were something like a ghost one wouldn't mind; but a fool of a ghost like this!"

Even as the words passed my lips I felt the touch of fingers against my throat. The touch increased my rage. I snatched at them, only to find that there was nothing there.

"Damn you!" I cried. "Funichon, you old fool, do you think that you can frighten me? You see those chessmen; they are mine, bought and paid for with my money – you dare to try and prevent me doing with them exactly as I please."

Again the touch against my throat. It made my rage the more. "As I live, I will smash them all to pieces, and grind them to powder beneath my heel."

My passion was ridiculous – childish even. But then the circumstances were exasperating – unusually so, one might plead. I was standing three or four feet from the table. I dashed forward. As I did so a hand was fastened on my throat. Instantly it was joined by another. They gripped me tightly. They maddened me. With a madman's fury I still pressed forward. I might as well have fought with fate. They clutched me as with bands of steel, and flung me to the ground.

III

When I recovered consciousness I found St Servan bending over me.

"What is the matter?" I inquired, when I found that I was lying on the floor.

"I think you must have fainted."

"Fainted! I never did such a thing in my life. It must have been a curious kind of faint, I think."

"It was a curious kind of faint."

With his assistance I staggered to my feet. I felt bewildered. I glanced round. There were the chessmen still upon the board, the hanging lamp above. I tried to speak. I seemed to have lost the use of my tongue. In silence he helped me to the door. He half led, half carried me – for I seemed to have lost the use of my feet as well as that of my tongue – to my bedroom. He even assisted me to undress, never leaving me till I was between the sheets. All the time not a word was spoken. When he went I believe he took the key outside and locked the door.

That was a night of dreams. I know not if I was awake or sleeping, but all sorts of strange things presented themselves to my mental eye. I could not shut them from my sight. One figure was prominent in all I saw – the figure of a man. I knew, or thought I knew, that it was M. Funichon. He was a lean old man, and what I noticed chiefly were his hands. Such ugly hands! In some fantastical way I seemed to be contending with them all through the night.

And yet in the morning when I woke – for I did wake up, and that from as sweet refreshing sleep as one might wish to have – it was all gone. It was bright day. The sun was shining into the great, ill-furnished room. As I got out of bed and began to dress, the humorous side of the thing had returned to me again. The idea of there being anything supernatural about a set of ivory chessmen appeared to me to be extremely funny.

I found St Servan had gone out. It was actually half-past ten! His table d'hôte at the Hôtel de Bretagne was at eleven, and before he breakfasted he always took a *petit verre* at the club. If he had locked the door overnight he had not forgotten to unlock it before he started. I went into the rambling, barnlike room which served us for a salon. The chessmen had disappeared. Probably St Servan had put them away – I wondered if the ghost had interfered with him. I laughed to myself as I went out – fancy St Servan contending with a ghost.

The proprietor of the Hôtel de Bretagne is Legitimist, so all the aristocrats go there – of course, St Servan with the rest. Presumably the landlord's politics is the point, to his cooking they are apparently indifferent – I never knew a worse table in my life! The landlord of the Hôtel de l'Europe may be a Communist for all I care – *his* cooking is first-rate, so I go there. I went there that morning. After I had breakfasted I strolled off towards the Grande Rue, to M. Bobineau.

When he saw me M. Bobineau was all smirks and smiles – he must have got those chessmen for *less* than five-and-twenty francs! I asked him if he had any more of the belongings of M. Funichon.

"But certainly! Three other sets of chessmen."

I didn't want to look at those, apparently one set was quite enough for me. Was that all he had?

"But no! There was an ancient bureau, very magnificent, carved" –

I thanked him – nor did I want to look at that. In the Grande Rue at Morlaix old bureaux carved about the beginning of the fifteenth century – if you listen to the vendors – are as plentiful as cobblestones.

"But I have all sorts of things of M. Funichon. It was I who bought them nearly all. Books, papers, and – "

M. Bobineau waved his hands towards a multitude of books and papers which crowded the shelves at the side of his shop. I took a volume down. When I opened it I found it was in manuscript.

"That work is unique!" explained Bobineau. "It was the intention of M. Funichon to give it to the world, but he died before his purpose was complete. It is the record of all the games of chess he ever played – in fifty volumes. Monsieur will perceive it is unique."

I should think it was unique! In fifty volumes! The one I held was a large quarto, bound in leather, containing some six or seven hundred pages, and was filled from cover to cover with matter in a fine, clear handwriting, written on both sides of the page. I pictured the face of the publisher to whom it was suggested that *he* should give to the world such a work as that.

I opened the volume at the first page. It was, as Bobineau said, apparently the record, with comments, of an interminable series of games of chess. I glanced at the initial game. Here are the opening moves, just as they were given there.

White	*Black*
Queen's Knight's Pawn, one square.	Queen's Knight's Pawn, one square.
King's Knight's Pawn, one square.	King's Knight's Pawn, one square.
Queen's Rook's Pawn, two squares.	Queen's Rook's Pawn, two squares.
King's Rook's Pawn, two squares.	King's Rook's Pawn, two squares.

They were exactly the moves of the night before. They were such peculiar moves, and made under such peculiar circumstances, that I was scarcely likely to mistake them. So far as we had gone, St Servan and I, assisted by the unseen hand, had reproduced M. Funichon's initial game in the first volume of his fifty – and a very peculiar game it seemed to be. I asked Bobineau what he would take for the volume which I held.

"Monsieur perceives that to part them would spoil the set, which is unique. Monsieur shall have the whole fifty" – I shuddered. I imagine Bobineau saw I did, he spoke so very quickly – "for a five-franc piece, which is less than the value of the paper and the binding."

I knew then that he had probably been paid for carting the rubbish away. However, I paid him his five-franc piece, and marched off with the volume under my arm, giving him to understand, to his evident disappointment, that at my leisure I would give him instructions as to the other forty-nine.

As I went along I thought the matter over. M. Funichon seemed to have been a singular kind of man – he appeared to have carried his

singularity even beyond the grave. Could it have been the cold-blooded
intention of his ghost to make us play the whole contents of the fifty
volumes through? What a fiend of a ghost his ghost must be!

I opened the volume and studied the initial game. The people were
right who had said that the man was mad. None but an imbecile would
have played such a game – his right hand against his left! – and none but
a raving madman would have recorded his imbecility in black and white,
as though it were a thing to be proud of! Certainly none but a criminal
lunatic would have endeavoured to foist his puerile travesty of the game
and study of chess upon two innocent men.

Still the thing was curious. I flattered myself that St Servan would be
startled when he saw the contents of the book I was carrying home. I
resolved that I would instantly get out the chessmen and begin another
game – perhaps the ghost of M. Funichon would favour us with a further
exposition of his ideas of things. I even made up my mind that I would
communicate with the Psychical Research Society. Not at all improbably
they might think the case sufficiently remarkable to send down a member
of their body to inquire into the thing upon the spot. I almost began to
hug myself on the possession of a ghost, a ghost, too, which might be
induced to perform at will – almost on the principle of "drop a coin into
the slot and the figures move"! It was cheap at a hundred francs. What a
stir those chessmen still might make! What vexed problems they might
solve! Unless I was much mistaken, the expenditure of those hundred
francs had placed me on the royal road to immortality.

Filled with such thoughts I reached our rooms. I found that St Servan
had returned. With him, if I may say so, he had brought his friends. Such
friends! Ye Goths! When I opened the door the first thing which greeted
me was a strong, not to say suffocating, smell of incense. The room was
filled with smoke. A fire was blazing on the hearth. Before it was St
Servan, on his knees, his hands clasped in front of him, in an attitude of
prayer. By him stood a priest, in his robes of office. He held what seemed
a pestle and mortar, whose contents he was throwing by handfuls on to
the flames, muttering some doggerel to himself the while. Behind him
were two acolytes,

> With nice clean faces, and nice white stoles,

who were swinging censers – hence the odour which filled the room. I
was surprised when I beheld all this. They appeared to be holding some

sort of religious service – and I had not bargained for that sort of thing when I had arranged with St Servan to share the rooms with him. In my surprise I unconsciously interrupted the proceedings.

"St Servan! Whatever is the meaning of this?"

St Servan looked up, and the priest looked round – that was all the attention they paid to me. The acolytes eyed me with what I conceived to be a grin upon their faces. But I was not to be put down like that.

"I must ask you, St Servan, for an explanation."

The priest turned the mortar upside down, and emptied the remainder of its contents into the fire.

"It is finished," he said.

St Servan rose from his knees and crossed himself.

"We have exorcised the demon," he observed.

"You have what?" I asked.

"We have driven out the evil spirit which possessed the chessmen."

I gasped. A dreadful thought struck me.

"You don't mean to say that you have dared to play tricks with my property?"

"Monsieur," said the priest, "I have ground it into dust."

He had. That fool of a St Servan had actually fetched his parish priest and his acolytes and their censers, and between them they had performed a comminatory service made and provided for the driving out of demons. They had ground my ivory chessmen in the pestle and mortar, and then burned them in the fire. And this in the days of the Psychical Research Society! And they had cost me a hundred francs! And that idiot of a ghost had never stretched out a hand or said a word!

Bram Stoker

The Judge's House

Bram Stoker (1847–1912), creator of the immortal Dracula, *wrote several compelling and horrific short tales in the 1880s and 1890s, notably "The Burial of the Rats", "The Squaw", and "The Dualitists". His best ghost story, "The Judge's House", first appeared in* Holly Leaves, the Christmas number of The Illustrated and Sporting Dramatic News *(5 December 1891).*

WHEN THE TIME for his examination drew near Malcolm Malcolmson made up his mind to go somewhere to read by himself. He feared the attractions of the seaside, and also he feared completely rural isolation, for of old he knew its charms, and so he determined to find some unpretentious little town where there would be nothing to distract him. He refrained from asking suggestions from any of his friends, for he argued that each would recommend some place of which he had knowledge, and where he had already acquaintances. As Malcolmson wished to avoid friends he had no wish to encumber himself with the attention of friends' friends, and so he determined to look out for a place for himself. He packed a portmanteau with some clothes and all the books he required, and then took a ticket for the first name on the local time-table which he did not know.

When at the end of three hours' journey he alighted at Benchurch, he felt satisfied that he had so far obliterated his tracks as to be sure of having a peaceful opportunity of pursuing his studies. He went straight to the one inn which the sleepy little place contained, and put up for the night. Benchurch was a market town, and once in three weeks was crowded to excess, but for the remainder of the twenty-one days it was as attractive as a desert. Malcolmson looked around the day after his arrival to try to find quarters more isolated than even so quiet an inn as The Good Traveller afforded. There was only one place which took his fancy, and it certainly satisfied his wildest ideas regarding quiet; in fact, quiet was not the proper word to apply to it – desolation was the only term conveying any suitable idea of its isolation. It was an old rambling, heavy-built house of the Jacobean style, with heavy gables and windows, unusually small, and set higher than was customary in such houses, and was surrounded with a high brick wall massively built. Indeed, on examination, it looked more like a fortified house than an ordinary dwelling. But all these things pleased Malcolmson. "Here," he thought, "is the very spot I have been looking for, and if I can only get opportunity of using it I shall be happy." His joy was increased when he realized beyond doubt that it was not at present inhabited.

From the post-office he got the name of the agent, who was rarely surprised at the application to rent a part of the old house. Mr Carnford, the local lawyer and agent, was a genial old gentleman, and frankly confessed his delight at anyone being willing to live in the house.

"To tell you the truth," said he, "I should be only too happy, on behalf of the owners, to let anyone have the house rent free for a term of years if only to accustom the people here to see it inhabited. It has been so long empty that some kind of absurd prejudice has grown up about it, and this can be best put down by its occupation – if only," he added with a sly glance at Malcolmson, "by a scholar like yourself, who wants it quiet for a time."

Malcolmson thought it needless to ask the agent about the "absurd prejudice"; he knew he would get more information, if he should require it, on that subject from other quarters. He paid his three months' rent, got a receipt, and the name of an old woman who would probably undertake to "do" for him, and came away with the keys in his pocket. He then went to the landlady of the inn, who was a cheerful and most kindly person, and asked her advice as to such stores and provisions as he would be likely to require. She threw up her hands in amazement when he told her where he was going to settle himself.

"Not in the Judge's House!" she said, and grew pale as she spoke. He explained the locality of the house, saying that he did not know its name. When he had finished she answered:

"Aye, sure enough – sure enough the very place! It is the Judge's House sure enough." He asked her to tell him about the place, why so called, and what there was against it. She told him that it was so called locally because it had been many years before – how long she could not say, as she was herself from another part of the country, but she thought it must have been a hundred years or more – the abode of a judge who was held in great terror on account of his harsh sentences and his hostility to prisoners at Assizes. As to what there was against the house itself she could not tell. She had often asked, but no one could inform her; but there was a general feeling that there was *something*, and for her own part she would not take all the money in Drinkwater's Bank and stay in the house an hour by herself. Then she apologized to Malcolmson for her disturbing talk.

"It is too bad of me, sir, and you – and a young gentleman, too – if you will pardon me saying it, going to live there all alone. If you were my boy – and you'll excuse me for saying it – you wouldn't sleep there a night, not if I had to go there myself and pull the big alarm bell that's on the roof!" The good creature was so manifestly in earnest, and was so kindly in her intentions, that Malcolmson, although amused, was touched. He told her kindly how much he appreciated her interest in him, and added:

"But, my dear Mrs Witham, indeed you need not be concerned about me! A man who is reading for the Mathematical Tripos has too much to think of to be disturbed by any of these mysterious 'somethings', and his work is of too exact and prosaic a kind to allow of his having any corner of his mind for mysteries of any kind. Harmonical Progression, Permutations and Combinations, and Elliptic Functions have sufficient mysteries for me!" Mrs Witham kindly undertook to see after his commissions, and he went himself to look for the old woman who had been recommended to him. When he returned to the Judge's House with her, after an interval of a couple of hours, he found Mrs Witham herself waiting with several men and boys carrying parcels, and an upholsterer's man with a bed in a cart, for she said, though tables and chairs might be all very well, a bed that hadn't been aired for mayhap fifty years was not proper for young bones to lie on. She was evidently curious to see the inside of the house; and though manifestly so afraid of the "somethings" that at the slightest sound she clutched on to Malcolmson, whom she never left for a moment, went over the whole place. After his examination of the house, Malcolmson decided to take up his abode in the great dining-room, which was big enough to serve for all his requirements; and Mrs Witham, with the aid of the charwoman, Mrs Dempster, proceeded to arrange matters. When the hampers were brought in and unpacked, Malcolmson saw that with much kind forethought she had sent from her own kitchen sufficient provisions to last for a few days. Before going she expressed all sorts of kind wishes; and at the door turned and said:

"And perhaps, sir, as the room is big and draughty it might be well to have one of those big screens put round your bed at night – though, truth to tell, I would die myself if I were to be so shut in with all kinds of – of 'things', that put their heads round the sides, or over the top, and look on me!" The image which she had called up was too much for her nerves, and she fled incontinently.

Mrs Dempster sniffed in a superior manner as the landlady disappeared, and remarked that for her own part she wasn't afraid of all the bogies in the kingdom.

"I'll tell you what it is, sir," she said; "bogies is all kinds and sorts of things – except bogies! Rats and mice, and beetles; and creaky doors, and loose slates, and broken panes, and stiff drawer handles, that stay out when you pull them and then fall down in the middle of the night. Look at the wainscot of the room! It is old – hundreds of years old! Do you think there's no rats and beetles there! And do you imagine, sir, that you won't see none of them! Rats is bogies, I tell you, and bogies is rats; and don't you get to think anything else!"

"Mrs Dempster," said Malcolmson gravely, making her a polite bow, "you know more than a Senior Wrangler! And let me say, that, as a mark of esteem for your indubitable soundness of head and heart, I shall, when I go, give you possession of this house, and let you stay here by yourself for the last two months of my tenancy, for four weeks will serve my purpose."

"Thank you kindly, sir!" she answered, "but I couldn't sleep away from home a night. I am in Greenhow's Charity, and if I slept a night away from my rooms I should lose all I have got to live on. The rules is very strict; and there's too many watching for a vacancy for me to run any risks in the matter. Only for that, sir, I'd gladly come here and attend on you altogether during your stay."

"My good woman," said Malcolmson hastily, "I have come here on purpose to obtain solitude; and believe me that I am grateful to the late Greenhow for having so organized his admirable charity – whatever it is – that I am perforce denied the opportunity of suffering from such a form of temptation! Saint Anthony himself could not be more rigid on the point!"

The old woman laughed harshly. "Ah, you young gentlemen," she said, "you don't fear for naught; and belike you'll get all the solitude you want here." She set to work with her cleaning; and by nightfall, when Malcolmson returned from his walk – he always had one of his books to study as he walked – he found the room swept and tidied, a fire burning in the old hearth, the lamp lit, and the table spread for supper with Mrs Witham's excellent fare. "This is comfort, indeed," he said, as he rubbed his hands.

When he had finished his supper, and lifted the tray to the other end of the great oak dining-table, he got out his books again, put fresh wood on the fire, trimmed his lamp, and set himself down to a spell of real hard work. He went on without pause till about eleven o'clock, when he knocked off for a bit to fix his fire and lamp, and to make himself a cup of tea. He had always been a tea-drinker, and during his college life had sat late at work and had taken tea late. The rest was a great luxury to him, and he enjoyed it with a sense of delicious, voluptuous ease. The renewed fire leaped and sparkled, and threw quaint shadows through the great old room; and as he sipped his hot tea he revelled in the sense of isolation from his kind. Then it was that he began to notice for the first time what a noise the rats were making.

"Surely," he thought, "they cannot have been at it all the time I was reading. Had they been, I must have noticed it!" Presently, when the noise increased, he satisfied himself that it was really new. It was evident that at first the rats had been frightened at the presence of a stranger, and the light of fire and lamp; but that as the time went on they had grown bolder and were now disporting themselves as was their wont.

How busy they were! and hark to the strange noises! Up and down behind the old wainscot, over the ceiling and under the floor they raced, and gnawed, and scratched! Malcolmson smiled to himself as he recalled to mind the saying of Mrs Dempster, "Bogies is rats, and rats is bogies!" The tea began to have its effect of intellectual and nervous stimulus, he saw with joy another long spell of work to be done before the night was past, and in the sense of security which it gave him, he allowed himself the luxury of a good look round the room. He took his lamp in one hand, and went all around, wondering that so quaint and beautiful an old house had been so long neglected. The carving of the oak on the panels of the wainscot was fine, and on and round the doors and windows it was beautiful and of rare merit. There were some old pictures on the walls, but they were coated so thick with dust and dirt that he could not distinguish any detail of them, though he held his lamp as high as he could over his head. Here and there as he went round he saw some crack or hole blocked for a moment by the face of a rat with its bright eyes glittering in the light, but in an instant it was gone, and a squeak and a scamper followed.

The thing that most struck him, however, was the rope of the great alarm bell on the roof, which hung down in a corner of the room on the right-hand side of the fireplace. He pulled up close to the hearth a great high-backed carved oak chair, and sat down to his last cup of tea. When this was done he made up the fire, and went back to his work, sitting at the corner of the table, having the fire to his left. For a while the rats disturbed him somewhat with their perpetual scampering, but he got accustomed to the noise as one does to the ticking of a clock or to the roar of moving water; and he became so immersed in his work that everything in the world, except the problem which he was trying to solve, passed away from him.

He suddenly looked up, his problem was still unsolved, and there was in the air that sense of the hour before the dawn, which is so dread to doubtful life. The noise of the rats had ceased. Indeed it seemed to him that it must have ceased but lately and that it was the sudden cessation which had disturbed him. The fire had fallen low, but still it threw out a deep red glow. As he looked he started in spite of his *sang froid*.

There on the great high-backed carved oak chair by the right side of the fireplace sat an enormous rat, steadily glaring at him with baleful eyes. He made a motion to it as though to hunt it away, but it did not stir. Then he made the motion of throwing something. Still it did not stir, but showed its great white teeth angrily, and its cruel eyes shone in the lamp-light with an added vindictiveness.

Malcolmson felt amazed, and seizing the poker from the hearth ran at it to kill it. Before, however, he could strike it, the rat, with a squeak that sounded like the concentration of hate, jumped upon the floor, and, running up the rope of the alarm bell, disappeared in the darkness beyond the range of the green-shaded lamp. Instantly, strange to say, the noisy scampering of the rats in the wainscot began again.

By this time Malcolmson's mind was quite off the problem; and as a shrill cock-crow outside told him of the approach of morning, he went to bed and to sleep.

He slept so sound that he was not even waked by Mrs Dempster coming in to make up his room. It was only when she had tidied up the place and got his breakfast ready and tapped on the screen which closed in his bed that he woke. He was a little tired still after his night's hard work, but a strong cup of tea soon freshened him up, and, taking his book, he went out for his morning walk, bringing with him a few sandwiches lest he should not care to return till dinner time. He found a quiet walk between high elms some way outside the town, and here he spent the greater part of the day studying his Laplace. On his return he looked in to see Mrs Witham and to thank her for her kindness. When she saw him coming through the diamond-paned bay-window of her sanctum she came out to meet him and asked him in. She looked at him searchingly and shook her head as she said:

"You must not overdo it, sir. You are paler this morning than you should be. Too late hours and too hard work on the brain isn't good for any man! But tell me, sir, how did you pass the night? Well, I hope? But, my heart! sir, I was glad when Mrs Dempster told me this morning that you were all right and sleeping sound when she went in."

"Oh, I was all right," he answered, smiling, "the 'somethings' didn't worry me, as yet. Only the rats; and they had a circus, I tell you, all over the place. There was one wicked looking old devil that sat up on my own chair by the fire, and wouldn't go till I took the poker to him, and then he ran up the rope of the alarm bell and got to somewhere up the wall or the ceiling – I couldn't see where, it was too dark."

"Mercy on us," said Mrs Witham, "an old devil, and sitting on a chair by the fireside! Take care, sir! take care! There's many a true word spoken in jest."

"How do you mean? 'Pon my word I don't understand."

"An old devil! The old devil, perhaps. There! sir, you needn't laugh," for Malcolmson had broken into a hearty peal. "You young folks thinks it easy to laugh at things that makes older ones shudder. Never mind, sir! never mind! Please God, you'll laugh all the time. It's what I wish you myself!" and the good lady beamed all over in sympathy with his enjoyment, her fears gone for a moment.

"Oh, forgive me!" said Malcolmson presently. "Don't you think me rude; but the idea was too much for me – that the old devil himself was on the chair last night!" And at the thought he laughed again. Then he went home to dinner.

This evening the scampering of the rats began earlier; indeed it had been going on before his arrival, and only ceased whilst his presence by its freshness disturbed them. After dinner he sat by the fire for a while and had a smoke; and then, having cleared his table, began to work as before. Tonight the rats disturbed him more than they had done on the previous night. How they scampered up and down and under and over! How they squeaked, and scratched, and gnawed! How they, getting bolder by degrees, came to the mouths of their holes and to the chinks and cracks and crannies in the wainscoting till their eyes shone like tiny lamps as the firelight rose and fell. But to him, now doubtless accustomed to them, their eyes were not wicked; only their playfulness touched him. Sometimes the boldest of them made sallies out on the floor or along the mouldings of the wainscot. Now and again as they disturbed him Malcolmson made a sound to frighten them, smiting the table with his hand or giving a fierce "hsh, hsh," so that they fled straightway to their holes.

And so the early part of the night wore on; and despite the noise Malcolmson got more and more immersed in his work.

All at once he stopped, as on the previous night, being overcome by a sudden sense of silence. There was not the faintest sound of gnaw, or scratch, or squeak. The silence was as of the grave. He remembered the odd occurrence of the previous night, and instinctively he looked at the chair standing close by the fireside. And then a very odd sensation thrilled through him.

There, on the great old high-backed carved oak chair beside the fireplace sat the same enormous rat, steadily glaring at him with baleful eyes.

Instinctively he took the nearest thing to his hand, a book of logarithms, and flung it at it. The book was badly aimed and the rat did not stir, so again the poker performance of the previous night was repeated; and again the rat, being closely pursued, fled up the rope of the alarm bell. Strangely too, the departure of this rat was instantly followed by the renewal of the noise made by the general rat community. On this occasion, as on the previous one, Malcolmson could not see at what part of the room the rat disappeared, for the green shade of his lamp left the upper part of the room in darkness, and the fire had burned low.

On looking at his watch he found it was close on midnight; and, not sorry for the *divertissement*, he made up his fire and made himself his nightly pot of tea. He had got through a good spell of work, and thought himself entitled to a cigarette; and so he sat on the great carved oak chair before the fire and enjoyed it. Whilst smoking he began to think that he would like to know where the rat disappeared to, for he had certain ideas for the morrow not entirely disconnected with a rat-trap.

Accordingly he lit another lamp and placed it so that it would shine well
into the right-hand corner of the wall by the fireplace. Then he got all
the books he had with him, and placed them handy to throw at the
vermin. Finally he lifted the rope of the alarm bell and placed the end of
it on the table, fixing the extreme end under the lamp. As he handled it
he could not help noticing how pliable it was, especially for so strong a
rope, and one not in use. "You could hang a man with it," he thought
to himself. When his preparations were made he looked around, and
said complacently:

"There now, my friend, I think we shall learn something of you this
time!" He began his work again, and though as before somewhat
disturbed at first by the noise of the rats, soon lost himself in his proposi-
tions and problems.

Again he was called to his immediate surroundings suddenly. This
time it might not have been the sudden silence only which took his attention; there was a slight movement of the rope, and the lamp moved.
Without stirring, he looked to see if his pile of books was within range,
and then cast his eye along the rope. As he looked he saw the great rat
drop from the rope on to the oak armchair and sit there glaring at him.
He raised a book in his right hand, and taking careful aim, flung it at the
rat. The latter, with a quick movement, sprang aside and dodged the
missile. He then took another book, and a third, and flung them one after
another at the rat, but each time unsuccessfully. At last, as he stood with
a book poised in his hand to throw, the rat squeaked and seemed afraid.
This made Malcolmson more than ever eager to strike, and the book flew
and struck the rat a resounding blow. It gave a terrified squeak, and
turning on its pursuer a look of terrible malevolence, ran up the chair-
back and made a great jump to the rope of the alarm bell and ran up it
like lightning. The lamp rocked under the sudden strain, but it was a
heavy one and did not topple over. Malcolmson kept his eyes on the rat,
and saw it by the light of the second lamp leap to a moulding of the wainscot and disappear through a hole in one of the great pictures which
hung on the wall, obscured and invisible through its coating of dirt and
dust.

"I shall look up my friend's habitation in the morning," said the
student, as he went over to collect his books. "The third picture from the
fireplace; I shall not forget." He picked up the books one by one,
commenting on them as he lifted them. "*Conic Sections* he does not mind,
nor *Cycloidal Oscillations*, nor the *Principia*, nor *Quaternions*, nor

Thermodynamics. Now for the book that fetched him!" Malcolmson took it up and looked at it. As he did so he started, and a sudden pallor overspread his face. He looked round uneasily and shivered slightly, as he murmured to himself:

"The Bible my mother gave me! What an odd coincidence." He sat down to work again, and the rats in the wainscot renewed their gambols. They did not disturb him, however; somehow their presence gave him a sense of companionship. But he could not attend to his work, and after striving to master the subject on which he was engaged gave it up in despair, and went to bed as the first streak of dawn stole in through the eastern window.

He slept heavily but uneasily, and dreamed much; and when Mrs Dempster woke him late in the morning he seemed ill at ease, and for a few minutes did not seem to realize exactly where he was. His first request rather surprised the servant.

"Mrs Dempster, when I am out today I wish you would get the steps and dust or wash those pictures – specially that one the third from the fireplace – I want to see what they are."

Late in the afternoon Malcolmson worked at his books in the shaded walk, and the cheerfulness of the previous day came back to him as the day wore on, and he found that his reading was progressing well. He had worked out to a satisfactory conclusion all the problems which had as yet baffled him, and it was in a state of jubilation that he paid a visit to Mrs Witham at The Good Traveller. He found a stranger in the cosy sitting-room with the landlady, who was introduced to him as Dr Thornhill. She was not quite at ease, and this, combined with the Doctor's plunging at once into a series of questions, made Malcolmson come to the conclusion that his presence was not an accident, so without preliminary he said:

"Dr Thornhill, I shall with pleasure answer you any question you may choose to ask me if you will answer me one question first."

The Doctor seemed surprised, but he smiled and answered at once. "Done! What is it?"

"Did Mrs Witham ask you to come here and see me and advise me?"

Dr Thornhill for a moment was taken aback, and Mrs Witham got very red and turned away; but the Doctor was a frank and ready man, and he answered at once and openly:

"She did: but she didn't intend you to know it. I suppose it was my clumsy haste that made you suspect. She told me that she did not like the idea of your being in that house all by yourself, and that she thought you took too much strong tea. In fact, she wants me to advise you if possible to give up the tea and the very late hours. I was a keen student in my time, so I suppose I may take the liberty of a college man, and without offence, advise you not quite as a stranger."

Malcolmson with a bright smile held out his hand. "Shake! as they say in America," he said. "I must thank you for your kindness and Mrs Witham too, and your kindness deserves a return on my part. I promise to take no more strong tea – no tea at all till you let me – and I shall go to bed tonight at one o'clock at latest. Will that do?"

"Capital," said the Doctor. "Now tell us all that you noticed in the old house," and so Malcolmson then and there told in minute detail all that had happened in the last two nights. He was interrupted every now and then by some exclamation from Mrs Witham, till finally when he told of the episode of the Bible the landlady's pent-up emotions found vent in a shriek; and it was not till a stiff glass of brandy and water had been administered that she grew composed again. Dr Thornhill listened with a face of growing gravity, and when the narrative was complete and Mrs Witham had been restored he asked:

"The rat always went up the rope of the alarm bell?"

"Always."

"I suppose you know," said the Doctor after a pause, "what the rope is?"

"No!"

"It is," said the Doctor slowly, "the rope which the hangman used for all the victims of the Judge's judicial rancour!" Here he was interrupted by another scream from Mrs Witham, and steps had to be taken for her recovery. Malcolmson having looked at his watch, and found that it was close to his dinner hour, had gone home before her complete recovery.

When Mrs Witham was herself again she almost assailed the Doctor with angry questions as to what he meant by putting such horrible ideas into the poor young man's mind. "He has quite enough there already to upset him," she added. Dr Thornhill replied:

"My dear madam, I had a distinct purpose in it! I wanted to draw his attention to the bell rope, and to fix it there. It may be that he is in a highly overwrought state, and has been studying too much, although I am bound to say that he seems as sound and healthy a young man, mentally and bodily, as ever I saw – but then the rats – and that suggestion of the devil." The doctor shook his head and went on. "I would have offered to go and stay the first night with him but that I felt sure it would have been a cause of offence. He may get in the night some strange fright or hallucination; and if he does I want him to pull that rope. All alone as he is it will give us warning, and we may reach him in time to be of service. I shall be sitting up pretty late tonight and shall keep my ears open. Do not be alarmed if Benchurch gets a surprise before morning."

"Oh, Doctor, what do you mean? What do you mean?"

"I mean this; that possibly – nay, more probably – we shall hear the great alarm bell from the Judge's House tonight," and the Doctor made about as effective an exit as could be thought of.

When Malcolmson arrived home he found that it was a little after his usual time, and Mrs Dempster had gone away – the rules of Greenhow's Charity were not to be neglected. He was glad to see that the place was bright and tidy with a cheerful fire and a well-trimmed lamp. The evening was colder than might have been expected in April, and a heavy wind was blowing with such rapidly-increasing strength that there was every promise of a storm during the night. For a few minutes after his entrance the noise of the rats ceased; but so soon as they became accustomed to his presence they began again. He was glad to hear them, for he felt once more the feeling of companionship in their noise, and his mind ran back to the strange fact that they only ceased to manifest themselves when that other – the great rat with the baleful eyes – came upon the scene. The reading-lamp only was lit and its green shade kept the ceiling and the upper part of the room in darkness, so that the cheerful light from the hearth spreading over the floor and shining on the white cloth laid over the end of the table was warm and cheery. Malcolmson sat down to his dinner with a good appetite and a buoyant spirit. After his dinner and a cigarette he sat steadily down to work, determined not to let anything disturb him, for he remembered his promise to the doctor, and made up his mind to make the best of the time at his disposal.

For an hour or so he worked all right, and then his thoughts began to wander from his books. The actual circumstances around him, the calls on his physical attention, and his nervous susceptibility were not to be denied. By this time the wind had become a gale, and the gale a storm. The old house, solid though it was, seemed to shake to its foundations, and the storm roared and raged through its many chimneys and its queer old gables, producing strange, unearthly sounds in the empty rooms and corridors. Even the great alarm bell on the roof must have felt the force of the wind, for the rope rose and fell slightly, as though the bell were moved a little from time to time, and the limber rope fell on the oak floor.

As Malcolmson listened to it he bethought himself of the doctor's words, "It is the rope which the hangman used for the victims of the Judge's judicial rancour," and he went over to the corner of the fireplace and took it in his hand to look at it. There seemed a sort of deadly interest in it, and as he stood there he lost himself for a moment in speculations as to who these victims were, and the grim wish of the Judge to have such a ghastly relic ever under his eyes. As he stood there the swaying of the bell on the roof still lifted the rope now and again; but presently there came a new sensation – a sort of tremor in the rope, as though something was moving along it.

Looking up instinctively Malcolmson saw the great rat coming slowly down towards him, glaring at him steadily. He dropped the rope and started back with a muttered curse, and the rat turning ran up the rope again and disappeared, and at the same instant Malcolmson became conscious that the noise of the rats, which had ceased for a while, began again.

All this set him thinking, and it occurred to him that he had not investigated the lair of the rat or looked at the pictures, as he had intended. He lit the other lamp without the shade, and, holding it up, went and stood opposite the third picture from the fireplace on the right-hand side where he had seen the rat disappear on the previous night.

At the first glance he started back so suddenly that he almost dropped the lamp, and a deadly pallor overspread his face. His knees shook, and heavy drops of sweat came on his forehead, and he trembled like an aspen. But he was young and plucky, and pulled himself together, and after the pause of a few seconds stepped forward again, raised the lamp, and examined the picture which had been dusted and washed, and now stood out clearly.

It was of a judge dressed in his robes of scarlet and ermine. His face was strong and merciless, evil, crafty, and vindictive, with a sensual mouth, hooked nose of ruddy colour, and shaped like the beak of a bird of prey. The rest of the face was of cadaverous colour. The eyes were of peculiar brilliance and with a terribly malignant expression. As he looked at them, Malcolmson grew cold, for he saw there the very counterpart of the eyes of the great rat. The lamp almost fell from his hand, he saw the rat with its baleful eyes peering out through the hole in the corner of the picture, and noted the sudden cessation of the noise of the other rats. However, he pulled himself together, and went on with his examination of the picture.

The Judge was seated in a great high-backed carved oak chair, on the right-hand side of a great stone fireplace where, in the corner, a rope hung down from the ceiling, its end lying coiled on the floor. With a feeling of something like horror, Malcolmson recognized the scene of the room as it stood, and gazed around him in an awe-struck manner as though he expected to find some strange presence behind him. Then he looked over to the corner of the fireplace – and with a loud cry he let the lamp fall from his hand.

There, in the Judge's armchair, with the rope hanging behind, sat the rat with the Judge's baleful eyes, now intensified and with a fiendish leer. Save for the howling of the storm without there was silence.

The fallen lamp recalled Malcolmson to himself. Fortunately it was of metal, and so the oil was not spilt. However, the practical need of attending to it settled at once his nervous apprehensions. When he had turned it out, he wiped his brow and thought for a moment.

"This will not do," he said to himself. "If I go on like this I shall become a crazy fool. This must stop! I promised the Doctor I would not take tea. Faith, he was pretty right! My nerves must have been getting into a queer state. Funny I did not notice it. I never felt better in my life. However, it is all right now, and I shall not be such a fool again."

Then he mixed himself a good stiff glass of brandy and water and resolutely sat down to his work.

It was nearly an hour when he looked up from his book, disturbed by the sudden stillness. Without, the wind howled and roared louder than ever, and the rain drove in sheets against the windows, beating like hail on the glass; but within there was no sound whatever save the echo of the wind as it roared in the great chimney, and now and then a hiss as a few raindrops found their way down the chimney in a lull of the storm. The fire had fallen low and had ceased to flame, though it threw out a red glow. Malcolmson listened attentively, and presently heard a thin, squeaking noise, very faint. It came from the corner of the room where the rope hung down, and he thought it was the creaking of the rope on the floor as the swaying of the bell raised and lowered it. Looking up, however, he saw in the dim light the great rat clinging to the rope and gnawing it. The rope was already nearly gnawed through – he could see the lighter colour where the strands were laid bare. As he looked the job was completed, and the severed end of the rope fell clattering on the oaken floor, whilst for an instant the great rat remained like a knob or tassel at the end of the rope, which now began to sway to and fro.

Malcolmson felt for a moment another pang of terror as he thought that
now the possibility of calling the outer world to his assistance was cut off,
but an intense anger took its place, and seizing the book he was reading
he hurled it at the rat. The blow was well aimed, but before the missile
could reach it the rat dropped off and struck the floor with a soft thud.
Malcolmson instantly rushed over towards it, but it darted away and
disappeared in the darkness of the shadows of the room. Malcolmson felt
that his work was over for the night, and determined then and there to
vary the monotony of the proceedings by a hunt for the rat, and took off
the green shade of the lamp so as to insure a wider spreading light. As he
did so the gloom of the upper part of the room was relieved, and in the
new flood of light, great by comparison with the previous darkness, the
pictures on the wall stood out boldly. From where he stood, Malcolmson
saw right opposite to him the third picture on the wall from the right of
the fireplace. He rubbed his eyes in surprise, and then a great fear began
to come upon him.

In the centre of the picture was a great irregular patch of brown
canvas, as fresh as when it was stretched on the frame. The background
was as before, with chair and chimney-corner and rope, but the figure of
the Judge had disappeared.

Malcolmson, almost in a chill of horror, turned slowly round, and then
he began to shake and tremble like a man in a palsy. His strength seemed
to have left him, and he was incapable of action or movement, hardly
even of thought. He could only see and hear.

There, on the great high-backed carved oak chair sat the Judge in his
robes of scarlet and ermine, with his baleful eyes glaring vindictively, and
a smile of triumph on the resolute, cruel mouth, as he lifted with his
hands a *black cap*. Malcolmson felt as if the blood was running from his
heart, as one does in moments of prolonged suspense. There was a
singing in his ears. Without, he could hear the roar and howl of the
tempest, and through it, swept on the storm, came the striking of
midnight by the great chimes in the market place. He stood for a space of
time that seemed to him endless, still as a statue and with wide-open,
horror-struck eyes, breathless. As the clock struck, so the smile of
triumph on the Judge's face intensified, and at the last stroke of midnight
he placed the black cap on his head.

Slowly and deliberately the Judge rose from his chair and picked up
the piece of rope of the alarm bell which lay on the floor, drew it through
his hands as if he enjoyed its touch, and then deliberately began to knot

one end of it, fashioning it into a noose. This he tightened and tested with his foot, pulling hard at it till he was satisfied and then making a running noose of it, which he held in his hand. Then he began to move along the table on the opposite side to Malcolmson, keeping his eyes on him until he had passed him, when with a quick movement he stood in front of the door. Malcolmson then began to feel that he was trapped, and tried to think of what he should do. There was some fascination in the Judge's eyes, which he never took off him, and he had, perforce, to look. He saw the Judge approach – still keeping between him and the door – and raise the noose and throw it towards him as if to entangle him. With a great effort he made a quick movement to one side, and saw the rope fall beside him, and heard it strike the oaken floor. Again the Judge raised the noose and tried to ensnare him, ever keeping his baleful eyes fixed on him, and each time by a mighty effort the student just managed to evade it. So this went on for many times, the Judge seeming never discouraged nor discomposed at failure, but playing as a cat does with a mouse. At last in despair, which had reached its climax, Malcolmson cast a quick glance round him. The lamp seemed to have blazed up, and there was a fairly good light in the room. At the many rat-holes and in the chinks and crannies of the wainscot he saw the rats' eyes; and this aspect, that was purely physical, gave him a gleam of comfort. He looked around and saw that the rope of the great alarm bell was laden with rats. Every inch of it was covered with them, and more and more were pouring through the small circular hole in the ceiling whence it emerged, so that with their weight the bell was beginning to sway.

Hark! it had swayed till the clapper had touched the bell. The sound was but a tiny one, but the bell was only beginning to sway, and it would increase.

At the sound the Judge, who had been keeping his eyes fixed on Malcolmson, looked up, and a scowl of diabolical anger overspread his face. His eyes fairly glowed like hot coals, and he stamped his foot with a sound that seemed to make the house shake. A dreadful peal of thunder broke overhead as he raised the rope again, whilst the rats kept running up and down the rope as though working against time. This time, instead of throwing it, he drew close to his victim, and held open the noose as he approached. As he came closer there seemed something paralysing in his very presence, and Malcolmson stood rigid as a corpse. He felt the Judge's icy fingers touch his throat as he adjusted the rope. The noose tightened – tightened. Then the Judge, taking the rigid form of the student in his arms, carried him over and placed him standing in the oak chair, and stepping up beside him, put his hand up and caught the end of the swaying rope of the alarm bell. As he raised his hand the rats fled squeaking, and disappeared through the hole in the ceiling. Taking the end of the noose which was round Malcolmson's neck he tied it to the hanging bell-rope, and then descending pulled away the chair.

When the alarm bell of the Judge's House began to sound a crowd soon assembled. Lights and torches of various kinds appeared, and soon a silent crowd was hurrying to the spot. They knocked loudly at the door, but there was no reply. Then they burst in the door, and poured into the great dining-room, the Doctor at the head.

There at the end of the rope of the great alarm bell hung the body of the student, and on the face of the Judge in the picture was a malignant smile.

Grant Allen

Pallinghurst Barrow

Grant Allen (1848–99) was a Canadian-born writer who spent most of his career in Britain. He became one of the most celebrated – and occasionally notorious – authors of the nineties, his most controversial works being The Evolution of the Idea of God *(1897) and* The Woman Who Did *(1895), a novel (in the Keynotes series) in which the title-figure decided that free love was less degrading than the bondage of marriage. He penned a variety of supernatural tales, often humorous but occasionally very grim, many of which were collected in* Strange Stories *(1884) and* Twelve Tales *(1899). "Pallinghurst Barrow" was originally written for the* Illustrated London News *(1892), and reprinted in his rare collection* Ivan Greet's Masterpiece *(1893).*

I

RUDOLPH REEVE SAT by himself on the Old Long Barrow on Pallinghurst Common. It was a September evening, and the sun was setting. The west was all aglow with a mysterious red light, very strange and lurid – a light that reflected itself in glowing purple on the dark brown heather and the dying bracken. Rudolph Reeve was a journalist and a man of science; but he had a poet's soul. He sat there long, watching the livid hues that incarnadined the sky – redder and fiercer than anything he ever remembered to have seen since the famous year of the Krakatoa sunsets – though he knew it was getting late, and he ought to have gone back long since to the manor-house to dress for dinner. Mrs Bouverie-Barton, his hostess, was always such a stickler for punctuality and dispatch. But, in spite of Mrs Bouverie-Barton, Rudolph Reeve sat on. There was something about that sunset and the lights on the bracken – something weird and unearthly – that positively fascinated him.

The view over the common, which stands high and exposed, a veritable waste of heath and gorse, is strikingly wide and expansive. Pallinghurst Ring, or the "Old Long Barrow", a well-known landmark, familiar by that name from time immemorial to all the countryside, crowns its actual summit, and commands from its top the surrounding hills far into the shadowy heart of Hampshire. On its terraced slope Rudolph sat and gazed out, in the exquisite flush of the dying reflections from the dying sun upon the dying heather. He sat and wondered to himself why death is always so much more beautiful, so much more poetical, so much calmer than life.

He was just going to rise, however, dreading the lasting wrath of Mrs Bouverie-Barton, when of a sudden a very weird yet definite feeling caused him for one moment to pause and hesitate. Why he felt it he knew not; but even as he sat there on the grassy tumulus, covered close with short sward of subterranean clover, he was aware, through no external sense, but by pure internal consciousness, of something living and moving within the barrow. He shut his eyes and listened. No; fancy, pure fancy! Not a sound broke the stillness of early evening, save the drone of insects – those dying insects, now beginning to fail fast before the first chill breath of approaching autumn. Rudolph opened his eyes again and looked down on the ground. In the little hollow by his feet innumerable plants of sundew spread their murderous rosettes of sticky red leaves, all bedewed with viscid gum, to catch and roll round the struggling flies that wrenched their tiny limbs in vain efforts to free themselves. But that was all. Nothing else was astir. In spite of sight and sound, however, he was still deeply thrilled by this strange consciousness as of something in the barrow underneath; something living and moving – or was it moving and dead? Something crawling and creeping as the long arms of the sundews crawled and crept around the helpless flies, whose juices they sucked out. A weird and awful feeling, yet strangely fascinating! He hated the vulgar necessity for going back to dinner. Why do people dine at all? So material! so commonplace! And the universe all teeming with strange secrets to unfold! He knew not why, but a fierce desire possessed his soul to stop and give way to this overpowering sense of the mysterious and the marvellous in the dark depths of the barrow.

With an effort he roused himself, and put on his hat, for his forehead was burning. The sun had now long set, and Mrs Bouverie-Barton dined at 7.30 p.m. punctually. He must rise and go home. Something unknown pulled him down to detain him. Once more he paused and hesitated. He was not a superstitious man, yet it seemed to him as if many strange shapes stood by unseen, and watched with great eagerness to see whether he would rise and go away, or yield to the temptation of stopping and indulging his curious fancy. Strange! – he saw and heard absolutely nothing; yet he dimly realized that unseen figures were watching him close with bated breath, and anxiously observing his every movement, as if intent to know whether he would rise and move on, or remain to investigate this causeless sensation.

For a minute or two he stood irresolute; and all the time he so stood the unseen bystanders held their breath and looked on in an agony of expectation. He could feel their outstretched necks; he could picture their strained attention. At last he broke away. "This is nonsense," he said aloud to himself, and turned slowly homeward. As he did so, a deep sigh, as of suspense relieved, but relieved in the wrong direction, seemed to rise – unheard, impalpable, spiritual – from the invisible crowd that gathered around him immaterial. Clutched hands seemed to stretch after him and try to pull him back. An unreal throng of angry and disappointed creatures seemed to follow him over the moor, uttering speechless imprecations on his head, in some unknown tongue – ineffable, inaudible. This horrid sense of being followed by unearthly foes took absolute possession of Rudolph's mind. It might have been merely the lurid redness of the afterglow, or the loneliness of the moor, or the necessity of being back not one minute late for Mrs Bouverie-Barton's dinner-hour; but, at any rate, he lost all self-control for the moment, and ran – ran wildly, at the very top of his speed, all the way from the barrow to the door of the manor-house garden. There he stopped and looked round with a painful sense of his own stupid cowardice. This was positively childish: he had seen nothing, heard nothing, had nothing definite to frighten him; yet he had run from his own mental shadow, like the veriest schoolgirl, and was trembling still from the profundity of his sense that somebody unseen was pursuing and following him. "What a precious fool I am," he said to himself, half angrily, "to be so terrified at nothing! I'll go back there by-and-by, just to recover my self-respect, and to show myself, at least, I'm not really frightened."

But even as he said it he was internally aware that his baffled foes,

standing grinning their disappointment with gnashed teeth at the garden
gate, gave a chuckle of surprise, delight, and satisfaction at his altered
intention.

II

There's nothing like light for dispelling superstitious terrors. Pallinghurst
Manor-house was fortunately supplied with electric light; for Mrs
Bouverie-Barton was nothing if not intensely modern. Long before
Rudolph had finished dressing for dinner, he was smiling once more to
himself at his foolish conduct. Never in his life before – at least, since he
was twenty – had he done such a thing; and he knew why he'd done it
now. It was a nervous breakdown. He had been overworking and Sir
Arthur Boyd, the famous specialist on diseases of the nervous system, had
recommended him "a week or two's rest and change in the country".
That was why he had accepted Mrs Bouverie-Barton's invitation to form
part of her autumn party at Pallinghurst Manor; and that was also doubtless why he had been so absurdly frightened at nothing at all just now on
the common.

He went down to dinner, however, in very good spirits. His hostess
was kind; she permitted him to take in that pretty American.
Conversation with the soup turned at once on the sunset. "You were on
the barrow, about seven, Mr Reeve," Mrs Bouverie-Barton observed
severely, when he spoke of the afterglow. "You watched that sunset close.
How fast you must have walked home! I was almost half afraid you were
going to be late for dinner."

Rudolph coloured slightly. "Oh dear no, Mrs Bouverie-Barton," he
answered gravely. "I may be foolish, but not, I hope, criminal. I know
better than to do anything so weak and wicked as that at Pallinghurst
Manor. I do walk rather fast, and the sunset – well, the sunset was just too
lovely."

"Elegant," the pretty American interposed.

"It always is, this night every year," little Joyce said quietly, with the
air of one who retails a well-known scientific fact. "It's the night, you
know, when the light burns bright on the Old Long Barrow."

Joyce was Mrs Bouverie-Barton's only child – a frail and pretty little creature, just twelve years old, very light and fairylike, but with a strange cowed look which, nevertheless, somehow curiously became her.

"What nonsense you talk, my child!" her mother exclaimed, darting a look at Joyce which made her relapse forthwith into instant silence. "I'm ashamed of her, Mr Reeve; they pick up such nonsense as this from their nurses."

But the child's words, though lightly whispered, had caught the quick ear of Archie Cameron, the distinguished electrician. He made a spring upon them at once; for the merest suspicion of the supernatural was to Cameron irresistible. "What's that, Joyce?" he cried, leaning forward across the table. "No, Mrs Bouverie-Barton, I really *must* hear it. What day is this today, and what's that you just said about the sunset and the light on the Old Long Barrow?"

Joyce glanced pleadingly at her mother, and then again at Cameron. A very faint nod gave her grudging leave to proceed with her tale, under maternal disapproval. Joyce hesitated and began. "Well, this is the night, you know," she said, "when the sun turns, or stands still, or crosses the tropic, or goes back again, or something."

Mrs Bouverie-Barton gave a little dry cough. "The autumnal equinox," she interposed severely, "at which, of course, the sun does nothing of the sort you suppose. We shall have to have your astronomy looked after, Joyce; such ignorance is exhaustive. But go on with your myth, please, and get it over quickly."

"The autumnal equinox; that's just it," Joyce went on, unabashed. "I remember that's the word, for old Rachel, the gipsy, told me so. Well, on this day every year, a sort of glow comes up on the moor; I know it does, for I've seen it myself; and the rhyme about it goes –

> *Every year on Michael's night*
> *Pallinghurst Barrow burneth bright*

Only the gipsy told me it was Baal's night before it was St Michael's; and it was somebody else's night, whose name I forget, before it was Baal's. And the somebody was a god to whom you must never sacrifice anything with iron, but always with flint or with a stone hatchet."

Cameron leaned back in his chair and surveyed the child critically. "Now, this is interesting," he said; "profoundly interesting. For here we get, what is always so much wanted, first-hand evidence. And you're quite sure, Joyce, you've really seen it?"

"Oh! Mr Cameron, how can you?" Mrs Bouverie-Barton cried, "I take the greatest trouble to keep all such rubbish out of Joyce's way; and then you men of science come down here and talk like this to her, and undo all the good I've taken months in doing."

"Well, whether Joyce has ever seen it or not," Rudolph Reeve said gravely, "I can answer for it myself that I saw a very curious light on the Long Barrow tonight; and, furthermore, I felt a most peculiar sensation."

"What was that?" Cameron asked, bending over towards him eagerly.

"Why, as I was sitting on the barrow," Rudolph began, "just after sunset, I was dimly conscious of something stirring inside, not visible or audible, but – "

"Oh, I know, I know!" Joyce put in, leaning forward with her eyes staring curiously; "a sort of a feeling that there was somebody somewhere, very faint and dim, though you couldn't see or hear them; they tried to pull you down, clutching at you like this: and when you ran away frightened, they seemed to follow you and jeer at you. Great gibbering creatures! Oh, I know what all that is! I've been there, and felt it."

"Joyce!" Mrs Bouverie-Barton put in, with a warning frown, "what nonsense you talk! You're really too ridiculous. How can you suppose Mr Reeve ran away – a man of science like him – from an imaginary terror?"

"Well, I won't quite say I ran away," Rudolph answered, somewhat sheepishly. "We never do admit these things, I suppose, after twenty. But I certainly did hurry home at the very top of my speed – not to be late for dinner, you know, Mrs Bouverie-Barton; and I *will* admit, Joyce, between you and me only, I was conscious all the way of something very much like your grinning followers behind me."

Mrs Bouverie-Barton darted him another look of intense displeasure. "I think," she said, in a chilly voice, "at a table like this and with such thinkers around, we might surely find something rather better to discuss than such worn out superstitions. Professor Spence, did you light upon any fresh palaeoliths in the gravel-pit this morning?"

III

Later in the drawing-room, a small group collected by the corner bay, remotest from Mrs Bouverie-Barton's own presidential chair, to hear Rudolph and Joyce compare experiences of the light above the barrow. When the two dreamers of dreams and seers of visions had finished, Mrs Bruce, the esoteric Buddhist, opened the flood-gates of her torrent speech with triumphant vehemence. "This is just what I should have expected," she said, looking round for a sceptic, that she might turn and rend him. "Novalis was right. Children are early men. They are freshest from the truth. They come straight to us from the Infinite. Little souls just let loose from the free expanse of God's sky see more than we adults do – at least, except a few of us. We ourselves, what are we but accumulated layers of phantasmata? Spirit-light rarely breaks in upon our grimed charnel of flesh. The dust of years overlies us. But the child, bursting new upon the dim world of Karma, trails clouds of glory from the beatific vision. So Wordsworth held; so the Masters of Tibet taught us, long ages before Wordsworth."

"It's curious," Professor Spence put in, with a scientific smile, restrained at the corners, "that all this should have happened to Joyce and to our friend Reeve at a long barrow. It has been shown conclusively that long barrows, which are the graves of the small, squat people who preceded the inroad of Aryan invaders, are the real originals of all the fairy hills and subterranean palaces of popular legend. You know the old story of how Childe Roland to the dark tower came, of course. Well, that dark tower was nothing more or less than a long barrow; perhaps Pallinghurst Barrow itself, perhaps some other; and Childe Roland went into it to rescue his sister, Burd Ellen, who had been stolen by the fairy king, after the fashion of his kind, for a human sacrifice. The Picts were a deeply religious people, who believed in human sacrifice. They felt they derived from it high spiritual benefit. And the queerest part of it all is that in order to see the fairies you must go round the barrow *widdershins* – that is the opposite way from the way of the sun – on this very night of all the year, Michaelmas Eve, which was the accepted old date of the autumnal equinox."

"All long barrows have a chamber of great stones in the centre, I believe," Cameron suggested tentatively.

"Yes, all or nearly all; megalithic, you know; unwrought; and that chamber's the subterranean palace, lit up with the fairy light that's so constantly found in old stories of the dead, and which Joyce and you, alone among the moderns, have been permitted to see, Reeve."

"It's a very odd fact," Dr Porter, the materialist, interposed musingly, "that the only ghosts people ever see are the ghosts of a generation very very close to them. One hears of lots of ghosts in eighteenth-century costumes, because everybody has a clear idea of wigs and small-clothes from pictures and fancy dresses. One hears of far fewer in Elizabethan dress, because the class most given to beholding ghosts are seldom acquainted with ruffs and farthingales; and one meets with none at all in Anglo-Saxon or Ancient British or Roman costumes, because those are only known to a comparatively small class of learned people; and ghosts, as a rule, avoid the learned – except you, Mrs Bruce – as they would avoid prussic acid. Millions of ghosts of remote antiquity must swarm about the world, though, after a hundred years or thereabouts they retire into obscurity and cease to annoy people with their nasty cold shivers. But the queer thing about these long-barrow ghosts is that they must be the spirits of men and women who died thousands and thousands of years ago, which is exceptional longevity for a spiritual being; don't you think so, Cameron?"

"Europe must be chock-full of them!" the pretty American assented, smiling; "though America hasn't had time, so far, to collect any consider-able population of spirits."

But Mrs Bruce was up in arms at once against such covert levity, and took the field in full force for her beloved spectres. "No, no," she said, "Dr Porter, there you mistake your subject. Man is the focus of the glass of his own senses. There are other landscapes in the fifth and sixth dimensions of space than the one presented to him. As Carlyle said, each eye sees in all things just what each eye brings with it the power of seeing. And this is true spiritually as well as physically. To Newton and Newton's dog Diamond what a different universe! One saw the great vision of universal gravitation, the other saw – a little mouse under a chair. Nursery rhymes summarize for us the gain of centuries. Nothing was ever destroyed, nothing was ever changed, and nothing new is ever created. All the spirits of all that is, or was, or ever will be people the universe everywhere, unseen, around us; and each of us sees of them

those only he himself is adapted to seeing. The rustic or the clown meets
no ghosts of any sort save the ghosts of the persons he knows about otherwise; if a man like yourself saw a ghost at all – which isn't likely for you
starve your spiritual side by blindly shutting your eyes to one whole
aspect of nature – you'd be just as likely to see the ghost of a Stone Age
chief as the ghost of a Georgian or Elizabethan."

"Did I catch the word 'ghost'?" Mrs Bouverie-Barton put in, coming
up unexpectedly with her angry glower. "Joyce, my child, go to bed. This
is not talk for you. And don't go chilling yourself by standing at the
window in your nightdress, looking out on the common to search for the
light on the Old Long Barrow, which is all pure moonshine. You nearly
caught your death of cold last year with that nonsense. It's always so.
These superstitions never do any good to anyone."

And, indeed, Rudolph felt a faint glow of shame himself at having
discussed such themes in the hearing of that nervous and high-strung
little creature.

IV

In the course of the evening, Rudolph's head began to ache, as it often
did. He knew that headache well; it was the worst neuralgic kind – the
wet-towel variety – the sort that keeps you tossing the whole night long
without hope of respite. About eleven o'clock, when the men went into
the smoking-room, the pain became unendurable. He called Dr Porter
aside, "Can't you give me anything to relieve it?" he asked piteously,
after describing his symptoms.

"Oh, certainly," the doctor answered, with brisk medical confidence.
"I'll bring you up a draught that will put that all right in less than half an
hour. What Mrs Bruce calls soma – the fine old crusted remedy of our
Aryan ancestor; there's nothing like it for cases of nervous inanition."

Rudolph went up to his room, and the doctor followed him a few
minutes later with a very small phial of a very thick green viscid liquid.
He poured ten drops carefully into a measured medicine-glass, and filled
it up with water. It amalgamated badly. "Drink that off," he said.
Rudolph drank it.

"I'll leave you the bottle," the doctor went on, laying it down on the dressing-table, "only use it with caution, ten drops in two hours if the pain continues. Not more than ten, recollect. It's a powerful narcotic – I dare say you know its name: it's Cannabis Indica."

Rudolph thanked him inarticulately, and flung himself on the bed without undressing. He had brought up a book with him – that delicious volume, Joseph Jacobs' *English Fairy Tales* – and he tried in some vague way to read the story of Childe Roland, to which Professor Spence had directed his attention. But his head ached so much he could hardly read it; he only gathered with difficulty that Childe Roland had been instructed by witch or warlock to come to a green hill surrounded with terrace-rings – like Pallinghurst Barrow – to walk round it thrice, *widdershins*, saying each time –

> *"Open door! open door!*
> *And let me come in,"*

and when the door opened to enter unabashed the fairy king's palace. And the third time the door did open, and Childe Roland entered a court, all lighted with a fairy light or gloaming; and then he went through a long passage, till he came at last to two side stone doors; and beyond them lay a hall – stately, glorious, magnificent – where Burd Ellen sat combing her golden hair with a comb of amber. And the moment she saw her brother, up she stood, and she said –

> *"Woe worth the day, ye luckless fool,*
> *Or ever that ye were born;*
> *For come the King of Elfland in*
> *Your fortune is forlorn."*

When Rudolph had read this far his head ached so much he could read no further; so he laid down the book, and reflected once more in some half-conscious mood on Mrs Bruce's theory that each man could see only the ghosts he expected. That seemed reasonable enough, for according to our faith is it unto us always. If so, then these ancient and savage ghosts of the dim old Stone Age, before bronze and iron, must still haunt the grassy barrows under the waving pines, where legend declared they were long since buried; and the mystic light over Pallinghurst moor must be the local evidence and symbol of their presence.

How long he lay there he hardly quite knew; but the clock struck twice, and his head was aching so fiercely now that he helped himself plentifully to a second dose of the thick green mixture. His hand shook too much to be puritanical to a drop or two. For a while it relieved him; then the pain grew worse again. Dreamily he moved over to the big north oriel to cool his brow with the fresh night air. The window stood open. As he gazed out a curious sight met his eye. At another oriel in the wing, which ran in an L-shaped bend from the part of the house where he had been put, he saw a child's white face gaze appealingly across at him. It was Joyce, in her white nightdress, peering with all her might, in spite of her mother's prohibition, at the mystic common. For a second she started. Her eyes met his. Slowly she raised one pale forefinger and pointed. Her lips opened to frame an inaudible word; but he read it by sight. "Look!" she said simply. Rudolph looked where she pointed.

A faint blue light hung lambent over the Old Long Barrow. It was ghostly and vague. It seemed to rouse and call him.

He glanced towards Joyce. She waved her hand to the barrow. Her lips said, "Go." Rudolph was now in that strange semi-mesmeric state of self-induced hypnotism when a command of whatever sort or by whomsoever given, seems to compel obedience. Trembling he rose, and taking his candle descended the stair noiselessly. Then, walking on tiptoe across the tile-paved hall, he reached his hat from the rack, and opening the front door stole out into the garden.

The soma had steadied his nerves and supplied him with false courage; but even in spite of it he felt a weird and creepy sense of mystery and the supernatural. Indeed, he would have turned back even now, had he not chanced to look up and see Joyce's pale face still pressed close against the window and Joyce's white hand still motioning him mutely onward. He looked once more in the direction where she pointed. The spectral light now burnt clearer and bluer, and more unearthly than ever, and the illimitable moor seemed haunted from end to end by innumerable invisible and uncanny creatures.

Rudolph groped his way on. His goal was the barrow. As he went, speechless voices seemed to whisper unknown tongues encouragingly in his ear; horrible shapes of elder creeds appeared to crowd round him and tempt him with beckoning fingers to follow them. Alone, erect, across the darkling waste, stumbling now and again over roots of gorse and heather, but steadied, as it seemed, by invisible hands, he staggered slowly forward, till at last, with aching head and trembling feet, he stood beside the immemorial grave of the savage chieftain. Away over in the east the white moon was just rising.

After a moment's pause, he began to walk round the tumulus. But something clogged and impeded him. His feet wouldn't obey his will; they seemed to move of themselves in the opposite direction. Then all at once he remembered he had been trying to go the way of the sun, instead of *widdershins*. Steadying himself, and opening his eyes, he walked in the converse sense. All at once his feet moved easily, and the invisible attendants chuckled to themselves so loud that he could almost hear them. After the third round his lips parted, and he murmured the mystic words: "Open door! Open door! Let me come in." Then his head throbbed worse than ever with exertion and giddiness, and for two or three minutes he was unconscious of anything.

When he opened his eyes again a very different sight displayed itself before him. Instantly he was aware that the age had gone back upon its steps ten thousand years, as the sun went back upon the dial of Ahaz; he stood face to face with a remote antiquity. Planes of existence faded; new sights floated over him; new worlds were penetrated; new ideas, yet very old, undulated centrically towards him from the universal flat of time and space and matter and motion. He was projected into another sphere and saw by fresh senses. Everything was changed, and he himself changed with it.

The blue light over the barrow now shone clear as day, though infinitely more mysterious. A passage lay open through the grassy slope into a rude stone corridor. Though his curiosity by this time was thoroughly aroused, Rudolph shrank with a terrible shrinking from his own impulse to enter this grim black hole, which led at once, by an oblique descent, into the bowels of the earth. But he couldn't help himself. For, O God! looking round him, he saw, to his infinite terror, alarm, and awe, a ghostly throng of naked and hideous savages. They were spirits, yet savages. Eagerly they jostled and hustled him, and crowded round him in wild groups, exactly as they had done to the spiritual sense a little earlier in the evening, when he couldn't see them. But now he saw them clearly with the outer eye; saw them as grinning and hateful barbarian shadows, neither black nor white, but tawny-skinned and low-browed; their tangled hair falling unkempt in matted locks about their receding foreheads; their jaws large and fierce; their eyebrows shaggy and protruding like a gorilla's, their loins just girt with a few scraps of torn skin; their whole mien inexpressibly repulsive and bloodthirsty.

They were savages, yet they were ghosts. The two most terrible and dreaded foes of civilized experience seemed combined at once in them. Rudolph Reeve crouched powerless in their intangible hands; for they seized him roughly with incorporeal fingers, and pushed him bodily into the presence of their sleeping chieftain. As they did so they raised loud peals of discordant laughter. It was hollow; but it was piercing. In that hateful sound the triumphant whoop of the Red Indian and the weird mockery of the ghost were strangely mingled into some appalling harmony.

Rudolph allowed them to push him in; they were too many to resist; and the soma had sucked all the strength out of his muscles. The women were the worst: ghastly hags of old, witches with pendant breasts and bloodshot eyes, they whirled round him in triumph, and shouted aloud in a tongue he had never before heard, though he understood it instinctively, "A victim! A victim! We hold him! We have him!"

Even in the agonized horror of that awful moment Rudolph knew why he understood those words, unheard till then. They were the first language of our race – the natural and instinctive mother-tongue of humanity.

They hauled him forward by main force to the central chamber, with hands and arms and ghostly shreds of buffalo-hide. Their wrists compelled him as the magnet compels the iron bar. He entered the palace. A dim phosphorescent light, like the light of a churchyard or of decaying paganism, seemed to illumine it faintly. Things loomed dark before him; but his eyes almost instantly adapted themselves to the gloom, as the eyes of the dead on the first night in the grave adapt themselves by inner force to the strangeness of their surroundings. The royal hall was built up of cyclopean stones, each as big as the head of some colossal stone, rudely piled on one another, and carved in relief with representations of serpents, concentric lines, interlacing zigzags, and the mystic swastika. But all these things Rudolph only saw vaguely, if he saw them at all; his attention was too much concentrated on devouring fear and the horror of his situation.

In the very centre a skeleton sat crouching on the floor in some loose, huddled fashion. Its legs were doubled up, its hands clasped round its knees, its grinning teeth had long been blackened by time or by the indurated blood of human victims. The ghosts approached it with strange reverence, in impish postures.

"See! We bring you a slave, great King!" they cried in the same barbaric tongue – all clicks and gutturals. "For this is the holy night of your father, the Sun, when he turns him about on his yearly course through the stars and goes south to leave us. We bring you a slave to renew your mouth. Rise! Drink this hot blood! Rise! Kill and eat him!"

The grinning skeleton turned its head and regarded Rudolph from its eyeless orbs with a vacant glance of hungry satisfaction. The sight of human meat seemed to create a soul beneath the ribs of death in some incredible fashion. Even as Rudolph, held fast by the immaterial hands of his ghastly captors, looked and trembled for his fate, too terrified to cry out or even to move and struggle, he beheld the hideous thing rise and assume a shadowy shape, all pallid blue light, like the shapes of his jailers. Bit by bit, as he gazed, the skeleton seemed to disappear, or rather to fade into some unsubstantial form, which was nevertheless more human, more corporeal, more horrible than the dry bones it had come from. Naked and yellow like the rest, it wore round its dim waist just an apron of dry grass, or, what seemed to be such, while over its shoulders hung the ghost of a bearskin mantle. As it rose, the other spectres knocked their foreheads low on the ground before it, and grovelled with their long locks in the ageless dust, and uttered elfin cries of inarticulate homage.

The great chief turned, grinning, to one of his spectral henchmen. "Give a knife!" he said curtly, for all that these strange shades uttered was snapped out in short, sharp sentences, and in a monosyllabic tongue, like the bark of jackals or the laugh of the striped hyena among the graves at midnight.

The attendant, bowing low once more, handed his liege a flint flake, very keen-edged, but jagged, a rude and horrible instrument of barbaric manufacture. But what terrified Rudolph most was the fact that this flake was no ghostly weapon, no immaterial shard, but a fragment of real stone, capable of inflicting a deadly gash or long torn wound. Hundreds of fragments, indeed, lay loose on the concreted floor of the chamber, some of them roughly chipped, others ground and polished. Rudolph had seen such things in museums many times before; with a sudden rush of horror, he recognized now for the first time in his life for what purpose the savages of that far off day had buried them with their dead in the chambered barrows.

With a violent effort he wetted his parched lips with his tongue, and cried out thrice in his agony the one word "Mercy!"

At that sound the savage king burst into a loud and fiendish laugh. It was a hideous laugh, halfway between a wild beast's and a murderous maniac's: it echoed through the long hall like the laughter of devils. "What does he say?" the king cried, in the same transparently natural words, whose import Rudolph could understand at once. "How like birds they talk, these white-faced men, whom we get for our only victims since the years grew foolish! 'Mu-mu-mu-moo!' they say; 'Mu-mu-mu-moo!' more like frogs than men and women!"

Then it came over Rudolph instinctively, through the maze of his terror, that he could understand the lower tongue of these elfin visions because he and his ancestors had once passed through it; but they could not understand his, because it was too high and too deep for them.

He had little time for thought, however. Fear bounded his horizon. The ghosts crowded round him, gibbering louder than before. With wild cries and heathen screams they began to dance about their victim. Two advanced with measured steps and tied his hands and feet with a ghostly cord. It cut into the flesh like the stab of a great sorrow. They bound him to a stake which Rudolph felt conscious was no earthly and material wood, but a piece of intangible shadow; yet he could no more escape from it than from the iron chain of an earthly prison. On each side of the stake two savage hags, long-haired, ill-favoured, inexpressibly cruel looking, set two small plants of Enchanter's Nightshade. Then a fierce orgiastic shout went up to the low roof from all the assembled people. Rushing forward together, they covered his body with what seemed to be oil and butter; they hung grave flowers round his neck; they quarrelled among themselves with clamorous cries for hairs and rags torn from his head and clothing. The women, in particular, whirled round him with frantic Bacchanalian gestures, crying aloud as they circled, "O great Chief! O my King! we offer you this victim; we offer you new blood to prolong your life. Give us in return sound sleep, dry graves, sweet dreams, fair seasons!"

They cut themselves with flint knives. Ghostly ichor streamed copious.

The king meanwhile kept close guard over his victim, whom he watched with hungry eyes of hideous cannibal longing. Then, at a given signal, the crowd of ghosts stood suddenly still. There was an awesome pause. The men gathered outside, the women crouched low in a ring close up to him. Dimly at that moment Rudolph noticed almost without noticing that each of them had a wound on the side of his own skull; and he understood why: they had themselves been sacrificed in the dim long ago to bear their king company to the world of spirits. Even as that thought struck him, the men and women with a loud whoop raised hands

aloft in unison. Each grasped a sharp flake, which they brandished
savagely. The king gave the signal by rushing at him with a jagged and
saw-like knife. It descended on Rudolph's head. At the same moment,
the others rushed forward, crying aloud in their own tongue, "Carve the
flesh from his bones! Slay him! hack him to pieces!"

Rudolph bent his head to avoid the blows. He cowered in abject
terror. Oh! what fear would any Christian ghost have inspired by the side
of these incorporeal pagan savages! Ah! mercy! mercy! They would tear
him limb from limb! They would rend him in pieces!

At that instant he raised his eyes, and, as by a miracle of fate, saw
another shadowy form floating vague before him. It was the form of a
man in sixteenth-century costume, very dim and uncertain. It might
have been a ghost – it might have been a vision – but it raised its shadowy
hand and pointed towards the door. Rudolph saw it was unguarded. The
savages were now upon him, their ghostly breath blew chill on his cheek.
"Show them iron!" cried the shadow in an English voice. Rudolph struck
out with both elbows and made a fierce effort for freedom. It was with
difficulty he roused himself, but at last he succeeded. He drew his pocket-
knife and opened it. At sight of the cold steel, which no ghost or troll or
imp can endure to behold, the savages fell back, muttering. But only for a
moment. Next instant with a howl of vengeance even louder than before,
they crowded round him and tried to intercept him. He shook them off
with wild energy, though they jostled and hustled him, and struck him
again and again with the sharp flint edges. Blood was flowing freely now
from his hands and arms – red blood of this world; but still he fought his
way out by main force with his sharp steel blade towards the door and
the moonlight. The nearer he got to the exit, the thicker and closer the
ghosts pressed around, as if conscious that their power was bounded by
their own threshold. They avoided the knife, meanwhile, with superstitious terror. Rudolph elbowed them fiercely aside, and lunging at them
now and again, made his way to the door. With one supreme effort he
tore himself madly out, and stood once more on the open heath, shivering like a greyhound. The ghosts thronged grinning by the open
vestibule, their fierce teeth, like wild beasts', confessing their impotent
anger. But Rudolph started to run, wearied as he was, and ran a few
hundred yards before he fell and fainted. He dropped on a clump of
white heather by a sandy ridge, and lay there unconscious till the
morning.

V

When the people from the manor house picked him up next day, he was hot and cold, terribly pale from fear, and mumbling incoherently. Dr Porter had him put to bed without a moment's delay. "Poor fellow!" he said, leaning over him, "he's had a very narrow escape indeed of a bad brain fever. I oughtn't to have prescribed Cannabis in his excited condition; or, at any rate, if I did, I ought, at least, to have watched its effect more closely. He must be kept very quiet now, and on no account whatever, nurse, must either Mrs Bruce or Mrs Bouverie-Barton be allowed to come near him."

But late in the afternoon Rudolph sent for Joyce.

The child came creeping in with an ashen face. "Well?" she murmured, soft and low, taking her seat by the bedside; "so the King of the Barrow very nearly had you!"

"Yes," Rudolph answered, relieved to find there was somebody to whom he could talk freely of his terrible adventure. "He nearly had me. But how did you come to know it?"

"About two by the clock," the child replied, with white lips of terror, "I saw the fires on the moor burn brighter and bluer: and then I remembered the words of a terrible old rhyme the gipsy woman taught me –

> *Pallinghurst Barrow – Pallinghurst Barrow!*
> *Every year one heart thou'lt harrow!*
> *Pallinghurst Ring – Pallinghurst Ring!*
> *A bloody man is thy ghostly king.*
> *Men's bones he breaks, and sucks their marrow,*
> *In Pallinghurst Ring on Pallinghurst Barrow.*

and just as I thought it, I saw the lights burn terribly bright and clear for a second, and I shuddered from horror. Then they died down low at once, and there was moaning on the moor, cries of despair, as from a great crowd cheated, and at that I knew that you were not to be the Ghost-king's victim."

E. Nesbit

The Mystery of the
Semi-Detached

Edith Nesbit (1858–1924) is best remembered for her children's classics, notably
Five Children and It *and* The Railway Children, *successively dramatized for
both television and cinema. Early in her career she contributed some excellent supernatural stories to the* Illustrated London News, Argosy, *and other magazines, and
the best of these were collected in* Grim Tales *(1893), including the classic "Man-
Size in Marble", "John Charrington's Wedding", and "The Mystery of the Semi-
Detached".*

HE WAS WAITING for her; he had been waiting an hour and a half in a
dusty suburban lane, with a row of big elms on one side and some eligible
building sites on the other – and far away to the south-west the twinkling
yellow lights of the Crystal Palace. It was not quite like a country lane, for
it had a pavement and lamp-posts, but it was not a bad place for a
meeting all the same: and farther up, towards the cemetery, it was really
quite rural, and almost pretty, especially in twilight. But twilight had long
deepened into the night, and still he waited. He loved her, and he was
engaged to be married to her, with the complete disapproval of every
reasonable person who had been consulted. And this half-clandestine
meeting was tonight to take the place of the grudgingly sanctioned
weekly interview – because a certain rich uncle was visiting at her house,
and her mother was not the woman to acknowledge to a moneyed uncle,
who might "go off" any day, a match so deeply ineligible as hers with
him.

So he waited for her, and the chill of an unusually severe May evening entered into his bones.

The policeman passed him with a surly response to his "Good night". The bicyclists went by him like grey ghosts with foghorns; and it was nearly ten o'clock, and she had not come.

He shrugged his shoulders and turned towards his lodgings. His road led him by her house – desirable, commodious, semi-detached – and he walked slowly as he neared it. She might, even now, be coming out. But she was not. There was no sign of movement about the house, no sign of life, no lights even in the windows. And her people were not early people.

He paused by the gate, wondering.

Then he noticed that the front door was open – wide open – and the street lamp shone a little way into the dark hall. There was something about all this that did not please him – that scared him a little, indeed. The house had a gloomy and deserted air. It was obviously impossible that it harboured a rich uncle. The old man must have left early. In which case –

He walked up the path of patent glazed tiles, and listened. No sign of life. He passed into the hall. There was no light anywhere. Where was everybody, and why was the front door open? There was no one in the drawing room, the dining room and the study (nine feet by seven) were equally blank. Everyone was out, evidently. But the unpleasant sense that he was, perhaps, not the first casual visitor to walk through that open door impelled him to look through the house before he went away and closed it after him. So he went upstairs, and at the door of the first bedroom he came to he struck a wax match, as he had done in the sitting rooms. Even as he did so he felt that he was not alone. And he was prepared to see *something*; but for what he saw he was not prepared. For what he saw lay on the bed, in a white loose gown – and it was his sweetheart, and its throat was cut from ear to ear. He doesn't know what happened then, nor how he got downstairs and into the street; but he got out somehow, and the policeman found him in a fit, under the lamp-post at the corner of the street. He couldn't speak when they picked him up, and he passed the night in the police cells, because the policeman had seen plenty of drunken men before, but never one in a fit.

The next morning he was better, though still very white and shaky. But the tale he told the magistrate was convincing, and they sent a couple of constables with him to her house.

There was no crowd about it as he had fancied there would be, and the blinds were not down.

As he stood, dazed, in front of the door, it opened, and she came out.

He held on to the door-post for support.

"*She's* all right, you see," said the constable, who had found him under the lamp. "I told you you was drunk, but you *would* know best –"

When he was alone with her he told her – not all – for that would not bear telling – but how he had come into the commodious semi-detached, and how he had found the door open and the lights out, and that he had been into that long back room facing the stairs, and had seen something – in even trying to hint at which he turned sick and broke down and had to have brandy given him.

"But, my dearest," she said, "I dare say the house was dark, for we were all at the Crystal Palace with my uncle, and no doubt the door was open, for the maids *will* run out if they're left. But you could not have been in that room, because I locked it when I came away, and the key was in my pocket. I dressed in a hurry and I left all my odds and ends lying about."

"I know," he said; "I saw a green scarf on a chair, and some long brown gloves, and a lot of hairpins and ribbons, and a prayerbook, and a lace handkerchief on the dressing table. Why, I even noticed the almanack on the mantelpiece – 21 October. At least it couldn't be that, because this is May. And yet it was. Your almanack is at 21 October, isn't it?"

"No, of course it isn't," she said, smiling rather anxiously; "but all the other things were just as you say. You must have had a dream, or a vision, or something."

He was a very ordinary, commonplace, City young man, and he didn't believe in visions, but he never rested day or night till he got his sweetheart and her mother away from that commodious semi-detached, and settled them in a quiet distant suburb. In the course of the removal he incidentally married her, and the mother went on living with them.

His nerves must have been a good bit shaken, because he was very queer for a long time, and was always enquiring if anyone had taken the desirable semi-detached; and when an old stockbroker with a family took it, he went the length of calling on the old gentleman and imploring him by all that he held dear, not to live in that fatal house.

"Why?" said the stockbroker, not unnaturally.

And then he got so vague and confused, between trying to tell why and trying not to tell why, that the stockbroker showed him out, and thanked his God he was not such a fool as to allow a lunatic to stand in the way of his taking that really remarkably cheap and desirable semi-detached residence.

Now the curious and quite inexplicable part of this story is that when she came down to breakfast on the morning of the 22 October she found him looking like death, with the morning paper in his hand. He caught hers – he couldn't speak, and pointed to the paper. And there she read that on the night of the 21st a young lady, the stockbroker's daughter, had been found, with her throat cut from ear to ear, on the bed in the long back bedroom facing the stairs of that desirable semi-detached.

Ralph Adams Cram

Sister Maddelena

Ralph Adams Cram (1863–1942), one of America's leading architects, initiated a revival of medieval Gothic forms, particularly in the design of churches. Among his many books are The Ruined Abbeys of Great Britain, The Gothic Quest *and* My Life in Architecture. *His first book was a collection of ghost stories,* Black Spirits and White *(1895), from which the following story is taken.*

ACROSS THE VALLEY of the Oreto from Monreale, on the slopes of the mountains just above the little village of Parco, lies the old convent of Sta Catarina. From the cloister terrace at Monreale you can see its pale walls and the slim campanile of its chapel rising from the crowded citron and mulberry orchards that flourish, rank and wild, no longer cared for by pious and loving hands. From the rough road that climbs the mountains to Assunto, the convent is invisible, a gnarled and ragged olive grove intervening, and a spur of cliffs as well, while from Palermo one sees only the speck of white, flashing in the sun, indistinguishable from the many similar gleams of desert monastery or pauper village.

Partly because of this seclusion, partly by reason of its extreme beauty, partly, it may be, because the present owners are more than charming and gracious in their pressing hospitality, Sta Catarina seems to preserve an element of the poetic, almost magical; and as I drove with the Cavaliere Valguanera one evening in March out of Palermo, along the garden valley of the Oreto, then up the mountain side where the warm light of the spring sunset swept across the Monreale, lying golden and mellow on the luxuriant growth of figs, and olives, and orange trees, and fantastic cacti, and so up to where the path of the convent swung off to the right round a dizzy point of cliff that reached out gaunt and gray from the olives below – as I drove thus in the balmy air, and saw of a sudden a vision of creamy walls and orange roofs, draped in fantastic festoons of roses, with a single curing palm tree stuck black and feathery against the gold sunset, it is hardly to be wondered at that I should slip into a mood of visionary enjoyment, looking for a time on the whole thing as the misty phantasm of a summer dream.

The Cavaliere had introduced himself to us – Tom Rendel and me – one morning soon after we reached Palermo, when, in the first bewilderment of architects in this paradise of art and colour, we were working nobly at our sketches in that dream of delight, the Capella Palatina. He was himself an amateur archaeologist, he told us, and passionately devoted to his island; so he felt impelled to speak to anyone whom he saw appreciating the almost – and in a way fortunately – unknown beauties of Palermo. In a little time we were fully acquainted, and talking like the oldest friends. Of course he knew acquaintances of Rendel's – someone always does: this time they were officers on the tubby U.S.S *Quinebug*, that, during the summer of 1888, was trying to uphold the maritime honour of the United States in European waters. Luckily for us, one of the officers was a kind of cousin of Rendel's, and came from Baltimore as well, so, as he had visited at the Cavaliere's place, we were soon invited to do the same. It was in this way that, with the luck that attends Rendel wherever he goes, we came to see something of domestic life in Italy, and that I found myself involved in another of those adventures for which I naturally sought so little.

I wonder if there is any other place in Sicily so faultless as Sta Catarina? Taormina is a paradise, an epitome of all that is beautiful in Italy – Venice expected. Girgenti is a solemn epic, with its golden temples between the sea and hills. Cefalu is wild and strange, and Monreale a vision out of a fairy tale; but Sta Catarina!

Fancy a convent of creamy stone and rose-red brick perched on a ledge of rock midway between earth and heaven, the cliff falling almost sheer to the valley two hundred feet and more, the mountain rising behind straight towards the sky; all the rocks covered with cactus and dwarf fig-trees, the convent draped in smothering roses, and in front a terrace with a fountain in the midst; and then – nothing – between you and the sapphire sea, six miles away. Below stretches the Eden valley, the "Concha d'Oro", gold-green fig orchards alternating with smoke-blue olives, the mountains rising on either hand and sinking undulously away towards the bay where, like a magic city of ivory and nacre, Palermo lies guarded by the twin mountains, Monte Pelligrino and Capo Zafferano, arid rocks like dull amethysts, rose in sunlight, violet in shadow: lions couchant, guarding the sleeping town.

Seen as we saw it for the first time that hot evening in March, with the golden lambent light pouring down through the valley, making it in verity a "shell of gold", sitting in Indian chairs on the terrace, with the perfume of roses and jasmines all around us, the valley of the Oreto, Palermo, Sta Catarina, Monreale – all were but parts of a dreamy vision, like the heavenly city of Sir Percivale, to attain which he passed across the golden bridge that burned after him as he vanished in the intolerable light of the Beatific Vision.

It was all so unreal, so phantasmal, that I was not surprised in the least when, late in the evening after the ladies had gone to their rooms, and the Cavaliere, Tom, and I were stretched out in chairs on the terrace, smoking lazily under the multitudinous stars, the Cavaliere said, "There is something I really must tell you both before you go to bed, so that you may be spared any unnecessary alarm."

"You are going to say that the place is haunted," said Rendel, feeling vaguely on the floor beside him for his glass of Amaro: "thank you; it is all it needs."

The Cavaliere smiled a little: "Yes, that is just it. Sta Catarina is really haunted; and much as my reason revolts against the ideas as superstitious and savoring of the priestcraft, yet I must acknowledge I see no way of avoiding the admission. I do not presume to offer any explanations, I only state the fact; and the fact is that tonight one or other of you will, in all human – or unhuman – probability, receive a visit from Sister Maddelena. You need not be in the least afraid, the apparition is perfectly gentle and harmless; and, moreover, having seen it once, you will never see it again. No one sees the ghost, or whatever it is, but once, and that usually the first night he spends in the house. I myself saw the thing eight – nine years ago, when I first bought the place from Marchese di Muxaro; all my people have seen it, nearly all my guests, so I think you may as well be prepared."

"Then tell us what to expect," I said; "what kind of a ghost is this nocturnal visitor?"

"It is simple enough. Some time tonight you will suddenly awake and see before you a Carmelite nun who will look fixedly at you, say distinctly and very sadly, 'I cannot sleep,' and then vanish. That is all, it is hardly

SISTER MADDELENA 315

worth speaking of, only some people are terribly frightened if they are
visited unwarned by strange apparitions; so I tell you this that you may
be prepared."

"This was a Carmelite convent, then?" I said.

"Yes; it was suppressed after the unification of Italy, and given to the
House of Muxaro; but the family died out, and I bought it. There is a
story about the ghostly nun, who was only a novice, and even that unwillingly, which gives an interest to an otherwise very commonplace and
uninteresting ghost."

"I beg that you will tell it us," cried Rendel.

"There is a storm coming," I added. "See, the lightning is flashing
already up among the mountains at the head of the valley; if the story is
tragic, as it must be, now is just the time for it. You will tell it, will you
not?"

The Cavaliere smiled that slow, cryptic smile of his that was so unfathomable.

"As you say, there is a shower coming, and as we have fierce tempests
here, we might not sleep; so perhaps we may as well sit up a little longer,
and I will tell you the story."

The air was utterly still, hot and oppressive: the rich, sick odor of the
oranges just bursting into bloom came up from the valley in a gently
rising tide. The sky, thick with stars, seemed mirrored in the rich foliage
below, so numerous were the glow worms under the still trees, and the
fireflies that gleamed in the hot air. Lightning flashed fitfully from the
darkening west; but as yet no thunder broke the heavy silence.

The Cavaliere lighted another cigar, and pulled a cushion under his
head so that he could look down to the distant lights of the city. "This is
the story," he said.

"Once upon a time, late in the last century, the Duca di Castiglione
was attached to the court of Charles III, King of the Two Sicilies, down
at Palermo. They tell me he was very ambitious, and, not content with
marrying his son to one of the ladies of the House of Tuscany, had
betrothed his only daughter, Rosalia, to Prince Antonio, a cousin of the
king. His whole life was wrapped up in the fame of his family, and he
quite forgot all domestic affection in his madness for dynastic glory. His
son was a worthy scion, cold and proud; but Rosalia was, according to
legend, utterly the reverse – a passionate, beautiful girl, wilful and head-
strong, and careless of her family and the world.

"The time had nearly come for her to marry Prince Antonio, a typical

roué of the Spanish court, when, through the treachery of a servant, the
Duke discovered that his daughter was in love with a young military
officer whose name I don't remember, and that an elopement had been
planned to take place the next night. The fury and dismay of the old
autocrat passed belief; he saw in a flash the downfall of all his hopes of
family aggrandizement through union with the royal house, and,
knowing well the spirit of his daughter, despaired of ever bringing her to
subjection. Nevertheless, he attacked her unmercifully, and, by bullying
and threats, by imprisonment, and even bodily chastisement, he tried to
break her spirit and bend her to his indomitable will. Through his power
at court he had the lover sent away to the mainland, and for more than a
year he held his daughter closely imprisoned in his palace on the Toledo
– that one, you may remember, on the right, just beyond the Via del
Collegio dei Gesuiti, with the beautiful iron-work grilles at all the
windows, and the painted frieze. But nothing could move her, nothing
bend her stubborn will; and at last, furious at the girl he could not
govern, Castiglione sent her to this convent, then one of the few houses of
barefoot Carmelite nuns in Italy. He stipulated that she should take the
name of Maddelena, that he should never hear of her again, and that she
should be held an absolute prisoner in this conventual castle.

"Rosalia – or Sister Maddelena, as she was now – believed her lover
dead, for her father had given her good proofs of this, and she believed
him; nevertheless she refused to marry another, and seized upon the
convent life as a blessed relief from the tyranny of her maniacal father.

"She lived here for four or five years; her name was forgotten at court
and in her father's palace. Rosalia di Castiglione was dead, and only
Sister Maddelena lived, a Carmelite nun, in her place.

"In 1798 Ferdinand IV found himself driven from his throne on the
mainland, his kingdom divided, and he himself forced to flee Sicily. With
him came the lover of the dead Rosalia, now high in military honour. He
on his part had thought Rosalia dead, and it was only by accident that he
found that she still lived, a Carmelite nun. Then began the second act of
the romance that until then had been only sadly commonplace, but now
became dark and tragic. Michele – Michele Biscari – that was his name;
I remember now – haunted the region of the convent, striving to
communicate with Sister Maddelena; and at last, from the cliffs over us,
up there among the citrons – you will see by the next flash of lightning –
he saw her in the great cloister, recognized her in her white habit, found
her the same dark and splendid beauty of six years before, only made

more beautiful by her white habit and her rigid life. By and by he found a day when she was alone, and tossed a ring to her as she stood in the midst of the cloister. She looked up, saw him, and from that moment lived only to love him in life as she had loved his memory in the death she had thought had overtaken him.

"With the utmost craft they arranged their plans together. They could not speak, for a word would have aroused the other inmates of the convent. They could make signs only when Sister Maddelena was alone. Michele could throw notes to her from the cliff – a feat demanding a strong arm, as you will see, if you measure the distances with your eye – and she could drop replies from the window over the cliff, which he picked up at the bottom. Finally he succeeded in casting into the cloister a coil of light rope. The girl fastened it to the bars of one of the windows, and – so great is the madness of love – Biscari actually climbed the rope from the valley to the window of the cell, a distance of almost two hundred feet, with but three little craggy resting places in all that height. For nearly a month these nocturnal visits were undiscovered, and Michele had almost completed his arrangements for carrying the girl from Sta Catarina and away to Spain, when unfortunately one of the sisters, suspecting some mystery, from the changed face of Sister Maddelena, began investigating, and at length discovered the rope neatly coiled up by the nun's window, and hidden under some clinging vines. She instantly told the Mother Superior; and together they watched from a window in the crypt of the chapel – the only place, as you will see tomorrow, from which one could see the window of Sister Maddelena's cell. They saw the figure of Michele daringly ascending the slim rope; watched hour after hour, the Sister remaining while the Superior went to say the hours in the chapel, at each of which Sister Maddelena was present; and at last, at prime, just as the sun was rising, they saw the figure slip down the rope, watched the rope drawn up and concealed, and knew that Sister Maddelena was in their hands for vengeance and punishment – a criminal.

"The next day, by the order of the Mother Superior, Sister Maddelena was imprisoned in one of the cells under the chapel, charged with her guilt, and commanded to make full and complete confession. But not a word would she say, although they offered her forgiveness if she would tell the name of her lover. At last the Superior told her that after this fashion would they act the coming night: she herself would be placed in the crypt, tied in front of the window, her mouth gagged; that the rope would be lowered, and the lover allowed to approach even to the sill of her window, and at that moment the rope would be cut, and before her eyes her lover would be dashed to death on the ragged cliffs. The plan was feasible, and Sister Maddelena knew that the Mother was perfectly capable of carrying it out. Her stubborn spirit was broken, and in the only way possible; she begged for mercy, for the sparing of her lover. The Mother Superior was deaf at first; at last she said, "It is your life or his. I will spare him on condition that you sacrifice your own life." Sister Maddelena accepted the terms joyfully, wrote a last farewell to Michele, fastened the note to the rope, and with her own hands cut the rope and saw it fall coiling down to the valley bed far below.

"Then she silently prepared for death; and at midnight, while her lover was wandering, mad with the horror of impotent fear, around the white wall of the convent, Sister Maddelena, for love of Michele, gave up her life. How, was never known. That she was indeed dead was only a suspicion, for when Biscari finally compelled the civil authorities to enter the convent, claiming that murder had been done there, they found no signs. Sister Maddelena had been sent to the parent house of the barefoot Carmelites at Avila in Spain, so the Superior stated, because of her incorrigible contumacy. The old Duke of Castiglione refused to stir hand or foot in the matter, and Michele, after fruitless attempts to prove that the Superior of Sta Catarina had caused the death, was forced to leave Sicily. He sought in Spain for very long; but no sign of the girl was to be found, and at last he died, exhausted with suffering and sorrow.

"Even the name of Sister Maddelena was forgotten, and it was not until the convents were suppressed, and this house came into the hands of the Muxaros, that her story was remembered. It was then that the ghost began to appear; and, an explanation being necessary, the story, or legend, was obtained from one of the nuns who still lived after the suppression. I think the fact – for it is a fact – of the ghost rather goes to prove that Michele was right, and that poor Rosalia gave her life as a sacrifice for love – whether in accordance with the terms of the legend or not, I cannot say. One or the other of you will probably see her tonight. You might ask her for the facts. Well, that is all the story of Sister Maddelena, known in the world as Rosalia di Castiglione. Do you like it?"

"It is admirable," said Rendel, enthusiastically. "But I fancy I should rather look on it simply as a story, and not as a warning of what is going to happen. I don't much fancy real ghosts myself."

"But the poor Sister is quite harmless," and Valguanera rose, stretching himself. "My servants say she wants a mass said over her, or something of that kind; but I haven't much love for such priestly hocus pocus – I beg your pardon" (turning to me), "I had forgotten that you were a Catholic: forgive my rudeness."

"My dear Cavaliere, I beg you not to apologize. I am sorry you cannot see things as I do; but don't for a moment think I am hypersensitive."

"I have an excuse – perhaps you will say only an explanation; but I live where I see all the absurdities and corruptions of the Church."

"Perhaps you let the accidents blind you to the essentials; but do not let us quarrel tonight – see, the storm is close on us. Shall we go in?"

The stars were blotted out through nearly all the sky; low, thunderous clouds, massed at the head of the valley, were sweeping over so close that they seemed to brush the black pines on the mountain above us. To the south and east the storm-clouds had shut down almost to the sea, leaving a space of black sky where the moon in its last quarter was rising just to the left of Monte Pellegrino – a black silhouette against the pallid moonlight. The rosy lightning flashed almost incessantly, and through the fitful darkness came the sound of bells across the valley, the rushing torrent below, and the full roar of the approaching rain, with a deep organ point of solemn thunder through it all.

We fled indoors from the coming tempest, and taking our candles, said "goodnight," and sought each his respective room.

My own was in the southern part of the old convent, giving on the terrace we had just quitted, and about over the main doorway. The rushing storm, as it swept down the valley with the swelling torrent beneath, was very fascinating, and after wrapping myself in a dressing gown I stood for some time by the deeply embrasured window, watching the blazing lightning and the beating rain whirled by fitful gusts of wind around the spurs of the mountains. Gradually the violence of the shower seemed to decrease, and I threw myself down on my bed in the hot air, wondering if I really was to experience the ghostly visit the Cavaliere so confidently predicted.

I had thought out the whole matter to my own satisfaction, and fancied I knew exactly what I should do, in case Sister Maddelena came to visit me. The story touched me: the thought of the poor faithful girl who sacrificed herself for her lover – himself, very likely, quite unworthy – and who now could never sleep for reason of her unquiet soul, sent out into the storm of eternity without spiritual aid or counsel. I could not sleep; for the still vivid lightning, the crowding thoughts of the dead nun, and the shivering anticipation of my possible visitation, made slumber quite out of the question. No suspicion of sleepiness had visited me, when, perhaps an hour after midnight, came a sudden vivid flash of lightning, and, as my dazzled eyes began to regain the power of sight, I saw her as plainly as in life – a tall figure, shrouded in the white habit of the Carmelites, her head bent, her hands clasped before her. In another flash of lightning she slowly raised her head and looked at me long and earnestly. She was very beautiful, like the *Virgin of Beltraffio* in the National Gallery – more beautiful than I had supposed possible, her deep, passionate eyes very tender and pitiful in their pleading, beseeching glance. I hardly think I was frightened, or even startled, but lay looking steadily at her as she stood in the beating lightning.

Then she breathed, rather than articulated, with a voice that almost brought tears, so infinitely sad and sorrowful was it, "I cannot sleep!" and the liquid eyes grew more pitiful and questioning as bright tears fell from them down the pale dark face.

The figure began to move slowly towards the door, its eyes fixed on mine with a look that was weary and almost agonized. I leaped from the bed and stood waiting. A look of utter gratitude swept over the face, and, turning, the figure passed through the doorway.

Out into the shadow of the corridor it moved, like a drift of pallid storm cloud, and I followed, all natural and instinctive fear or nervousness quite blotted out by the part I felt I was to play in giving rest to a tortured soul. The corridors were velvet black; but the pale figure floated before me always, an unerring guide, now but a thin mist on the utter night, now white and clear in the bluish lightning through some window or doorway.

Down the stairway into the lower hall, across the refectory, where the great frescoed Crucifixion flared into sudden clearness under the fitful lightning, out into the silent cloister.

It was very dark. I stumbled along the heaving bricks, now guiding myself by a hand on the whitewashed wall, now by a touch on a column wet with the storm. From all the eaves the rain was dripping on to the pebbles at the foot of the arcade: a pigeon, startled from the capital where it was sleeping, beat its way into the cloister close. Still the white thing drifted before me to the farther side of the court, then along the cloister at right angles, and paused before one of the many doorways that led to the cells.

A sudden blaze of fierce lightning, the last now of the fleeting trail of storm, leaped around us, and in the vivid light I saw the face turned again with the look of overwhelming desire, of beseeching pathos, that had choked my throat with an involuntary sob when first I saw Sister Maddelena. In the brief interval that ensued after the flash, and before the roaring thunder burst like the crash of battle over the trembling convent, I heard again the sorrowful words, "I cannot sleep," come from the impenetrable darkness. And when the lightning came again, the white figure was gone.

I wandered around the courtyard, searching in vain for Sister Maddelena, even until the moonlight broke through the torn and sweeping fringes of the storm. I tried the door where the white figure vanished: it was locked; but I had found what I sought, and, carefully noting its location, went back to my room, but not to sleep.

In the morning the Cavaliere asked Rendel and me which of us had seen the ghost, and I told him my story; then I asked him to grant me permission to sift the thing to the bottom; and he courteously gave the whole matter into my charge, promising that he would consent to anything.

I could hardly wait to finish breakfast; but no sooner was this done than, forgetting my morning pipe, I started with Rendel and the Cavaliere to investigate.

"I am sure there is nothing in that cell," said Valguanera, when we came in front of the door I had marked. "It is curious that you should have chosen the door of the very cell that tradition assigns to Sister Maddelena; but I have often examined that room myself, and I am sure that there is no chance for anything to be concealed. In fact, I had the floor taken up once, soon after I came here, knowing the room was that of the mysterious Sister, and thinking that there, if anywhere, the monastic crime would have taken place; still, we will go in, if you like."

He unlocked the door, and we entered, one of us, at all events, with a beating heart. The cell was very small, hardly eight feet square. There certainly seemed no opportunity for concealing a body in the tiny place; and although I sounded the floor and walls, all gave a solid, heavy answer – the unmistakable sound of masonry.

For the innocence of the floor the Cavaliere answered. He had, he said, had it all removed, even to the curving surfaces of the vault below; yet somewhere in this room the body of the murdered girl was concealed – of this I was certain. But where? There seemed no answer; and I was

compelled to give up the search for the moment, somewhat to the amusement of Valguanera, who had watched curiously to see if I could solve
the mystery.

But I could not forget the subject, and towards noon started on
another tour of investigation. I procured the keys from the Cavaliere,
and examined the cells adjoining; they were apparently the same, each
with its window opposite the door, and nothing – Stay, were they the
same? I hastened into the suspected cell; it was as I thought: this cell,
being on the corner, could have had two windows, yet only one was
visible, and that to the left, at right angles with the doorway. Was it imagination? As I sounded the wall opposite the door, where the other
window should be, I fancied that the sound was a trifle less solid and dull.
I was becoming excited. I dashed back to the cell on the right, and,
forcing open the little window, thrust my head out.

It was found at last! In the smooth surface of the yellow wall was a
rough space, following approximately the shape of the other cell
windows, not plastered like the rest of the wall, but showing the shapes of
bricks through its thick coatings of whitewash. I turned with a gasp of
excitement and satisfaction: yes, the embrasure of the wall was deep
enough; what a wall it was! Four feet at least, and the opening of the
window reached to the floor, though the window itself was hardly three
feet square. I felt absolutely certain that the secret was solved, and called
the Cavaliere and Rendel, too excited to give them an explanation of my
theories.

They must have thought me mad when I suddenly began scraping
away at the solid wall in front of the door; but in a few minutes they
understood what I was about, for under the coatings of paint and plaster
appeared the original bricks; and as my architectural knowledge had led
me rightly, the space I had cleared was directly over a vertical joint
between firm, workmanlike masonry on one hand, and rough
amateurish work on the other, bricks laid anyway, and without order or
science.

Rendel seized a pick, and was about to assail the rude wall, when I
stopped him.

"Let us be careful," I said; "who knows what we may find?" So we set
to work digging out the mortar around the brick at about the level of our
eyes.

How hard the mortar had become! But a brick yielded at last, and
with trembling fingers I detached it. Darkness within, yet beyond ques-

tion there was a cavity there, not a solid wall; and with infinite care we removed another brick. Still the hole was too small to admit enough light from the dimly illuminated cell. With a chisel we pried at the sides of a large block of masonry, perhaps eight bricks in size. It moved, and we softly slid it from its bed.

Valguanera, who was standing watching us as we lowered the bricks to the floor, gave a sudden cry, a cry like that of a frightened woman – terrible, coming from him. Yet there was cause.

Framed by the ragged opening of the bricks, hardly seen in the dim light, was a face, an ivory image, more beautiful than any antique bust, but drawn and distorted by unspeakable agony; the lovely mouth half open, as though gasping for breath; the eyes cast upward; and below, slim chiselled hands crossed on the breast, but clutching the folds of the white Carmelite habit, torture and agony visible in every tense muscle, fighting against the determination of the rigid pose.

We stood there breathless, staring at the pitiful sight, fascinated, bewitched. So this was the secret. With fiendish ingenuity, the rigid ecclesiastics had blocked up the window, then forced the beautiful creature to stand in the alcove, while with remorseless hands and iron hearts they had shut her into a living tomb. I had read of such things in romance; but to find the verity here, before my eyes –

Steps came down the cloister, and with a simultaneous thought we sprang to the door and closed it behind us. The room was sacred; that awful sight was not for curious eyes. The gardener was coming to ask some trivial question of Valguanera. The Cavaliere cut him short. "Pietro, go down to Parco and ask Padre Stefano to come here at once." (I thanked with a glance.) "Stay!" He turned to me; "Signore, it is already two o'clock and too late for mass, is it not?"

I nodded.

Valguanera thought a moment, then he said, "Bring two horses; the Signor Americano will go with you – do you understand?" Then, turning to me, "You will go, will you not? I think you can explain matters to Padre Stefano better than I."

"Of course I will go, more than gladly."

So it happened that after a hasty luncheon I wound down the mountain to Parco, found Padre Stefano, explained my errand to him, found him intensely eager and sympathetic, and by five o'clock had him back at the convent with all that was necessary for the resting of the soul of the dead girl.

In the warm twilight, with the last light of the sunset pouring into the little cell through the window where almost a century ago Rosalia had for the last time said farewell to her lover, we gathered together to speed her tortured soul on its journey, so long delayed. Nothing was omitted; all the needful offices of the Church were said by Padre Stefano, while the light in the window died away, and the flickering flames of the candles carried by two of the acolytes from San Francisco threw fitful flashes of pallid light into the dark recess where the white face had prayed to Heaven for a hundred years.

Finally, the Padre took the asperge from the hands of one of the acolytes, and with a sign of the cross in benediction while he chanted the *Asperges*, gently sprinkled the holy water on the upturned face. Instantly the whole vision crumbled to dust, the face was gone, and where once the candlelight had flickered on the perfect semblance of the girl dead so very long, it now fell only on the rough bricks which closed the window, bricks laid with frozen hearts by pitiless hands.

But our task was not done yet. It had been arranged that Padre Stefano should remain at the convent all night, and that as soon as midnight made it possible he should say the first mass for the repose of the girl's soul. We sat on the terrace talking over the strange events of the last crowded hours, and I noted with satisfaction that the Cavaliere no longer spoke of the Church with that hardness, which had hurt me so often. It is true that the Padre was with us nearly all the time; but not only was Valguanera courteous, he was almost sympathetic; and I wondered if it might not prove that more than one soul benefited by the untoward events of the day.

With the aid of the astonished and delighted servants, and no little help as well from Signora Valguanera, I fitted up the long cold altar in the chapel, and by midnight we had the gloomy sanctuary beautiful with flowers and candles. It was a curiously solemn service, in the first hour of the new day, in the midst of blazing candles and the thick incense, the odor of the opening orange-blooms drifting up in the fresh morning air, and mingling with the incense smoke and the perfume of flowers within. Many prayers were said that night for the soul of the dead girl, and I think many afterwards; for after the benediction I remained for a little time in my place, and when I rose from my knees and went towards the chapel door, I saw a figure kneeling still, and, with a start, recognized the form of the Cavaliere. I smiled with quiet satisfaction and gratitude, and went away softly, content with the chain of events that now seemed finished.

The next day the alcove was again walled up, for the precious dust could not be gathered together for transportation to consecrated ground; so I went down to the little cemetery at Parco for a basket of earth, which we cast in over the ashes of Sister Maddelena.

By and by, when Rendel and I went away, with great regret, Valguanera came down to Palermo with us; and the last act that we performed in Sicily was assisting him to order a tablet of marble, whereon was carved this simple inscription:

HERE LIES THE BODY OF
ROSALIA DI CASTIGLIONÉ,
CALLED
SISTER MADDELENA.
HER SOUL
IS WITH HIM WHO GAVE IT.

To this I added in thought:
"Let him that is without sin among you cast the first stone."

Lettice Galbraith

The Trainer's Ghost

Lettice Galbraith's New Ghost Stories *(1897) was one of the best collections in the genre published in the late nineteenth century (unjustly forgotten today).*

THE CAT AND COMPASS was shut in for the night. The front of the house was dark and silent, for it was long past closing time, but from one of the rear ground-floor windows a thin shaft of yellow light gleamed through the falling rain, and indicated that behind the shutters of the snug bar-parlour, in a cheerful atmosphere of tobacco smoke and the odorous steam of hot "Scotch" Mr Samuel Vicary, licensed victualler, and two other congenial spirits, were "making a night of it".

"It's too late for Downey now," the landlord remarked, with a glance at the clock, as he leaned forward to knock out his pipe on the hob. "Twenty past twelve, and raining like blazes. Damn the weather; if it holds on like this, 'The Ghoul' will have his work cut out to get round the old course on Thursday with 8 stone 9."

"Not with that lot behind him," rejoined a seedy individual who sat on the farther side of the table. "I've watched them pretty careful. The race lies between us and the favourite, and with Downey up, she's safe enough. It's real jam this time – eh, Mr Davis?"

The gentleman indicated drained his glass with an unctuous smile. His exterior suggested the prosperous undertaker. As a matter of fact he was a bookmaker in a big way of business, and suspected, moreover, of having considerable interest in a stable notorious for the in and out running of its horses.

"That's about the size of it," he answered, drawing in his thick lips with a gentle, sucking sound, expressive of inward satisfaction.

"Prime whisky this, Vicary! I'll take another tot. Yes, it is a big thing, and, after this, Davis, Smiles, and Co. must lie quiet for a bit. There'll be plenty of fools to cry over burnt fingers by Monday, and what with stewards meddling where they've no cause to interfere, and the press writing up a lot of rot about 'rings' and such like, and the Jockey Club holding inquiries, a man must mind his P's and Q's in these days. Racing is going to the dogs, and soon there'll be no making a decent living on the turf. How it does rain to be sure! I shouldn't care to find myself abroad tonight."

"Here's some poor devil as has got to face it," said the tout, as the sound of horse-hoofs echoed down the quiet road. "Ain't he coming a lick, too! He's not afraid of bustling his cattle."

"Small blame to him either in weather like this," grunted the landlord, removing his pipe to listen. "Why, that's Downey's hack. I'd swear to her gallop among a thousand. To think, now, of his turning up at this time of night!"

The clatter of hoofs ceased, and the men sprang to their feet. In the silence that followed they heard the muffled slam of a closing gate, and the clink of shoes on the stones of the yard outside. Vicary snatched up the lamp and hurried to the door, while the visitors looked at each other.

"'Tis Downey sure enough," said the bookmaker, spitting energetically into the fire. "Now, what brings him here so late? He hasn't pelted over from Hawkhurst in the teeth of this storm for the pleasure of our company, I'll go bail."

The newcomer had swung himself off his horse before the landlord could unfasten the door.

"Yes, it's me – Downey," was his answer to that worthy's cautious challenge. "Look sharp with that chain and let me get under cover. I'm stiff with the cold, I can tell you, and the mare is about beat."

The chain fell with a clank, and Vicary flung back the door.

"Come in, come in," he cried, holding the lamp above his head to get a better view of his visitor. "Lord! how it do rain! Get out of that coat and put a tot of whisky inside you, while I see to the mare. 'Tis all right," he added, as the other jerked his head interrogatively in the direction of the bar-parlour, "there's only me and Slimmy and Davis. Go right in and help yourself."

Thus assured, the fresh arrival went forward, the water dripping from his soaked hat and covert coat, and trickling in little black streams over the well-stoned passage; while Vicary, flinging a rug across his shoulders, led the tired horse round to the stables. When he returned to the parlour Downey was drying himself before the fire, a smoking tumbler in his hand, and a good cigar between his lips.

"Well?" inquired the landlord, setting down the lamp with a keen glance at the disturbed countenances of the three men. "I take it, you did not come through this rain for nothing. Is aught the matter?"

"Matter enough," ejaculated Slimmy. "Here's Coulson got a rod in pickle that is going to upset our pot."

Vicary laughed.

"Go on with you," he said derisively, "they've nothing at Malton as can collar the Ghoul."

"Don't you be so precious sharp," the tout retorted. "Wait till you hear what Downey's got to say."

The jockey shifted his cigar to the other side of his mouth. "It is this way," he began. "One of Coulson's lads was at our place this afternoon, and he let on to me in confidence that they have a colt over there they think a real good thing for the Ebor. It is entered in Berkeley's name – the Captain, him as sold the Malton place to Coulson."

"The Captain's been stony broke this three year," put in Vicary. "How did he come by the colt?"

"Picked him up in the dales, from what I gather (he'd always a rare eye for a horse had the Captain), and fancied him so that he got young Alick to take half-share, and lend the purchase-money into the bargain, I reckon. The Coulsons always thought a lot of the old family. It wouldn't be the first time one of them had helped a Berkeley out of a tight place."

"That's true," assented the landlord. "Markham told me old Alick held enough of the squire's paper to cover a room. There wasn't anything he'd have stuck at to keep him on his legs. I remember him saying once in that very bar there, 'I'd come from hell,' he says, 'to stand by one of the old stock.' Fifteen years ago this very day it was, just before the Ebor, and the last time I ever saw the old chap alive, for Blue Ruin kicked the life out of him in his box at Malton on the morning of the race. Nothing would serve the squire but the horse must be shot the same night. Lord, what a shindy there was! And if it weren't like one of old Berkeley's fool's-tricks to 'blue' twelve hundred pounds that way, and him not knowing where to turn for the ready! But about this colt; if he's such a clipper, how is it nobody's heard of him before this?"

"Coulson has kept him dark. He's been trained at Beverley, and they only brought him to Malton three weeks back. The lad tells me he has been doing very good work, and he is to be tried in the morning with Cream Cheese – that is schoolmaster to the Leger crack. Now look here, if the colt can beat Cream Cheese at a stone, he's a mortal for the Ebor. On a heavy course he'll walk right away from the Ghoul, and put us in the cart."

The landlord whistled.

"You are sure the lad's square?"

"I'd peel the flesh off his bones if I thought he was putting the double on me; but he daren't try it. Coulson as good as swore the boys over to hold their tongues, but Tom says the stable is that sweet on his chance, they'll put their shirts on the colt at starting-price."

"Who's to ride him?"

"Alick's head lad. The brute has a temper, and won't stand much 'footling' about; but Jevons and he understand each other, and his orders are to get him off well, and sit still."

"I suppose now," suggested the bookmaker, "this Jevons ain't a reasonable sort of chap?"

Downey grinned. "As well try to square Coulson himself. He is one of your Sunday-school-and-ten-commandments sort, is Jevons. Besides, his father was the old squire's second horseman, and the lad was brought up in the stables. He swears by the Berkeleys, and would never lend a hand to put a spoke in the Captain's wheel."

"Do you know what time the trial is to come off?"

"About six. I reckoned on Slimmy's being within call, for there is precious little time to lose. It is light by four."

"I'm game," said the tout, "if Mr Vicary will lend me something to take me over."

The landlord consulted his watch. "Half-past one," he said. "Let's see; it's close on fifteen mile to Coulson's. I'll drop you at the Pig and Whistle. You can get over the fields from Gunny's corner in twenty minutes."

"You know your way?" queried Davis, uneasily.

"Every yard of it, guv'nor. Coulson and me is old friends so long as we don't happen to meet. There is a nice bit of cover at the end of the ground where I can lie snug. Will you wait for me, Mr Vicary?"

"Aye, I'll be on the road by Gunny's at seven. What for you, Downey; can we give you a shakedown here?"

"No thank you; I'm off," answered the jockey, laughing; "you're altogether too warm in this corner for a nice young man like me. I'm putting up at the Great Northern, and shall see you and Davis for the first time on the course, and not more than I can help of you then."

The rain had cleared off, and the first pale rifts in the eastern sky were broadening into grey dawn before Slimmy, from the convenient elevation of a friendly elder-bush, caught sight of a line of dark specks moving across the wold, and gradually resolving themselves into a string of horses.

"Here they come," he murmured, pocketing the flat bottle from which he had been refreshing his inner man, and working himself cautiously forward on the stout bough, while he parted the leaves with his left hand to command a better view. "And here's young Alick and the Captain. I thought as much," he added, triumphantly, for the trainer and Berkeley had cantered up and reined in their hacks within ten paces of his hiding-place.

In a very few minutes the horses were stripped and got into line. "They will start themselves," said Coulson, "and take it easy for the first half mile. Then you'll see, Captain, that there is very little fear but what the colt will give a good account of himself tomorrow. There they go, and a good start too."

The horses jumped off together, a big chestnut, which even in the half light Slimmy had recognized as Cream Cheese, coming to the front, with a clear lead. The soft drum of the hoofs on the moist ground died away, and the two men stood up in their stirrups, following with keen eyes the dim outline of the horses as they rounded the curve and swept into the straight, the chestnut still showing the way, with his stable companion and a powerful-looking bay in close attendance. "There he goes!" was the tout's mental ejaculation, for, at the bend for home, a dark horse crept up on the inside, and, taking up the running at half distance, came on and finished easily with a couple of lengths to spare.

Coulson turned to his companion with a smile.

"He'll do, Captain. The money is as good as banked. You can put on his clothes, Jevons, and take him home. He's a clipper, and no mistake. He came up the straight like a – "

"Rocket," suggested Berkeley. "How's that for a name? By Gunpowder out of Falling Star – not bad, I think."

"Couldn't be better," was the hearty answer.

"A few more of his sort, and we'll soon have you back at the Hall, Master Charles. I shall live to lead in a Derby winner for you yet. Lord! I think it would almost bring the old man out of his grave to know the Berkeleys had their own again."

The words were hardly past his lips when a crack, like the report of a pistol, close behind them, made both men jump as if they had been shot.

Mr Slimmy, who, having heard and seen all he wanted, was in the act of beating a masterly retreat, had unfortunately set his foot on a rotten branch, which instantly snapped beneath his weight. Taken by surprise, the tout lost his foothold and his balance at the same time, made an ineffectual grab at the swinging boughs, pitched forward, and, despite his wild endeavours to recover himself, descended precipitately in a shower of leaves and dry twigs on the wrong side of the hedge.

"Where the deuce did the fellow come from?" ejaculated Berkeley, as he gazed blankly at the heap on the ground. Coulson's only answer was to swing himself off his horse and fling the bridle to his companion. The quick-witted trainer had reckoned up the situation in a moment, and before the luckless Slimmy could gather himself together Coulson's hand was on his collar, and Coulson's "crop" was cracking and curling about his person, picking out the tenderest parts with a scientific precision that made him writhe and twist in frantic efforts to free himself from that iron grip. But the trainer stood six feet in his socks, and was well built. He held his victim like a rat, while his strong right arm brought the lash whistling down again and again with a force that cut through the tout's seedy clothing like a knife.

"For God's sake, Coulson," cried Captain Berkeley, "hold hard, or you will kill the man."

"And a good thing, too," said the trainer, relinquishing his hold on Slimmy with a suddenness that sent him sprawling into the muddy ditch. "I know him, and I'll have no touting on my place. If he shows his face here again, he'll find himself in the horsepond. Stop that row," he went on, turning to where Slimmy lay in the ditch, crying and cursing alternately; "and get off my ground before I chuck you over the fence."

White with rage and pain, the tout picked himself up and scrambled through the gap in the hedge as fast as his aching limbs could carry him. But when he had put a safe distance between himself and Coulson, he turned and shook his fist at the trainer's retreating figure.

"Curse you," he said, with a horrible imprecation. "I'll pay you out for this. I'll be even with you, if I swing for it, swelp me if I ain't."

Owner and trainer rode home in silence.

Coulson was a good deal upset by the discovery that his horse was being watched. He had recognized Slimmy, and Slimmy was known to be in the employ of a party popularly supposed to stick at nothing, and quite capable of trying to get at a horse that threatened to upset their game. Then, again, the arrangements and time of the trial had been kept so quiet that it seemed impossible the tout could get wind of it, except from one directly connected with the stables. Altogether Coulson felt uneasy, and, after some consideration, he mentioned his suspicions to his head lad, in whom he had the most implicit confidence. Jevons thought things over for a bit. Then he suggested the colt's box should be changed, and that he should sit up with him.

"Put him in the end box next the saddle-room, sir; it is so seldom used that an outsider would not think of trying it, and there isn't many of the lads as would like to rux about in there tonight, leastways not one as has a bad conscience."

Coulson knew what he meant. In the box next the saddle-room his father, old Alick Coulson, had come by his end, kicked to death by the Ebor favourite on the very eve of the race. A training-stable is not exactly a hot-bed of superstition, but, without doubt, a feeling did exist in connection with that particular box, and, as Jevons had said, it was very rarely used.

"Shall you like to sit up there yourself?" the trainer asked bluntly.

Jevons did not mind at all. He said he did not hold with ghosts and such like, and he was sure a sportsman like the old master would know better than to come upsetting the colt and spoiling his, Jevons's, nerve just before the race. Still, as there was gas in the saddle-room and a fire, if Mr Coulson had no objection, he might as well sit there, and look in every now and again to see his charge next door was getting on all right.

The trainer readily agreed. He had a high opinion of the lad's coolness and common sense, but he also felt that to pass the night alone and without a light in a place which, however undeservedly, had the reputation of being haunted, and that, too, on the very anniversary of the tragedy from which the superstition took its rise, was a performance calculated to try the strongest nerves, and he preferred that Jevons should not face the ordeal.

Indeed, it struck him as he left the lad for the night that he would scarcely have cared to undertake the watch himself. It might be fancy, but there was a queer feel about the place.

"Fifteen years ago tonight," thought Coulson, "since an Ebor crack stood in that box. It was a dark horse, too, and owned by the squire. It is a coincidence anyway. No, I shouldn't care to take on Jevons's job."

Nor was he alone in his conclusions. Several other people expressed a similar conviction, notably Jevons's subordinate, who had heard of the arrangement in the morning.

"I wouldn't be in Bill's shoes tonight – no, not for fifty down," he said, and slipped off unobserved to the nearest box to post a letter.

The communication he despatched was addressed to "S Downey, Esq., Great Northern Hotel, York," and was marked "immediate". The lad was going over to the races in the afternoon, and felt tolerably certain of getting speech with the jockey; but he was a careful young man, and wisely left nothing to chance.

It wanted fifteen minutes to midnight. Outside, the night was as black as your hat: not a vestige of a moon, not a single star to break the uniform darkness of the sky. With sunset a noisy blustering wind had sprung up, rattling about the chimneys, clashing the wet branches, and deadening the sound of cautious footfalls creeping across the paddock in the direction of the stables. Jevons was sitting over the saddle-room fire, with his pipe and the *Sporting Life* for company, and the remains of his supper-beer on the table beside him. From time to time he took a lantern and went to look at his charge. The colt had been quiet enough all the earlier part of the evening, but for the last half-hour Jevons fancied he could hear him fidgeting about on the other side of the wall.

"What ails the brute?" he said to himself, laying down his pipe to listen.

The wind dropped suddenly, making the silence all the more intense by contrast with the previous roar; and through the stillness Jevons heard the clink of a bucket, and the sound of someone moving about in the loose-box.

He sprang to his feet and snatched up the lantern. His sole idea was that someone was trying to get at the horse, and his hand was on the revolver in his breast-pocket when he opened the door. So strong was the impression that he was positively surprised to find no sign of an intruder. The colt was lying in the farthest corner and perfectly quiet. Jevons looked all round. There was certainly nothing to see, but it struck him that the air felt very cold, and he shut the door. The instant it closed behind him, a dark shadow fell across the square of light issuing from the entrance to the saddle-room.

"Now's your time, Slimmy," whispered Mr Vicary. "Nip in and doctor his liquor. This is getting precious slow."

The beer stood on a table barely two paces from the door. Stretching out his arm, the tout emptied the contents of a small bottle into the jug, and crept noiselessly back to his hiding-place.

"There's a deuce of a draught in here," said Jevons to himself, "and where it comes from fairly beats me."

He held up his hand at different heights, trying to test the direction of the chill current of air. But it seemed to come from every quarter at once, and shifted continually.

The lad struck a lucifer, and held it level with his shoulder. To his utter astonishment the flame burned clear and steady, though he could feel the cold draught blowing on his face, and even stirring the hair on his closely cropped head.

"That's a rum go," he said, staring at the match as it died out. He backed a few steps towards the wall, the draught was fainter; when he came level with the horse it ceased altogether.

"You are wise, my lad, to stick to this corner," Jevons remarked as he looked at the colt; "it's enough to blow your head off on the other side. Well, it must have been the wind I heard, for there ain't nothing here."

He locked the door and went back to the saddle-room. The hands of the American clock on the narrow mantelpiece pointed to twelve. Jevons loaded his pipe, poured out the rest of the beer, and took a long pull. Then he kicked the fire together, and looked about for a match.

"Now, where did I put that box," he said, staring stupidly round. "Where did I put that – what is it I'm looking for? What's got my head? It's all of a swim."

He felt for a chair and sat down, holding his hand to his heavy eyes. The lids felt as if they were weighted with lead. The gas danced in a golden mist that blinded him, and the whole room was spinning round and round. Then the pipe dropped from his nerveless fingers, and his head forward on the table.

"He's safe," muttered Vicary, as he softly pushed the door ajar and surveyed the unconscious lad. "That's prime stuff to keep the baby quiet. Here's the key, Slimmy; I'll bring the light. When we've damped the powder in that there rocket, Coulson will wish he hadn't been so handy with his crop this morning."

Slimmy turned the key in the lock and looked into the box; then he gave a slight start, and drew quickly back.

"What's up?" inquired the landlord. "Go on, it's all right."

"Sh!" whispered the tout, "he might hear you."

"Hear us? not he, nor the last day neither, if it come now."

He was thinking of Jevons, but Slimmy pulled to the door and held it.

"There's someone in there," he muttered, "an old chap. He's sitting on a bucket right in front of the horse."

"Did he see you?"

"I don't know, his back was turned and he looked asleep like."

He leaned forward, listening intently, but not a sound came from behind the closed door.

"Coulson didn't mean to be caught napping," said Vicary, under his breath. "Is it a stable hand?"

"A cut above that," returned the other, in the same tone.

" 'Tis queer he should keep so quiet."

They waited a few minutes, but everything was still.

"See here," whispered Slimmy, untwisting the muffler he wore round his neck, "there ain't no manner of use standing here all night. Give me the stick. If I can get past him quiet, I will; but if he moves, you be ready to slip the handkerchief over his head. He can't make much of a fight agen the two of us, and we ain't got this far to be stalled off by an old crock like him; keep well behind him. Never mind the lantern. He's got a light inside."

There was a light inside, but where it came from would have been difficult to say. It fell clear as a limelight over half the box, and beyond the shadow lay black and impenetrable, a wall of darkness.

As he crossed the threshold Slimmy felt a blast of cold air sweep towards him, striking a strange chill into his very bones.

Straight opposite stood a horse, and before him an old man was sitting on a reversed bucket, his elbow resting on his knee, his head on his hand. To all appearances he was asleep. But even in that intense stillness the tout could catch no sound of breathing. His own heart was thumping against his ribs with the force of a sledge-hammer. He felt his flesh creeping with a sensation of fear that was almost sickening. Fear? Yes, that was the word; he was horribly afraid. And of what? Of a weak old man, for whom he would have been more than a match single-handed, and they were two to one. What a fool he was, to be sure! With desperate effort he pulled himself together and went forward, his eye warily fixed on the silent figure. Neither man nor horse moved. Slimmy thrust his hand into his pocket and felt for the bottle which was to settle the

Rocket's chances for the Ebor! His fingers were on the cork, when the silence was broken by a sound that brought a cold sweat out on his forehead and lifted the hair on his head. It was a low chuckling laugh. The man on the bucket was looking at him. The gleaming eyes fixed on him with a sort of mesmeric power, and the bottle fell from his trembling fingers.

"Quick with the rag, Sam," he gasped, "he's seen me." But Vicary stood like one turned to stone. His gaze fastened on the seated figure, taking in every item of the quaint dress, the high gill collar and ample bird's-eye stock, the drab coat and antiquated breeches and gaiters. His mouth was open, but for the life of him he could not speak. He was waiting in the helpless fascination of horror to see the face of a man who had been dead and buried for fifteen years.

Slowly, like an automaton, that strange watcher turned his head. The square, resolute mouth was open as if to speak; the shrunken skin was a greenish yellow colour, like the skin of a corpse; along the temple ran a dull blue mark in the shape of a horse's hoof; but the eyes burned like two living coals, as they fixed themselves on the face of the terrified publican.

With a single yell of "Lord ha' mercy on us! 'tis old Alick himself!" Vicary turned and fled.

Slimmy heard the crash of the lantern on the stones and the sound of his flying feet, and an awful terror came upon him, a great fear, which made his teeth chatter in his head and curdled the blood in his veins.

The place seemed full of an unnatural light – the blue flames that dance at night over deserted graveyards. The air was foul with the horrible odours of decay. Above all, he felt the fearful presence of that which was neither living nor dead – the semblance of a man whose human body had for fifteen years been rotting in the grave. It was not living, but it moved. Its cold, shining eyes were looking into his, were coming nearer. Now they were close to him. With the energy of despair, Slimmy grasped his stick by the thin end and struck with his full force at the horror before him. The loaded knob whistled through empty air, and, overbalanced by the force of his own blow, the wretched tout pitched forward, and with one piercing shriek fell prone on the straw.

"Did you hear that?"

"What the deuce was it?"

The two men, who were sitting over the fire in the comfortable smoking-room, sprang to their feet. Coulson put down his pipe and went into the hall. Some one was moving about in the kitchen.

"Is that you, Martin?" he called. "What was that row?"

The man came out at once.

"Did you hear it too, sir? It made me jump, it came so sudden. Sounded like some one hollering out in the stables."

"Get a lantern. I must go across and see what it was. Are you coming, too, Captain? Then bring that shillelagh in your hand. It might be useful."

Martin unbolted the side door, which opened on the garden, and the three men crossed the gravel path and went through the yard. Here they saw the gleam of another lantern. Some one was running towards them. It was one of the lads, half dressed, and evidently just out of bed.

"Is that you, Mr Coulson?" he said breathlessly. "Did you hear that scream? It woke us all up. Bryant can see the saddle-room from his window, and he says the door is wide open."

"Come on," was Coulson's answer, as they hurried across to the stables. The square of light from the saddle-room showed clearly through the darkness.

"Here's Jevons," said the trainer, who was the first to enter. "He is only asleep," he added, as he lifted the lad's head and listened to the regular breathing. He shook him roughly, trying to arouse him, but Jevons was beyond being awakened by any ordinary method; he made an inarticulate grunt, and dropped back into his former attitude.

"Drunk?" ejaculated Martin, blankly.

"Drugged, by gad!" Captain Berkeley had taken the empty jug from the table and smelt it. The sickly odour of the powerful opiate clung about the pitcher and told its own tale.

"Then," cried the trainer, "as I'm a living man, they've got at the colt." His face was white and set as he seized the lantern and ran to the loose-box. The door was open; the key was in the lock. The men crowded up. There was scarcely a doubt in their minds but that the mischief was already done. Coulson held up the lantern and looked round. The colt was standing up in the corner, snorting and sniffing the air. He, too, had been startled by that terrible cry.

On the ground, straight in front of the door, a man lay prone on his face. There was no mistaking the look of that helpless body, the limp flaccidity of those outstretched arms.

"He's dead, sir," said Martin, as he turned up the white face; "hold the light down; his coat's all wet with – something."

It was not blood, only a sticky, dark-coloured fluid, the contents of a broken bottle lying underneath the body. Just beyond the reach of the clenched right hand was a heavy loaded-stick, and near the door they found a thick woollen handkerchief. Berkeley bent down and looked at the drawn features.

"Surely," he said, in a low voice, "it is the same man you thrashed this morning?"

Coulson nodded. "He meant squaring accounts with me and he has had to settle his own instead. It is strange that there should be no marks of violence about him, and yet he looks as if he had died hard."

And truly, the dead man's face was terrible in its fixed expression of mortal fear. The eyes were staring and wide open, the teeth clenched, a little froth hung about the blue lips. It was a horrid sight. They satisfied themselves that life was absolutely extinct. Then Coulson gave orders for the colt to be taken back to his old box, locked the door on the corpse until the police could arrive, and spent the remainder of the night in the saddle-room, waiting until Jevons should have slept off the effects of the opiate.

But when the lad awoke he could throw very little light on the matter. He swore positively there was no one in the box when he paid his last visit at five minutes to twelve, and he could remember nothing after returning to the saddle-room. How the tout had effected an entrance, by what means his purpose had been frustrated and his life destroyed, remained for ever a mystery. The only living man who knew the truth held his tongue, and the dead can tell no tales. But Mr Vicary, as he watched Captain Berkeley's colt walk away from his field next day, and, cleverly avoiding a collision with the favourite on the rails, pass the post a winner by three lengths, was struck by the fact that the "Rocket" had grown smaller during the night, and he could have sworn the horse he saw in the loose-box had some white about him somewhere.

"He's one o' raight sort," exclaimed a stalwart Yorkshireman who stood at Vicary's elbow. "When aa seed him i' t' paddock, aa said aa'l hev a pound on th' squoire's 'oss for t' sake of ould toimes, for he's strange and loike Blue Ruin, as won th' Ebor in seventy-foive. 'Twas fust race as iver aa'd clapped eyes on, and aa'd backed him for ivery penny aa'd got."

The publican turned involuntarily to the speaker, "Did you say yon colt was like Blue Ruin?" he asked hoarsely.

"The very moral of him, barring he ain't quite so thick, and ain't got no white stocking. I reckon you'll remember Blue Ruin," added the farmer, referring to a friend on the other side, "him as killed ould Coulson?"

Vicary was a strong man, but at the mention of that name a strange, sickly sensation crept over him. The colour forsook his face, and when, a few minutes later he called for a brandy "straight", the hand he stretched out for the glass was shaking visibly.

Once, and once only, did the landlord allude to the events of that fatal night. It was when Mr David, loudly deploring his losses, expressed an opinion that Slimmy was "a clumsy fool, and matters would have come out very differently if he had been there."

"You may thank your stars," was Vicary's energetic rejoinder, "that you never set foot in the cursed place. The poor chap is dead, and there ain't no call for me to get myself mixed up in the business. Least said, soonest mended, say I; but you mind the story I told you the night Downey brought the news of that blooming colt, about ould Coulson swearing he'd come back from the dead, if need be, to do a Berkeley a good turn."

"I remember right enough. What's that got to do with it?"

The landlord glanced nervously over his shoulder. "Only this," he answered, sinking his voice to a whisper, "*he kept his word!*"

W. C. Morrow

An Original Revenge

William Chambers Morrow (1853–1923) was an American writer based for many years in San Francisco. This story is taken from his celebrated collection of bizarre supernatural tales The Ape, the Idiot & Other People *(1897).*

ON A CERTAIN DAY I received a letter from a private soldier, named Gratmar, attached to the garrison of San Francisco. I had known him but slightly, the acquaintance having come about through his interest in some stories which I had published, and which he had a way of calling "psychological studies." He was a dreamy, romantic, fine-grained lad, proud as a tiger-lily and sensitive as a blue-bell. What mad caprice led him to join the army I never knew; but I did know that there he was wretchedly out of place, and I foresaw that his rude and repellant environment would make of him in time a deserter, or a suicide, or a murderer. The letter at first seemed a wild outpouring of despair, for it informed me that before it should reach me its author would be dead by his own hand. But when I had read farther I understood its spirit, and realized how coolly formed a scheme it disclosed and how terrible its purport was intended to be. The worst of the contents was the information that a certain officer (whom he named) had driven him to the deed, and that *he was committing suicide for the sole purpose of gaining thereby the power to revenge himself upon his enemy!* I learned afterward that the officer had received a similar letter.

This was so puzzling that I sat down to reflect upon the young man's peculiarities. He had always seemed somewhat uncanny, and had I proved more sympathetic he doubtless would have gone farther and told me of certain problems which he professed to have solved concerning the life beyond this. One thing that he had said came back vividly: "If I could only overcome that purely gross and animal love of life that makes us all shun death, I would kill myself, for I know how far more powerful I could be in spirit than in flesh."

The manner of the suicide was startling, and that was what might have been expected from this odd character. Evidently scorning the flummery of funerals, he had gone into a little canyon near the military reservation and blown himself into a million fragments with dynamite, so that all of him that was ever found was some minute particles of flesh and bone.

I kept the letter a secret, for I desired to observe the officer without rousing his suspicion of my purpose; it would be an admirable test of a dead man's power and deliberate intention to haunt the living, for so I interpreted the letter. The officer thus to be punished was an oldish man, short, apoplectic, overbearing, and irascible. Generally he was kind to most of the men in a way; but he was gross and mean, and that explained sufficiently his harsh treatment of young Gratmar, whom he could not understand, and his efforts to break that flighty young man's spirit.

Not very long after the suicide certain modifications in the officer's conduct became apparent to my watchful oversight. His choler, though none the less sporadic, developed a quality which had some of the characteristics of senility; and yet he was still in his prime, and passed for a sound man. He was a bachelor, and had lived always alone; but presently he began to shirk solitude at night and court it in daylight. His brother-officers chaffed him, and thereupon he would laugh in rather a forced and silly fashion, quite different from the ordinary way with him, and would sometimes, on these occasions, blush so violently that his face would become almost purple. His soldierly alertness and sternness relaxed surprisingly at some times and at others were exaggerated into unnecessary acerbity, his conduct in this regard suggesting that of a drunken man who knows that he is drunk and who now and then makes a brave effort to appear sober. All these things, and more, indicating some mental strain, or some dreadful apprehension, or perhaps something worse than either, were observed partly by me and partly by an intelligent officer whose watch upon the man had been secured by me.

To be more particular, the afflicted man was observed often to start suddenly and in alarm, look quickly round, and make some unintelligent monosyllabic answer, seemingly to an inaudible question that no visible person had asked. He acquired the reputation, too, of having taken lately to nightmares, for in the middle of the night he would shriek in the most dreadful fashion, alarming his room-mates prodigiously. After these attacks he would sit up in bed, his ruddy face devoid of color, his eyes glassy and shining, his breathing broken with gasps, and his body wet with a cold perspiration.

Knowledge of these developments and transformations spread throughout the garrison; but the few (mostly women) who dared to express sympathy or suggest a tonic encountered such violent rebuffs that they blessed Heaven for escaping alive from his word-volleys. Even the garrison surgeon, who had a kindly manner, and the commanding general, who was constructed on dignified and impressive lines, received little thanks for their solicitude. Clearly the doughty old officer, who had fought like a bulldog in two wars and a hundred battles, was suffering deeply from some undiscoverable malady.

The next extraordinary thing which he did was to visit one evening (not so clandestinely as to escape my watch) a spirit medium – extraordinary, because he always had scoffed at the idea of spirit communications. I saw him as he was leaving the medium's rooms. His face was purple, his eyes were bulging and terrified, and he tottered in his walk. A policeman, seeing his distress, advanced to assist him; whereupon the soldier hoarsely begged –

"Call a hack."

Into it he fell, and asked to be driven to his quarters. I hastily ascended to the medium's rooms, and found her lying unconscious on the floor. Soon, with my aid, she recalled her wits, but her conscious state was even more alarming than the other. At first she regarded me with terror, and cried –

"It is horrible for you to hound him so!"

I assured her that I was hounding no one.

"Oh, I thought you were the spir – I mean – I – oh, but it was standing exactly where you are!" she exclaimed.

"I suppose so," I agreed, "but you can see that I am not the young man's spirit. However, I am familiar with this whole case, madam, and if I can be of any service in the matter I should be glad if you would inform me. I am aware that our friend is persecuted by a spirit, which visits him frequently, and I am positive that through you it has informed him that the end is not far away, and that our elderly friend's death will assume some terrible form. Is there anything that I can do to avert the tragedy?"

The woman stared at me in a horrified silence. "How did you know these things?" she gasped.

"That is immaterial. When will the tragedy occur? Can I prevent it?"

"Yes, yes!" she exclaimed. "It will happen this very night! But no earthly power can prevent it!"

She came close to me and looked at me with an expression of the most acute terror.

"Merciful God! what will become of me? He is to be murdered, you understand – murdered in cold blood by a spirit – and he knows it and *I know it*! If he is spared long enough he will tell them at the garrison, and they will all think that I had something to do with it! Oh, this is terrible, terrible, and yet I dare not say a word in advance – nobody there would believe in what the spirits say, and they will think that I had a hand in the murder!" The woman's agony was pitiful.

"Be assured that he will say nothing about it," I said; "and if you keep your tongue from wagging you need fear nothing."

With this and a few other hurried words of comfort, I soothed her and hastened away.

For I had interesting work on hand: it is not often that one may be in at such a murder as that! I ran to a livery stable, secured a swift horse, mounted him, and spurred furiously for the reservation. The hack, with its generous start, had gone far on its way, but my horse was nimble, and his legs felt the pricking of my eagerness. A few miles of this furious pursuit brought me within sight of the hack just as it was crossing a dark ravine near the reservation. As I came nearer I imagined that the hack swayed somewhat, and that a fleeing shadow escaped from it into the tree-banked further wall of the ravine. I certainly was not in error with regard to the swaying, for it had roused the dull notice of the driver. I saw him turn, with an air of alarm in his action, and then pull up with a heavy swing upon the reins. At this moment I dashed up and halted.

"Anything the matter?" I asked.

"I don't know," he answered, getting down. "I felt the carriage sway, and I see that the door's wide open. Guess my load thought he'd sobered up enough to get out and walk, without troubling me or his pocket-book."

Meanwhile I too had alighted; then struck a match, and by its light we discovered, through the open door, the "load" huddled confusedly on the floor of the hack, face upward, his chin compressed upon his breast by his leaning against the further door, and looking altogether vulgar, misshapen, and miserably unlike a soldier. He neither moved nor spoke when we called. We hastily clambered within and lifted him upon the seat, but his head rolled about with an awful looseness and freedom, and another match disclosed a ghastly dead face and wide eyes that stared horribly at nothing.

"You would better drive the body to headquarters," I said.

Instead of following, I cantered back to town, housed my horse, and went straightway to bed; and this will prove to be the first information that I was the "mysterious man on a horse," whom the coroner could never find.

About a year afterwards I received the following letter (which is observed to be in fair English) from Stockholm, Sweden:

> DEAR SIR, For some years I have been reading your remarkable psychological studies with great interest, and I take the liberty to suggest a theme for your able pen. I have just found in a library here a newspaper, dated about a year ago, in which is an account of the mysterious death of a military officer in a hack.

Then followed the particulars, as I have already detailed them, and the very theme of post-mortem revenge which I have adopted in this setting out of facts. Some persons may regard the coincidence between my correspondent's suggestion and my private and exclusive knowledge as being a very remarkable thing; but there are likely even more wonderful things in the world, and at none of them do I longer marvel. More extraordinary still is his suggestion that in the dynamite explosion a dog or a quarter of beef might as well have been employed as a suicide-minded man; that, in short, the man may not have killed himself at all, but might have employed a presumption of such an occurrence to render more effective a physical persecution ending in murder by the living man who had posed as a spirit. The letter even suggested an arrangement with a spirit medium, and I regard that also as a queer thing.

The declared purpose of this letter was to suggest material for another of my "psychological studies"; but I submit that the whole affair is of too grave a character for treatment in the levity of fiction. And if the facts and coincidences should prove less puzzling to others than to me, a praiseworthy service might be done to humanity by the presentation of whatever solution a better understanding than mine might evolve.

The only remaining disclosure which I am prepared now to make is that my correspondent signed himself "Ramtarg," – an odd-sounding name, but for all I know it may be respectable in Sweden. And yet there is something about the name that haunts me unceasingly, much as does some strange dream which we know we have dreamt and yet which it is impossible to remember.

Alice Perrin

Caulfield's Crime

Alice Perrin (1867–1934) was a very popular novelist who spent many years in India. Among her books are The Spell of the Jungle, The Waters of Destruction, Star of India, *and a study of* The Anglo-Indians. *Her first collection,* East of Suez *(1901), contained several weird supernatural tales including "In the Next Room", "Chunia, Ayah", and "Caulfield's Crime".*

CAULFIELD WAS A SULKY, bad-tempered individual who made no friends and was deservedly unpopular, but he had the reputation of being the finest shot in the Punjab, and of possessing a knowledge of sporting matters that was almost superhuman. He was an extremely jealous shot, and hardly ever invited a companion to join him on his shooting trips, so it may be understood that I was keenly alive to the honour conferred on me when he suddenly asked me to go out for three days' small game shooting with him.

"I know a string of *jheels*,"[1] he said, "about thirty miles from here, where the duck and snipe must swarm. I marked the place down when I was out last month, and I've made arrangements to go there next Friday morning. You can come, too, if you like."

I readily accepted the ungracious invitation, though I could hardly account for it, knowing his solitary ways, except that he probably thought I was unlikely to assert myself, being but a youngster, and also he knew me better than he did most people, for our houses were next door, and I often strolled over to examine his enormous collection of skins and horns and other sporting trophies.

[1] Tract of marshy ground.

I bragged about the coming expedition in the club that evening, and was well snubbed by two or three men who would have given anything to know the whereabouts of Caulfield's string of jheels, and who spitefully warned me to be careful that Caulfield did not end by shooting *me*.

"I believe he'd kill any chap who annoyed him," said one of them, looking round to make sure that Caulfield was not at hand. "I never met such a nasty-tempered fellow, I believe he's mad. But he can shoot, and what he doesn't know about game isn't worth knowing."

Caulfield and I rode out the thirty miles early on the Friday morning, having sent our camp on ahead the previous night. We found our tents pitched in the scanty shade of some stunted *dâk* jungle trees with thick dry bark, flat, shapeless leaves, that clattered together when stirred by the wind, and wicked-looking red blossoms. It was not a cheerful spot, and the soil was largely mixed with salt which had worked its way in white patches to the surface, and only encouraged the growth of the rankest of grass.

Before us stretched a dreary outlook of shallow lake and swampy ground, broken by dark patches of reeds and little bushy islands, while on the left a miserable mud village overlooked the water. The sun had barely cleared away the thick, heavy mist, which was still slowly rising here and there, and the jheel birds were wading majestically in search of their breakfast of small fish, and uttering harsh, discordant cries.

To my astonishment, Caulfield seemed a changed man. He was in excellent spirits, his eyes were bright, and the sullen frown had gone from his forehead.

"Isn't it a lovely spot?" he said, laughing and rubbing his hands. "Beyond that village the snipe ought to rise in thousands from the rice fields. We shan't be able to shoot it all in three days, worse luck, but we'll keep it dark, and come again. Let's have breakfast. I don't want to lose any time."

Half an hour later we started, our guns over our shoulders, and a couple of servants behind us carrying the luncheon and cartridge bags. My spirits rose with Caulfield's, for I felt we had the certainty of an excellent day's sport before us.

But the birds were unaccountably wild and few and far between, and luck seemed dead against us. "Some brutes" had evidently been there before us and harried the birds, was Caulfield's opinion, delivered with disappointed rage, and after tramping and wading all day, we returned, weary and crestfallen, with only a few couple of snipe and half a dozen teal between us. Caulfield was so angry he could hardly eat any dinner, and afterwards sat cursing his luck and the culprits who had forestalled us, till we could neither of us keep awake any longer.

The next morning we took a different route from the previous day, but with no better result. On and on, and round and round we tramped, with only an occasional shot here and there, and at last, long after midday, we sat wearily down to eat our luncheon. I was ravenously hungry, and greedily devoured my share of the provisions, but Caulfield hardly touched a mouthful, and only sat moodily examining his gun, and taking long pulls from his whisky flask. We were seated on the roots of a large tamarind tree, close to the village, and the place had a dreary, depressing appearance. The yellow mud walls were ruined and crumbling, and the inhabitants seemed scanty and poverty-stricken. Two ragged old women were squatting a short distance off, watching us with dim, apathetic eyes, and a few naked children were playing near them, while some nigger boys were driving two or three lean buffaloes towards the water.

Presently another figure came in sight – a fakir, or mendicant priest, as was evident by the tawny masses of wool woven amongst his own black locks and hanging in ropes below his shoulders, the ashes smeared over the almost naked body, and the hollow gourd for alms which he held in his hand. The man's face was long and thin, and his pointed teeth glistened in the sunlight as he demanded money in a dismal monotone. Caulfield flung a pebble at him and told him roughly to be off, with the result that the man slowly disappeared behind a clump of tall, feathery grass.

"Did you notice that brute's face?" said Caulfield as we rose to start again. "He must have been a pariah dog in a former existence. He was exactly like one!"

"Or a jackal perhaps," I answered carelessly. "He looked more like a wild beast."

Then we walked on, skirting the village and plunging into the damp, soft rice fields. We put up a wisp of snipe, which we followed till we had shot them nearly all, and then, to our joy, we heard a rush of wings overhead, and a lot of duck went down into the corner of a jheel in front of us.

"We've got 'em!" said Caulfield, and we hurried on till we were almost within shot of the birds, and could hear them calling to each other in their fancied security. But suddenly they rose again in wild confusion, and with loud cries of alarm were out of range in a second. Caulfield

swore, and so did I, and our rage was increased ten-fold when the
disturber of the birds appeared in sight, and proved to be the fakir who
had paid us a visit at luncheon-time. Caulfield shook his fist at the man
and abused him freely in Hindustani, but without moving a muscle of his
dog-like face the fakir passed us and continued on his way.

Words could not describe Caulfield's vexation.

"They were pin-tail, all of them," he said, "and the first decent chance
we've had since we came out. To think of that beastly fakir spoiling the
whole show, and I don't suppose he had the least idea what he had done."

"Probably not," I replied, "unless there was some spite in it because
you threw a stone at him that time."

"Well, come along," said Caulfield, with resignation, "we must make
haste as it will be dark soon, and I want to try a place over by those palms
before we knock off. We may as well let the servants go back as they've
had a hard day. Have you got some cartridges in your pocket?"

"Yes, plenty," I answered, and after despatching the two men back to
the camp with what little game we had got, we walked on in silence.

The sun was sinking in a red ball and the air was heavy with damp, as
the white mist stole slowly over the still, cold jheels. Far overhead came
the first faint cackle of the wild geese returning home for the night, and
presently as we approached the clump of palms we saw more water glistening between the rough stems, and on it, to our delight, a multitude of
duck and teal.

But the next moment there was a whir-r-r of wings like the rumble of
thunder, and a dense mass of birds flew straight into the air and wheeled
bodily away, while the sharp, cold atmosphere resounded with their startled cries. Caulfield said nothing, but he set his jaw and walked rapidly
forward, while I followed. We skirted the group of palms, and on the
other side we came upon our friend the fakir, who had again succeeded
in spoiling our sport. The long, lanky figure was drawn to its full height,
the white eyeballs and jagged teeth caught the red glint of the setting sun,
and he waved his hand triumphantly in the direction of the vanishing
cloud of birds.

Then there came the loud report of a gun, and the next thing I saw
was a quivering body on the ground, and wild eyes staring open in the
agony of death. Caulfield had shot the fakir, and now he stood looking
down at what he had done, while I knelt beside the body and tried hopelessly to persuade myself that life was not extinct. When I got up we
gazed at each other for a moment in silence.

"What are we to do?" I asked presently.

"Well, you know what it means," Caulfield said in a queer, hard voice. "Killing a native is no joke in these days, and I should come out of it pretty badly."

I glanced at the body in horror. The face was rigid, and seemed more beast-like than ever. I looked at Caulfield again before I spoke, hesitatingly.

"Of course the whole thing was unpremeditated – an accident."

"No, it wasn't," he said defiantly. "I meant to shoot the brute, and it served him right. And you can't say anything else if it comes out. But I don't see why anyone should know about it but ourselves."

"It's a nasty business," I said, my heart sinking at the suggestion of concealment.

"It will be nastier still if we don't keep it dark, and you won't like having to give me away, you know. Either we must bury the thing here and say nothing about it, or else we must take it back to the station and stand the devil's own fuss. Probably I shall be kicked out of the service."

"Of course I'll stand by you," I said with an effort, "but we can't do anything this minute. We'd better hide it in that long grass and come back after dinner. We must have something to dig with."

Caulfield agreed sullenly, and between us we pushed the body in amongst the thick, coarse grass, which completely concealed it, and then made our way back to the camp. We ordered dinner and pretended to eat it, after which we sat for half an hour smoking, until the plates were cleared away and the servants had left the tent. Then I put my hunting-knife into my pocket, and Caulfield picked up a kitchen chopper that his bearer had left lying on the floor, after hammering a stiff joint of a camp chair, and we quitted the tent casually as though intending to have a stroll in the moonlight, which was almost as bright as day. We walked slowly at first, gradually increasing our pace as we left the camp behind us, and Caulfield never spoke a word until we came close to the tall grass that hid the fakir's body. Then he suddenly clutched my arm.

"God in heaven!" he whispered, pointing ahead, "what is that?"

I saw the grass moving, and heard a scraping sound that made my heart stand still. We moved forward in desperation and parted the grass with our hands. A large jackal was lying on the fakir's body, grinning and snarling at being disturbed over his hideous meal.

"Drive it away," said Caulfield, hoarsely. But the brute refused to move, and as it lay there showing its teeth, its face reminded me horribly of the wretched man dead beneath its feet. I turned sick and faint, so Caulfield shouted and shook the grass and threw clods of soil at the animal, which rose at last and slunk slowly away. It was an unusually large jackal, more like a wolf, and had lost one of its ears. The coat was rough and mangy and thickly sprinkled with grey.

For more than an hour we worked desperately with the chopper and hunting-knife, being greatly aided in our task by a rift in the ground where the soil had been softened by water running from the jheel, and finally we stood up with the sweat pouring from our faces, and stamped down the earth which now covered all traces of Caulfield's crime. We had filled the grave with some large stones that were lying about (remnants of some ancient temple, long ago deserted and forgotten), thus feeling secure that it could not easily be disturbed by animals.

The next morning we returned to the station, and Caulfield shut himself up more than ever. He entirely dropped his shooting, which before had been his one pleasure, and the only person he ever spoke to, unofficially, was myself.

The end of April came with its plague of insects and scorching winds. The hours grew long and weary with the heat, and dust storms howled and swirled over the station, bringing perhaps a few tantalizing drops of rain, or more often leaving the air thick with a copper-coloured haze.

One night when it was too hot to sleep, Caulfield suddenly appeared on my verandah and asked me to let him stay the night in my bungalow. "I know I'm an ass," he said in awkward apology, "but I can't stay by myself. I get all sorts of beastly ideas."

I asked no questions, but gave him a cheroot and tried to cheer him up, telling him scraps of gossip, and encouraging him to talk, when a sound outside made us both start. It proved to be only the weird, plaintive cry of a jackal, but Caulfield sprang to his feet, shaking all over. "There it is again!" he exclaimed. "It has followed me over here. Listen!" turning his haggard, sleepless eyes on me. "Every night that brute comes and howls round my house, and I tell you, on my oath, it's the same jackal we saw eating the poor devil I shot."

"Nonsense, my dear chap," I said, pushing him back into the chair, "you must have got fever. Jackals come and howl round my house all night. That's nothing."

"Look here," said Caulfield, very calmly, "I have no more fever than you have, and if you imagine I am delirious you are mistaken." He lowered his voice. "I looked out one night and saw the brute. It had only one ear!"

In spite of my own common sense and the certainty that Caulfield was not himself, my blood ran cold, and after I had succeeded in quieting him and he had dropped off to sleep on the couch, I sat in my long chair for hours, going over in my mind every detail of that horrible night in the jungle.

Several times after this Caulfield came to me and repeated the same tale. He swore he was being haunted by the jackal we had driven away from the fakir's body, and finally took it into his head that the spirit of the murdered man had entered the animal and was bent on obtaining vengeance.

Then he suddenly ceased coming over to me, and when I went to see him he would hardly speak, and only seemed anxious to get rid of me. I urged him to take leave or see a doctor, but he angrily refused to do either, and said he wished I would keep away from him altogether. So I left him alone for a couple of days, but on the third evening my conscience pricked me for having neglected him, and I was preparing to go over to his bungalow, when his bearer rushed in with a face of terror and besought me to come without delay. He said he feared his master was dying, and he had already sent for the doctor. The latter arrived in Caulfield's verandah simultaneously with myself, and together we entered the sick man's room. Caulfield was lying unconscious on his bed.

"He had a sort of fit, sahib," said the frightened bearer, and proceeded to explain how his master had behaved.

The doctor bent over the bed. "Do you happen to know if he had been bitten by a dog lately?" he asked, looking up at me.

"Not to my knowledge," I answered, while the faint wail of a jackal out across the plain struck a chill to my heart.

For twenty-four hours we stayed with Caulfield, watching the terrible struggles we were powerless to relieve, and which lasted till the end came. He was never able to speak after the first paroxysm, which had occurred before we arrived, so we could not learn from him whether he had been bitten or not, neither could the doctor discover any scar on his body which might have been made by the teeth of an animal. Yet there was no shadow of doubt that Caulfield's death was due to hydrophobia.

As we stood in the next room when all was over, drinking the dead man's whisky and soda, which we badly needed, we questioned the bearer closely, but he could tell us little or nothing. His master, he said, did not keep dogs, nor had the bearer ever heard of his having been bitten by one; but there had been a mad jackal about the place nearly three weeks ago which his master had tried to shoot but failed.

"It couldn't have been that," said the doctor; "he would have come to me if he had been bitten by a jackal."

"No," I answered mechanically, "it could not have been that." And I went into the bedroom to take a last look at poor Caulfield's thin, white face with its ghastly, hunted expression, for there was now nothing more that I could do for him.

Then I picked up a lantern and stepped out into the dark verandah, intending to go home. As I did so, something came silently round the corner of the house and stood in my path. I raised my lantern and caught a glimpse of a mass of grey fur, two fiery yellow eyes, and bared, glistening teeth. It was only a stray jackal, and I struck at it with my stick, but instead of running away it slipped past me and entered Caulfield's room. The light fell on the animal's head, and I saw that it had only one ear.

In a frenzy I rushed back into the house calling for the doctor and servants.

"I saw a jackal come in here," I said, searching round the bedroom, "hunt it out at once."

Every nook and corner was examined, but no jackal was found.

"Go home to bed, my boy, and keep quiet till I come and see you in the morning," said the doctor, looking at me keenly. "This business has shaken your nerves, and your imagination is beginning to play you tricks. Goodnight."

"Goodnight," I answered, and went slowly back to my bungalow, trying to persuade myself that he was right.

Robert W. Chambers

The Bridal Pair

At the turn of the century, Robert William Chambers was one of America's most widely-read writers of supernatural fiction following the great success of his first collection The King in Yellow, *1895. "The Bridal Pair" was first published in the Christmas number of* Harper's Monthly Magazine *(December 1902).*

I

"IF I WERE YOU," said the elder man, "I should take three months' solid rest."

"A month is enough," said the younger man. "Ozone will do it; the first brace of grouse I bag will do it – " He broke off abruptly, staring at the line of dimly lighted cars, where negro porters stood by the vestibuled sleepers, directing passengers to state-rooms and berths.

"Dog all right, doctor?" inquired the elder man, pleasantly.

"All right, doctor," replied the younger; "I spoke to the baggage-master."

There was a silence; the elder man chewed an unlighted cigar reflectively, watching his companion with keen narrowing eyes.

The younger physician stood full in the white electric light, his head lowered, apparently preoccupied with a study of his own shadow swimming and quivering on the asphalt at his feet.

"So you fear I may break down?" he observed, without raising his head.

"I think you're tired out," said the other.

"That's a more agreeable way of expressing it," said the young fellow. "I hear" – he hesitated, with a faint trace of irritation – "I understand that Forbes Stanly thinks me mentally unsound."

"He probably suspects what you're up to," said the elder man, soberly.

"Well, what will he do when I announce my germ theory? Put me in a strait-jacket?"

"He'll say you're mad, until you prove it; every physician will agree with him – until your radium test shows us the microbe of insanity."

"Doctor," said the young man, abruptly. "I'm going to admit something – to *you*."

"All right; go ahead and admit it."

"Well, I *am* a bit worried about my own condition."

"It's time you were," observed the other. "Yes – it's about time."

"Doctor, I am seriously affected."

The elder man looked up sharply.

"Yes, I'm – in love."

"Ah!" muttered the elder physician, amused and a trifle disgusted – "so that's your malady, is it?"

"A malady – yes; – not explainable by our germ theory, not affected by radio-activity. Doctor, I'm speaking lightly enough, but there's no happiness in it."

"Never is," commented the other, striking a match and lighting his ragged cigar. After a puff or two the cigar went out. "All I have to say," he added, "is, don't do it just now. Show me a scale of pure radium and I'll give you leave to marry every spinster in New York. In the meantime go and shoot a few dozen harmless, happy grouse; they can't shoot back. But let love alone. . . . By the way, who is she?"

"I don't know."

"You know her name, I suppose?"

The young fellow shook his head. "I don't even know where she lives," he said, finally.

After a pause the elder man took him gently by the arm: "Are you subject to this sort of thing! Are you susceptible?"

"No, not at all."

"Ever before in love?"

"Yes – once."

"When."

"When I was about ten years old. Her name was Rosamund – aged eight. I never had the courage to speak to her. She died recently, I believe."

The reply was so quietly serious, so destitute of any suspicion of humor, that the elder man's smile faded; and again he cast one of his swift keen glances at his companion.

"Won't you stay away three months?" he asked, patiently.

But the other only shook his head, tracing with the point of his walking-stick the outline of his own shadow on the asphalt. A moment later he glanced at his watch, closed it with a snap, silently shook hands with his equally silent friend, and stepped aboard the sleeping-car.

Neither had noticed the name of the sleeping-car.

It happened to be the "*Rosamund.*"

II

Loungers and passengers on Wildwood station drew back from the platform's edge as the towering locomotive shot by them, stunning their ears with the clangor of its melancholy bell.

Slower, slower glided the dusty train, then stopped, jolting; eddying circles of humanity closed around the cars, through which descending passengers pushed.

"Wildwood! Wildwood!" cried the trainmen; trunks tumbling out of the forward car descended with a bang! – a yelping, wagging setter dog landed on the platform, hysterically grateful to be free; and at the same moment a young fellow in tweed shooting-clothes, carrying a gripsack and gun-case, made his way forward toward the baggage-master, who was being jerked all over the platform by the frantic dog.

"Much obliged; I'll take the dog," he said, slipping a bit of silver into the official's hand, and receiving the dog's chain in return.

"Hope you'll have a good sport," replied the baggage-master. "There's a lot o' birds in this country, they tell me. You've got a good dog there."

The young man smiled and nodded, released the chain from his dog's collar, and started off up the dusty village street, followed by an urchin carrying his luggage.

The landlord of the Wildwood Inn stood on the veranda, prepared to receive guests. When a young man, a white setter dog, and a small boy loomed up, his speculative eyes became suffused with benevolence."How-de-do, sir?" he said, cordially. "Guess you was with us three year since – stayed to supper. Ain't that so?"

"It certainly is," said his guest, cheerfully. "I am surprised that you remember me."

"Be ye?" rejoined the landlord, gratified. "Say! I can tell the name of every man, woman, an' child that has ever set down to eat with us. You was here with a pair o' red bird-dawgs; shot a mess o' birds before dark, come back pegged out, an' took the ten-thirty to Noo York. Hey? Yaas, an' you was cussin' round because you couldn't stay an' shoot for a month."

"I had to work hard in those days," laughed the young man. "You are right; it was three years ago this month."

"Times a flyer; it's fitted with triple screws these days," said the landlord. "Come right in an' make yourself to home. Ed! Oh, Ed! Take this bag to 13! We're all full, sir. You ain't scared at No.13, be ye? Say, if I ain't a liar you had 13 three years ago! Waal, now! – ain't that the dumb-dest – But you can have what you want Monday. How long was you calk-erlatin' to stay?"

"A month – if the shooting is good."

"It's all right. Orrin Plummer come in last night with a mess o' pa'tridges. He says the woodcock is droppin' in to the birches south o' Sweetbrier Hill."

The young man nodded, and began to remove his gun from the service-worn case of sole-leather.

"Ain't startin' right off, be ye?" inquired his host, laughing.

"I can't begin too quickly," said the young man, busy locking barrels to stock, while the dog looked on, thumping the veranda floor with his plumy tail.

The landlord admired the slim, polished weapon. "That's the instroo-ment!" he observed. "That there's a slick bird-dog, too. Guess I'd better fill my ice-box. Your limit's thirty of each – cock an' pa'tridge. After that there's ducks."

"It's a good, sane law," said the young man, dropping his gun under one arm.

The landlord scratched his ear reflectively. "Lemme see," he mused; "wasn't you a doctor? I heard tell that you made up pieces for the papers about the idjits an'loonyticks of Rome an' Roosia an' furrin climes."

"I have written a little on European and Asiatic insanity," replied the doctor, good-humoredly.

"Was you over to them parts?"

"For three years." He whistled the dog in from the road, where several yellow curs were walking round and round him, every hair on end.

The landlord said: "You look a little peaked yourself. Take it easy the fust, is my advice."

His guest nodded abstractedly, lingering on the veranda, preoccupied with the beauty of the village street, which stretched away westward under tall elms. Autumn-tinted hills closed the vista; beyond them spread the blue sky.

"The cemetery lies that way, does it not?" inquired the young man.

"Straight ahead," said the landlord. "Take the road to the Holler."

"Do you" – the doctor hesitated – "do you recall a funeral there three years ago?"

"Whose?" asked his host, bluntly.

"I don't know."

"I'll ask my woman; she saves them funeral pieces an' makes a album . . . Friend o' yours buried there?"

"No."

The landlord sauntered toward the bar-room, where two fellow-taxpayers stood shuffling their feet impatiently.

"Waal, good-luck, Doc," he said, without intentional offence: "supper's at six. We'll try an' make you comfortable."

"Thank you," replied the doctor, stepping out into the road, and motioning the white setter to heel

"I remember now," he muttered, as he turned northward, where the road forked; "the cemetery lies to the westward; – there should be a lane at the next turning – "

He hesitated and stopped, then resumed his course, mumbling to himself: "I can pass the cemetery later; she would not be there; – I don't think I shall ever see her again . . . I – I wonder whether I am – perfectly – well – "

The words were suddenly lost in a sharp indrawn breath; his heart ceased beating, fluttered, then throbbed on violently; and he shook from head to foot.

There was a glimmer of a summer gown under the trees; a figure passed from shadow to sunshine, and again into the cool dusk of a leafy lane.

The pallor of the young fellow's face changed; a heavy flush spread from forehead to neck; he strode forward, dazed, deafened by the tumult of his drumming pulses. The dog, alert, suspicious, led the way, wheeling into the bramble-bordered lane, only to halt, turn back and fall in behind his master again.

In the lane ahead the light summer gown fluttered under the foliage, bright in the sunlight, almost lost in the shadows. Then he saw her on the hill's breezy crest, poised for a moment against the sky.

When at length he reached the hill, he found her seated in the shade of a pine. She looked up serenely, as though she had expected him, and they faced each other. A moment later his dog left him, sneaking away without a sound.

When he strove to speak, his voice had an unknown tone to him. Her upturned face was his only answer. The breeze in the pine-tops, which had been stirring monotonously, ceased.

III

Her delicate face was like a blossom lifted in the still air; her upward glance chained him to silence. The first breeze broke the spell; he spoke a word, then speech died on his lips; he stood twisting his shooting-cap, confused, not daring to continue.

The girl leaned back, supporting her weight on one arm, fingers almost buried in the deep green moss.

"It is three years today," he said, in the dull voice of one who dreams – "three years today. May I not speak?"

In her lowered head and eyes he read acquiescence; in her silence, consent. "Three years ago, today," he repeated; "the anniversary has given me courage to speak to you. Surely you will not take offence – we have travelled so far together! – from the end of the world to the end of it, and back again, here – to this place of all places in the world! And now to find you here on this day of all days – here within a step of our first meeting-place – three years ago today! And all the world we have travelled over since, never speaking, yet ever passing on paths parallel – paths which for thousands of miles ran almost within arm's distance – "

She raised her head slowly, looking out from the shadows of the pines

into the sunshine. Her dreamy eyes rested on acres of golden-rod and
hill-side brambles quivering in the September heat; on fern-choked
gullies edged with alder; on brown and purple grasses; on pine thickets
where slim silver-birches glimmered.

"Will you speak to me?" he asked. "I have never even heard the sound
of your voice."

She turned and looked at him, touching with idle fingers the soft hair
curling on her temples. Then she bent her head once more, the faintest
shadow of a smile in her eyes.

"Because," he said, humbly, "these long years of silent recognition
count for something! And then the strangeness of it! – the fate of it, – the
quiet destiny that ruled our lives, – that rules them now – now as I am
speaking, weighting every second with its tiny burden of fate."

She straightened up, lifting her half-buried hand from the moss; and
he saw the imprint there where the palm and fingers had rested.

"Three years that end today – end with the new moon," he said. "Do
you remember?"

"Yes," she said. He quivered at the sound of her voice. "You were
there, just beyond those oaks," he said, eagerly: "we can see them from
here. The road turns there – "

"Turns by the cemetery," she murmured.

"Yes, yes, by the cemetery! You had been there, I think."

"Do you remember that?" she asked.

"I have never forgotten – never!" he repeated, striving to hold her eyes
to his own; "it was not twilight; there was a glimmer of day in the west,
but the woods were darkening, and the new moon lay in the sky, and the
evening was very clear and still."

Impulsively he dropped on one knee beside her to see her face; and as
he spoke, curbing his emotion and impatience with that subtle deference
which is inbred in men or never acquired, she stole a glance at him; and
his worn visage brightened as though touched with sunlight.

"The second time I saw you was in New York," he said – "only a
glimpse of your face in the crowd – but I knew you."

"I saw you," she mused.

"Did you?" he cried, enchanted. "I dared not believe that you recognized me."

"Yes, I knew you . . . Tell me more."

The thrilling voice set him aflame; faint danger-signals tinted her face
and neck.

"In December," he went on, unsteadily, "I saw you in Paris – I saw only you amid the thousand faces in the candle-light of Notre Dame."

"And I saw you . . . And then?"

"And then two months of darkness. . . . And at last a light – moonlight – and you on the terrace at Amara."

"There was only a flower-bed – a few spikes of white hyacinths between us," she said, dreamily.

He strove to speak coolly. "Day and night have built many a wall between us; – was that you who passed me in the starlight; so close that our shoulders touched, in that narrow street in Samarkand? And the dark figure with you – "

"Yes, it was I and my attendant."

"And . . . you, there in the fog – "

"At Archangel? Yes, it was I."

"On the Goryn?"

"It was I . . . And I am here at last – with you. It is our destiny."

So, kneeling there beside her in the shadow of the pines, she absolved him in their dim confessional, holding him guiltless under the destiny that awaits us all.

Again that illumination touched his haggard face as though brightened by a sun ray stealing through the still foliage above. He grew younger under the level beauty of her gaze; care fell from him like a mask; the shadows that had haunted his eyes faded; youth awoke, transfiguring him and all his eyes beheld.

Made prisoner by love, adoring her, fearing her, he knelt beside her, knowing already that she had surrendered, though fearful yet by word or gesture or a glance to claim what destiny was holding for him – holding securely, inexorably, for him alone.

IV

He spoke of her kindness in understanding him, and of his gratitude; of her generosity, of his wonder that she had ever noticed him on his way through the world.

"I cannot believe that we have never before spoken to each other," he said – "that I do not even know your name. Surely there was once a corner in the land of childhood where we sat together when the world was younger."

She said, dreamily, "Have you forgotten?"

"Forgotten?"

"That sunny corner in the land of childhood."

"Had you been there, I should not have forgotten," he replied, troubled.

"Look at me," she said. Her lovely eyes met his; under the penetrating sweetness of her gaze his heart quickened and grew restless and his uneasy soul stirred, awaking memories.

"There was a child," she said – "years ago; a child at school. You sometimes looked at her; you never spoke. Do you remember?"

He rose to his feet, staring down at her.

"Do you remember?" she asked again.

"Rosamund! Do you mean Rosamund? How should you know that?" he faltered.

The struggle for memory focused all his groping senses; his eyes seemed to look her through and through.

"How can you know?" he repeated, unsteadily. "You are not Rosamund. . . . Are you? . . . She is dead. I heard that she was dead . . . *Are you Rosamund?*"

"Do you not know?"

"Yes; you are not Rosamund . . . What do you know of her?"

"I think she loved you."

"Is she dead?"

The girl looked up at him, smiling, following with delicate perception the sequence of his thoughts; and already his thoughts were far from the child Rosamund, a sweetheart of a day long since immortal – already he had forgotten his question, though the question was of life or death. Sadness and unrest and the passing of souls concerned not him; she knew that all his thoughts were centred on her; that he was already living over once more the last three years, with all their mystery and charm, savoring their fragrance anew in the exquisite enchantment of her presence.

Through the autumn silence the pines began to sway in a wind unfelt below. She raised her eyes and saw their green crests shimmering and swimming in a cool current; a thrilling sound stole out, and with it floated the pine perfume, exhaling in the sunshine. He heard the dreamy

harmony above, looked up; then, troubled, sombre, moved by he knew
not what, he knelt once more in the shadow beside her – close beside her.
She did not stir. Their destiny was close upon them. It came in the guise
of love.

He bent nearer. "I love you," he said. "I loved you from the first. And
shall forever. You knew it long ago."

She did not move.

"You knew I loved you?"

"Yes, I knew it."

The emotion in her voice, in every delicate contour of her face,
pleaded for mercy. He gave her none, and she bent her head in silence,
clasped hands tightening.

And when at last he had had his say, the burning words still rang in her
ears through the silence. A curious faintness stole upon her, coming
stealthily like a hateful thing. She strove to put it from her, to listen, to
remember and understand the words he had spoken, but the dull confusion grew with the sound of the pines.

"Will you love me? Will you try to love me?"

"I love you," she said; "I have loved you so many, many years – I – I
am Rosamund – "

She bowed her head and covered her face with both hands.

"Rosamund! Rosamund!" he breathed, enraptured.

She dropped her hands with a little cry; the frightened sweetness of her
eyes held back his outstretched arms. "Do not touch me," she whispered;
"you will not touch me, will you? – not yet – not now. Wait till I understand!" She pressed her hands to her eyes, then again let them fall,
staring straight at him.

"I loved you so!" she whispered. "Why did you wait!"

"Rosamund! Rosamund!" he cried, sorrowfully, "what are you saying?
I do not understand; I can understand nothing save that I worship you.
May I not touch you? – touch your hand, Rosamund? I love you so."

"And I love you. I beg you not to touch me, – not yet. There is something – some reason why – "

"Tell me, sweetheart."

"Do you not know?"

"By Heaven, I do not!" he said, troubled and amazed.

She cast one desperate, unhappy glance at him, then rose to her full
height, gazing out over the hazy valleys to where the mountains began,
piled up like dim sun-tipped clouds in the north.

The hill wind stirred her hair and fluttered the white ribbons at waist and shoulder. The golden-rod swayed in the sunshine. Below, amid yellow tree-tops, the roofs and chimneys of the village glimmered.

"Dear, do you not understand?" she said. "How can I make you understand that I love you – too late?"

"Give yourself to me, Rosamund; let me touch you – let me take you – "

"Will you love me always?"

"In life, in death, which cannot part us. Will you marry me, Rosamund?"

She looked straight into his eyes. "Dear, do you not understand? Have you forgotten? I died three years ago today."

The unearthly sweetness of her white face startled him. A terrible light broke in on him; his heart stood still.

In his dull brain words were sounding – his own words, written years ago: "When God takes the mind and leaves the body alive, there grows in it, sometimes, a beauty almost supernatural."

He had seen it in his practice. A thrill of fright penetrated him, piercing every vein with its chill. He strove to speak; his lips seemed frozen; he stood there before her, a ghastly smile stamped on his face, and in his heart terror. "What do you mean, Rosamund?" he said at last.

"That I am dead, dear. Did you not understand that? I – I thought you knew it – when you first saw me at the cemetery, after all those years since childhood . . . Did you not know it?" she asked, wistfully. "I must wait for my bridal."

Misery whitened his face as he raised his head and looked out across the sunlit world. Something had smeared and marred the fair earth; the sun grew gray as he stared.

Stupefied by the crash, the ruins of life around him, he stood mute, erect, facing the west.

She whispered. "Do you understand?"

"Yes," he said; "we will wed later. You have been ill, dear; but it is all right now – and will always be – God help us! Love is stronger than all – stronger than death."

"I know it is stronger than death," she said, looking out dreamily over the misty valley.

He followed her gaze, calmly, serenely reviewing all that he must renounce, the happiness of wedlock, children – all that a man desires.

Suddenly instinct stirred, awaking man's only friend – hope. A lifetime for the battle! For a cure! Hopeless? He laughed in his excitement. Despair? – when the cure lay almost within his grasp! The work he had given his life to! A month more in the laboratory – two months – three – perhaps a year. What of it? It must surely come – how could he fail when the work of his life meant all in life for her?

The light of exaltation slowly faded from his face; ominous foreboding thoughts crept in; fear laid a shaky hand on his head, which fell heavily forward on his breast.

Science and man's cunning and the wisdom of the world!

"O God," he groaned, "for Him who cured by laying on His hands!"

V

Now that he had learned her name, and that her father was alive, he stood mutely beside her, staring steadily at the chimneys and stately dormered roof almost hidden behind the crimson maple foliage across the valley – her home.

She had seated herself once more upon the moss, hands clasped upon one knee, looking out into the west with dreamy eyes.

"I shall not be long," he said, gently. "Will you wait here for me? I will bring your father with me."

"I will wait for you. But you must come before the new moon. Will you? I must go when the new moon lies in the west."

"Go, dearest? Where?"

"I may not tell you," she sighed, "but you will know very soon – very soon now. And there will be no more sorrow. I think," she added, timidly.

"There will be no more sorrow," he repeated, quietly.

"For the former things are passing away," she said.

He broke the heavy spray of golden-rod and laid it across her knees; she held out a blossom to him – a blind gentian, blue as her eyes. He kissed it.

"Be with me when the new moon comes," she whispered. "It will be so sweet. I will teach you how divine is death, if you will come."

"You shall teach me the sweetness of life," he said, tremulously.

"Yes – life. I did not know you called it by its truest name."

So he went away, trudging sturdily down the lane, gun glistening on his shoulder.

Where the lane joins the shadowy village street his dog skulked up to him, sniffing at his heels.

A mill whistle was sounding; through the red rays of the setting sun people were passing. Along the row of village shops loungers followed him with vacant eyes. He saw nothing, heard nothing, though a kindly voice called after him, and a young girl smiled at him on her short journey through the world.

The landlord of the Wildwood Inn sat sunning himself in the red evening glow.

"Well, doctor," he said, "you look tired to death. Eh? What's that you say?"

The young man repeated his question in a low voice. The landlord shook his head. "No, sir. The big house on the hill is empty – been empty these three years. No, sir, there ain't no family there now. The old gentleman moved away three years ago."

"You are mistaken," said the doctor; "his daughter tells me he lives there."

"His – his daughter?" repeated the landlord. "Why, doctor, she's dead." He turned to his wife, who sat sewing by the open window: "Ain't it three years, Marthy?"

"Three years today," said the woman, biting off her thread. "She's buried in the family vault over the hill. She was a right pretty little thing, too."

"Turned nineteen," mused the landlord, folding his newspaper reflectively.

VI

The great gray house on the hill was closed, windows and doors boarded over, lawn, shrubbery, and hedges tangled with weeds. A few scarlet poppies glimmered above the brown grass. Save for these, and clumps of tall wild phlox, there were no blossoms among the weeds.

His dog, which had sneaked after him, cowered as he turned northward across the fields. Swifter and swifter he strode; and as he stumbled on, the long sunset clouds faded, the golden light in the west died out, leaving a calm, clear sky tinged with faintest green.

Pines hid the west as he crept toward the hill where she awaited him. As he climbed through dusky purple grasses, higher, higher, he saw the new moon's crescent tipping above the hills; and he crushed back the deathly fright that clutched at him and staggered on. "Rosamund!"

The pines answered him.

"Rosamund!"

The pines replied, answering together. Then the wind died away, and there was no answer when he called.

East and south the darkening thickets, swaying, grew still. He saw the slim silver-birches glimmering like the ghosts of young trees dead; he saw on the moss at his feet a broken stalk of golden-rod.

The new moon had drawn a veil across her face; sky and earth were very still.

While the moon lasted he lay, eyes open, listening, his face pillowed on the moss. It was long after sunrise when his dog came to him; later still when men came.

And at first they thought he was asleep.

Robert Benson

The Watcher

Like his eldest brother (A. C. Benson), Robert Hugh Benson (1871–1914) – who became the private chamberlain to Pope Pius X in 1911 – also wrote two fine collections of weird tales: The Light Invisible *(1903) including "The Watcher", and* A Mirror of Shalott *(1907). "I have always felt that the ghost stories of the late Monsignor Benson never received their just meed of appreciation," observed Montague Summers, connoisseur of gothic and supernatural fiction.*

ONE MORNING, the priest and I went out soon after breakfast and walked up and down a grass path between two yew hedges; the dew was not yet off the grass that lay in shadow; and thin patches of gossamer still hung like torn cambric on the yew shoots on either side. As we passed for the second time up the path, the old man suddenly stooped and, pushing aside a dock-leaf at the foot of the hedge, lifted a dead mouse, and looked at it as it lay stiffly on the palm of his hand. I saw that his eyes filled slowly with the ready tears of old age.

"He had chosen his own resting-place," he said. "Let him lie there. Why did I disturb him?" – And he laid him gently down again; and then gathering a fragment of wet earth he sprinkled it over the mouse. "Earth to earth, ashes to ashes," he said, "in sure and certain hope" – and then he stopped; and straightening himself with difficulty walked on, and I followed him.

"You once expressed an interest," he said, "in my tales of the visions of Nature I have seen. Shall I tell you how once I saw a very different sight?

"I was eighteen years old at the time, that terrible age when the soul

seems to have dwindled to a spark overlaid by a mountain of ashes –
when blood and fire and death and loud noises seem the only things of
interest, and all tender things shrink back and hide from the dreadful
noonday of manhood. Someone gave me one of those shot-pistols that
you may have seen, and I loved the sense of power that it gave me, for I
had never had a gun. For a week or two in the summer holidays I was
content with shooting at a mark, or at the level surface of water, and
delighted to see the cardboard shattered, or the quiet pool torn to shreds
along its mirror where the sky and green lay sleeping. Then that ceased
to interest me, and I longed to see a living thing suddenly stop living at
my will. Now," and he held up a deprecating hand, "I think sport is
necessary for some natures. After all, the killing of creatures is necessary
for man's food, and sport as you will tell me is a survival of man's delight
in obtaining food, and it requires certain noble qualities of endurance
and skill. I know all that, and I know further that for some natures it is a
relief – an escape for humours that will otherwise find an evil outlet. But I
do know this – that for me it was not necessary.

"However, there was every excuse, and I went out in good faith one
summer evening, intending to shoot some rabbits as they ran to cover
from the open field. I walked along the inside of a fence with a wood
above me and on my left, and the green meadow on my right. Well,
owing probably to my own lack of skill, though I could hear the patter
and rush of the rabbits all round me, and could see them in the distance
sitting up listening with cocked ears, as I stole along the fence, I could not
get close enough to fire at them with any hope of what I fancied was
success; and by the time that I had arrived at the end of the wood I was in
an impatient mood.

"I stood for a moment or two leaning on the fence looking out of that
pleasant coolness into the open meadow beyond; the sun had at that
moment dipped behind the hill before me and all was in shadow except
where there hung a glory about the topmost leaves of a beech that still
caught the sun. The birds were beginning to come in from the fields, and
were settling one by one in the wood behind me, staying here and there
to sing one last line of melody. I could hear the quiet rush and then the
sudden clap of a pigeon's wings as he came home, and as I listened I
heard pealing out above all other sounds the long liquid song of a thrush
somewhere above me. I looked up idly and tried to see the bird, and after
a moment or two caught sight of him as the leaves of the beech parted in
the breeze, his head lifted and his whole body vibrating with the joy of

life and music. As someone has said, his body was one beating heart. The last radiance of the sun over the hill reached him and bathed him in golden warmth. Then the leaves closed again as the breeze dropped, but still his song rang out.

"Then there came on me a blinding desire to kill him. All the other creatures had mocked me and run home. Here at least was a victim, and I would pour out the sullen anger that had been gathering during my walk, and at least demand this one life as a substitute. Side by side with this I remembered clearly that I had come out to kill for food: that was my one justification. Side by side I saw both these things, and I had no excuse — no excuse.

"I turned my head every way and moved a step or two back to catch sight of him again, and, although this may sound fantastic and over-wrought, in my whole being was a struggle between light and darkness. Every fibre of my life told me that the thrush had a right to live. Ah! he had earned it, if labour were wanting, by this very song that was guiding death towards him, but black sullen anger had thrown my conscience, and was now struggling to hold it down till the shot had been fired. Still I waited for the breeze, and then it came, cool and sweet-smelling like the breath of a garden, and the leaves parted. There he sang in the sunshine and in a moment I lifted the pistol and drew the trigger.

"With the crack of the cap came silence overhead, and after what seemed an interminable moment came the soft rush of something falling and the faint thud among last year's leaves. Then I stood half terrified, and stared among the dead leaves. All seemed dim and misty. My eyes were still a little dazzled by the bright background of sunlit air and rosy clouds on which I had looked with such intensity, and the space beneath the branches was a world of shadows. Still I looked a few yards away, trying to make out the body of the thrush, and fearing to hear a struggle of beating wings, among the dry leaves.

"And then I lifted my eyes a little, vaguely. A yard or two beyond where the thrush lay was a rhododendron bush. The blossoms had fallen and the outline of dark, heavy leaves was unrelieved by the slightest touch of colour. As I looked at it, I saw a face looking down from the higher branches.

"It was a perfectly hairless head and face, the thin lips were parted in a wide smile of laughter, there were innumerable lines about the corners of the mouth, and the eyes were surrounded by creases of merriment. What was perhaps most terrible about it all was that the eyes were not looking

at me, but down among the leaves; the heavy eyelids lay drooping, and
the long, narrow, shining slits showed how the eyes laughed beneath
them. The forehead sloped quickly back, like a cat's head. The face was
the colour of earth, and the outlines of the head faded below the ears and
chin into the gloom of the dark bush. There was no throat, or body or
limbs so far as I could see. The face just hung there like a down-turned
Eastern mask in an old curiosity shop. And it smiled with sheer delight,
not at me, but at the thrush's body. There was no change of expression so
long as I watched it, just a silent smile of pleasure petrified on the face. I
could not move my eyes from it.

"After what I suppose was a minute or so, the face had gone. I did not
see it go, but I became aware that I was looking only at leaves.

"No; there was no outline of leaf, or play of shadows that could
possibly have been taken for form of a face. You can guess how I tried to
force myself to believe that that was all; how I turned my head this way
and that to catch it again; but there was no hint of a face.

"Now, I cannot tell you how I did it; but although I was half beside
myself with fright, I went forward towards the bush and searched furiously among the leaves for the body of the thrush; and at last I found it,
and lifted it. It was still limp and warm to the touch. Its breast was a little
ruffled, and one tiny drop of blood lay at the root of the beak below the
eyes, like a tear of dismay and sorrow at such an unmerited, unexpected
death.

"I carried it to the fence and climbed over, and then began to run in
great steps, looking now and then awfully at the gathering gloom of the
wood behind, where the laughing face had mocked the dead. I think,
looking back as I do now, that my chief instinct was that I could not leave
the thrush there to be laughed at, and that I must get it out into the clean,
airy meadow. When I reached the middle of the meadow I came to a
pond which never ran quite dry even in the hottest summer. On the bank
I laid the thrush down, and then deliberately but with all my force
dashed the pistol into the water; then emptied my pockets of the
cartridges and threw them in too.

"Then I turned again to the piteous little body, feeling that at least I
had tried to make amends. There was an old rabbit hole near, the grass
growing down in its mouth, and a tangle of web and dead leaves behind.
I scooped a little space out among the leaves, and then laid the thrush
there; gathered a little of the sandy soil and poured it over the body,
saying, I remember, half unconsciously, 'Earth to earth, ashes to ashes, in

sure and certain hope' – and then I stopped, feeling I had been a little profane, though I do not think so now. And then I went home.

"As I dressed for dinner, looking out over the darkening meadow where the thrush lay, I remember feeling happy that no evil thing could mock the defenceless dead out there in the clean meadow where the wind blew and the stars shone down."

Thomas Nelson Page

The Spectre in the Cart

*Thomas Nelson Page (1853–1922) was an American writer, lawyer and diplomat, best known for his stories about Virginia (*Red Ruck, In Ole Virginia, *etc.) and many important social studies including* The Old South, The Negro, *and* Social Life in Old Virginia. *During the First World War he served as US Ambassador to Italy. This tale appeared in his collection* Bred in the Bone *(1904).*

I HAD NOT SEEN my friend Stokeman since we were at college together, and now naturally we fell to talking of old times. I remembered him as a hard-headed man without a particle of superstition, if such a thing be possible in a land where we are brought up on superstition, from the bottle. He was at that time full of life and of enjoyment of whatever it brought. I found now that his wild and almost reckless spirits had been tempered by the years which had passed as I should not have believed possible, and that gravity had taken place of the gaiety for which he was then noted.

He used to maintain, I remember, that there was no apparition or supernatural manifestation, or series of circumstances pointing to such a manifestation, however strongly substantiated they appeared to be, that could not be explained on purely natural grounds.

During our stay at college a somewhat notable instance of what was by many supposed to be a supernatural manifestation occurred in a deserted house on a remote plantation in an adjoining county.

It baffled all investigation, and got into the newspapers, recalling the Cock Lane ghost, and many more less celebrated apparitions. Parties were organized to investigate it, but were baffled. Stokeman, on a bet of a box of cigars, volunteered to go out alone and explode the fraud; and did so, not only putting the restless spirit to flight, but capturing it and dragging it into town as the physical and indisputable witness both of the truth of his theory and of his personal courage. The exploit gave him immense notoriety in our little world.

I was, therefore, no little surprised to hear him say seriously now that he had come to understand how people saw apparitions.

"I have seen them myself," he added gravely.

"You do not mean it!" I sat bolt upright in my chair in my astonishment. I had myself, largely through his influence, become a sceptic in matters relating to the supernatural.

"Yes, I have seen ghosts. They not only have appeared to me, but were as real to my ocular vision as any other external physical object which I saw with my eyes."

"Of course, it was an hallucination. Tell me; I can explain it."

"I explained it myself," he said, dryly. "But it left me with a little less conceit and a little more sympathy with the hallucinations of others not so gifted."

It was a fair hit.

"In the year – ," he went on, after a brief period of reflection, "I was the State's Attorney for my native county, to which office I had been elected a few years after I left college, and the year we emancipated ourselves from carpet-bag rule, and I so remained until I was appointed to the bench. I had a personal acquaintance, pleasant or otherwise, with every man in the county. The district was a close one, and I could almost have given the census of the population. I knew every man who was for me and almost every one who was against me. There were few neutrals. In those times much hung on the elections. There was no border-land. Men were either warmly for you or hotly against you.

"We thought we were getting into smooth water, where the sailing was clear, when the storm suddenly appeared about to rise again. In the canvass of that year the election was closer than ever and the contest hotter.

"Among those who went over when the lines were thus sharply drawn was an old negro named Joel Turnell, who had been a slave of one of my nearest neighbours, Mr Eaton, and whom I had known all my life as an easy-going, palavering old fellow with not much principle, but with kindly manners and a likable way. He had always claimed to be a supporter of mine, being one of the two or three negroes in the county who professed to vote with the whites.

"He had a besetting vice of pilfering, and I had once or twice defended him for stealing and gotten him off, and he appeared to be grateful to me. I always doubted him a little; for I believed he did not have force of character enough to stand up against his people, and he was a chronic liar. Still, he was always friendly with me, and used to claim the emoluments and privileges of such a relation. Now, however, on a sudden, in this campaign he became one of my bitterest opponents. I attributed it to the influence of a son of his, named Absalom who had gone off from the county during the war when he was only a youth, and had stayed away for many years without anything being known of him, and had now returned unexpectedly. He threw himself into the fight. He claimed to have been in the army, and he appeared to have a deep-seated animosity against the whites, particularly against all those whom he had known in boyhood. He was a vicious-looking fellow, broad-shouldered and bow-legged, with a swagger in his gait. He had an ugly scar on the side of his throat, evidently made by a knife, though he told the negroes, I understood, that he had got it in the war, and was ready to fight again if he but got the chance. He had not been back long before he was in several rows, and as he was of brutal strength, he began to be much feared by the negroes. Whenever I heard of him it was in connection with some fight among his own people, or some effort to excite race animosity. When the canvass began he flung himself into it with fury, and I must say with marked effect. His hostility appeared to be particularly directed against myself, and I heard of him in all parts of the district declaiming against me. The negroes who, for one or two elections, had appeared to have quieted down and become indifferent as to politics were suddenly revivified. It looked as if the old scenes of the Reconstruction period, when the two sides were like hostile armies, might be witnessed again. Night meetings, or "camp-fires," were held all through the district, and from many of them came the report of Absalom Turnell's violent speeches stirring up the blacks and arraying them against the whites. Our side was equally aroused and the whole section was in a ferment. Our effort was to prevent any outbreak and tide over the crisis.

"Among my friends was a farmer named John Halloway, one of the best men in my county, and a neighbor and friend of mine from my boyhood. His farm, a snug little homestead of fifty or sixty acres, adjoined our plantation on one side; and on the other, that of the Eatons, to whom Joel Turnell and his son Absalom had belonged, and I remember that as a boy it was my greatest privilege and reward to go over on a Saturday and be allowed by John Halloway to help him plough, or cut his hay. He was a big, ruddy-faced, jolly boy, and even then used to tell me about being in love with Fanny Peel, who was the daughter of another farmer in the neighborhood, and a Sunday-school scholar of my mother's. I thought him the greatest man in the world. He had a fight once with Absalom Turnell when they were both youngsters, and, though Turnell was rather older and much the heavier, whipped him completely. Halloway was a good soldier and a good son, and when he came back from the war and won his wife, who was a belle among the young farmers, and settled down with her on his little place, which he proceeded to make a bower of roses and fruit-trees, there was not a man in the neighborhood who did not rejoice in his prosperity and wish him well. The Halloways had no children and, as is often the case in such instances, they appeared to be more to each other than are most husbands and wives. He always spoke of his wife as if the sun rose and set in her. No matter where he might be in the county, when night came he always rode home, saying that his wife would be expecting him. 'Don't keer whether she's asleep or not,' he used to say to those who bantered him, 'she knows I'm a-comin', and she always hears my click on the gate-latch, and is waitin' for me.'

"It came to be well understood throughout the county.

" 'I believe you are hen-pecked,' said a man to him one night.

" 'I believe I am, George,' laughed Halloway, 'and by Jings! I like it, too.'

"It was impossible to take offence at him, he was so good-natured. He would get out of his bed in the middle of the night, hitch up his horse and pull his bitterest enemy out of the mud. He had on an occasion ridden all night through a blizzard to get a doctor for the wife of a negro neighbor in a cabin near by who was suddenly taken ill. When someone expressed admiration for it, especially as it was known that the man had not long before been abusing Halloway to the provost-marshal, who at that time was in supreme command, he said:

" 'Well, what's that got to do with it? Wa'n't the man's wife sick? I don't deserve no credit, though; if I hadn't gone, my wife wouldna' 'a' let me come in her house.'

"He was an outspoken man, too, not afraid of the devil, and when he believed a thing he spoke it, no matter whom it hit. In this way John had been in trouble several times while we were under 'gun-rule'; and this, together with his personal character, had given him great influence in the county, and made him a power. He was one of my most ardent friends and supporters, and to him, perhaps, more than to any other two men in the county, I owed my position.

"Absalom Turnell's rancorous speeches had stirred all the county, and the apprehension of the outbreak his violence was in danger of bringing might have caused trouble but for John Halloway's coolness and level-headedness. John offered to go around and follow Absalom up at his meetings. He could 'spike his guns,' he said.

"Some of his friends wanted to go with him. 'You'd better not try that,' they argued. 'That fellow, Ab Turnell's got it in for you.' But he said no. The only condition on which he would go was that he should go alone.

" 'They ain't any of 'em going to trouble me. I know 'em all and I git along with 'em first rate. I don't know as I know this fellow Ab; he's sort o' grown out o' my recollection; but I wan't to see. He knows me, I know. I got my hand on him once when he was a boy – about my age, and he ain't forgot that, I know. He was a blusterer; but he didn't have real grit. He won't say nothin' to my face. But I must go alone. You all are too flighty.'

"So Halloway went alone and followed Ab up at his 'camp-fires,' and if report was true his mere presence served to curb Ab's fury, and take the fire out of his harangues. Even the negroes got to laughing and talking about it. 'Ab was jest like a dog when a man faced him,' they said; 'he could n' look him in the eye.'

"The night before the election there was a meeting at one of the worst places in the county, a country store at a point known as Burley's Fork, and Halloway went there, alone – and for the first time in the canvass thought it necessary to interfere. Absalom, stung by the taunts of some of his friends, and having stimulated himself with mean whiskey, launched out in a furious tirade against the whites generally, and me in particular; and called on the negroes to go to the polls next day prepared to 'wade in blood to their lips.' For himself, he said, he had 'drunk blood' before, both of white men and women, and he meant to drink it again. He whipped out and flourished a pistol in one hand and a knife in the other. His language exceeded belief, and the negroes, excited by his violence, were showing the effect on their emotions of his wild declamation, and were beginning to respond with shouts and cries when Halloway rose and walked forward. Absalom turned and started to meet him, yelling his fury and threats, and the audience were rising to their feet when they were stopped. It was described to me afterward.

"Halloway was in the midst of a powder magazine, absolutely alone, a single spark would have blown him to atoms and might have caused a catastrophe which would have brought untold evil. But he was as calm as a May morning. He walked through them, the man who told me said, as if he did not know there was a soul in a hundred miles of him, and as if Absalom were only something to be swept aside.

" 'He wa'n't exac'ly laughin', or even smilin', said my informant, 'but he jest looked easy to his mine.'

"They were all waiting, he said, expecting Absalom to tear him to pieces on the spot; but as Halloway advanced, Absalom faltered and stopped. He could not stand his calm eye.

" 'It was jest like a dog givin' way before a man who ain't afraid of him,' my man said. 'He breshed Absalom aside as if he had been a fly, and began to talk to us, and I never heard such a speech.'

"I got there just after it happened; for some report of what Absalom intended to do had reached me that night and I rode over hastily, fearing that I might arrive too late. When, however, I arrived at the place everything was quiet, Absalom had disappeared. Unable to face his downfall, he had gone off, taking old Joel with him. The tide of excitement had changed and the negroes, relieved at the relaxing of the tension, were laughing among themselves at their champion's defeat and disavowing any sympathy with his violence. They were all friendly with Halloway.

" 'Dat man wa'n' nothin' but a' outside nigger, nohow,' they said. 'And he always was more mouth than anything else,' etc.

" 'Good Lord! He say he want to drink *blood*!' declared one man to another, evidently for us to hear, as we mounted our horses.

" 'Drink *whiskey*!' replied the other, drily, and there was a laugh of derision.

"I rode home with Halloway.

"I shall never forget his serenity. As we passed along, the negroes were lining the roads on their way homeward, and were shouting and laughing among themselves; and the greetings they gave us as we passed were as civil and good-humored as if no unpleasantness had ever existed. A little after we set out, one man, who had been walking very fast just ahead of us, and had been keeping in advance all the time, came close to

Halloway's stirrup and said something to him in an undertone. All I caught was, 'layin' up something against him.'

" 'That's all right, Dick; let him lay it up, and keep it laid up,' Halloway laughed.

" 'Dat's a bad feller!' the negro insisted, uneasily, his voice kept in an undertone. 'You got to watch him. I'se knowed him from a boy.'

"He added something else in a whisper which I did not catch.

" 'All right; certainly not! Much obliged to you, Dick. I'll keep my eyes open. Goodnight.'

" 'Goodnight, gent'men'; and the negro fell back and began to talk with the nearest of his companions effusively.

" 'Who is that?' I asked, for the man had kept his hat over his eyes."

" 'That's Dick Winchester. You remember that old fello 't used to belong to old Mr Eaton – lived down in the pines back o' me, on the creek 't runs near my place. His wife died the year of the big snow.'

"It was not necessary for him to explain further. I remembered the negro for whom Halloway had ridden through the storm that night.

"I asked Halloway somewhat irrelevantly, if he carried a pistol. He said no, he had never done so.

" 'Fact is, I'm afraid of killin' somebody. And I don't want to do that, I know. Never could bear to shoot my gun even durin' o' the war, though I shot her 'bout as often as any of 'em, I reckon – always used to shut my eyes right tight whenever I pulled the trigger. I reckon I was a mighty pore soldier,' he laughed. I had heard that he was one of the best in the army.

" 'Besides, I always feel sort o' cowardly if I've got a pistol on. Looks like I was afraid of somebody – an' I ain't. I've noticed if two fellows have pistols on and got to fightin', mighty apt to one git hurt, maybe both. Sort o' like two dogs growling – long as don't but one of 'em growl it's all right. If don't but one have a pistol, t'other feller always has the advantage and sort o' comes out top, while the man with the pistol looks mean.'

"I remember how he looked in the dim moonlight as he drawled his quaint philosophy.

" 'I'm a man o' peace, Mr Johnny, and I learnt that from your mother – I learnt a heap o' things from her,' he added, presently, after a little period of reflection. 'She was the lady as used always to have a kind word for me when I was a boy. That's a heap to a boy. I used to think she was an angel. You think it's *you* I'm a fightin' for in this canvass? 'Tain't. I like you well enough, but I ain't never forgot your mother, and her kindness to my old people durin' the war when I was away. She give me this hand-kerchief for a weddin' present when I was married after the war – said 'twas all she had to give, and my wife thinks the world and all of it; won't let me have it 'cept as a favor; but this mornin' she told me to take it – said 'twould bring me luck.' He took a big bandanna out of his pocket and held it up in the moonlight. I remembered it as one of my father's.

" 'She'll make me give it up tomorrow night when I git home,' he chuckled.

"We had turned into a road through the plantations, and had just come to the fork where Halloway's road turned off toward his place.

" 'I lays a heap to your mother's door – purty much all this, I reckon.' His eye swept the moon-bathed scene before him. 'But for her I mightn't 'a got *her*. And ain't a man in the world got a happier home, or as good a wife.' He waved his hand toward the little homestead that was sleeping in the moonlight on the slope the other side of the stream, a picture of peace.

"His path went down a little slope, and mine kept along the side of the hill until it entered the woods. A great sycamore tree grew right in the fork, with its long, hoary arms extending over both roads, making a broad mass of shadow in the white moonlight.

"The next day was the day of the election. Halloway was at one poll and I was at another; so I did not see him that day. But he sent me word that evening that he had carried his poll, and I rode home knowing that we should have peace.

"I was awakened next morning by the news that both Halloway and his wife had been murdered the night before. I at once galloped over to his place, and was one of the first to get there. It was a horrible sight. Halloway had evidently been waylaid and killed by a blow of an axe just as he was entering his yard gate, and then the door of the house had been broken open and his wife had been killed, after which Halloway's body had been dragged into the house, and the house had been fired with the intention of making it appear that the house had burned by accident. But by one of those inscrutable fatalities, the fire, after burning half of two walls, had gone out.

"It was a terrible sight, and the room looked like a shambles. Halloway had plainly been caught unawares while leaning over his gate. The back of his head had been crushed in with the eye of an axe, and he had died instantly. The pleasant thought which was in his mind at the instant – perhaps, of the greeting that always awaited him on the click of his latch;

perhaps, of his success that day; perhaps, of my mother's kindness to him when he was a boy – was yet on his face, stamped there indelibly by the blow that killed him. There he lay, face upwards, as the murderer had thrown him after bringing him in, stretched out his full length on the floor, with his quiet face upturned, looking in that throng of excited, awe-stricken men, just what he had said he was: a man of peace. His wife, on the other hand, wore a terrified look on her face. There had been a terrible struggle. She had lived to taste the bitterness of death, before it took her."

Stokeman, with a little shiver, put his hand over his eyes as though to shut out the vision that recurred to him. After a long breath he began again.

"In a short time there was a great crowd, there white and black. The general mind flew at once to Absalom Turnell. The negroes present were as earnest in their denunciation as the whites; perhaps, more so, for the whites were past threatening. I knew from the grimness that trouble was brewing, and I felt that if Absalom were caught and any evidence were found on him, no power on earth could save him. A party rode off in search of him, and went to old Joel's house. Neither Absalom nor Joel were there; they had not been home since the election, one of the women said.

"As a law officer of the county I was to a certain extent in charge at Halloway's, and in looking around for all the clues to be found, I came on a splinter of 'light-wood,' not as large or as long as one's little finger, stuck in a crack in the floor near the bed: a piece of a stick of 'fat-pine,' such as negroes often carry about, and use as tapers. One end had been burned; but the other end was clean and was jagged just as it had been broken off. There was a small scorched place on the planks on either side, and it was evident that this was one of the splinters that had been used in firing the house. I called a couple of the coolest, most level-headed men present and quietly showed them the spot, and they took the splinter out and I put it in my pocket.

"By one of those fortuitous chances which so often happen in every lawyer's experience, and appear inexplicable, Old Joel Turnell walked up to the house just as we came out. He was as sympathetic as possible, appeared outraged at the crime, professed the highest regard for Halloway, and the deepest sorrow at his death. The sentiment of the crowd was rather one of sympathy with him, that he should have such a son as Absalom.

"I took the old man aside to have a talk with him, to find out where his son was and where he had been the night before. He was equally vehement in his declarations of his son's innocence, and of professions of regard for Halloway. And suddenly to my astonishment he declared that his son had spent the night with him and had gone away after sunrise.

"Then happened one of those fatuous things – Joel took a handkerchief out of his pocket and wiped his face, and as he did so I recognized the very handkerchief Halloway had shown me the night before. With the handkerchief, Joel drew out several splinters of light-wood, one of which had been broken off from a longer piece. I picked it up and it fitted exactly into the piece that had been stuck in the crack in the floor. At first, I could scarcely believe my own senses. Of course, it became my duty to have Joel arrested immediately. But I was afraid to have it done there, the crowd was so deeply incensed. So I called the two men to whom I had shown the light-wood splinter, told them the story, and they promised to get him away and arrest him quietly and take him safely to jail, which they did.

"Even then we did not exactly believe that the old man had any active complicity in the crime, and I was blamed for arresting the innocent old father and letting the guilty son escape. The son, however, was arrested shortly afterward.

"The circumstances from which the crime arose gave the case something of a political aspect, and the prisoners had the best counsel to be procured, both at our local bar and in the capital. The evidence was almost entirely circumstantial, and when I came to work it up, I found, as often occurs, that although the case was plain enough on the outside, there were many difficulties in the way of fitting all the circumstances to prove the guilt of the accused and to make out every link in the chain. Particularly was this so in the prosecution of the young man, who was supposed to be the chief criminal, and in whose case there was a strong effort to prove an alibi.

"As I worked, I found to my surprise that the guilt of the old man, though based wholly on circumstantial evidence, was established more clearly than that of his son – not indeed, as to the murders, but as to the arson, which served just as well to convict on. The handkerchief, which Joel had not been able to resist the temptation to steal, and the splinter of light-wood in his pocket, which fitted exactly into that found in the house, together with other circumstances, proved his guilt conclusively. But although there was an equal moral certainty of the guilt of the young man, it was not so easy to establish it by law.

"Old Dick Winchester was found dead one morning and the alibi was almost completely proved, and only failed by the incredibility of the witnesses for the defence. Old Joel persistently declared that Absalom was innocent, and but for a confession by Absalom of certain facts intended to shift the suspicion from himself to his father, I do not know how his case might have turned out.

"I believed him to be the instigator as well as the perpetrator of the crime.

"I threw myself into the contest, and prosecuted with all the vigor I was capable of. And I finally secured the conviction of both men. But it was after a hard fight. They were the only instances in which, representing the Commonwealth, I was ever conscious of strong personal feeling, and of a sense of personal triumph. The memory of my last ride with Halloway, and of the things he had said to me; the circumstances under which he and his wife were killed; the knowledge that in some sort it was on my account; and the bitter attacks made on me personally (for in some quarters I was depicted as a bloodthirsty ruffian, and it was charged that I was for political reasons prosecuting men whom I personally knew to be innocent), all combined to spur me to my utmost effort. And when the verdicts were rendered, I was conscious of a sense of personal triumph so fierce as to shock me.

"Not that I did not absolutely believe in the guilt of both prisoners; for I considered that I had demonstrated it, and so did the jurors who tried them.

"The day of the execution was set. An appeal was at once taken in both cases and a stay was granted, and I had to sustain the verdicts in the upper court. The fact that the evidence was entirely circumstantial had aroused great interest, and every lawyer in the State had his theory. The upper court affirmed in both cases and appeals were taken to the highest court, and again stay of execution was granted.

"The prisoners' counsel had moved to have the prisoners transferred to another county, which I opposed. I was sure that the people of my county would observe the law. They had resisted the first fierce impulse, and were now waiting patiently for justice to take its course. Months passed, and the stay of execution had to be renewed. The road to Halloway's grew up and I understood that the house had fallen in, though I never went that way again. Still the court hung fire as to its conclusion.

"The day set for the execution approached for the third time without the court having rendered its decision.

"On the day before that set for the execution, the court gave its decision. It refused to interfere in the case of old Joel, but reversed, and set aside the verdict in that of the younger man. Of a series of over one hundred bills of exception taken by his counsel as a 'drag-net,' one held; and owing to the admission of a single question by a juror, the judgment was set aside in Absalom's case and a new trial was ordered.

"Being anxious lest the excitement might increase, I felt it my duty to stay at the county-seat that night, and as I could not sleep I spent the time going over the records of the two cases; which, like most cases, developed new points every time they were read.

"Everything was perfectly quiet all night, though the village was filling up with people from the country to see the execution, which at that time was still public. I determined next morning to go to my home in the country and get a good rest, of which I began to feel the need. I was detained, however, and it was well along in the forenoon before I mounted my horse and rode slowly out of town through a back street. The lane kept away from the main road except at one point just outside of town, where it crossed it at right angles.

"It was a beautiful spring day – a day in which it is a pleasure merely to live, and as I rode along through the quiet lane under the leafy trees I could not help my mind wandering and dwelling on the things that were happening. I am not sure, indeed, that I was not dozing; for I reached the highway without knowing just where I was.

"I was recalled to myself by a rush of boys up the street before me, with a crowd streaming along behind them. It was the head of the procession. The sheriff and his men were riding, with set faces, in front and on both sides of a slowly moving vehicle; a common horse-cart in which in the midst of his guards, and dressed in his Sunday clothes, with a clean white shirt on, seated on his pine coffin, was old Joel. I unconsciously gazed at him, and at the instant he looked up and saw me. Our eyes met as naturally as if he had expected to find me there, and he gave me as natural and as friendly a bow – not a particle reproachful; but a little timid, as though he did not quite know whether I would speak to him.

"It gave me a tremendous shock. I had a sudden sinking of the heart, and nearly fell from my horse.

"I turned and rode away; but I could not shake off the feeling. I tried to reassure myself with the reflection that he had committed a terrible crime. It did not compose me. What insisted on coming to my mind was the eagerness with which I had prosecuted him and the joy I had felt at my success.

"Of course, I know now it was simply that I was overworked and needed rest; but at that time the trouble was serious.

"It haunted me all day, and that night I could not sleep. For many days afterwards, it clung to me, and I found myself unable to forget it, or to sleep as I had been used to do.

"The new trial of Absalom came on in time, and the fight was had all over again. It was longer than before, as every man in our county had an opinion, and a jury had to be brought from another county. But again the verdict was the same. And again an appeal was taken; was refused by the next higher court; and allowed by the highest; this time because a talesman had said he had expressed an opinion, but had not formed one. In time the appeal was heard once more, and after much delay, due to the number of cases on the docket and the immense labor of studying carefully so huge a record it was decided. It was again reversed, on the technicality mentioned, and a new trial was ordered.

"That same day the court adjourned for the term.

"Having a bedroom adjoining my office, I spent that night in town. I did not go to sleep until late, and had not been asleep long when I was awakened by the continual repetition of a monotonous sound. At first I thought I was dreaming, but as I aroused it came to me distinctly: the sound of blows in the distance struck regularly. I awaked fully. The noise was in the direction of the jail. I dressed hastily and went down on the street. I stepped into the arms of a half-dozen masked men who quietly laid me on my back, blindfolded me and bound me so that I could not move. I threatened and struggled; but to no purpose, and finally gave it up and tried expostulation. They told me that they intended no harm to me; but that I was their prisoner and they meant to keep me. They had come for their man, they said, and they meant to have him. They were perfectly quiet and acted with the precision of old soldiers.

"All the time I could hear the blows at the jail as the mob pounded the iron door with sledges, and now and then a shout or cry from within.

"The blows were on the inner door, for the mob had quickly gained access to the outer corridor. They had come prepared and, stout as the door was, it could not resist long. Then one great roar went up and the blows ceased suddenly, and then one cry.

"In a little while I heard the regular tramp of men, and in a few minutes the column came up the street, marching like soldiers. There must have been five hundred of them. The prisoner was in the midst, bare-headed and walking between two mounted men, and was moaning and pleading and cursing by turns.

"I asked my captors if I might speak, and they gave me ten minutes. I stood up on the top step of the house, and for a few minutes I made what I consider to have been the best speech I ever made or shall make. I told them in closing that I should use all my powers to find out who they were, and if I could do so I should prosecute them, every one, and try and have them hanged for murder.

"They heard me patiently, but without a word, and when I was through, one of the leaders made a short reply. They agreed with me about the law; but they felt that the way it was being used was such as to cause a failure of justice. They had waited patiently, and were apparently no nearer seeing justice executed than in the beginning. So they proposed to take the law into their own hands. The remedy was, to do away with all but proper defences and execute the law without unreasonable delay.

"It was the first mob I had ever seen, and I experienced a sensation of utter powerlessness and insignificance; just as in a storm at sea, a hurricane, or a conflagration. The individual disappeared before the irresistible force.

"An order was given and the column moved on silently.

"A question arose among my guards as to what should be done with me.

"They wished to pledge me to return to my rooms and take no steps until morning, but I would give no pledges. So they took me along with them.

"From the time they started there was not a word except the orders of the leader and his lieutenants and the occasional outcry of the prisoner, who prayed and cursed by turns.

"They passed out of the village and turned in at Halloway's place.

"Here the prisoner made his last struggle. The idea of being taken to Halloway's place appeared to terrify him to desperation. He might as well have struggled against the powers of the Infinite. He said he would confess everything if they would not take him there. They said they did not want his confession. He gave up, and from this time was quiet; and he soon began to croon a sort of hymn.

"The procession stopped at the big sycamore under which I had last parted from Halloway.

"I asked leave to speak again; but they said no. They asked the prisoner if he wanted to say anything. He said he wanted something to eat. The leader said he should have it; that it should never be said that any man – even he – had asked in vain for food in that county.

"Out of a haversack food was produced in plenty, and while the crowd waited, amidst profound silence the prisoner squatted down and ate up the entire plateful.

"Then the leader said he had just five minutes more to live, and he had better pray.

"He began a sort of wild incoherent ramble; confessed that he had murdered Halloway and his wife, but laid the chief blame on his father, and begged them to tell his friends to meet him in heaven.

"I asked leave to go, and it was given me on condition that I would not return for twenty minutes. This I agreed to.

"I went to my home and aroused someone, and we returned. It was not much more than a half hour since I had left, but the place was deserted. It was all as silent as the grave. There was no living creature there. Only under the great sycamore, from one of its long, pale branches that stretched across the road, hung that dead thing with the toes turned a little in, just out of our reach, turning and swaying a little in the night wind.

"We had to climb to the limb to cut the body down.

"The outside newspapers made a good deal of the affair. I was charged with indifference, with cowardice, with venality. Some journals even declared that I had instigated the lynching and participated in it, and said that I ought to be hanged.

"I did not mind this much. It buoyed me up, and I went on with my work without stopping for a rest, as I had intended to do.

"I kept my word and ransacked the county for evidence against the lynchers. Many knew nothing about the matter; others pleaded their privilege and refused to testify on the ground of self-incrimination.

"The election came on again, and almost before I knew it I was in the midst of the canvass.

"I held that election would be an indorsement of me, and defeat would be a censure. After all, it is the indorsement of those about our own home that we desire.

"The night before the election I spoke to a crowd at Burley's Fork.

The place had changed since Halloway checked Absalom Turnell there. A large crowd was in attendance. I paid Halloway my personal tribute that night, and it met with a deep response. I denounced the lynching. There was a dead silence. I was sure that in my audience were many of the men who had been in the mob that night.

"When I rode home quite a company started with me.

"The moon, which was on the wane, was, I remember, just rising as we set out. It was a soft night, rather cloudy, but not dark, for the sad moon shone a little now and then, looking wasted and red. The other men dropped off from time to time as we came to the several roads that led to their homes and at last I was riding alone. I was dead tired, and after I was left by my companions sat loungingly on my horse. My mind ran on the last canvass and the strange tragedy that had ended it, with its train of consequences. I was not aware when my horse turned off from the main road into the by-lane that led through the Halloway place to my own home. My horse was the same I had ridden that night. I awakened suddenly to a realization of where I was, and regretted for a second that I had come by that road. The next moment I put the thought away as a piece of cowardice and rode on, my mind perfectly easy. My horse presently broke into a canter and I took a train of thought distinctly pleasant. I mention this to account for my inability to explain what followed. I was thinking of old times and of a holiday I had once spent at Halloway's when old Joel came through on his way to his wife's house. It was the first time I remembered ever seeing Joel. I was suddenly conscious of something white moving on the road before me. At the same second my horse suddenly wheeled with such violence as to break my stirrup-leather and almost throw me over his neck. I pulled him up and turned him back, and there before me, coming along the unused road up the hill from Halloway's, was old Joel, sitting in a cart, looking at me, and bowing to me politely just as he had done that morning on his way to the gallows; while dangling from the white limb of the sycamore, swaying softly in the wind, hung the corpse of Absalom. At first I thought it was an illusion and I rubbed my eyes. But there they were. Then I thought it was a delusion; and I reined in my horse and reasoned about it. But it was not; for I saw both men as plainly as I saw my stirrup-leather lying there in the middle of the road, and in the same way. My horse saw them too, and was so terrified that I could not keep him headed to them. Again and again I pulled him around and looked at the men and tried to reason about them; but every time I looked there they were, and my horse snorted and wheeled in terror. I could see the clothes they wore: the clean, white shirt and neat Sunday suit old Joel had on, and the striped, hickory shirt, torn on the shoulders, and the gray trousers that the lynched man wore – I could see the white rope wrapped around the limb and hanging down, and the knot at his throat; I remembered them perfectly. I could not get near the cart, for the road down to Halloway's, on which it moved steadily without ever approaching, was stopped up. But I rode right under the limb on which the other man hung, and there he was just above my head. I reasoned with myself, but in vain. There he still hung silent and limp, swinging gently in the night wind and turning a little back and forth at the end of the white rope.

"In sheer determination to fight it through I got off my horse and picked up my stirrup. He was trembling like a leaf. I remounted and rode back to the spot and looked again, confident that the spectres would not have disappeared. But there they were, Old Joel, sitting in his cart, bowing to me civilly with timid, sad, friendly eyes, as much alive as I was, and the dead man, with his limp head and arms and his toes turned in, hanging in mid-air.

"I rode up under the dangling body and cut at it with my switch. At the motion my horse bolted. He ran fully a mile before I could pull him in.

"The next morning I went to my stable to get my horse to ride to the polls. The man at the stable said:

" 'He ain't fit to take out, sir. You must 'a gi'n him a mighty hard ride last night – he won't tetch a moufful; he's been in a cold sweat all night.'

"Sure enough, he looked it.

"I took another horse and rode out by Halloway's to see the place by daylight.

"It was quiet enough now. The sycamore shaded the grass-grown track, and a branch, twisted and broken by some storm, hung by a strip of bark from the big bough that stretched across the road above my head, swaying, with limp leaves, a little in the wind; a dense dog-wood bush in full bloom among the young pines, filled a fence-corner down the disused road where old Joel had bowed to me from his phantom cart the night before. But it was hard to believe that these were the things which had created such impressions on my mind – as hard to believe as that the quiet cottage peering out from amid the mass of peach-bloom on the other slope was one hour the home of such happiness, and the next the scene of such a tragedy."

Once more he put his hands suddenly before his face as though to shut out something from his vision.

"Yes, I have seen apparitions," he said, thoughtfully, "but I have seen what was worse."

Sabine Baring-Gould

H.P.

Sabine Baring-Gould (1834–1924), long-serving squire-parson of Lew Trenchard in Devon, will always be remembered for the great hymns he wrote, especially "Onward, Christian Soldiers"; but he was also amazingly prolific in other branches of literature, including biographies, travel books, folklore, novels, and ghost stories. "H.P.", reflecting his interest in French history and archaeology, is taken from A Book of Ghosts *(1904).*

THE RIVER VÉZÈRE leaps to life among the granite of the Limousin, forms a fine cascade, the Saut de la Virolle, then after a rapid descent over mica-schist, it passes into the region of red sandstone at Brive, and swelled with affluents it suddenly penetrates a chalk district, where it has scooped out for itself a valley between precipices some two to three hundred feet high.

These precipices are not perpendicular, but overhang, because the upper crust is harder than the stone it caps; and atmospheric influences, rain and frost, have gnawed into the chalk below, so that the cliffs hang forward as penthouse roofs, forming shelters beneath them. And these shelters have been utilized by man from when the first occupants of the district arrived at a vastly remote period, almost uninterruptedly to the present day. When peasants live beneath these roofs of nature's providing, they simply wall up the face and ends to form houses of the cheapest description of construction, with the earth as the floor, and one wall and the roof of living rock, into which they burrow to form cupboards, bedplaces, and cellars.

The refuse of all ages is superposed, like the leaves of a book, one stratum above another in orderly succession. If we shear down through these beds, we can read the history of the land, so far as its manufacture goes, beginning at the present day and going down, down to the times of primeval man. Now, after every meal, the peasant casts down the bones he has picked, he does not stoop to collect and cast forth the sherds of a broken pot, and if a sou falls and rolls away, in the dust of these gloomy habitations it gets trampled into the soil, to form another token of the period of occupation.

When the first man settled here the climatic conditions were different. The mammoth or woolly elephant, the hyaena, the cave bear, and the reindeer ranged the land. Then naked savages, using only flint tools, crouched under these rocks. They knew nothing of metals and of pottery. They hunted and ate the horse; they had no dogs, no oxen, no sheep. Glaciers covered the centre of France, and reached down the Vézère valley as far as to Brive.

These people passed away, whither we know not. The reindeer retreated to the north, the hyena to Africa, which was then united to Europe. The mammoth became extinct altogether.

After long ages another people, in a higher condition of culture, but who also used flint tools and weapons, appeared on the scene, and took possession of the abandoned rock shelters. They fashioned their implements in a different manner by flaking the flint in place of chipping it. They understood the art of the potter. They grew flax and wove linen. They had domestic animals, and the dog had become the friend of man. And their flint weapons they succeeded in bringing to a high polish by incredible labour and perseverance.

Then came in the Age of Bronze, introduced from abroad, probably from the East, as its great depot was in the basin of the Po. Next arrived the Gauls, armed with weapons of iron. They were subjugated by the Romans, and Roman Gaul in turn became a prey to the Goth and the Frank. History has begun and is in full swing.

The medieval period succeeded, and finally the modern age, and man now lives on top of the accumulation of all preceding epochs of men and stages of civilization. In no other part of France, indeed of Europe, is the story of man told so plainly, that he who runs may read; and ever since the middle of last century, when this fact was recognized, the district has been studied, and explorations have been made there, some slovenly, others scientifically.

A few years ago I was induced to visit this remarkable region and to

examine it attentively. I had been furnished with letters of recommendation from the authorities of the great Museum of National Antiquities at
St German, to enable me to prosecute my researches unmolested by
over-suspicious gendarmes and ignorant mayors.

Under one overhanging rock was a cabaret or tavern, announcing that
wine was sold there, by a withered bush above the door.

The place seemed to me to be a probable spot for my exploration. I
entered into an arrangement with the proprietor to enable me to dig, he
stipulating that I should not undermine and throw down his walls. I
engaged six labourers, and began proceedings by driving a tunnel some
little way below the tavern into the vast bed of debris.

The upper series of deposits did not concern me much. The point I
desired to investigate, and if possible to determine, was the
approximate length of time that had elapsed between the
disappearance of the reindeer hunters and the coming on the scene of
the next race, that which used polished stone implements and had
domestic animals.

Although it may seem at first sight as if both races had been savage, as
both lived in the Stone Age, yet an enormous stride forward had been
taken when men had learned the arts of weaving, of pottery, and had
tamed the dog, the horse, and the cow. These new folk had passed out of
the mere wild condition of the hunter, and had become pastoral and to
some extent agricultural.

Of course, the data for determining the length of a period might be
few, but I could judge whether a very long or a very brief period had
elapsed between the two occupations by the depth of debris – chalk fallen
from the roof, brought down by frost, in which were no traces of human
workmanship.

It was with this distinct object in view that I drove my adit into the
slope of rubbish some way below the cabaret, and I chanced to have hit
on the level of the deposits of the men of bronze. Not that we found much
bronze – all we secured was a broken pin – but we came on fragments of
pottery marked with the chevron and nail and twisted thong ornament
peculiar to that people and age.

My men were engaged for about a week before we reached the face of
the chalk cliff. We found the work not so easy as I had anticipated.
Masses of rock had become detached from above and had fallen, so that
we had either to quarry through them or to circumvent them. The soil
was of that curious coffee colour so inseparable from the chalk forma-

tion. We found many things brought down from above, a coin commemorative of the storming of the Bastille, and some small pieces of the later Roman emperors. But all of these were, of course, not in the solid ground below, but near the surface.

When we had reached the face of the cliff, instead of sinking a shaft I determined on carrying a gallery down an incline, keeping the rock as a wall on my right, till I reached the bottom of all.

The advantage of making an incline was that there was no hauling up of the earth by a bucket let down over a pulley, and it was easier for myself to descend.

I had not made my tunnel wide enough, and it was tortuous. When I began to sink, I set two of the men to smash up the masses of fallen chalk rock, so as to widen the tunnel, so that I might use barrows. I gave strict orders that all the material brought up was to be picked over by two of the most intelligent of the men, outside in the blaze of the sun. I was not desirous of sinking too expeditiously; I wished to proceed slowly, cautiously, observing every stage as we went deeper.

We got below the layer in which were the relics of the Bronze Age and of the men of polished stone, and then we passed through many feet of earth that rendered nothing, and finally came on the traces of the reindeer period.

To understand how that there should be a considerable depth of the debris of the men of the rude stone implements, it must be explained that these men made their hearths on the bare ground, and feasted around their fires, throwing about them the bones they had picked, and the ashes, and broken and disused implements, till the ground was inconveniently encumbered. Then they swept all the refuse together over their old hearth, and established another on top. So the process went on from generation to generation.

For the scientific results of my exploration I must refer the reader to the journals and memoirs of learned societies. I will not trouble him with them here.

On the ninth day after we had come to the face of the cliff, and when we had reached a considerable depth, we uncovered some human bones. I immediately adopted special precautions, so that these should not be disturbed. With the utmost care the soil was removed from over them, and it took us half a day to completely clear a perfect skeleton. It was that of a full-grown man, lying on his back, with the skull supported against the wall of chalk rock. He did not seem to have been buried. Had he been so, he would doubtless have been laid on his side in a contracted posture, with the chin resting on the knees.

One of the men pointed out to me that a mass of fallen rock lay beyond his feet, and had apparently shut him in, so that he had died through suffocation, buried under the earth that the rock had brought down with it.

I at once despatched a man to my hotel to fetch my camera, that I might by flashlight take a photograph of the skeleton as it lay; and another I sent to get from the chemist and grocer as much gum arabic and isinglass as could be procured. My object was to give to the bones a bath of gum to render them less brittle when removed, restoring to them the gelatine that had been absorbed by the earth and lime in which they lay.

Thus I was left alone at the bottom of my passage, the four men above being engaged in straightening the entrance and sifting the earth.

I was quite content to be alone, so that I might at my ease search for traces of personal ornament worn by the man who had thus met his death. The place was somewhat cramped, and there really was not room in it for more than one person to work freely.

Whilst I was thus engaged, I suddenly heard a shout, followed by a crash, and, to my dismay, an avalanche of rubble shot down the inclined passage of descent. I at once left the skeleton, and hastened to effect my exit, but found that this was impossible. Much of the super-incumbent earth and stone had fallen, dislodged by the vibrations caused by the picks of the men smashing up the chalk blocks, and the passage was completely choked. I was sealed up in the hollow where I was, and thankful that the earth above me had not fallen as well, and buried me, a man of the present enlightened age, along with the primeval savage of eight thousand years ago.

A large amount of matter must have fallen, for I could not hear the voices of the men.

I was not seriously alarmed. The workmen would procure assistance and labour indefatigably to release me; of that I could be certain. But how much earth had fallen? How much of the passage was choked, and how long would they take before I was released? All that was uncertain. I had a candle, or, rather, a bit of one, and it was not probable that it would last till the passage was cleared. What made me most anxious was the question whether the supply of air in the hollow in which I was enclosed would suffice.

My enthusiasm for prehistoric research failed me just then. All my interests were concentrated on the present and I gave up groping about the skeleton for relics. I seated myself on a stone, set the candle in a socket of chalk I had scooped out with my pocket-knife, and awaited events with my eyes on the skeleton.

Time passed somewhat wearily. I could hear an occasional thud, thud, when the men were using the pick; but they mostly employed the shovel, as I supposed. I set my elbows on my knees and rested my chin in my hands. The air was not cold, nor was the soil damp; it was dry as snuff. The flicker of my light played over the man of bones, and especially illumined the skull. It may have been fancy on my part, it probably was fancy, but it seemed to me as though something sparkled in the eye-sockets. Drops of water possibly lodged there, or crystals formed within the skull; but the effect was much as of eyes leering and winking at me. I lighted my pipe, and to my disgust found that my supply of matches was running short. In France the manufacture belongs to the state, and one gets but sixty *allumettes* for a penny.

I had not brought my watch with me below ground, fearing lest it might meet with an accident; consequently I was unable to reckon how time passed. I began counting and ticking off the minutes on my fingers, but soon tired of doing this.

My candle was getting short; it would not last much longer, and then I should be in the dark. I consoled myself with the thought that with the extinction of the light the consumption of the oxygen in the air would be less rapid. My eyes now rested on the flame of the candle, and I watched the gradual diminution of the composite. It was one of those abominable *bougies* with holes in them to economize the wax, and which consequently had less than the proper amount of material for feeding and maintaining a flame. At length the light went out, and I was left in total darkness. I might have used up the rest of my matches, one after another, but to what good? – they would prolong the period of illumination for but a very little while.

A sense of numbness stole over me, but I was not as yet sensible of deficiency of air to breathe. I found that the stone on which I was seated was pointed and hard, but I did not like to shift my position for fear of getting among and disturbing the bones, and I was still desirous of having them photographed *in situ* before they were moved.

I was not alarmed at my situation; I knew that I must be released eventually. But the tedium of sitting there in the dark and on a pointed stone was becoming intolerable.

Some time must have elapsed before I became, dimly at first, and then distinctly, aware of a bluish phosphorescent emanation from the skeleton. This seemed to rise above it like a faint smoke, which gradually gained consistency, took form, and became distinct; and I saw before me the misty, luminous form of a naked man, with wolfish countenance, prognathous jaws, glaring at me out of eyes deeply sunk under projecting brows. Although I thus describe what I saw, yet it gave me no idea of substance; it was vaporous, and yet it was articulate. Indeed, I cannot say at this moment whether I actually saw this apparition with my eyes, or whether it was a dream-like vision of the brain. Though luminous, it cast no light on the walls of the cave; if I raised my hand it did not obscure any portion of the form presented to me. Then I heard:"I will tear you with the nails of my fingers and toes, and rip you with my teeth."

"What have I done to injure and incense you?" I asked.

And here I must explain. No word was uttered by either of us; no word could have been uttered by this vaporous form. It had no material lungs, nor throat, nor mouth to form vocal sounds. It had but the semblance of a man. It was a spook, not a human being. But from it proceeded thought-waves, odylic force which smote on the tympanum of my mind or soul, and thereon registered the ideas formed by it. So in like manner I thought my replies, and they were communicated back in the same manner. If vocal words had passed between us neither would have been intelligible to the other. No dictionary was ever compiled, or would be compiled, of the tongue of prehistoric man; moreover, the grammar of the speech of that race would be absolutely incomprehensible to man now. But thoughts can be interchanged without words. When we think we do not think in any language. It is only when we desire to communicate our thoughts to other men that we shape them into words and express them vocally in structural grammatical sentences. The beasts have never attained to this, yet they can communicate with one another, not by language, but by thought vibrations.

I must further remark that when I give what ensued as a conversation, I have to render the thought intercommunication that passed between the Homo Praehistoricus – the prehistoric man – and me, in English as best I can render it. I knew as we conversed that I was not speaking to him in English, nor in French, nor Latin, nor in any tongue whatever. Moreover, when I use the words "said" or "spoke", I mean no more than that the impression was formed by my brain-pan or the receptive drum of my soul, was produced by the rhythmic, orderly sequence of thought-waves. When, however, I express the words "screamed" or "shrieked," I signify that those vibrations came sharp and swift; and when I say "laughed," that they came in a choppy, irregular fashion, conveying the idea, not the sound of laughter.

"I will tear you! I will rend you to bits and throw you in pieces about this cave!" shrieked the Homo Praehistoricus, or primeval man.

Again I remonstrated, and inquired how I had incensed him. But yelling with rage, he threw himself upon me. In a moment I was enveloped in a luminous haze, strips of phosphorescent vapour laid themselves about me, but I received no injury whatever, only my spiritual nature was subjected to something like a magnetic storm. After a few moments the spook disengaged itself from me, and drew back to where it was before, screaming broken exclamations of meaningless rage, and jabbering savagely. It rapidly cooled down.

"Why do you wish me ill?" I asked again.

"I cannot hurt you. I am spirit, you are matter, and spirit cannot injure matter; my nails are psychic phenomena. Your soul you can lacerate yourself, but I can effect nothing, nothing."

"Then why have you attacked me? What is the cause of your impotent resentment?"

"Because you are a son of the twentieth century, and I lived eight thousand years ago. Why are you nursed in the lap of luxury? Why do you enjoy comforts, a civilization that we knew nothing of? It is not just. It is cruel on us. We had nothing, nothing, literally nothing, not even lucifer matches!"

Again he fell to screaming, as might a caged monkey rendered furious by failure to obtain an apple which he could not reach.

"I am very sorry, but it is no fault of mine."

"Whether it be your fault or not does not matter to me. You have these things – we had not. Why, I saw you just now strike a light on the sole of your boot. It was done in a moment. We had only flint and ironstone, and it took half a day with us to kindle a fire, and then it flayed our knuckles with continuous knocking. No! we had nothing, nothing – no lucifer matches, no commercial travellers, no Benedictine, no pottery, no metal, no education, no elections, no *chocolat menier*."

"How do you know about these products of the present age, here, buried under fifty feet of soil for eight thousand years?"

"It is my spirit which speaks with your spirit. My spook does not always remain with my bones. I can go up; rocks and stones and earth heaped over me do not hold me down. I am often above. I am in the tavern overhead. I have seen men drink there. I have seen a bottle of Benedictine. I have applied my psychical lips to it, but I could taste, absorb nothing. I have seen commercial travellers there, cajoling the patron into buying things he did not want. They are mysterious, marvellous beings, their powers of persuasion are little short of miraculous. What do you think of doing with me?"

"Well, I propose first of all photographing you, then soaking you in gum arabic, and finally transferring you to a museum."

He screamed as though with pain, and gasped: "Don't! don't do it. It will be torture insufferable."

"But why so? You will be under glass, in a polished oak or mahogany box."

"Don't! You cannot understand what it will be to me – a spirit more or less attached to my body, to spend ages upon ages in a museum with fibulae, triskelli, palstaves, celts, torques, scarabs. We cannot travel very far from our bones – our range is limited. And conceive of my feelings for centuries condemned to wander among glass cases containing prehistoric antiquities, and to hear the talk of scientific men alone. Now here, it is otherwise. Here I can pass up when I like into the tavern, and can see men get drunk, and hear commercial travellers hoodwink the patron, and then when the taverner finds he has been induced to buy what he did not want, I can see him beat his wife and smack his children. There is something human, humorous, in that, but fibulae, palstaves, torques – bah!"

"You seem to have a lively knowledge of antiquities," I observed.

"Of course I have. There come archaeologists here and eat their sandwiches above me, and talk prehistoric antiquities till I am sick. Give me life! Give me something interesting!"

"But what do you mean when you say that you cannot travel far from your bones?"

"I mean that there is a sort of filmy attachment that connects our psychic nature with our mortal remains. It is like a spider and its web. Suppose the soul to be the spider and the skeleton to be the web. If you break the thread the spider will never find its way back to its home. So it is with us; there is an attachment, a faint thread of luminous spiritual matter that unites us to our earthly husk. It is liable to accidents. It sometimes gets broken, sometimes dissolved by water. If a black beetle crawls across it it suffers a sort of paralysis. I have never been to the other side of the river, I have feared to do so, though very anxious to look at that creature like a large black caterpillar called the Train.".

"This is news to me. Do you know of any case of rupture of connection?"

"Yes," he replied. "My old father, after he was dead some years, got his link of attachment broken, and he wandered about disconsolate. He could not find his own body, but he lighted on that of a young female of seventeen, and he got into that. It happened most singularly that her spook, being frolicsome and inconsiderate, had got its bond also broken, and she, that is her spirit, straying about in quest of her body, lighted on that of my venerable parent, and for want of a better took possession of it. It so chanced that after a while they met and became chummy. In the world of spirits there is no marriage, but there grow up spiritual attachments, and these two got rather fond of each other, but never could puzzle it out which was which and what each was; for a female soul had entered into an old male body, and a male soul had taken up its residence in a female body. Neither could riddle out of which sex each was. You see they had no education. But I know that my father's soul became quite sportive in that young woman's skeleton."

"Did they continue chummy?"

"No; they quarrelled as to which was which, and they are not now on speaking terms. I have two great-uncles. Theirs is a sad tale. Their souls were not wandering one day, and inadvertently they crossed and recrossed each other's tracks so that their spiritual threads of attachment got twisted. They found this out, and that they were getting tangled up. What one of them should have done would have been to have stood still and let the other jump over and dive under his brother's thread till he had cleared himself. But my maternal great-uncles – I think I forgot to say they were related to me through my mother – they were men of peppery tempers and they could not understand this. They had no education. So they jumped one this way and one another, each abusing the other, and made the tangle more complete. That was about six thousand years ago, and they are now so knotted up that I do not suppose they will be clear of one another till time is no more."

He paused and laughed.

Then I said: "It must have been very hard for you to be without pottery of any sort."

"It was," replied H.P. (this stands for Homo Praehistoricus, not for

House-Parlourmaid or Hardy Perennial), "very hard. We had skins for water and milk – "

"Oh! you had milk. I supposed you had no cows."

"Nor had we, but the reindeer were beginning to get docile and be tamed. If we caught young deer we brought them up to be pets for our children. And so it came about that as they grew up we found out that we could milk them into skins. But that gave it a smack, and whenever we desired a fresh draught there was nothing for it but to lie flat on the ground under a doe reindeer and suck for all we were worth. It was hard. Horses were hunted. It did not occur to us that they could be tamed and saddled and mounted. Oh! it was not right. It was not fair that you should have everything and we nothing – nothing – nothing! Why should you have all and we have had naught?"

"Because I belong to the twentieth century. Thirty-three generations go to a thousand years. There are some two hundred and sixty-four or two hundred and seventy generations intervening between you and me. Each generation makes some discovery that advances civilization a stage, the next enters on the discoveries of the preceding generations, and so culture advances stage by stage. Man is infinitely progressive, the brute beast is not."

"That is true," he replied. "I invented butter, which was unknown to my ancestors, the unbuttered man."

"Indeed!"

"It was so," he said, and I saw a flush of light ripple over the emanation. I suppose it was a glow of self-satisfaction. "It came about thus. One of my wives had nearly let the fire out. I was very angry, and catching up one of the skins of milk, I banged her about the head with it till she fell insensible to the earth. The other wives were very pleased and applauded. When I came to take a drink, for my exertions had heated me, I found that the milk was curdled into butter. At first I did not know what it was, so I made one of my other wives taste it, and as she pronounced it to be good, I ate the rest myself. That was how butter was invented. For four hundred years that was the way it was made, by banging a milk-skin about the head of a woman till she was knocked down insensible. But at last a woman found out that by churning the milk with her hand butter could be made equally well, and then the former process was discontinued except by some men who clung to ancestral customs."

"But," said I, "nowadays you would not be suffered to knock your wife about, even with a milk-skin."

SABINE BARING-GOULD

"Why not?"

"Because it is barbarous. You would be sent to gaol."

"But she was my wife."

"Nevertheless it would not be tolerated. The law steps in and protects women from ill-usage."

"How shameful! Not allowed to do what you like with your own wife!"

"Most assuredly not. Then you remarked that this was how you dealt with one of your wives. How many did you possess?"

"Off and on, seventeen."

"*Now*, no man is suffered to have more than one."

"What – one at a time?"

"Yes," I replied.

"Ah, well. Then if you had an old and ugly wife, or one who was a scold, you could not kill her and get another, young and pretty."

"That would not be allowed."

"Not even if she were a scold?"

"No, you would have to put up with her to the bitter end."

"Humph!" H.P. remained silent for a while wrapped in thought. Presently he said: "There is one thing I do not understand. In the wineshop overhead the men get very quarrelsome, others drunk, but they never kill one another."

"No. If one man killed another he would have his head cut off – here in France – unless extenuating circumstances were found. With us in England he would be hanged by the neck till he was dead."

"Then – what is your sport?"

"We hunt the fox."

"The fox is bad eating. I never could stomach it. If I did kill a fox I made my wives eat it, and had some mammoth meat for myself. But hunting is business with us – or was so – not sport."

"Nevertheless with us it is our great sport."

"Business is business and sport is sport," he said. "Now, we hunted as business, and had little fights and killed one another as our sport."

"We are not suffered to kill one another."

"But take the case," said he, "that a man has a nose-ring, or a pretty wife, and you want one or the other. Surely you might kill him and possess yourself of what you so ardently covet?"

"By no means. Now, to change the topic," I went on, "you are totally destitute of clothing. You do not even wear the traditional garment of fig leaves."

"What avail fig leaves? There is no warmth in them."

"Perhaps not – but one of delicacy."

"What is that? I don't understand." There was clearly no corresponding sensation in the vibrating tympanum of his psychic nature.

"Did you never wear clothes?" I inquired.

"Certainly, when it was cold we wore skins, skins of the beasts we killed. But in summer what is the use of clothing? Besides, we only wore them out of doors. When we entered our homes, made of skins hitched up to the rock overhead, we threw them off. It was hot within, and we perspired freely."

"What, were naked in your homes! you and your wives?"

"Of course we were. Why not? It was very warm within with the fire always kept up."

"Why – good gracious me!" I exclaimed, "that would never be tolerated nowadays. If you attempted to go about the country unclothed, even get out of your clothes freely at home, you would be sent to a lunatic asylum and kept there."

"Humph!" He again lapsed into silence.

Presently he exclaimed: "After all, I think that we were better off as we were eight thousand years ago, even without your matches, Benedictine, education, *chocolat menier*, and commercials, for then we were able to enjoy real sport – we could kill one another, we could knock old wives on the head, we could have a dozen or more squaws according to our circumstances, young and pretty, and we could career about the country or sit and enjoy a social chat at home, stark naked. We were best off as we were. There are compensations in life at every period of man. *Vive la liberté!*"

At that moment I heard a shout – saw a flash of light. The workmen had pierced the barrier. A rush of fresh air entered. I staggered to my feet.

"*O! mon Dieu! Monsieur vit encore!*"

I felt dizzy. Kind hands grasped me. I was dragged forth. Brandy was poured down my throat. When I came to myself I gasped: "Fill in the hole! Fill it all up. Let H.P. lie where he is. He shall not go to the British Museum. I have had enough of prehistoric antiquities. *Adieu, pour toujours la Vézère.*"

Lafcadio Hearn

Yuki-Onna

Lafcadio Hearn (1850–1904) settled in Japan in 1890 after living for twenty years in America. Always fascinated by legends and mythology (especially from India, China and Japan), his collections of tales – Some Chinese Ghosts *(1887),* In Ghostly Japan *(1899),* Kotto *(1902),* Kwaidan *(1904), and* Fantastics *(1914) – have been admired and reprinted regularly in the ninety years since his death. This tale is taken from* Kwaidan *(1904, subject of one of Japan's greatest "ghost" anthology films). Hearn wrote (in January 1904) that "Yuki-Onna" was "told me by a farmer of Chofu, Nishitama-gori, in Musashi province, as a legend of his native village. Whether it has ever been written in Japanese I do not know; but the extraordinary belief which it records used certainly to exist in most parts of Japan, and in many curious forms . . . "*

IN A VILLAGE of Musashi Province, there lived two woodcutters; Mosaku and Minokichi. At the time of which I am speaking, Mosaku was an old man; and Minokichi, his apprentice, was a lad of eighteen years. Every day they went together to a forest situated about five miles from their village. On the way to that forest there is a wide river to cross; and there is a ferry-boat. Several times a bridge was built where the ferry is; but the bridge was each time carried away by a flood. No common bridge can resist the current there when the river rises.

Mosaku and Minokichi were on their way home, one very cold evening, when a great snowstorm overtook them. They reached the ferry; and they found that the boatman had gone away, leaving his boat on the other side of the river. It was no day for swimming; and the woodcutters took shelter in the ferryman's hut – thinking themselves lucky to find any shelter at all. There was no brazier in the hut, nor any place in which to make a fire: it was only a two-mat¹ hut, with a single door, but no window. Mosaku and Minokichi fastened the door, and lay down to rest, with their straw rain-coats over them. At first they did not feel very cold; and they thought that the storm would soon be over.

The old man almost immediately fell asleep; but the boy, Minokichi, lay awake a long time, listening to the awful wind, and the continual slashing of the snow against the door. The river was roaring; and the hut swayed and creaked like a junk at sea. It was a terrible storm; and the air was every moment becoming colder; and Minokichi shivered under his rain-coat. But at last, in spite of the cold, he too fell asleep.

He was awakened by a showering of snow in his face. The door of the hut had been forced open; and, by the snow-light (yuki-akari), he saw a woman in the room – a woman all in white. She was bending above Mosaku, and blowing her breath upon him – and her breath was like a bright white smoke. Almost in the same moment she turned to Minokichi, and stooped over him. He tried to cry out, but found that he could not utter any sound. The white woman bent down over him, lower and lower, until her face almost touched him; and he saw that she was very beautiful – though her eyes made him afraid. For a little time she continued to look at him – then she smiled, and she whispered: "I intended to treat you like the other man. But I cannot help feeling some pity for you – because you are so young . . . You are a pretty boy, Minokichi; and I will not hurt you now. But, if you ever tell anybody – even your own mother – about what you have seen this night, I shall know it; and then I will kill you . . . Remember what I say!"

With these words, she turned from him, and passed through the doorway. Then he found himself able to move; and he sprang up, and looked out. But the woman was nowhere to be seen; and the snow was driving furiously into the hut. Minokichi closed the door, and secured it by fixing several billets of wood against it. He wondered if the wind had blown it open – he thought that he might have been only dreaming, and might have mistaken the gleam of the snow-light in the doorway for the

¹That is to say, with a floor-surface of about six feet square.

figure of a white woman: but he could not be sure. He called to Mosaku, and was frightened because the old man did not answer. He put out his hand in the dark, and touched Mosaku's face, and found that it was ice! Mosaku was stark and dead . . .

By dawn the storm was over; and when the ferryman returned to his station, a little after sunrise, he found Minokichi lying senseless beside the frozen body of Mosaku. Minokichi was promptly cared for, and soon came to himself; but he remained a long time ill from the effects of the cold of that terrible night. He had been greatly frightened also by the old man's death; but he said nothing about the vision of the woman in white. As soon as he got well again, he returned to his calling – going alone every morning to the forest, and coming back at nightfall with his bundles of wood, which his mother helped him to sell.

One evening, in the winter of the following year, as he was on his way home, he overtook a girl who happened to be travelling by the same road. She was a tall, slim girl, very good-looking; and she answered Minokichi's greeting in a voice as pleasant to the ear as the voice of a song-bird. Then he walked beside her; and they began to talk. The girl said that her name was O-Yuki; that she had lately lost both of her parents; and that she was going to Yedo, where she happened to have some poor relations, who might help her to find a situation as servant. Minokichi soon felt charmed by this strange girl; and the more that he looked at her, the handsomer she appeared to be. He asked her whether she was yet betrothed; and she answered, laughingly, that she was free. Then, in her turn, she asked Minokichi whether he was married, or pledged to marry; and he told her that, although he had only a widowed mother to support, the question of an "honourable daughter-in-law" had not yet been considered, as he was very young . . . After these confidences, they walked on for a long while without speaking; but, as the proverb declares, *Ki ga aréba, mé mo kuchi hodo ni mono wo iu*: "When the wish is there, the eyes can say as much as the mouth." By the time they reached the village, they had become very much pleased with each other; and then Minokichi asked O-Yuki to rest awhile at his house. After some shy hesitation, she went there with him; and his mother made her welcome, and prepared a warm meal for her. O-Yuki behaved so nicely that Minokichi's mother took a sudden fancy to her, and persuaded her to delay her journey to Yedo. And the natural end of the matter was that

O-Yuki never went to Yedo at all. She remained in the house, as an "honourable daughter-in-law."

O-Yuki proved a very good daughter-in-law. When Minokichi's mother came to die – some five years later – her last words were words of affection and praise for the wife of her son. And O-Yuki bore Minokichi ten children, boys and girls – handsome children all of them, and very fair of skin.

The country-folk thought O-Yuki a wonderful person, by nature different from themselves. Most of the peasant-women age early; but O-Yuki, even after having become the mother of ten children, looked as young and fresh as on the day when she had first come to the village.

One night, after the children had gone to sleep, O-Yuki was sewing by the light of a paper lamp; and Minokichi, watching her, said:

"To see you sewing there, with the light on your face, makes me think of a strange thing that happened when I was a lad of eighteen. I then saw somebody as beautiful and white as you are now – indeed, she was very like you."

Without lifting her eyes from her work, O-Yuki responded:

"Tell me about her . . . Where did you see her?"

Then Minokichi told her about the terrible night in the ferryman's hut – and about the White Woman that had stopped above him, smiling and whispering – and about the silent death of old Mosaku. And he said:

"Asleep or awake, that was the only time that I saw a being as beautiful as you. Of course, she was not a human being; and I was afraid of her – very much afraid – but she was so white! . . . Indeed, I have never been sure whether it was a dream that I saw, or the Woman of the Snow."

O-Yuki flung down her sewing, and arose, and bowed above Minokichi where he sat, and shrieked into his face:

"It was I – I – I! Yuki it was! And I told you then that I would kill you if you ever said one word about it! . . . But for those children asleep there, I would kill you this moment! And now you had better take very, very good care of them; for if ever they have reason to complain of you, I will treat you as you deserve!"

Even as she screamed, her voice became thin, like a crying of wind – then she melted into a bright white mist that spired to the roof-beams, and shuddered away through the smoke-hole . . . Never again was she seen.

M. R. James

The Ash-Tree

Montague Rhodes James succeeded – more than any other writer – in reviving and restyling the fine art of the ghost story at the turn of the century. "The Ash-Tree" comes from his first, and greatest, collection, Ghost Stories of an Antiquary *(1904), widely regarded as the single most important and influential (and most reprinted) supernatural title of the past hundred years.*

EVERYONE WHO HAS travelled over eastern England knows the smaller country-houses with which it is studded – the rather dank little buildings, usually in the Italian style, surrounded with parks of some eighty to a hundred acres. For me they have always had a very strong attraction: with the grey paling of split oak, the noble trees, the meres with their reed-beds, and the line of distant woods. Then, I like the pillared portico – perhaps stuck on to a red-brick Queen Anne house which has been faced with stucco to bring it into line with the "Grecian" taste of the end of the eighteenth century; the hall inside, going up to the roof, which hall ought always to be provided with a gallery and a small organ. I like the library, too, where you may find anything from a psalter of the thirteenth century to a Shakespeare quarto. I like the pictures, of course; and perhaps most of all I like fancying what life in such a house was when it was first built, and in the piping times of landlords' prosperity, and not least now, when, if money is not so plentiful, taste is more varied and life quite as interesting. I wish to have one of these houses, and enough money to keep it together and entertain my friends in it modestly.

But this is a digression. I have to tell you of a curious series of events which happened in such a house as I have tried to describe. It is

Castringham Hall in Suffolk. I think a good deal has been done to the building since the period of my story, but the essential features I have sketched are still there – Italian portico, square block of white house, older inside than out, park with fringe of woods, and mere. The one feature that marked out the house from a score of others is gone. As you looked at it from the park, you saw on the right a great old ash-tree growing within half a dozen yards of the wall, and almost or quite touching the building with its branches. I suppose it had stood there ever since Castringham ceased to be a fortified place, and since the moat was filled in and the Elizabethan dwelling-house built. At any rate, it had wellnigh attained its full dimensions in the year 1690.

In that year the district in which the Hall is situated was the scene of a number of witch-trials. It will be long, I think, before we arrive at a just estimate of the amount of solid reason – if there was any – which lay at the root of the universal fear of witches in old times. Whether the persons accused of this offence really did imagine that they were possessed of unusual powers of any kind; or whether they had the will at least, if not the power, of doing mischief to their neighbours; or whether all the confessions, of which there are so many, were extorted by the mere cruelty of the witch-finders – these are questions which are not, I fancy, yet solved. And the present narrative gives me pause. I cannot altogether sweep it away as mere invention. The reader must judge for himself.

Castringham contributed a victim to the *auto-da-fé*. Mrs Mothersole was her name, and she differed from the ordinary run of village witches only in being rather better off and in a more influential position. Efforts were made to save her by several reputable farmers of the parish. They did their best to testify to her character, and showed considerable anxiety as to the verdict of the jury.

But what seems to have been fatal to the woman was the evidence of the then proprietor of Castringham Hall – Sir Matthew Fell. He deposed to having watched her on three different occasions from his window, at the full of the moon, gathering sprigs "from the ash-tree near my house". She had climbed into the branches, clad only in her shift, and was cutting off small twigs with a peculiarly curved knife, and as she did so she seemed to be talking to herself. On each occasion Sir Matthew had done his best to capture the woman, but she had always taken alarm at some accidental noise he had made, and all he could see when he got down to the garden was a hare running across the park in the direction of the village.

On the third night he had been at pains to follow at his best speed, and had gone straight to Mrs Mothersole's house; but he had had to wait a quarter of an hour battering at her door, and then she had come out very cross, and apparently very sleepy, as if just out of bed; and he had no good explanation to offer of his visit.

Mainly on this evidence, though there was much more of a less striking and unusual kind from other parishioners, Mrs Mothersole was found guilty and condemned to die. She was hanged a week after the trial, with five or six more unhappy creatures, at Bury St Edmunds.

Sir Matthew Fell, then Deputy-Sheriff, was present at the execution. It was a damp, drizzly March morning when the cart made its way up the rough grass hill outside Northgate, where the gallows stood. The other victims were apathetic or broken down with misery; but Mrs Mothersole was, as in life so in death, of a very different temper. Her "poysonous Rage," as a reporter of the time puts it, "did so work upon the Bystanders – yea, even upon the Hangman – that it was constantly affirmed of all that saw her that she presented the living Aspect of a mad Divell. Yet she offer'd no Resistance to the Officers of the Law; onely she looked upon those that laid Hands upon her with so direfull and venomous an Aspect that – as one of them afterwards assured me – the meer Thought of it preyed inwardly upon his Mind for six Months after."

However, all that she is reported to have said was the seemingly meaningless words: "There will be guests at the Hall." Which she repeated more than once in an undertone.

Sir Matthew Fell was not unimpressed by the bearing of the woman. He had some talk upon the matter with the vicar of his parish, with whom he travelled home after the assize business was over. His eviddence at the trial had not been very willingly given; he was not specially infected with the witch-finding mania, but he declared, then and afterwards, that he could not give any other account of the matter than that he had given, and that he could not possibly have been mistaken as to what he saw. The whole transaction had been repugnant to him, for he was a man who liked to be on pleasant terms with those about him; but he saw a duty to be done in this business, and he had done it. That seems to have been the gist of his sentiments, and the vicar applauded it, as any reasonable man must have done.

A few weeks after, when the moon of May was at the full, vicar and squire met again in the park, and walked to the Hall together. Lady Fell was with her mother, who was dangerously ill, and Sir Matthew was alone at home; so the vicar, a Mr Crome, was easily persuaded to take a late supper at the Hall.

Sir Matthew was not very good company this evening. The talk ran chiefly on family and parish matters, and, as luck would have it, Sir Matthew made a memorandum in writing of certain wishes or intentions of his regarding his estates, which afterwards proved exceedingly useful.

When Mr Crome thought of starting for home, about half-past nine o'clock, Sir Matthew and he took a preliminary turn on the gravelled walk at the back of the house. The only incident that struck Mr Crome was this: they were in sight of the ash-tree which I described as growing near the windows of the building, when Sir Matthew stopped and said;

"What is that that runs up and down the stem of the ash? It is never a squirrel? They will all be in their nests by now."

The vicar looked and saw the moving creature, but he could make nothing of its colour in the moonlight. The sharp outline, however, seen for an instant, was imprinted on his brain, and he could have sworn, he said, though it sounded foolish, that, squirrel or not, it had more than four legs.

Still, not much was to be made of the momentary vision, and the two men parted. They may have met since then, but it was not for a score of years.

Next day Sir Matthew Fell was not downstairs at six in the morning, as was his custom, nor at seven, nor yet at eight. Hereupon the servants went and knocked at his chamber door. I need not prolong the description of their anxious listenings and renewed batterings on the panels. The door was opened at last from the outside, and they found their master dead and black. So much you have guessed. That there were any marks of violence did not at the moment appear; but the window was open.

One of the men went to fetch the parson, and then by his directions rode on to give notice to the coroner. Mr Crome himself went as quick as he might to the Hall, and was shown to the room where the dead man lay. He has left some notes among his papers which show how genuine a respect and sorrow was felt for Sir Matthew, and there is also this passage, which I transcribe for the sake of the light it throws upon the course of events, and also upon the common beliefs of the time:

"There was not any the least Trace of an Entrance having been forc'd to the Chamber: but the Casement stood open, as my poor Friend would always have it in this Season. He had his Evening Drink of small Ale in a

silver vessel of about a pint measure and tonight had not drunk it out.
This Drink was examined by the Physician from Bury, a Mr Hodgkins,
who could not, however, as he afterwards declar'd upon his Oath, before
the Coroner's quest, discover that any matter of a venomous kind was
present in it. For, as was natural, in the great Swelling and Blackness of
the Corpse, there was talk made among the Neighbours of Poyson. The
Body was very much Disorder'd as it laid in the Bed, being twisted after
so extream a sort as gave too probable Conjecture that my worthy Friend
and Patron had expir'd in great Pain and Agony. And what is as yet
unexplain'd, and to myself the Argument of some Horrid and Artfull
Designe in the Perpetrators of this Barbarous Murther, was this, that the
Women which were entrusted with the lay-out of the Corpse and
washing it, being both sad Persons and very well Respected in their
Mournfull Profession, came to me in a great Pain and Distress both of
Mind and Body, saying, what was indeed confirmed upon the first View,
that they had no sooner touch'd the Breast of the Corpse with their
naked Hands than they were sensible of a more than ordinary violent
Smart and Acheing in their Palms, which, with their whole Forearms, in
no long time swell'd so immoderately the Pain still continuing, that, as
afterwards proved, during many weeks they were forc'd to lay by the
exercise of their Calling; and yet no mark seen on the Skin.

   "Upon hearing this, I sent for the Physician, who was still in the
House, and we made as carefull a proof as we were able by the Help of a
small Magnifying Lens of Crystal of the condition of the Skinn on this
Part of the Body: but could not detect with the Instrument we had any
Matter of Importance beyond a couple of small Punctures or Pricks,
which we then concluded were the Spotts by which the Poyson might be
introduced, remembering that Ring of *Pope Borgia*, with other known
Specimens of the Horrid Art of the Italian Poysoners of the last age.

   "So much is to be said of the Symptoms seen on the Corpse. As to
what I am to add, it is meerly my own Experiment, and to be left to
Posterity to judge whether there be anything of Value therein. There was
on the Table by the Beddside a Bible of the small size, in which my
Friend – punctuall as in Matters of less Moment, so in this more weighty
one – used nightly, and upon his First Rising, to read a sett Portion. And
I taking it up – not without a Tear duly paid to him which from the Study
of this poorer Adumbration was now pass'd to the contemplation of its
great Originall – it came into my Thoughts, as at such moments of
Helplessness we are prone to catch at any the least Glimmer that makes

promise of Light, to make trial of that old and by many accounted Superstitious Practice of drawing the *Sortes*: of which a Principall Instance, in the case of his late Sacred Majesty the Blessed Martyr King *Charles* and my Lord *Falkland*, was now much talked of. I must needs admit that by my Trial not much Assistance was afforded me: yet, as the Cause and Origin of these Dreadful Events may hereafter be search'd out, I set down the Results, in the case it may be found that they pointed the true Quarter of the Mischief to a quicker Intelligence than my own. "I made, then, three trials, opening the Book and placing my Finger upon certain Words: which gave in the first these words, from Luke xiii. 7, *Cut it down*; in the second, Isaiah xiii. 20, *It shall never be inhabited*; and upon the third Experiment, Job xxxix. 30, *Her young ones also suck up blood.*"

This is all that need be quoted from Mr Crome's papers. Sir Matthew Fell was duly coffined and laid into the earth, and his funeral sermon, preached by Mr Crome on the following Sunday, has been printed under the title of "The Unsearchable Way; or, England's Danger and the Malicious Dealings of Anti-christ," it being the vicar's view, as well as that most commonly held in the neighbourhood, that the squire was the victim of a recrudescence of the Popish Plot.

His son, Sir Matthew the second, succeeded to the title and estates. And so ends the first act of the Castringham tragedy. It is to be mentioned, though the fact is not surprising, that the new baronet did not occupy the room in which his father had died. Nor, indeed, was it slept in by anyone but an occasional visitor during the whole of his occupation. He died in 1735, and I do not find that anything particular marked his reign, save a curiously constant mortality among his cattle and livestock in general, which showed a tendency to increase slightly as time went on.

Those who are interested in the details will find a statistical account in a letter to the *Gentleman's Magazine* of 1772, which draws the facts from the baronet's own papers. He put an end to it at last by a very simple expedient, that of shutting up all his beasts in sheds at night, and keeping no sheep in his park. For he had noticed that nothing was ever attacked that spent the night indoors. After that the disorder confined itself to wild birds, and beasts of chase. But as we have no good account of the symptoms, and as all-night watching was quite unproductive of any clue, I do not dwell on what the Suffolk farmers called the "Castringham sickness."

The second Sir Matthew died in 1735, as I said, and was duly succeeded by his son, Sir Richard. It was in his time that the great family pew was built out on the north side of the parish church. So large were the squire's ideas that several of the graves on that unhallowed side of the building had to be disturbed to satisfy his requirements. Among them was that of Mrs Mothersole, the position of which was accurately known, thanks to a note on a plan of the church and yard, both made by Mr Crome.

A certain amount of interest was excited in the village when it was known that the famous witch, who was still remembered by a few, was to be exhumed. And the feeling of surprise, and indeed disquiet, was very strong when it was found that, though her coffin was fairly sound and unbroken, there was no trace whatever inside it of body, bones, or dust. Indeed, it is a curious phenomenon, for at the time of her burying no such things were dreamt of as resurrection-men, and it is difficult to conceive any rational motive for stealing a body otherwise than for the uses of the dissecting-room.

The incident revived for a time all the stories of witch-trials and of the exploits of the witches, dormant for forty years, and Sir Richard's orders that the coffin should be burnt were thought by a good many to be rather foolhardy, though they were duly carried out.

Sir Richard was a pestilent innovator, it is certain. Before his time the Hall had been a fine block of the mellowest red brick; but Sir Richard had travelled in Italy and become infected with the Italian taste, and, having more money than his predecessors, he determined to leave an Italian palace where he had found an English house. So stucco and ashlar masked the brick; some indifferent Roman marbles were planted about in the entrance-hall and gardens; a reproduction of the Sibyl's temple at Tivoli was erected on the opposite bank of the mere; and Castringham took on an entirely new, and, I must say, a less engaging, aspect. But it was much admired, and served as a model to a good many of the neighbouring gentry in after-years.

One morning (it was in 1754) Sir Richard woke after a night of discomfort. It had been windy, and his chimney had smoked persistently, and yet it was so cold that he must keep up a fire. Also something had so rattled about the window that no man could get a moment's peace. Further, there was the prospect of several guests of position arriving in the course of the day, who would expect sport of some kind, and the inroads of the distemper (which continued among his game) had been lately so serious that he was afraid for his reputation as a game-preserver. But what really touched him most nearly was the other matter of his sleepless night. He could certainly not sleep in that room again.

That was the chief subject of his meditations at breakfast, and after it he began a systematic examination of the rooms to see which would suit his notions best. It was long before he found one. This had a window with an eastern aspect and that with a northern; this door the servants would be always passing, and he did not like the bedstead in that. No, he must have a room with a western look-out, so that the sun could not wake him early, and it must be out of the way of the business of the house. The housekeeper was at the end of her resources.

"Well, Sir Richard," she said, "you know that there is but one room like that in the house."

"Which may that be?" said Sir Richard.

"And that is Sir Matthew's – the West Chamber."

"Well, put me in there, for there I'll lie tonight," said her master. "Which way is it? Here, to be sure"; and he hurried off.

"Oh, Sir Richard, but no one has slept there these forty years. The air has hardly been changed since Sir Matthew died there."

Thus she spoke, and rustled after him.

"Come, open the door, Mrs Chiddock. I'll see the chamber, at least."

So it was opened, and, indeed, the smell was very close and earthy. Sir Richard crossed to the window, and, impatiently, as was his wont, threw the shutters back, and flung open the casement. For this end of the house was one which the alterations had barely touched, grown up as it was with the great ash-tree, and being otherwise concealed from view.

"Air it, Mrs Chiddock, all today, and move my bed-furniture in in the afternoon. Put the Bishop of Kilmore in my old room."

"Pray, Sir Richard," said a new voice, breaking in on his speech, "might I have the favour of a moment's interview?"

Sir Richard turned round and saw a man in black in the doorway, who bowed.

"I must ask your indulgence for this intrusion, Sir Richard. You will, perhaps, hardly remember me. My name is William Crome, and my grandfather was vicar here in your grandfather's time."

"Well, sir," said Sir Richard, "the name of Crome is always a passport to Castringham. I am glad to renew a friendship of two generations' standing. In what can I serve you? for your hour of calling – and, if I do not mistake you, your bearing – shows you to be in some haste."

"That is no more than the truth, sir. I am riding from Norwich to Bury St Edmunds with what haste I can make, and I have called in on my way to leave with you some papers which we have but just come upon in looking over what my grandfather left at his death. It is thought you may find some matters of family interest in them."

"You are mighty obliging, Mr Crome, and, if you will be so good as to follow me to the parlour, and drink a glass of wine, we will take a first look at these same papers together. And you, Mrs Chiddock, as I said, be about airing this chamber . . . Yes, it is here my grandfather died . . . Yes, the tree, perhaps, does make the place a little dampish . . . No; I do not wish to listen to any more. Make no difficulties, I beg. You have your orders – go. Will you follow me, sir?"

They went to the study. The packet which young Mr Crome had brought – he was then just become a Fellow of Clare Hall in Cambridge, I may say, and subsequently brought out a respectable edition of Polyaenus – contained among other things the notes which the old vicar had made upon the occasion of Sir Matthew Fell's death. And for the first time Sir Richard was confronted with the enigmatical *Sortes Biblicae* which you have heard. They amused him a good deal.

"Well," he said, "my grandfather's Bible gave one prudent piece of advice – *Cut it down.* If that stands for the ash-tree, he may rest assured I shall not neglect it. Such a nest of catarrhs and agues was never seen."

The parlour contained the family books, which, pending the arrival of a collection which Sir Richard had made in Italy, and the building of a proper room to receive them, were not many in number.

Sir Richard looked up from the papers to the book-case.

"I wonder," says he, "whether the old prophet is there yet? I fancy I see him."

Crossing the room, he took out a dumpy Bible, which, sure enough, bore on the flyleaf the inscription: *To Matthew Fell, from his Loving Godmother, Anne Aldous, 2 September, 1659.*

"It would be no bad plan to test him again, Mr Crome. I will wager we get a couple of names in the Chronicles. H'm! what have we here? 'Thou shalt seek me in the morning, and I shall not be.' Well, well! Your grandfather would have made a fine omen of that, hey? No more prophets for me! They are all in a tale. And now, Mr Crome, I am infinitely obliged to you for your packet. You will, I fear, be impatient to get on. Pray allow me – another glass."

So with offers of hospitality, which were genuinely meant (for Sir

Richard thought well of the young man's address and manner), they parted.

In the afternoon came the guests – the Bishop of Kilmore, Lady Mary Hervey, Sir William Kentfield, etc. Dinner at five, wine, cards, supper, and dispersal to bed.

Next morning Sir Richard is disinclined to take his gun with the rest. He talks with the Bishop of Kilmore. This prelate, unlike a good many of the Irish Bishops of his day, had visited his see, and, indeed, resided there for some considerable time. This morning, as the two were walking along the terrace and talking over the alterations and improvements in the house, the Bishop said, pointing to the window of the West Room:

"You could never get one of my Irish flock to occupy that room, Sir Richard."

"Why is that, my lord? It is, in fact, my own."

"Well, our Irish peasantry will always have it that it brings the worst of luck to sleep near an ash-tree, and you have a fine growth of ash not two yards from your chamber window. Perhaps," the Bishop went on, with a smile, "it has given you a touch of its quality already, for you do not seem, if I may say it, so much the fresher for your night's rest as your friends would like to see you."

"That, or something else, it is true, cost me my sleep from twelve to four, my lord. But the tree is to come down tomorrow, so I shall not hear much more from it."

"I applaud your determination. It can hardly be wholesome to have the air you breathe strained, as it were, through all that leafage."

"Your lordship is right there, I think. But I had not my window open last night. It was rather the noise that went on – no doubt from the twigs sweeping the glass – that kept me open-eyed."

"I think that can hardly be, Sir Richard. Here – you see it from this point. None of these nearest branches even can touch your casement unless there were a gale, and there was none of that last night. They miss the panes by a foot."

"No, sir, true. What, then, will it be, I wonder, that scratched and rustled so – Ay, and covered the dust on my sill with lines and marks?"

At last they agreed that the rats must have come up through the ivy. That was the Bishop's idea, and Sir Richard jumped at it.

So the day passed quietly, and night came, and the party dispersed to their rooms, and wished Sir Richard a better night.

And now we are in his bedroom, with the light out and the Squire in bed. The room is over the kitchen, and the night outside still and warm, so the window stands open.

There is very little light about the bedstead, but there is a strange movement there; it seems as if Sir Richard were moving his head rapidly to and fro with only the slightest possible sound. And now you would guess, so deceptive is the half-darkness, that he had several heads, round and brownish, which move back and forward, even as low as his chest. It is a horrible illusion. Is it nothing more? There! something drops off the bed with a soft plump, like a kitten, and is out of the window in a flash; another – four – and after that there is quiet again.

Thou shalt seek me in the morning, and I shall not be.

As with Sir Matthew, so with Sir Richard – dead and black in his bed!

A pale and silent party of guests and servants gathered under the window when the news was known. Italian poisoners, Popish emissaries, infected air – all these and more guesses were hazarded, and the Bishop of Kilmore looked at the tree, in the fork of whose lower boughs a white tom-cat was crouching, looking down the hollow which years had gnawed in the trunk. It was watching something inside the tree with great interest.

Suddenly it got up and craned over the hole. Then a bit of the edge on which it stood gave way, and it went slithering in. Everyone looked up at the noise of the fall.

It is known to most of us that a cat can cry; but few of us have heard, I hope, such a yell as came out of the trunk of the great ash. Two or three screams there were – the witnesses are not sure which – and then a slight and muffled noise of some commotion or struggling was all that came. But Lady Mary Hervey fainted outright, and the housekeeper stopped her ears and fled till she fell on the terrace.

The Bishop of Kilmore and Sir William Kentfield stayed. Yet even they were daunted, though it was only at the cry of a cat; and Sir William swallowed once or twice before he could say:

"There is something more than we know of in that tree, my lord. I am for an instant search."

And this was agreed upon. A ladder was brought, and one of the gardeners went up, and, looking down the hollow, could detect nothing but a few dim indications of something moving. They got a lantern, and let it down by a rope.

"We must get at the bottom of this. My life upon it, my lord, but the secrets of these terrible deaths is there."

Up went the gardener again with the lantern, and let it down the hole cautiously. They saw the yellow light upon his face as he bent over, and saw his face struck with an incredulous terror and loathing before he cried out in a dreadful voice and fell back from the ladder – where, happily, he was caught by two of the men – letting the lantern fall inside the tree.

He was in a dead faint, and it was some time before any word could be got from him.

By then they had something else to look at. The lantern must have broken at the bottom, and the light in it caught upon dry leaves and rubbish that lay there, for in a few minutes a dense smoke began to come up, and then flame; and, to be short, the tree was in a blaze.

The bystanders made a ring at some yards' distance, and Sir William and the Bishop sent men to get what weapons and tools they could; for, clearly, whatever might be using the tree as its lair would be forced out by the fire.

So it was. First, at the fork, they saw a round body covered with fire – the size of a man's head – appear very suddenly, then seem to collapse and fall back. This, five or six times; then a similar ball leapt into the air and fell on the grass, where after a moment it lay still. The Bishop went as near as he dared to it, and saw – what but the remains of an enormous spider, veinous and seared! And, as the fire burned lower down, more terrible bodies like this began to break out from the trunk, and it was seen that these were covered with greyish hair.

All that day the ash burned, and until it fell to pieces the men stood about it, and from time to time killed the brutes as they darted out. At last there was a long interval when none appeared, and they cautiously closed in and examined the roots of the tree.

"They found," says the Bishop of Kilmore, "below it a rounded hollow place in the earth, wherein were two or three bodies of these creatures that had plainly been smothered by the smoke; and, what is to me more curious, at the side of this den, against the wall, was crouching the anatomy or skeleton of a human being, with the skin dried upon the bones, having some remains of black hair, which was pronounced by those that examined it to be undoubtedly the body of a woman, and clearly dead for a period of fifty years."

Allen Upward

The Story of the Green House, Wallington

Allen Upward (1863–1926) was a prolific bestselling author of mysteries and novels and short stories, including Secrets of the Courts of Europe *(1897),* The Wonderful Career of Ebenezer Cobb *(1900),* The Accursed Princess *(1900) and a weird occult novel* The Discovery of the Dead *(1910). This story was the first in a series called "The Ghost Hunters" commissioned by C. Arthur Pearson for the* Royal *magazine, where it first appeared in the Christmas number, 1905. This series (which has never been reprinted in book form) emulated the very successful "Flaxman Low" series by K. & H. Prichard which Pearson had published six years earlier.*

IN UNDERTAKING TO relate some of my experiences in connection with the purchase and sale of haunted houses, I desire to make it clear that I have no theories to put forward on the subject of what is called the "occult".

I was successful in this class of business, but some of the adventures I went through were of such a character that I dared not continue. My nerves are fairly strong, but there are some things which I never wish to face again.

I was first tempted to dabble in this unlucky class of business by the Green House, Wallington.

My partner, Mr Mortimer – our firm is Mortimer & Hargreaves – mentioned to me one day that he had had a client in to see him who was very anxious to obtain an immediate offer, at almost any price, for a house situated in what was then the rural district of Wallington.

"He says he cannot sell the house because people think it is haunted. It is all nonsense of course; but the people in the neighbourhood have got the idea firmly into their heads; and now if any tenants come they are sure to hear of it directly, and get frightened. The result is that he has lost tenant after tenant, and now the reputation of the house is so bad that he cannot sell it."

"What sort of a house is it?" I asked. "And what will he take for it?"

"He says he will take anything – £500 if he can't get more; though the house cost £1,500 to build. You had better see the man yourself."

I therefore dropped a line to Mr Giltstrap, the owner of the Green House, requesting him to go down with me to see the property.

On the way to Wallington I put some questions about the house to Giltstrap, whose manner was rather reserved. He assured me it was in thorough repair, but he seemed reluctant to answer when I asked him about the ghost.

"Is there any story about the house? Anything to account for its being haunted?"

"No; no. What story should there be? It's a modern house – hardly been built ten years."

"And how long has it been your property?"

"I bought it as soon as it was put up."

"And how long has it been haunted?"

Mr Giltstrap frowned as though he disliked to hear this word.

"The house has been talked about for some years now – four or five."

His disinclination to speak was so evident that I did not care to pursue the subject.

We got out at Wallington Station, and as we passed a house agent's on the road Giltstrap said abruptly:

"I must step in here and get the keys. Wait a moment."

As a house-agent myself, I could understand that he did not wish to introduce me to the local man, lest it should lead to any dispute about commission. But my curiosity about the Green House was so strong that I could not resist the temptation to walk in after him.

I was just in time to hear the owner say curtly:

"I have called for the keys of the Green House, if you please."

The local agent was evidently a man in a small way, for we found him seated at a desk in the outer office, in his shirtsleeves. He gave a cross look at Giltstrap, and a suspicious one at me, and then rose and reached down the keys from a nail.

"I haven't been able to find a caretaker yet," he said with a touch of malice. "They say you must pay them for living in such a house."

Giltstrap reddened at this speech, which was calculated to put off an intending purchaser. He glared first at the agent and then at me, snatched the keys without a word, and hurried out.

The Green House was a modern, red-brick one, standing in a road with several others, and certainly not looking at all the kind of place to have a supernatural legend attached to it.

As soon as we got inside I saw that the house was partly furnished. Giltstrap explained that he had been trying to get someone to come and occupy it rent free for a time in order to live down its reputation.

I asked if there was any room particularly connected with the ghostly rumours.

After what struck me as a momentary hesitation, he led me upstairs into what was clearly the principal bedroom, overlooking the front garden and the road outside.

"Is this where the ghost walks?" I asked as I glanced round the empty room. The paper on the walls was in good condition, and the ceiling had been newly white-washed.

The owner of the Green House was plainly annoyed by my insistence.

"There is no ghost, and it does not walk anywhere," he said irritably. "But the people who sleep in this room complain."

"What do they complain of?"

He fidgeted and again showed some reluctance in answering.

"Oh, nothing except some nonsense or other. They say they do not sleep well, and they dream things. Fancies, you know – fancies."

"Well, what sort of fancies?" I persisted. "If they dream, they must dream of something."

Giltstrap glanced up at the ceiling, and swiftly withdrew his eyes with a nervous tremor. I was now firmly persuaded that he himself had been the victim of some spectral horror, though he was anxious to conceal it for fear of frightening me off.

"Perhaps I had better not tell you anything," he said, after considering a moment. "There is a great deal in the influence of suggestion, so it is said. If I were to tell you what the people who have slept in this room have seen, or dreamt they have seen, that might be enough to make you dream the same. Whereas, if a sensible man without any notions came and slept here, he would most likely never be disturbed."

I thought there was something in what he said, and did not press him further.

There was a staircase outside leading to a second floor, and I moved towards it.

"Oh, do you want to see the other rooms?" Giltstrap snapped, as he prepared to follow.

"I want to see everything," I said decidedly.

Upstairs I found another room which had been left unfurnished. The prospect from the window showed me that it was situated over the haunted chamber.

"Is there something wrong with this room, as well?" I demanded.

"The servants don't like sleeping in it," was the grudging admission. "It does very well as a boxroom."

I saw that it was useless to try and extract any more information from Giltstrap.

After a thorough inspection, I decided that the house would be well worth £1200, apart from its evil reputation. I went back to town with the owner, and bargained with him on the way.

I was very anxious to secure an option to purchase the Green House at the end of a month, during which time I was to occupy it, but this proposal the owner obstinately refused.

"I want to sell it outright or not at all. If you live in it a month and have no trouble, I shall then be able to ask a reasonable price."

Anxious to secure a bargain, I gave way, and got out at Victoria the owner of the Green House, at the price of £500.

When I told my partner the next day what I had done, he declined to commit himself.

"I shall know whether it is a good bargain or not when I hear what you have sold it for," he observed grimly.

My next step was to secure some attendance, and to send down some furniture for the two empty rooms round which the mystery appeared to cling.

In the course of the negotiations I had occasion for the services of my lady secretary.

I was accustomed to discuss business matters with her, and as soon as she learned the character of the present transaction, she surprised me by displaying an unusual interest in it. She even volunteered her assistance.

"I wonder if you would mind my going to see the Green House, Mr Hargreaves? I am very much interested in psychical research."

"Do you mean that you really believe there is something in it?" I exclaimed in dismay. I had grown to look on Miss Sargent as a young lady of great intelligence, and I was not very well pleased at the idea of taking the ghost seriously.

"I know that there are things in Nature which ordinary rules do not explain," was the grave answer. "I have seen things myself which could not be accounted for by natural means."

This was rather alarming. I recalled the strange, uneasy manner of the late owner of the Green House, and asked myself whether he had not been a secret believer in some occult happenings.

"I am what is called a sensitive," Miss Sargent proceeded to explain. "I have a peculiar faculty for seeing any abnormal manifestations."

A thought struck me.

"Would it be possible for you to go and pass a night or two there?" I inquired. "I don't mind telling you that if the apparition, or whatever it is, can be exorcized I hope to sell the house at a considerable profit; and I should be glad to pay a small commission."

Miss Sargent appeared to welcome the suggestion. She was a good girl, the chief support of a widowed mother and three little sisters, and I knew she would like to earn something for them.

The question was referred to her mother, who arranged to come with her, it being understood that I should form one of the party. I engaged a respectable woman to come in by the day, and, on the evening agreed upon, we went down together to take possession of the haunted house.

Miss Sargent and her mother were installed in the haunted room, and I decided to occupy the attic overhead.

After a pleasant supper the two ladies retired at about eleven o'clock. I sat up a little later, smoking a cigar and contrasting the cheerful evening I had just passed with the lonely ones I was accustomed to in my West End chambers.

Towards twelve I went upstairs, intending to go to bed. But whether it was the sensation of being in a strange house under such circumstances, or a secret apprehension of which I was hardly conscious, no sooner did I find myself in the room I had chosen than I was seized with an overmastering reluctance to get into the bed.

I took off my coat merely, rolled myself well up in the blankets, and tried to go to sleep. I am an old traveller, and have never experienced any difficulty in sleeping in my clothes in trains, or under similar circumstances.

But on this occasion the attempt was hopeless; I lay on the bed literally shivering, and not from cold. I neither saw nor heard anything, I was not alarmed in the ordinary sense, and yet if I had known there was a murderer lurking in the room ready to spring on me and stab me the moment I closed my eyes I could not have felt more wretchedly afraid.

Suddenly I heard a low moan – the moan of a creature in mortal terror, drawn out till it became a muffled scream.

I flung off the blankets, raised my head, and listened with a beating heart.

The moan was repeated, coming distinctly from underneath me. In an instant I had grasped the truth. It came from the room below.

I sprang from the bed, and, without stopping to put on my coat, lit the candle I had brought up with me, and flew downstairs.

As I reached the first floor landing the moan was repeated in a more terrible key – the key of horror instead of terror. At the same moment the door of the haunted room was thrown open, and Mrs Sargent appeared on the threshold, with a cloak thrown over her shoulders, and a look of fear and distress on her face.

"What is it?" I gasped.

"It is Alwyne!" she cried in answer, "She is seeing something horrible in her sleep, *and I can't wake her!*"

Without stopping to consider questions of etiquette, I dashed into the room. The gas had been turned full on, and by its light I saw the girl lying stretched on a couch at the foot of the bed, her features frozen into the expression of one who looks upon some horrid sight, while from her parted lips there issued those appalling sounds which wounded like the stabs of a knife.

I caught her by the shoulders and shook her, without making the slightest change in her swoon-like condition.

"Water!" I called out to the mother, who stood wringing her hands, too dazed to act.

The water was brought, and I dashed half a glassful in the face of the sufferer. At first it had no more effect than if she had been dead.

Then came a startling change.

The moans suddenly ceased, the victim opened her eyes, which showed the dull glassy stare of a somnambulist, and sitting half up, she commenced muttering so quickly and indistinctly that it was difficult to catch the words.

"The-blood-the-blood-the-blood-the-blood-dripping-dripping-dripping-dripping-from-the-red-leak-in-the-ceiling-the-red-leak-the-red-leak-in-the-ceiling-in-the-ceiling-dripping-on-me-dripping-on-me-dripping-on-ME!"

The words rose into a wild shriek as her blank eyes were turned full on the ceiling overhead, the ceiling between her room and mine.

Involuntarily I looked up. The ceiling did not show the slightest mark. As I had noticed when I went over the house with Giltstrap, it was newly whitewashed – I thought I now knew why.

But the moment was not for reflection.

"Help me to carry her out of this – quick!" I called out to the mother.

Between us we lifted up the unconscious girl and carried her out of the accursed room, and into one adjoining, where we laid her on the bed.

Hardly had she passed the doorway of the haunted chamber when the dreadful ejaculations began to die away, and the rigidity of the features to relax. In a short time the trance condition passed away into a deep sleep, and I was able to leave Miss Sargent in her mother's care.

When she woke in the morning, her mother told me, she remembered nothing whatever of what had passed in the night. She was barely conscious of having had a bad dream.

At her own request, I described to her at breakfast what had occurred, as minutely as possible. She was profoundly impressed.

"I am certain," she declared with conviction, "that what I saw represents something that actually happened in this house. Dreadful as it sounds, I firmly believe that somebody has been murdered in that attic in which you slept, and that his blood did drip through the ceiling of the room below, as I saw it last night."

Reluctant as I was for many reasons to entertain such a suggestion, I dared not neglect it altogether. I determined at all events to do whatever could be done to solve the mystery.

As soon as Miss Sargent and her mother had left the house, in which the elder lady would not hear of their passing another night, though her daughter did not seem in the least afraid, I went straight to a builder's in the neighbourhood, and engaged him to send some men to examine the flooring between the two haunted rooms.

The builder received my order with marked interest.

"I knew there was something the matter with that house," he observed. "It ain't likely that tenant after tenant would come away scared without something was wrong. Why, do you know, sir, in the last five years, since Mr Giltstrap gave it up, I've white-washed one ceiling in that house *nine times*!"

"Then Mr Giltstrap once lived in it himself, did he?" I exclaimed.

"Seeing that I built it for him, I can say he did," was the answer.

"And why did he leave it?" I demanded, fairly roused.

But the builder could not or would not satisfy my curiosity on that head.

"Mr Giltstrap was a good customer of mine; he always paid me regular; and I ain't got nothing to say against him."

The builder's interest led him to accompany his men, a carpenter and a plasterer, to the scene of action.

I pointed out the place on the ceiling, as nearly as I could judge it, from which the ghostly dew had appeared to fall.

The men took measurements, and then, proceeding to the attic above, located a spot under the bed in which I had tried to sleep.

The bed was quickly removed, the flooring stripped off, and in the space between the joists there was exposed a mass of lime.

Both the men, as well as their master, were quick to declare that the lime could not have been left there when the house was completed.

"That lime has been put there for no good," the builder asserted. "If you want some things hidden away and destroyed, there's nothing better than what lime is when it's fresh. It burns as well as fire, and makes no smoke."

"You mean a dead body?" I said shuddering.

"I don't say nothing about that," the builder answered, pulling himself up. "It ain't for me to say what that lime's been used for. All I say is it wasn't me that left it there, nor yet my men."

The two men began clearing the stuff away. The volatile element had evidently evaporated long ago. As they struck downward with their tools, one of them went through the plaster of the ceiling below, and a shaft of light came up.

An exclamation from one of the men followed. I bent down and peered into the cavity.

On a large beam which here crossed the floor I saw a deep black stain, the stain of long-dried blood!

A moment after the carpenter stooped suddenly, groped about with one hand amid the woodwork, and drew forth to the light a small sharp stiletto, rusted with the same dismal stain.

Nothing more was found. I gave the builder an order to entirely renew the flooring between the two haunted rooms; and from the time that was done, there has never again been the slightest complaint from any occupier of the property.

I let the Green House almost immediately to a respectable tenant, a retired schoolmaster, who changed its name; and before a year was out I was able to dispose of it to a purchaser at the price of £1,250, a sum which enabled me to compensate Miss Sargent for her trying experience.

The most extraordinary part of the story remains to be told.

The report of what had taken place having got abroad in Wallington, the local police came to me to obtain the stiletto, which I had been careful to preserve. By its means they were enabled to unearth a crime which had gone unsuspected till that hour, and to extort a confession from the murderer.

Into the details of this terrible case I do not mean to enter. It is sufficient to say that the victim had perished while asleep in the attic, and that his blood had actually soaked through the ceiling into the room below, which was that of his murderer – Giltstrap!

A. C. Benson

The Slype House

Arthur Christopher Benson (1862–1925), eldest of the three celebrated writer-brothers, is best remembered today for his poem "Land of Hope and Glory", set to music by Elgar. He was a very prolific author and diarist. The bulk of his supernatural stories were published in the collections The Hill of Trouble *(1903) and* The Isles of Sunset *(1905). "The Slype House" comes from the latter volume.*

IN THE TOWN OF Garchester, close to St Peter's Church, and near the river, stood a dark old house called the Slype House, from a narrow passage of that name that ran close to it, down to a bridge over the stream. The house showed a front of mouldering and discoloured stone to the street, pierced by small windows, like a monastery; and indeed, it was formerly inhabited by a college of priests. It abutted at one angle upon the aisle of the church, and there was a casement window that looked out from a room in the house, formerly the infirmary, into the aisle; it had been so built that any priest that was sick might hear the Mass from his bed, without descending into the church. Behind the house lay a little garden, closely grown up with trees and tall weeds, that ran down to the stream. In the wall that gave on the water, was a small door that admitted to an old timbered bridge that crossed the stream, and had a barred gate on the further side, which was rarely seen open; though if a man had watched attentively he might sometimes have seen a small lean person, much bowed and with a halting gait, slip out very quietly about dusk, and walk, with his eyes cast down among the shadowy byways.

The name of the man who dwelt in the Slype House was Anthony

Purvis. He was of an ancient family, and had inherited wealth. He had been a sickly child, an only son, his father a man of substance, who lived very easily in the country; his mother had died when he was still a child, and this sorrow had been borne very heavily by his father, who had loved her tenderly, and after her death had become morose and sullen, withdrawing himself from all company and exercise, and brooding angrily over his loss, as though God had determined to vex him. He had never cared much for the child, who had been peevish and fretful; and the boy's presence had done little but remind him of the wife he had lost; so that the child had lived alone, nourishing his own fancies, and reading much in a library of curious books that was in the house. The boy's health had been too tender for him to go to school; but when he was eighteen, he seemed stronger, and his father sent him to a university, more for the sake of being relieved of the boy's presence than for his good. And there, being unused to the society of his equals, he had been much flouted and despised for his feeble frame; till a certain bitter ambition sprang up in his mind, like a poisonous flower, to gain power and make himself a name; and he had determined that as he could not be loved he might still be feared; so he bided his time in bitterness, making great progress in his studies; then, when those days were over, he departed eagerly, and sought and obtained his father's leave to attend a university of Italy, where he fell into somewhat evil hands; for he made friends with an old doctor of the college, who feared not God and thought ill of man, and spent all his time in dark researches into the evil secrets of nature, the study of dangerous poisons and many other hidden works of darkness, such as intercourse with spirits of evil, and the black influences that lie in wait for the soul; and he found Anthony an apt pupil. There he lived for some years till he was nearly thirty, seldom visiting his home, and writing but formal letters to his father, who supplied him gladly with a small revenue, so long as he kept away and troubled him not.

Then his father died, and Anthony came home to take up his inheritance, which was a plentiful one; he sold his land, and visiting the town of Garchester, by chance, for it lay near his home, he had lighted upon the Slype House, which lay very desolate and gloomy; and as he needed a large place for his instruments and devices, he had bought the house, and had now lived there for twenty years in great loneliness, but not ill-content.

To serve him he had a man and his wife, who were quiet and simple people and asked no questions; the wife cooked his meals, and kept the rooms, where he slept and read, clean and neat; the man moved his machines for him, and arranged his phials and instruments, having a light touch and a serviceable memory.

The door of the house that gave on the street opened into a hall; to the right was a kitchen, and a pair of rooms where the man and his wife lived. On the left was a large room running through the house; the windows on to the street were walled up, and the windows at the back looked on the garden, the trees of which grew close to the casements, making the room dark, and in a breeze rustling their leaves or leafless branches against the panes. In this room Anthony had a furnace with bellows, the smoke of which discharged itself into the chimney; and here he did much of his work, making mechanical toys, as a clock to measure the speed of wind or water, a little chariot that ran a few yards by itself, a puppet that moved its arms and laughed – and other things that had wiled away his idle hours; the room was filled up with dark lumber, in a sort of order that would have looked to a stranger like disorder, but so that Anthony could lay his hand on all that he needed. From the hall, which was paved with stone, went up the stairs, very strong and broad, of massive oak; under which was a postern that led to the garden; on the floor above was a room where Anthony slept, which again had its windows to the street boarded up, for he was a light sleeper, and the morning sounds of the awakening city disturbed him.

The room was hung with a dark arras, sprinkled with red flowers; he slept in a great bed with black curtains to shut out all light; the windows looked into the garden; but on the left of the bed, which stood with its head to the street, was an alcove, behind the hangings, containing the window that gave on the church. On the same floor were three other rooms; in one of these, looking on the garden, Anthony had his meals. It was a plain, panelled room. Next was a room where he read, filled with books, also looking on the garden; and next to that was a little room of which he alone had the key. This room he kept locked, and no one set foot in it but himself. There was one more room on this floor, set apart for guests (who never came), with a great bed and a press of oak. And that looked on the street. Above, there was a row of plain plastered rooms, in which stood furniture for which Anthony had no use, and many crates in which his machines and phials came to him; this floor was seldom visited, except by the man, who sometimes came to put a box there; and the spiders had it to themselves; except for a little room where stood an optic glass through which on clear nights Anthony sometimes looked at the moon and stars, if there was any odd misadventure among them, such as an eclipse; or when a fiery-tailed comet went his way silently in the heavens.

Anthony had but two friends who ever came to see him. One was an old physician who had ceased to practise his trade, which indeed was never abundant, and who would sometimes drink a glass of wine with Anthony, and engage in curious talk of men's bodies and diseases, or look at one of Anthony's toys. Anthony had come to know him by having called him in to cure some ailment, which needed a surgical knife; and that had made a kind of friendship between them; but Anthony had little need thereafter to consult him about his health, which indeed was now settled enough, though he had but little vigour; and he knew enough of drugs to cure himself when he was ill. The other friend was a foolish priest of the college, that made belief to be a student but was none, who thought Anthony a very wise and mighty person, and listened with open mouth and eyes to all that he said or showed him. This priest, who was fond of wonders, had introduced himself to Anthony by pretending to borrow a volume of him; and then had grown proud of the acquaintance, and bragged greatly of it to his friends, mixing up much that was fanciful with a little that was true. But the result was that gossip spread wide about Anthony, and he was held in the town to be a very fearful person, who could do strange mischief if he had a mind to; Anthony never cared to walk abroad, for he was of a shy habit, and disliked to meet the eyes of his fellows; but if he did go about, men began to look curiously after him as he went by, shook their heads and talked together with a dark pleasure, while children fled before his face and women feared him; all of which pleased Anthony mightily, if the truth were told; for at the bottom of his restless and eager spirit lay a deep vanity unseen, like a lake in woods; he hungered not indeed for fame, but for repute – and he cared little in what repute he was held, so long as men thought him great and marvellous; and as he could not win renown by brave deeds and words, he was rejoiced to win it by keeping up a certain darkness and mystery about his ways and doings; and this was very clear to him, so that when the silly priest called him Seer and Wizard, he frowned and looked sideways; but he laughed in his heart and was glad.

Now, when Anthony was near his fiftieth year, there fell on him a heaviness of spirit which daily increased upon him. He began to question his end and what lay beyond. He had always made pretence to mock at religion, and had grown to believe that in death the soul was extinguished like a burnt-out flame. He began, too, to question his life and what he had done. He had made a few toys, he had filled vacant hours, and he had gained an ugly kind of fame – and this was all. Was he so certain, he began to think, after all, that death was the end? Were there not, perhaps, in the vast house of God, rooms and chambers beyond that in which he was set for awhile to pace to and fro? About this time he began to read in a Bible that had lain dusty and unopened on a shelf. It was his mother's book, and he found therein many little tokens of her presence. Here was a verse underlined; at some gracious passages the page was much fingered and worn; in one place there were stains that looked like the mark of tears; then again, in one page, there was a small tress of hair, golden hair, tied in a paper with a name across it, that seemed to be the name of a little sister of his mother's that died a child; and again there were a few withered flowers, like little sad ghosts, stuck through a paper on which was written his father's name – the name of the sad, harsh, silent man whom Anthony had feared with all his heart. Had those two, indeed, on some day of summer, walked to and fro, or sat in some woodland corner, whispering sweet words of love together? Anthony felt a sudden hunger of the heart for a woman's love, for tender words to soothe his sadness, for the laughter and kisses of children – and he began to ransack his mind for memories of his mother; he could remember being pressed to her heart one morning when she lay abed, with her fragrant hair falling about him. The worst was that he must bear his sorrow alone, for there were none to whom he could talk of such things. The doctor was as dry as an old bunch of herbs, and as for the priest, Anthony was ashamed to show anything but contempt and pride in his presence.

For relief he began to turn to a branch of his studies that he had long neglected; this was a fearful commerce with the unseen spirits. Anthony could remember having practised some experiments of this kind with the old Italian doctor; but he remembered them with a kind of disgust, for they seemed to him but a sort of deadly juggling; and such dark things as he had seen seemed like a dangerous sport with unclean beings, more brute-like than human. Yet now he read in his curious books with care, and studied the tales of necromancers, who had indeed seemed to have some power over the souls of men departed. But the old books gave him but little faith, and a kind of angry disgust at the things attempted. And he began to think that the horror in which such men as made these books lived, was not more than the dark shadow cast on the mirror of the soul by their own desperate imaginings and timorous excursions.

One Sunday he was strangely sad and heavy; he could settle to nothing, but threw book after book aside, and when he turned to some work of construction, his hand seemed to have lost its cunning. It was a grey and sullen day in October; a warm wet wind came buffeting up from the west, and roared in the chimneys and eaves of the old house. The shrubs in the garden plucked themselves hither and thither as though in pain. Anthony walked to and fro after his midday meal, which he had eaten hastily and without savour; at last, as though with a sudden resolution, he went to a secret cabinet and got out a key; and with it he went to the door of the little room that was always locked.

He stopped at the threshold for a while, looking hither and thither; and then he suddenly unlocked it and went in, closing and locking it behind him. The room was as dark as night, but Anthony going softly, his hands before him, went to a corner and got a tinder-box which lay there, and made a flame.

A small dark room appeared, hung with a black tapestry; the window was heavily shuttered and curtained; in the centre of the room stood what looked like a small altar, painted black; the floor was all bare, but with white marks upon it, half effaced. Anthony looked about the room, glancing sidelong, as though in some kind of doubt; his breath went and came quickly, and he looked paler than usual.

Presently, as though reassured by the silence and calm of the place, he went to a tall press that stood in a corner, which he opened, and took from it certain things – a dish of metal, some small leather bags, a large lump of chalk, and a book. He laid all but the chalk down on the altar, and then opening the book, read in it a little; and then he went with the chalk and drew certain marks upon the floor, first making a circle, which he went over again and again with anxious care; at times he went back and peeped into the book as though uncertain. Then he opened the bags, which seemed to hold certain kinds of powder, this dusty, that in grains; he ran them through his hands, and then poured a little of each into his dish, and mixed them with his hands. Then he stopped and looked about him. Then he walked to a place in the wall on the further side of the altar from the door, and drew the arras carefully aside, disclosing a little alcove in the wall; into this he looked fearfully, as though he was afraid of what he might see.

In the alcove, which was all in black, appeared a small shelf, that stood but a little way out from the wall. Upon it, gleaming very white against the black, stood the skull of a man, and on either side of the skull were the bones of a man's hand. It looked to him, as he gazed on it with a sort of curious disgust, as though a dead man had come up to the surface of a black tide, and was preparing presently to leap out. On either side stood two long silver candlesticks, very dark with disuse; but instead of holding candles, they were fitted at the top with flat metal dishes; and in these he poured some of his powders, mixing them as before with his fingers. Between the candlesticks and behind the skull was an old and dark picture, at which he gazed for a time, holding his taper on high. The picture represented a man fleeing in a kind of furious haste from a wood, his hands spread wide, and his eyes staring out of the picture; behind him everywhere was the wood, above which was a star in the sky – and out of the wood leaned a strange pale horned thing, very dim. The horror in the man's face was skilfully painted, and Anthony felt a shudder pass through his veins. He knew not what the picture meant; it had been given to him by the old Italian, who had smiled a wicked smile when he gave it, and told him that it had a very great virtue. When Anthony had asked him of the subject of the picture, the old Italian had said, "Oh, it is as appears; he hath been where he ought not, and he hath seen something he doth not like." When Anthony would have liked to have known more, and especially what the thing was that leaned out of the wood, the old Italian had smiled cruelly and said, "Know you not? Well, you will some day when you have seen him"; and never a word more would he say.

When Anthony had put all things in order, he opened the book at a certain place, and laid it upon the altar; and then it seemed as though his courage failed him, for he drew the curtain again over the alcove, unlocked the door, set the tinder-box and the candle back in their place, and softly left the room.

He was very restless all evening. He took down books from the shelves, turned them over, and put them back again. He addressed himself to some unfinished work, but soon threw it aside; he paced up and down, and spent a long time, with his hands clasped behind him, looking out into the desolate garden, where the red sunset burnt behind the leafless trees. He was like a man who has made up his mind to a grave decision, and shrinks back upon the brink. When his food was served he could hardly touch it, and he drank no wine as his custom was to do, but only water, saying to himself that his head must be clear. But in the evening he went to his bedroom, and searched for something in a press there; he found at last what he was searching for, and unfolded a long black robe, looking gloomily upon it, as though it aroused unwelcome thoughts; while he was pondering, he heard a hum of music behind the arras; he put the robe down, and stepped through the hangings, and stood awhile in the little oriel that looked down into the church. Vespers were proceeding; he saw the holy lights dimly through the dusty panes, and heard the low preluding of the organ; then, solemn and slow, rose the sound of a chanted psalm on the air; he carefully unfastened the casement which opened inward, standing for a while to listen, while the air, fragrant with incense smoke, drew into the room along the vaulted roof. There were but a few worshippers in the church, who stood below him; two lights burnt stilly upon the altar, and he saw distinctly the thin hands of a priest who held a book close to his face. He had not set foot within a church for many years, and the sight and sound drew his mind back to his childhood's days. At last with a sigh he put the window to very softly, and went to his study, where he made pretence to read, till the hour came when he was wont to retire to his bed. He sent his servant away, but instead of lying down, he sat, looking upon a parchment, which he held in his hand, while the bells of the city slowly tolled the creeping hours.

At last, a few minutes before midnight, he rose from his place; the house was now all silent, and without the night was very still, as though all things slept tranquilly. He opened the press and took from it the black robe, and put it round him, so that it covered him from head to foot, and then gathered up the parchment, and the key of the locked room, and went softly out, and so came to the door. This he undid with a kind of secret and awestruck haste, locking it behind him. Once inside the room, he wrestled awhile with a strong aversion to what was in his mind to do, and stood for a moment, listening intently, as though he expected to hear some sound. But the room was still, except for the faint biting of some small creature in the wainscot.

Then with a swift motion he took up the tinder-box and made a light; he drew aside the curtain that hid the alcove; he put fire to the powder in the candlesticks, which at first spluttered, and then swiftly kindling sent up a thick smoky flame, fragrant with drugs, burning hot and red. Then he came back to the altar; cast a swift glance round him to see that all was ready; put fire to the powder on the altar, and in a low voice began to recite words from the book, and from the parchment which he held in his hand; once or twice he glanced fearfully at the skull, and the skeleton hands which gleamed luridly through the smoke; the figures in the picture wavered in the heat; and now the powders began to burn clear, and throw up a steady light; and still he read, sometimes turning a page, until at last he made an end; and drawing something from a silver box which lay beside the book, he dropped it in the flame, and looked straight before him to see what might befall. The thing that fell in the flame burned up brightly, with a little leaping of sparks, but soon it died down; and there was a long silence in the room, a breathless silence, which, to Anthony's disordered mind, was not like the silence of emptiness, but such silence as may be heard when unseen things are crowding quietly to a closed door, expecting it to be opened, and as it were holding each other back.

Suddenly, between him and the picture, appeared for a moment a pale light, as of moonlight, and then with a horror which words cannot attain to describe, Anthony saw a face hang in the air a few feet from him, that looked in his own eyes with a sort of intent fury, as though to spring upon him if he turned either to the right hand or to the left. His knees tottered beneath him, and a sweat of icy coldness sprang on his brow; there followed a sound like no sound that Anthony had ever dreamed of hearing; a sound that was near and yet remote, a sound that was low and yet charged with power, like the groaning of a voice in grievous pain and anger, that strives to be free and yet is helpless. And then Anthony knew that he had indeed opened the door that looks into the other world, and that a deadly thing that held him in enmity had looked out. His reeling brain still told him that he was safe where he was, but that he must not step or fall outside the circle; but how he should resist the power of the wicked face he knew not. He tried to frame a prayer in his heart; but there swept such a fury of hatred across the face that he dared not. So he closed his eyes and stood dizzily waiting to fall, and knowing that if he fell it was the end.

Suddenly, as he stood with closed eyes, he felt the horror of the spell relax; he opened his eyes again, and saw that the face died out upon the air, becoming first white and then thin.

Then there fell a low and sweet music upon the air, like a concert of flutes and harps, very far away. And then suddenly, in a sweet radiance, the face of his mother, as she lived in his mind, appeared in the space, and looked at him with a kind of heavenly love; then beside the face appeared two thin hands which seemed to wave a blessing towards him, which flowed like healing into his soul.

The relief from the horror, and the flood of tenderness that came into his heart, made him reckless. The tears came into his eyes, not in a rising film, but a flood hot and large. He took a step forwards round the altar; but as he did so, the vision disappeared, the lights shot up into a flare and went out; the house seemed to be suddenly shaken; in the darkness he heard the rattle of bones, and the clash of metal, and Anthony fell all his length upon the ground and lay as one dead.

But while he thus lay, there came to him in some secret cell of the mind a dreadful vision, which he could only dimly remember afterwards with a fitful horror. He thought that he was walking in the cloister of some great house or college, a cool place, with a pleasant garden in the court. He paced up and down, and each time that he did so, he paused a little before a great door at the end, a huge blind portal, with much carving about it, which he somehow knew he was forbidden to enter. Nevertheless, each time that he came to it, he felt a strong wish, that constantly increased, to set foot therein. Now in the dream there fell on him a certain heaviness, and the shadow of a cloud fell over the court, and struck the sunshine out of it. And at last he made up his mind that he would enter. He pushed the door open and with much difficulty, and found himself in a long blank passage, very damp and chilly, but with a glimmering light; he walked a few paces down it. The flags underfoot were slimy, and the walls streamed with damp. He then thought that he would return; but the great door was closed behind him, and he could not open it. This made him very fearful; and while he considered what he should do, he saw a tall and angry-looking man approaching very swiftly down the passage. As he turned to face him, the other came straight to him, and asked him very sternly what he did there; to which Anthony replied that he had found the door open. To which the other replied that it was fast now, and that he must go forward. He seized Anthony as he spoke by the arm, and urged him down the passage. Anthony would fain have resisted, but he felt like a child in the grip of a giant, and went forward in great terror and perplexity. Presently they came to a door in the side of the wall, and as they passed it, there stepped out an ugly shadowy thing, the nature of which he could not clearly discern, and marched softly behind them. Soon they came to a turn in the passage, and in a moment the way stopped on the brink of a dark well, that seemed to go down a long way into the earth, and out of which came a cold fetid air, with a hollow sound like a complaining voice. Anthony drew back as far as he could from the pit, and set his back to the wall, his companion letting go of him. But he could not go backward, for the thing behind him was in the passage, and barred the way, creeping slowly nearer. Then Anthony was in a great agony of mind, and waited for the end.

But while he waited, there came someone very softly down the passage and drew near; and the other, who had led him to the place, waited, as though ill-pleased to be interrupted; it was too murky for Anthony to see the newcomer, but he knew in some way that he was a friend. The stranger came up to them, and spoke in a low voice to the man who had drawn Anthony thither, as though pleading for something; and the man answered angrily, but yet with a certain dark respect, and seemed to argue that he was acting in his right, and might not be interfered with. Anthony could not hear what they said, they spoke so low, but he guessed the sense, and knew that it was himself of whom they discoursed, and listened with a fearful wonder to see which would prevail. The end soon came, for the tall man, who had brought him there, broke out into a great storm of passion; and Anthony heard him say, "He hath yielded himself to his own will; and he is mine here; so let us make an end." Then the stranger seemed to consider; and then with a quiet courage, and in a soft and silvery voice like that of a child, said, "I would that you would have yielded to my prayer; but as you will not, I have no choice." And he took his hand from under the cloak that wrapped him, and held something out; then there came a great roaring out of the pit, and a zigzag flame flickered in the dark. Then in a moment the tall man and the shadow were gone; Anthony could not see whither they went, and he would have thanked the stranger; but the other put his finger to his lip as though to order silence, and pointed to the way he had come, saying, "Make haste and go back; for they will return anon with others; you know not how dear it hath cost me." Anthony could see the stranger's face in the gloom, and he was surprised to see it so youthful; but he saw also that tears stood in the eyes of the stranger, and that something dark like blood trickled down his brow; yet he looked very lovingly at him. So Anthony made haste to go back, and found the door ajar; but as he reached it, he heard a horrible din behind him, of cries and screams; and it was with a sense of gratitude, that he could not put into words, but which filled all his heart, that he found himself back in the cloister again. And then the vision all fled away, and with a shock coming to himself, he found that he was lying in his own room; and then he knew that a battle had been fought out over his soul, and that the evil had not prevailed.

He was cold and aching in every limb; the room was silent and dark, with the heavy smell of the burnt drugs all about it. Anthony crept to the door, and opened it; locked it again, and made his way in the dark very feebly to his bed-chamber; he had just the strength to get into his bed, and then all his life seemed to ebb from him, and he lay, and thought that he was dying. Presently from without there came the crying of cocks, and a bell beat the hour of four; and after that, in his vigil of weakness, it was strange to see the light glimmer in the crevices, and to hear the awakening birds that in the garden bushes took up, one after another, their slender piping song, till all the choir cried together.

But Anthony felt a strange peace in his heart; and he had a sense, though he could not say why, that it was as once in his childhood, when he was ill, and his mother had sat softly by him while he slept.

So he waited, and in spite of his mortal weakness that was a blessed hour.

When his man came to arouse him in the morning, Anthony said that he believed that he was very ill, that he had had a fall, and that the old doctor must be fetched to him. The man looked so strangely upon him, that Anthony knew that he had some fear upon his mind. Presently the doctor was brought, and Anthony answered such questions as were put to him, in a faint voice, saying, "I was late at my work, and I slipped and fell." The doctor, who looked troubled, gave directions; and when he went away he heard his man behind the door asking the doctor about the strange storm in the night, that had seemed like an earthquake, or as if a thunder-bolt had struck the house. But the doctor said very gruffly, "It is no time to talk thus, when your master is sick to death." But Anthony knew in himself that he would not die yet.

It was long ere he was restored to a measure of health; and indeed he never rightly recovered the use of his limbs; the doctor held that he had suffered some stroke of palsy; at which Anthony smiled a little, and made no answer.

When he was well enough to creep to and fro, he went sadly to the dark room, and with much pain and weakness carried the furniture out of it. The picture he cut in pieces and burnt; and the candles and dishes, with the book, he cast into a deep pool in the stream; the bones he buried in the earth; the hangings he stored away for his own funeral.

Anthony never entered his workroom again; but day after day he sat in his chair, and read a little, mostly the Bible; he made a friend of a very wise old priest, to whom he opened all his heart, and to whom he conveyed much money to be bestowed on the poor; there was a great calm in his spirit, which was soon written in his face, in spite of his pain, for he often suffered sorely; but he told the priest that something, he knew not certainly what, seemed to dwell in him, waiting patiently for his coming; and so Anthony awaited his end.

Bernard Capes

A Ghost-Child

Bernard Capes (1854–1918) produced many excellent supernatural tales, notably "An Eddy on the Floor", "The Moon Stricken", and "The Black Reaper". One of his most touching short stories, "A Ghost-Child", was specially written for the Pall Mall Magazine *in January 1906, and was reprinted later that year in his* Loaves and Fishes.

IN MAKING THIS confession public, I am aware that I am giving a butterfly to be broken on a wheel. There is so much of delicacy in its subject, that the mere resolve to handle it at all might seem to imply a lack of the sensitiveness necessary to its understanding; and it is certain that the more reverent the touch, the more irresistible will figure its opportunity to the common scepticism which is bondslave to its five senses. Moreover one cannot, in the reason of things, write to publish for Aristarchus alone; but the gauntlet of Grub Street must be run in any bid for truth and sincerity.

On the other hand, to withhold from evidence, in these days of what one may call a zetetic psychology, anything which may appear elucidatory, however must be pronounced, I think, a sin against the Holy Ghost.

All in all, therefore, I decided to give, with every passage to personal identification safeguarded, the story of a possession, or visitation, which is signified in the title to my narrative.

Tryphena was the sole orphaned representative of an obscure but gentle family which had lived for generations in the east of England. The spirit of the fens, of the long gray marshes, whose shores are the neutral ground of two elements, slumbered in her eyes. Looking into them, one seemed to see little beds of tiny green mosses luminous under water, or stirred by the movement of microscopic life in their midst. Secrets, one felt, were shadowed in their depths, too frail and sweet for understanding. The pretty love-fancy of babies seen in the eyes of maidens, was in hers to be interpreted into the very cosmic dust of sea-urchins, sparkling like chrysoberyls. Her soul looked out through them, as if they were the windows of a water-nursery.

She was always a child among children, in heart and knowledge most innocent, until Jason came and stood in her field of vision. Then, spirit of the neutral ground as she was, inclining to earth or water with the sway of the tides, she came wondering and dripping, as it were, to land, and took up her abode for final choice among the daughters of the earth. She knew her woman's estate, in fact, and the irresistible attraction of all completed perfections to the light that burns to destroy them.

Tryphena was not only an orphan, but an heiress. Her considerable estate was administered by her guardian, Jason's father, a widower, who was possessed of this single adored child. The fruits of parental infatuation had come early to ripen on the seedling. The boy was self-willed and perverse, the more so as he was naturally of a hot-hearted disposition. Violence and remorse would sway him in alternate moods, and be made, each in its turn, a self-indulgence. He took a delight in crossing his father's wishes, and no less in atoning for his gracelessness with moving demonstrations of affection.

Foremost of the old man's most cherished projects was, very naturally, a union between the two young people. He planned, manoeuvred, spoke for it with all his heart of love and eloquence. And, indeed, it seemed at last as if his hopes were to be crowned. Jason, returning from a lengthy voyage (for his enterprising spirit had early decided for the sea, and he was a naval officer), saw, and was struck amazed before, the transformed vision of his old child-play-fellow. She was an opened flower whom he had left a green bud – a thing so rare and flawless that it seemed a sacrilege for earthly passions to converse of her. Familiarity, however, and some sense of reciprocal attraction, quickly dethroned that eucharist. Tryphena could blush, could thrill, could solicit, in the sweet ways of innocent womanhood. She loved him dearly, wholly, it was plain – had found the realization of her old formless dreams in this wondrous birth of a desire for one, in whose new-impassioned eyes she had known herself reflected hitherto only for the most patronized of small gossips. And, for her part, fearless as nature, she made no secret of her love. She was absorbed in, a captive to, Jason from that moment and for ever.

He responded. What man, however perverse, could have resisted, on first appeal, the attraction of such beauty, the flower of a radiant soul? The two were betrothed; the old man's cup of happiness was brimmed.

Then came clouds and a cold wind, chilling the garden of Hesperis. Jason was always one of those who, possessing classic noses, will cut them off, on easy provocation, to spite their faces. He was so proudly independent, to himself, that he resented the least assumption of proprietorship in him on the part of other people – even of those who had the best claim to his love and submission. This pride was an obsession. It stultified the real good in him, which was considerable. Apart from it, he was a good, warm-tempered fellow, hasty but affectionate. Under its dominion, he would have broken his own heart on an imaginary grievance.

He found one; it is to be supposed, in the privileges assumed by love; in its exacting claims upon him; perhaps in its little unreasoning jealousies. He distorted these into an implied conceit of authority over him on the part of an heiress who was condescending to his meaner fortunes. The suggestion was quite base and without warrant; but pride has no balance. No doubt, moreover, the rather childish self-depreciations of the old man, his father, in his attitude towards a match he had so fondly desired, helped to aggravate this feeling. The upshot was that, when within a few months of the date which was to make his union with Tryphena eternal, Jason broke away from a restraint which his pride pictured to him as intolerable, and went on a yachting expedition with a friend.

Then, at once, and with characteristic violence, came the reaction. He wrote, impetuously, frenziedly, from a distant port, claiming himself Tryphena's, and Tryphena his, for ever and ever and ever. They were man and wife before God. He had behaved like an insensate brute, and he was at that moment starting to speed to her side, to beg her forgiveness and the return of her love.

He had no need to play the suitor afresh. She had never doubted or questioned their mutual bondage, and would have died a maid for his sake. Something of sweet exultation only seemed to quicken the leap in her body, that her faith in her dear love was vindicated.

But the joy came near to upset the reason of the old man, already tottering to its dotage; and what followed destroyed it utterly.

The yacht, flying home, was lost at sea, and Jason was drowned.

I once saw Tryphena about this time. She lived with her near mindless charge, lonely in an old gray house upon the borders of a salt mere, and had little but the unearthly cries of seabirds to answer to the questions of her widowed heart. She worked, sweet in charity, among the marsh folk, a beautiful unearthly presence; and was especially to be found where infants and the troubles of child-bearing women called for her help and sympathy. She was a wife herself, she would say quaintly; and some day perhaps, by grace of the good spirits of the sea, would be a mother. None thought to cross her statement, put with so sweet a sanity; and indeed, I have often noticed that the neighbourhood of great waters breeds in souls a mysticism which is remote from the very understanding land-dwellers.

How I saw her was thus:

I was fishing, on a day of chill calm, in a dinghy off the flat coast. The stillness of the morning had tempted me some distance from the village where I was staying. Presently a sense of bad sport and healthy famine "plumped" in me, so to speak, for luncheon, and I looked about for a spot picturesque enough to add a zest to sandwiches, whisky, and tobacco. Close by, a little creek or estuary ran up into a mere, between which and the sea lay a cluster of low sand-hills; and thither I pulled. The spot, when I reached it, was calm, chill desolation manifest – lifeless water and lifeless sand, with no traffic between them but the dead inter-change of salt. Low sedges, at first, and behind them low woods were mirrored in the water at a distance, with an interval between me and them of sheeted glass; and right across this shining pool ran a dim, half-drowned causeway – the sea-path, it appeared, to and from a lonely house which I could just distinguish squatting among trees. It was Tryphena's house.

Now, paddling dispiritedly, I turned a cold dune, and saw a mermaid before me. At least, that was my instant impression. The creature sat coiled on the strand, combing her hair – that was certain, for I saw the gold-green tresses of it whisked by her action into rainbow threads. It appeared as certain that her upper half was flesh and her lower fish, and it was only on my nearer approach that this latter resolved itself into a pale green skirt, roped, owing to her posture, about her limbs, and the hem fanned out at her feet into a tail fin. Thus also her bosom, which had appeared naked, became a bodice, as near to her flesh in colour and texture as a smock is to a lady's-smock, which some call a cuckoo-flower. It was plain enough now; yet the illusion for the moment had quite startled me.

As I came near, she paused in her strange business to canvass me. It was Tryphena herself, as after-inquiry informed me. I have never seen so lovely a creature. Her eyes, as they regarded me passing, were something to haunt a dream: so great in tragedy – not fathomless, but all in motion near their surfaces, it seemed, with green and rooted sorrows. They were the eyes, I thought, of an Undine late-humanized, late awakened to the rapturous and troubled knowledge of the woman's burden. Her forehead was most fair, and the glistening thatch divided on it like a golden cloud revealing the face of a wondering angel.

I passed, and a sand-heap stole my vision foot by foot. The vision was gone when I returned. I have reason to believe it was vouchsafed me within a few months of the coming of the ghost-child.

On the morning succeeding the night of the day on which Jason and Tryphena were to have been married, the girl came down from her bedroom with an extraordinary expression of still rapture on her face. After breakfast she took the old man into her confidence. She was childish still; her manner quite youthfully thrilling; but now there was a new-born wonder in it that hovered on the pink of shame.

"Father! I have been under the deep waters and found him. He came to me last night in my dreams – so sobbing, so impassioned – to assure me that he had never really ceased to love me, though he had near broken his own heart pretending it. Poor boy! poor ghost! What could I do but take him to my arms? And all night he lay there, blest and forgiven, till in the morning he melted away with a sigh that woke me; and it seemed to me that I came up dripping from the sea."

"My boy! He has come back!" chuckled the old man. "What have you done with him, Tryphena?"

"I will hold him tighter the next time," she said.

But the spirit of Jason visited her dreams no more.

That was in March. In the Christmas following, when the mere was locked in stillness, and the wan reflection of snow mingled on the ceiling with the red dance of firelight, one morning the old man came hurrying and panting to Tryphena's door.

"Tryphena! Come down quickly! My boy, my Jason, has come back! It was a lie that they told us about his being lost at sea!"

Her heart leapt like a candle-flame! What new delusion of the old man's was this? She hurried over her dressing and descended. A garrulous old voice mingled with a childish treble in the breakfast-room.

Hardly breathing, she turned the handle of the door, and saw Jason before her.

But it was Jason, the prattling babe of her first knowledge; Jason, the flaxen-haired, apple-cheeked cherub of the nursery; Jason, the confiding, the merry, the loving, before pride had come to warp his innocence. She fell on her knees to the child, and with a burst of ecstasy caught him to her heart.

She asked no question of the old man as to when or whence this apparition had come, or why he was here. For some reason she dared not. She accepted him as some waif, whom an accidental likeness had made glorious to their hungering hearts. As for the father, he was utterly satisfied and content. He had heard a knock at the door, he said, and had opened it and found this. The child was naked, and his pink, wet body glazed with ice. Yet he seemed insensible to the killing cold. It was Jason – that was enough. There is no date nor time for imbecility. Its phantoms spring from the clash of ancient memories. This was just as actually his child as – more so, in fact, than – the grown young figure which, for all its manhood, had dissolved into the mist of waters. He was more familiar with, more confident of it, after all. It had come back to be unquestioningly dependent on him; and that was likest the real Jason, flesh of his flesh.

"Who are you, darling?" said Tryphena.

"I am Jason," answered the child.

She wept, and fondled him rapturously.

"And who am I?" she asked. "If you are Jason, you must know what to call me."

"I know," he said; "but I mustn't, unless you ask me."

"I won't," she answered, with a burst of weeping. "It is Christmas Day, dearest, when the miracle of a little child was wrought. I will ask you nothing but to stay and bless our desolate home."

He nodded, laughing.

"I will stay, until you ask me."

They found some little old robes of the baby Jason, put away in lavender, and dressed him in them. All day he laughed and prattled; yet it was strange that, talk as he might, he never once referred to matters familiar to the childhood of the lost sailor.

In the early afternoon he asked to be taken out – seawards, that was his wish. Tryphena clothed him warmly, and, taking his little hand, led him away. They left the old man sleeping peacefully. He was never to wake again.

As they crossed the narrow causeway, snow, thick and silent, began to fall. Tryphena was not afraid for herself or the child. A rapture upheld her; a sense of some compelling happiness, which she knew before long must take shape on her lips.

They reached the seaward dunes – mere ghosts of foothold in that smoke of flakes. The lap of vast waters seemed all around them, hollow and mysterious. The sound flooded Tryphena's ears, drowning her senses. She cried out, and stopped.

"Before they go," she screamed – "before they go, tell me what you were to call me!"

The child sprang a little distance, and stood facing her. Already his lower limbs seemed dissolving in the mists.

"I was to call you 'mother'!" he cried, with a smile and toss of his hand.

Even as he spoke, his pretty features wavered and vanished. The snow broke into him, or he became part with it. Where he had been, a gleam of iridescent dust seemed to show one moment before it sank and was extinguished in the falling cloud. Then there was only the snow, heaping an eternal chaos with nothingness.

Tryphena made this confession, on a Christmas Eve night, to one who was a believer in dreams. The next morning she was seen to cross the causeway, and thereafter was never seen again. But she left the sweetest memory behind her, for human charity, and an elf-like gift of loveliness.

Alice Perrin

The Bead Necklace

Alice Perrin followed East of Suez *with another fine collection,* Red Records *(1906), which included several bizarre tales of the supernatural; among them the best of these are "Footsteps in the Dust", "Powers of Darkness", "The Sistrum", and "The Bead Necklace".*

WHEN IT BECAME known in the village of Hayfield that Adela Roscoe was engaged to be married, everyone inquired if the man had money; nobody thought of asking if he were nice till afterwards, because the Major had repeatedly shouted abroad the fact that he intended his daughter to marry a rich man or to be an old maid. Only a few months ago he had sworn himself voiceless and turned the colour of a beetroot for the reason that Chris Mortimer, who was merely the son of a poor clergyman in the next parish, had dared to propose to Adela.

"What! Marry my daughter to a beggarly puppy in the Merchant Service!" he roared at the culprit. "What do you take me for? Let me tell you that the man who marries her must be able to keep a father-in-law in style as well as a wife. Do you hear? The girl's an investment, and one that is going to pay me a thousand per cent too. You clear out of this, you young jackanapes, and if I catch you hanging round, or trying to speak to her, I'll break every bone in your wretched body," etc. etc.

And with such rigid precaution did the unpleasant old gentleman guard his treasure for the next fortnight, that young Mortimer was forced to join his ship and sail away to the South Sea Islands without the opportunity of a word or a look from Adela; and the farewell note he tried to smuggle in via the garden boy, was returned to him by post, torn to shreds, in an envelope (unstamped) which bore the Major's crest. The note had contained a passionate assurance of his undying love, and entreaty that she would be true to him, a vow that he would come back with a fortune to claim her – a fortune so large that even her father would be satisfied.

"There is money to be made where I am going," he wrote; "a pal of mine has let me into a secret – it's a dead certainty. Only wait for me and love me, and never think that I shall not return."

But, as we know, Adela did not receive her letter, and the garden boy, who had failed in his best endeavours to deliver it, would have summonsed the Major for knocking out his front teeth, only that Mortimer's bribe had rendered him impervious to suffering.

Then one day, when the ineligible suitor had long been safely on the ocean, a tall, black-haired stranger suddenly appeared in company with the Major and his daughter, and the interested public subsequently discovered that he was a baronet, that he was staying with the Roscoes, and that he had been a friend of the Major's before debt and discredit had driven the latter to a remote and cheap country district.

Adela detested their guest – the first they had entertained since her return from the inexpensive French boarding-school where she had been educated, and where she had spent all her holidays from the time of her mother's death. Sir Bennet Falcon frightened and disgusted her; he would stare into her face with his heavy bloodshot eyes until her cheeks grew crimson, and then he would laugh and say it was so refreshing to see a blush. When he was not playing cards or drinking with her father, he would follow her about, talking to her in a way that she did not understand; or he would tease her as if she were a child – pull her bright hair, pinch her cheeks, and chuckle with evil satisfaction when she flew into a rage. He always smelt of whisky; his very clothes seemed to have been steeped in spirit; his face reminded her of a gargoyle; his husky voice rasped her nerves; his odious touch made her shiver. But his presence apparently had a soothing effect upon the Major, who now assumed a fatherly attitude towards his only child, sent for a new hat and parasol for her from London, made a fuss about her health and comfort, and insisted that she should retire to bed early. This she was quite ready to do, for as the evening advanced Sir Bennet's attentions grew increasingly nauseating, and she was thankful to escape to her room, though the loud voices and coarse laughter below invariably kept her awake till long after midnight.

The girl was thoroughly miserable. She had given her love to Chris Mortimer, and her tender heart ached for a sight of the young sailor's frank face and direct grey eyes. The future without him seemed dark and hopeless, and she was also tormented with a fearful suspicion, which was justified one sunny morning, when her father called her into the dining-room and said that Sir Bennet wished to marry her.

"Oh! I couldn't," she cried, with horror in her brown eyes. "I couldn't – I couldn't!" She put out both her hands as though to ward off the revolting suggestion.

"Now, my good girl," – the Major began to walk up and down the room blowing out his loose red cheeks, and flapping behind him the tail of his rough shooting coat – "I'm not going to have any nonsense. Sir Bennet is waiting for you at the bottom of the garden, and you'll just go straight and tell him you will be his wife, and say 'Thank you' as well. What the devil can a miserable chit like you want more? You'll be My Lady; he stinks of money; even *he* can't get through his income, and if you let him go on as he's doing now, you'll be a rich widow in no time, and free to marry your fool of a cabin-boy, or whatever he may be."

But Adela only sank into a chair and cried despairingly. She was gentle and timid by nature, and utterly incapable of openly defying her father's orders.

"Get up and stop that noise," he continued, halting before her. "What do you suppose I asked the man down here for? Why have I let him drink me out of house and home? Why have I allowed him to clear me out at poker? Because I meant him to marry *you*, of course, and now he's hooked, you've got to keep him. Gad! To think what this marriage means – " the Major slapped his thigh, shut his eyes, and drew a long breath. "It means Life and the World once more! Do you think I'm going to stay and rot in this infernal hole, when there's an easy way out like this? No; I've made a damned good bargain, and you're not going to upset the apple-cart, my lady, I can tell you. Come along – "

He dragged her to her feet, giving her an impatient shake, and with a storm of bad language he drove her before him through the little hall and out of the front door; then he stood in the porch, his legs apart, and menace in his attitude, while with bowed head and faltering footsteps the girl went blindly towards the figure that waited in the distance.

There followed a week of misery for Adela. She felt as though she had committed some horrible crime; she had broken her promise to the man she loved; she was Sir Bennet's promised wife, and there was no chance of escape – for Chris was hundreds of miles away across the seas and could not help her. What would he think when he came back and found she was Lady Falcon? Would he ever understand and forgive? The wedding day was fixed; Sir Bennet wrote by every post for presents for his fiancée; he was even paying for her trousseau, a proceeding that gratified the father as much as it annoyed the daughter; the two men were boisterous and triumphant, and apparently quite unaffected by the white face, despairing eyes, and spiritless manner of their victim.

Then it became necessary for Sir Bennet to go to London that he might interview lawyers and tailors, arrange about settlements, and the opening of his town and country houses. He was away for three weeks, and Adela felt almost happy by contrast when relieved of his hateful company, though the thought of the future hung like a dark cloud over her mind. The days flew by, and the end of her respite was at hand; this evening Sir Bennet would return with his evil face, his atmosphere of dissipation, and his noxious love-making. She sat at the open window of her little drawing-room, her hands lying limp in her lap, her wistful eyes gazing out at the wealth of summer flowers, the hovering butterflies, the happy birds; she was thinking of Chris as one thinks of a dear, dead friend, with a dumb regret, a finality of sorrow, an absence of hope.

The garden gate clicked and the village postman hurried up the drive. She took the letters from him through the window and nodded pleasantly as the man touched his cap and turned away. There were some bills for the Major, and a curious-looking packet for herself sewn up with red cotton in dirty wax-cloth. The address was blurred and indistinct, but the handwriting brought the colour flooding over her face and neck, and she put it to her lips with a gasp of pleasure. Then she tore it open with shaking fingers and searched desperately for the letter that she felt convinced would be inside, but only a barbaric-looking necklace of faded beads fell on to her lap, and apparently Chris had sent it to her without a word. It was a bitter disappointment, and the tears ran down her cheeks as she examined again and again the wrappings of her strange present. She held the necklace up, and wondered why Chris had wanted her to have it; the beads were common glass, and were strung on to something that looked like stiff brown thread, but they were arranged in squares with curious lines and patterns, and she had certainly never seen anything quite like it before. At any rate it had come from Chris, his dear fingers had held it, his hands had packed it up; she would treasure the wrapper on which he had written her name, and tonight she would wear the necklace, hideous though it might be, as a charm to give her strength for the ordeal of Sir Bennet's return.

She looked enchanting when she came down to the drawing-room that evening before dinner: her cheeks were flushed with emotion; her eyes dreamy with memories of her lost lover; her white gown threw up the brilliance of her hair and added to the shapeliness of her slight figure; the quaint bead necklace lay round her delicate throat. Sir Bennet stood on the hearth-rug; he had asked for a fire, though the summer night was warm to closeness, and he spread his shaking fingers over the flames; his eyes were dull, and his swollen lips twitched as he greeted the girl and kissed her unwilling face. He had evidently been drinking more heavily than usual during his absence.

"What's that ugly thing round your neck?" he asked, and as he peered at the beads a look came into his face as though some unpleasant recollection had been awakened. Adela murmured an incoherent reply. She wished now she had not worn the necklace, and she felt relieved that her father was not in the room to ask further questions. She could hear him in the dining-room drawing corks.

"Come and sit here," said Sir Bennet, flinging himself into a corner of the sofa. She tried to evade his clutch, but he pulled her down into the vacant place by his side.

"See what I've brought for my little white bird." He fumbled in his pocket and produced a long morocco case. "Open it! I'll bet you've never seen anything to equal what's inside."

She pressed the spring without any feeling of pleasurable curiosity, and beheld a diamond necklace that startled her with its brilliance – it seemed to be made of captive lightning.

"There!" croaked Sir Bennet. "What d'ye think of that? Take that dirty little bead thing off your pretty neck and put this on."

He dragged at the beads as though he would break the fastening, but it held firm.

"Oh! don't," cried Adela; "you'll break it."

"Well, and what then? Who gave it to you?" he asked with sudden fierceness.

Adela, fearful of being pressed on the subject, nervously undid the string and let him take her treasure from her, and again the look of uneasy recollection, almost fear, came into the man's eyes.

"I've seen these things before," he said shortly; "natives wear 'em in the South Sea Islands – " He put it in his pocket, then clasped the diamonds round her neck and regarded the effect with satisfied complacence. "There!" he added, "that's better."

"May I have my beads back?" she asked timidly, when she had thanked him for his gift with forced gratitude.

"No," he answered, and set his jaw. "I don't want to see a thing like that on your neck again; it's only fit for savages, and it reminds me of a deuced bad time I had once in my life which I prefer to forget. There's the gong." He rose and offered her his arm.

During dinner he was inclined to be sullen and quarrelsome; he ate little, but drank freely of the Major's whisky; and when Adela left the room he got up with difficulty to open the door for her. She passed him swiftly, avoiding his gaze, and fled to her room, where she railed in helpless bitterness against the cruelty of her lot, cried over the loss of her necklace, and kissed the wrapping it had travelled in.

Later, she heard the two men leave the dining-room and come stumbling up the staircase. Her father was laughing, foolishly, and Sir Bennet was talking fast in a curious high-pitched tone.

"But didn't you see the fellow, Roscoe?" he was saying as they passed her room, and his voice reminded her of a day when she had visited a large hospital and the raving of a delirious patient had reached her ears through a half-closed door. "He looked into the dining-room twice, and then, when we came out, he was hiding behind the curtain in the hall – Lord! he's coming up the stairs now – keep him back, Roscoe, for the love of Heaven – stop him – give me time to lock my door – "

There was a rush of unsteady footsteps down the passage, a loud slam, a helpless giggling laugh from the Major as he blundered into his own room, and then all was quiet. Adela shuddered and turned wearily to the open window; she leaned out and inhaled the fragrance of the flowers beneath, the cool sweetness of the night air; little white moths brushed past her face, and now and then a bird called from the trees at the end of the garden. A faint hint of the rising moon was stealing over the sky, and Adela sat motionless and inert while the weird light slowly increased and clove the darkness into blocks of shadow.

Suddenly the sound of a muffled cry within the house made her start and draw back her head. Again she heard it, and her heart beat quickly with apprehension. She opened the door and listened; in his room at the end of the passage Sir Bennet seemed to be running violently to and fro and calling hoarsely for help, but before she could dart across to rouse her father, a dishevelled figure with a white terrified face and wild eyes rushed past her and down the stairs. She heard the hall-door bang, and the thud of running feet over the lawn.

In a moment she was at her father's bedside. "Get up – get up!" she shouted, shaking him desperately, "Sir Bennet must have gone mad – he has rushed out of the house half dressed – Father! Father!"

But the Major snored on; she was powerless to rouse him from his heavy stupor, and she ran in bewilderment back to her open window. The moonlight was streaming over the smooth grass; and, in and out among the bushes, as though pursued by a relentless enemy, ran Sir Bennet, stooping, doubling, dodging. His heavy steps and panting breath throbbed on the night air, and once or twice he half fell, recovering himself with a low hunted cry.

It was a sickening sight, but the girl's courage rose unexpectedly, as sometimes happens with timid natures in a sudden crisis. She leant out of the window and called to him. At the sound of her voice he stopped, then hurried towards her and held up his hands. His face, in the moonlight, drawn with terror and delusion, was ghastly.

"Come down!" he called, "come down and help me drive him away – he is waiting there under the trees. If you are with me perhaps he will go, but alone I cannot escape from him, and he will hunt me to my death. After all these years he has come for his revenge – Adela! Adela!"

The fear and supplication in his voice were pitiable; she braced her nerves and prepared to go down. Perhaps her presence would soothe and influence him – even if he should kill her in his delirium it would be better than living to be his wife.

"Wait," she cried softly, "I am coming." And presently her hand was on his trembling arm, and she was firmly reassuring him that he was safe from his imaginary pursuer. She led him to a garden bench under the dining-room window, and he sat down a shaking, huddled heap.

"It was that cursed necklace you were wearing," he stammered; "it made me think of him – the natives on the island used to wear them – " He stopped and drew his hand across his wet forehead. "Of course I didn't really see him – he has been dead for years," he glanced about him fearfully, "and yet he looked into the dining-room, he followed me up the stairs – he was in my room," his voice rose and he gripped her hands, "I am going to tell you all about it – the whole truth – perhaps that will keep him away and satisfy him?"

"Yes," said Adela soothingly, "yes – tell me."

His grasp tightened on her hands, and he began to speak in a harsh, monotonous key, staring intently all the while into the surrounding shadows.

"Years ago I had a friend – a friend who stuck to me when I was under a cloud and people were cutting me; we went away together yachting – he sacrificed a lot to go with me. We cruised about in warm climates and stopped at ports we had never heard of, and at last we got among the South Sea Islands. Then there was a storm – my God; what a storm! – it was like the end of the world – and the yacht went down. All night Horsley and I clung to the same piece of wreckage, and in the morning we were washed ashore, the only survivors. It was a long low island, and the natives were cannibals – we saw them at it one night, watched them through the cocoa-nut palms by the light of the fire they had made, and then we knew what they were keeping us for. We were guarded day and night, though they let us wander within certain limits, and gave us a hut to live in. We saw no ships, we had no chance to build a boat, or escape by swimming, and day by day we waited for our death. Then Horsley ran a poisonous thorn into his foot and had to stay in the hut, and one morning when I went down as usual to the shore in the hope of seeing a sail, there seemed to be no natives on the watch. All night they had been singing and tom-toming, and I suppose the guards had got careless and were asleep, for I saw none of them about. Just as I was thinking of going back through the palm grove to the hut to tell Horsley there might be a chance to take to the sea, a ship came round the corner of the island. She was only a small trading vessel that had got out of her course, but she meant rescue if the natives didn't spot her. I looked all round – there wasn't a soul in sight, the ship was only a few hundred yards off, the water was calm, and I could swim well. I thought if I went back for Horsley, who couldn't walk with his bad foot, the natives would have time to see the ship, and the chances were we should be intercepted and killed. The ship's captain would never send a boat ashore and risk the lives of his crew, I knew that – and I knew if I got away I should be leaving Horsley to a cruel death. I swear I fought the temptation, but all the same I took off my clothes and swam for my life. I reached the ship, I told them about Horsley, but they refused to do more than give me shelter, because the natives of that island were known to be savagely hostile; and we steamed away into safety while Horsley was left there alone – "

He ceased abruptly, his mouth open, his breath coming in quick gasps; he pointed towards the trees:

"There! Don't you see him? Over by the bushes – he hasn't gone, I've done no good by telling the truth – he is coming out into the moonlight on the lawn – Ah! I can't bear to see his face. Go back, Horsley!" he shouted; "I never meant to leave you, I meant to get the ship's boat and fetch you – I swear I did"; he pushed past Adela's restraining hand, and ran with superhuman swiftness down the path.

She heard him crash through the old wooden gate, and his rapid foot-steps rang clear on the hard road; faster, faster they sped into the distance, until the echo died away on the still night air.

Extract from a local newspaper:

An inquest was held yesterday on the body of Sir Bennet Falcon, Baronet, who was found drowned in a pond two miles from the village of Hayfield, where he had been staying on a visit to his friends, Major and Miss Roscoe. The jury returned a verdict of suicide whilst temporarily insane; and much sympathy is felt in the neighbourhood for Miss Roscoe, to whom the deceased gentleman was engaged to be married. We regret to learn that the young lady is at present lying dangerously ill from the effects of the shock, and grave doubts are entertained as to her recovery.

But Adela was called back from the borders of death by news which gave her the promise of a happy future. The secret that had been imparted to Chris Mortimer by his obliging friend had lived up to its character of "a dead certainty", and Chris would be arriving home in a few months' time a comparatively rich man. The precious life-giving letter rested day and night beneath Adela's pillow, but in it there was one paragraph which shocked and startled her, and which she never willingly re-read:

"I wonder if you ever received a rum kind of necklace I sent you? I know you didn't get the letter I wrote at the same time, because the fellow who took it on shore confessed afterwards that he had lost the letter, though he swore he posted the little parcel. I saw an old native wearing the necklace, and it struck me as being rather curious, so I persuaded him to sell the thing, though he made an awful fuss about parting with it, and said it was a most powerful charm against ill-luck; so, being a superstitious sailor, I thought I'd send it to you! – but I'm sorry I did, because I heard later that it had a nasty history. The beads were supposed to be strung on the sinews of a white man who was killed some years ago on one of these islands before the savages were routed out and taught better manners, and though it's probably only a yarn, you'd better throw it away or give it to someone who has a taste for gruesome curiosities. You shall have pearls instead, my darling, and soon I shall be home to fasten them round your neck myself . . ."

Clive Pemberton

A Dead Man's Bargain

Clive Pemberton was an Edwardian journalist with a penchant for mystery stories. His books include The Harvest of Deceit, The Valliscourt Mystery, Her Own Secret, A Member of Tattersall's, *and* The Weird o' it *(1906), a collection of ten supernatural horror stories.*

THE CONVERSATION IN the smoke-room had flowed unflaggingly, as conversation will when a cosmopolitan gathering comes together, and the pipes are drawing well and none is a laggard with the glass. There were a dozen grouped round the blazing log fire – men from all parts and in diverse walks of life. Topic after topic was broached, descanted upon at length or dismissed with a word, and at last the subject of supernatural agency was started.

"I can't and don't believe in what some people call supernatural agencies," said a stout, jovial faced man, drawing briskly at a mammoth briar. "I remember a man telling me once of a visitation he had from his mother-in-law – deceased ten years – and it nearly killed him – the shock of seeing her again, I suppose," and he laughed ponderously into his glass.

"I don't believe in spirits or such things either," chimed in a matter-of-fact commercial. "You see, I'm one to only believe in what my eyes show me, and spirits that come to worry folk and frighten them out of their wits always – "

"Yet supernatural happenings are on record whether you believe in them or not."

All turned simultaneously to learn from whom the interruption had come. It proceeded from a man who was sitting somewhat apart from the group round the fireplace. At the first glance, all noticed the same strange thing about him. The face was that of a young man, but the hair, which grew somewhat long and dishevelled, was snow-white, and in the eyes there lurked an expression such as is only seen in those having once undergone some shock or never-to-be-forgotten ordeal. There was a moment of silence, then the first speaker addressed the stranger, who, after his quietly-spoken words, had retired into the background again as though embarrassed at having spoken.

"I don't think any of us but are open to conviction," said the commercial, looking invitingly round. He turned to the stranger. "If you have a story to tell, sir, you will not have to complain of inattention. What do you say, gentlemen?"

The affirmative was unanimous, and the stranger slowly drew his chair forward into the circle. Amid a flattering silence he commenced his story.

You ask yourselves why I, young in years, should have the face of a worn old man and hair whiter than Time could ever bleach it? Listen to the true story of my awful and inexplicable experience – an experience that in one short hour changed the colour of my hair from brown to white, and carved lines on my face that nothing will ever erase while memory lasts to haunt me with the recollection of the most fearful ordeal mortal man ever went through and emerged alive to speak of.

At the time of which I speak – some five years ago – I was living in a remote little town in the Midlands, which I will call L—. From my earliest years, the passion of my life had been music, and an annuity of two hundred a year allowed me to follow my natural inclinations without fear of being harassed by financial difficulties. Insignificant and even unimportant though L— was, it yet possessed one object of interest and antiquity – the Parish Church. This was a fine old building erected in the reign of Elizabeth – rich in stained glass and well preserved stone frescoes. But its greatest attraction – to me, at any rate – was the organ – a superb instrument combining the immortal work of Father Smith with the modern improvements in mechanism by the latter-day builders. The whole instrument had been reconstructed and made perfect by the generosity of a rich patron some two years before, and on the completion of the work a new organist was appointed – a stranger to L– named Reuben Chelston. I suppose it was our equal enthusiasm in the one pursuit that drew us together, for, in a very short time, Reuben Chelston and I were firm and inseparable companions. As an executant on the organ I have never heard his equal; but as time went on and I got to know him better, I found that he was a man possessed of some very extraordinary theories regarding the supernatural, and in the creed of spiritualism he thoroughly believed. At first his extraordinary doctrines – delivered at lightning speed and with a kind of hysterical excitement that invariably seized him when on the subject – astonished me not a little, and would have led many to incline towards the belief that he was mad; but constant and close contact with the man had given me a deeper insight into his temperament than others possessed, and as I never attempted to argue the matter with him or try to convince him to the contrary, no harm was done. There was seldom an evening that I did not spend with him in the empty church, listening while he played as only he could play. In my mind's eye I can see him now, his great shaggy head thrown back, eyes closed in a sort of ecstatic trance, and the most wonderful melodies ravishing the air as his hands swept over the keys.

Strange melodies they were sometimes that his fancy would conceive, and if some of those extemporaneous pieces he played to me could be reproduced, they would, I am convinced, rank with some of the finest compositions the world has ever heard. It was about a year after the beginning of our somewhat curious intimacy that I first noticed the beginning of a strange change in my friend. He had repeatedly told me that he had confided in me as in no other living person, for, indeed, I was his only companion and he seemed to possess no other friends or acquaintances. He was always a man of moods, now grave, now gay, and subject to curious lapses of sullenness when he appeared to be thinking deeply over something known only to himself. It was summer time, and after the usual practice in the church one evening, he returned with me to my rooms. Once or twice I was on the point of asking him what was amiss, for he seemed to be labouring under some excitement that he found difficult to suppress. For a long time after we had finished the meal he sat silent, his eyes fixed vacantly on the wall and his lips moving rapidly as though he were repeating some set formula to himself over and over again. Suddenly he turned to me – his voice wonderfully quiet and well under control.

"Harold," he said; "I am going away for a while."

"Going away?" I repeated. "Where to? what for?"

"I am going away from here," he went on, not appearing to notice my questions, "because I cannot do what I have to do here."

"What have you to do which cannot be done here?" I asked, curiously. He was silent for a moment, then he seemed to rouse himself, and his voice sounded clear and distinct.

"As you know," he said, fixing his eyes – the most wonderful eyes ever set in a man's head – on mine, "I have confided things to you that nobody save myself knows of. Have you noticed that I have been away every Wednesday night for the past six weeks?"

"Why – yes," I replied, quickly, "but I did not like to – "

"Quite so," he said, lifting his thin white hand; "but I want you to know why I have been away and what took me away. I have been attending seances – spiritualistic seances!"

I was silent as I heard this, and he went on again quickly after a short pause.

"Harold, why cannot you think as I do?" he cried, a note of pettish irritation in his voice. "I tell you that great marvels can be unfolded by those who return for a fleeting space from the other side. Something will be revealed to me tomorrow night, and then – and then – "

My thoughts had been wandering a little when he commenced speaking, but as he said this my attention was arrested in an instant.

"How can anything be revealed to you tomorrow night?" I said, looking closely at him. "You don't mean that you – that you – ?"

I broke off as he leaned swiftly towards me.

"This I do tell you," he said, in a kind of awed whisper. "Tomorrow night, myself and one medium will await that which I have been told will be given to me. Such a melody as the world has never yet heard the equal of will be given to me, note by note, by – "

"By whom?" I said sharply, as he suddenly checked himself. He sat silent and thoughtful for a moment.

"That I cannot tell you," he replied, at last. "But this I do promise you, Harold. You shall be the first to hear the wonderful melody, be it what it is." He dropped his voice to a thrilling whisper. "What if it should be so stupendously unearthly as to be unfit for mortal ears?"

The suddenly conceived idea seemed to move him to ungovernable excitement. He rose and paced the floor with eager, nervous strides. For my part I sat silent and thoughtful. The idea was preposterous, even fraught with a vague suggestion of evil that struck a warning note within my prosaic being.

"Chelston," I said suddenly, looking up at him; "I am going to ask you to do – or rather, *not* to do – something."

He paused and looked at me with dilated eyes.

"Well?" he said, quickly.

"I want you not to do what you – you have just told me you are going to do!"

He made a quick movement with his hands.

"Why do you ask me such an impossible thing?" he said, half angrily.

"Because I instinctively feel that some evil will come of it," I rejoined, boldly. "If we were meant to – to – "

"Enough!" he interposed, peremptorily. "What I have told you I *shall* do! Remember, I promise you that you shall be the first to hear it. Nothing shall prevent you hearing it first! Think of me tomorrow night! . . ."

The following day he left L— before anybody was up and about. It was a blistering hot day – the hottest of that summer – and, situated in a cup-like valley as the town was, it was almost insufferable. All that never-to-be-forgotten day, I felt strangely depressed and restless. I could not settle to anything, and though I tried hard to interest myself in a composition I was at work on, I could not shake off the vague foreboding of a nameless disaster that seemed hanging over me. During the afternoon, the barometer fell with that sudden and ominous rush that always heralds an approaching thunder-storm. Tired with doing nothing all day and still over-shadowed by that same feeling of depression, I determined to walk to the church in the cool of the evening and spend an hour at the organ. The air was still humid and oppressive when I started, although the great heat had gone with the hazing of the sun by a bank of black, uprising clouds. I noticed them as I waited outside the verger's cottage while he fetched the keys.

"It looks as if a storm was brewing, Trench," I said, pointing to the sullen bank of clouds.

"Ay!" he replied, shading his eyes with his hand – "It dew that, to be sure, an' it'll be on us afore we expect it, I reckon. I wouldn't be too long if I were you, sir. It *will* be rain when it does come down!"

I agreed with him, and having taken the keys, went on to the church. Having let myself in, I locked the door behind me and mounted the gallery steps to the organ loft. The church – even in bright daylight – was always dim and somewhat gloomy, owing to every window being composed of richly coloured stained glass. Now, with the gathering murky gloom without, the interior was almost completely dark, only the white stone pillars and alabaster statues gleaming white and indistinct at the far end below. I should here explain that when the instrument had been renovated and enlarged, a water-driven engine had been installed, thereby rendering the services of a bellows man unnecessary. Afterwards, I would have given the world if another had been with me . . . But I am anticipating. Having lighted the desk lamps and uncovered the keyboards, I pulled down the lever that controlled the engine, and from the vault far below, I heard the dull thud! thud! of the pistons as they drove the air into the bellows. In a few moments I was lost in a world of melody, and as I put fancy after fancy into execution, the minutes slipped on into long after the hour I had intended to stop. Suddenly I lifted my hands from the keys, and closed my eyes as the gilt music support on the desk before me glinted like an electric spark. It was a gleaming flash of lightning that had stealthily darted from the window on my left and had been reflected in the brass rest. With my hands grasping the stops I listened intently. The rain was pattering down on the roof above with harsh force, and yes! faint but unmistakable was the distant mutter and roll of thunder. Quite suddenly – more suddenly than I can describe – I was seized with that strange sensation which everybody has felt at some time when in an empty building – the sensation that I was not *alone* and was being *watched*! I sat perfectly rigid, straining my ears to hear – what? I do not know, but while I would have given anything to have looked behind me, I found myself powerless to move my head or even glance in the slanting mirror that commanded a view of the gallery and well behind and below me. How long I sat thus I do not know, but a second gleam of lightning – far more vivid than the first – recalled me to action. Seizing the handle that controlled the engine, I turned it off, then pulled the knob of the ledge that covered the keyboards. It would not *move*! Something seemed to be holding it back! I tugged and pulled at it but to no purpose, and as my strange nervousness – it was positive *fear* by this time! – kept momentarily increasing, I at last desisted, for my one desire was to get outside despite the avalanche of rain that was descending on the roof above me. The last breath of wind ebbed out of the empty bellows with a curious ticking sound; then, amid a strange, deathly still lull both within and without, I turned out one of the gas jets. As I did so, a peculiar thing happened. A draught – faint, yet perfectly distinct – swept behind me; but, with an indescribable feeling of terror, I noticed that the flame beside me did not flicker or become actuated by it in the slightest degree. A kind of frantic desire seized me to tear madly down the steps and out into the raging storm, for fragments of Reuben Chelston's strange conversations recurred to me, and, try as I would, I could not shut them out. With a sudden effort I turned out the remaining gas-jet, and in black darkness groped my way to the door. I had just reached it when I again distinctly felt a slight stirring of the air – just what a draught would be if caused by somebody passing! Down the steps I crept, one by one, the lightning blazing in at the windows with blinding brilliancy and alarming rapidity. To get to the door, I had to walk the whole length of the aisle, and, with my heart wildly beating, I sped up it, twisting my head round mechanically at every yard. I was about two-thirds up, perhaps, when I suddenly stopped. What was that? I strained my ears, my heart-beats humming in my head. It came again, sending a thrill of horror through me, for clearly enough I heard the sudden throb of the engine far below and then the sound of the bellows filling. Like the crash of brazen cymbals in my ears it was borne in upon me that I was *not alone*! Somebody had started the engine – somebody was in the building with me. Summoning all my presence of mind, I called out – "Who is there?"

The echo of my voice was drowned in an appalling crash of thunder; but as it died away, I fancied that a wild laugh came from the gallery! And then – and then – How can I describe what followed? I cannot – simply cannot, for my brain reels at the recollection of it. The storm seemed to suddenly subside – the rain ceased to clatter on the roof, and in an unbroken silence, the organ began to sound. If I could command the language and descriptive power of the greatest mind that ever lived, I could not convey the faintest conception of the weird music that flooded the empty building and poured into my shivering ears; but instinctively I knew that it was a dead march – unearthly and of such sombre grandeur as no living brain of man ever conceived. It seemed to tell of phases that are faintly imagined and seen, shadow-like as in a dream, and awe-struck and bewildered I crouched down on the cold stone floor, covering my ears, for I knew such melody was never meant for human ears to hear. How long it lasted I cannot say, but it gradually died away as gently and imperceptibly as a summer breeze, and as it did so, the clock in the tower slowly struck nine. Then action came to me, and springing to my feet, I flew to the door and fumbled with the key. The rain was falling heavily without as I tore open the door, and I felt that strange soft wind I had felt twice before pass me from behind! It passed me – passed me into the night and was gone! . . .

The man with the white hair ceased speaking, and lifting his hand to his forehead, brushed away a gleam of sweat that shone there. He lifted his glass and drank a little.

"A strange thing," said one, breaking the silence; "but – "

"How I got home I never knew," he continued, appearing not to notice the interruption; "but the sequel to that strange night's experience came two hours later. A telegram came for me with the news that Reuben Chelston had died suddenly at half past eight at the conclusion of a spiritualistic seance. And, as the last notes of that terrible dead march died away and I opened the door, the clock in the tower struck nine, and – and I felt that wind pass me! . . ."

There was silence in the room – a silence that remained unbroken.

Tom Gallon

The House that was Lost

Tom Gallon (1866–1914), after a series of badly paid jobs, went on a long tramp through England in pursuit of inspiration and adventure before settling in London earning "stray guineas in Grub Street". He found popularity with his plays and stories about low-life, emulating both Dickens and W. W. Jacobs, mixing comedy with the macabre. His books include Comethup *(1899),* The Kingdom of Hate *(1899) and* The Charity Ghost *(1902). This tale first appeared in* The Story-Teller, *May 1908.*

THE EVENTS I set down here occurred some three years ago, and I write of them now with as much wonderment as I regarded them then. Let me say at the outset that I have puzzled and puzzled over the mystery, and have arrived at no actual solution of it, nor do I know whether any solution will ever be arrived at, or whether, even if such is the case, I shall ever hear of it.

I am a commercial clerk, earning a small salary sufficient to keep my wife and two children and myself in modest comfort. My name is Paul Jenner, and I live at No.—, Drawbridge Crescent, —. Well, never mind the precise locality. I give you these particulars in order that you may understand that I am a very ordinary and commonplace person, not given to romancing. I want you to understand that I am setting down in bald and simple language what actually happened to me on a certain night in January three years ago.

It was on a Saturday night, and I had, as usual, come home on that day from the City early in the afternoon. It had been a black and foggy day, and I remember that the gas had been lighted in the streets and in the office where I worked from early morning. The fog was very bad at the time I returned home, and I congratulated myself on the fact that I had not to go out again that night. I sat with my wife and the two children in our little sitting-room all the evening, with that comfortable feeling that I was my own master until Monday morning, and that I need trouble about nothing outside the house. In due course the children went to bed, and then it was Mary reminded me of a letter that must be written and posted that night. Sufficient is it for me to say that the letter was to an elderly relative of some means who lived in the country, and who had taken great interest in the children. My wife (prudent woman) remembered that the following day was the birthday of this relative, and that she should receive proper greeting by the Sunday morning post in the country town in which she lived.

Frankly, I did not want the bother of it; but Mary always knows best in these matters, and so I wrote my note and sealed it up. Let me add here that I had read nothing exciting during the evening – nothing to stir my imagination in any way.

I stamped the letter and proceeded to the front door. Judge of my astonishment when, on throwing it open, I saw nothing but the grey wall of fog coming up to the very house; even the railings, not ten yards in front of our little house, were blotted out completely, I called softly back into the house to my wife to come and look.

"Don't lose yourself, Paul," she said, half laughing. "What a terrible night!"

"I shan't lose myself," I replied, laughing in turn. "The pillar-box is only at the end of the crescent; if I stick to the railings, I can't possibly miss it. Don't wait here," I added solicitously. "I'll leave the door ajar, so that I can slip in easily when I come back. I've left my keys on my writing desk."

Mary went in, and I pulled the door close, and then stepped out boldly for the front gate. Imagine me standing there, just outside my own gate, and with my back to the crescent, knowing that I had to go to the left to find the pillar-box which was at the end of the crescent. There are nine houses, and mine is the third, so that I knew I had to pass six more before reaching the pillar-box. I knew also that the gate of each house had an ornamental centre-piece standing up above it, and that I must touch six of those ornamental centre-pieces before I stepped away from the crescent at the end to reach the pillar-box. That I knew would be something of an adventure, for the fog was the densest I have ever seen; I could only see the faint glow of the lamp in the centre of the crescent above me when I came opposite to the lamp-post; the post itself was invisible.

I counted the six gates, and then stood at the end of the last line of railings. I knew that the pillar-box was exactly opposite me. I took three quick steps, and literally cannoned into it. I was a little proud of my own judgment in getting it so nicely. Then I fumbled for the mouth of it, and dropped in my letter.

All this may sound very commonplace and ordinary; but you shall hear what followed. I am an observant man, and I had noticed always that the mouth of the pillar-box faced directly along the crescent, thus standing at right angles to the road. At the moment that I had my right hand in that mouth, therefore, I argued that if I stood out at the stretch of my arm I must be facing the crescent; I had but to move straight forward again to touch the friendly railings. I was putting that plan into operation, and had let go of the mouth of the pillar-box, when a man, coming hurriedly round the corner, ran straight into me, muttered a gruff apology, and was lost in the fog again in a moment. And in that accidental collision he had spun me round and tossed me aside – and I was lost!

That is literally true. I took a step and found myself slipping off the kerbstone into the road; stumbled back again, and strove to find my way along by sticking to the edge of the pavement. After a minute or two I was so sure of myself that I ventured to cross the pavement, and by great good luck touched in a moment one of those ornamental centre-pieces of one of the gates – or so, at least, it seemed. I went on with renewed confidence until I saw certain bushes which topped the railings of one particular house, and then I knew that the next house must be mine. I pushed open the gate with confidence, stepped quickly up the little path, and reached the door. I was right; the door yielded to my touch, and I went hurriedly in.

I had taken off my hat, and had held it towards the familiar hat-stand before I realized that it was not a familiar hat-stand at all; it was one I did not know. I looked round in some confusion, meaning to make good my escape without being observed, and yet wondering into what house I could have come so near my own, when I stopped stock still, with the hat held in my hand, listening. From a room near at hand I heard the sound of a low, long-drawn moan, as from someone in pain. More than that, it was almost the wail of someone in acute terror.

Now I am a mild and inoffensive man, and I confess that my first instinct was to fly. There was the door within a foot of me; I could open it again noiselessly and slip out, and leave whoever was moaning to his or her own trouble. My next instinct, however, was a braver one; I might be able to help. Putting my hat on, and so leaving my hands free, I moved cautiously towards the sound, which was coming intermittently.

I found that the house was built in exactly the same fashion that mine was; there was the same number of steps leading to a room downstairs, which in my case was used as a playroom for the children. I went down these steps slowly and cautiously, with my flesh creeping a little, I must admit, as that weird moaning went on, and almost inclined to turn back with every step I took. But at last I got into the basement, and came to the door of the room from which the sound proceeded. I was in the very act of recklessly thrusting open the door when another sound broke upon my ears that held me still. The sound of someone singing in a raucous voice.

It was a sea song I remembered to have heard when a boy, and the words of which I have forgotten; it was something about "Blow the man down". The door of the room was open a little way, and through the crack of it I was able to peer in; and there I saw a sight that for a moment made me doubt my own eyes. I remember that I rubbed my eyes in a stupid way and looked again, and this is what I saw:

The room was in a neglected state, with strips of wallpaper hanging down from the walls and with a blackened ceiling. There was a table in the centre of it, and at that table a man was seated, with a square black bottle and a glass before him, and a candle burning near his left hand. I can see the whole room now as plainly and as clearly as I saw it then. He was a man so villainously ugly that I had a thought that he was not a man at all, but some hideous thing out of a nightmare. He had very long arms – so long that they were stretched across the table, and his hands gripped the opposite edge of it; a great heavy head, crowned with a mass of red hair, was set low between enormously broad shoulders; his eyes, half closed, were high up and close together on either side of a nose that was scarcely a nose at all; the lips were thick and heavy.

But it was not the man that I looked at first, it was at two other figures in the room. These figures were seated on chairs facing the table at which the man was, and the strangeness of them lay in the fact that each was securely bound to the chair on which he and she sat, for it was a man and a woman. The man, who was quite young was not only bound, but gagged securely also; the woman was more lightly tied to her chair by the arms only, and her mouth was free. She was leaning back, with her eyes closed, and it was from her lips that that strange wailing sound was coming, and mingling with the raucous singing of the man at the table. My first impression was that the man at the table was some sort of unclean, bestial judge, and the others his prisoners.

He stopped his singing to pour some liquor from the square bottle into his glass and to drink it off; then he resumed his former attitude, with his fingers locked over the edge of the table. And now I noticed that while the woman, who was, by the way, quite young and very pretty, with a fair, dainty prettiness, still kept her eyes closed, the eyes of the bound man never left that dreadful figure seated at the other side of the table.

"Wouldn't you like to speak, you dog?" said the red-haired man. "What would you give now to have the use of your limbs – the free wagging of your tongue? What would you say to me; what would you do to me?"

The man who was bound could, of course, answer nothing. I saw his face flush and darken, and I guessed what his thoughts were. For myself, I was too fascinated by the scene before me to do anything else than peer through the crack and watch what was going on.

"Lovers – eh?" exclaimed the man at the table. "You thought I was unsuspicious; you thought I knew nothing and suspected nothing – didn't you? While I was safely out of the way you could meet, the pair of you – day after day, and week after week; and this puppy could steal from me what was mine by right."

The woman opened her eyes for the first time and spoke. "It isn't true," she said, a sob breaking her voice. "It was all innocent. Dick and I have done no wrong."

"You lie!" thundered the man, bringing his fist down upon the table with a blow that might have split it. "You've always lied – lied from the moment your father gave you to me – from the very hour I married you. You always hated me; I've seen you shudder many and many a time at the mere sight of me. Don't I know it; haven't I felt you stab me a thousand times more deeply than you could have stabbed me with any weapon? You white devil! I've come at last to hate you as much as you hate me."

The woman turned her head slowly and looked at the younger man; a faint smile crossed her lips. In an instant the red-haired man had leapt to his feet, showing me astonishingly enough that he was a dwarf, with the shortest legs surely ever a man had. But the bulk of him was enormous, and I could guess, with a shudder, at his strength. He caught up the glass, crossed the room, and flung the contents in the face of the man.

"It's a waste of good liquor – but that's for the look she gave you. I wish there was some death more horrible than any invented yet that I could deal out to you," he added, standing with the glass in his hand and glaring at his victim. "The death I mean for you is too easy."

He walked across to the fireplace in a curious purposeless way, and stirred a great fire that was blazing there. Then from a corner of the room he dragged with ease a great sack that appeared to contain wood and shavings; so much I saw in a rent in the side of it. This he dropped down near the fire, as if in readiness for something, and then went back to his seat, applying himself again to the drink that was on the table. And still I watched, as a man may watch a play, wondering how it will end.

"I got the best of you tonight," he said presently. "You might have been too much for me if I hadn't come upon you from behind; but I was ready and waiting. I've been watching longer than you think; I had everything mapped out clearly days ago. Tonight sees the end of all things for the pair of you; tomorrow sees me miles away from here. You came in secret, you dog; you'll go in secret."

"We have done no wrong," said the woman again. "We loved each other years ago, when we were boy and girl; there was no sin in that."

"Bah! – I don't believe a word of it. Don't I know that in your black heart you've compared the two of us every day of your life since first I saw you. His straightness for my crookedness; his sleek, black hair for my red; his prettiness for this face of mine" – he struck his own face relentlessly with one hand as he spoke – "that women shudder at. Don't I know all that?"

It was the strangest and most pitiful thing that the creature sitting there before his victims suddenly covered his face with his hands and groaned. If ever I had seen a soul in torment, I saw it then, and though I loathed him I could have wept for him. After a moment or two he dropped his hands and seized the bottle, and poured out the last drops into the glass and drank them off; then flung the bottle and glass crashing into the fireplace, as though there was an end to that business. And now, as he got down again from the chair, I saw the eyes of the woman open wide and follow his every movement with a dreadful look of terror in them.

"I'll kill you both – here in the place where you've met – and then I'll fire the house," went on the dwarf. "I've planned it all. Look your last on each other, for tonight you die – and this house shall be your funeral pyre!"

"I swear to you," panted the woman eagerly, "by all I hold most holy and most dear, that if you'll let us go, we'll never see each other again. For pity's sake! – for the sake of Dick!"

"For the sake of Dick!" sneered the dwarf. "That shows you in your true colours; that shows who you are and what you are. There's one poor satisfaction left to you; you'll die together."

What held me then it would be impossible to say. I can only plead that in the dreadful thing that followed I was as a man who sits at a play, wondering what will happen next, and with never a thought in him of interfering. I think in my anxiety I had pressed open the door a little to get a clearer view, so that I saw every movement of the dwarf. For myself, I had forgotten everything – my own home, and my wife, and the babies who slept in their quiet room above. It was as though I had stepped straight into a new world.

I saw the dwarf advance towards the man in the chair, carrying his right hand stiff and straight beside him, gripping something, I could not tell what it was that he held. I saw him come straight at him, and I saw the eyes of the woman in the opposite chair watching him as one fascinated. Then I saw two movements; one with the left hand of the dwarf, when he struck the other man on the face; then with the right hand, when he raised something that gleamed in the light of the candle and brought it down with a sound that was new and horrible to me on the breast of the other man. And I saw the face of the man change, and start as it were into new life, and then fall as it were into death. And I saw his head drop forward, and his eyes were closed.

Then, above it all, and yet seeming as a sort of dreadful chorus to it all, rang out the scream from the woman in the other chair. I do not think that the dwarf heard it; he had drawn back from what had been the living man, and was staring like one mad upon what he had done. And still piercing the air of the place rang the scream of the woman – not for her lover alone, but for herself.

That sound seemed at last to break in upon the senses of the dwarf and to call him partially to himself. I had watched him to the point where he drew himself together and crouched like a wild beast ready to spring, with that in his hand that dripped red, when, in some fashion, I flung myself round the partially open door and stumbled into the room. I think I must have been a little mad myself; otherwise, frail and commonplace creature that I was, I could not have battled with this madman. I came upon him from behind and gripped him, seizing him by the throat and by the head, and all the while shouting something to him quite unintelligible.

The attack had been so sudden and so unexpected that I had him, in a sense, at my mercy. He could not know who had attacked him; he struggled madly, not alone to get away from me, but also to discover who I was. I struggled to keep his face away from me, gripped him by the neck and by the hair, and fought with him for what I knew then was my own life. And so struggling we stumbled at last horribly against that still figure bound in the chair and brought it over crashing with us to the floor. And then in a sudden I felt the dwarf inert in my hands, and knew that I had conquered.

What I must have looked like in that room, kneeling there, panting and struggling to get my breath, I cannot now tell; the whole business was so like a nightmare. I remember seeing the dwarf lying there – huddled up and very still. I remember that other figure, bound grotesquely in the chair and lying, still bound, upon its side; and I remember, too, the woman, with her arms close fastened behind her, sitting there and sobbing wildly.

The dwarf must have been stunned; he lay there quite still, with the knife that was dreadfully red fallen from his hand, and lying beside him. When at last I staggered to my knees I saw that the girl was staring at me with a face that seemed to suggest that here, perhaps, was another ruffian come to kill her.

"Who – who are you?" she asked in a frightened whisper.

"A friend – one who stumbled in by accident," I panted.

"Look at the man that's tied to the chair," she whispered hoarsely. "He can't be dead."

I knew that he was, but still I looked, as she bade me. I had no need to look twice; the poor fellow was quite dead. The blow had been strong and sure. On my knees beside him, I looked up and nodded slowly to her; there was no need for words.

She leaned back in her chair again and closed her eyes. "Set me free," she said in a faint voice.

I could not touch that knife that lay there; in a mechanical, methodical way I took from my waistcoat pocket the decent, respectable little bone-handled penknife I carried always with me. With that I cut her bonds, noting as I did so how cruelly they had cut into the white flesh; and after a moment or two she swung her arms listlessly against her sides and opened her eyes, and then, with an effort raised her hands and pressed them against her temples.

"What will you do?" I asked, looking at her curiously.

"I – I don't know," she said; and then, breaking into weeping, sobbed out: "Oh – dear God – that it should have come to this! What shall I do – what shall I do?"

"You must get away," I said, watching the dwarf, who was beginning to stir a little. "If he wakes, you know what will happen."

"I know – I know," she said; and got to her feet and began to move towards that bound figure still lying tied to the chair.

But at that I got before her, and with my hands against her shoulders held her back, and pleaded passionately to her that she should go, and leave the dead alone. She listened, with that strange look in her eyes of a child wakened from sleep and not clearly understanding; but she yielded to me, and stumbled under my guidance to the door.

We had reached it, and I had opened it for her to pass out, when suddenly the dwarf twisted over on to his hands and knees, and then raised himself upright. He did not seem to realize for a moment what had happened; then he caught sight of the woman, and, with a snarl, crawled forward and gripped the hilt of the knife. At that she pushed suddenly past me and fled like a hare up the stairs. I heard the swift passage of her footsteps in the little hall of the house – then the slamming of the outer door.

And now I had to look to myself, for I saw in the eyes of the man that he would not let this witness escape if he could catch him. I had managed to get through the door by the time that he had got to his feet, and in a dazed fashion was stumbling towards me, knife in hand. With a sudden swoop he reached the table and blew out the candle, and at the same moment I ran up the stairs, and in the darkness stumbled along the hall and fumbled with the catch of the door. By great good fortune I got the door open, and literally fell out into the fog.

I could not see him as he tore after me; in a faintness I had fallen to my knees, and I heard him, as he raced past me, panting heavily. Then the fog swallowed him up, and I knelt there on the pavement alone, shaking from head to foot.

I had, of course, no means of knowing exactly which house it was in which I had had my adventure; I could only judge roughly that it must be about the middle of the crescent. I started along again, in the right direction, as I hoped, and thought to find my own house; missed the railings, after going what seemed to be an interminable distance, and came up hard against a pillar-box. Scarcely knowing what I did, I set my right hand in the mouth of it, and performed the same manoeuvre I had done before; advanced three paces, and touched railings again. Stumbling along these, I came blindly to a house that I thought might be mine, walked up the path, and pushed open a door that yielded; and there, with the face of my Mary looking at me in alarm and wonderment, I fell in a dead faint at her feet.

It has to be recorded that I never found the house again. I know everyone that lives in Drawbridge Crescent – all highly respectable people, of humdrum lives. Over and over again, in clear weather, I have walked to that pillar-box and have closed my eyes, and have tried to remember what steps I took on that particular night, after a stranger had cannoned into me and twisted me round; but all in vain. Whether in some house in some other road nearby lies the body of a man who was foully murdered on that particular night; or whether in one of the innocent-looking houses of the Crescent itself the crime was committed; or whether, in some strange supernatural fashion, I saw that night a deed committed that had been committed long before, I shall never know. That it is no mere figment of the imagination, and that something really happened that night, is proved by one fact. My wife, in raising me from the floor that night when I fell at her feet, found my fingers locked close upon something, and, forcing them open, disclosed what it was.

A tuft of red hair!

Henry James

The Jolly Corner

Henry James's last major ghost story, "The Jolly Corner", was first published in the English Review, *December, 1908. It was written soon after he revisited New York after an absence of twenty years. James observed about this tale: "I was moved to adopt as my motive an analysis of some one of the conceivably rarest and intensest grounds for an 'unnatural' anxiety, a* malaise *so incongruous and discordant, in the given prosaic prosperous conditions, as almost to be compromising. Spencer Brydon's adventure however is one of those finished fantasies that, achieving success or not, speak best even to the critical sense for themselves – which I leave it to do . . ."*

I

"EVERYONE ASKS ME what I 'think' of everything," said Spencer Brydon; "and I make answer as I can – begging or dodging the question, putting them off with any nonsense. It wouldn't matter to any of them really," he went on, "for, even were it possible to meet in that stand-and-deliver way so silly a demand on so big a subject, my thoughts would still be almost altogether about something that concerns only myself." He was talking to Miss Staverton, with whom for a couple of months now he had availed himself of every possible occasion to talk; this disposition and this resource, this comfort and support, as the situation in fact presented itself, having promptly enough taken the first place in the considerable array of rather unattenuated surprises attending his so strangely belated return to America. Everything was somehow a surprise; and that might be natural when one had so long and so consistently neglected everything, taken pains to give surprises so much margin for play. He had given them more than thirty years – thirty-three, to be exact; and they now seemed to him to have organized their performance quite on the scale of that license. He had been twenty-three on leaving New York – he was fifty-six today; unless indeed he were to reckon as he had sometimes, since his repatriation, found himself feeling; in which case he would have lived longer than is often allotted to man. It would have taken a century, he repeatedly said to himself and said also to Alice Staverton, it would have taken a longer absence and a more averted mind than those even of which he had been guilty, to pile up the differences, the newness, the queerness, above all the bignesses, for the better or the worse, that at present assaulted his vision wherever he looked.

The great fact all the while however had been the incalculability; since he *had* supposed himself, from decade to decade, to be allowing, and in the most liberal and intelligent manner, for brilliancy of change. He actually saw that he had allowed for nothing; he missed what he would have been sure of finding, he found what he would never have imagined. Proportions and values were upside-down; the ugly things he had expected, the ugly things of his far-away youth, when he had too promptly waked up to a sense of the ugly – these uncanny phenomena placed him rather, as it happened, under the charm; whereas the "swagger" things, the modern, the monstrous, the famous things, those he had more particularly, like thousands of ingenuous enquirers every year, come over to see, were exactly his sources of dismay. They were as so many set traps for displeasure, above all for reaction, of which his rest-less tread was constantly pressing the spring. It was interesting, doubtless, the whole show, but it would have been too disconcerting hadn't a certain finer truth saved the situation. He had distinctly not, in this steadier light, come over all for the monstrosities; he had come, not only in the last analysis but quite on the face of the act, under an impulse with which they had nothing to do. He had come – putting the thing pompously – to look at his "property", which he had thus for a third of a century not been within four thousand miles of; or, expressing it less sordidly, he had yielded to the humour of seeing again his house on the jolly corner, as he usually, and quite fondly, described it – the one in which he had first seen the light, in which various members of his family had lived and had died, in which the holidays of his overschooled boyhood had been passed and the few social flowers of his chilled adoles-cence gathered, and which, alienated then for so long a period, had, through the successive deaths of his two brothers and the termination of old arrangements, come wholly into his hands. He was the owner of another, not quite so "good" – the jolly corner having been, from far back, superlatively extended and consecrated; and the value of the pair represented his main capital, with an income consisting, in these later years, of their respective rents which (thanks precisely to their original excellent type) had never been depressingly low. He could live in "Europe", as he had been in the habit of living, on the product of these flourishing New York leases, and all the better since, that of the second structure, the mere numbers in its long row, having within a twelve-month fallen in, renovation at a high advance had proved beautifully possible.

These were items of property indeed, but he had found himself since his arrival distinguishing more than ever between them. The house within the street, two bristling blocks westward, was already in course of reconstruction as a tall mass of flats; he had acceded, some time before, to overtures for this conversion – in which, now that it was going forward, it had been not the least of his astonishment to find himself able, on the spot, and though without a previous ounce of such experience, to participate with a certain intelligence, almost with a certain authority. He had lived his life with his back so turned to such concerns and his face addressed to those of so different an order that he scarce knew what to make of this lively stir, in a compartment of his mind never yet penetrated, of a capacity for business and a sense for construction. These virtues, so common all round him now, had been dormant in his own organism – where it might be said of them perhaps that they had slept the sleep of the just. At present, in the splendid autumn weather – the autumn as least was a pure boon in the terrible place – he loafed about his "work" undeterred, secretly agitated; not in the least "minding" that the whole proposition, as they said, was vulgar and sordid, and ready to climb ladders, to walk the plank, to handle materials and look wise about them, to ask questions, in fine, and challenge explanations and really "go into" figures.

It amused, it verily quite charmed him; and, by the same stroke, it amused, and even more, Alice Staverton, though perhaps charming her perceptibly less. She wasn't however going to be better off for it, as *he* was – and so astonishingly much: nothing was now likely, he knew, even to make her better-off than she found herself, in the afternoon of life, as the delicately frugal possessor and tenant of the small house in Irving Place to which she had subtly managed to cling through her almost unbroken New York career. If he knew the way to it now better than to any other address among the dreadful multiplied numberings which seemed to him to reduce the whole place to some vast ledger-page, overgrown, fantastic, of ruled and criss-crossed lines and figures – if he had formed, for his consolation, that habit, it was really not a little because of the charm of his having encountered and recognized, in the vast wilderness of the wholesale, breaking through the mere gross generalization of wealth and force and success, a small still scene where items and shades, all delicate things, kept the sharpness of the notes of a high voice perfectly trained, and where economy hung about like the scent of a garden. His old friend lived with one maid and herself dusted her relics and trimmed her lamps and polished her silver; she stood off in the awful modern crush, when she could, but she sallied forth and did battle when the challenge was really to "spirit," the spirit she after all confessed to, proudly and a little shyly, as to that of the better time, that of *their* common, their quite far-away and antediluvian social period and order. She made use of the street-cars when need be, the terrible things that people scrambled for as the panic-stricken at sea scramble for the boats; she affronted, inscrutably, under stress, all the public concussions and ordeals; and yet, with that slim mystifying grace of her appearance, which defied you to say if she were a fair young woman who looked older through trouble, or a fine smooth older one who looked young through successful indifference; with her precious reference, above all, to memories and histories into which he could enter, she was as exquisite for him as some pale pressed flower (a rarity to begin with), and, failing other sweetnesses, she was a sufficient reward of his effort. They had communities of knowledge, "their" knowledge (this discriminating possessive was always on her lips) of presences of the other age, presences all overlaid, in his case, by the experience of a man and the freedom of a wanderer, overlaid by pleasure, by infidelity, by passages of life that were strange and dim to her, just by "Europe" in short, but still unobscured, still exposed and cherished, under that pious visitation of the spirit from which she had never been diverted.

She had come with him one day to see how his "apartment house" was rising; he had helped her over gaps and explained to her plans, and while they were there had happened to have, before her, a brief but lively discussion with the man in charge, the representative of the building-firm that had undertaken his work. He had found himself quite "standing-up" to this personage over a failure on the latter's part to observe some detail of one of their noted conditions, and had so lucidly argued his case that, besides ever so prettily flushing, at the time, for sympathy in his triumph, she had afterwards said to him (though to a slightly greater effect of irony) that he had clearly for too many years neglected a real gift. If he had but stayed at home he would have anticipated the inventor of the skyscraper. If he had but stayed at home he would have discovered his genius in time really to start some new variety of awful architectual hare and run it till it burrowed in a gold-mine. He was to remember these words, while the weeks elapsed, for the small silver ring they had sounded over the queerest and deepest of his own lately most disguised and most muffled vibrations.

It had begun to be present to him after the first fortnight, it had broken out with the oddest abruptness, this particular wanton wonderment; it met him there – and this was the image under which he himself judged the matter, or at least, not a little, thrilled and flushed with it – very much as he might have been met by some strange figure, some unexpected occupant, at a turn of one of the dim passages of an empty house. The quaint analogy quite hauntingly remained with him, when he didn't indeed rather improve it by a still intenser form: that of his opening a door behind which he would have made sure of finding nothing, a door into a room shuttered and void, and yet so coming, with a great suppressed start, on some quite erect confronting presence, sometimes planted in the middle of the place and facing him through the dusk. After that visit to the house in construction he walked with his companion to see the other and always so much the better one, which in the eastward direction formed one of the corners, the "jolly" one precisely, of the street now so generally dishonoured and disfigured in its westward reaches, and of the comparatively conservative Avenue. The Avenue still had pretensions, as Miss Staverton said, to decency; the old people had mostly gone, the old names were unknown, and here and there an old association seemed to stray, all vaguely, like some very aged person, out too late, whom you might meet and feel the impulse to watch or follow, in kindness, for safe restoration to shelter.

They went in together, our friends; he admitted himself with his key, as he kept no one there, he explained, preferring, for his reasons, to leave the place empty, under a simple arrangement with a good woman living in the neighbourhood and who came for a daily hour to open windows and dust and sweep. Spencer Brydon had his reasons and was growingly aware of them; they seemed to him better each time he was there, though he didn't name them all to his companion, any more than he told her as yet how often, how quite absurdly often, he himself came. He only let her see for the present, while they walked through the great blank rooms, that absolute vacancy reigned and that, from top to bottom, there was nothing but Mrs Muldoon's broomstick, in a corner, to tempt the burglar. Mrs Muldoon was then on the premises, and she loquaciously attended the visitors, preceding them from room to room and pushing back shutters and throwing up sashes – all to show them, as she remarked, how little there was to see. There was little indeed to see in the great gaunt shell where the main dispositions and the general apportion-ment of space, the style of and age of ampler allowances, had neverthe-less for its master their honest pleading message, affecting him as some good old servant's, some lifelong retainer's appeal for a character, or even for a retiring-pension; yet it was also a remark of Mrs Muldoon's that, glad as she was to oblige him by her noonday round, there was a request she greatly hoped he would never make of her. If he should wish her for any reason to come in after dark she would just tell him, if he "plased," that he must ask it of somebody else.

The fact that there was nothing to see didn't militate for the worthy woman against what one *might* see, and she put it frankly to Miss Staverton that no lady could be expected to like, could she? "scraping up to thim top storeys in the ayvil hours." The gas and electric light were off the house, and she fairly evoked a gruesome vision of her march through the great grey rooms – so many of them as there were too! – with her glimmering taper. Miss Staverton met her honest glare with a smile and the profession that she herself certainly would recoil from such an adven-ture. Spencer Brydon meanwhile held his peace – for the moment; the question of the "evil" hours in his old home had already become too grave for him. He had begun some time since to "crape," and he knew just why a packet of candles addressed to that pursuit had been stowed by his own hand, three weeks before, at the back of a drawer of the fine old sideboard that occupied, as a "fixture," the deep recess in the dining-room. Just now he laughed at his companions – quickly however changing the subject; for the reason that, in the first place, his laugh struck him even at that moment as starting the odd echo, the conscious human resonance (he scarce knew how to qualify it) that sounds made while he was there alone sent back to his ear or his fancy; and that, in the second, he imagined Alice Staverton for the instant on the point of asking him, with a divination, if he ever so prowled. There were divinations he was unprepared for, and he had at all events averted enquiry by the time Mrs Muldoon had left them, passing on to other parts.

There was happily enough to say, on so consecrated a spot, that could be said freely and fairly; so that a whole train of declarations was precipitated by his friend's having herself broken out, after a yearning look round: "But I hope you don't mean they want you to pull *this* to pieces!" His answer came, promptly, with his re-awakened wrath: it was of course exactly what they wanted, and what they were "at" him for, daily, with the iteration of people who couldn't for their life understand a man's liability to decent feelings. He had found the place, just as it stood and beyond what he could express, an interest and a joy. There were values other than the beastly rent-values, and in short, in short – ! But it was thus Miss Staverton took him up. "In short you're to make so good a thing of your sky-scraper that, living in luxury on *those* ill-gotten gains, you can afford for a while to be sentimental here!" Her smile had for him, with the words, the particular mild irony with which he found half her talk suffused; an irony without bitterness and that came exactly, from her having so much imagination – not, like the cheap sarcasm with which one heard most people, about the world of "society," bid for the reputation of cleverness, from nobody's really having any. It was agreeable to him at this very moment to be sure that when he had answered, after a brief demur, "Well yes: so, precisely, you may put it!" her imagination would still do him justice. He explained that even if never a dollar were to come to him from the other house he would nevertheless cherish this one; and he dwelt, further, while they lingered and wandered, on the fact of the stupefaction he was already exciting, the positive mystification he felt himself create.

He spoke of the value of all he read into it, into the mere sight of the walls, mere shapes of the rooms, mere sound of the floors, mere feel, in his hand, of the old silver-plated knobs of the several mahogany doors, which suggested the pressure of the palms of the dead; the seventy years of the past in fine that these things represented, the annals of nearly three generations, counting his grandfather's, the one that had ended there, and the impalpable ashes of his long-extinct youth, afloat in the very air like microscopic motes. She listened to everything; she was a woman who answered intimately but who utterly didn't chatter. She scattered abroad therefore no cloud of words; she could assent, she could agree, above all she could encourage, without doing that. Only at the last she went a little further than he had done himself. "And then how do you know? You may still, after all, want to live here." It rather indeed pulled him up, for it wasn't what he had been thinking, at least in her sense of the words. "You mean I may decide to stay on for the sake of it?"

"Well, *with* such a home – !" But, quite beautifully, she had too much tact to dot so monstrous an *i*, and it was precisely an illustration of the way she didn't rattle. How could any one – of any wit – insist on anyone else's "wanting" to live in New York?

"Oh," he said, "I *might* have lived here (since I had my opportunity early in life); I might have put in here all these years. Then everything would have been different enough – and, I dare say, 'funny' enough. But that's another matter. And then the beauty of it – I mean of my perversity, of my refusal to agree to a 'deal' – is just in the total absence of a reason. Don't you see that if I had a reason about the matter at all it would have to be the other way, and would then be inevitably a reason of dollars? There are no reasons here but of dollars. Let us therefore have none whatever – not the ghost of one."

They were back in the hall then for departure, but from where they stood the vista was large, through an open door, into the great square main saloon, with its almost antique felicity of brave spaces between windows. Her eyes came back from that reach and met his own a moment. "Are you very sure the 'ghost' of one doesn't, much rather, serve – ?"

He had a positive sense of turning pale. But it was as near as they were then to come. For he made answer, he believed, between a glare and a grin: "Oh ghosts – of course the place must swarm with them! I should be ashamed of it if it didn't. Poor Mrs Muldoon's right, and it's why I haven't asked her to do more than look in."

Miss Staverton's gaze again lost itself, and things she didn't utter, it was clear, came and went in her mind. She might even for the minute, off there in the fine room, have imagined some element dimly gathering. Simplified like the death-mask of a handsome face, it perhaps produced for her just then an effect akin to the stir of an expression in the "set" commemorative plaster. Yet whatever her impression may have been she produced instead a vague platitude. "Well, if it were only furnished and lived in – !"

She appeared to imply that in case of its being still furnished he might have been a little less opposed to the idea of a return. But she passed straight into the vestibule, as if to leave her words behind her, and the next moment he had opened the house-door and was standing with her on the steps. He closed the door and, while he re-pocketed his key, looking up and down, they took in the comparatively harsh actuality of the Avenue, which reminded him of the assault of the outer light of the Desert on the traveller emerging from an Egyptian tomb. But he risked before they stepped into the street his gathered answer to her speech. "For me it is lived in. For me it is furnished." At which it was easy for her to sigh "Ah yes – !" all vaguely and discreetly; since his parents and his favourite sister, to say nothing of other kin, in numbers, had run their course and met their end there. That represented, within the walls, ineffaceable life.

It was a few days after that, during an hour passed with her again, he had expressed his impatience of the too flattering curiosity – among the people he met – about his appreciation of New York. He had arrived at none at all that was socially producible, and as for that matter of his "thinking" (thinking the better or the worse of anything there) he was wholly taken up with one subject of thought. It was mere vain egoism, and it was moreover, if she liked a morbid obsession. He found all things come back to the question of what he personally might have been, how he might have led his life and "turned out," if he had not so, at the outset, given it up. And confessing for the first time to the intensity within him of this absurd speculation – which but proved also, no doubt, the habit of too selfishly thinking – he affirmed the impotence there of any other source of interest, any other native appeal. "What would it have made of me, what would it have made of me? I keep for ever wondering, all idiotically; as if I could possibly know! I see what it has made of dozens of others, those I meet, and it positively aches within me, to the point of exasperation, that it would have made something of me as well. Only I can't make out *what*, and the worry of it, the small rage of curiosity never to be satisfied, brings back what I remember to have felt, once or twice, after judging best, for reasons, to burn some important letter unopened. I've been sorry, I've hated it – I've never known what was in the letter. You may of course say it's a trifle – !"

"I don't say it's a trifle," Miss Staverton gravely interrupted.

She was seated by her fire, and before her, on his feet and restless, he turned to and fro between this intensity of his idea and a fitful and unseeing inspection, through his single eye-glass, of the dear little old objects on her chimney-piece. Her interruption made him for an instant look at her harder. "I shouldn't care if you did!" he laughed, however;

"and it's only a figure, at any rate, for the way I now feel. *Not* to have followed my perverse young course – and almost in the teeth of my father's curse, as I may say; not to have kept it up, so, 'over there' from that day to this, without a doubt or a pang; not, above all, to have liked it, to have loved it, so much, loved it, no doubt, with such an abysmal conceit of my own preference: some variation from *that*, I say, must have produced some different effect for my life and for my 'form.' I should have stuck here – if it had been possible; and I was too young, at twenty-three, to judge, *pour deux sous*, whether it *were* possible. If I had waited I might have seen it was, and then I might have been, by staying here, something nearer to one of these types who have been hammered so hard and made so keen by their conditions. It isn't that I admire them so much – the question of any charm in them, or of any charm, beyond that of the rank money-passion, exerted by their conditions *for* them, has nothing to do with the matter; it's only a question of what fantastic, yet perfectly possible, development of my own nature I mayn't have missed. It comes over me that I had then a strange *alter ego* deep down somewhere within me, as the full-blown flower is in the small tight bud, and that I just took the course, I just transferred him to the climate, that blighted him for once and for ever."

"And you wonder about the flower," Miss Staverton said. "So do I, if you want to know; and so I've been wondering these several weeks. I believe in the flower," she continued, "I felt it would have been quite splendid, quite huge and monstrous."

"Monstrous above all!" her visitor echoed; "and I imagine, by the same stroke, quite hideous and offensive."

"You don't believe that," she returned; "if you did you wouldn't wonder. You'd know, and that would be enough for you. What you feel – and what I feel for you – is that you'd have had power."

"You'd have liked me that way?" he asked.

She barely hung fire. "How should I not have liked you?"

"I see. You'd have liked me, have preferred me, a billionaire!"

"How should I not have liked you?" she simply again asked.

He stood before her still – her question kept him motionless. He took it in, so much there was of it; and indeed his not otherwise meeting it testified to that. "I know at least what I am," he simply went on; "the other side of the medal's clear enough. I've not been edifying – I believe I'm thought in a hundred quarters to have been barely decent. I've followed strange paths and worshipped strange gods; it must have come to you again and again – in fact you've admitted to me as much – that I was leading, at any time these thirty years, a selfish frivolous scandalous life. And you see what it has made of me."

She just waited, smiling at him. "You see what it has made of *me*."

"Oh you're a person whom nothing can have altered. You were born to be what you are, anywhere, anyway; you've the perfection nothing else could have blighted. And don't you see how, without my exile, I shouldn't have been waiting till now – ?" But he pulled up for the strange pang.

"The great thing to see," she presently said, "seems to me to be that it has spoiled nothing. It hasn't spoiled your being here at last. It hasn't spoiled this. It hasn't spoiled your speaking – " She also however faltered.

He wondered at everything her controlled emotion might mean. "Do you believe then – too dreadfully! – that I am as good as I might ever have been?"

"Oh no! Far from it!" With which she got up from her chair and was nearer to him. "But I don't care," she smiled.

"You mean I'm good enough?"

She considered a little. "Will you believe it if I say so? I mean will you let that settle your question for you?" And then as if making out in his face that he drew back from this, that he had some idea which, however absurd, he couldn't yet bargain away: "Oh you don't care either – but very differently: you don't care for anything but yourself."

Spencer Brydon recognized it – it was in fact what he had absolutely professed. Yet he importantly qualified. "*He* isn't myself. He's the just so totally other person. But I do want to see him," he added. "And I can. And I shall."

Their eyes met for a minute while he guessed from something in hers that she divined his strange sense. But neither of them otherwise expressed it, and her apparent understanding, with no protesting shock, no easy derision, touched him more deeply than anything yet, constituting for his stifled perversity, on the spot, an element that was like breathable air. What she said however was unexpected. "Well, *I've* seen him."

"You – ?"

'I've seen him in a dream."

"Oh a 'dream' – !" It let him down.

"But twice over," she continued. "I saw him as I see you now."

"You've dreamed the same dream – ?"

"Twice over," she repeated. "The very same."

This did somehow a little speak to him, as it also gratified him. "You dream about me at that rate?"

"Ah about *him*!" she smiled.

His eyes again sounded her. "Then you know all about him." And as she said nothing more: "What's the wretch like?"

She hesitated, and it was as if he were pressing her so hard that, resisting for reasons of her own, she had to turn away. "I'll tell you some other time!"

II

It was after this that there was most of a virtue for him, most of a cultivated charm, most of a preposterous secret thrill, in the particular form of surrender to his obsession and of address to what he more and more believed to be his privilege. It was what in these weeks he was living for – since he really felt life to begin but after Mrs Muldoon had retired from the scene and, visiting the ample house from attic to cellar, making sure he was alone, he knew himself in safe possession and, as he tacitly expressed it, let himself go. He sometimes came twice in the twenty-four hours; the moments he liked best were those of gathering dusk, of the short autumn twilight; this was the time of which, again and again, he found himself hoping most. Then he could, as seemed to him, most intimately wander and wait, linger and listen, feel his fine attention, never in his life before so fine, on the pulse of the great vague place: he preferred the lampless hour and only wished he might have prolonged each day the deep crepuscular spell. Later – rarely much before midnight, but then for a considerable vigil – he watched with his glimmering light; moving slowly, holding it high, playing it far, rejoicing above all, as much as he might, in open vistas, reaches of communication between rooms and by passages; the long straight chance or show, as he would have called it, for the revelation he pretended to invite. It was a practice he found he could perfectly "work" without exciting remark; no one was in the least the wiser for it; even Alice Staverton, who was moreover a well of discretion, didn't quite fully imagine.

He let himself in and let himself out with the assurance of calm proprietorship; and accident so far favoured him that, if a fat Avenue "officer" had happened on occasion to see him entering at eleven-thirty, he had never yet, to the best of his belief, been noticed as emerging at two. He walked there on the crisp November nights, arrived regularly at the evening's end; it was as easy to do this after dining out as to take his way to a club or to his hotel. When he left his club, if he hadn't been dining out, it was ostensibly to go to his hotel; and when he left his hotel, if he had spent a part of the evening there, it was ostensibly to go to his club. Everything was easy in fine: everything conspired and promoted: there was truly even in the strain of his experience something that glossed over, something that salved and simplified, all the rests of consciousness. He circulated, talked, renewed, loosely and pleasantly, old relations – met indeed, so far as he could, new expectations and seemed to make out on the whole that in spite of the career, of such different contacts, which he had spoken of to Miss Staverton as ministering so little, for those who might have watched it, to edification, he was positively rather liked than not. He was a dim secondary social success – and all with people who had truly not an idea of him. It was all mere surface sound, this murmur of their welcome, this popping of their corks – just as his gestures of response were the extravagant shadows, emphatic in proportion as they meant little, of some game of *ombres chinoises*. He projected himself all day, in thought, straight over the bristling line of hard unconscious heads and into the other, the real, the waiting life; the life that, as soon as he had heard behind him the click of his great house-door, began for him, on the jolly corner, as beguilingly as the slow opening bars of some rich music follows the tap of the conductor's wand.

He always caught the first effect of the steel point of his stick on the old marble of the hall pavement, large black-and-white squares that he remembered as the admiration of his childhood and that had then made in him, as he now saw, for the growth of an early conception of style. This effect was the dim reverberating tinkle as of some far-off bell hung who should say where? – in the depths of the house, of the past, of that mystical other world that might have flourished for him had he not, for weal or woe, abandoned it. On this impression he did ever the same thing; he put his stick noiselessly away in a corner – feeling the place once more in the likeness of some great glass bowl, all precious concave crystal, set delicately humming by the play of a moist finger round its edge. The concave crystal held, as it were, this mystical other world, and the indescribably fine murmur of its rim was the sigh there, the scarce audible pathetic wail to his trained ear, of all the old baffled forsworn possibilities. What he did therefore by this appeal of his hushed presence was to wake them into such measure of ghostly life as they might still enjoy. They were shy, all but unappeasably shy, but they weren't really sinister; at least they weren't as he had hitherto felt them – before they had taken the Form he so yearned to make them take, the Form he at moments saw himself in the light of fairly hunting on tiptoe, the points of his evening-shoes, from room to room and from storey to storey.

That was the essence of his vision – which was all rank folly, if one would, while he was out of the house and otherwise occupied, but which took on the last verisimilitude as soon as he was placed and posted. He knew what he meant and what he wanted; it was as clear as the figure on a cheque presented in demand for cash. His *alter ego* "walked" – that was the note of his image of him, while his image of his motive for his own odd pastime was the desire to waylay him and meet him. He roamed, slowly, warily, but all restlessly, he himself did – Mrs Muldoon had been right, absolutely, with her figure of their "craping"; and the presence he watched for would roam restlessly too. But it would be as cautious and as shifty; the conviction of its probable, in fact its already quite sensible, quite audible evasion of pursuit grew for him from night to night, laying on him finally a rigour to which nothing in his life had been comparable. It had been the theory of many superficially-judging persons, he knew, that he was wasting that life in a surrender to sensations, but he had tasted of no pleasure so fine as his actual tension, had been introduced to no sport that demanded at once the patience and the nerve of this stalking of a creature more subtle, yet at bay perhaps more formidable, than any beast of the forest. The terms, the comparisons, the very practices of the chase positively came again into play; there were even moments when passages of his occasional experience as a sportsman, stirred memories, from his younger time, of moor and mountain and desert, revived for him – and to the increase of his keenness – by the tremendous force of analogy. He found himself at moments – once he had placed his single light on some mantel-shelf or in some recess – stepping back into shelter or shade, effacing himself behind a door or in an embrasure, as he had sought of old the vantage of rock and tree; he found himself holding his breath and living in the joy of an instant, the supreme suspense created by big game alone.

He wasn't afraid (though putting himself the question as he believed gentlemen on Bengal tiger-shoots or in close quarters with the great bear of the Rockies had been known to confess to having put it); and this indeed – since here at least he might be frank! – because of the impression, so intimate and so strange, that he himself produced as yet a dread, produced certainly a strain, beyond the liveliest he was likely to feel. They fell for him into categories, they fairly became familiar, the signs for his own perception, of the alarm his presence and his vigilance created; though leaving him always to remark, portentously, on his probably having formed a relation, his probably enjoying a consciousness, unique in the experience of man. People enough, first and last, had been in terror of apparitions, but who had ever before so turned the tables and become himself, in the apparitional world, an incalculable terror? He might have found this sublime had he quite dared to think of it; but he didn't too much insist, truly, on that side of his privilege. With habit and repetition he gained to an extraordinary degree the power to penetrate the dusk of distances and the darkness of corners, to resolve back into their innocence the treacheries of uncertain light, the evil-looking forms taken in the gloom by mere shadows, by accidents of the air, by shifting effects of perspective; putting down his dim luminary he could still wander on without it, pass into other rooms and, only knowing it was there behind him in case of need, see his way about, visually project for his purpose a comparative clearness. It made him feel, this acquired faculty, like some monstrous stealthy cat; he wondered if he would have glared at these moments with large shining yellow eyes, and what it mightn't verily be, for the poor hard-pressed *alter ego*, to be confronted with such a type.

He liked however the open shutters; he opened everywhere those Mrs Muldoon had closed, closing them as carefully afterwards, so that she shouldn't notice: he liked – oh this he did like, and above all in the upper rooms! – the sense of the hard silver of the autumn stars through the window-panes, and scarcely less the flare of the street-lamps below, the white electric lustre which it would have taken to keep out. This was human actual social; this was of the world he had lived in, and he was more at his ease certainly for the countenance, coldly general and impersonal, that all the while and in spite of his detachment it seemed to give him. He had support of course mostly in the rooms at the wide front and the prolonged side; it failed him considerably in the central shades and the parts at the back. But if he sometimes, on his rounds, was glad of his optical reach, so none the less often the rear of the house affected him as the very jungle of his prey. The place was there more subdivided; a large "extension" in particular, where small rooms for servants had been multiplied, abounded in nooks and corners, in closets and passages, in the ramifications especially of an ample back staircase over which he leaned, many a time, to look far down – not deterred from his gravity even while aware that he might, for a spectator, have figured some solemn simpleton playing at hide-and-seek. Outside in fact he might himself make that ironic rapprochement; but within the walls, and in spite of the clear windows, his consistency was proof against the cynical light of New York.

It had belonged to that idea of the exasperated consciousness of his victim to become a real test for him; since he had quite put it to himself from the first that, oh distinctly! he could "cultivate" his whole perception. He had felt it as above all open to cultivation – which indeed was but another name for his manner of spending his time. He was bringing it on, bringing it to perfection, by practice; in consequence of which it had grown so fine that he was now aware of impressions, attestations of his general postulate, that couldn't have broken upon him at once. This was the case more specifically with a phenomenon at last quite frequent for him in the upper rooms, the recognition – absolutely unmistakable, and by a turn dating from a particular hour, his resumption of his campaign after a diplomatic drop, a calculated absence of three nights – of his being definitely followed, tracked at a distance carefully taken and to the express end that he should the less confidently, less arrogantly, appear to himself merely to pursue. It worried, it finally quite broke him up, for it proved, of all the conceivable impressions, the one least suited to his book. He was kept in sight while remaining himself – as regards the essence of his position – sightless, and his only recourse then was in abrupt turns, rapid recoveries of ground. He wheeled about, retracing his steps, as if he might so catch in his face at least the stirred air of some other quick revolution. It was indeed true that his fully dislocalized thought of these manoeuvres recalled to him Pantaloon, at the Christmas farce, buffeted and tricked from behind by ubiquitous Harlequin; but it left intact the influence of the conditions themselves each time he was re-exposed to them, so that in fact this association, had he suffered it to become constant, would on a certain side have but ministered to his intenser gravity. He had made, as I have said, to create on the premises the baseless sense of a reprieve, his three absences; and the result of the third was to confirm the after-effect of the second.

On his return, that night – the night succeeding his last intermission –

he stood in the hall and looked up the staircase with a certainty more intimate than any he had yet known. "He's *there*, at the top, and waiting – not, as in general, falling back for disappearance. He's holding his ground, and it's the first time – which is a proof, isn't it? that something has happened for him." So Brydon argued with his hand on the banister and his foot on the lowest stair; in which position he felt as never before the air chilled by his logic. He himself turned cold in it, for he seemed of a sudden to know what now was involved. "Harder pressed? – yes, he takes it in, with its thus making clear to him that I've come, as they say, 'to stay.' He finally doesn't like and can't bear it, in the sense, I mean, that his wrath, his menaced interest, now balances with his dread. I've hunted him till he has 'turned': that, up there, is what has happened – he's the fanged or the antlered animal brought at last to bay." There came to him, as I say – but determined by an influence beyond my notation! – the acuteness of this certainty; under which however the next moment he had broken into a sweat that he would as little have consented to attribute to fear as he would have dared immediately to act upon it for enterprise. It marked none the less a prodigious thrill, a thrill that represented sudden dismay, no doubt, but also represented, and with the self-same throb, the strangest, the most joyous, possibly the next minute almost the proudest, duplication of consciousness.

"He has been dodging, retreating, hiding, but now, worked up to anger, he'll fight!" – this intense impression made a single mouthful, as it were, of terror and applause. But what was wondrous was that the applause, for the felt fact, was so eager, since, if it was his other self he was running to earth, this ineffable identity was thus in the last resort not unworthy of him. It bristled there – somewhere near at hand, however unseen still – as the hunted thing, even as the trodden worm of the adage *must* at last bristle; and Brydon at this instant tasted probably of a sensation more complex than had ever before found itself consistent with sanity. It was as if it would have shamed him that a character so associated with his own should triumphantly succeed in just skulking, should to the end not risk the open, so that the drop of this danger was, on the spot, a great lift of the whole situation. Yet with another rare shift of the same subtlety he was already trying to measure by how much more he himself might now be in peril of fear; so rejoicing that he could, in another form, actively inspire that fear, and simultaneously quaking for the form in which he might passively know it.

The apprehension of knowing it must after a little have grown in him,

and the strangest moment of his adventure perhaps, the most memorable
or really most interesting, afterwards, of his crisis, was the lapse of certain
instants of concentrated conscious *combat*, the sense of a need to hold on
to something, even after the manner of a man slipping and slipping on
some awful incline; the vivid impulse, above all, to move, to act, to
charge, somehow and upon something – to show himself, in a word, that
he wasn't afraid. The state of "holding-on" was thus the state to which he
was momentarily reduced; if there had been anything, in the great
vacancy, to seize, he would presently have been aware of having clutched
it as he might under a shock at home have clutched the nearest chair-
back. He had been surprised at any rate – of this he was aware – into
something unprecedented since his original appropriation of the place;
he had closed his eyes, held them tight, for a long minute, as with that
instinct of dismay and that terror of vision. When he opened them the
room, the other contiguous rooms, extraordinarily, seemed lighter – so
light, almost, that at first he took the change for day. He stood firm,
however that might be, just where he had paused; his resistance had
helped him – it was as if there were something he had tided over. He
knew after a little what this was – it had been in the imminent danger of
flight. He had stiffened his will against going: without this he would have
made for the stairs, and it seemed to him that, still with his eyes closed, he
would have descended them, would have known how, straight and
swiftly, to the bottom.

Well, as he had held out, here he was – still at the top, among the more
intricate upper rooms and with the gauntlet of the others, of all the rest of
the house, still to run when it should be his time to go. He would go at his
time – only at his time; didn't he go every night very much at the same
hour? He took out his watch – there was light for that; it was scarcely a
quarter past one, and he had never withdrawn so soon. He reached his
lodgings for the most part at two – with his walk of a quarter of an hour.
He would wait for the last quarter – he wouldn't stir till then; and he kept
his watch there with his eyes on it, reflecting while he held it that this
deliberate wait, a wait with an effort which he recognized, would serve
perfectly for the attestation he desired to make. It would prove by his
budging at last from his place. What he mainly felt now was that, since he
hadn't originally scuttled, he had his dignities – which had never in his
life seemed so many – all to preserve and to carry aloft. This was before
him in truth as a physical image, an image almost worthy of an age of
greater romance. That remark indeed glimmered for him only to glow

the next instant with a finer light; since what age of romance, after all, could have matched either the state of his mind or, "objectively," as they said, the wonder of his situation? The only difference would have been that, brandishing his dignities over his head as in a parchment scroll, he might then – that is in the heroic time – have proceeded downstairs with a drawn sword in his other grasp.

At present, really, the light he had set down on the mantel of the next room would have to figure his sword; which utensil, in the course of a minute, he had taken the requisite number of steps to possess him self of. The door between the rooms was open, and from the second another door opened to a third. These rooms, as he remembered, gave all three upon a common corridor as well, but there was a fourth, beyond them, without issue save through the preceding. To have moved, to have heard his step again, was appreciably a help; though even in recognizing this he lingered once more a little by the chimney-piece on which his light had rested. When he next moved, just hesitating where to turn, he found himself considering a circumstance that, after his first and comparatively vague apprehension of it, produced in him the start that often attends some pang of recollection, the violent shock of having ceased happily to forget. He had come into sight of the door in which the brief chain of communication ended and which he now surveyed from the nearer threshold, the one not directly facing it. Placed at some distance to the left of this point, it would have admitted him to the last room of the four, the room without other approach or egress, had it not, to his intimate conviction been closed *since* his former visitation, the matter probably of a quarter of an hour before. He stared with all his eyes at the wonder of the fact, arrested again where he stood and again holding his breath while he sounded its sense. Surely it had been *subsequently* closed – that is it had been on his previous passage indubitably open!

He took it full in the face that something had happened between – that he couldn't not have noticed before (by which he meant on his original tour of all the rooms that evening) that such a barrier had exceptionally presented itself. He had indeed since that moment undergone an agitation so extraordinary that it might have muddled for him any earlier view; and he tried to convince himself that he might perhaps then have gone into the room and, inadvertently, automatically, on coming out, have drawn the door after him. The difficulty was that this exactly was what he never did; it was against his whole policy, as he might have said, the essence of which was to keep vistas clear. He had them from the first,

as he was well aware, quite on the brain: the strange apparition, at the far
end of one of them, of his baffled "prey" (which had become by so sharp
an irony so little the term now to apply!) was the form of success his imagination had most cherished, projecting into it always a refinement of
beauty. He had known fifty times the start of perception that had afterwards dropped; had fifty times gasped to himself "There!" under some
fond brief hallucination. The house, as the case stood, admirably lent
itself; he might wonder at the taste, the native architecture of the particular time, which could rejoice so in the multiplication of doors – the
opposite extreme to the modern, the actual almost complete proscription
of them; but it had fairly contributed to provoke this obsession of the
presence encountered telescopically, as he might say, focussed and
studied in diminishing perspective and as by a rest for the elbow.

It was with these considerations that his present attention was charged
– they perfectly availed to make what he saw portentous. He *couldn't*, by
any lapse, have blocked that aperture; and if he hadn't, if it was unthink-
able, why what else was clear but that there had been another agent?
Another agent? – he had been catching, as he felt, a moment back, the
very breath of him; but when had he been so close as in this simple, this
logical, this completely personal act? It was so logical, that is, that one
might have *taken* it for personal; yet for what did Brydon take it, he asked
himself, while, softly panting, he felt his eyes almost leave their sockets.
At this time at last they were, the two, the opposed projections of him, in
presence; and this time, as much as one would, the question of danger
loomed. With it rose, as not before, the question of courage – for what he
knew the blank face of the door to say to him was "Show us how much
you have!" It stared, it glared back at him with that challenge; it put to
him the two alternatives; should he just push it open or not? Oh to have
this consciousness was to *think* – and to think, Brydon knew, as he stood
there, was, with the lapsing moments, not to have acted! Not to have
acted! – that was the misery and the pang – was even still not to act; was
in fact *all* to feel the thing in another, in a new and terrible way. How
long did he pause and how long did he debate? There was presently
nothing to measure it; for his vibration had already changed – as just by
the effect of its intensity. Shut up there, at bay, defiant, and with the
prodigy of the thing palpably proveably *done*, thus giving notice like some
stark sign-board – under that accession of accent the situation itself had
turned; and Brydon at last remarkably made up his mind on what it had
turned to.

It had turned altogether to a different admonition; to a supreme hint, for him, of the value of Discretion! This slowly dawned, no doubt – for it could take its time; so perfectly, on his threshold, had he been stayed, so little as yet had he either advanced or retreated. It was the strangest of all things that now when, by his taking ten steps and applying his hand to a latch, or even his shoulder and his knee, if necessary, to a panel, all the hunger of his prime need might have been met, his high curiosity crowned, his unrest assuaged – it was amazing, but it was also exquisite and rare, that insistence should have, at a touch, quite dropped from him. Discretion – he jumped at that; and yet not, verily, at such a pitch, because it saved his nerves or his skin, but because, much more valuably, it saved the situation. When I say he "jumped" at it I feel the consonance of this term with the fact that – at the end indeed of I know not how long – he did move again, he crossed straight to the door. He wouldn't touch it – it seemed now that he might *if* he would: he would only just wait there a little, to show, to prove, that he wouldn't. He had thus another station, close to the thin partition by which revelation was denied him; but with his eyes bent and his hands held off in a mere intensity of still-ness. He listened as if there had been something to hear, but this attitude, while it lasted, was his own communication. "If you won't then – good; I spare you and I give up. You affect me as by the appeal positively for pity; you convince me that for reasons rigid and sublime – what do I know? – we both of us should have suffered. I respect them then, and, though moved and privileged as, I believe, it has never been given to man, I retire, I renounce – never, on my honour, to try again. So rest for ever – and let *me*!"

That, for Brydon was the deep sense of his last demonstration – solemn, measured, directed, as he felt it to be. He brought it to a close, he turned away; and now verily he knew how deeply he had been stirred. He retraced his steps, taking up his candle, burnt, he observed, well-nigh to the socket, and marking again, lighten it as he would, the distinctness of his football; after which, in a moment, he knew himself at the other side of the house. He did here what he had not yet done at these hours – he opened half a casement, one of those in the front, and let in the air of the night; a thing he would have taken at any time previous for a sharp rupture of his spell. His spell was broken now, and it didn't matter – broken by his concession and his surrender, which made it idle hence-forth that he should ever come back. The empty street – its other life so marked even the great lamplit vacancy – was within call, within touch;

he stayed there as to be in it again, high above it though he was still perched; he watched as for some comforting common fact, some vulgar human note, the passage of a scavenger or a thief, some night-bird however base. He would have blessed that sign of life; he would have welcomed positively the slow approach of his friend the policeman, whom he had hitherto only sought to avoid, and was not sure that if the patrol had come into sight he mightn't have felt the impulse to get into relation with it, to hail it, on some pretext, from his fourth floor.

The pretext that wouldn't have been too silly or too compromising, the explanation that would have saved his dignity and kept his name, in such a case, out of the papers, was not definite to him: he was so occupied with the thought of recording his Discretion – as an effect of the vow he had just uttered to his intimate adversary – that the importance of this loomed large and something had overtaken all ironically his sense of proportion. If there had been a ladder applied to the front of the house, even one of the vertiginous perpendiculars employed by painters and roofers and sometimes left standing overnight, he would have managed somehow, astride of the window-sill, to compass by outstretched leg and arm that mode of descent. If there had been some such uncanny thing as he had found in his room at hotels, a workable fire-escape in the form of notched cable or a canvas shoot, he would have availed himself of it as a proof – well, of his present delicacy. He nursed that sentiment, as the question stood, a little in vain, and even – at the end of he scarce knew, once more, how long – found it, as by the action on his mind of the failure of response of the outer world, sinking back to vague anguish. It seemed to him he had waited an age for some stir of the great grim hush; the lie of the town was itself under a spell – so unnaturally, up and down the whole prospect of known and rather ugly objects, the blankness and the silence lasted. Had they ever, he asked himself, the hard-faced houses, which had begun to look livid in the dim dawn, had they ever spoken so little to any need of his spirit? Great builded voids, great crowded stillnesses put on, often, in the heart of cities, for the small hours, a sort of sinister mask, and it was of this large collective negation that Brydon presently became conscious – all the more that the break of day was, almost incredibly, now at hand, proving to him what a night he had made of it.

He looked again at his watch, saw what had become of his time-values (he had taken hours for minutes – not, as in other tense situations, minutes for hours) and the strange air of the streets was but the weak, the

sullen flush of a dawn in which everything was still locked up. His choked
appeal from his own open window had been the sole note of life, and he
could but break off at last as for a worse despair. Yet while so deeply
demoralized he was capable again of an impulse denoting – at least by
his present measure – extraordinary resolution; of retracing his steps to
the spot where he had turned cold with the extinction of his last pulse of
doubt as to there being in the place another presence than his own. This
required an effort strong enough to sicken him; but he had his reason,
which over-mastered for the moment everything else. There was the
whole of the rest of the house to traverse, and how should he screw
himself to that if the door he had seen closed were at present open? He
could hold to the idea that the closing had practically been for him an act
of mercy, a chance offered him to descend, depart, get off the ground
and never again profane it. This conception held together, it worked; but
what it meant for him depended now clearly on the amount of forbear-
ance his recent action, or rather his recent inaction, had engendered.
The image of the "presence," whatever it was, waiting there for him to
go – this image had not yet been so concrete for his nerves as when he
stopped short of the point at which certainty would have come to him.
For, with all his resolution, or more exactly with all his dread, he did stop
short – he hung back from really seeing. The risk was too great and his
fear too definite; it took at this moment an awful specific form.

He knew – yes, as he had never known anything – that, *should* he see
the door open, it would all too abjectly be the end of him. It would mean
that the agent of his shame – for his shame was the deep abjection – was
once more at large and in general possession; and what glared him thus in
the face was the act that this would determine for him. It would send him
straight about to the window he had left open, and by that window, be
long ladder and dangling rope as absent as they would, he saw himself
uncontrollably insanely fatally take his way to the street. The hideous
chance of this he at least could avert; but he could only avert it by
recoiling in time from assurance. He had the whole house to deal with,
this fact was still there; only he now knew that uncertainty alone could
start him. He stole back from where he had checked himself – merely to
do so was suddenly like safety – and, making blindly for the greater staircase, left gaping rooms and sounding passages behind. Here was the top
of the stairs, with a fine large dim descent and three spacious landings to
mark off. His instinct was all for mildness, but his feet were harsh on the
floors, and, strangely, when he had in a couple of minutes become aware

of this, it counted somehow for help. He couldn't have spoken, the tone of his voice would have scared him, and the common conceit or resource of "whistling in the dark" (whether literally or figuratively) have appeared basely vulgar; yet he liked none the less to hear himself go, and when he had reached his first landing – taking it all with no rush, but quite steadily – that stage of success drew from him a gasp of relief.

The house, withal, seemed immense, the scale of space again inordinate; the open rooms, to no one of which his eyes deflected, gloomed in their shuttered state like mouths of caverns; only the skylight that formed the crown of the deep well created for him a medium in which he could advance, but which might have been, for queerness of colour, some watery under-world. He tried to think of something noble, as that his property was really grand, a splendid possession; but this nobleness took the form too of the clear delight with which he was finally to sacrifice it. They might come in now, the builders, the destroyers – they might come as soon as they would. At the end of two flights he had dropped to another zone, and from the middle of the third, with only one more left, he recognized the influence of the lower windows, of half-drawn blinds, of the occasional gleam of street-lamps, of the glazed spaces of the vestibule. This was the bottom of the sea, which showed an illumination of its own and which he even saw paved – when at a given moment he drew up to sink a long look over the banisters – with the marble squares of his childhood. By that time indubitably he felt, as he might have said in a commoner cause, better; it had allowed him to stop and draw breath, and the ease increased with the sight of the old black-and-white slabs. But what he most felt was that now surely, with the element of impunity pulling him as by hard firm hands, the case was settled for what he might have seen above had he dared that last look. The closed door, blessedly remote now, was still closed – and he had only in short to reach that of the house.

He came down further, he crossed the passage forming the access to the last flight; and if here again he stopped an instant it was almost for the sharpness of the thrill of assured escape. It made him shut his eyes – which opened again to the straight slope of the remainder of the stairs. Here was impunity still, but impunity almost excessive; inasmuch as the side-lights and the high fan-tracery of the entrance were glimmering straight into the hall; an appearance produced, he the next instant saw, by the fact that the vestibule gaped wide, that the hinged halves of the inner door had been thrown far back. Out of that again the *question* sprang at him, making his eyes, as he felt, half-start from his head, as they had done, at the top of the house, before the sign of the other door. If he had left that one open, hadn't he left this one closed, and wasn't he now in *most* immediate presence of some inconceivable occult activity? It was as sharp, the question, as a knife in his side, but the answer hung fire still and seemed to lose itself in the vague darkness to which the thin admitted dawn, glimmering archwise over the whole outer door, made a semicircular margin, a cold silvery nimbus that seemed to play a little as he looked – to shift and expand and contract.

It was as if there had been something within it, protected by indistinctness and corresponding in extent with the opaque surface behind, the painted panels of the last barrier to his escape, of which the key was in his pocket. The indistinctness mocked him even while he stared, affected him as somehow shrouding or challenging certitude, so that after faltering an instant on his step he let himself go with the sense that here was at last something to meet, to touch, to take, to know – something all unnatural and dreadful, but to advance upon which was the condition for him either of liberation or of supreme defeat. The penumbra, dense and dark, was the virtual screen of a figure which stood in it as still as some image erect in a niche or as some black-vizored sentinel guarding a treasure. Brydon was to know afterwards, was to recall and make out, the particular thing he had believed during the rest of his descent. He saw, in its great grey glimmering margin, the central vagueness diminish, and he felt it to be taking the very form toward which, for so many days, the passion of his curiosity had yearned. It gloomed, it loomed, it was something, it was somebody, the prodigy of a personal presence.

Rigid and conscious, spectral yet human, a man of his own substance and stature waited there to measure himself with his power to dismay. This only could it be – this only till he recognized, with his advance, that what made the face dim was the pair of raised hands that covered it and in which, so far from being offered in defiance, it was buried as for dark deprecation. So Brydon, before him, took him in; with every fact of him now, in the higher light, hard and acute – his planted stillness, his vivid truth, his grizzled bent head and white masking hands, his queer actuality of evening-dress, of dangling double eye-glass, of gleaming silk lappet and white linen, of pearl button and gold watch-guard and polished shoe. No portrait by a great modern master could have presented him with more intensity, thrust him out of his frame with more art, as if there had been "treatment," of the consummate sort, in his every shade and salience. The revulsion, for our friend, had become, before he knew it, immense – this drop, in the act of apprehension, to the sense of his adversary's inscrutable manoeuvre. That meaning at least, while he gaped, it offered him; for he could but gape at his other self in this other anguish, gape as a proof that *he*, standing there for the achieved, the enjoyed, the triumphant life, couldn't be faced in his triumph. Wasn't the proof in the splendid covering hands, strong and completely spread? – so spread and so intentional that, in spite of a special verity that surpassed every other, the fact that one of these hands had lost two fingers, which were reduced to stumps, as if accidentally shot away, the face was effectually guarded and saved.

"Saved," though, *would* it be? – Brydon breathed his wonder till the very impunity of his attitude and the very insistence of his eyes produced, as he felt, a sudden stir which showed the next instant as a deeper portent, which the head raised itself, the betrayal of a braver purpose. The hands, as he looked, began to move, to open; then, as if deciding in a flash, dropped from the face and left it uncovered and presented. Horror, with the sight, had leaped into Brydon's throat, gasping there in a sound he couldn't utter; for the bared identity was too hideous as *his* and his glare was the passion of his protest. The face, *that* face, Spencer Brydon's? – he searched it still, but looking away from it in dismay and denial, falling straight from his height of sublimity. It was unknown, inconceivable, awful, disconnected from any possibility – ! He had been "sold", he inwardly moaned, stalking such game as this: the presence before him was a presence, the horror within him a horror, but the waste of his nights had been only grotesque and the success of his adventure an irony. Such an identity fitted his at no point, made its alternative monstrous. A thousand times yes, as it came upon him nearer now – the face was the face of a stranger. It came upon him nearer now, quite as one of those expanding fantastic images projected by the magic lantern of childhood; for the stranger, whoever he might be, evil, odious, blatant, vulgar, had advanced as for aggression, and he knew himself give ground. Then harder pressed still, sick with the force of his shock, and falling back as under the hot breath and the roused passion of a life larger than his own, a rage of personality before which his own collapsed, he felt the whole vision turn to darkness and his very feet give way. His head went round; he was going; he had gone.

III

What had next brought him back, clearly – though after how long? – was Mrs Muldoon's voice, coming to him from quite near, from so near that he seemed presently to see her as kneeling on the ground before him while he lay looking up at her; himself not wholly on the ground, but half-raised and upheld – conscious, yes, of tenderness of support and, more particularly, of a head pillowed in extraordinary softness and faintly refreshing fragrance. He considered, he wondered, his wit but half at his service; then another face intervened, bending more directly over him, and he finally knew that Alice Staverton had made her lap an ample and perfect cushion to him, and that she had to this end seated herself on the lowest degree of the staircase, the rest of his long person remaining stretched on his old black-and-white slabs. They were cold, these marble squares of his youth; but *he* somehow was not, in this rich return of consciousness – the most wonderful hour, little by little, that he had ever known, leaving him, as it did, so gratefully, so abysmally passive, and yet as with a treasure of intelligence waiting all round him for quiet appropriation; dissolved, he might call it, in the air of the place and producing the golden glow of a late autumn afternoon. He had come back, yes – come back from further away than any man but himself had ever travelled; but it was strange how with this sense what he had come back *to* seemed really the great thing, and as if his prodigious journey had been all for the sake of it. Slowly but surely his consciousness grew, his vision of his state thus completing itself: he had been miraculously *carried* back – lifted and carefully borne as from where he had been picked up, the uttermost end of an interminable grey passage. Even with this he was suffered to rest, and what had now brought him to the knowledge was the break in the long mild motion.

It had brought him to knowledge, to knowledge – yes, this was the beauty of his state; which came to resemble more and more that of a man who has gone to sleep on some news of a great inheritance, and then, after dreaming it away, after profaning it with matters strange to it, has waked up again to serenity of certitude and has only to lie and watch it grow. This was the drift of his patience – that he had only to let it shine on him. He must moreover, with intermissions, still have been lifted and borne; since why and how else should he have known himself, later on,

with the afternoon glow intenser, no longer at the foot of his stairs – situated as these now seemed at that dark other end of his tunnel – but on a
deep window-bench of his high saloon, over which had been spread,
couch-fashion, a mantle of soft stuff lined with grey fur that was familiar
to his eyes and that one of his hands kept fondly feeling as for its pledge of
truth. Mrs Muldoon's face had gone, but the other, the second he had
recognized, hung over him in a way that showed how he was still
propped and pillowed. He took it all in, and the more he took it the more
it seemed to suffice; he was as much at peace as if he had had food and
drink. It was the two women who had found him, on Mrs Muldoon's
having plied, at her usual hour, her latch-key – and on her having above
all arrived while Miss Staverton still lingered near the house. She had
been turning away, all anxiety, from worrying the vain bell-handle – her
calculation having been of the hour of the good woman's visit; but the
latter, blessedly, had come up while she was still there, and they had
entered together. He had then lain, beyond the vestibule, very much as
he was lying now – quite, that is, as he appeared to have fallen, but all so
wondrously without bruise or gash; only in a depth of stupor. What he
most took in, however, at present, with the steadier clearance, was that
Alice Staverton had for a long unspeakable moment not doubted he was
dead.

  "It must have been that I *was*." He made it out as she held him. "Yes –
I can only have died. You brought me literally to life. Only," he
wondered, his eyes rising to her, "only, in the name of all the benedic-
tions, how?"

  It took her but an instant to bend her face and kiss him, and something
in the manner of it, and in the way her hands clasped and locked his head
while he felt the cool charity and virtue of her lips, something in all this
beatitude somehow answered everything. "And now I keep you," she
said.

  "Oh keep me, keep me!" he pleaded while her face still hung over
him: in response to which it dropped again and stayed close, clingingly
close. It was the seal of their situation – of which he tasted the impress for
a long blissful moment in silence. But he came back. "Yet how did you
know – ?"

  "I was uneasy. You were to have come, you remember – and you had
sent no word."

  "Yes, I remember – I was to have gone to you at one today." It caught
on to their "old" life and relation – which were so near and so far. "I was

still out there in my strange darkness – where was it, what was it? I must have stayed there so long." He could but wonder at the depth and the duration of his swoon.

"Since last night?" she asked with a shade of fear for her possible indiscretion.

"Since this morning – it must have been: the cold dim dawn of today. Where have I been," he vaguely wailed, "where have I been?" He felt her hold him close, and it was as if this helped him now to make in all security his mild moan. "What a long dark day!"

All in her tenderness she had waited a moment. "In the cold dim dawn?" she quavered.

But he had already gone on piecing together the parts of the whole prodigy. "As I didn't turn up you came straight – ?"

She barely cast about. "I went first to your hotel – where they told me of your absence. You had dined out last evening and hadn't been back since. But they appeared to know you had been at your club."

"So you had the idea of *this* – ?"

"Of what?" she asked in a moment.

"Well – of what has happened."

"I believed at least you'd have been here. I've known, all along," she said, "that you've been coming."

" 'Known' it – ?"

"Well, I've believed it. I said nothing to you after that talk we had a month ago – but I felt sure. I knew you would," she declared.

"That I'd persist, you mean?"

"That you'd see him."

"Ah but I didn't!" cried Brydon with his long wail. "There's somebody – an awful beast; whom I brought, too horribly, to bay. But it's not me."

At this she bent over him again, and her eyes were in his eyes. "No – it's not you." And it was as if, while her face hovered, he might have made out in it, hadn't it been so near, some particular meaning blurred by a smile. "No, thank heaven," she repeated – "it's not you! Of course it wasn't to have been."

"Ah but it *was*," he gently insisted. And he stared before him now as he had been staring for so many weeks. "I was to have known myself."

"You couldn't!" she returned consolingly. And then reverting, and as if to account further for what she had herself done, "But it wasn't only *that*, that you hadn't been at home," she went on. "I waited till the hour at which we had found Mrs Muldoon that day of my going with you; and she arrived, as I've told you, while, failing to bring anyone to the door, I lingered in my despair on the steps. After a little, if she hadn't come, by such a mercy, I should have found means to hunt her up. But it wasn't," said Alice Staverton, as if once more with her fine intention – "it wasn't only that."

His eyes, as he lay, turned back to her. "What more then?"

She met it, the wonder she had stirred. "In the cold dim dawn, you say? Well, in the cold dim dawn of this morning I too saw you."

"Saw *me* – ?"

"Saw *him*," said Alice Staverton. "It must have been at the same moment."

He lay an instant taking it in – as if he wished to be quite reasonable. "At the same moment?"

"Yes – in my dream again, the same one I've named to you. He came back to me. Then I knew it for a sign. He had come to you."

At this Brydon raised himself; he had to see her better. She helped him when she understood his movement, and he sat up, steadying himself beside her there on the window-bench and with his right hand grasping her left. "*He* didn't come to me."

"You came to yourself," she beautifully smiled.

"Ah I've come to myself now – thanks to you, dearest. But this brute, with his awful face – this brute's a black stranger. He's none of *me*, even as I *might* have been," Brydon sturdily declared.

But she kept the clearness that was like the breath of infallibility. "Isn't the whole point that you'd have been different?"

He almost scowled for it. "As different as *that* – ?"

Her look again was more beautiful to him than the things of this world. "Haven't you exactly wanted to know *how* different? So this morning," she said, "you appeared to me."

"Like *him*?"

"A black stranger!"

"Then how did you know it was I?"

"Because, as I told you weeks ago, my mind, my imagination, had worked so over what you might, what you mightn't have been – to show you, you see, how I've thought of you. In the midst of that you came to me – that my wonder might be answered. So I knew," she went on; "and believed that, since the question held you too so fast, as you told me that day, you too would see for yourself. And when this morning I again saw I knew it would be because you had – and also then, from the first moment, because you somehow wanted me. *He* seemed to tell me of that. So why," she strangely smiled, "shouldn't I like him?"

It brought Spencer Brydon to his feet. "You 'like' that horror – ?"

"I *could* have liked him. And to me," she said, "he was no horror. I had accepted him."

" 'Accepted' – ?" Brydon oddly sounded.

"Before, for the interest of his difference – yes. And as I didn't disown him, as I knew him – which you at last, confronted with him in his difference, so cruelly didn't, my dear – well, he must have been, you see, less dreadful to me. And it may have pleased him that I pitied him."

She was beside him on her feet, but still holding his hand – still with her arm supporting him. But though it all brought for him thus a dim light, "You 'pitied' him?" he grudgingly, resentfully asked.

"He has been unhappy; he has been ravaged," she said.

"And haven't I been unhappy? Am not I – you've only to look at me! – ravaged?"

"Ah I don't say I like him *better*," she granted after a thought. "But he's grim, he's worn – and things have happened to him. He doesn't make shift, for sight, with your charming monocle."

"No" – it struck Brydon: "I couldn't have sported mine 'down-town.' They'd have guyed me there."

"His great convex pince-nez – I saw it, I recognized the kind – is for his poor ruined sight. And his poor right hand – !"

"Ah!" Brydon winced – whether for his proved identity or for his lost fingers. Then, "He has a million a year," he lucidly added, "But he hasn't you."

"And he isn't – no, he isn't – *you!*" she murmured as he drew her to his breast.

F. Marion Crawford

The Doll's Ghost

*F. Marion Crawford (1854–1909) achieved enormous worldwide popularity in the
1880s and 1890s with a long series of novels, endlessly reprinted (and still seen in
every secondhand bookshop today in great quantities). However, these are little read
today – unlike a small core of seven marvellous weird uncanny tales: "The Dead
Smile", "The Screaming Skull", "Man Overboard!", "By the Waters of Paradise",
"For the Blood is the Life", "The Upper Berth" (one of the most anthologized ghost
stories of all time), and the gem which follows here: "The Doll's Ghost" (1908).*

IT WAS A TERRIBLE accident, and for one moment the splendid
machinery of Cranston House got out of gear and stood still. The butler
emerged from the retirement in which he spent his elegant leisure, two
grooms of the chambers appeared simultaneously from opposite directions, there were actually house-maids on the grand staircase, and those
who remember the facts most exactly assert that Mrs Pringle herself positively stood upon the landing. Mrs Pringle was the housekeeper. As for
the head nurse, the under nurse, and the nursery maid, their feelings
cannot be described. The head nurse laid one hand upon the polished
marble balustrade and stared stupidly before her, the under nurse stood
rigid and pale, leaning against the polished marble wall, and the nursery-
maid collapsed and sat down upon the polished marble step, just beyond
the limits of the velvet carpet, and frankly burst into tears.

The Lady Gwendolen Lancaster-Douglas-Scroop, youngest daughter
of the ninth Duke of Cranston, and aged six years and three months,
picked herself up quite alone, and sat down on the third step from the
foot of the grand staircase in Cranston House.

"Oh!" ejaculated the butler, and he disappeared again.

"Ah!" responded the grooms of the chambers, as they also went away.

"It's only that doll," Mrs Pringle was distinctly heard to say, in a tone of contempt.

The under nurse heard her say it. Then the three nurses gathered round Lady Gwendolen and patted her, and gave her unhealthy things out of their pockets, and hurried her out of Cranston House as fast as they could, lest it should be found out upstairs that they had allowed the Lady Gwendolen Lancaster-Douglas-Scroop to tumble down the grand staircase with her doll in her arms. And as the doll was badly broken, the nursery-maid carried it, with the pieces, wrapped up in Lady Gwendolen's little cloak. It was not far to Hyde Park, and when they had reached a quiet place they took means to find out that Lady Gwendolen had no bruises. For the carpet was very thick and soft, and there was thick stuff under it to make it softer.

Lady Gwendolen Douglas-Scroop sometimes yelled, but she never cried. It was because she had yelled that the nurse had allowed her to go downstairs alone with Nina, the doll, under one arm, while she steadied herself with her other hand on the balustrade, and trod upon the polished marble steps beyond the edge of the carpet. So she had fallen, and Nina had come to grief.

When the nurses were quite sure that she was not hurt, they unwrapped the doll and looked at her in her turn. She had been a very beautiful doll, very large, and fair, and healthy, with real yellow hair, and eyelids that would open and shut over very grown-up dark eyes. Moreover, when you moved her right arm up and down she said "Pa-pa," and when you moved the left she said "Ma-ma" very distinctly.

"I heard her say 'Pa' when she fell," said the under nurse, who heard everything. "But she ought to have said 'Pa-pa.'"

"That's because her arm went up when she hit the step," said the head nurse. "She'll say the other 'Pa' when I put it down again."

"Pa," said Nina, as her right arm was pushed down, and speaking through her broken face. It was cracked right across, from the upper corner of the forehead, with a hideous gash, through the nose and down to the little frilled collar of the pale green silk Mother Hubbard frock, and two little three-cornered pieces of porcelain had fallen out.

"I'm sure it's a wonder she can speak at all, being all smashed," said the under nurse.

"You'll have to take her to Mr Puckler," said her superior. "It's not far, and you'd better go at once."

Lady Gwendolen was occupied in digging a hole in the ground with a little spade, and paid no attention to the nurses.

"What are you doing?" enquired the nursery-maid, looking on.

"Nina's dead, and I'm diggin' her a grave," replied her ladyship thoughtfully.

"Oh, she'll come to life again all right," said the nursery-maid.

The under nurse wrapped Nina up again and departed. Fortunately a kind soldier, with very long legs and a very small cap, happened to be there; and as he had nothing to do, he offered to see the under nurse safely to Mr Puckler's and back.

Mr Bernard Puckler and his little daughter lived in a little house in a little alley, which led out off a quiet little street not very far from Belgrave Square. He was the great doll doctor, and his extensive practice lay in the most aristocratic quarter. He mended dolls of all sizes and ages, boy dolls and girl dolls, baby dolls in long clothes, and grown-up dolls in fashionable gowns, talking dolls and dumb dolls, those that shut their eyes when they lay down, and those whose eyes had to be shut for them by means of a mysterious wire. His daughter Else was only just over twelve years old, but she was already very clever at mending dolls' clothes, and at doing their hair, which is harder than you might think, though the dolls sit quite still while it is being done.

Mr Puckler had originally been a German, but he had dissolved his nationality in the ocean of London many years ago, like a great many foreigners. He still had one or two German friends, however, who came on Saturday evenings, and smoked with him and played picquet or "skat" with him for farthing points, and called him "Herr Doctor," which seemed to please Mr Puckler very much.

He looked older than he was, for his beard was rather long and ragged, his hair was grizzled and thin, and he wore horn-rimmed spectacles. As for Else, she was a thin, pale child, very quiet and neat, with dark eyes and brown hair that was plaited down her back and tied with a bit of black ribbon. She mended the dolls' clothes and took the dolls back to their homes when they were quite strong again.

The house was a little one, but too big for the two people who lived in it. There was a small sitting-room on the street, and the workshop was at the back, and there were three rooms upstairs. But the father and daughter lived most of their time in the workshop, because they were generally at work, even in the evenings.

Mr Puckler laid Nina on the table and looked at her a long time, till the tears began to fill his eyes behind the horn-rimmed spectacles. He was a very susceptible man, and he often fell in love with the dolls he mended, and found it hard to part with them when they had smiled at him for a few days. They were real little people to him, with characters and thoughts and feelings of their own, and he was very tender with them all. But some attracted him especially from the first, and when they were brought to him maimed and injured, their state seemed so pitiful to him that the tears came easily. You must remember that he had lived among dolls during a great part of his life, and understood them.

"How do you know that they feel nothing?" he went on to say to Else. "You must be gentle with them. It costs nothing to be kind to the little beings, and perhaps it makes a difference to them."

And Else understood him, because she was a child, and she knew that she was more to him than all the dolls.

He fell in love with Nina at first sight, perhaps because her beautiful brown glass eyes were something like Else's own, and he loved Else first and best, with all his heart. And, besides, it was a very sorrowful case. Nina had evidently not been long in the world; for her complexion was perfect, her hair was smooth where it should be smooth, and curly where it should be curly, and her silk clothes were perfectly new. But across her face was that frightful gash, like a sabre-cut, deep and shadowy within, but clean and sharp at the edges. When he tenderly pressed her head to close the gaping wound, the edges made a fine grating sound, that was painful to hear, and the lids of the dark eyes quivered and trembled as though Nina were suffering dreadfully.

"Poor Nina!" he exclaimed sorrowfully. "But I shall not hurt you much, though you will take a long time to get strong."

He always asked the names of the broken dolls when they were brought to him, and sometimes the people knew what the children called them, and told him. He liked "Nina" for a name. Altogether and in every way she pleased him more than any doll he had seen for many years, and he felt drawn to her, and made up his mind to make her perfectly strong and sound, no matter how much labour it might cost him.

Mr Puckler worked patiently a little at a time, and Else watched him. She could do nothing for poor Nina, whose clothes needed no mending. The longer the doll doctor worked, the more fond he became of the yellow hair and the beautiful brown glass eyes. He sometimes forgot all the other dolls that were waiting to be mended, lying side by side on a shelf, and sat for an hour gazing at Nina's face, while he racked his ingenuity for some new invention by which to hide even the smallest trace of the terrible accident.

She was wonderfully mended. Even he was obliged to admit that; but the scar was still visible to his keen eyes, a very fine line right across the face, downwards from right to left. Yet all the conditions had been most favourable for a cure, since the cement had set quite hard at the first attempt and the weather had been fine and dry, which makes a great difference in a dolls' hospital.

At last he knew that he could do no more, and the under nurse had already come twice to see whether the job was finished, as she coarsely expressed it.

"Nina is not quite strong yet," Mr Puckler had answered each time, for he could not make up his mind to face the parting.

And now he sat before the square deal table at which he worked, and Nina lay before him for the last time with a big brown-paper box beside her. It stood there like her coffin, waiting for her, he thought. He must put her into it, and lay tissue paper over her dear face, and then put on the lid and at the thought of tying the string his sight was dim with tears again. He was never to look into the glassy depths of the beautiful brown eyes any more, nor to hear the little wooden voice say "Pa-pa" and "Ma-ma." It was a very painful moment.

In the vain hope of gaining time before the separation, he took up the little sticky bottles of cement and glue and gum and colour, looking at each one in turn, and then at Nina's face. And all his small tools lay there, neatly arranged in a row, but he knew that he could not use them again for Nina. She was quite strong at last, and in a country where there should be no cruel children to hurt her she might live a hundred years, with only that almost imperceptible line across her face, to tell of the fearful thing that had befallen her on the marble steps of Cranston House.

Suddenly Mr Puckler's heart was quite full and he rose abruptly from his seat and turned away.

"Else," he said unsteadily, "you must do it for me. I cannot bear to see her go into the box."

So he went and stood at the window with his back turned, while Else did what he had not the heart to do.

"Is it done?" he asked, not turning round. "Then take her away, my dear. Put on your hat, and take her to Cranston House quickly, and when you are gone I will turn round."

Else was used to her father's queer ways with the dolls, and though she had never seen him so much moved by a parting, she was not much surprised.

"Come back quickly," he said, when he heard her hand on the latch. "It is growing late, and I should not send you at this hour. But I cannot bear to look forward to it any more."

When Else was gone, he left the window and sat down in his place before the table again, to wait for the child to come back. He touched the place where Nina had lain, very gently, and he recalled the softly-tinted pink face, and the glass eyes, and the ringlets of yellow hair, till he could almost see them.

The evenings were long, for it was late in the spring. But it began to grow dark soon, and Mr Puckler wondered why Else did not come back. She had been gone an hour and a half, and that was much longer than he had expected, for it was barely half a mile from Belgrave Square to Cranston House. He reflected that the child might have been kept waiting, but as the twilight deepened he grew anxious, and walked up and down in the dim workshop, no longer thinking of Nina, but of Else, his own living child, whom he loved.

An indefinable, disquieting sensation came upon him by fine degrees, a chilliness and a faint stirring of his thin hair, joined with a wish to be in any company rather than to be alone much longer. It was the beginning of fear.

He told himself in strong German-English that he was a foolish old man, and he began to feel about for the matches in the dusk. He knew just where they should be, for he always kept them in the same place, close to the little tin box that held bits of sealing-wax of various colours, for some kinds of mending. But somehow he could not find the matches in the gloom.

Something had happened to Else, he was sure, and as his fear increased, he felt as though it might be allayed if he could get a light and see what time it was. Then he called himself a foolish old man again, and the sound of his own voice startled him in the dark. He could not find the matches.

The window was grey still; he might see what time it was if he went close to it, and he could go and get matches out of the cupboard afterwards. He stood back from the table, to get out of the way of the chair, and began to cross the board floor.

Something was following him in the dark. There was a small pattering, as of tiny feet upon the boards. He stopped and listened, and the roots of his hair tingled. It was nothing, and he was a foolish old man. He made two steps more, and he was sure that he heard the little pattering again. He turned his back to the window, leaning against the sash so that the panes began to crack, and he faced the dark. Everything was quite still, and it smelt of paste and cement and wood-filings as usual.

"Is that you, Else?" he asked, and he was surprised by the fear in his voice.

There was no answer in the room, and he held up his watch and tried to make out what time it was by the grey dusk that was just not darkness. So far as he could see, it was within two or three minutes of ten o'clock. He had been a long time alone. He was shocked, and frightened for Else, out in London so late, and he almost ran across the room to the door. As he fumbled for the latch, he distinctly heard the running of the little feet after him.

"Mice!" he exclaimed feebly, just as he got the door open.

He shut it quickly behind him, and felt as though some cold thing had settled on his back and were writhing upon him. The passage was quite dark, but he found his hat and was out in the alley in a moment, breathing more freely, and surprised to find how much light there still was in the open air. He could see the pavement clearly under his feet, and far off in the street to which the alley led he could hear the laughter and calls of children, playing some game out of doors. He wondered how he could have been so nervous, and for an instant he thought of going back into the house to wait quietly for Else. But instantly he felt that nervous fright of something stealing over him again. In any case it was better to walk up to Cranston House and ask the servants about the child. One of the women had perhaps taken a fancy to her, and was even now giving her tea and cake.

He walked quickly to Belgrave Square, and then up the broad streets, listening as he went, whenever there was no other sound, for the tiny footsteps. But he heard nothing, and was laughing at himself when he rang the servants' bell at the big house. Of course, the child must be there.

The person who opened the door was quite an inferior person – for it was a back door – but affected the manners of the front, and stared at Mr Puckler superciliously under the strong light.

No little girl had been seen, and he knew "nothing about no dolls."

"She is my little girl," said Mr Puckler tremulously, for all his anxiety was returning tenfold, "and I am afraid something has happened."

The inferior person said rudely that "nothing could have happened to her in that house, because she had not been there, which was a jolly good reason why"; and Mr Puckler was obliged to admit that the man ought to know, as it was his business to keep the door and let people in. He wished to be allowed to speak to the under nurse, who knew him; but the man was ruder than ever, and finally shut the door in his face.

When the doll doctor was alone in the street he steadied himself by the railing, for he felt as though he were breaking in two, just as some dolls break, in the middle of the backbone.

Presently he knew that he must be doing something to find Else, and that gave him strength. He began to walk as quickly as he could through the streets, following every highway and byway which his little girl might have taken on her errand. He also asked several policemen in vain if they had seen her, and most of them answered him kindly, for they saw that he was a sober man and in his right senses, and some of them had little girls of their own.

It was one o'clock in the morning when he went up to his own door again, worn out and hopeless and broken-hearted. As he turned the key in the lock, his heart stood still, for he knew that he was awake and not dreaming, and that he really heard those tiny footsteps pattering to meet him inside the house along the passage.

But he was too unhappy to be much frightened any more, and his heart went on again with a dull regular pain, that found its way all through him with every pulse. So he went in, and hung up his hat in the dark, and found the matches in the cupboard and the candlestick in its place in the corner.

Mr Puckler was so much overcome and so completely worn out that he sat down in his chair before the work-table and almost fainted, as his face dropped forward upon his folded hands. Beside him the solitary candle burned steadily with a low flame in the still warm air.

"Else! Else!" he moaned against his yellow knuckles. And that was all he could say, and it was no relief to him. On the contrary, the very sound of the name was a new and sharp pain that pierced his ears and his head and his very soul. For every time he repeated the name it meant that little Else was dead, somewhere out in the streets of London in the dark.

He was so terribly hurt that he did not even feel something pulling gently at the skirt of his old coat, so gently that it was like the nibbling of a tiny mouse. He might have thought that it was really a mouse if he had noticed it.

"Else! Else!" he groaned, right against his hands.

Then a cool breath stirred his thin hair, and the low flame of the one candle dropped down almost to a mere spark, not flickering as though a draught were going to blow it out, but just dropping down as if it were tired out. Mr Puckler felt his hands stiffening with fright under his face; and there was a faint rustling sound, like some small silk thing blown in a gentle breeze. He sat up straight, stark and scared, and a small wooden voice spoke in the stillness.

"Pa-pa," it said, with a break between the syllables.

Mr Puckler stood up in a single jump, and his chair fell over backwards with a smashing noise upon the wooden floor. The candle had almost gone out.

It was Nina's doll-voice that had spoken, and he should have known it among the voices of a hundred other dolls. And yet there was something more in it, a little human ring, with a pitiful cry and a call for help, and the wail of a hurt child. Mr Puckler stood up, stark and stiff, and tried to look round, but at first he could not, for he seemed to be frozen from head to foot.

Then he made a great effort, and he raised one hand to each of his temples, and pressed his own head round as he would have turned a doll's. The candle was burning so low that it might as well have been out altogether, for any light it gave, and the room seemed quite dark at first. Then he saw something. He would not have believed that he could be more frightened than he had been just before that. But he was, and his knees shook, for he saw the doll standing in the middle of the floor, shining with a faint and ghostly radiance, her beautiful glassy brown eyes fixed on his. And across her face the very thin line of the break he had mended shone as though it were drawn in light with a fine point of white flame.

Yet there was something more in the eyes, too; there was something human, like Else's own, but as if only the doll saw him through them, and not Else. And there was enough of Else to bring back all his pain and to make him forget his fear.

"Else! My little Else!" he cried aloud.

The small ghost moved, and its doll-arm slowly rose and fell with a stiff, mechanical motion.

"Pa-pa," it said.

It seemed this time that there was even more of Else's tone echoing somewhere between the wooden notes that reached his ears so distinctly, and yet so far away. Else was calling him, he was sure.

His face was perfectly white in the gloom, but his knees did not shake any more, and he felt that he was less frightened.

"Yes, child! But where? Where?" he asked. "Where are you, Else?"

"Pa-pa!"

The syllables died away in the quiet room. There was a low rustling of silk, the glassy brown eyes turned slowly away, and Mr Puckler heard the pitter-patter of the small feet in the bronze kid slippers as the figure ran straight to the door. Then the candle burned high again, the room was full of light, and he was alone.

Mr Puckler passed his hand over his eyes and looked about him. He could see everything quite clearly, and he felt that he must have been dreaming, though he was standing instead of sitting down, as he should have been if he had just waked up. The candle burned brightly now. There were the dolls to be mended, lying in a row with their toes up. The third one had lost her right shoe, and Else was making one. He knew that, and he was certainly not dreaming now. He had not been dreaming when he had come in from his fruitless search and had heard the doll's footsteps running to the door. He had not fallen asleep in his chair. How could he possibly have fallen asleep when his heart was breaking? He had been awake all the time.

He steadied himself, set the fallen chair upon its legs, and said to himself again very emphatically that he was a foolish old man. He ought to be out in the streets looking for his child, asking questions, and enquiring at the police stations, where all accidents were reported as soon as they were known, or at the hospitals.

"Pa-pa!"

The longing, wailing, pitiful little wooden cry rang from the passage, outside the door, and Mr Puckler stood for an instant with white face, transfixed and rooted to the spot. A moment later his hand was on the latch. Then he was in the passage, with the light streaming from the open door behind him.

Quite at the other end he saw the little phantom shining clearly in the shadow, and the right hand seemed to beckon to him as the arm rose and fell once more. He knew all at once that it had not come to frighten him but to lead him, and when it disappeared, and he walked boldly towards the door, he knew that it was in the street outside, waiting for him. He forgot that he was tired and had eaten no supper, and had walked many miles, for a sudden hope ran through and through him, like a golden stream of life.

And sure enough, at the corner of the alley, and at the corner of the street, and out in Belgrave Square, he saw the small ghost flitting before him. Sometimes it was only a shadow, where there was other light, but then the glare of the lamps made a pale green sheen on its little Mother Hubbard frock of silk; and sometimes, where the streets were dark and silent, the whole figure shone out brightly, with its yellow curls and rosy neck. It seemed to trot along like a tiny child, and Mr Puckler could almost hear the pattering of the bronze kid slippers on the pavement as it ran. But it went very fast, and he could only just keep up with it, tearing along with his hat on the back of his head and his thin hair blown by the night breeze, and his horn-rimmed spectacles firmly set up on his broad nose.

On and on he went, and he had no idea where he was. He did not even care, for he knew certainly that he was going the right way.

Then at last, in a wide, quiet street, he was standing before a big, sober-looking door that had two lamps on each side of it, and a polished brass bell-handle, which he pulled.

And just inside, when the door was opened, in the bright light, there was the little shadow, and the pale green sheen of the little silk dress, and once more the small cry came to his ears, less pitiful, more longing.

"Pa-pa!"

The shadow turned suddenly bright, and out of the brightness the beautiful brown glass eyes were turned so happily to his, while the rosy mouth smiled so divinely that the phantom doll looked almost like a little angel just then.

"A little girl was brought in soon after ten o'clock," said the quiet voice of the hospital doorkeeper. "I think they thought she was only stunned. She was holding a big brown-paper box against her, and they could not get it out of her arms. She had a long plait of brown hair that hung down as they carried her."

"She is my little girl," said Mr Puckler, but he hardly heard his own voice.

He leaned over Else's face in the gentle light of the children's ward, and when he had stood there a minute the beautiful brown eyes opened and looked up to his.

"Pa-pa!" cried Else softly, "I knew you would come!"

Then Mr Puckler did not know what he did or said for a moment, and what he felt was worth all the fear and terror and despair that had almost killed him that night. But by and by Else was telling her story, and the nurse let her speak, for there were only two other children in the room, who were getting well and were sound asleep.

"They were big boys with bad faces," said Else, "and they tried to get Nina away from me, but I held on and fought as well as I could till one of them hit me with something, and I don't remember any more, for I tumbled down, and I suppose the boys ran away, and somebody found me there. But I'm afraid Nina is all smashed."

"Here is the box," said the nurse. "We could not take it out of her arms till she came to herself. Should you like to see if the doll is broken?"

And she undid the string cleverly, but Nina was all smashed to pieces. Only the gentle light of the children's ward made a pale green sheen in the folds of the little Mother Hubbard frock.

Ambrose Bierce

The Moonlit Road

The supernatural horror stories of Ambrose Bierce (1842–?1914) were usually very short and pithy, and always memorable. He is generally regarded as the greatest American writer in the genre, in the long gap between Edgar Allan Poe and Fitz-James O'Brien, and the twentieth-century masters like H. P. Lovecraft. This fine tale (linked by three separate short narratives) appeared in the new expanded edition of Can Such Things Be (US, 1909; and revised, UK, 1926).

I: Statement of Joel Hetman, Jr

I AM THE MOST unfortunate of men. Rich, respected, fairly well educated and of sound health – with many other advantages usually valued by those having them and coveted by those who have them not – I sometimes think that I should be less unhappy if they had been denied me, for then the contrast between my outer and my inner life would not be continually demanding a painful attention. In the stress of privation and the need of effort I might sometimes forget the sombre secret ever baffling the conjecture that it compels.

I am the only child of Joel and Julia Hetman. The one was a well-to-do country gentleman, the other a beautiful and accomplished woman to whom he was passionately attached with what I now know to have been a jealous and exacting devotion. The family home was a few miles from Nashville, Tennessee, a large, irregularly built dwelling of no particular order of architecture, a little way off the road, in a park of trees and shrubbery.

At the time of which I write I was nineteen years old, a student at Yale. One day I received a telegram from my father of such urgency that in compliance with its unexplained demand I left at once for home. At the railway station in Nashville a distant relative awaited me to apprise me of the reason for my recall: my mother had been barbarously murdered – why and by whom none could conjecture, but the circumstances were these:

My father had gone to Nashville, intending to return the next afternoon. Something prevented his accomplishing the business in hand, so he returned on the same night, arriving just before the dawn. In his testimony before the coroner he explained that having no latchkey and not caring to disturb the sleeping servants, he had, with no clearly defined intention, gone round to the rear of the house. As he turned an angle of the building, he heard a sound as of a door gently closed, and saw in the darkness, indistinctly, the figure of a man, which instantly disappeared among the trees of the lawn. A hasty pursuit and brief search of the grounds in the belief that the trespasser was someone secretly visiting a servant proving fruitless, he entered at the unlocked door and mounted the stairs to my mother's chamber. Its door was open, and stepping into black darkness he fell headlong over some heavy object on the floor. I may spare myself the details; it was my poor mother, dead of strangulation by human hands!

Nothing had been taken from the house, the servants had heard no sound, and excepting those terrible finger-marks upon the dead woman's throat – dear God! that I might forget them! – no trace of the assassin was ever found.

I gave up my studies and remained with my father, who, naturally, was greatly changed. Always of a sedate, taciturn disposition, he now fell into so deep a dejection that nothing could hold his attention, yet anything – a footfall, the sudden closing of a door – aroused in him a fitful interest; one might have called it an apprehension. At any small surprise of the senses he would start visibly and sometimes turn pale, then relapse into a melancholy apathy deeper than before. I suppose he was what is called a 'nervous wreck.' As to me, I was younger then than now – there is much in that. Youth is Gilead, in which is balm for every wound. Ah, that I might again dwell in that enchanted land! Unacquainted with grief, I knew not how to appraise my bereavement; I could not rightly estimate the strength of the stroke.

One night, a few months after the dreadful event, my father and I walked home from the city. The full moon was about three hours above the eastern horizon; the entire countryside had the solemn stillness of a summer night; our footfalls and the ceaseless song of the katydids were the only sound, aloof. Black shadows of bordering trees lay athwart the road, which, in the short reaches between, gleamed a ghostly white. As we approached the gate to our dwelling, whose front was in shadow, and in which no light shone, my father suddenly stopped and clutched my arm, saying, hardly above his breath:

"God! God! what is that?"

"I hear nothing," I replied.

"But see – see!" he said, pointing along the road, directly ahead.

I said: "Nothing is there. Come, father, let us go in – you are ill."

He had released my arm and was standing rigid and motionless in the centre of the illuminated roadway, staring like one bereft of sense. His face in the moonlight showed a pallor and fixity inexpressibly distressing. I pulled gently at his sleeve, but he had forgotten my existence. Presently he began to retire backward, step by step, never for an instant removing his eyes from what he saw, or thought he saw. I turned half round to follow, but stood irresolute. I do not recall any feeling of fear, unless a sudden chill was its physical manifestation. It seemed as if an icy wind had touched my face and enfolded my body from head to foot; I could feel the stir of it in my hair.

At that moment my attention was drawn to a light that suddenly streamed from an upper window of the house: one of the servants, awakened by what mysterious premonition of evil who can say, and in obedience to an impulse that she was never able to name, had lit a lamp. When I turned to look for my father he was gone, and in all the years that have passed no whisper of his fate has come across the borderland of conjecture from the realm of the unknown.

II: Statement of Caspar Grattan

Today I am said to live; tomorrow, here in this room, will lie a senseless shape of clay that all too long was I. If anyone lift the cloth from the face of that unpleasant thing it will be in gratification of a mere morbid curiosity. Some, doubtless, will go further and inquire, "Who was he?"

In this writing I supply the only answer that I am able to make – Caspar Grattan. Surely, that should be enough. The name has served my small need for more than twenty years of a life of unknown length. True, I gave it to myself, but lacking another I had the right. In this world one must have a name; it prevents confusion, even when it does not establish identity. Some, though, are known by numbers, which also seem inadequate distinctions.

One day, for illustration, I was passing along a street of a city, far from here, when I met two men in uniform, one of whom, half pausing and looking curiously into my face, said to his companion, "That man looks like 767." Something in the number seemed familiar and horrible. Moved by an uncontrollable impulse, I sprang into a side street and ran until I fell exhausted in a country lane.

I have never forgotten that number, and always it comes to memory attended by gibbering obscenity, peals of joyless laughter, the clang of iron doors. So I say a name, even if self-bestowed, is better than a number. In the register of the potter's field I shall soon have both. What wealth!

Of him who shall find this paper I must beg a little consideration. It is not the history of my life; the knowledge to write that is denied me. This is only a record of broken and apparently unrelated memories, some of them as distinct and sequent as brilliant beads upon a thread, others remote and strange, having the character of crimson dreams with interspaces blank and black – witch fires glowing still and red in a great desolation.

Standing upon the shore of eternity, I turn for a last look landward over the course by which I came. There are twenty years of footprints fairly distinct, the impressions of bleeding feet. They lead through poverty and pain, devious and unsure, as of one staggering beneath a burden –

Remote, unfriended, melancholy, slow.

Ah, the poet's prophecy of Me – how admirable, how dreadfully admirable!

Backward beyond the beginning of this via dolorosa – this epic of suffering with episodes of sin – I see nothing clearly; it comes out of a cloud. I know that it spans only twenty years, yet I am an old man.

One does not remember one's birth – one has to be told. But with me it was different; life came to me full-handed and dowered me with all my faculties and powers. Of a previous existence I know no more than others, for all have stammering intimations that may be memories and may be dreams. I know not only that my first consciousness was of maturity in body and mind – a consciousness accepted without surprise or conjecture. I merely found myself walking in a forest, half-clad, footsore, unutterably weary and hungry. Seeing a farmhouse, I approached and asked for food, which was given me by one who inquired my name. I did not know, yet knew that all had names. Greatly embarrassed, I retreated, and night coming on, lay down in the forest and slept.

The next day I entered a large town which I shall not name. Nor shall I recount further incidents of the life that is now to end – a life of wandering, always and everywhere haunted by an overmastering sense of crime in punishment of wrong and of terror in punishment of crime. Let me see if I can reduce it to narrative.

I seem once to have lived near a great city, a prosperous planter, married to a woman whom I loved and distrusted. We had, it sometimes seems, one child, a youth of brilliant parts and promise. He is at all times a vague figure, never clearly drawn, frequently altogether out of the picture.

One luckless evening it occurred to me to test my wife's fidelity in a vulgar, commonplace way familiar to everyone who has acquaintance with the literature of fact and fiction. I went to the city, telling my wife that I should be absent until the following afternoon. But I returned before daybreak and went to the rear of the house, purposing to enter by a door which I had secretly so tampered that it would seem to lock, yet not actually fasten. As I approached it, I heard it gently open and close, and saw a man steal away into the darkness. With murder in my heart, I sprang after him, but he had vanished without even the bad luck of identification. Sometimes now I cannot even persuade myself that it was a human being.

Crazed with jealousy and rage, blind and bestial with all the elemental passions of insulted manhood, I entered the house and sprang up the stairs to the door of my wife's chamber. It was closed, but having tampered with its lock also, I easily entered, and despite the black darkness soon stood by the side of her bed. My groping hands told me that although disarranged it was unoccupied.

"She is below," I thought, "and terrified by my entrance has evaded me in the darkness of the hall."

With the purpose of seeking her I turned to leave the room, but took a wrong direction – the right one! My foot struck her, cowering in a corner of the room. Instantly my hands were at her throat, stifling a shriek, my knees were upon her struggling body; and there in the darkness, without a word of accusation or reproach, I strangled her till she died!

There ends the dream. I have related it in the past tense, but the present would be the fitter form, for again and again the sombre tragedy re-enacts itself in my consciousness – over and over I lay the plan, I suffer the confirmation, I redress the wrong. Then all is blank; and afterward the rains beat against the grimy window panes, or the snow falls upon my scant attire, the wheels rattle in the squalid street where my life lies in poverty and mean employment. If there is ever sunshine I do not recall it; if there are birds they do not sing.

There is another dream, another vision of the night. I stand among the shadows in a moonlit road. I am aware of another presence, but whose I cannot rightly determine. In the shadow of a great dwelling I catch the gleam of white garments; then the figure of a woman confronts me in the road – my murdered wife! There is death in the face; there are marks upon the throat. The eyes are fixed on mine with an infinite gravity which is not reproach, nor hate, nor menace, nor anything less terrible than recognition. Before this awful apparition I retreat in terror – a terror that is upon me as I write. I can no longer rightly shape the words. See! they –

Now I am calm, but truly there is no more to tell: the incident ends where it began – in darkness and in doubt.

Yes, I am again in control of myself; "the captain of my soul." But that is not respite; it is another stage and phase of expiation. My penance, constant in degree, is mutable in kind: one of its variants is tranquillity. After all, it is only a life sentence. "To Hell for life" – that is a foolish penalty: the culprit chooses the duration of his punishment. Today my term expires.

To each and all, the peace that was not mine.

III: Statement of the Late Julia Hetman, through the Medium Bayrolles

I had retired early and fallen almost immediately into a peaceful sleep, from which I awoke with that indefinable sense of peril which is, I think, a common experience in that other, earlier life. Of its unmeaning character, too, I was entirely persuaded, yet that did not banish it. My husband, Joel Hetman, was away from home; the servants slept in another part of the house. But these were familiar conditions; they had never distressed me. Nevertheless, the strange terror grew so insupportable that conquering my reluctance to move I sat up and lit the lamp at my bedside. Contrary to my expectation this gave me no relief; the light seemed rather an added danger, for I reflected that it would shine out under the door, disclosing my presence to whatever evil thing might lurk outside. You that are still in the flesh, subject to horrors of the imagination, think what a monstrous fear that must be which seeks in darkness security from malevolent existences of the night. That is to spring to close quarters with an unseen enemy – the strategy of despair!

Extinguishing the lamp I pulled the bedclothing about my head and lay trembling and silent, unable to shriek, forgetful to pray. In this pitiable state I must have lain for what you call hours – with us there are no hours, there is no time.

At last it came – a soft, irregular sound of footfalls on the stairs! They were slow, hesitant, uncertain, as of something that did not see its way; to my disordered reason all the more terrifying for that, as the approach of some blind and mindless malevolence to which is no appeal. I even thought that I must have left the hall lamp burning and the groping of this creature proved it a monster of the night. This was foolish and inconsistent with my previous dread of the light, but what would you have? Fear has no brains; it is an idiot. The dismal witness that it bears and the cowardly counsel that it whispers are unrelated. We know this well, we who have passed into the Realm of Terror, who skulk in eternal dusk among the scenes of our former lives, invisible even to ourselves, and one another, yet hiding forlorn in lonely places; yearning for speech with our loved ones, yet dumb, and as fearful of them as they of us. Sometimes the disability is removed, the law suspended: by the deathless power of love or hate we break the spell – we are seen by those whom we would warn, console, or punish. What form we seem to them to bear we know not; we know only that we terrify even those whom we most wish to comfort, and from whom we most crave tenderness and sympathy.

Forgive, I pray you, this inconsequent digression by what was once a woman. You who consult us in this imperfect way – you do not understand. You ask foolish questions about things unknown and things forbidden. Much that we know and could impart in our speech is meaningless in yours. We must communicate with you through a stammering intelligence in that small fraction of our language that you yourselves can speak. You think that we are of another world. No, we have knowledge of no world but yours, though for us it holds no sunlight, no warmth, no music, no laughter, no song of birds, nor any companionship. O God! what a thing it is to be a ghost, cowering and shivering in an altered world, a prey to apprehension and despair!

No, I did not die of fright: the Thing turned and went away. I heard it go down the stairs, hurriedly, I thought, as if itself in sudden fear. Then I rose to call for help. Hardly had my shaking hand found the doorknob when – merciful heaven! – I heard it returning. Its footfalls as it remounted the stairs were rapid, heavy and loud; they shook the house. I fled to an angle of the wall and crouched upon the floor. I tried to pray. I tried to call the name of my dear husband. Then I heard the door thrown open. There was an interval of unconsciousness, and when I revived I felt a strangling clutch upon my throat – felt my arms feebly beating against something that bore me backward – felt my tongue thrusting itself from between my teeth! And then I passed into this life.

No, I have no knowledge of what it was. The sum of what we knew at death is the measure of what we know afterward of all that went before. Of this existence we know many things, but no new light falls upon any page of that; in memory is written all of it that we can read. Here are no heights of truth overlooking the confused landscape of that dubitable domain. We still dwell in the Valley of the Shadow, lurk in its desolate places, peering from brambles and thickets at its mad, malign inhabitants. How should we have new knowledge of that fading past?

What I am about to relate happened on a night. We know when it is night, for then you retire to your houses and we can venture from our places of concealment to move unafraid about our old homes, to look in at the windows, even to enter and gaze upon your faces as you sleep. I had lingered long near the dwelling where I had been so cruelly changed to what I am, as we do while any that we love or hate remain. Vainly I had sought some method of manifestation, some way to make my continued existence and my great love and poignant pity understood by my husband and son. Always if they slept they would wake, or if in my desperation I dared approach them when they were awake, would turn toward me the terrible eyes of the living, frightening me by the glances that I sought from the purpose that I held.

On this night I had searched for them without success, fearing to find them; they were nowhere in the house, nor about the moonlit dawn. For, although the sun is lost to us for ever, the moon, full-orbed or slender, remains to us. Sometimes it shines by night, sometimes by day, but always it rises and sets, as in that other life.

I left the lawn and moved in the white light and silence along the road, aimless and sorrowing. Suddenly I heard the voice of my poor husband in exclamations of astonishment, with that of my son in reassurance and dissuasion; and there by the shadow of a group of trees they stood – near, so near! Their faces were toward me, the eyes of the elder man fixed upon mine. He saw me – at last, at last, he saw me! In the consciousness of that, my terror fled as a cruel dream. The death spell was broken: Love had conquered law! Mad with exultation I shouted – I must have shouted, "He sees, he sees: he will understand!" Then, controlling myself, I moved forward, smiling and consciously beautiful, to offer myself to his arms, to comfort him with endearments, and, with my son's hand in mine, to speak words that should restore the broken bonds between the living and the dead.

Alas! alas! his face went white with fear, his eyes were those of a hunted animal. He backed away from me, as I advanced, and at last turned and fled into the wood – whither, it is not given to me to know.

To my poor boy, left doubly desolate, I have never been able to impart a sense of my presence. Soon he, too, must pass to this Life Invisible and be lost to me for ever.

Alexander Harvey

The Forbidden Floor

Alexander Harvey was a Belgian-born American author, and editor of the journals Current Opinion *and* American Monthly. *His pleasantly erotic tale, "The Forbidden Floor", was one of a number of ghost stories printed in* The Cavalier *magazine, in the early 1900s.*

I

It may be – I do not say that it is – but it may be that it is as unreasonable to require a ghost to appear in an atmosphere of cold skepticism as to require a photograph to be developed in a blaze of sunlight.

Mgr R. H. Benson

"THIS STAIRWAY," she concluded, with the graceful movement of her long, white arm, which seemed no less natural than the musical quaver in her tone – "this stairway leads to my son's rooms."

For the first time in my brief experience of Mrs Bowers the quiet serenity of expression which constituted one of the many charms of her beautiful face left it utterly.

The large, deep blue eyes were visible to me now only through the screen of drooping lashes. The coils of her glorious white hair were beneath my eyes. She had bent her head with the manifest purpose of concealing some too poignant emotion.

For the space of a minute I had to gaze vacantly at the sudden whiteness of her smooth brow, the quick curl of her exquisite red lip. The change from the repose of manner which made the mere presence of this lady soothing disconcerted me.

I felt a sudden wonder that one so fair to behold should have remained a widow. Then I glanced over my shoulder at the stairway.

Access to the wide flight of waxed wood steps was denied by a barred gate of curiously wrought bronze reaching from the floor to perhaps the height of my waist. My eye followed the stairway to the landing above. It was that of the top floor.

Like everything connected with this old colonial mansion, the banisters were built upon a massive scale. They wound about the turn of the stairway at the top floor and were lost to view behind heavy green curtains of velvet. As I gazed curiously, I heard the notes of one of Beethoven's most mystical compositions.

My ears had but begun to drink in the rhythm when I experienced an uncanny shock of what I can only call suspicion. It was the sort of sensation I had had when, years before, I felt intuitively the presence of a person hiding in my room. The instinct had not misled me then. I was sure it did not mislead me now.

There was no shadow of doubt in my mind that behind the curtain above us at the head of those stairs lurked an eavesdropper. There seems to linger in things material some trace of the personality of him or of her by whose daily contact they once derived their atmosphere or their essence.

I know not what term may best denote the subtle influence of the individual upon surrounding objects. A suggestion of it came vividly into my mind as my eye roved up the stair and was halted by the curtain. All objects here conveyed their messages as plainly as a whisper in the ear.

The half light seemed charged with intimations of an unrevealed but not unsuspected presence. The very floor beneath my feet, like the ceiling overhead, was telling some story, and telling it in a way that thrilled. But that lady at my side was moved, apparently, only by the music floating to us from behind the curtain.

"That is Arthur himself playing," I heard her whisper.

I withdrew my eyes from the stairway and gazed once more at the widow's pale face. Mrs Bowers was always lovely to look upon, but each time she alluded to her son the light in her deep blue eyes made her seem young despite the snowy hair massed upon her brow.

She withdrew noiselessly from the gate at the foot of the stairway, and

I had no alternative but to follow. We were in the library below before she said another word.

"You shall meet my son at dinner; that is, if he comes down to dinner."

She hesitated. Her soft hand clutched the handkerchief she held.

"You will not mention that gate to my son?"

Her eyes framed a piteous appeal to me as she asked that. I bowed my head, fearing lest a word might wound her.

"My son is a little – fanciful." She brought out that last word by a visible effort. "No one goes to the top floor – not even myself – except the housekeeper."

I had no time to reply before she fled, leaving me to work among the books. Instead of delving at once among the mass of papers upon the library table, I mused for some minutes upon the mystery of the forbidden floor.

I had never seen the young man who held such undisturbed possession there. My own connection with this household had begun only a day or two before. My presence in the mansion was due to the anxiety of Mrs Bowers to give the world an authentic biography of her late distinguished husband.

His career had been no less varied than it seemed brilliant. This splendour of his Civil War record caused his election to conspicuous public posts. He had served his native land in her diplomatic corps. Great financial enterprises owed their success to his administrative genius.

One of his speeches was so perfect a specimen of a certain kind of oratory as to have found a place in the school readers.

The widow of this brilliant man had been shocked by what purported to be accurate versions of her husband's career. These had been exploited in various periodicals and newspapers in a fashion calculated to discredit the motives of the dead man at one great crisis in the nation's destiny.

Mrs Bowers burned to vindicate the good name of him whose memory was to her so sacred. The executors of her husband's estate had made me a most flattering offer to undertake the task of a biographer.

The prospect of a few months in the country amid surroundings so conducive to my personal comfort was too tempting to resist, quite apart from all considerations respecting the liberal stipend offered by the widow.

This was the second day of my residence in the Bowers mansion. I had

no clue to the character of the widow's son. I gathered from the somewhat vague details supplied by the reticent lawyer who engaged me in
the city that Arthur Bowers was a gifted but somewhat fantastic young
man, who wrote poetry and painted.

From the elderly housekeeper who showed me to my room on the
night of my arrival I derived the additional impression that he kept much
to himself. It now appeared that he barred himself against 'intrusion
behind a gate. For the extreme beauty of the widow I had been totally
unprepared.

I had expected to find an ancient dame living in the past. I found,
instead, a gracious lady, white-haired, to be sure, but seductive in the
willowy lightness of her figure and irresistible through the fresh beauty of
her face.

It was time to dress for dinner when my preliminary inspection of the
late general's correspondence was completed. The intimacy of the relations revealed in the letters with men who have made our country's
history was astounding.

It was obvious that a biography of the eminent statesman would prove
highly sensational, disclosing, as it must, unsuspected factors in the
growth of our republic from an isolated nation to a position of supreme
importance among the great powers of the world.

One or two episodes of historical importance with which these letters
were concerned made it imperative to consult not only the widow, but
the son, before any details could be made public. I had not spent two
hours in a study of the documents before me, yet I was already in possession of political secrets for which many a sensational publication would
pay considerable sums. My appreciation of this fact made me a little
uncomfortable. What if the facts now in my possession were disclosed
prematurely through someone's indiscretion? I might be accused of
betraying a confidence. In much perplexity I restored the bundles of
letters to the great desk at which I worked. I must consult the dead man's
son without delay.

As I left the library for the dining room my ear caught the strains of
music from the top of the house. I halted at the head of the stairs. The
keys of a piano were evidently responding to the hand of a master. I
could have listened for an hour.

The air was quite unknown to me, although the rhythm vaguely
suggested the Italian school. The thought flashed through my mind that I
might be listening to one of the young man's own compositions. In that

event, Arthur Bowers was a genius. My eye met that of the old house-keeper.

She stood mutely and with the rigidity of a statue, gazing down at my upturned face. I felt a moment's annoyance. This old lady might be one of those disagreeable people whose aptitude for watching unobserved suggests a tendency to be sly.

"Master Arthur won't be down tonight, sir," she said.

Her tone was hushed. Her manner was respectful enough. I could not help thinking, as I studied her lined face, that she alone had access to the forbidden floor. With her last word she disappeared, and I went on down.

Whatever intentions I had formed to discuss the matter perplexing me with Mrs Bowers herself were foiled by the presence of guests. One of these was a graceful young lady, dark-eyed and tall, with a becoming gravity of manner. The other was her father, a local judge, pompous and little, with that self-assertiveness which a career on the bench does so much to develop in a man.

"So you're Mr Roegers, are you?" he snapped, seizing my hand. "Glad to meet you. I hope you'll turn out a right account of my old friend, the Senator."

With that he dropped my hand, or rather flung it from him. I was so extremely amused by his swelling port that I at once forgave the brusque-ness of this little judge. One could have forgiven anything in a man with such a daughter.

Miss Miggs soothed where her father ruffled. She deferred where he played the bully. But she was hopelessly eclipsed by the dazzling beauty of the white haired woman. Mrs Bowers wore a *decolleté* dress of black and gold, from which her shoulders emerged like the petals of a lily. Her perfect arms were in fluttering motion.

Her manifest regret at the absence of her son lent to the smile with which she favored us in turn an inexpressible melancholy that sweetened her face like a perfume. I understood that the judge was a widower. I wondered if he could be courting our hostess.

"So Arthur won't come down from the top of the house!" I heard the judge say as he finished his fish. "Gad! He's behaving like his ancestress."

He looked about him at the rest of us while a broad grin creased his jowl on both sides. I had been exchanging ideas with Miss Miggs on the subject of Venice, but the loud tones in which His Honor proclaimed his impression challenged our attention.

"His ancestress!" I repeated blankly, no one else having volunteered
an observation.

"His ancestress!" repeated Judge Miggs, attacking the game just set in
front of him. "She was to have been married from this very house to an
officer of Washington's army."

"Odd that I never heard of that."

Mrs Bowers proffered this observation in her musical tone. She had
not shown much interest in the conversation until now.

"The Senator told me the story," proceeded the judge. "The
Revolutionary War was raging at that time."

I glanced at the countenance of Mrs Bowers. A flush which heightened
her beauty a moment before had left her cheeks entirely.

"Did the marriage of Arthur's ancestress take place?" she inquired
faintly.

"Gad, no!" cried the judge. "Her betrothed came to this very house a
day or two before the wedding was to take place – "

He hesitated.

"And the British captured him?" I suggested.

"They captured her," replied the judge with a laugh. "Her lover
caught her kissing Lord Howe's aide-de-camp on the top floor."

"Then she married the Briton instead of the Yankee!"

I made the observation as gaily as I could for the sake of lifting the pall
which seemed to have dropped upon the subject. My effort was vain, for
the retort of the judge seemed to extinguish us completely.

"She married neither," he said shortly.

"Until the day of her death she never left the top floor."

I exchanged glances with Miss Miggs. Mrs Bowers took a sip of vichy.
The judge, unaware of the mischief he had done stuck to the theme all
night. He was still pointing the moral of the legend when his car arrived
to take him home.

I heard him taking his noisy leave of his hostess at the door, his loud
voice relieved at intervals by a brief remark from his daughter.

II

In the matter of apparitions . . . popular and simple human testimony is of more considerable weight than is the purely scientific testimony.

Mgr R. H. Benson

Mrs Bowers was still very pale when she came back to the dining-room.

"I think I will say good night," she observed faintly.

I saw her clutch the back of the chair. In a moment I was at her side.

"It is nothing," I heard her murmur.

"I am afraid our conversation this evening upset you," I ventured.

But she shook her head.

"Arthur's absence upset me." I could just catch her whisper. "He seemed very much attached to her – once. Now he will not even come downstairs for a sight of her."

I understood. I could only gaze in silent sympathy into her face. Then she extended her hand, bade me good night, and left the room. I lit a cigar and made my way to the library.

It was close upon midnight as I sank into a great leather chair, yet the thought of bed made me restless. My purpose in coming to this house seemed defeated already. I smoked on in the darkness until I heard a clock behind me chime the hour.

The silver strokes beat the air one after another, until the toll of twelve reminded me that a new day was bringing me a new duty. I got upon my feet with a disconcerting sense that the location of the electric button that switched on the light was a mystery to be solved.

I took a single step toward the window, when a moving something drew my eye to the great bookcase looming in the shadow against an opposite wall. Slowly and steadily the object grew luminous as I watched it.

The wraith of a feminine form defined itself to my staring eyes with a loveliness so appealing that, in spite of the thrill, I felt at the root of each hair on my head I would not have sold the sight before me for a bag of gold.

I saw a pair of sloping shoulders beneath a firmly chiseled neck. I saw a rounded waist and a delicate hand pressed to a smooth cheek. The long robe forming the vestment of this apparition was twined about the curves of the figure after the fashion favored by all sculptors of Greek goddesses. Only the face was kept from me.

I remained for the first few minutes of this experience as motionless as the fantom at which I stared. I did not stir until I saw it glide. The apparition darted and halted, darted and halted, making, it seemed, for the wide door at the extremity of the vast apartment.

As I kept pace with its advance I marveled at the ethereal grace revealed in every stage of this mute progress. The restless clock seemed eager to accompany us through the darkness, so quick was its ticking to my ear.

I had never quivered with so icy a chill as now galvanized my limbs into a kind of movement so like that of the ghost before me that I seemed unearthly to myself.

On, on we went, through the door and out upon the rug beyond. Not until the staircase halted the spectre for a moment did it turn. For the first time I looked into the face.

Prepared though I was by the unspeakable perfection of form before me for a loveliness of feature which could alone accompany a presence so angelic, the countenance upon which I was allowed to gaze at last transformed me for the instant into a living statue.

The chin, rounded with a beauty that told also of strength; the nose, straight, firm, positive, yet delicate, sensitive, tremulous; the brow, noble and serene – these details blended themselves into an expressiveness that caught its quality from a pair of eyes into which I could not look. They did not seem to evade me. The figure kept its gaze upon the floor.

The light radiated from the eyes was that, I saw now, which lent its effulgence to the fantom. I realized by a species of intuition that one glance of these orbs meant the loss of consciousness for any upon whom it fell. No one could have endured the delicious shock of so much beauty.

I followed to the very top of the next flight of stairs. The fantom climbed another storey, and on I stole. It made for the gate that afforded access to the forbidden floor.

There it halted, and turned to beckon me. I saw the folds of its vesture broaden like a wide white wing as the moving arm it waved pointed on and upward. Then it climbed the stair. I was at the gate, too, now, and I could have leaped the obstacle easily.

An instant recollection of the mother's warning words enabled me to take my eyes from the fantom for the first time. I could not scale the bars of the bronzed gate without becoming guilty of a breach of trust.

Yet I could no more have gazed at all this grace and beauty, fantom and thing of shadow though it was, without slavish obedience to its least behest than Paris and the men on the walls of Troy could contemplate the loveliest of women without falling in homage at her feet.

I put a hand to my brow as I stole guiltily down to the library with all the silence of the ghost I had just beheld. The spacious apartment allotted to me was directly off the library itself. I had but to grope my way to a corner familiar now and find my bed. I fell upon it like a log.

The staring sun roused me with my clothes still on and the vapors of an indescribable intoxication in my head. I made haste to change my clothes. The water of my bath seemed oddly warm, although I took it cold. I was in the dining-room before it occurred to me to look at my watch. It was nearly noon.

An accusing something within me was silenced by the housekeeper's assurance that I was the first member of the household to appear that day at the breakfast table.

"I should like to talk over some matters with Mr Bowers," I hazarded, gulping some coffee to avoid meeting the eye of this dame.

"Master Arthur will not leave the top floor this day," was her answer, uttered shortly – so shortly, in fact, that I understood from her manner how useless it would be to continue the subject.

"How well you look, Mr Roegers! Good morning!"

There was no mistaking the tones. The sweet widow was looking in from the garden through the window, a nosegay in one hand. I left the table at once.

"I was afraid you might grow fanciful after that anecdote the judge told us last night," she began, as I crossed the lawn to where she stood plucking roses. "Do you believe in ghosts, Mr Roegers?"

I gazed keenly into her eyes for a minute. She was smiling.

"Do I look as if I had seen a ghost?"

I put the question gaily, but I could feel the beating of my heart.

"There is a ghost in the family, you know," she proceeded, following the train of her own thought rather than the drift of my question. "It is a sort of heirloom."

I could feel that thrill at the roots of my hair.

"And what is this ghost like?"

"Oh, I never saw it!"

At that moment my eye caught the glance of the ancient housekeeper. She was standing at the window. Our eyes met with the instantaneity of a flash of light and dropped the gaze as quickly. I put another question to Mrs Bowers:

"The ghost – is it not that of the lady the judge told us of?"

The charming widow shook the masses of her white hair as she inserted a flower above her brow.

"Who knows?"

It was impossible to pursue the topic. I withdrew to the library without even introducing the subject of that interview with Arthur Bowers for which I longed. He did not descend from the forbidden floor.

Until I had taken the measure of this young man, I hesitated to discuss with his mother the delicate themes arising from my brief experience of this unusual household. I had the dining-room to myself that evening. Mrs Bowers, or so the housekeeper said, was indisposed.

As I seated myself in the library, after a solitary stroll through the shrubbery of the lawn, it occurred to me that, as the authorized biographer of the late General Bowers, I ought to look into his ancestry.

It was an easy matter to find the family genealogy among the volumes on the well-stocked shelves. One county history dealt exclusively with the very mansion in which I was now at work. The edifice was venerable – for America – and, inevitably, had served George Washington as one of his innumerable headquarters.

I was so deeply immersed in my historical reading as to let three full hours slip by. The stroke of twelve had caught me unawares. I thought of the night before and shivered. Then I switched off the light.

The fantom arose from the ground at my very feet!

III

I am entirely convinced of the existence of the spiritual world – that there are real intelligences in that world, and that it is possible for them under certain circumstances to communicate with this world.

Mgr R. H. Benson

Only the fevered ticking of the little clock reached my ear as I stood rigid in the fantom's radiant presence.

There is a famous passage consecrated by Burke to a confession, in his most glorious prose, of his sheer incapacity to describe Marie Antoinette reigning in sovereign beauty over the fascinated court of Versailles.

Homer, too, dared not trust his powers when the beauty of Helen demanded a supreme display of his genius. I can but follow the poet's example in setting down, not an account of the feminine loveliness that now held me as his rapt contemplation of Eve held Adam when first his eye devoured her, but a description of the effect this loveliness had upon my sensibilities.

It seemed, then, as if the whole veil of woman was rent aside to my dazzled vision from the mere circumstance that I gazed at the fantom. I was myself and not myself – myself in knowing that I was the same man as ever, not myself in feeling weirdly, supernaturally energized.

The incompleteness of my life was extinguished in the full tide of a holier love than mortals have thrilled to. In the inspiring presence of this wraith I felt capable of that faith which moves mountains.

The fleshly and the spiritual ceased to contend as I contemplated with reverence the haunting sweetness before me. I could have conquered the world, founded empires – then I became the greatest of poets, endowed with a genius breathed into me by this irresistible ghost.

There surged through me all imaginable ecstasies, glorious powers, finer perceptions than ever mortal had. I understood in a flash whatever in my past had baffled me with its mystery. Strains of exquisite music floated through my brain.

How inadequate is the statement that one has seen a ghost! That thought filled my consciousness then like a light streaming from its beacon to the mariner caught in fogs. One does not see a ghost, but surrenders to it as the wax yields to the flame.

I did not come out of this trance until a movement of the fantom intimated subtly to me that I was to emerge from its enchantment. I grew aware that I was following the vision once again through the portal.

The transcendent object of my infatuation conducted me straight to the forbidden floor. I was favored as before with its beauteous gesture. No thought of the ban so recently placed upon my presence here was in my mind, even had I left any power to oppose my mortal will to this immortal spirit.

I followed it unceasingly, unquestioningly. There was no physical obstacle to my progress anywhere. The bronze gate affording access to the forbidden floor had been thrown open.

I set foot boldly upon the lowest step of the stair. The first contact seemed to afford me a definite sensation of personality in the very air. I can liken this feeling only to that bitter blast, that vague uneasiness, which is said to disseminate itself through the night as some vast iceberg skirts the coast of a northern isle. I had caught a chill, and I shivered.

Nor for an instant did I halt. The stairway did not creak. By the time I had set foot upon its summit I was thrilling to some excitation, breathing in impressions like those one derives from moving passages of poetry or strong scenes in a play.

I touched the wall only to find my feelings keener, my sensitiveness to the stimulation increased. All material objects exhaled the mystery stamped upon them by a person or an event in times past of which I was now absorbing impressions. I did not feel that murder had been done here.

The tragedy was all of the heart, of the grief of a soul, of the perpetual and impotent longing of one who, loving, poured out an agony of sorrow to walls that caught the mood. The heart that had been crushed was a woman's. This message, too, I was given by the impregnated air.

The curtain at the summit of the stairway was pushed aside as if by a breath from some other world. I had attained a great quadrangular vestibule, tenantless except for the apparition and myself.

The ghost, preceding me at an interval of some feet, was kneeling beside a wide window through which the warm night air came gently. I beheld a mass of flowers in a vase upon a carved mahogany table. I became conscious of the softness of rugs beneath my feet. I moved as silently as the thing I followed.

No attitude could express the forlornness of an indomitable grief more appealingly than that of the kneeling fantom. Magnetized by an attraction that made me daring, I touched the shoulder of the ghost.

The whiteness of one arm extended itself to my face. Slowly the vision grew toward me, folding itself closely about my neck and breast until the ghost literally rested in my arms. I could not see the features of my beloved as her unreal lips sought mine.

I could not feel the long tresses I tried to stroke. I spoke no word as I vowed to cherish her in this world and prayed for death that I might be with her in the next.

The tired moon that drooped prettily in the sky had sent a curious beam down here. My eye, habituated more and more to the sweet obscurity, caught now a sharper outline of the vase filled with flowers. The heavy table showed its carved proportions less reservedly.

A mahogany chair, resting as a sleeping monster might rest, upon the floor entered the enlarging field of my vision. The impression made by all these upon my spirits was one of personality radiating palpably from them.

Not, indeed, that the objects had themselves this quality. I mean no more than that they emitted or effected suggestions of a personality with which they had been formerly in intimate contact. The darkness of that apartment, pierced by the beams from the window, seemed laden with such revelations.

The great chair told of one who had reposed, and reposed gracefully, in its arms. The vase betrayed a secret it had caught concerning her who once delighted in its shapeliness.

I have always been sensitive to impressions made after this manner upon things by persons. I have caught often enough from the disused furniture of a neglected room verifiable details of the character and life of one associated with it. Never was this sense so receptive in me as at present. But every emanation from the things around me was of evil purport. I was being warned.

"And you will cherish me forever, beloved?"

How I understood that she had put this question I can never tell. The words were not spoken. The language was not earthly. A something within registered the appeal and responded to it. I told of my own unworthiness to be made the object of a celestial passion.

I confessed my longing to reach the confines of the universe in some high quest of a Holy Grail for her sake. I received the outpourings of her passionate regret that in an earthly form years before she had cherished thoughts gross and material, the memory of which left her too sullied for the purity of my faith in her now.

And her fantom arms were wreathed about my neck still, and her bowed head pillowed itself against me, and she quivered with ecstasies of which I partook as a leaf rises and falls with the breeze of a summer's day.

I besought her now to look into my eyes. I saw her head denying that petition. I received some mysterious intimation that the meeting of our gaze must entail an indescribable fatality, not to her but to me.

I conveyed my sense of joy in such a circumstance. Here was the proof of my devotion awaiting her acceptance. Let me but gaze into those eyes and I would wander forever through the universe a blissful spirit. But she only kept her face buried upon my shoulder and held my head with her arms.

I had begun a more impassioned plea when she rushed from my embrace, reeling to the window. I saw her fall upon her knees cowering. She covered her face with one hand, while, extending the other, she pointed to some object behind me.

I turned and beheld – Arthur Bowers!

There was no mistaking those eyes, that proud forehead, the delicacy of each refined feature. He was his mother's son. For a terrible moment he and I glared into each other's faces. I saw him raise an arm. He rushed forward. I threw myself between him and the fantom, but when I directed my gaze to its refuge the object of my infatuation had disappeared.

The next moment Arthur Bowers had me by the throat. Then consciousness left me, but not for long. I was prone upon the floor when my senses returned and the arm of Arthur Bowers was about my head.

"I saw her with you!"

He spoke in the musical accents of his own mother, but grief never found utterance so wild. His tone was a revelation. I cried my reply with the voice of a man in panic.

"She made you vows of an eternal love and you pledged yours in return."

He bowed his head once more. I realized the sense of betrayal that tortured him. The ghost had proved unfaithful. I was torn with his own jealousy, but he proved to me that his ordeal had been worse than mine.

"I saw her with you!" he said. "One torture has been spared you. You never saw her when her gaze rested upon – me!"

I hated him for a second of time. Then I conquered my worst self and pitied him. He had removed his arm from my head and was assisting me to my feet.

"We shall never see her again."

It was I who said this. He buried his face in his hands.

"She was too timid," he murmured faintly, "to let us look into her eyes."

The question elicited from me by this remark led to further revelations.

He, too, had held mysterious communion with the infatuating wraith; had confessed a longing to reach the confines of the universe for her sake.

To him, too, she had professed regret that in an earthly form years before her thoughts were gross and material.

"It was from love of that fantom, then," said I, "that you remained shut up here so much?"

"Yes, yes," was his tragic whisper, "I have been haunted by her presence here by day as well as by night. Your glimpse of her was fleeting. She has haunted me always."

He was forced to bow his head to hide his grief. But in a moment I heard him speak afresh:

"I have seemed to hear her whisper in my ear by day – not once, but always. If your mere sight of her has made you what you seem to me now, what must I be after my long subjection to her spell? You know now why I loathe you!"

We exchanged a glance as he confessed so much. I became suddenly aware of a change in the atmosphere of the forbidden floor. The emanations of personality from things material here had ceased.

The atmosphere was laden no longer with psychical impressions caught from walls and floor. The vase was no more to me now than a work of art. Its mystery had fled. The great carved table had forfeited its subtle gift of communication.

The terrific emotion which first charged the air with its vibration had been neutralized at last. No visual image of the departed wraith could precipitate itself upon my consciousness in this purged atmosphere again. My mind reverted to the brilliant hypothesis which that explorer of the world of fantasm, Mgr R. H. Benson, has constructed to fit cases of this kind.

It is conceivable to him that emotions generated by a passed and passing life may be conditioned by the state of mind at dissolution. The living and the dying set up vibrations in "the emotional atmosphere." These continue in agitation. The place grows haunted. An appropriate or corresponding vibration can alone break the spell.

"When that meets this," to quote the words of Benson, "the suspended chord is complete and comes to a full close." Or, to borrow the image of the same high authority, "an emotional scene which has translated itself, so to speak, into terms of a material plane can, like music in a phonograph, retranslate itself back again."

I felt now that I had the clue to my ghost.

The lady in seclusion on the forbidden floor so long ago had been true to her lover – in her fashion. He had, indeed, surprised her in the arms of another. It was a sentimental accident in her life.

She had been denied all opportunity to explain. She was possibly the victim of a man's sudden impulse. My own infatuation with the rare and beauteous spirit had led me far.

In any event the longing of the human soul to be understood – the craving of this lady to vindicate herself – persisted while she lived. It was her most vehement desire as she passed away.

The very walls, the chair she sat in, the vase in which she arranged her daily nosegay, grew sick with this discarded lady's longing.

"If telepathy from living mind to living mind," asks Mgr Benson, in the course of his study of fantasms, "is a force so mighty as to convey a visual image from France to England, is it not perfectly conceivable that a telepathic force which has been stored, so to speak, in a kind of material battery for years – stored there by the terrific emotional impulse of the original crime – may be powerful enough also to produce a visual image?"

It was so with me.

I did not cease my scrutiny of the countenance of Arthur Bowers as these thoughts ran riot in my head. His mind was too manifestly overwhelmed by the shock it had sustained. He paled slightly and spoke at last in low tones.

"I have nothing to live for."

The words I would have spoken in reply were cut short by the entry of the old housekeeper. She and I exchanged another such swift glance as had given me one shock already. Arthur Bowers did not seem to heed. He merely repeated:

"I have nothing to live for."

"Ah! I cried, "you forget Miss Miggs."

"True!" he exclaimed. "I had forgotten Miss Miggs."

Their wedding did, in fact, follow speedily.

I should note as well that the old housekeeper is no other than that Mrs Murray, whose materializations prove so interesting to students of the occult.

May I add without egotism that my account of the late Senator's career has placed me, if I may trust the book reviewers, among the few great biographers of the age?

The widow was so pleased with the work that she consented to reward me with the inestimable gift of herself.

E. Nesbit

The Shadow

Edith Nesbit continued to write a large number of ghost and horror stories after her
early Grim Tales *(1893), and the best of these (including "The Shadow") were*
collected and published together in the suitably titled Fear *(1910).*

THIS IS NOT an artistically rounded off ghost story, and nothing is
explained in it, and there seems to be no reason why any of it should have
happened. But that is no reason why it should not be told. You must have
noticed that all the real ghost stories you have ever come close to, are like
this in these respects – no explanation, no logical coherence. Here is the
story.

There were three of us and another, but she had fainted suddenly at the
second extra of the Christmas dance, and had been put to bed in the
dressing-room next to the room which we three shared. It had been one
of those jolly, old-fashioned dances where nearly everybody stays the
night, and the big country house is stretched to its utmost containing –
guests harbouring on sofas, couches, settees, and even mattresses on
floors. Some of the young men actually, I believe, slept on the great
dining-table. We had talked of our partners, as girls will, and then the
stillness of the manor house, broken only by the whisper of the wind in
the cedar branches, and the scraping of their harsh fingers against our
window panes, had pricked us to such luxurious confidence in our
surroundings of bright chintz and candle-flame and fire-light, that we
had dared to talk of ghosts – in which, we all said, we did not believe one
bit. We had told the story of the phantom coach, and the horribly strange
bed, and the lady in the sacque, and the house in Berkeley Square.

We none of us believed in ghosts, but my heart, at least, seemed to leap to my throat and choke me there, when a tap came to our door – a tap faint, not to be mistaken.

"Who's there?" said the youngest of us, craning a lean neck towards the door. It opened slowly, and I give you my word the instant of suspense that followed is still reckoned among my life's least confident moments. Almost at once the door opened fully, and Miss Eastwich, my aunt's housekeeper, companion and general stand-by, looked in on us.

We all said "Come in," but she stood there. She was, at all normal hours, the most silent woman I have ever known. She stood and looked at us, and shivered a little. So did we – for in those days corridors were not warmed by hot-water pipes, and the air from the door was keen.

"I saw your light," she said at last, "and I thought it was late for you to be up – after all this gaiety. I thought perhaps – " her glance turned towards the door of the dressing-room.

"No," I said, "she's fast asleep." I should have added a goodnight, but the youngest of us forestalled my speech. She did not know Miss Eastwich as we others did; did not know how her persistent silence had built a wall round her – a wall that no one dared to break down with the commonplaces of talk, or the littlenesses of mere human relationship. Miss Eastwich's silence had taught us to treat her as a machine; and as other than a machine we never dreamed of treating her. But the youngest of us had seen Miss Eastwich for the first time that day. She was young, crude, ill-balanced, subject to blind, calf-like impulses. She was also the heiress of a rich tallow-chandler, but that has nothing to do with this part of the story. She jumped up from the hearth-rug, her unsuitably rich silk lace-trimmed dressing-gown falling back from her thin collar-bones, and ran to the door and put an arm round Miss Eastwich's prim, lisse-encircled neck. I gasped. I should as soon have dared to embrace Cleopatra's Needle. "Come in," said the youngest of us – "come in and get warm. There's lots of cocoa left." She drew Miss Eastwich in and shut the door.

The vivid light of pleasure in the housekeeper's pale eyes went through my heart like a knife. It would have been so easy to put an arm round her neck, if one had only thought she wanted an arm there. But it was not I who had thought that – and indeed, my arm might not have brought the light evoked by the thin arm of the youngest of us.

"Now," the youngest went on eagerly, "you shall have the very biggest, nicest chair, and the cocoa-pot's here on the hob as hot as hot –

and we've all been telling ghost stories, only we don't believe in them a bit; and when you get warm you ought to tell one too."

Miss Eastwich – that model of decorum and decently done duties – tell a ghost story!

"You're sure I'm not in your way," Miss Eastwich said, stretching her hands to the blaze. I wondered whether housekeepers have fires in their rooms even at Christmas time. "Not a bit" – I said it, and I hope I said it as warmly as I felt it. "I – Miss Eastwich – I'd have asked you to come in other times – only I didn't think you'd care for girls' chatter."

The third girl, who was really of no account, and that's why I have not said anything about her before, poured cocoa for our guest. I put my fleecy Madeira shawl round her shoulders. I could not think of anything else to do for her, and I found myself wishing desperately to do something. The smiles she gave us were quite pretty. People can smile prettily at forty or fifty, or even later, though girls don't realize this. It occurred to me, and this was another knife-thrust, that I had never seen Miss Eastwich smile – a real smile, before. The pale smiles of dutiful acquiescence were not of the same blood as this dimpling, happy, transfiguring look.

"This is very pleasant," she said, and it seemed to me that I had never before heard her real voice. It did not please me to think that at the cost of cocoa, a fire, and my arm round her neck, I might have heard this new voice any time these six years.

"We've been telling ghost stories," I said. "The worst of it is, we don't believe in ghosts. No one one knows has ever seen one."

"It's always what somebody told somebody, who told somebody you know," said the youngest of us, "and you can't believe that, can you?"

"What the soldier said, is not evidence," said Miss Eastwich. Will it be believed that the little Dickens quotation pierced one more keenly than the new smile or the new voice?

"And all the ghost stories are so beautifully rounded off – a murder committed on the spot – or a hidden treasure, or a warning . . . I think that makes them harder to believe. The most horrid ghost-story I ever heard was one that was quite silly."

"Tell it."

"I can't – it doesn't sound anything to tell. Miss Eastwich ought to tell one."

"Oh do," said the youngest of us, and her salt cellars loomed dark, as she stretched her neck eagerly and laid an entreating arm on our guest's knee.

"The only thing that I ever knew of was – was hearsay," she said slowly, "till just the end."

I knew she would tell her story, and I knew she had never before told it, and I knew she was only telling it now because she was proud, and this seemed the only way to pay for the fire and the cocoa, and the laying of that arm round her neck.

"Don't tell it," I said suddenly. "I know you'd rather not."

"I daresay it would bore you," she said meekly, and the youngest of us, who after all, did not understand everything, glared resentfully at me.

"We should just love it," she said. "Do tell us. I'm certain anything you think ghostly would be quite too beautifully horrid for anything."

Miss Eastwich finished her cocoa and reached up to set the cup on the mantelpiece.

"I can't do any harm," she said half to herself, "they don't believe in ghosts, and it wasn't exactly a ghost either. And they're all over twenty – they're not babies."

There was a breathing time of hush and expectancy. The fire crackled and the gas suddenly flared higher because the billiard lights had been put out. We heard the steps and voices of the men going along the corridors.

"It is really hardly worth telling," Miss Eastwich said doubtfully, shading her faded face from the fire with her thin hand.

We all said "Go on – oh, go on – do!"

"Well," she said, "twenty years ago – and more than that – I had two friends, and I loved them more than anything in the world. And they married each other – "

She paused, and I knew just in what way she had loved each of them. The youngest of us said –

"How awfully nice for you. Do go on."

She patted the youngest's shoulder, and I was glad that I had understood, and that the youngest of all hadn't. She went on.

"Well, after they were married, I did not see much of them for a year or two; and then he wrote and asked me to come and stay, because his wife was ill, and I should cheer her up, and cheer him up as well; for it was a gloomy house, and he himself was growing gloomy too."

I knew, as she spoke, that she had every line of that letter by heart.

"Well, I went. The address was in Lee, near London; in those days there were streets and streets of new villa-houses growing up round old brick mansions standing in their own grounds, with red walls round, you know, and a sort of flavour of coaching days, and post chaises, and Blackheath highwaymen about them. He had said the house was gloomy, and it was called 'The Firs', and I imagined my cab going through a dark, winding shrubbery, and drawing up in front of one of these sedate, old, square houses. Instead, we drew up in front of a large, smart villa, with iron railings, gay encaustic tiles leading from the iron gate to the stained-glass-panelled door, and for shrubbery only a few stunted cypresses and aucubas in the tiny front garden. But inside it was all warm and welcoming. He met me at the door."

She was gazing into the fire, and I knew she had forgotten us. But the youngest girl of all still thought it was to us she was telling her story.

"He met me at the door," she said again, "and thanked me for coming, and asked me to forgive the past."

"What past?" said that high priestess of the *inàpropos*, the youngest of all.

"Oh – I suppose he meant because they hadn't invited me before, or something," said Miss Eastwich worriedly, "but it's a very dull story, I find, after all, and – "

"Do go on," I said – then I kicked the youngest of us, and got up to rearrange Miss Eastwich's shawl, and said in blatant dumb show, over the shawled shoulder: "Shut up, you little idiot – "

After another silence, the housekeeper's new voice went on.

"They were very glad to see me, and I was very glad to be there. You girls, now, have such troops of friends, but these two were all I had – all I had ever had. Mabel wasn't exactly ill, only weak and excitable. I thought he seemed more ill than she did. She went to bed early and before she went, she asked me to keep him company through his last pipe, so we went into the dining-room and sat in the two armchairs on each side of the fireplace. They were covered with green leather I remember. There were bronze groups of horses and a black marble clock on the mantelpiece – all wedding-presents. He poured out some whisky for himself, but he hardly touched it. He sat looking into the fire. At last I said:

"What's wrong? Mabel looks as well as you could expect."

"He said, 'Yes – but I don't know from one day to another that she won't begin to notice something wrong. That's why I wanted you to come. You were always so sensible and strong-minded, and Mabel's like a little bird on a flower.'

"I said yes, of course, and waited for him to go on. I thought he must be in debt, or in trouble of some sort. So I just waited. Presently he said:

"'Margaret, this is a very peculiar house' – he always called me Margaret. You see we'd been such old friends. I told him I thought the house was very pretty, and fresh, and homelike – only a little too new – but that fault would mend with time. He said:

"'It *is* new: that's just it. We're the first people who've ever lived in it. If it were an old house, Margaret, I should think it was haunted.'

"I asked if he had seen anything. 'No,' he said 'not yet.'

"'Heard then?' said I.

"'No – not heard either,' he said, 'but there's a sort of feeling: I can't describe it – I've seen nothing and I've heard nothing, but I've been so near to seeing and hearing, just near, that's all. And something follows me about – only when I turn round, there's never anything, only my shadow. And I always feel that I *shall* see the thing next minute – but I never do – not quite – it's always just not visible.'

"I thought he'd been working rather hard – and tried to cheer him up by making light of all this. It was just nerves, I said. Then he said he had thought I could help him, and did I think anyone he had wronged could have laid a curse on him, and did I believe in curses. I said I didn't – and the only person anyone could have said he had wronged forgave him freely, I knew, if there was anything to forgive. So I told him this too."

It was I, not the youngest of us, who knew the name of that person, wronged and forgiving.

"So then I said he ought to take Mabel away from the house and have a complete change. But he said No; Mabel had got everything in order, and he could never manage to get her away just now without explaining everything – 'and, above all,' he said, 'she mustn't guess there's anything wrong. I daresay I shan't feel quite such a lunatic now you're here.'

"So we said goodnight."

"Is that all the story!" said the third girl, striving to convey that even as it stood it was a good story.

"That's only the beginning," said Miss Eastwich. "Whenever I was alone with him he used to tell me the same thing over and over again, and at first when I began to notice things, I tried to think that it was his talk that had upset my nerves. The odd thing was that it wasn't only at night – but in broad daylight – and particularly on the stairs and passages. On the staircase the feeling used to be so awful that I have had to bite my lips till they bled to keep myself from running upstairs at full speed. Only I knew if I did I should go mad at the top. There was always something behind me – exactly as he had said – something that one could just not see. And a sound that one could just not hear. There was a long corridor at the top of the house. I have sometimes almost seen something – you know how one sees things without looking – but if I turned round, it seemed as if the thing drooped and melted into my shadow. There was a little window at the end of the corridor.

"Downstairs there was another corridor, something like it, with a cupboard at one end and the kitchen at the other. One night I went down into the kitchen to heat some milk for Mabel. The servants had gone to bed. As I stood by the fire, waiting for the milk to boil, I glanced through the open door and along the passage. I never could keep my eyes on what I was doing in that house. The cupboard door was partly open; they used to keep empty boxes and things in it. And, as I looked, I knew that now it was not going to be 'almost' any more. Yet I said, 'Mabel?' not because I thought it could be Mabel who was crouching down there, half in and half out of the cupboard. The thing was grey at first, and then it was black. And when I whispered, 'Mabel,' it seemed to sink down till it lay like a pool of ink on the floor, and then its edges drew in, and it seemed to flow, like ink when you tilt up the paper you have spilt it on; and it flowed into the cupboard till it was all gathered into the shadow there. I saw it go quite plainly. The gas was full on in the kitchen. I screamed aloud, but even then, I'm thankful to say, I had enough sense to upset the boiling milk, so that when he came downstairs three steps at a time, I had the excuse for my scream of a scalded hand. The explanation satisfied Mabel, but next night he said:

"'Why didn't you tell me? It was that cupboard. All the horror of the house comes out of that. Tell me – have you seen anything yet? Or is it only the nearly seeing and nearly hearing still?'

"I said, 'You must tell me first what you've seen. He told me, and his eyes wandered, as he spoke, to the shadows by the curtains, and I turned up all three gas lights, and lit the candles on the mantelpiece. Then we looked at each other and said we were both mad, and thanked God that Mabel at least was sane. For what he had seen was what I had seen.

"After that I hated to be alone with a shadow, because at any moment I might see something that would crouch, and sink, and lie like a black pool, and then slowly draw itself into the shadow that was nearest. Often that shadow was my own. The thing came first at night, but afterwards there was no hour safe from it. I saw it at dawn and at noon, in the firelight, and always it crouched and sank, and was a pool that flowed into some shadow and became part of it. And always I saw it with a straining of the eyes – a pricking and aching. It seemed as though I could only just see it, as if my sight, to see it, had to be strained to the uttermost. And still the sound was in the house – the sound that I could just not hear. At last, one morning early, I did hear it. It was close behind me, and it was only a sigh. It was worse than the thing that crept into the shadows.

"I don't know how I bore it. I couldn't have borne it, if I hadn't been so fond of them both. But I knew in my heart that, if he had no one to whom he could speak openly, he would go mad, or tell Mabel. His was not a very strong character; very sweet, and kind, and gentle, but not strong. He was always easily led. So I stayed on and bore up, and we were very cheerful, and made little jokes, and tried to be amusing when Mabel was with us. But when we were alone, we did not try to be amusing. And sometimes a day or two would go by without our seeing or hearing anything, and we should perhaps have fancied that we had fancied what we had seen and heard – only there was always the feeling of there being something about the house, that one could just not hear and not see. Sometimes we used to try not to talk about it, but generally we talked of nothing else at all. And the weeks went by, and Mabel's baby was born. The nurse and the doctor said that both mother and child were doing well. He and I sat late in the dining-room that night. We had neither of us seen or heard anything for three days; our anxiety about Mabel was lessened. We talked of the future – it seemed then so much brighter than the past. We arranged that, the moment she was fit to be moved, he should take her away to the sea, and I should superintend the moving of their furniture into the new house he had already chosen. He was gayer than I had seen him since his marriage – almost like his old self. When I said goodnight to him, he said a lot of things about my having been a comfort to them both. I hadn't done anything much, of course, but still I am glad he said them.

"Then I went upstairs, almost for the first time without that feeling of something following me. I listened at Mabel's door. Everything was quiet. I went on towards my own room, and in an instant I felt that there *was* something behind me. I turned. It was crouching there; it sank, and the black fluidness of it seemed to be sucked under the door of Mabel's room.

I went back. I opened the door a listening inch. All was still. And then I heard a sigh close behind me. I opened the door and went in. The nurse and the baby were asleep. Mabel was asleep too – she looked so pretty – like a tired child – the baby was cuddled up into one of her arms with its tiny head against her side. I prayed then that Mabel might never know the terrors that he and I had known. That those little ears might never hear any but pretty sounds, those clear eyes never see any but pretty sights. I did not dare to pray for a long time after that. Because my prayer was answered. She never saw, never heard anything more in this world. And now I could do nothing more for him or for her.

"When they had put her in her coffin, I lighted wax candles round her, and laid the horrible white flowers that people will send near her, and then I saw he had followed me. I took his hand to lead him away.

"At the door we both turned. It seemed to us that we heard a sign. He would have sprung to her side, in I don't know what mad, glad hope. But at that instant we both saw it. Between us and the coffin, first grey, then black, it crouched an instant, then sank and liquefied – and was gathered together and drawn till it ran into the nearest shadow. And the nearest shadow was the shadow of Mabel's coffin. I left the next day. His mother came. She had never liked me."

Miss Eastwich paused. I think she had quite forgotten us.

"Didn't you see him again?" asked the youngest of us all.

"Only once," Miss Eastwich answered, "and something black crouched then between him and me. But it was only his second wife, crying beside the coffin. It's not a cheerful story is it? And it doesn't lead anywhere. I've never told anyone else. I think it was seeing his daughter that brought it all back."

She looked towards the dressing-room door.

"Mabel's baby?"

"Yes – and exactly like Mabel, only with his eyes."

The youngest of all had Miss Eastwich's hands, and was petting them.

Suddenly the woman wrenched her hands away, and stood at her gaunt height, her hands clenched, eyes straining. She was looking at something that we could not see, and I know what the man in the Bible meant when he said: "The hair of my flesh stood up."

What she saw seemed not quite to reach the height of the dressing-room door handle. Her eyes followed it down, down – widening and widening. Mine followed them – all the nerves of them seemed strained to the uttermost – and I almost saw – or did I quite see? I can't be certain. But we all heard the long-drawn, quivering sigh. And to each of us it seemed to be breathed just behind us.

It was I who caught up the candle – it dripped all over my trembling hand – and was dragged by Miss Eastwich to the girl who had fainted during the second extra. But it was the youngest of all whose lean arms were round the housekeeper when we turned away, and that have been round her many a time since, in the new home where she keeps house for the youngest of us.

The doctor who came in the morning said that Mabel's daughter had died of heart disease – which she had inherited from her mother. It was that that had made her faint during the second extra. But I have sometimes wondered whether she may not have inherited something from her father. I had never been able to forget the look on her dead face.

William Hope Hodgson

The Gateway of
the Monster

The last months of the Edwardian decade saw the debut of a series in The Idler *magazine featuring the legendary occult detective, Carnacki. He was created by William Hope Hodgson (1877–1918), best-known today for his monumental fantasy novels* The Night Land *and* The House on the Borderland. *"The Gateway of the Monster" launched the Carnacki series (in which some of the later plots were disappointingly rationalized as criminal hoaxes) in January 1910.*

IN RESPONSE TO Carnacki's usual card of invitation to have dinner and listen to a story, I arrived promptly at Cheyne Walk, to find the three others who were always invited to these happy little times there before me. Five minutes later Carnacki, Arkright, Jessop, Taylor and I were all engaged in the "pleasant occupation" of dining.

"You've not been long away this time," I remarked as I finished my soup, forgetting momentarily, Carnacki's dislike of being asked even to skirt the borders of his story until such time as he was ready. Then he would not stint words.

"No," he replied with brevity, and I changed the subject, remarking that I had been buying a new gun, to which piece of news he gave an intelligent nod and a smile, which I think showed a genuinely good-humoured appreciation of my intentional changing of the conversation.

Later, when dinner was finished, Carnacki snugged himself comfortably down in his big chair, along with his pipe, and began his story, with very little circumlocution:

"As Dodgson was remarking just now, I've only been away a short time, and for a very good reason too – I've only been away a short distance. The exact locality I am afraid I must not tell you; but it is less than twenty miles from here; though, except for changing a name, that won't spoil the story. And it *is* a story too! One of the most extraordinary things I have ever run against.

"I received a letter a fortnight ago from a man I will call Anderson, asking for an appointment. I arranged a time and when he turned up I found that he wished me to look into, and see whether I could not clear up, a long-standing and well authenticated case of what he termed "haunting". He gave me very full particulars and, finally, as the thing seemed to present something unique, I decided to take it up.

"Two days later I drove up to the house late in the afternoon and discovered it a very old place, standing quite alone in its own grounds.

"Anderson had left a letter with the butler, I found, pleading excuses for his absence, and leaving the whole house at my disposal for my investigations.

"The butler evidently knew the object of my visit and I questioned him pretty thoroughly during dinner, which I had in rather lonely state. He is an elderly and privileged servant, and had the history of the Grey Room exact in detail. From him I learned more particulars regarding two things that Anderson had mentioned in but a casual manner. The first was that the door of the Grey Room would be heard in the dead of night to open, and slam heavily, and this even when the butler knew it was locked and the key on the bunch in his pantry. The second was that the bedclothes would always be found torn off the bed and hurled in a heap into a corner.

"But it was the door slamming that chiefly bothered the old butler. Many and many a time, he told me, had he lain awake and just shivered with fright, listening; for a time the door would be slammed time after time thud! thud! thud! so that sleep was impossible.

"From Anderson, I knew already that the room had a history extending back over a hundred and fifty years. Three people had been strangled in it – an ancestor of his and his wife and child. This is authentic, as I had taken very great pains to make sure, so that you can imagine it was with a feeling that I had a striking case to investigate, that I went upstairs after dinner to have a look at the Grey Room.

"Peters, the butler, was in rather a state about my going, and assured me with much solemnity that in all the twenty years of his service, no one had ever entered that room after nightfall. He begged me in quite a fatherly way to wait till the morning when there could be no danger and then he could accompany me himself.

"Of course, I told him not to bother. I explained that I should do no more than look around a bit and perhaps fix a few seals. He need not fear, I was used to that sort of thing. But he shook his head when I said that.

"'There isn't many ghosts like ours, sir,' he assured me with mournful pride. And by Jove he was right, as you will see.

"I took a couple of candles and Peters followed with his bunch of keys. He unlocked the door, but would not come inside with me. He was evidently in quite a fright and renewed his request that I would put off my examination until daylight. Of course I laughed at him, and told him he could stand sentry at the door and catch anything that came out.

"'It never comes outside, sir,' he said, in his funny, old solemn manner. Somehow he managed to make me feel as if I were going to have the creeps right away. Anyway, it was one to him, you know.

"I left him there and examined the room. It is a big apartment and well furnished in the grand style, with a huge four-poster which stands with its head to the end wall. There were two candles on the mantelpiece and two on each of the three tables that were in the room. I lit the lot and after that the room felt a little less inhumanly dreary, though, mind you, it was quite fresh and well kept in every way.

"After I had taken a good look round I sealed lengths of *bebe* ribbon across the windows, along the walls, over the pictures, and over the fireplace and the wall-closets. All the time, as I worked, the butler stood just without the door and I could not persuade him to enter, though I jested with him a little as I stretched the ribbons and went here and there about my work. Every now and again he would say: 'You'll excuse me, I'm sure, sir; but I do wish you would come out, sir. I'm fair in a quake for you.'

"I told him he need not wait, but he was loyal enough in his way to what he considered his duty. He said he could not go away and leave me all alone there. He apologized, but made it very clear that I did not realize the danger of the room; and I could see, generally, that he was getting into a really frightened state. All the same I had to make the room so that I should know if anything material entered it, so I asked him not to bother me unless he really heard something. He was beginning to fret my nerves and the 'feel' of the room was bad enough already, without making things any nastier.

"For a time further, I worked, stretching ribbons across a little above the floor and sealing them so that the merest touch would break the seals, were anyone to venture into the room in the dark with the intention of playing the fool.

"All this had taken me far longer than I had anticipated and, suddenly, I heard a clock strike eleven. I had taken off my coat soon after commencing work; now however, as I had practically made an end of all that I intended to do, I walked across to the settee and picked it up. I was in the act of getting into it when the old butler's voice (he had not said a word for the last hour) came sharp and frightened: 'Come out, sir, quick! There's something going to happen!' Jove! but I jumped, and then in the same moment, one of the candles on the table to the left of the bed went out. Now whether it was the wind, or what, I do not know; but just for a moment I was enough startled to make a run for the door; though I am glad to say that I pulled up before I reached it. I simply could not bunk out with the butler standing there after having, as it were, read him a sort of lesson on 'bein' brave, y'know'. So I just turned right round, picked up the two candles off the mantelpiece, and walked across to the table near the bed. Well, I saw nothing. I blew out the candle that was still alight; then I went to those on the two other tables and blew them out. Then, outside of the door, the old man called again: 'Oh! sir, do be told! Do be told!'

"'All right, Peters,' I said, and by Jove, my voice was not as steady as I should have liked! I made for the door and had a bit of work not to start running. I took some thundering long strides, though, as you can imagine. Near the entrance I had a sudden feeling that there was a cold wind in the room. It was almost as if the window had been suddenly opened a little. I got to the door and the old butler gave back a step, in a sort of instinctive way.

"'Collar the candles, Peters!' I said, pretty sharply, and shoved them into his hands. I turned and caught the handle and slammed the door shut with a crash. Somehow, do you know, as I did so I thought I felt something pull back on it, but it must have been only fancy. I turned the key in the lock, and then again, double-locking the door.

"I felt easier then and set-to and sealed the door. In addition I put my card over the keyhole and sealed it there, after which I pocketed the key and went downstairs – with Peters who was nervous and silent, leading the way. Poor old beggar! It had not struck me until that moment that he had been enduring a considerable strain during the last two or three hours.

"About midnight I went to bed. My room lay at the end of the corridor upon which opens the door of the Grey Room. I counted the doors between it and mine and found that five rooms lay between. And I am sure you can understand that I was not sorry.

"Just as I was beginning to undress an idea came to me and I took my candle and sealing-wax and sealed the doors of all the five rooms. If any door slammed in the night, I should know just which one.

"I returned to my room, locked myself in and went to bed. I was waked suddenly from a deep sleep by a loud crash somewhere out in the passage. I sat up in bed and listened, but heard nothing. Then I lit my candle. I was in the very act of lighting it when there came the bang of a door being violently slammed along the corridor.

"I jumped out of bed and got my revolver. I unlocked the door and went out into the passage, holding my candle high and keeping the pistol ready. Then a queer thing happened. I could not go a step towards the Grey Room. You all know I am not really a cowardly chap. I've gone into too many cases connected with ghostly things, to be accused of that; but I tell you I funked it, simply funked it, just like any blessed kid. There was something precious unholy in the air that night. I backed into my bedroom and shut and locked the door. Then I sat on the bed all night and listened to the dismal thudding of a door up the corridor. The sound seemed to echo through all the house.

"Daylight came at last and I washed and dressed. The door had not slammed for about an hour, and I was getting back my nerve again. I felt ashamed of myself, though in some ways it was silly, for when you're meddling with that sort of thing your nerve is bound to go, sometimes. And you just have to sit quiet and call yourself a coward until the safety of the day comes. Sometimes it is more than just cowardice, I fancy. I believe at times it is Something warning you and fighting *for* you. But all the same, I always feel mean and miserable after a time like that.

"When the day came properly I opened my door and keeping my revolver handy, went quietly along the passage. I had to pass the head of the stairs on the way, and who should I see coming up but the old butler, carrying a cup of coffee. He had merely tucked his nightshirt into his trousers and he'd an old pair of carpet slippers on.

"'Hullo, Peters!' I said, feeling suddenly cheerful, for I was as glad as any lost child to have a live human being close to me. 'Where are you off to with the refreshments?'

"The old man gave a start and slopped some of the coffee. He stared up at me and I could see that he looked white and done-up. He came on up the stairs and held out the little tray to me.

" 'I'm very thankful indeed, sir, to see you safe and well,' he said. 'I feared one time you might risk going into the Grey Room, sir. I've lain awake all night, with the sound of the Door. And when it came light I thought I'd make you a cup of coffee. I knew you would want to look at the seals, and somehow it seems safer if there's two, sir.'

" 'Peters,' I said, 'you're a brick. This is very thoughtful of you.' And I drank the coffee. 'Come along,' I told him, and handed him back the tray. 'I'm going to have a look at what the Brutes have been up to. I simply hadn't the pluck to in the night.'

" 'I'm very thankful, sir,' he replied. 'Flesh and blood can do nothing, sir, against devils, and that's what's in the Grey Room after dark.'

"I examined the seals on all the doors as I went along and found them right, but when I got to the Grey Room, the seal was broken, though the visiting-card over the keyhole was untouched. I ripped it off and unlocked the door and went in, rather cautiously, as you can imagine; but the whole room was empty of anything to frighten one; and there was heaps of light. I examined all my seals, and not a single one was disturbed. The old butler had followed me in, and suddenly he said, 'The bedclothes, sir!'

"I ran up to the bed and looked over, and surely, they were lying in the corner to the left of the bed. Jove! you can imagine how queer I felt. Something *had* been in the room. I stared for a while from the bed to the clothes on the floor. I had a feeling that I did not want to touch either. Old Peters, though, did not seem to be affected that way. He went over to the bed-coverings and was going to pick them up, as doubtless he had done every day these twenty years back, but I stopped him. I wanted nothing touched until I had finished my examination. This I must have spent a full hour over and then I let Peters straighten up the bed, after which we went out and I locked the door, for the room was getting on my nerves.

"I had a short walk and then breakfast, which made me feel more my own man. Then to the Grey Room again, and with Peters' help and one of the maids, I had everything taken out except the bed, even the very pictures.

"I examined the walls, floor and ceiling then with probe, hammer and magnifying glass, but found nothing unusual. I can assure you I began to realize in very truth that some incredible thing had been loose in the room during the past night.

"I sealed up everything again and went out, locking and sealing the door as before.

"After dinner that night, Peters and I unpacked some of my stuff and I fixed up my camera and flashlight opposite to the door of the Grey Room with a string from the trigger of the flashlight to the door. You see, if the door really opened, the flashlight would blare out and there would be, possibly, a very queer picture to examine in the morning.

'The last thing I did before leaving was to uncap the lens and after that I went off to my bedroom and to bed, for I intended to be up at midnight, and to insure this, I set my little alarm to call me; also I left my candle burning.

"The clock woke me at twelve and I got up and into my dressing-gown and slippers. I shoved my revolver into my right side-pocket and opened my door. Then I lit my darkroom lamp and withdrew the slide so that it would give a clear light. I carried it up the corridor about thirty feet and put it down on the floor, with the open side away from me, so that it would show me anything that might approach along the dark passage. Then I went back and sat in the doorway of my room, with my revolver handy, staring up the passage towards the place where I knew my camera stood outside of the door of the Grey Room.

"I should think I had watched for about an hour and a half, when suddenly I heard a faint noise away up the corridor. I was immediately conscious of a queer prickling sensation about the back of my head and my hands began to sweat a little. The following instant the whole end of the passage flicked into sight in the abrupt glare of the flashlight. Then came the succeeding darkness and I peered nervously up the corridor, listening tensely, and trying to find what lay beyond the faint, red glow of my dark-lamp, which now seemed ridiculously dim by contrast with the tremendous blaze of the flash-powder . . . And then, as I stooped forward, staring and listening, there came the crashing thud of the door of the Grey Room. The sound seemed to fill the whole of the large corridor and go echoing hollowly through the house. I tell you, I felt horrible – as if my bones were water. Simply beastly. Jove! how I did stare and how I listened. And then it came again, thud, thud, thud, and then a silence that was almost worse than the noise of the door, for I kept fancying that some brutal thing was stealing upon me along the corridor.

"Suddenly, my lamp was put out, and I could not see a yard before me. I realized all at once that I was doing a very silly thing, sitting there and I jumped up. Even as I did so, I *thought* I heard a sound in the passage, quite *near* to me. I made one backward spring into my room and slammed and locked the door.

"I sat on my bed and stared at the door. I had my revolver in my hand, but it seemed an abominably useless thing. Can you understand? I felt that there was something the other side of my door. For some unknown reason, I *knew* it was pressed up against the door, and it was soft. That was just what I thought. Most extraordinary thing to imagine, when you come to think of it!

"Presently I got hold of myself a bit and marked out a pentacle hurriedly with chalk on the polished floor and there I sat in it until it was almost dawn. And all the time, away up the corridor, the door of the Grey Room thudded at solemn and horrid intervals. It was a miserable, brutal night.

"When the day began to break, the thudding of the door came gadually to an end, and at last I grabbed together my courage and went along the corridor in the half light, to cap the lens of my camera. I can tell you, it took some doing; but if I had not gone my photograph would have been spoilt, and I was tremendously keen to save it. I got back to my room and then set-to and rubbed out the five-pointed star in which I had been sitting.

"Half an hour later there was a tap at my door. It was Peters, with my coffee. When I had drunk it we both walked along to the Grey Room. As we went, I had a look at the seals on the other doors, but they were untouched. The seal on the door of the Grey Room was broken, as also was the string from the trigger of the flashlight, but the visiting-card over the keyhole was still there. I ripped it off and opened the door.

"Nothing unusual was to be seen, until we came to the bed; then I saw that as on the previous day, the bedclothes had been torn off, and hurled into the left-hand corner, exactly where I had seen them before. I felt very queer, but I did not forget to look at the seals, only to find that not one had been broken.

"Then I turned and looked at old Peters and he looked at me, nodding his head.

" 'Let's get out of here!' I said, 'It's no place for any living human to enter without proper protection.'

"We went out then and I locked and sealed the door, again.

"After breakfast I developed the negative, but it showed only the door of the Grey Room, half opened. Then I left the house, as I wanted to get certain matters and implements that might be necessary to life, perhaps to the spirit, for I intended to spend the coming night in the Grey Room.

"I got back in a cab about half past five with my apparatus, and this Peters and I carried up to the Grey Room where I piled it carefully in the centre of the floor. When everything was in the room, including a cat which I had brought, I locked and sealed the door and went towards my bedroom, telling Peters I should not be down to dinner. He said 'Yes, sir', and went downstairs, thinking that I was going to turn-in, which was what I wanted him to believe, as I knew he would have worried both himself and me if he had known what I intended.

"But I merely got my camera and flashlight from my bedroom and hurried back to the Grey Room. I entered and locked and sealed myself in and set-to for I had a lot to do before it got dark.

"First I cleared away all the ribbons across the floor; then I carried the cat – still fastened in its basket – over towards the far wall and left it. I returned then to the centre of the room and measured out a space twenty-one feet in diameter which I swept with a 'broom of hyssop'. About this I drew a circle of chalk, taking care never to step over the circle.

"Beyond this I smudged, with a bunch of garlic, a broad belt right around the chalked circle, and when this was complete I took from among my stores in the centre a small jar of a certain water. I broke away the parchment and withdrew the stopper. Then, dipping my left forefinger in the little jar I went round the circle again, making upon the floor, just within the line of chalk, the Second Sign of the Saaamaaa Ritual, and joining each Sign most carefully with the left handed crescent. I can tell you, I felt easier when this was done and the 'water-circle' complete.

"Then I unpacked some more of the stuff that I had brought and placed a lighted candle in the 'valley' of each crescent. After that I drew a pentacle so that each of the five points of the defensive star touched the chalk circle. In the five points of the star I placed five portions of a certain bread, each wrapped in linen; and in the five 'vales', five opened jars of the water I had used to make the 'water-circle'. And now I had my first protective barrier complete.

"Now anyone, except you who know something of my methods of investigation, might consider all this a piece of useless and foolish superstition; but you all remember the Black Veil case, in which I believe my life was saved by a very similar form of protection; whilst Aster, who sneered at it and would not come inside, died.

'I got the idea from the *Sigsand MS*, written, so far as I can make out, in the fourteenth century. At first, naturally, I imagined it was just an expression of the superstition of his time, and it was not until long after my first reading that it occurred to me to test his 'Defence', which I did, as I've just said, in that horrible Black Veil business. You know how *that* turned out. Later I used it several times and always I came through safe, until that Noving Fur case. It was only a partial 'Defence' there and I nearly died in the pentacle. After that I came across Professor Garder's 'Experiments with a Medium'. When they surrounded the Medium with a current of a certain number of vibrations in vacuum, he lost his position – almost as if it cut him off from the Immaterial.

"That made me think, and led eventually to the Electric Pentacle, which is a most marvellous 'Defence' against certain manifestations. I used the shape of the defensive star for this protection because I have, personally, no doubt at all but that there is some extraordinary virtue in the old magic figure. Curious thing for a twentieth century man to admit, is it not? But then, as you all know, I never did, and never will allow myself to be blinded by a little cheap laughter. I ask questions and keep my eyes open!

"In this last case I had little doubt that I had run up against an abnatural monster, and I meant to take every possible care, for the danger is abominable.

"I turned-to now to fit the Electric Pentacle, setting it so that each of its 'points' and 'vales' coincided exactly with the 'points' and 'vales' of the drawn pentagram upon the floor. Then I connected up the battery and the next instant the pale blue glare from the intertwining vacuum tubes shone out.

"I glanced about me then, with something of a sigh of relief, and realized suddenly that the dusk was upon me, for the window was grey and unfriendly. Then I stared round at the big, empty room, over the double-barrier of electric and candle light, and had an abrupt, extraordinary sense of weirdness thrust upon me – in the air, you know, it seemed; as it were a sense of something inhuman impending. The room was full of the stench of bruised garlic, a smell I hate.

"I turned now to my camera, and saw that it and the flashlight were in order. Then I tested the action of my revolver carefully, though I had little thought that it would be needed. Yet, to what extent materialisation of an ab-natural creature is possible, given favourable conditions, no one can say, and I had no idea what horrible thing I was going to see or feel the presence of. I might, in the end, have to fight with a material thing. I did not know and could only be prepared. You see, I never forgot that three people had been strangled in the bed close to me, and the fierce slamming of the door I had heard myself. I had no doubt that I was investigating a dangerous and ugly case.

"By this time the night had come (though the room was very light with the burning candles) and I found myself glancing behind me constantly and then all round the room. It was nervy work waiting for that thing to come into the room.

'Suddenly I was aware of a little, cold wind sweeping over me, coming from behind. I gave one great nerve-thrill and a prickly feeling went all over the back of my head. Then I hove myself round with a sort of stiff jerk and stared straight against that queer wind. It seemed to come from the corner of the room to the left of the bed – the place where both times I had found the heaped and tossed bedclothes. Yet I could see nothing unusual, no opening – nothing! . . .

"Abruptly I was aware that the candles were all a-flicker in that unnatural wind . . . I believe I just squatted there and stared in a horribly frightened, wooden way for some minutes. I shall never be able to let you know how disgustingly horrible it was sitting in that vile, cold wind! And then – flick! flick! flick! all the candles round the outer barrier went out, and there was I, locked and sealed in that room and with no light beyond the weakish blue glare of the Electric Pentacle.

"A time of abominable tenseness passed and still that wind blew upon me, and then suddenly I knew that something stirred in the corner to the left of the bed. I was made conscious of it rather by some inward, unused sense, than by either sight or sound, for the pale, short-radius glare of the Pentacle gave but a very poor light for seeing by. Yet, as I stared, something began slowly to grow upon my sight – a moving shadow, a little darker than the surrounding shadows. I lost the thing amid the vagueness and for a moment or two I glanced swiftly from side to side with a fresh, new sense of impending danger. Then my attention was directed to the bed. All the coverings were being drawn steadily off, with a hateful, stealthy sort of motion. I heard the slow, dragging slither of the clothes, but I could see nothing of the thing that pulled. I was aware in a funny, subconscious, introspective fashion that the 'creep' had come upon me, prickling all over my head, yet I was cooler mentally than I had been for some minutes; sufficiently so to feel that my hands were sweating coldly and to shift my revolver, half-consciously, whilst I rubbed my right hand dry upon my knee; though never for an instant taking my gaze or my attention from those moving clothes.

"The faint noises from the bed ceased once and there was a most intense silence, with only the dull thudding of the blood beating in my head. Yet immediately afterwards I heard again the slurring sound of the bedclothes being dragged off the bed. In the midst of my nervous tension I remembered the camera and reached out for it, but without looking away from the bed. And then, you know, all in a moment, the whole of the bed-coverings were torn off with extraordinary violence and I heard the flump they made as they were hurled into the corner.

"There was a time of absolute quietness then for perhaps a couple of minutes and you can imagine how horrible I felt. The bedclothes had been thrown with such savageness! And then again the abominable unnaturalness of the thing that had just been done before me!

"Suddenly, over by the door, I heard a faint noise – a sort of crickling sound and then a pitter or two upon the floor. A great nervous thrill swept over me, seeming to run up my spine and over the back of my head, for the seal that secured the door had just been broken. Something was there. I could not see the door; at least, I mean to say that it was impossible to say how much I actually saw and how much my imagination supplied. I made it out only as a continuation of the grey walls . . . And then it seemed to me that something dark and indistinct wavered there among the shadows.

"Abruptly I was aware that the door was opening and with an effort I reached again for my camera; but before I could aim in the door was slammed with a terrific crash that filled the whole room with a sort of hollow thunder. I jumped like a frightened child. There seemed such a power behind the noise, as if a vast, wanton Force were 'out'. Can you understand?

"The door was not touched again; but, directly afterwards I heard the basket in which the cat lay creak. I tell you, I fairly pringled all along my back. I knew that I was going to learn definitely whether what was abroad was dangerous to Life. From the cat there rose suddenly a hideous caterwaul that ceased abruptly, and then – too late – I snapped on the flashlight. In the great glare I saw that the basket had been over-turned and the lid was wrenched open, with the cat lying half in and half out upon the floor. I saw nothing else, but I was full of the knowledge that I was in the presence of some Being or Thing that had power to destroy.

"During the next two or three minutes there was an odd, noticeable quietness in the room, and you must remember I was half-blinded for the time because of the flashlight, so that the whole place seemed to be pitchy dark just beyond the shine of the pentacle. I tell you it was most horrible. I just knelt there in the star and whirled round on my knees, trying to see whether anything was coming at me.

"My power of sight came gradually and I got a little hold of myself, and abruptly I saw the thing I was looking for, close to the 'water-circle'. It was big and indistinct and wavered curiously as though the shadow of a vast spider hung suspended in the air, just beyond the barrier. It passed swiftly round the circle and seemed to probe ever towards me, but only to draw back with extraordinary jerky movements, as might a living person who touched the hot bar of a grate.

"Round and round it moved and round and round I turned. Then just opposite to one of the 'vales' in the pentacles it seemed to pause as though preliminary to a tremendous effort. It retired almost beyond the glow of the vacuum light and then came straight towards me, appearing to gather form and solidity as it came. There seemed a vast malign deter-mination behind the movement that must succeed. I was on my knees and I jerked back, falling on to my left hand and hip, in a wild endeavour to get back from the advancing thing. With my right hand I was grabbing madly for my revolver which I had let slip. The brutal thing came with one great sweep straight over the garlic and the 'water-circle', almost to the vale of the pentacle. I believe I yelled. Then, just as suddenly as it had swept over it seemed to be hurled back by some mighty, invisible force.

"It must have been some moments before I realized that I was safe, and then I got myself together in the middle of the pentacles, feeling horribly done and shaken and glancing round and round the barrier, but the thing had vanished. Yet I had learnt something, for I knew now that the Grey Room was haunted by a monstrous hand.

"Suddenly as I crouched there I saw what had so nearly given the monster an opening through the barrier. In my movements within the pentacle I must have touched one of the jars of water, for just where the thing had made its attack the jar that guarded the 'deep' of the 'vale' had been moved to one side and this had left one of the 'five doorways' unguarded. I put it back quickly and felt almost safe again, for I had found the cause and the 'Defence' was still good. I began to hope again that I should see the morning come in. When I saw that thing so nearly succeed I'd had an awful, weak, overwhelming feeling that the 'barriers' could never bring me safe through the night against such a Force. You can understand?

"For a long time I could not see the hand; but presently I thought I saw, once or twice, an odd wavering over among the shadows near the door. A little later, as though in a sudden fit of malignant rage, the dead body of the cat was picked up and beaten with dull, sickening blows against the solid floor. That made me feel rather queer.

"A minute afterwards the door was opened and slammed wide with tremendous force. The next instant the thing made one swift, vicious dart at me from out of the shadows. Instinctively I started sideways from it and so plucked my hand from upon the Electric Pentacle, where – for a wickedly careless moment – I had placed it. The monster was hurled off from the neighbourhood of the pentacles, though – owing to my inconceivable foolishness – it had been enabled for a second time to pass the outer barriers. I can tell you I shook for a time with sheer funk. I moved right to the centre of the pentacles again and knelt there, making myself as small and compact as possible.

"As I knelt, I began to have presently, a vague wonder at the two 'accidents' which had so nearly allowed the brute to get at me. Was I being *influenced* to unconscious voluntary actions that endangered me? The thought took hold of me and I watched my every movement. Abruptly I stretched a tired leg and knocked over one of the jars of water. Some was spilled, but because of my suspicious watchfulness, I had it upright and back within the vale while yet some of the water remained. Even as I did so the vast, black half-materialized hand beat up at me out of the shadows and seemed to leap almost into my face, so nearly did it approach, but for the third time it was thrown back by some altogether enormous, over-mastering force. Yet, apart from the dazed fright in which it left me, I had for a moment that feeling of spiritual sickness as if some delicate, beautiful, inward grace had suffered which is felt only upon the too near approach of the ab-human and is more dreadful in a strange way than any physical pain that can be suffered. I knew by this more of the extent and closeness of the danger, and for a long time I was simply cowed by the butt-headed brutality of that Force upon my spirit. I can put it no other way.

'I knelt again in the centre of the pentacles, watching myself with as much fear almost, as the monster, for I knew now that unless I guarded myself from every sudden impulse that came to me I might simply work my own destruction. Do you see how horrible it all was?

"I spent the rest of the night in a haze of sick fright and so tense that I could not make a single movement naturally. I was in such fear that any desire for action that came to me might be prompted by the Influence that I knew was at work on me. And outside of the barrier that ghastly thing went round and round, grabbing and grabbing in the air at me. Twice more was the body of the dead cat molested. The second time I heard every bone in its body scrunch and crack. And all the time the horrible wind was blowing upon me from the corner of the room to the left of the bed.

"Then, just as the first touch of dawn came into the sky the unnatural wind ceased in a single moment and I could see no sign of the hand. The dawn came slowly and presently the wan light filled all the room and made the pale glare of the Electric Pentacle look more unearthly. Yet it was not until the day had fully come that I made any attempt to leave the barrier, for I did not know but that there was some method abroad in the sudden stopping of that wind to entice me from the pentacles.

"At last, when the dawn was strong and bright, I took one last look round and ran for the door. I got it unlocked in a nervous, clumsy fashion; then locked it hurriedly and went to my bedroom where I lay on the bed and tried to steady my nerves. Peters came presently with the coffee and when I had drunk it I told him I meant to have a sleep, as I had been up all night. He took the tray and went out quietly, and after I had locked my door I turned in properly and at last got to sleep.

"I woke about midday and after some lunch went up to the Grey Room. I switched off the current from the Pentacle, which I had left on in my hurry; also, I removed the body of the cat. You can understand, I did not want anyone to see the poor brute.

"After that I made a very careful search of the corner where the bedclothes had been thrown. I made several holes through the wood-work and probed, but found nothing. Then it occurred to me to try with my instrument under the skirting. I did so and heard my wire ring on metal. I turned the hook-end of the probe that way and fished for the thing. At the second go I got it. It was a small object and I took it to the window. I found it to be a curious ring made of some greyish metal. The curious thing about it was that it was made in the form of a pentagon;

that is, the same shape as the inside of the magic pentacle, but without the 'mounts' which form the points of the defensive star. It was free from all chasing or engraving.

'You will understand that I was excited when I tell you that I felt sure I held in my hand the famous Luck Ring of the Anderson family which, indeed, was of all things the most intimately connected with the history of the haunting. This ring had been handed on from father to son through generations, and always – in obedience to some ancient family tradition – each son had to promise never to wear the ring. The ring, I may say, was brought home by one of the Crusaders under very peculiar circumstances, but the story is too long to go into here.

"It appears that young Sir Hulbert, an ancestor of Anderson's, made a bet one evening, in drink, you know, that he would wear the ring that night. He did so, and in the morning his wife and child were found strangled in the bed in the very room in which I stood. Many people, it would seem, thought young Sir Hulbert was guilty of having done the thing in drunken anger and he, in an attempt to prove his innocence, slept a second night in the room. He also was strangled.

"Since then no one has spent a night in the Grey Room until I did so. The ring had been lost so long that its very existence had become almost a myth, and it was most extraordinary to stand there with the actual thing in my hand, as you can understand.

"It was whilst I stood there looking at the ring that I got an idea. Supposing that it were, in a way, a doorway – you see what I mean? A sort of gap in the world-hedge, if I may so phrase my idea. It was a queer thought, I know, and possibly was not my own, but one of those mental nudgings from the Outside.

"You see, the wind had come from that part of the room where the ring lay. I pondered the thought a lot. Then the shape – the inside of a pentacle. It had no 'mounts', and without mounts, as the *Sigsand MS.* has it: 'Thee mownts wych are thee Five Hills of safetie. To lack is to gyve pow'r to thee daemon; and surlie to fayvor thee Evill Thynge'. You see, the very shape of the ring was significant. I determined to test it.

"I unmade my pentacle, for it must be 'made' afresh *and around* the one to be protected. Then I went out and locked the door, after which I left the house to get certain matters, for neither 'yarbs nor fyre not water' must be used a second time. I returned about seven-thirty and as soon as the things I had brought had been carried up to the Grey Room I dismissed Peters for the night, just as I had done the evening before.

When he had gone downstairs I let myself into the room and locked and sealed the door. I went to the place in the centre of the room where all the stuff had been packed and set to work with all my speed to construct a barrier about me and the ring.

"I do not remember whether I explained to you, but I had reasoned that if the ring were in any way a 'medium of admission', and it were enclosed with me in the Electric Pentacle it would be, to express it loosely, insulated. Do you see? The Force which had visible expression as a Hand would have to stay beyond the Barrier which separates the Ab from the Normal, for the 'gateway' would be removed from accessibility.

"As I was saying, I worked with all my speed to get the barrier completed about me and the ring for it was already later than I cared to be in that room 'unprotected'. Also, I had a feeling that there would be a last effort made that night to regain the use of the ring. For I had the strongest conviction that the ring was a necessity to materialisation. You will see whether I was right.

"I completed the barriers in about an hour and you can imagine something of the relief I felt when I saw the pale glare of the Electric Pentacle once more all about me. From then onwards, for about two hours, I sat quietly facing the corner from which the wind came.

'About eleven o'clock I had a queer knowledge that something was near to me, yet nothing happened for a whole hour after that. Then suddenly I felt the cold, queer wind begin to blow upon me. To my astonishment it seemed now to come from behind me and I whipped round with a hideous quake of fear. The wind hit me in the face. It was flowing up from the floor close to me. I stared in a sickening maze of new frights. What on earth had I done now! The ring was there, close beside me, where I had put it. Suddenly, as I stared, bewildered, I was aware that there was something queer about the ring – funny shadowy movements and convolutions. I looked at them stupidly. And then, abruptly, I knew that the wind was blowing up at me from the ring. A queer indistinct smoke became visible to me, seeming to pour upwards through the ring and mix with the moving shadows. Suddenly I realized that I was in more than any mortal danger, for the convoluting shadows about the ring were taking shape and the death-hand was forming *within* the Pentacle. My goodness, do you realize it? I had brought the 'gateway' into the pentacles and the brute was coming through – pouring into the material world, as gas might pour out from the mouth of a pipe.

"I should think that I knelt for a couple of moments in a sort of stunned fright. Then with a mad, awkward movement I snatched at the ring, intending to hurl it out of the pentacle. Yet, it eluded me as though some invisible, living thing jerked it hither and thither. At last I gripped it, but in the same instant it was torn from my grasp with incredible and brutal force. A great black shadow covered it and rose into the air and came at me. I saw that it was the Hand, vast and nearly perfect in form. I gave one crazy yell and jumped over the pentacle and the ring of burning candles and ran despairingly for the door. I fumbled idiotically and ineffectually with the key, and all the time I stared, with the fear that was like insanity, toward the Barriers. The Hand was plunging towards me; yet, even as it had been unable to pass into the pentacle when the ring was without; so, now that the ring was within it had no power to pass out. The monster was chained, as surely as any beast would be, were chains riveted upon it.

"Even then, in that moment, I got a flash of this knowledge, but I was too utterly shaken with fright to reason and the instant I managed to get the key turned I sprang into the passage and slammed the door with a crash. I locked it and got to my room, somehow; for I was trembling so that I could hardly stand, as you can imagine. I locked myself in and managed to get the candle lit; then I lay down on the bed and kept quiet for an hour or two, and so I grew steadier.

"I got a little sleep later, but woke when Peters brought my coffee. When I had drunk it I felt altogether better and took the old man along with me whilst I had a look into the Grey Room. I opened the door and peeped in. The candles were still burning wan against the daylight and behind them was the pale, glowing star of the Electric Pentacle. And there in the middle was the ring – the gateway of the monster, lying demure and ordinary.

"Nothing in the room was touched and I knew that the brute had never managed to cross the pentacles. Then I went out and locked the door.

"After a further sleep of some hours I left the house. I returned in the afternoon in a cab. I had with me an oxy-hydrogen jet and two cylinders, containing the gases. I carried the things to the Grey Room and there, in the centre of the Electric Pentacle, I erected the little furnace. Five minutes later the Luck Ring, once the 'luck' but now the 'bane' of the Anderson family, was no more than a little splash of hot metal."

Carnacki felt in his pocket and pulled out something wrapped in tissue paper. He passed it to me. I opened it and found a small circle of greyish metal something like lead, only harder and rather brighter.

"Well," I asked, at length, after examining it and handing it round to the others, "did that stop the haunting?"

Carnacki nodded. "Yes," he said. "I slept three nights in the Grey Room before I left. Old Peters nearly fainted when he knew that I meant to, but by the third night he seemed to realize that the house was just safe and ordinary. And you know, I believe in his heart he hardly approved."

Carnacki stood up and began to shake hands. "Out you go!" he said, genially.

And, presently, we went pondering to our various homes.